MONEY MARKS

OR

THE HIGHWAYMAN OF THE SEAS

With Twenty Original Illustrations

LONDON

GEORGE VICKERS, ANGEL COURT, STRAND

CONTENTS.

LIST OF ILLUSTRATIONS.

MONEY MARKS

OR THE

Highwayman of the Seas

MONEY MARKS AND THE OLD SALT FIND THEMSELVES IN A TRAP.

CHAPTER I.

RATCLIFF HIGHWAY.

"Hurrah! more rum here. Jolly dogs—we're all jolly dogs! Slap bang! set him up again. More rum! We're all jolly dogs! I say and mean to be merry to-night, if we never are again!"

These random exclamations proceeded from a rough-looking man, who was dressed in the garb of a sailor.

He was more than three-parts drunk, and was amusing himself with trying to dance a very shaky hornpipe.

In one hand he held a glass of rum, in the other a bad, evil-smelling cigar, in the composition of which lettuce-leaves had more to do than tobacco.

He was singing at the top of his voice, and making night hideous with loud lion-like roars.

In very truth, he had the lungs of a stentor.

This man was well known in the district of Ratcliff Highway as Bob Cannon, the drunken sailor. He had spent most of his life on the sea, and when he came home after a year's or a two years' voyage, as the case might be, with his money rattling in his pocket, he went in for what he called a spree.

He was a tall, thick-set fellow, strong as a horse, with a fist like a sledge-hammer, and a leg that could kick a horse's lower jaw off.

The place in which Bob Cannon was enjoying himself, after his own peculiar fashion, was in the very centre of Ratcliff Highway.

It was a public-house known as the "Pint of Porter." Downstairs the house was fitted up with a bar, parlour, and tap-room.

Upstairs there was what is called a long room—that is to say, a room more remarkable for length than breadth—in which were a few tables, benches, and a small rudely-constructed box, in which sat three musicians—a fiddler, a fifer, and a trumpeter, or, more strictly speaking, a player on the cornet.

These hard-worked and badly-payed sons of Orpheus, did their best to amuse the motley group which nightly resorted to the "Pint of Porter."

The company consisted of men and women. The former were for the most part sailors; the latter consisted of those frail and degraded specimens of humanity which are to be met with in all large cities, and every seaport town.

Everybody drank, and everybody danced, and a great many sang.

The uproar was tremendous.

The musicians played until they could play no longer. Then they left off with aching cheeks, tired fingers, and heaving breasts.

Having imbibed some liquor, they recommenced.

The waiter in the long room was a tall, smartly-built young fellow, of some twenty, or may be one-and-twenty, summers, who was known as Money Marks.

This name had been given him by the landlord of the "Pint of Porter" when he was a baby. Mr. Samkin, the landlord, had been astonished one night by the apparition of a well-dressed, lady-like woman, who came into his bar and demanded a bottle of the best champagne.

Mr. Samkin had to go into the cellar to get it. When he returned he was surprised to find the lady-like woman gone.

She had vanished, as if by magic.

But lying on the counter was what Mr. Samkin was pleased to call a "hinfant."

The woman had evidently taken it from beneath her shawl, and placed it on the counter while the landlord's back was turned, almost immediately afterwards making her escape, and going no one knew whither.

Mr. Samkin rushed into the street, and cried—

"Hi! Stop! I say, stop! You've left your babby! Stop, I say! Hi, mum! you've left your precious babby."

But he received no answer. The passers-by came up to him and laughed at him, and Mr. Samkin returned to his bar, and examined the "hinfant."

It was well dressed, and was tolerably good looking. By its side lay a purse of gold.

Mr. Samkin was married, and had two children of his own; so that he did not dislike the little innocents.

In a loud voice he called his wife out of the bar-parlour. He trembled violently, dreading a storm.

"What have we here?" asked Mrs. Samkin.

"A—a baby, my dear."

"Baby!" repeated Mrs. Samkin, horrified.

"Yes."

"Oh, Samkin! what have you been a doing of?"

"Doing, my dear!"

"Yes, you wretch!"

"Nothing."

"You'll swear it, I suppose?"

"I will."

"Here is your guilt brought home to you, Samkin."

"My guilt!" stammered Samkin.

"Of course. Oh, that I should live to see this day, and be insulted in my own house! Where is the hussey that brought it?"

"That's just what I wish I knew."

"Wait till I see her!" continued Mrs. Samkin, clenching her fists, grating her teeth, and shaking her head from one side to the other viciously; "I'll baby her! I'll teach her how to bring disgrace on respectable people!"

"What do you mean?"

"What I say."

"But——"

"Don't talk to me. Look at the child, and be ashamed of your wicked self! It's awful, Samkin; and where you expect to go to when you die is more than I can tell. Heaven wont have you!"

"Listen to me."

"I wont!" cried Mrs. Samkin, with a stamp of the foot.

"But you must."

"I tell you I wont! Where's the hussey?"

"Gone."

"I know that; but where does she live?"

"How should I know?"

"Don't tell me you are ignorant. Oh, Samkin! I have felt for months past you didn't love me as you used to. There was none of your old tenderness about you—no 'my dears,' and 'my loves'—and never a kiss in the dark, or when going upstairs."

Mr. Samkin got in a furious rage—he foamed at the mouth, and cried—

"Do you want to drive me frantic, missis? It ain't no child of mine!"

"Whose then?"

"That's it! That's where it is!"

"Explain yourself."

"I will."

Mrs. Samkin sank into a chair, and putting her pocket-handkerchief to her eyes, prepared to listen to her degenerate husband's explanation.

"I was a standing in the bar."

"Well!"

"A decent, almost stylish sort of a feemayle comes in, and she says, showing a half-sovereign, 'A bottle of champagne, if you please, and mind it is of your best.'"

"Yes."

"I had gone after the lush, and while I was gone, I'm blowed if she didn't step it—leaving of the poor hinfant on the counter."

"You ain't telling of me no lies, Samkin?"

"It's gospel—if it ain't I wish I may drop down dead, and be buried by the parish."

"It beats me," murmured Mrs. Samkin.

"And me too; all into fits. But I say——"

"What?"

"Just cast your eyes over here."

"Where?"

"On the counter. What's that?"

"A purse."

"Look at it."

Mrs. Samkin got up, went to the counter, and took up the purse, which she emptied into her lap.

"Oh, my!" she cried; "it's gold."

"How much?"

They both eagerly counted the glittering pieces.

"Twenty, thirty, forty, fifty pounds," said Samkin. "Bless me! what a mint o' money."

"Samkin, forgive me," said his wife.

"What for?"

"I've wronged you."

"Oh, it don't matter."

"Kiss and be friends. We'll keep the poor child, and perhaps we may be rewarded for it some day."

"P'raps," said Samkin, dubiously.

"There is no writing about him, is there?"

"Not a scrap."

"What shall we call him?" asked Mrs. Samkin.

"He's marked well."

"Where?"

"Got three moles on his forehead over the right eyebrow."

"So he has."

"I say."

"What?"

"I've got it."

"Got what?"

"Why a name for him," said Mr. Samkin.

"You have?"

"Yes."

"Let's have it."

"He's got money, and he's got marks; let's call him Money Marks."

"So we will. Samkin, you's a genus," replied his wife. And that was how the child became Money Marks.

He was duly christened and brought up by the Samkins', who heard nothing about his parentage from anybody.

They gave him the rudiments of a plain education, teaching him to read and write and cipher, and, when he was old enough, made what use they could of him, thinking they were justified in so doing.

At first he ran errands and did what he could.

When he got older, he was made potboy, afterwards barman, and, in a word, he made himself generally useful.

He was a fine high-spirited fellow, and a favourite with everybody. He was curious about his mother and father, and often said he would find them out, though how he intended to do so was a mystery which neither himself nor those about him could solve.

Money Marks rather liked Bob Cannon—he had frequently befriended him—for Bob was a generous fellow, though quarrelsome when in his cups.

"Rum, here!" cried Bob Cannon; "I can't stomach your table-beer."

In order to give force to his words, he took up a pewter pot, hurled it violently against the wall, and made it as flat as a pancake.

"Ha, ha!" he laughed; "that's the way to do it—that's the way, my merry lads all—that's how I used to poise and throw the harpoon when I went to the North Pole with Sir Charles McClintock, a searching after poor Johnny Franklin."

The landlord of the house did not like quite so much uproar, as the police had been paying him overmuch delicate attention lately, and he went upstairs to remonstrate with noisy Bob.

"Mr. Cannon!" he exclaimed.

"What cheer, my hearty?"

"You are making a very considerable tumult—excuse me for using strong language, but the noise is dreadful."

"Noise!" echoed Bob Cannon. "Haw, haw! Out of the way, ye land-lubber. Bob Cannon was born at sea, and when he's ashore his sea legs aint of no use to him—he flounders about like a lobster or a porpoise. I'm a plain-spoken fellow, and no sea-gull to steady myself by my wings."

"I really must——" began Mr. Samkin.

"No you mustn't. I run what rig I like when I'm on *terror former*."

An old salt who was sitting in the corner got up and said—

"Belay, belay, Bob."

"Not I," replied Bob.

"Mr. Cannon," said the landlord, persuasively.

"Your honour."

"Pray be a little quiet."

"He's only a fresh-water sailor," exclaimed Money Marks, with a laugh.

"Eh! what's that, my little counter-jumper?" cried Bob.

"A fresh-water sailor."

"Fresh-water! not a bit of it. Yo, ho! there—yo, ho! Tauten reef tackles, haul out your weather earing; after-points taut. Yo, ho! reef away, yo, ho! my lads, yo, ho! steady there, yo, ho!"

"Give us a song, Bob," cried somebody.

"Yes, yes, a song."

"He'll sing us all deaf and silly," remarked another.

"Sing! I'll sing to you. I can sing so as to make all the whales in the sea listen to me," replied Bob Cannon. "Belay there; pipe all hands."

"Ay, ay, sir," replied the old salt in the corner, getting up and demanding silence.

Bob cleared his throat, and began—

"Aboard of a British ship I'll sail
　Where gallant hearts abide;
With my love to cruise through the stormy gale,
　And over the swelling tide."

Here he gave a lurch and fell over a table, carrying everything to the ground; pipes, glasses, pots and bottles tumbling on the floor in the midst of the havoc.

"Oh Lord! oh Lord!" cried the landlord, wringing his hands. "Here's a disaster; sure I'm the most unlucky devil that ever lived."

"My eyes," cried the old salt, "only listen how he pipes; there's jawing tackle for you."

Money Marks rushed forward to help the inebriated seaman up, but Bob wouldn't allow that he was drunk.

"Avast there—avast," he said.

"I want to bear a hand."

"Ah, my boy, you should be a sailor; it's a glorious life," said Bob Cannon, with drunken gravity.

"I wasn't brought up to the sea."

"What matter."

"Come. get up."

"I'm all right; avast, avast. I'd teach you how to knot a reef point and pass a gasket. I've seen chaps who couldn't take two hatches when they came aboard expert in less than a month. The only difficulty is the weather; there the landlubbers get licked. It takes a lifetime to larn the weather."

"Come, Bob, get up; you can't lie here all night."

"I'm going to sleep."

"Shall I bring you your nightcap?"

"I don't want no land-lubbering rubbish."

"Pull him into a corner," said the landlord. "Take hold of him by his heels. He'll be better after an hour's sleep."

Money Marks took hold of the blunt but honest tar, and dragged him with some difficulty into a corner, where he was soon sleeping soundly and snoring heavily.

Mr. Samkin made a sign to the musicians, who struck up a lively air.

Then he beckoned to Money Marks, who came to his side and said—

"What is it, sir?"

"Has he much money in his pocket?"

"A few pounds."

"Oh, very well; just see that none of the girls get hold of him until this breakage is paid for."

"Right, sir; I'll see to it," replied Money Marks, with a sagacious shake of the head.

At twelve o'clock the lights were put out and the company departed. Bob Cannon, the jovial sailor, alone remained in a state of drunken stupor. It was not at all an unusual thing for drunken men to sleep on the floor of the long room.

If it was possible to move them they were moved, but sometimes they were so helplessly drunk that it was out of the question to think of doing so.

Very often the ladies to whom the sailors when on shore attached themselves might be seen carrying their admirers off to their lodgings, so that they might not fall into the hands of other spoilers.

The police were used to the spectacle of drunken sailors on wheelbarrows going through the streets late at night.

One constable, in the Exhibition year, saw no less than twelve pass him on his beat; and the only reply to his question, "Who goes there?" was, "Common sailor drunk on a wheelbarrow."

Occasionally the fiddler would get intoxicated and sleep on one of the tables in the long room, but Bob Cannon was alone in his glory. At half-past twelve, Money Marks put the lights out, and left Bob Cannon by himself in the long room of the "Pint of Porter."

CHAPTER II.

THE GHOST ON TOWER HILL.

THE night was dark, and the wind moaned in that peculiar fashion which denotes a storm.

The sky was lowering, and occasionally a bright vivid gleam shot athwart it. So bright, so vivid, as to be almost blinding.

Then there was a rumbling as of distant thunder. Assuredly the elements were convulsed at some distance from London, and there was every chance of the storm spreading and reaching the metropolis.

Bob Cannon slept till two o'clock.

Then the fumes of the liquor he had imbibed wore off.

He woke up and looked around him; all was dark, pitchy dark.

"Black as h——," he muttered between his teeth.

The noise of the whistling wind broke upon his ear, and he added, "like enough to be a dirty night."

Rising to his feet he groped his way to the door. Nothing annoyed him so much as darkness; he didn't care about it so very much if he were not alone in it, but to be alone in the dark was more than honest old Bob Cannon could bear.

He came in contact with a table.

There was a crash and a fall, the noise of which aroused Mr. Samkin, who had just fallen into his first sleep.

"What on earth's that?" said Mrs. Samkin, who awoke at the same time.

"That drunken sailor, I suppose. Who else do you think it is?"

"Well, I'm sure, Samkin, you needn't snap me up like that, as if I were a brute beast, and of no account whatever."

"My dear."

"I'm not your dear."

"Well, then, you are not; anyhow hold your noise, I'm not in the humour for it. We shall have no sleep if this sort of game's to continue all night," said Mr. Samkin, surlily.

"Call Marks, then."

"All right!" said the landlord.

"Marks!" he shouted.

Money was fast asleep, and the summons had to be repeated, before the loud voice of his master roused him. Hastily striking a light, he as hastily donned his clothes, and ascended the stairs to his master's bed-room.

He did not go in but stood outside the door.

"What is it, sir?"

"Can't you come in?"

"The missis, sir," said Money, hesitatingly.

"Oh, hang that! the missis wont look at you."

"It isn't that, sir; I might look at the missis."

"It wont kill her you if you do. Come in."

Money Marks thus adjured, entered the bed-room. Mrs. Samkin immediately dived under the bed-clothes, like a frightened beaver under the water.

"There's that sailor fellow loose again," said Mr. Samkin.

"Loose, sir?"

"Yes."

"I thought he had taken rum enough to floor him for a fortnight."

"Never mind what you thought, my good fellow, the fact is as I state it to you."

"What shall I do?"

"Oh! go and quiet him."

"Get him out of the house?"

"If you can."

"Very well, but——"

"But what?"

"There's the damage."

"Ah! so there is; he must pay for that."

"How much?"

"Say thirty shillings."

"I'll get it, sir," said Money Marks.

"Very well, off you go. Don't let me be disturbed anymore, if I am I shan't sleep all night."

Money Marks nodded his head, and went on his errand; when he reached the dancing-room he shaded the candle with his hand, and saw Bob Cannon sitting up with a rueful expression of countenance.

"What cheer, mate?" exclaimed the sailor.

"I've come to look after you. The governor says he can't have this infernal row in the middle of the night."

"What row?"

"The row you've been kicking up."

"Oh! I'm the lad for a bit of a bobbery, as the old song says," sung Bob Cannon.

"What's the matter with you?"

"Why just this, I found myself in the dark, and I can't stand it. I've tumbled over a table, and barked my shins. I want to get out of the place and go home."

"Where?"

"Rotherhithe."

"Is that where you lodge?"

"Yes."

"Well, you can go as soon as you like, if——"

"If what?"

"You pay for the damage."

"What damage?"

"The damage you did when you fell over the table."

"Oh! shiver my timbers, I forgot all about that."

"You ought to say smash my iron plates in these days."

"What's the shot?"

"Thirty shillings."

"You're like the rest of the land-sharks; here's the money, take it."

"The petticoats are your ruin, Bob," said Money Marks with a shrewd smile.

"And so they are of all of us before we die. But come, bear a hand. Let's get out of this. Do you want to earn half-a-crown?"

"It 'll be welcome if it comes."

"Come it shall, then; if so be as you're willing."

"Explain yourself."

"Why look'ee here, my lad, I've sprung a leak, and feel three sheets in the wind. I'm that bad, I can't get home by myself. If you will give me a prop up as far as the Sailors' Home I'll say thank'ee, for I don't want to be picked up to-night by any of the flash molls, who are always prowling about after Jack when he has had a drop too much."

"Oh, I see what you mean, but I say——"

"What?"

"It's so late, and I'm dead beat."

"Are you so?"

"Yes, as tired as a dog."

"Never mind, you'll lend a friend a helping hand. I wont stop here—I can't; and if I go by myself, mate, it'll be a case for me, for I shall lose all my money. I'd better turn my pockets out, make a clean sweep, and give all I have to you."

"Well, give me your money," said Marks; "I'll take care of it for you, if you are afraid of losing it, and make it up to you in the morning to the uttermost farthing."

"I'd do that with pleasure, my lad," replied the sailor, "becos' I know you, and I'd swear against anybody that you'd do what's right with me, but it's this way. I've lost my centre of gravity. I'm not what I used to be—that is, what I was afore I came ashore for my spree, and got on the drink."

"Well, I suppose I must see you home? That's what comes of being good-natured."

"They all say you're a good sort."

"Yes, and take care to prove it. Wait here while I go and get my coat and hat. I'll be with you directly, and then I'm your man—d'ye hear?"

"I hear right enough, my boy. Off you go, and God bless you for your kindness to a poor drunken sailor!"

Money Marks went away to don his habiliments, presently returning fully equipped. Bob Cannon descended the stairs, and reached the street by Money Marks' assistance.

Ratcliff Highway was asleep, and the street presented a deserted appearance. A solitary policeman was to be descried making his midnight round, and looking as miserable as a midnight policeman can look.

The clouds, heavy, dark, and funereal, were collecting together, and looking more sombre every minute.

Occasionally a big drop of rain plashed upon the pavement, and heralded the storm which was about to commence.

"If we go by the Tower," said Money Marks, "as like as not we shall see the ghost."

"Ghost!" echoed Bob Cannon, in astonishment.

"Yes."

"What ghost?"

"I don't know whose ghost it is—probably that of some nobleman whose head was cut off on Tower Hill some hundreds of years ago."

"But, I say, is there really a ghost?" exclaimed Bob Cannon, clinging rather nervously to his companion's arm.

"So goes the report. I will not vouch for the truth of it."

"Let's go round by the Tower, and take—yes, take a peep at the ghost."

"If you like—I'm game," replied Money Marks. "Now I am out I don't care much what I do. It may be all an invention about the ghost, but I've heard tell of it from lots of people. I'm surprised you haven't heard."

"Not a word, my lad."

They passed a lamp-post, and Money Marks noticed that the sailor looked very pale. He could hardly believe that he was frightened, and yet it would appear so. He determined to ask him.

"Are you afraid?" he said.

"I can't say I'm not a little bit afraid, my lad," rejoined Bob Cannon. "You see it's this way with me. I once saw a ghost—or something like one—but it wasn't the ghost of a man, nor yet the ghost of an animal."

"What was it then?"

"Why, it was the ghost of a ship!"

"A ship?"

"Yes," replied Bob Cannon, solemnly.

"You don't mean to tell me that you believe in that nonsense?" said Money Marks, derisively. "I thought all that was exploded. You must have seen some mist."

"It wasn't mist either."

"Then it was nonsense."

"Not all nonsense."

"The *Flying Dutchman* I suppose you mean?"

"That's it, my lad. That's just what we did see. It was Vanderdecken, and no mistake. If I tell a lie, I wish I may sink, and go to Davy Jones's locker the next voyage I take!"

The sailor spoke emphatically, as if he had perfect faith and confidence in what he said. Money Marks, however, was not convinced. He went to Tower Hill more to test the truth of the rumour than anything else, and, if possible, to expose an imposition. Everybody knows that Tower Hill is a large open space, like a square, without trees or shrubs. On the right, as you come from Lower Thames Street, is the Tower of London, an irregular pile of buildings protected by cannon and a moat, which is of great depth but quite dry. It has had no water in it for many years, though some people say a moat full of water would improve the appearance of the Tower wonderfully.

As they debouched upon the hill, the storm which had been threatening so long burst in all its fury. The lightning flashed; the thunder crashed loud enough to awaken the dead; and the rain descended in torrents.

"This is remarkably pleasant," said Money Marks, shrugging his shoulders—"more especially as I have left my umbrella at home."

"Does the water hurt thee, lad?" inquired Bob Cannon.

"I don't know that it hurts me, but it wets me through; and I don't care about having rheumatic fever."

"I should think not. If you went to sea, you would soon get hardened—and no wet would injure you."

"I have sometimes thought I should like to go to sea," replied Money Marks, musingly.

"Say you so?"

"Yes. Am I not too old?"

"A man is never too old for a fine profession. Make a voyage to the China Seas, my lad, and see a little of the world. That's your game, that's what you ought to do, and if you don't like it stop at Shanghai, where there are plenty of English, and settle down as a clerk."

"Your advice sounds well."

"Ay, and believe me it's good."

"I'll think it over."

"Do so, boy."

"I don't see the ghost," said Money Marks, abruptly turning the subject.

"Nor I."

"Perhaps it is afraid to come out in such dreadful weather!"

"Not it. If it be a ghost it will come, rain or shine. The phantom-ship can ride out any storm that ever was heard of. I have seen her trying to round the Cape when it was blowing so heavens hard, that we had to go before the blast with bare poles, and trust to its mercy."

"That was agreeable."

"It was so agreeable that I don't care if I never do it again, my lad," replied Bob Cannon, shaking his head with solemnity.

"Let us stand here, in the open space," said Money Marks, "and give the poor devil of a ghost a chance. If it comes out to-night, we are safe to see it here."

"We have nothing to fear together."

"No, I never heard of a ghost doing one any harm."

"If it be so disposed, I can fight, and you're no lob-lolly boy."

"Not I. I can handle my mawleys with any of them. Why else have I lived all my life in Ratcliff Highway? It does rain confounded hard though."

"That it does; but we're not sugar."

"Nor yet salt."

"If I am not, it isn't the fault of the sea," replied Bob Cannon, with a loud laugh.

"Hush!" suddenly cried Money Marks.

"What is it?" nervously exclaimed the sailor.

"There! there! do you not see it?—the ghost!" replied Money Marks, in tones which trembled not a little.

"No; where?"

The sailor, strong man though he was, trembled excessively, and clung to his companion's arm for support. Although naval men are brave, they are for the most part superstitious. They are at the mercy of the wind and the waves, and never know when some catastrophe may overtake them. They lead a solitary and an isolated life, which inclines them to be mistrustful and credulous. They will believe in anything mystical and which cannot easily be explained.

Bob Cannon fully believed that a ghost was near them, and for that matter so did Money Marks.

The latter, however, had too much good sense to take any thing for granted; he wished to prove actually, and beyond the power of contradiction, that such things as ghosts existed before he placed implicit credence in them.

Pointing straight before him, and in the direction of the gateway leading into the Tower, near the lodge in which the visitor waits the arrival of the gaily decked beefeater or warder.

Bob Cannon followed his young friend's gesture, and saw a tall figure dressed entirely in white.

It moved slowly.

Its eyes resembled glowing coals, at least so it appeared to the inflamed imaginations of the beholders.

When it got opposite the two men it stopped and beckoned to them with its right hand.

Bob Cannon groaned in an agony of terror, his knees knocked together, and he was the picture of abject fear.

"What, man, turning woman?" whispered Money Marks; "wake up."

"I can't. My God, it's a ghost! I—I say, let's go; Lord, wasn't I a fool to come."

The rain still descended in torrents, and the thunder and lightning prevailed at intervals. The light from the gas-lamps which fringed Tower Hill rendered the figure of the apparition visible, though it was much more indistinct and much fainter than it would have been had the stars appeared in the heavens, or had the moon shown her bright though pallid countenance.

Money Marks did not participate in his friend's fear.

He was alarmed and puzzled, but that was all.

"If it is a ghost," he said, "it is a remarkably plucky one, and as it evidences a desire to make our acquaintance, I vote we gratify it; what do you say?"

"Say," cried Bob Cannon, "that you must be mad."

"Mad?"

"Yes, to think of such a thing."

"It can't hurt us."

"We don't know that."

"I shouldn't like to try."

"You a British seaman, and afraid of a shadow?"

"It is more than that."

"How do you know? have you felt it—spoken to it?"

"No."

"Then you are not in a position to form an opinion upon its nature and composition," returned Money Marks. "What I propose, is simply this—the ghost beckons us, let us follow it at a respectful distance, keep it in sight, and find out where it leads us."

"I'd rather go home. I'm not afraid of any *man* living, but when it comes to *spirits*, why I strike my colours without firing a gun," replied Bob Cannon.

"You shall not do so this time at all events," cried Money Marks; "I have made up my mind to follow that figure, and follow it I will."

"Are you in earnest?"

"Rather! Such being my determination, you can't desert a pal and call yourself a man, can you?"

"If you go," said the sailor, "I must go with you, my lad, though I swear by the piper that played before Moses, that I would rather be tied up and receive six dozen laid well on by the bo'san—I would, so help me bob."

The ghost had continued to make its signals, waiting patiently for a response, and when the men began to move forward, it pursued the even tenour of its way, walking rather more quickly, however, than it had previously done.

It skirted the railings which protect passengers from falling into the moat, and reached that part which, like the slopes at Windsor, is well laid out, beautifully wooded, and intersected by neatly gravelled walks.

It stopped at a gate.

This gate was always kept locked; it had been constructed for the convenience of the governor of the Tower.

The ghost experienced no difficulty in passing through this gate, which opened as if by magic.

At the entrance to the garden in the moat, Bob Cannon hung back.

"Come along; who's afraid?" exclaimed Money Marks, who was becoming blithe under the influence of excitement.

"I'd rather not."

"What's the matter now?"

"It's going into the Tower."

"What of that?"

"I've heard speak of the Spirit of the Bloody Tower; p'raps it's that."

"And perhaps it isn't—any how, we'll find out. Come on, old heart of oak."

"I believe I was born in cucumber month, for I'm watery-headed to-night," replied the sailor.

Money Marks pulled him by main force to the gate, and having passed through they halted.

The top of a flight of steps was to be seen dimly, but everything beyond was dark and dismal, so much so indeed that the form of the ghost became invisible.

They appeared to be on the brink of Tartarus, so Cimmerian was the darkness.

All at once a light appeared half-way down the steps; it seemed to be emitted from a lantern, and sufficed to show the pursuers the way.

"Hang me!" said Money Marks, "if it isn't the most polite ghost I ever heard of."

Bob Cannon seemed to have given himself into his companion's hands unreservedly.

They descended the steps together, and the ghost led the way with unerring precision.

CHAPTER III.

IN A TRAP.

THE ghost entered the garden and traversed one of the gravelled paths. Suddenly turning to the right at a sharp angle, it walked into a thicket of laurel trees and privet.

Through the leaves Money Marks saw the bull's-eye of the lantern glimmering.

The sailor hung back.

"It is a device to destroy us," he said.

"Not it," replied Money Marks. "There is something mysterious about that shadowy being, and unravel the mystery I will."

"Nay, then——"

"Not a word. Follow me."

So saying, the courageous young man plunged into the thicket, with a determination to solve the problem or perish in the attempt.

Bob Cannon would not be thought a coward, and he followed him, though his old trembling recurred and made him feel very uncomfortable.

The branches of the shrubs and small trees yielded before the pressure which was put upon them, and the two men found themselves in an open space, in the middle of which a trap-door was raised.

The ghost stood upon the topmost steps of a ladder, and beckoned to Money Marks to descend.

"That's a nice sort of a Jacob's ladder, anyhow," said Bob Cannon; "I should think the ghost had been brought up at sea. You must mind how you descend, or you may knock your daylights in."

"Never fear," replied Money Marks, who was all impatience to solve the mystery.

The sailor would not go first; he allowed Marks to do that. He was afraid of some delicate attention on the part of the ghost.

Up to the present time that latter personage had been inoffensive enough, but would he remain so, that was the question.

The ladder was short; it did not consist of more than five-and-twenty steps.

Having arrived at the end of it, a flight of stone steps was revealed, down which the party went. Money Marks exhibited a courageous disposition and a blind faith in the good intentions of the ghost, which was highly creditable to his young, innocent, and unsophisticated nature.

At the end of the flight of steps was a passage which was evidently under the moat, and which clearly led into some vaults or excavations below the basement of the fortifications.

Perhaps the trap-door in the thicket was a secret entrance to some hidden dungeons, the mystery of which was not generally known. It was undoubtedly the custom of the governors of prisons in the Middle Ages to confine their prisoners in the most loathsome places, therefore these vaults beneath the Tower of London were, in all probability, the relics of barbarism.

The passage was of great length, and devious and winding. The moisture hung upon the walls in beads, and falling on the floor formed into little puddles in which the foot sometimes sank over the ankle.

Frogs hopped about in little droves and occasionally a shrill croak denoted that the foot of the invader of these time-honoured domains had trodden upon one of the crawling or jumping reptiles.

There were doors in the walls which spoke of dungeons, and Money Marks shuddered as he saw them.

Without giving the least warning of its intention, the ghost stood still in the centre of a large apartment, the dimensions of which Money Marks could only guess at.

It stamped its foot upon the pavement three times in a violent manner.

A door slammed violently behind Marks and the sailor.

Money Marks gnashed his teeth with rage—he saw he had been duped.

The ghost threw off its white covering and a strong stalwart man was revealed, who, bursting into a hoarse laugh, exclaimed—

"Ha, ha! my fine fellows; how do you feel after your ghost-hunt, eh? I flatter myself I've taken the wind out of your sails pretty neatly."

"Scoundrel!" hissed Money Marks between his teeth.

"Well, blow me!" exclaimed Bob Cannon. "Blow me tight!"

Marks could only think that he had been entrapped into the hideous and dismal-looking vaults beneath the Tower of London for some foul purpose; probably the rascal who had so cleverly deluded them was desirous of robbing them of whatever they had about them—ready money, watches, and so forth, afterwards intending to cast their bodies headlong into a sewer, where they would rot or be devoured by rats.

Truly they were in an agreeable situation!

Money Marks thought it was just possible that he could effect a retreat by the way he had entered, but he was grievously deceived.

Turning round abruptly, he found himself face to face with a gigantic negro, who was standing sentry over the door he had just closed.

"Stand on one side," cried Money Marks.

The negro shook his wool-covered head, and opening his mouth grinned a ghastly grin.

"It's no good your kicking against the pricks, my fine fellows," cried the fellow who had acted the part of the ghost; "you are in for it, and you may as well submit quietly."

"In for what?" inquired Money Marks.

"That you will know all about when the proper time comes; at present you are my prisoners."

"Prisoners!"

"Yes."

"How is that?"

"Can't you see?"

"Would you rob us?"

"Oh, no; I don't care particularly about robbing you, but I shall treat you so well while you stay with me that I have no doubt you will gladly make me a present of whatever you may have about you."

"This is infamous!" cried Money Marks, in a rage.

"So I have been told before," replied the ghost.

"I will take care to punish you when I get out."

"When you do; but you must recollect that at present you are boxed up."

"Confusion!"

"What's the meaning of all this 'ere rumpus, messmate?" cried Bob Cannon.

"That's what I want to know," replied the man who had captured him.

"Who are you?"

"A ghost, I suppose."

"Avast! I don't want none of your jokes."

"Well, you took me for a ghost, anyhow."

"Yes, that's right enough."

"What's my name—I suppose you want to know?"

"That's about the size of it."

"Well, I'm Charleston Jack, the Fire-eater."

"Secesh?"

"To my backbone."

"How came you here?" demanded Money Marks.

"That's another thing; you want to know too much."

"You wont say?"

"Perhaps I'll enlighten you to-morrow."

"Are we to sleep here?"

"To be sure."

"In this place?"

"That depends upon how you behave yourself. If you're saucy you may have the floor to lie upon, but if you're civil and take things easy as they come, I'll toss you a bundle of straw and perhaps give you a drop of liquor to keep the cold out," replied Charleston Jack.

Money Marks said no more; he thought that any discussion before the morning would be worse than useless, and he affected to fall into the humours of his capturer, whom he began to think was a Confederate agent in England for the purpose of enlisting, or otherwise capturing, recruits for the navy of the Southern States.

Charleston Jack gave each of his prisoners a glass of raw rum and a truss of straw to sleep on. Then he left them for the night, telling them to be good boys and to mind and say their prayers.

"Here's a pretty go, I don't think," cried Bob Cannon, when they were left alone in the dark together.

"We've been done," replied Money Marks, dolefully.

"What's the little game, think you?"

"Oh, we're in for something as safe as houses, though what that something is I can't quite make out at this moment. We're not to be murdered, that's certain, nor yet robbed, though the latter would make little difference to me as I have nothing to be robbed of. You have a few pounds though."

"Yes, I'll hide that away in my boot."

Bob Cannon stowed his gold away as he said, and declared he felt more at his ease now that he knew the plundering villains would have some difficulty in discovering his hoard.

"You know the old song?" said Money Marks.

"What old song?"

"The nigger melody."

"What's the use of asking, when there's such lots of em?"

"Why this one—'I'm off to Charleston with my banjo on my knee.'"

"Yes."

"Well, I'm blessed if I don't think that's the fakement we're in for."

"Off to Charleston?"

"That's it."

"Why, the port's blockaded," said Bob Cannon.

"I know it is, but there is such a thing as blockade running, isn't there?" replied Money Marks.

"Ah! I take you now. I see."

"Well, listen to me, and I will explain it to you altogether. The trade of blockade running is so tarnation risky, that though they offer immense sums as bounties, the sailors wont go, and there are lots of things that must be smuggled into the States, so the running the blockade must go on. Well, the agents kidnap men as we've been kidnapped, and we shall have to go in a day or two to Old Virginny."

"I don't care as long as it's on the sea. What matter what flag you sail under?" exclaimed Bob Cannon.

"I don't care so much as I thought I should at first," murmured Money Marks. "I have long been tired of the miserably quiet life I lived in the Highway. It was simply chronicling small beer with a vengeance. My soul has always panted for action, and if my surmises are correct, we shall have action enough and to spare."

"So you wont mind a life on the sea, my lad," cried Bob Cannon.

"I have always loved the sea from my very childhood," said Money Marks, with kindling enthusiasm; "there is an inexpressible charm about the ocean which has always captivated my imaginative mind. Perhaps being amongst sailors so much as I have may have contributed to this result."

"Possibly it may," said Bob Cannon, who added, "so you think we are in for a cruise together?"

"I feel sure of it."

"Isn't it kidnapping British subjects?"

"Of course it is; but the rogues are so clever that we shall never have an opportunity of telling our grievances."

"Not say good-bye to our friends?"

"Not a bit of it."

"That's a pity; there's Sall Lomax of the Marsh-gate who'll cry her poor little eyes out about me till she picks up somebody else. I promised her whatever loose cash I might have about me, and she'll miss it."

"More than she will you, perhaps," said Money Marks, with a sly smile.

"Ha, ha! like enough, my lad—like enough," replied Bob Cannon, goodnaturedly; "but an old sailor like myself, who has been married in nearly every part of the globe, must not be hard on the women. Lord love 'em, what should us poor mortals do without them?"

"Well I shall see if I can't get forty winks," cried Money Marks; "we shall have our work cut out for us in the morning, I'll be bound."

"Say you so? Then I'll e'en follow your example," said Bob Cannon.

Turning over, the two men nestled into the trusses of straw as well as they could, and soon fell into a sound slumber. In the meantime Charleston Jack was engaged in an important conversation, which the reader must be initiated in.

CHAPTER IV.

THE SWAMP SNAKE.

ONE of the vaults or dungeons some little distance from the particular one in which Money Marks and his companions were calmly sleeping away the weary hours of their confinement, had been fitted up as a sitting-room by Charleston Jack and his friends, who on this evening of thunder, rain, and lightning, were four in number.

All were fierce, indomitable-looking men; fine fellows, strongly made and well put together, handsome and honest as to their faces; muscular to a degree, and having highly intellectual foreheads.

Charleston Jack was sitting at the head of a deal table, upon which stood glasses, bottles, and some cold meat. Some candles were burning in common brass sticks, and shed a sickly glare around the room, for, as a matter of course, everyone was smoking.

"Well, captain," exclaimed Charleston Jack, "I think we've about got our complement."

"You think we have," replied Johnston Arlee, who was captain of a steam-vessel, at that moment lying off the Tower, supposed to be a vessel devoted to the merchant service, and intended to ply between London and Cadiz.

This vessel, however, was soon destined to become famous as the *Swamp Snake*. Its armament was waiting for it at Calais, and consisted of one pivot gun, to be placed on the forecastle, and four broadside guns, constructed on the Armstrong principle.

"'Od snakes," continued Charleston Jack; "how our chaps will laugh at the ghost dodge. It's one way of getting men, captain, but I'll go bail they're as fine a set of men as ever trod a deck."

"That they are. We shall make something of them in time."

"In time," said Charleston Jack, indignantly: "why they're all ready made to you—hard old salts, every man Jack of them."

"Are they so?"

"See them and judge for yourself."

"I will in the morning," replied Captain Arlee. "Are they at all mutinous, or do they resign themselves to their lot?"

"They all take it easy, and make no objection to sign the articles of enlistment."

"That's good."

"I know how to manage sailors, I give them plenty of rum and plenty of 'bacca, and such 'bacca, too, as they are not usually in the habit of getting—real honeydew and of the best quality. I have laughed to see some of the old stagers wink as they chewed it."

"Get them all ready," said Captain Arlee, "to sail in four-and-twenty hours. Let all be embarked to-morrow night; take them through the vaults to the flight of steps opening into the river, then put them into boats and row to the *Snake*. Do you fully understand?"

Charleston Jack replied in the affirmative, and the party soon after separated.

Captain Arlee had been a gentleman planter in Western Virginia before the war in the United States broke out, but he sacrificed everything, for what he thought the patriotic cause, and selling his property, equipped a vessel for the express purpose of running the blockade, and bearing aid to his distressed countrymen.

The other men were his lieutenants and officers, all men of family and possessions, with the exception of Charleston Jack the Fire-eater, who was a younger son of a good stock, but had nothing except his daring to recommend him; this, however, was more than sufficient.

Captain Arlee did not wish to have his ship detained for a breach of the Foreign Enlistment Act, and he did not enlist men openly, he preferred to trick and deceive them in the first instance, and enlist their sympathies afterwards as well as themselves.

Charleston Jack had on a former occasion been in London, and had during his stay in the capital of the world, made the acquaintance of an officer quartered in the Tower of London.

This gentleman had asked him to dine at the Tower.

It was summer.

After dinner Charleston Jack took a stroll by himself in the garden in the moat, and by the purest accident discovered the trap-door, the flight of stone steps, and the vast series of subterranean chambers which he afterwards turned to such good account.

Like a sensible man, he told no one of his discovery; intending to make use of it at some future day.

The time arrived, when it was of the utmost use to him and his compatriots. His fertile brain suggested the ghost scheme, which answered so well that in less than a fortnight he entrapped no less than a hundred men, all of whom willingly agreed, after their first burst of chagrin was over, to join the Confederate cause, and fight beneath the stars and bars, which are symbolical of the flag of that country.

The next day Charleston Jack sought Bob Cannon and Money Marks at an early hour, and accosted them with these words—

"Morning, my men. No harm is intended you. I have merely come to talk to you on matters of business. You have nothing to be alarmed at. Will you hear me now or have your breakfast first?"

"Well, sir," replied Bob Cannon, "if it's all the same to you, I shouldn't object to a little matter of breakfast, but of course, you will please yourself."

"Cuffy!" cried Charleston Jack.

"Comin', massa," replied the gigantic negro, who had astonished Money Marks the night before.

"Bring something to eat; some herrings and coffee, a haddock, or whatever you've got."

Cuffy was the cook; he cooked over a charcoal fire, which emitted no smoke, and had a vault all to himself. The coffee was ready in a very short space of time, and he returned with a plate of haddocks done to a turn.

The men eat ravenously and thought that they were being very well treated.

"Are you satisfied, my men?" exclaimed Charleston Jack.

"Yes, very much so," replied Money Marks. "Now tell us what you intend doing."

"Just what I was coming to. Listen to me. I am an agent of the Confederate States of America, and an officer holding a commission in the navy. We want sailors, and we have used stratagem and cunning to get them; if you will join us willingly, you shall be well paid, we will give you twelve pounds a month and a fair share of prize money, should we come across a merchantman richly laden, and worth the trouble of overhauling.

"You promise that?"

"Most faithfully."

"When do we sail?"

"At once."

"What's the vessel's name?"

"The *Swamp Snake*."

"Where is she lying?"

"In the Pool."

"Is she a man-of-war?"

"No; but she will be armed."

"What is her complement?"

"A hundred and ten men."

"All told?"

"Yes, all told."

"Have you the required number?"

"With yourselves we have."

"Shall we be engaged with the enemy?"

"In all likelihood you will. Come my men, give me your answer; will you go?"

"Here's my hand on it, messmate," cried Bob Cannon; "and I don't think our young game-cock here will hold out."

"You agree?"

"We do."

Bob Cannon and Money Marks spoke at the same moment.

"That is well."

"What are we to do now?"

"You had better join your companions in arms who are jollifying in a huge vault, some little distance off."

"How did you find out these catacombs?"

"Ah! that is another thing altogether. I don't open my mouth to fill other people's. Follow me."

They followed Charleston Jack, who conducted them along a winding passage, to a spacious hall in which the crew of the *Swamp Snake* were grouped. Part of their pay had been advanced them, and cards liberally distributed. Rum and tobacco were plentiful, and drinking, gambling, and smoking went on all day long.

Two Confederate officers were on guard at all hours, with loaded pistols, to prevent an outbreak, or a dangerous quarrel.

Bob Cannon soon made himself at home, he discovered amongst the prisoners one or two friends of his own, men whom he had sailed with in former times, and the party soon became rumoured that the crew were to go on board the next day, and much rejoicing thereat ensued.

A sailor always thinks it legitimate to get drunk before he sails; and Charleston Jack had a great deal of trouble to prevent all his men lying on their backs and becoming incapable.

One tall man made himself especially obnoxious to everybody, he was prodigiously powerful, and fully capable, in his own opinion, of coercing at least four ordinary men.

He was known by the name of Bully Bolivar.

Bully Bolivar was a man who thought he could carry everything by storm. He imagined that he only had to bluster to conquer, and he took care never to lose an opportunity of hearing himself speak.

He always made a point of attacking new comers, and he went up to Bob Cannon and Money Marks, and said, in a rough coarse tone of voice—

"What cheer, my hearties?—what cheer?"

"Oh, pretty tidy!" replied Money Marks; "we're none so flourishing. How's yourself?"

"First chop—as usual. How long have you been to sea?"

"Never saw salt water yet."

"A green hand!"

"Yes."

"You must pay your footing, then, amongst old salts."

"What do you mean?"

"You give me a sovereign, and you'll see."

"I've got no money."

"No money!"

"Not a halfpenny."

"Oh, that wont do! I want some cash; and if you don't part, I'll knock you down and jump on you."

"Will you?" said Money Marks, whose nether lip quivered a little with nervous emotion.

"Will I?—yes, as soon as look at you."

Money Marks allowed his hand to slide into the pocket of his coat, where he carried a knife; for he was determined to use that dangerous though rather cowardly weapon, if the bully attacked him.

"Do you hear, you young cub, when you're spoken to?" shouted Bully Bolivar.

"I hear you fast enough."

"Well, then, shell out, or I'll punch your head into a jelly!"

"No you wont," said Marks, decisively.

"I wont?" said the sailor, with that repetition so peculiar to common men, "who's to prevent me?"

VIOLA'S GRIEF AT THE DEATH OF HER FATHER.

"I will."

"You—you shrimp! Why I'd eat you for breakfast without salt!"

"You'd find me rather indigestible."

"I'd run the risk of that. Now where's that money?"

"I tell you I have none."

"Hand it up."

"I can't."

"You mean you wont?"

"I mean what I say."

"If you stand there and give me any of your sauce, I'll fetch you a wipe on the side of the head which you wont forget in a hurry, I'll swear."

Money Marks smiled complacently.

A large crowd of idlers had collected around the two disputants, expecting to see some fun. Any row is a source of amusement to those who are idle, and have nothing better to do than to look on at and listen to a silly altercation.

"Now then, my sucking Nelson," said Bully Bolivar, "pay me that money you owe me!"

"I owe you no money," returned Money Marks.

"Oh, don't you! we'll see about that. I suppose you never sailed on board the *Arethusa?*"

"No—that I never did!"

"Ha! ha! that's a good 'un to begin with."

And as he laughed, the crowd also laughed.

"You weren't paid off at Plymouth?"

"No."

"And you didn't get picked up, and taken into a 'case' where you got eased of all your money?"

"No."

"And you didn't come to me for the loan of a five-pun' note?"

"No."

"Oh my! lying 's nothing to you," cried Bully Bolivar, holding up his hands.

The fellow spoke in so plausible a way that he made those who heard him believe the truth of what he said.

"Come, give us that money," continued Bolivar, "or I'll knock you on your beam-ends!"

"You can try."

"It wont take me long to do it, I can tell you."

"Wont it?"

"No."

"Perhaps you may find yourself mistaken."

"I'll take my chance of that. Pay me my money. I only want what I am entitled to."

"Yes, yes, pay him his money!" shouted the crowd.

"But I owe him nothing."

"Oh, that's all my eye!"

"Pay him! pay him!"

"Gentlemen!" cried Bully Bolivar.

"Sir to you," replied some one.

"It's a fair and honest debt."

"Of course it is. Who says it isn't?"

"I do!" cried Money Marks. "He's trying to best me, and if I had a heap of money I wouldn't submit to it; but I haven't got any."

"Don't believe him. I see him with a handful of gold," said Bolivar.

"It's a lie!"

"Who says it's a lie?"

"I do!" replied Money Marks, fiercely.

"I'll teach you to give me the lie!" cried the ruffian, clenching his fists, and squaring up to the young man.

"Beware!" shouted Money Marks.

"Of what?"

"The weapon I hold in my hand. I'll knife you!"

"He says he'll stick a knife into me," said Bully Bolivar. "Mates, what do you say to that? Do you hear it? He wont pay me the money he owes me, and says he'll stick a knife into me if I ask for it. That's fine treatment, that is. I wont sail with scums of the earth. Give it him. Knock him down. The cowardly rascal. Send his eye into his boot."

The mob seemed very much disposed to do as the bully recommended them, but an elderly man interposed, saying—

"Does anyone here know this young man? We know Bolivar—and he's an old stager—but this young fellow does not look as if he had been to sea much."

"I never saw the sea in my life!" cried Money Marks; "and although I have accepted service under the Confederate flag, I shouldn't be here if I had not been kidnapped like the rest of you."

"Does anyone know him?" again repeated the old man.

"No one spoke.

"Call Bob Cannon—he knows me," said Money Marks.

"Bob Cannon!"

"Ay, ay, sir!"

"You're wanted."

"And I'm to the fore. What is it?" said Bob, coming forward.

"Do you know this young man?"

"I do."

"Well?"

"Yes, very well."

"How long have you known him?"

"This fifteen years."

"Has he ever been to sea?"

"No, that I'll take my oath he hasn't!"

"Then he can't have served on board the *Arethusa*?"

"Not he."

"Nor yet have been paid off at Portsmouth?"

"Certainly not."

"Nor can he have borrowed five pounds of Bully Bolivar?"

"Not a rap."

"You're sure of that?"

"Certain."

"What was he on shore?"

"Potman at the 'Pint of Porter,' in Ratcliff Highway," replied Bob Cannon.

"Mr. Samkin's?"

"Yes."

"Oh! I remember him now. That's the young fellow, is it?" said the grey-headed old man.

Bully Bolivar looked confused, but tried to brazen the matter out.

"You're all a lot of liars!" he said, between his teeth.

"What's that?" inquired Bob Cannon, who was game to the backbone.

"You're all a lot of liars!" repeated the fellow.

"Do you mean me?"

"I don't suppose you're much better than the rest of them?"

"If you say that again I'll squelch you!"

"I'll squelch *you*. It's more than any of you can do single-handed! I'll fight a dozen of you—one down and t'other come on!"

"Not you, not you," resounded on all sides.

"You'd have your work cut out for you if you were to fight me," said Bob Cannon.

"I don't think so."

"Will you try?"

"Will I? I should think so; it will keep my hand in. I'm Yankee, I am—Yankee born and bred—and nothing would please me more than to whip a tarnation Britisher. I'm your man, master; we'll try conclusions."

The prospect of a fight was pleasing to all parties; the officers on guard did not consider it their business to interfere with so trifling a matter as a stand-up hand-to-hand fight.

If knives or other offensive weapons had been employed, they would have promptly suppressed the dangerous disturbance, but, as a rule, sailors' faces are neither remarkably handsome nor remarkably tender, and a little knocking about is not calculated to do them much harm.

A well-directed blow may now and then put an ill-shaped feature into its proper place.

Money Marks interposed.

"It is my quarrel," he said; "let me fight the man."

"No, no, my little cock; you're not big enough," replied Bob Cannon. "I'll do my best, and if I'm beaten you shall try."

"I can fight," said Money Marks; "I have turned some of the best and strongest of you out of my master's bar when you've been noisy."

"Bolivar's the best fighter out," said some one.

"Can he wrestle?"

"No."

"There I'd have him, then; a Cornish man taught me," said Money Marks.

"Wrestling ain't English."

"Isn't it? Then I should like to know what is," replied Money Marks, scornfully.

"Come, I say you blokes," cried Bully Bolivar; "is there to be a free fight, or is it to be nothing but words? I want to know what you are a going to do. If anyone means fighting, I'm ready. I'll fight any one, from the able-bodied seaman down to the game-cock potman."

"Come on," said Bob Cannon.

The two men instantly stripped and faced one another.

The most intense excitement reigned everywhere.

Men ceased gambling, cards were picked up, and the spectators jumped upon tables and chairs, and leant upon one another's shoulders, standing on tiptoe to see the battle.

A ring was formed.

Betting was very brisk.

The odds were two to one, four to one, and finally six to one on Bully Bolivar before a blow was struck.

Bob Cannon stepped forward in a plucky manner, and faced his herculean antagonist.

Money Marks got a bowl of water and a rag, for he was going to second his friend.

Cannon struck the first blow, and got well on Bolivar, hitting him a tremendous blow in the mouth, which caused all his teeth to rattle like castanets.

"Well hit, well hit," shouted every one.

The odds turned in favour of Bob Cannon, and the betting was immediately four to one on Bully Bolivar, instead of six, as it had been previously.

Bully Bolivar shook his head and assumed the offensive, fighting scientifically, and striking his adversary once on the nose and once on the chest.

First blood was claimed for Bolivar, but disallowed, as his mouth was bleeding; consequently the honour of drawing first blood remained the property of Bob Cannon and his friends.

Time was called.

Money Marks went down on one knee and supported Bob on the other, while he sponged his face and encouraged him with friendly words and timely counsel.

"Hit him hard, Bob," he said; "don't be afraid of him. He's big, but he's tender; walk into him and show him that a Britisher's as good as a Yankee."

"Come on, Bunker's Hill," cried Bob Cannon, once more entering the lists.

"I'm all here," replied Bolivar; "but it is more than you know where you'll be in five minutes."

"A top of you scrouging your eyes out, p'raps," said a voice.

"It is p'raps, and a d—— poor p'raps, too," replied Bolivar, with a knowing wink. "I wouldn't give you much for it."

The fight now commenced in earnest, and was waged for some time with varying fortune. Bolivar had confessedly the best of it. Twice was Bob Cannon knocked nearly senseless on the floor, and twice did he come to the scratch with his innate fortitude and endurance.

But the enemy was too strong for him—he hit too hard, and put his blows in too straight. Bob was not a skilful fighter—he could hit hard when any remissness on the part of his adversary allowed him to get in, but this of course was only seldom.

In the fourth round he contrived to hit Bully Bolivar a blow behind the ear, and then to follow up his success by a blow in the pit of the stomach.

Bolivar dropped, and his friends cried foul, but the referee decided that both hits were fair.

When Bully Bolivar again came to the scratch he looked a little pale and staggered a little, but he speedily recovered himself, and had his revenge in knocking Bob Cannon head-over-heels to where Money Marks was waiting for him.

Bob Cannon was stunned and did not come to time, therefore Bully Bolivar was adjudged the winner, and not at all sorry was that worthy that the battle had terminated so suddenly in his favour, for he had found Bob Cannon a tremendous hitter, and an awkward customer. Had the sailor only possessed a little scientific acumen, the result would have been very different—when brute force and science are united, the result cannot be doubted for an instant.

"That wasn't much of a spell," said Bully Bolivar, rubbing his hands together, and looking like Goliath of Gath in front of the Jewish army.

"No," said Cuffy, the black, who was a friend of Bolivar's, and who had entered with some rum and some tobacco; "you know how to do it, Massa Bolivar."

"We can warm 'em, eh, Cuffy?"

"Yes, massa; you and me together."

"I'll take a sup of something short after that bit of a ball," said Bolivar.

Some rum was handed him, and he drank half a tumbler-full without winking.

"Are there any more of you?" he asked, in a vain-glorious manner.

No one spoke.

"You've had enough, eh? and I'm cock of the walk?"

Money Marks felt stung to the quick at this remark, and springing to his feet, he handed his senseless friend over to the care of another, who promised to apply restoratives and look after him.

"No, you're not," he cried.

"What, my little barman, is it you?" said Bolivar, dancing about in a mocking manner.

"Yes, it is I."

"Do you want to be made mincemeat of?"

"Do you?"

"If you can do it. It would be a pity to punch your head—you look so pretty."

"That's more than you will do when I take you in hand," replied Money Marks.

A general laugh arose at the expense of the bully.

At this juncture Charleston Jack entered, and looking around him perceived that there was an unusual commotion.

"Well, boys," he said, "can you manage to kill time? We go on board to-night."

"Hurrah! hurrah!" cried the men.

"What have we here?"

"It's a fair fight."

"Whom between?"

"Bully Bolivar and a new hand."

"Oh, all right. Let me see fair play."

Charleston Jack stood on one side. The ring was formed again, and the second fight began.

Money Marks was more cautious and twice as nimble as Bob Cannon had been; he stood well on his toes and danced round his antagonist with a marvellous quickness. Every now and then Bully Bolivar received a blow unexpectedly, and when he endeavoured to return it, his opponent was yards away, springing up and down in an elastic manner, which made Bolivar fume with rage and disappointment.

Marks knew how to draw back to avoid a blow; he could also drop and bend his back, and dart into corners.

His plan was to exhaust Bolivar's supply of wind, and when, by continuous exertions, he had visibly distressed him, he intended to grapple with and throw him.

For half-an-hour this strange sort of fighting continued, and Bolivar blew and panted like a grampus.

Money Marks saw that his opportunity was arriving, and he watched for it carefully. Bolivar's face was streaming with blood from a dozen blows, and he fought recklessly, exposing himself continually.

Once he succeeded in hitting Marks on the face, but he did not do him much injury; there was an abrasion of the skin and that was all.

At the conclusion of a long round, just when Money Marks expected time to be called, he rushed at Bully Bolivar, struck him in the face and the stomach simultaneously, and then summoning up all his strength, grappled with his formidable enemy, and after a terrible contest threw him with awful force.

The bully fell on the back of his head upon the hard flag-stones with which the place was paved, and giving a deep groan lapsed into a state of insensibility.

Had not the enthusiasm of the spectators been checked it would have found vent in a loud cheer, but suppressing their emotions, they crowded round Money Marks, patted him on the back and grasped him by the hand, shaking it most cordially.

"Well done, my fine fellow," cried Charleston Jack; "that was done bravely. We shall make something of you one of these days."

Money Marks smiled proudly.

"What is your name?"

"Money Marks."

"Have you ever been to sea?"

"No."

"Can you write and read?"

"Yes."

"The captain is in want of a secretary, I will speak to him of you."

"Thank you, sir," replied Money Marks, looking up thankfully.

Bob Cannon was not much hurt; he was used to knocking about. He soon recovered his serenity, and was very much pleased to hear that Marks had so ably punished the bullying rascal who had boasted so much and in the end done so little.

That evening the entire crew of the *Swamp Snake* were conveyed through a secret passage to a doorway opening upon the river. Boats were in readiness to take them off, and by five o'clock in the morning the *Swamp Snake* was steaming down the Thames with the tide, fully manned and only wanting her armament.

In six hours they made Calais, where they took their cannon on board, filled their powder magazine, and sailed for Nassau.

Money Marks could not help feeling the oddness of his new situation. The captain employed him as a secretary or amanuensis, but still he was expected to do some little work on deck, although he was spared the indignity of swabbing and holystoning.

But three days before he had been leading a sober and prosaic existence as potman in a London public house.

Now he was an adventurer in the fullest sense of the word, sailing under a flag which was not recognised by foreign nations, and which was not nearly so powerful on the sea as the opponent it had to contend with.

As he laid his head down in his hammock he breathed a fervent inspiration that his new lot might lead to something great and glorious.

The *Swamp Snake* was a splendid vessel, beautifully built by one of the best shipwrights in the Clyde. She was as near perfection as she possibly could be.

Money Marks "took" to his new life at once; he conceived a fondness for the sea, and promised to become an excellent sailor. He was not above gleaning information from anyone who was disposed to give it to him, the natural consequence of which was that he got on wonderfully, whilst another would have stood still.

Bob Cannon initiated him into the mysteries of practical seamanship, and he became a favourite with everyone except Bully Bolivar, who hated him like poison for overthrowing him in the great contest which took place in the vaults beneath the Tower of London.

CHAPTER V.

A PRIZE.

WHEN the *Swamp Snake* was about ten days from London, having taken the journey easy, doing little more than three knots an hour, to save coal, a ship was sighted from the north-west.

Captain Arlee sent for Charleston Jack, and expressed his conviction that the approaching vessel was a North American merchantman, probably richly laden and worth the trouble of capturing.

"You know," exclaimed Captain Arlee, "that we are instructed to make captures if we can; we are duly commissioned, so that it will not be an act of piracy, and I propose that we attack the brig and appropriate her merchandize. What say you?"

"You know that nothing would please me better," replied Charleston Jack; "shall I pipe all hands to quarters?"

"Not yet; just be so good as to hint at what is likely to happen, so that every man may be prepared— that is all I would do at present."

"Very well, sir."

"Are the guns shotted and primed?"

"They are."

"Hoist the English colours."

"Ay, ay, sir."

"And hail the brig."

Charleston Jack took his departure, and as he went from deck to deck the faces of the men flushed with pleasure as the prospect of an engagement dawned upon them.

As the brig drew nearer it was noticed that she was a simple merchantman, unarmed, and therefore incapable of offering any resistance.

The Stars and Stripes flew from her masthead, plainly denoting her nationality.

Money Marks and Bob Cannon were leaning over the taffrail, conversing together.

"Is there likely to be a fight?" inquired Money Marks.

"Fight, my lad! Not they; don't you see she's unarmed?"

"What shall we do with her?"

"Take what merchandize we can carry out of her, seize the passengers and crew, and burn the ship."

"Scuttle her?"

"I suppose so."

"Then we conduct war upon civilized principles."

"Of course we do, my lad."

"I thought at first we were pirates."

"No! Did you?" said Bob Cannon, in admiring astonishment.

"I did, indeed."

"I have often thought I should have liked to be a pirate and have sailed with the buccaneers, and Captain Kidd and Paul Jones, and all that lot."

"There seems something very horrible about it," said Money Marks, musingly.

"Well, there is that."

"I don't think a man could become a pirate unless he was at war with his fellow-creatures."

"Don't you?"

"No; and for this reason he would have to be guilty of many cruelties and atrocities, of which he would not dream, were not his mind soured by some great wrong."

"It may be so?"

The American brig was hailed, and approached to within speaking distance.

"What ship?" shouted Captain Arlee through a trumpet.

"The *Glorious Republic*."

"Where from?"

"Boston, Massachusetts."

"To what port bound?"

"Liverpool."

"Cargo?"

"Cotton."

"Stand to!" said Captain Arlee, in reply.

This answer frightened the Yankees, who are celebrated for their 'cuteness, and they endeavoured to make way, but they had not sail enough flying.

A second summons more peremptory than the first having been disregarded, Captain Arlee said to his lieutenant—

"Hoist the Confederate flag!"

It was instantly done.

A cry of dismay broke from the Yankees.

They redoubled their efforts at escape.

"Fire a shotted gun over their heads," said the captain.

The word of command travelled to the proper quarter: there was a flash, a puff of smoke, and then a loud report.

The ball struck the brig amidships, doing considerable damage.

It had had its muzzle depressed by accident. The captain was angry at the ship's being struck, but he said nothing, except—

"Let me have the name of the man who fired that gun in contravention of my orders."

This determined proceeding on the part of the *Swamp Snake* speedily caused the *Glorious Republic* to lower sail and stand to.

She was boarded by Charleston Jack and Money Marks.

The captain was a greyheaded old man of sixty and upwards. The passengers were grouped upon the deck aft, while the crew were standing forward. Amongst the former was a young lady of great beauty. She could not have numbered more than sixteen summers, but her face and features were perfect; her feet small, her hands tiny; her bosom round and voluptuous, her mouth of little size, her lips full and rosy, her hair of a bright yellow, glittering in the sunshine as if gold-dust had been sprinkled over it.

Money Marks' eyes rested on her countenance in a moment; he saw nothing else. He fancied that he had never seen so lovely a creature in his life; she captivated and enthralled him at first sight.

In truth she was a lovely girl—an anchorite might have been pardoned for forgetting his vows of chastity, and falling down on his knees before so beautiful an idol.

The captain approached Charleston Jack, and said in a voice which quivered with anger—

"By what right, sir, human or divine, do you attack my vessel?"

"I sail under the flag of the Confederate Government, with which Confederacy your country is at war——"

"Vile rebels!"

"We do not think so. However, might is right here on the high seas, if not on the banks of the Potomac. I will trouble you for your papers previous to my taking possession of the ship in a formal manner."

"Sir, think of what you are doing," said the old man, trembling.

"I have thought, or, more properly, my captain has thought for me."

"This ship is my own."

"Sorry for you."

"You should not war against individuals."

"Your generals burn the houses of private persons."

"But I have taken no part in the war."

"No more had those private persons of whom I am speaking."

"This ship, with its cargo, is my all."

"I can't help that."

"I care not for myself," continued the captain; "but my daughter who stands by my side has no one to look to but me."

"That is sad."

"Pursue your way and you will find a foe more worthy of your steel."

"I cannot do so."

"Why not?"

"I simply obey my orders."

"And they are——"

"To command you to evacuate your ship in an hour's time. The passengers and crew will be taken on board the Confederate ship, *Swamp Snake*, and will be landed at the first convenient opportunity; the cargo, as far as is practicable, will be appropriated, and the ship will be destroyed."

"Destroy my ship!" cried the captain, wringing his hands; "oh! miserable day. Alas! that I should ever have lived to see this dreadful day. My daughter, God help her! what will become of her? It is too much."

"Calm yourself," said Charleston Jack; "you will be luckier, perhaps, next voyage."

"No, no, no!"

"I say, yes."

"I am ruined beyond redemption."

"Oh, no! it is not so bad as that."

The old man was not to be comforted; he fell down upon the deck of the ship, and writhed about in great pain; a ruby-coloured foam collected round his lips, and he appeared to be in strong convulsions.

All this time Money Marks had continued to stare at the young lady who had in the first instance rivetted his attention.

When the old man fell on the deck, she rushed forward, exclaiming—

"My father—my father! he is dying! Mercy—mercy! he is dying!"

The old gentleman had apparently suffered from disease of the heart, for before his daughter could reach him he had breathed his last, and was still in the embrace of death.

When this fact was ascertained beyond a doubt, a heavy sadness fell around, and no one breathed a word.

The wretched girl, uttering a despairing cry, threw herself upon her father's body, and gave way to the most passionate grief.

The tears sprang to Money Marks' eyes, and he brushed them away with the back of his hand.

It was a melancholy scene.

CHAPTER VI.

VIOLA.

WHEN the crew of the *Glorious Republic* had been transferred to the blockade-runner and privateer, the vessel was thoroughly overhauled and everything of value taken from her.

The cotton, of course, was too bulky, and took up too much room to be transferred to the privateer, so it was condemned to be burnt. It was fortunate for the old man that he was not alive to witness the almost wanton destruction of his dearly-loved vessel. He had expected to get a good deal of money in Liverpool for his merchandize, and so he would have done.

The fire raged fiercely, and in an hour's time the *Glorious Republic* was a complete wreck, burnt down to the water's edge.

Viola was treated as tenderly as possible. Her grief for the death of her only parent was respected by all, but the dimensions of the ship would not permit of her having a private cabin all to herself. She was obliged to mix with those who had been her friends on the ill-fated vessel, but they were for the most part so taken up with their own griefs that they could not give her much sympathy.

Money Marks always contrived to be on deck when Viola was there. He had learnt her name from one of the passengers—a garrulous old man, who was disposed to talk about everything and anybody to the first one who would take the trouble to listen to him.

From this old man Marks had discovered the lovely girl's name to be Viola Cathcart. She belonged to a good old Virginian family, but her father had served with the North when hostilities commenced with the bombardment of Fort Sumter in Charleston harbour, and they had gone to New York.

Viola had many friends in the South, and wished to return to them; but her more prudent father deemed it inadvisable to do so.

One evening Money Marks saw Viola sitting by herself on deck. She was holding a book in her hand and pretending to read, but the lines were invisible to her; she was weeping, and the words ran into one another as she gazed upon them through a misty haze.

For some minutes Money Marks gazed silently upon her with as much rapture as he would have contemplated a beautiful image of a sorrowing nymph.

All at once her instinct told Viola that she was being watched, and she started up. When she saw Money Marks she blushed and her face became the colour of a deep scarlet.

"A fine evening," Money Marks ventured to say.

"Yes, it is," she replied, shading her eyes as if the sun hurt them, but in reality she did not care for the setting sun—she merely wished to hide the traces of tears.

She rose to go.

"Pray do not go: I have often wished to talk to you."

"To me?"

"Yes."

"And why?"

"To comfort you in your great sorrow."

"That is kind of you, but you must remember that you were the cause of my grief."

"I?" said Money Marks, in astonishment.

"If not you yourself, you belong to the marauding party."

"We merely do our duty."

"Your duty in this case, sir, killed my father."

Here her tears flowed afresh.

"Have you no friends?"

"Not one."

"No mother?"

"Alas! no."

"No relations; no brothers, sisters? You may think me rude, but I take the deepest interest in you."

"I am alone in the world. I'm ruined utterly. I have no one to care for and I have nothing to live upon."

"That is very sad."

"Very," she echoed, with a despairing wail.

"What shall you do?"

"God in heaven only knows," she said, turning her eyes piteously towards heaven.

"Would that I could be a brother to you," said Money Marks, getting red and pale by turns.

"To me. You a brother to me?"

"Yes, why not?"

"We are strangers."

"Comparative strangers to one another, but is there not a bond of sympathy between us?"

"How?"

"I, too, am alone in the world, and never knew my father or my mother. There is a great similarity between our situations. Oh, I conjure you, let us be as brother and sister."

"Oh! no, you know not what you ask. I'm heavily laden with grief and bowed down with sorrow," she said in a sad voice.

"But——"

"Nay, hear me out; I do not wish to involve any one else in my sorrowful career. You are young—may meet with a splendid fortune."

"Ah! that would be worthless without you," replied Money Marks.

"Sir," she said, rebukingly, "that is almost equivalent to a declaration of love, which I do not feel myself gratified in listening to; as long as you confined yourself to a declaration of friendship, I was your patient, and I trust, courteous listener; now, I must beg you to excuse me as I wish to go."

"To go?"

"Yes, I may not stay to be insulted."

"Gracious heavens!" cried Money Marks, "I would die sooner than insult you!"

She moved away.

"Viola—Miss Cathcart."

But ere the words had left his lips she had vanished like a child of mist."

Money Marks was confounded; he was afraid that he had offended the idol of his heart beyond the power of forgiveness, and he was disconsolate in consequence.

The next day a still more burning sun fell upon them, and the cabins were so hot as to absolutely intolerable; the ladies were for the most part on deck, sitting under an awning. The steward of the ship had procured some fishing tackle, and some of the monsters of the deep were expected to bite at a piece of pork or salt junk, but they disappointed the anglers in not doing so.

Viola brought her book with her as usual on deck, and leant over the taffrail.

Some one inadvertently pushed up against her, and knocked the book out of her hand into the water.

Viola stretched forward to reach it, but in so doing fell forward, and was precipitated into the ocean.

A terrible shriek rent the air.

All was confusion and dismay.

The passengers stared blankly at one another, while Charleston Jack threw a life-buoy overboard.

Money Marks was below when he heard the shriek, and he rushed on deck, meeting Bob Cannon by the main hatchway.

"What is it ?" he demanded.

"Girl overboard."

"Which girl ?"

"One of the passengers."

"Yes."

"Whom ?"

"Cappen's daughter."

"God help us," said Money Marks, staggering against the mizen-mast.

"Save her ! save her !" cried somebody. "Is there no one man enough to risk his life to save that of a woman."

No one moved.

But the passionate appeal acted like a shock of electricity upon Money Marks, who sprang forward, dashed over the benches, stood on the side of the ship, marked the floating body of the girl gradually drawing astern, put his hands above his head, and darted into the briny element without a moment's loss of time, or the least hesitation.

There was a momentary pause. Then a loud ringing shout rent the air. Both passengers and crew admired this act of spontaneous heroism.

Captain Arlee gave his orders in a prompt and decisive manner ; determined that all that he could do to meet the emergency, should be done as well as circumstances would permit.

"Reverse the engines," he said.

This was instantly done, and the way of the vessel stopped.

"Lower the boat," he added.

This was also done.

In the meantime Money Marks was swimming vigorously towards Viola, who had contrived to seize a life-buoy, which had floated near to her.

In spite of her grief and her misfortunes, life was dear to her ; at the early age of sixteen she did not like to leave the world, of which she had seen but little, but which appeared fair to her.

Money Marks reached her at length, after a hard swim. The sea was calm and quiet as a mill-pond.

"Miss Cathcart," cried Money Marks, "I am here to save you."

"You," she said, as if she were grieved at her deliverer being the man whom the day before she had dismissed in so summary a manner.

"Yes, pardon me for putting my arm round your waist ; I must bear you up until the boat arrives."

He encircled her waist with his arm, and looking on her pale face, and dishevelled hair, fancied that Venus rising from the sea could not be more beautiful.

"What a long way off the ship seems," said Viola.

"Yes, we are drifting ; but you hear that ?"

"What ?"

"That measured sound."

"Yes."

"That is the sound of the oars in the rowlocks ; the ship's boat is launched, and we shall soon be rescued."

"That is a comfort."

"Do you feel faint ?"

"A little."

"Bear up a few moments longer."

"Oh, yes," she replied, feeling grateful to him for his support, without which she must inevitably have given way.

Suddenly the water was disturbed a little to the left of Money Marks, who wondered what the cause of so unusual a circumstance was.

He looked carefully in that direction, and was horrified to see the black fin of a shark protruding above the water.

It was an awful moment.

He scarcely knew how to act, and yet if he did act his action must be prompt.

A shark is a terrible foe—he makes a dash at you, your bones crash and crack, and you are drawn beneath the water, to lie in an aqueous grave.

It was not for himself that he cared.

With the chivalry of youth, he felt that he could die happy, were it permitted him to save the life of his incomparable Viola.

"What is that ?" she asked, catching sight of the monster's fin, about the same time that he did.

Money Marks did not like to say what the fish really was so he said—

"It is what is called a dog-fish ; hold on to the buoy, and I will go and kill it. It will be a trophy to take back to the ship. Do you think that you can support yourself for a couple of minutes ?"

"I think so. Do not run into any danger."

"Oh, no ! it is harmless enough. (God forgive me for lying," muttered Money Marks to himself).

The boat was still some thirty or forty yards off.

Charleston Jack shouted repeatedly to those in the water to keep their courage up and hold on.

Money Marks saw that if something was not done, the monster would be upon them before the boat would have time to reach them.

Like all sailors, he carried a knife at his girdle or belt.

It was a clasp-knife.

This he drew, and resolved to assume the defensive with it.

He was an accomplished swimmer and diver. In these days of swimming-baths and cheap excursions to the sea-side, most Londoners are.

In his opinion he had very little chance of escaping with his life from the contest with the shark. Yet he felt a positive pleasure in sacrificing his life for Viola ; if he could preserve her safety, he did not care a straw for his own.

Such is the power of love.

Love can do anything. There is no passion so powerful as love. Money is able to do a great deal, but love can do more.

Can money buy the priceless affection of a virgin's heart ?

No.

Can money purchase domestic felicity ?

No.

Can money open the gates of Heaven to believers.

No ; but love can. It has been well named the master-passion. Here was a young man, courting death as it were—seeking instant destruction, and rushing into the jaws of death.

And why ?

Because he loved.

This simple answer contains the key to many a social problem which has been designated the work of the hands of a madman.

Love is ecstatic insanity.

The shark was rapidly approaching.

Money Marks watched his position well, and calculated where he would be in the space of ten seconds. Then bending down his head and throwing up his legs, he dived, keeping his eyes open, and holding the knife well in his hand.

It was a perilous venture.

Upon its success everything depended.

The poor fellow's heart beat as it had never beaten before. To be devoured alive by a shark is probably of all deaths the most painful ; when dragged beneath the water it is true that insensibility soon comes to your relief, but to feel the teeth of the monster in your flesh, to hear your bones crack, to suffer excruciating agony, is surely a foretaste of the pains of hell.

As Money Marks had sagaciously surmised, he came up directly under the belly of the shark.

Now was his time.

Not a moment was to be lost.

Choosing his opportunity, he threw his hand upwards, and pierced the belly of the shark with his knife, carrying his hand forward, and ripping up the monster's intestines.

The sea became darkened with blood of a deep purple colour.

The shark beat the sea with his fins, and lashed the waves with his tail, and made a futile effort to turn round and annihilate Money Marks, who, however, had risen to the surface to get breath, and was preparing for a fresh encounter.

Providentially this was not necessary. He had dealt the shark its death-blow ; and just as he was preparing to dive a second time, the fish rolled over on its back, struggling convulsively.

Those in the boat had now arrived. They were not acquainted with the whole of the facts, but they could guess what had occurred, and when the dead body of the shark floated on the surface of the water, Charleston Jack exclaimed—

"As fine a deed as ever I witnessed in all my life! Bravo! young man. Well done!"

Viola was taken into the boat in a fainting condition. Money Marks was exhausted. One of the seamen struck the iron point of a boat-hook in the body of the shark, and it was drawn along after the boat to the ship.

The state of the case was soon made known to those on board the *Swamp Snake*, and a vociferous cheer was given for Money Marks, who, after imbibing a restorative, was himself again.

Viola was confined to her berth until the next day.

The captain of the ship publicly complimented Money Marks on his heroism, which was a theme of admiration with everybody, except Bully Bolivar, who hated the young man more than ever for his success.

"I could have done the same thing, and have done it better," he said, "only I didn't have the chance."

Chances generally come to people who look after and lay themselves out for them.

Bob Cannon was especially delighted with his young friend's success. He shook him by the hand, and insisted upon his taking half his allowance of grog that evening.

"I always said you'd be somebody, and do something," he exclaimed, "but you wouldn't believe me. I'm blessed if I don't think that there ghost on Tower Hill was the best thing that ever happened to you."

"If you think so I will not contradict you," replied Money Marks, with a smile.

"You'll be a great man."

"I hope so, I'm sure."

"I'll stick to you."

"Thank you."

"I'll never leave you; when you get a ship I'll sail under you."

"Will you?"

"Yes, my lad. You've got more in your upper story than I have, and I shall see you at the top of the tree before long. You've got it in you. You know how to do it."

Money Marks accepted his friend's prediction as if it were oracular, and drinking the rum he offered him, went upstairs to the captain's room, to do some work which Captain Johnson Arlee had in readiness for him.

Marks had never felt so happy in all his life before. He had saved Viola's life, and if that did not give him a claim upon her gratitude, what in the name of fortune would? Nothing.

Moreover, he had twice risked his life—once in jumping overboard, the second time in fighting the shark.

He waited about on deck all the next morning, expecting Viola to make her appearance. At last she came, looking pale but radiantly beautiful. Oh! so lovely, so soul-enchanting, so bewitching, that the heart of the most stoical saint that ever lived would have been moved to thoughts of love, on witnessing her enchanting charms.

Viola was the queen of Money Marks' soul. She was his first love, and we all know how intense, how fervid, how absorbing, and engrossing, a first love is.

It seems to our unsophisticated natures to be a glimpse of Paradise—a foretaste of Heaven.

Viola advanced towards him with outstretched hand, her face beamed gratitude, her eyes spoke thankfulness, and she shook him by the hand in a friendly manner.

They might have been acquaintances of long standing, so familiar was her manner.

Her timidity had wholly vanished—she was free and abandoned.

"I have to thank you very, very much, Mr. Marks," she said, "for your gallantry and devotion to me yesterday."

"Oh! that is nothing," he said, with a careless laugh.

"Indeed, but it is, though. When I think of that dreadful shark I shut my eyes and shudder involuntarily. It was too awful."

"Not at all."

"You might have swam away, and left me to my fate."

"Oh, no! a shark always pursues a flying victim," said Money Marks, drawing upon his imagination for a pleasant fiction.

"Is it so?"

"Undoubtedly."

"Nevertheless, I owe my life to you."

"You are very good to say so."

They were walking side by side, and contrived to get to the extreme end of the ship, close to the binnacle and the wheel at which the helmsman was standing; in this place they were removed from the rest of the passengers, and could talk freely without fear of interruption.

"Do you really feel grateful to me?" said Money Marks.

"Do I?"

"Yes."

"Can you ask?"

"I shall be so happy if you will tell me you mean what you say, and that the phrases you make use of are not mere conventional phrases," said Money Marks, looking very silly and sentimental, but thoroughly meaning every word he said.

"I do, indeed, mean it."

"Will you in your turn do something to oblige me?"

"If I may."

Viola cast down her eyes at this question, and looked more fascinating than usual.

"Shall I tell you what it is?"

"If you please."

"It is—you remember what we were talking about the last time I had the pleasure of conversing with you?"

"Oh! yes, perfectly."

"Very well. Will you try and call to mind what I asked you to do?"

"What do you mean?"

"What I asked you to be to me."

"Oh, yes! Now I recollect, you asked me to be your sister."

"I did, dear Miss Cathcart. Will you—will you be my sister?" cried Money Marks, in impassioned accents. "Some day I may ask you to be something nearer and dearer, now I only ask you to be my sister. If you say 'yes' you will make me intensely happy."

Viola looked the earnest young man in the face, and said—

"You wish this—do you?"

"More than anything I ever wished in my life."

She held out her hand, and said—

"My answer is in the affirmative. I will be your sister."

"My own darling sister," cried Money Marks, rapturously; "bless you for this—bless you—bless you!"

He was about to raise her hand rapturously to his lips when he remembered that it was not the fashion for a brother to kiss a sister's hand, so he refrained from doing so.

"I believe," continued Viola, "that Providence has sent you to console me for the loss of my father, and I am fully prepared to look upon you as my guardian."

"Nothing would please me more than to undertake the trust."

"You are too kind to me," said Viola, as the tears sprang to her eyes. "You saved my life, and, not satisfied with that, you try and kill my melancholy, and save me from myself."

"We are friends, then?" said Money Marks.

"Oh, yes! dear, fast friends—friends for ever and ever. I have longed so for some one to whom I could talk, and in whom I could confide."

"May I ask what you intend to do?"

"When?"

"When the vessel arrives at Nassau."

"I suppose I must land there, and work for my living as best I can. Your captain has despoiled me of my patrimony."

"That is a poor prospect."

"What else can I do? Where are you going after leaving Nassau."

"I believe, we run the blockade."

"Indeed! at Charleston or Wilmington?"

"Charleston."

"I have friends in Virginia."

"At all events you could find a refuge in Charleston, and yet there is the danger of running the blockade."

"Oh! I am not afraid of that."

"In that case," said Money Marks, "tell the captain that you wish to go to Charleston, and I have little doubt that he will take you. If you wish it, and will permit me to do so, I will plead your cause myself, and Captain Arlee has a great deal of confidence in me."

"I shall feel proud if you will do so," replied Viola. "At Nassau I know not a soul, and I should, in all probability, experience the greatest difficulty in getting a living at dressmaking, which is the only branch of industry with which I am acquainted."

"That is your only resource?" said Money Marks, with a commiserating look.

" My only one.'

" Then by all means go to Charleston. I, your brother, advise you to do so."

It was under cover of the cabin hatchway, but Money Marks took up Viola Cathcart's hand, raised it to his lips and kissed it fervently.

Viola blushed, withdrew her hand, and ran down the stairs into the saloon, where dinner was awaiting her.

CHAPTER VII.

CHARLESTON.

THE *Swamp Snake* soon made Nassau, and there landed the crew of the *Glorious Republic*.

Money Marks, as he had promised, interested himself about Viola.

The captain was dictating a letter to him one day when he exclaimed—

" I want to speak to you, if you please, sir, before we land our prisoners."

" About whom ?"

" Miss Cathcart."

" The captain's daughter ?"

" The same."

" What of her ?"

" She is desirous of going to Charleston, where she has friends, and as you were the cause of her father's death——"

" The cause ?"

" You know what I mean, sir."

" Well, well ; go on."

" She thinks that you may be induced to take her to Charleston, if we succeed in running the blockade."

" I have no objection to doing that, but——"

" What, sir ?"

" I say, my boy, you must take care you are not running a muck," said Captain Arlee, severely.

" What do you mean, sir ?" demanded Money Marks, turning very red, and guessing what the captain was going to say.

" I speak to you as a friend."

" Of course, sir."

" Very well ; and you must not be offended at what I say."

" Certainly not, sir."

" I am afraid you are falling in love."

" In love !"

" Yes."

" With whom ?"

" That penniless girl," said Captain Arlee.

" Penniless !" echoed Money Marks, indignantly. " If she is penniless, who made her so ?"

" That is foreign to the present question," said the captain, sternly. " I take an interest in you, and I should not like to see you throw yourself away so early in life."

" She is a lady, sir," replied Money Marks, " and I have never even spoken to her of love. I chanced to save her life, and she is grateful for it—that is the only cause of her civility to me."

" Very possibly ; but take my advice, and beware," replied Captain Arlee.

Money Marks bowed. He gained permission for Viola Cathcart to stay on board, and that was all he cared about. The captain's strictures on his conduct were nothing to him ; all he feared was that he should be separated from Viola. If she determined to stay at Charleston, Marks made up his mind to desert from the ship rather than leave her behind him for an indefinite period—perhaps for ever.

During the whole of that day he thought over the captain's behaviour, and could not help coming to the conclusion that he was in love with Viola himself.

Money Marks had not remarked any overt act of love— he had not seen the captain speak to Miss Cathcart, but when his suspicions were fully aroused he remembered seeing him look in her direction in a fascinated manner.

After a time Money Marks became jealous ; but he said nothing, not considering it safe or advisable to do so.

He had some cause to fear, because Viola had not told him she loved him, or plighted her faith to him in any way ; she had merely accepted him as a brother, therefore she could marry anyone else without committing a breach of faith.

A captain in Mr. Arlee's position was not exactly a desirable match for any girl, but still he was better than

nothing. If he went through the vicissitudes of the war and came out unscathed, he might be rewarded and honoured afterwards. Women, however, look more to the present than the future.

The *Swamp Snake* took a quantity of cargo in at Nassau, and amongst other things a supply of lint and surgical stores for the wounded, lint and chemicals being scarce in the Confederacy.

In three days she was ready for sea, and prepared for the voyage to Charleston, which was a very hazardous one, and the chances were the ship would be captured.

They had an experienced pilot on board, and Captain Arlee was fully prepared to fight, if it were necessary to do so.

When they were within fifteen miles of Charleston, the pilot came to Captain Arlee, and said—

" How many knots an hour, sir, can your vessel do ?"

" Her average speed is eleven knots an hour, but she can do thirteen," replied the captain.

" Then let all steam be put on, for two Federal vessels are in the offing ; they have evidently sighted us, and will most probably dispute our passage before we have gone many yards further."

The *Swamp Snake* carried no canvas, and she was hull down in the water. What there was of her was painted black.

She burned the best and purest coke, which emitted a white smoke totally different from the volumes of dark vapour emitted by those vessels which use coal to feed their engines with.

It will be seen that to sight the *Swamp Snake* was a difficult operation, but the Yankee ships were well provided with telescopes, and they were so accustomed to the *ruses* of the blockade-runners that they could almost see a fly on the horizon with the naked eye.

The fires were banked up and the crew called to quarters. The guns were all double-shotted, and Charleston Jack stood by the pivot himself, ready to send her murderous and destructive fire in whichever direction it was most needed.

The hulls of several vessels could be distinctly seen at half-past eleven o'clock at night ; before one, if they ever hoped to be in Charleston, they would have arrived at that city. There is a doubt about all human affairs, and the captain of the *Swamp Snake* could not predict with any certainty that he should avoid capture ; and yet he felt sanguine as to the result of his rash enterprise, and so did his men.

At a quarter to twelve the lights in the forts in Charleston harbour were to be seen, but at twelve o'clock a dense mist arose, and the pilot, holding up his hands, said—

" Thank God !"

He liked nothing better than a mist to run the blockade in. He was a famous fellow, and had carried six vessels out and seven vessels in to Charleston successfully, so that his reputation was pretty well made. In a word, his services were invaluable.

The engines of the *Swamp Snake* were groaning beneath the pressure put upon them, and the sides of the ship were creaking ; every timber and every bolt was strained to its utmost.

The men stood by their guns with lighted matches, and conversed with one another in undertones and with bated breath.

Suddenly, and at a moment when nobody was expecting such a contingency, a most brilliant light was to be seen on the larboard bow. It gradually expanded and got larger and larger until all within a certain radius was rendered light as day.

Of course the *Swamp Snake* labouring away was discovered by the enemy, who had employed this ingenious device to find out the whereabouts of a suspected blockade-runner.

Before the crew of the *Snake* had time to think of this novel phenomenon, crash came a ball over the decks.

The captain of the *Snake* gave orders for the fires to be stimulated with pitch and tallow so as to make the screws revolve faster if possible.

This order was promptly obeyed.

Then he commanded the gunners to let fly at the enemy. The broadside of two guns was first fired, and damaged the enemy's rigging, for the light she showed made her an excellent mark.

Charleston Jack, however, attacked her smoke-stack and

MONEY MARKS ATTACKS CAPTAIN ARLEE.

smashed it to pieces with a well-delivered discharge from his pivot-gun.

He loaded again as soon as possible, and an exciting action, resulting in various insignificant casualties on each side, ensued.

The pace of the *Swamp Snake* was increased to the extraordinary speed of fourteen miles an hour, and she soon drew ahead.

The forts and the people of Charleston heard the discharge of guns, and were intensely anxious to know the result of the contest.

At half-past twelve the *Swamp Snake* steamed past Fort Sumter, with three men killed and fourteen wounded, with two holes through her hull and one amidships; but she had run the blockade and arrived safely with her valuable cargo, which was a source of triumph to the inhabitants of the proud but hard-pressed City of Charleston.

The captain was *fêted* and made much of by all those with whom he came in contact, and he took Money Marks out

with him : the latter was pleased to find that a very old friend of Viola Cathcart's father resided in Charleston, and that he was inclined to behave with the greatest kindness to the girl.

He offered her an asylum in the house, and undertook to provide for her. Marks called frequently upon her, and Mr. Dalgren, the old gentleman above alluded to, received him courteously as the preserver of Viola.

Cuffy, the black, met Money Marks in the street one day and said—

"Mornin', Massa."

"Good-morning, Cuffy," replied Money Marks.

"Ha, ha!" said the negro; "you go to Massa Dalgren's to see Missy Viola."

"Well, what of that?"

"You not the oly one, Massa Marks."

"Eh?"

Money Marks stood still in startled perplexity.

"No; some other one he go too."

"Who is he?"

"Ha, ha! Give Cuffy a greenback, and he will tell."

"There are no greenbacks here, but I'll give you a dollar."

"Gold?"

"Yes, all in gold."

"Then Cuffy will tell Massa Marks who goes to see Missy Viola."

The negro grinned, showed his teeth, and held out his hand for the money which had been promised him. When he had received it, he spat upon it for luck, and placed it in his breeches pocket.

"Now tell me," said Money Marks.

"Oh, Massa Marks, how red your cheek flush."

"Never mind that."

"And how your hand trembles."

"That is nothing. Speak of——"

"All right, Massa Marks; Cuffy will tell who go to see Missy Viola—it is captain of *Swamp Snake*."

"What, our captain?"

"Yes, him the man."

"May lightnings blast him!"

"Ha, ha!" laughed Cuffy.

"How many times has he been? Come, tell me."

Cuffy counted on his fingers, and said—

"One—two—three—three times, Massa Marks."

"Three times," said Money Marks; "you are sure you are speaking the truth?"

"Certain, sure."

"If you deceive me——"

"This nigger never tell no lies," replied Cuffy, proudly.

"Where is Captain Arlee now?"

"At Massa Dalgren's."

"There now?"

"Him walk up dat way."

"He may have gone on business."

"No, no; he go to see Missy Viola, Cuffy watch him and know it all."

"He is a scoundrel," cried Money Marks, who was about to walk quickly in the direction of Mr. Dalgren's, when Cuffy laid his hand upon his shoulder, saying—

"Stop bit, Massa Marks."

Some one wearing a large-brimmed palmetto hat, who was going by, noticed the action, and gave Cuffy a violent kick, saying—

"How dare you lay a finger on a white man, you black cuss?"

Cuffy glared, but said nothing. Money Marks looked surprised.

"What's that for?" he inquired, as the assailant passed on.

"Oh, that nothing," replied Cuffy; "this Charleston is a great place for slavery; poor slave of no account in Charleston. If I had said a word, that man would have had me whip for more'n half-an-hour."

"Comfortable state of things, certainly. I suppose you wont be sorry if the North conquers the South, then you will have abolition."

"Ah! bobilition's the thing for us; but where you going?"

"To Mr. Dalgren's."

"What for?"

"To see if I can find Captain Arlee."

"Suppose you find?"

"Well, in that case I shall chastise him summarily."

"You will?"

"Undoubtedly."

"But you forget."

"What?"

"He your master, he your captain, Massa Marks; a sailor on board ship is as much a slave as Cuffy on coffee-plantation."

"Ha!" said Money Marks, starting as if a snake had stung him, "you speak the truth, but I am not now on board."

"That true enough, but if you touch captain he will put you in prison for mutiny."

"I wish I had a friend," said Money Marks, with a despairing look, as if he was talking to himself.

"You have friend, Massa Marks."

"Who have I?"

"You forget Cuffy."

"You my friend?"

"Yes, if nigger not too bad to be friend of anybody."

"Thank you for the offer."

"What you saying? you not accept?"

"Yes I will accept your friendship, Cuffy," said Money Marks, "and there's my hand upon it."

He extended his right hand, and black and white man greeted one another cordially.

"God bless you, Massa Marks! you one fine fellow," said Cuffy.

"Good-bye for the present."

"What for good-bye?"

"I am going."

"Where?"

"To Mr. Dalgren's."

"Cuffy go with you; now he your friend he never leave you."

Seeing that any opposition on his part would be worse than useless, Money Marks acquiesced in the proposition of his dusky companion, followed by whom he threaded some of the best streets of the proud city of Charleston, and at length arrived at the door of the house inhabited by Mr. Dalgren.

Money Marks was in an intense rage to think that the captain of the *Swamp Snake* should dare to call upon Viola, who, although she had consented to be his sister, was in reality much dearer to him. He loved her with all the force of a fiery and passionate nature, and he could not bear the idea of Captain Arlee having stolen interviews with a young and lovely girl whom he had already, with the sanguine mind of youth, come to look upon as peculiarly and altogether his own.

His own!

With this happy and rapturous consummation he would have reached the pinnacle of his joy and the summit of his delight.

He was about to knock at the door, when Cuffy retained him by saying—

"Massa Marks."

"Well?"

"'Xcuse me, but——"

"What?"

"It not safe to knock at door."

"Why not? I am admitted whenever I wish for admittance."

"Ah! that all very well, but captain of *Swamp Snake* will know you then, and you will see nothing."

"There is truth in that."

"To be sure there is. Cuffy no fool."

"What do you propose?" said Money Marks, anxiously.

"What I propose is this," replied Cuffy. "I know the nigs downstairs — Sambo, the gardener; he my foster-brother. Come into the garden."

"Very well; so be it. Lead the way," replied Money Marks.

The weather was very hot, and all the blinds in the house were down, so that the intense heat of the sun might be excluded. Consequently if Viola had been at one of the windows she could not have seen him.

Suddenly a strange noise was heard a little way down the street.

It was like the sound of a comet dashing in electric haste through illimitable space.

Money Marks trembled violently, not knowing what it might portend.

Cuffy caught him by the arm, and shouted hoarsely in his ear—

"Down, down—flat on your face; down, or you dead man."

They both threw themselves down where they were, one in the gutter, the other upon the blazing hot pavement, which was so hot as to scorch and blister the flesh if it were unprotected.

In an instant there was a crash, an explosion, and the sound of falling bricks and mortar, mingled with the heart-rending cries such as women and children in an extremity of terror give utterance to.

Money Marks was still at a loss to account for this strange phenomenon, and lay where he was without offering to move a muscle.

Cuffy waited about half-a-minute before he stirred, then he jumped up with a wild laugh, crying—

"Ha, ha! Massa Yankee; you clever, but you no hurt Cuffy; he tough old nig and know a dodge or two."

Finding that his faithful attendant had risen, Money

Marks followed his example, and stood upon his legs once more.

"What was that?" he asked, "and what is the meaning of all the noise, smoke, and confusion? Has our world come in contact with another world and had a collision?"

"No kolishun, Massa Marks," replied Cuffy, with a broad grin, "it only shell from Federal fleet. See the house over there burning? That Greek fire, noting put that out."

"Nothing?"

"No, Massa Marks, noting in the 'varsal world. It sort of phosphorus, and burn, burn, burn, till everyting burnt up."

Money Marks looked down the street, which was full of flames and smoke.

A shell from the Federal fleet at that time blockading Charleston and riding at anchor in the mouth of the harbour had entered the city.

The principal occupation of the hostile fleet was to bombard Fort Sumter and Morris Island, but occasionally it made war on the women and children, and launched from its immense Parrot guns destructive shells filled with that awful compound known as Greek fire, which all civilized nations had tabooed in warfare.

The Yankees, however, were not content with fair fighting, they abandoned all instincts of humanity, and revived the ineffable barbarisms of the middle ages, making them ten times more abominable by the improvements of modern science.

Their hatred to Charleston was, and is, unutterable. They hold it to be the first city which began the civil war by the bombardment, bloodless though it was, and capture of Sumter. They hate Charleston because she was the flourishing centre of the Southern trade, the headquarters of slavery, and the abode of the proudest planters and slaveowners of which the Confederacy can boast.

The shell had fallen against the wall of a private house, making a great rent in the brickwork, and setting the house on fire in several places.

Many pieces or splinters of the shell had flown into the street, and had not Money Marks and Cuffy laid down in the prompt manner which on that occasion, if on no other, distinguished their actions, they would have stood a strong chance of being struck.

The advent of the missile had been signalised by three deaths.

An old man and a young woman lay side by side in the roadway, wrapped in a long slumber. Their bodies were horribly mutilated, and presented a shocking spectacle, from which all but the most hardened shrunk tremblingly.

Who was there in that gallant and devoted city who was not hardened? A long familiarity with death, and scenes of violence, had curdled the milk of human nature, and made stoics of those who a few short years before had all the innocence and gentleness of babes and sucklings.

A little further on, the decapitated body of a negro lay in the gutter; a fragment of the shell had struck him, carrying off his head, and the headless trunk lay upon the ground, while the head was being curiously regarded by a mob of negro children, who had come out to see "what dis hyar shindy was." It being a "kick-up" of the most interesting nature to them.

The house which had been set on fire now began to blaze brightly; but the municipal arrangements were so perfect that in less than ten minutes from the bursting of the shell, their fire-engines, attended by their respective brigades, were upon the spot.

In another five minutes, the water-cocks had been turned on, a good supply of the liquid element was secured, and six jets were playing upon the flames.

The hose was well directed, and extinguished the fire in every place, except where the Greek fire had fallen, and that defied the efforts of the firemen to put it out.

After regarding this curious scene for some little time, Money Marks requested Cuffy to take him to the garden-entrance of Mr. Dalgren's residence.

The bursting of the shell did not seem to excite much amazement or indignation amongst the somewhat fiery inhabitants of Charleston. The fact was they were used to it, and use is second nature.

Cuffy led Money Marks to the garden, and obtained admittance through Sambo's instrumentality. He spoke for some time in a low tone to Sambo, and then coming to Money Marks, said—

"Sambo tell me that Missy Viola and Cappen Arlee in the garden, sitting under large palm-tree; been there some time—Sambo think two hour. Mr. Arlee he smoke, and Missy Viola she drink ice-water."

"Confound them both!" cried Money Marks, grating his teeth together.

"We can go to palm-tree, and then Massa Marks you hear for yourself."

"Very well, and if——"

He broke off abruptly.

"If what?"

"If I hear him utter one word of love, which is responded to by her, I will tear his heart out where he stands!"

"That would be murder."

"Well, what of it?"

"We should be hung up."

"We?"

"Yes, Cuffy help Massa Marks, and if Massa hang, Cuffy hang too," replied the faithful fellow, looking up in his new master's face with moisture in his eyes, arising from natural emotion, caused by his attachment to the young sailor.

"But, Cuffy, suppose I were in a passionate moment to kill the captain?"

"Yes."

"It doesn't follow that we are to remain here quietly for the police of Charleston to arrest us."

"No, it not follow."

"Why not escape into the swamps?"

"We can do that, but not live long in swamps."

"What then?"

"What then do!" said Cuffy, "then go 'cross country to Wilmington—not more'n eighty or ninety mile—and take ship there. What you say, Massa Marks?"

"I think it is a good plan, but I hope to goodness that there will be no necessity for it."

"I hope so, too, but it impossible to tell."

With that he walked along a neatly gravelled path, and passed many tropical shrubs and plants of the greatest beauty. Presently they came to a dense coppice, at the back of which was the palm-tree, under the shelter of which Captain Johnson Arlee and Miss Viola Cathcart were conversing.

Cuffy entered the thicket with a practised hand and foot. He had entered many a cane-brake, and was fully accomplished in the art of making tracks anywhere.

He had been a slave down south for a great many years, but at last he was sold to an aged master, who died in the days of the John Brown excitement. John Brown, as the song tells us, now lies mouldering in the grave. But Cuffy's master on his death-bed thought it his duty to emancipate his slaves and disinherit his nephew, which he did.

Cuffy then took service on board a ship, and went to England with Charleston Jack and Captain Johnson Arlee.

The thicket, into which the two men had penetrated, was so thick as to resemble a jungle, but they contrived to make their way through it noiselessly and with discretion, until they reached a certain spot, from which they could see the lovers—if they were lovers—and overhear what they had to say.

Money Marks was in a fume of excitement. He loved Viola Cathcart most passionately, but as he had never declared his passion he had no right to ask her to refuse the visits of other men. He had saved her life, and placed her under an obligation, but that was nothing, comparatively speaking.

As a reward for what he had done, he had asked her permission to be her brother, and in reply to this request, she had consented to regard him in a fraternal light, and to be his sister.

His sister!

That was not what he wanted. It was well enough for a beginning, but he wanted something more than that—he wanted to be her lover, and afterwards to become her husband.

If she were really in love with Captain Arlee, this end would be impossible, and he hated Arlee with all the strength of which his nature was capable. When they were within a short distance of the lovers he laid his hand upon Cuffy's arm, and said in a tremulous whisper—

"Halt!"

They both came to a stand-still, crouched down in the

underwood, and listened intently to the conversation which fell upon their ears.

Viola was sitting on the ground by the side of Captain Johnson Arlee, who held one of her unresisting hands in his.

They were talking to one another in a low tone of voice.

Money Marks felt that if he heard Viola confess any love for Arlee, the confession would sour his disposition for ever, and throw a cloud over the whole period, whether long or short, of his future existence. He felt that to lose Viola's love would make a demon of him, and send him irresistibly to the bad.

This being the case it is no wonder that he put his hand to his ear with trembling eagerness, so as to catch every word which might fall from the lips of the two people upon whom he was playing the spy.

Captain Arlee was a fine handsome fellow, possessed of a handsome face; his eyes particularly arrested the attention of the beholder, though there was more of sin than thoughts of heaven in them. He was, in short, the *beau idéal* of a privateersman; just the dashing sort of sailor of fortune whom it was the interest of the Confederacy to employ, and keep in their service; he was bold, courageous, daring, a good executor, and tolerably lucky. In his manners to ladies, he was polished and gentle—two qualities which at all times ensure the possessor the regard of the fair sex.

Money Marks heard him say—" Oh, my angel, if you would only give me some token of your regard, so that I could remember you when far, far away upon the stormy ocean, and say, 'this was her's, this was Viola's; she gave it me as a love-token, and bade me hope.' "

" Could you not remember me without that, Captain Arlee?" replied Viola, in a low, sweet voice, which contrasted strangely with his wild, thrilling, passionate tone.

" Do not call me Captain Arlee," he said, evading her question.

" Why not ?"

" It seems so very stiff and formal."

" Not to me; you must recollect that our acquaintance is very slight."

" I feel as if I had known you a thousand years."

" That is a long time," she said, with a smile of incredulity.

" My love for you——"

" I will not listen to words of love, sir," she cried.

" Pardon me."

" No, I will not pardon you. I was imprudent to grant you this interview; if you were a man of any delicacy of sentiment and refinement, you would see at once that I cannot, with any decency and respect to myself, listen to words of love and passion, from any man so soon after the terrible bereavement which has so recently overtaken me."

" I did not forget the dreadful calamity to which you allude, Miss Cathcart," returned the captain, with dignity; " but I wished to stand to you in the place of a parent. You are young."

" But not friendless," said Viola, with dignity.

" You allude to that fellow on board my ship ?"

" Whom do you mean ?"

" Money Marks."

" Well."

" I will tie the scoundrel up and give him a round dozen on the voyage home."

" For what, Captain Arlee ?"

Cuffy had the greatest difficulty to hold Money Marks in his place. The fiery, spirited young man wished to jump up, and dash forward with a view of instantly annihilating the vindictive captain of the *Swamp Snake.*

" For his presumption in loving you."

" Is it more presumption in him than in you ?"

" Look at the difference in our relative positions."

" What is the difference? you are both sailors of fortune."

" Ay, ay, but he is nobody knows whom, and I am a gentleman. It is true I have no money, but what of that ? I have every opportunity of doing my country good service, and when the war is over I shall in all probability be rewarded in the most handsome manner by my Government."

" Your Government, Captain Arlee," said Viola, impressively, " is fighting in a bad cause."

" Ah! say you so ?"

" I do."

" Explain."

" It is fighting for slavery, and for the maintenance of slavery."

" Not so."

" I say it is, and Heaven will never prosper the arms of the South until unconditional abolition has been declared."

" These remarks are traitorous, young lady," said Captain Arlee.

" Possibly they are so," replied Viola, quietly.

" You echo your father's well-known dangerous sentiments."

" Not altogether; I sympathize with the South, because it was the home of my mother, and is now the abode of many of my friends. I have relatives in both armies, two under Lee, one under Sherman, another under Johnston, and three are fighting under Hood; yours is a gallant struggle, nobly conducted by a gallant and brave people."

" Miss Cathcart," said Captain Arlee, looking steadily at her.

" Sir."

" Are you aware that your remark just now is treasonable ?"

" I did not think of it in a political light."

" You did not ?"

" No, I thought I was talking to a friend or——"

" What?"

" A gentleman."

He winced at this reply.

" I am a friend, but it is in your power to make me an enemy, and if I am that, I am relentless and remorseless."

" Indeed."

" Yes, it is in my power now to lay an information against you, and have you committed to prison in this town."

" What, do you threaten me ?" said Viola.

" The villain," said Money Marks, between his teeth.

" I merely hint at what it is in my power to do," said the captain.

" Then I can only tell you, sir, that the bare hinting of such a thing does you infinite discredit, and I beg that you will permit me to go to Mr. Dalgren, before whom I will lay the whole state of the case, and ask his protection. I am poor and lonely, and bowed down with sorrow, but I will let you see that I am spirited and proud, and that I am not to be trampled upon, and insulted with impunity."

" I do not wish to insult you, but you have been guilty of using treasonable language."

" Well, sir, if I have done so, was it not said in confidence ?"

" There was no stipulation to that effect."

" If you wish to betray me, do so."

" Will you purchase my forbearance ?"

" At what price ?" she demanded, while her eyes flashed fire.

" The price of your love."

" You ask me to love you ?"

" I do."

" Have I not already told you that I cannot do so ?"

" You have not said so in so many words."

" I gave you to understand that I do not consider myself at liberty to listen to words of love from anybody, until after a certain time; that is, until I have paid a tribute to my dear father, which his shade has a right to expect, and which I would rather die than not render."

" Yes, yes, I understand that," said Captain Arlee, " but in these days so many accidents occur, that we do not think of death as we did in times of peace. It is nearer to us, and we have looked upon its face so often, that it has lost its terror for us. By all means pay respect to your father's memory, and mourn decently, but do not for months and months give yourself up to grief; that will never do. I sail for England soon."

" I am the judge, and the best judge, of my own actions."

" Perhaps not."

" You are insolent."

" Unintentionally so."

" I will not listen to you."

" You must."

" Must, sir ?"

" Ay, I said so."

" What mean you ?"

" Give me some hope; your stony conduct and cool behaviour drive me frantic. Oh! Miss Cathcart, oh! Viola, you do not, cannot guess the force of my devotion for you; I would do anything to please you."

"Allow me to go then," said Viola. "It is easy to put your love to the test; suffer me to depart."

"Not yet."

"That shows me the utter worthlessness of your vows."

"Give me some hope."

"I cannot."

"Oh! Viola, do you wish to drive me mad?" said Captain Arlee, sinking on one knee, and grasping her unwilling hand in one of his own.

"I wish to do nothing that is injurious to you. It is yourself that threatens me with harm."

"No, no, you mistake me—you misconstrue my motives. I will not have you say so. Viola, Viola, do you wish to distract me? Do you not know that this is the country of impassioned love, and mingling of hearts, the union of kindred souls? If you are ignorant of this fact, look above you! Consult the burning sun in the fair cerulean sky, and become a convert to the doctrine of sudden love and hasty marriages."

"Never. Leave me, Captain Arlee."

"I will not until I hear from you that you will be mine. Let those full red lips utter words of love, and tell me that I am dear to them, and——"

"Never, I say; unhand me, Captain Arlee, I will not suffer this."

"Dearest Viola."

"Do you wish to compromise me beyond redemption?"

"Answer me."

"I have done so."

"Tell me you love me."

"Never!"

"Speak the gracious words, or drive me mad for ever."

"You are mad already."

"Then 'tis your fault. Love me, tell me so, and make me sane."

"I will not listen to you."

"You shall."

"I say I will not."

"Once for all, Miss Cathcart," said Captain Arlee, "let me entreat you to listen to me. I want you to understand that I cannot be your *friend*."

"Why not?"

"Because I must be your enemy or your lover."

"Oh! monstrous; you frighten me with your threats."

He attempted to say something, but Viola broke from him, and ran with the fleetness of a deer across the lawn, and gained the shelter of the house before Captain Arlee could recover from the surprise and astonishment into which her precipitate and unexpected conduct had thrown him.

He threw himself upon the ground and lay there lamenting Viola's obduracy in no measured terms.

"She shall be mine," he said, in an impassioned tone, "yes—yes, she shall be mine, if I have to sin for her beyond redemption. Mine! mine! mine! Once mine, or once in my power, and all the rest will be easy. If she will not listen to me, I will employ force, for I love her beyond anything. I will take her from home and—but it is useless to talk of what I will do; I have the determination to do great things, but all depends upon accident and circumstances."

He paused a moment, and then resumed—

"That low rascal, Money Marks, is attached to the girl, or I am much mistaken; if it be so I will see him hanging to the yard-arm before I will suffer him to triumph over me. The scoundrel!—to dare to interfere with me. But his presumption shall be quickly and severely punished. Ah, yes! I promise him a speedy reward for his unheard-of insolence."

Suddenly a dark shadow fell upon him and a tall figure stood before him. It was the figure of a fine stalwart man, whose demeanour was almost majestic.

"No time like the present, Captain Arlee," exclaimed the figure.

The captain looked up, and, to his confusion, beheld Money Marks.

The latter had broken away from Cuffy, who would have restrained him, but the strength of the young man exceeded that of the negro, and he had his own way.

"You here?" cried Captain Arlee.

"I am."

"You dare to dog my footsteps, and play the spy upon my actions?"

"It would appear so."

"You are bold, young man."

"I have been told so before."

"Ha! you would insult me. I can see your motive in thus confronting me. You have witnessed my interview with Miss Cathcart; you are jealous, you—but I see it all. Well, it shall be my business to punish your presumption at a more fitting time. You are under my command."

"I was."

"And are; so now back to your ship; I order you."

"And I refuse to obey," said Money Marks, folding his arms and confronting his commander with all the consummate coolness he could summon to his aid.

"I order you under arrest."

"And I defy you."

"Ha! beware!"

"Of what, or whom?"

"Of me," replied Captain Arlee, rising to his feet.

"I think no more of you than I would of a worm I trample heedlessly under my feet," said Money Marks.

"This insolence shall not go unrewarded."

"Reward it now."

"No, no; not now: a time will come, and shortly. You shall hear from me."

Captain Arlee attempted to make off, but was seized by Money Marks, who dragged him back to the copse, saying—

"Your last hour is come. You are a monster, and I must rid the earth of you. Defend yourself, for I mean to battle for the right."

Captain Arlee turned deadly pale; his cheeks became the colour of ashes, and he trembled most violently.

"What would you do with me?" said the captain.

"Kill you."

"No, no! spare my life. I—I was not in earnest; my threats were not meant——"

"I cannot believe that. I know you too well, Captain Arlee—I know you to be a villain."

"I have done you no wrong."

"You have attempted to do so, and I am about to prevent your carrying your designs into execution. I have overheard your conversation with Vi—with Miss Cathcart and I have overheard your remarks made when you thought yourself alone."

"You are a low-minded wretch to stoop to such base methods of gaining information," said Captain Arlee, plucking up a spirit.

"Possibly; but when my interests are attacked I defend myself how I can."

"You will be sorry for this some day."

"Of the future I never think; the present alone concerns me," said Money Marks, with assurance.

Cuffy, not knowing what the issue of this contest would be, and not caring a straw what became of the captain, remained in concealment, always prepared to dash out and take the part of his new friend, Money Marks, for whom he conceived the greatest attachment; he was ready at all times to serve him with the utmost fidelity.

"Let me go; I will give you money," said Captain Arlee.

"I want it not."

"I shall call for help."

"Utter a sound and you are a dead man."

Captain Arlee would have remained silent had he been a wise man. It did not require much intelligence to read the determination for evil which was so clearly expressed in those flashing eyes, in the twitching of that finely cut nostril, and the contemptuous curl of that well-chiselled and full lip.

But he disregarded those signs, and attempted to cry out. The motion was fatal to him.

No sooner had he opened his mouth than Money Marks dashed his fist into his face and felled him to the earth with a blow that would have prostrated an ox.

Captain Arlee lay on his back upon the green sward, breathing heavily and groaning at short intervals.

Cuffy emerged from his place of concealment, and said, in a whisper—

"Massa Marks, Massa Marks, what you do now?"

Money Marks' eyes were flashing with awful rage, and so insensate was he that he did not hear Cuffy's question until he had repeated it three times. When he did fully understand it he replied to it in a practical manner by taking up a stone and battering the head of the prostrate man with it.

When he had beaten him to his satisfaction, he said to Cuffy—

"Do you think he is dead?"

"Him dead sure enough, massa; him dead as stone you hit with," said Cuffy.

"Pick up the body, then, and throw it into the thicket."

Captain Arlee's face was not disfigured: he had been beaten about the temples and the upper part of his head, and this part was covered with clotted blood and flowing blood, and hair matted with the sanguinary fluid. His face was pale although sprinkled here and there with blood.

Money Marks took one vindictive glance at him, and then Cuffy seized his late commander in his arms and threw him into the bushes, amidst which he fell with a crash.

"That do, massa?" inquired Cuffy.

"Yes, that will do. There is some carrion for the vultures."

"That serve him right. Cuffy never like Massa Arlee, him too proud; him think nothing of poor nig; him like all Southern peoples."

It was Money Marks' first murder, for he could not doubt that he had killed the captain; he had struck him repeatedly and administered very many heavy blows to him.

A strange feeling took possession of him—he felt that he wished to get away from the spot; that he *must* get away, or that he should die of suffocation where he stood.

He prepared to leave the spot, with the brand of Cain upon his brow; he had broken God's law, and he had infringed the law of man; he had no mercy to expect from Heaven or earth.

When his passion cooled a little he regretted what he had done, and wished that he had been less hasty. Yet he had to congratulate himself upon the removal of a rival.

He walked towards the garden-gate at which he had entered, when a loud shouting and holloaing saluted his ears.

Turning to Cuffy, he said—

"What is that?"

"I think it Massa Dalgren."

"In search of whom?"

"Of us, I suppose; he must have seen the—the murder."

Money Marks turned faint, and hesitated, not knowing what to do.

CHAPTER VIII.

THE ANACONDA.

MONEY MARKS thought it was incumbent upon him to make his escape as quickly as possible. He could not be sure that Mr. Dalgren had witnessed his attack upon the captain of the *Swamp Snake*, but it was just possible that he had done so, and, if that was the case, Charleston was no place for him.

Turning to Cuffy, he said—

"Follow me."

Cuffy replied in an earnest manner—

"To the end of de world, Massa Marks. Cuffy follow you anywhere."

Money Marks took to his heels, and ran as fast as he could to the garden-door at which he had entered.

It was unlocked. Opening it, he entered the street, and walked quickly along, followed by Cuffy.

At length they reached one of those cellars in which spirits were stored. Going down the steps they had something to drink, and, sitting in a corner by themselves, discussed their future plans.

"What shall we do now, Cuffy?" said Money Marks.

"Skedaddle, massa, like Yankees at Bull Run."

"Do you think the man's dead?"

"Cappen Arlee?"

"Yes."

"Oh! sure him dead enough—dead as mutton."

"What will they do?"

"Offer reward for your capture."

"And then?"

"Hang you up by the neck, and kill you, Massa Marks."

"That would not be very pleasant, certainly. I think we had better get out of this. What is your opinion?"

"Cuffy think so, too."

"Where shall we go?"

"Into the country, where the rice-plantations are, and live in swamp."

"Live in the swamps!" said Money Marks.

"Yes."

"You surprise me. I thought it was impossible to do so."

"Only one thing to fear, and that the fever. Oh, yes! two more things."

"What are they?"

"Snakes and alligators; one great beast they call cayman, him man-eater."

"Ah, I understand; but how are we to live in the swamps?"

"Take pistol and kill birds, and carry little biscuit with us. Shan't be long in swamp—go on to Wilmington. Take Cuff's advice, massa, and go through swamps to Wilmington."

"Very well," replied Money Marks, after some consideration, "we will do as you suggest. Do you know the way?"

"Yes, massa," said Cuffy. "Me slave down south once and me run away, and live in swamps one, two, three, four, week."

It was arranged between the two men that they should leave the city under cover of night, and steal into the swamps which lay to the south of Charleston. They provided themselves with pistols and ammunition, and prepared themselves for a march of ten days' duration. This scheme was both wild and imprudent, but they were both young, and youth is the season of imprudence and hazardous adventure; as we get older the blood gets cooler, and our adventurous instincts pass away.

Besides all this, it was absolutely necessary for Money Marks to fly from justice. He had broken the law, and in all likelihood the law would retaliate, and string him up to the nearest gibbet.

After walking nearly fifteen miles, they camped under a leafy tree, and, climbing into the boughs, slept till morning. The next day they pursued their journey. Money Marks got a shot at a gaily plumaged bird— of the name of which he was ignorant, but which Cuffy declared to be good eating—and at one o'clock, in the heat of the day, when the rage of the sun was most severe, they halted, and Cuffy prepared a fire to cook the bird by, while Money Marks expressed his intention of lying down under a tree and smoking a pipe, during the time his attached servant was engaged in cooking the dinner.

With a careless indifference, which was one of his characteristics, he sat himself down upon what appeared to be a log. Drawing his pipe from his pocket, he took out his pouch, and leisurely filled the bowl with what was really worthy the name of Old Virginia. A fusee lighted the tobacco, and he allowed the burning match to fall upon the log, where it settled.

Suddenly the log began to heave and move.

Money Marks sprang to his feet with a cry of alarm—his hair became erect, and perspiration started from every pore in his skin.

It was an awful moment.

Such a moment as he had never experienced before, and he hoped it might be his lot never to see again.

Instead of a log, that which he had so confidingly been sitting upon was a huge snake of the anaconda tribe.

It had crawled out of a thicket to bask in the sun, and the sun had stupified it, and sent it to sleep.

Its head was in the thicket when Money Marks made its acquaintance, though its body, or the best part of it, was in the open air.

Turning quickly round, the hideous reptile raised itself up until its spiral coils enabled it to stand and rear its crest about six feet from the ground.

It then turned its eyes full upon Money Marks, dazzling and fascinating him with its awful gaze.

Every now and then its jaws opened and its forked tongue darted in and out, as if in anticipation of a feast upon human flesh.

Oh, the pain, the agony, the indescribable torture of that terrible instant.

Money Marks trembled from head to foot, but he stood rooted to the spot, incapable of action and unable to move; his gaze was riveted upon that of the snake, and unless Heaven came to his rescue by the interposition of some miracle, his case was indeed hopeless.

His first impulse was to call aloud to Cuffy, who would promptly render him assistance, but when he attempted to cry out his tongue clove to the roof of his mouth.

The snake did not seem inclined to be offensively active just at present; it contented itself with moving its head backwards and forwards in an undulating manner, as if it felt perfectly sure of its prey, and wished to play with the wretched victim, as a cat plays with a mouse which it has caught, and which it has under its paw.

Cuffy was busy cooking: he had just finished picking the feathers off the bird which Money Marks had shot, and he was taking out the inside.

A cheerful fire burned close by. His back was turned to Money Marks, whom he imagined to be enjoying himself at a short distance.

Consequently he had no more idea of the dreadful and imminent peril in which his master stood than the child unborn.

Money Marks endeavoured to pray to Heaven for assistance, but he was too much agitated to remember the words which soothed his hours in the days of his infancy.

All at once the serpent narrowed the space between it and its victim, and drawing back its head, seemed ready to strike. Its body was inflated and swollen, and puffed up to an unnatural size.

Money Marks gave himself up for lost; he cursed the hour in which he had been born, and wished that Cuffy had been at the bottom of the sea before he had persuaded him to take refuge in the swamps, and leave Charleston on a perilous journey to Wilmington.

If he had remained in Charleston, it now occurred to him, in this, his dire extremity, that he might have found some place of refuge in so large a city, numbering for its population more than a hundred thousand souls.

Oh, that he had never been so foolhardy as to seek the shelter of the swamps, for then the awful fate which menaced him would have been averted.

Alas, regrets were vain, and wishes were equally useless.

Rather the hangman's rope, the jeers of the populace, the naked scaffold, and the cruel drop, than the poisoned fangs of the deadly anaconda.

Just as the creature appeared prepared to do battle, Cuffy oddly enough began to hum a well-known nigger melody.

The snake was pleased with the rough music, restrained its inclination to dart at Money Marks, and drew back, listening with evident delight to the words as they fell from Cuffy's lips.

Money Marks was reprieved, and the spell which had hitherto lain upon him, impeding his actions and paralyzing his arms, was removed.

His hand sought his girdle, and he drew a pistol therefrom.

To level it at the anaconda and pull the trigger was the work of an instant.

The ball entered the snake's eye, and a terrible hiss proclaimed the fact that the ball had gone crashing into the monster's brain.

Not trusting himself to deliver another shot, Money Marks ran towards Cuffy, who, alarmed at hearing the shot, was hastening up to the scene of action.

The snake was desperately injured, but not as yet killed. It lashed the earth with its tail, and twining around several young trees tore them up by the roots, doing great havoc and mischief, as if some convulsion of nature was taking place.

"Oh! Massa Marks," cried Cuffy; "what was the matter? You like as if see 'nother Tower Hill ghost."

Money Marks fell on his knees from excess of emotion, and pointed with his outstretched hand in the direction of the writhing snake.

"Um!" exclaimed Cuffy, as he perceived the monster; "big snake—Cuffy and snakes have met before; him ugly customer. Plague take him—hard hit, though; not dead yet. Cuffy give him 'nother shot."

So saying he levelled his pistol at the snake, and shot him through the head. Then he picked up one of the saplings he had torn up in his furious struggles, and running up to the dying reptile began to belabour his tail with the primitive weapon with which he had armed himself in the absence of anything better.

After violently belabouring the serpent for sometime he desisted from his efforts and went back to Money Marks, saying—

"Him ugly beast, Massa Marks; very ugly beast, but him dead now. No fear now; soon get used to snakes, plenty in swamp—an' good thing. Shall have better dinner —snake good eating."

"Good to eat?" repeated Money Marks, who was slowly recovering himself.

"Yes."

"Well, I never heard that before."

"Oh, yes! him true," said Cuffy, who went back to the still struggling snake.

The monster was dead however; the gyrations and contortions were nothing more than muscular writhings.

Cuffy fearlessly approached the snake, and, in spite of a few jerks given out by the moving body, he cut off three or four slices from the back, with which he returned to the camp in triumph.

It was some little time before Money Marks recovered his serenity sufficiently to be able to eat, but when he did he preferred the bird to the serpent steaks which Cuffy devoured with great relish, declaring that he had found a delicacy which he knew how to appreciate.

After dinner they once more pursued their way, and after a weary march of more than a fortnight they found themselves in Wilmington, footsore, tired, and longing for rest.

They were not without money, but the small stock they had could not be expected to last for ever. If they had expected such a thing they would have been greatly disappointed.

Three weeks after their arrival at this great port of the Confederacy, Money Marks said to Cuffy—

"How much money have you got?"

"One dollar," replied Cuffy, with a lugubrious look.

"And I have two. We must do something, or else we shall be starving."

"Suppose we go to sea again, Massa Marks?"

"To sea?"

"Yes; plenty ship come in here. Come down to the quay with me, and we soon find good ship."

"I think that is the wisest thing we can do."

"I'm sartin sure of it," replied Cuffy.

They accordingly walked down to the docks. Cuffy did not walk by his young master's side, he walked behind him at a respectful distance, only coming up when he was told to do so, and when Money Marks stopped and spoke to him. All sailors as a rule are fond of drinking, and there was a place near the docks called the "Waterlogged Craft" where most of the old salts assembled. Here at the same bar stood captains, lieutenants, and common seamen.

Money Marks ordered some rum, and said to some one standing near him—

"Do you happen to know of any ship about to sail?"

"I know of two or three."

"Have they got their full complement of hands?"

"All but one," replied the stranger, who was a dark, scowling, morose-looking man.

He fixed his keen black eyes, looking so potent for evil, full upon Money Marks, and seemed desirous of reading his heart, if he could dive far enough into his intervening thoughts to do so.

"Which one is that?"

"The Ocean Queen."

"Can you give me any particulars respecting the vessel?" said Money Marks.

"Yes, plenty," replied the stranger, with a significant smile which was full of meaning.

"I shall be much obliged to you."

"Never thank any one, young man, until you have gained your favour."

"I did not say I was much obliged, but that I should be," replied Money Marks, with dignity.

"Well, well, what are your questions?—what do you want to know?"

"What is the burden of the Ocean Queen?"

"A thousand tons."

"Then she is a decent sized vessel."

"If you knew anything about tonnage you would not be in doubt, and ask that question."

"What is her trade?"

"She does a little business occasionally between Africa and Cuba."

"Rice and palm oil, I suppose?"

"You are not far wrong."

"What is the number of the crew?"

"Thirty men, three lieutenants, two mates—forty men, in short, all told."

"When does she sail?"

"In a week's time."

"What is the captain's name?"

"Monkhouse."

"When can he be seen?"

"At almost any time."

"Where is he now?"

"Standing before you."

"Where?"

"Under your nose."

"Yourself!"

"The same, my man, and at your service," exclaimed the captain, lighting a cigar in an unconcerned manner.

———

CHAPTER IX.

CAPTAIN MONKHOUSE.

"So you want to join, eh?" inquired Monkhouse.

"Yes, sir," replied Money Marks.

"Have you been a sailor all your life?"

"No, sir, not all my life."

"Do you know your duty?"

"I hope so."

"Well, I'll take you for a year, if you like to join."

"Thank you, sir."

"You look a likely fellow."

"I can be smartish when I like."

"Come to me on board the *Queen* to-morrow, and I will talk to you."

"Very well, sir."

"Who is that black fellow with you?"

"We always sail together."

"Indeed!"

"Yes, we are old friends and comrades."

"Does he ship as cook?"

"No, as ship's carpenter."

"Ah! that will just do. Our carpenter has deserted—left us at Bahia." Turning to Cuffy, the captain said: "Nigger!"

"Yes, cappen," replied Cuffy, with a grin.

"Are you tough?"

"Guess I am."

"Can you stand nigger's pay?"

"What's that?"

"More kicks than halfpence."

"Calc'late can, cappen."

"Then you're the boy for me. Where do you hail from?"

"Where was I raised?"

"Yes."

"Down in Tennessee."

"Ah! you were raised too far south to be honest, but I'll try you both—never like to see men out of work. Call on me to-morrow at my hotel."

"I thought you said you would be on board the ship, sir?" said Money Marks.

"Ah! so I did. Come on board about ten o'clock in the morning. The *Queen* is lying off the harbour mouth. Good day to you."

"Good day, cappen," said Cuffy.

"None of your cheek, sambo, or I have a bit of bamboo which will tickle the soles of your feet!" said Monkhouse, with a savage look.

Cuffy's countenance fell, and he looked grave.

The captain of the *Ocean Queen* turned on his heel, left the bar of the "Water-logged Craft," and walked away in the direction of the custom-house.

"Me no like that man," said Cuffy to Money Marks.

"Not like him—why?"

"I not know exactly, but he bad mans."

"H'm—p'raps you're right, but beggars mustn't be choosers," said Money Marks, "and I think we had better accept his offer."

"You're a fool if you do!" cried a voice at his elbow.

"Oh! and who are you that knows so much more than anybody else?" inquired Money Marks.

"Who am I!" replied a fine handsome-looking fellow, who had addressed him.

"Yes, and who are you?"

"My name's what you'll be, if you ain't civil."

"What's that?"

"Walker!"

"I don't know about that."

"But I do—howsomever it ain't worth one's while to quarrel over a fellow like that d—— blackguard, who has just gone out. I was going to give you a bit of good advice. The cap'n of the *Ocean Queen* is a duffer—he's not true metal—he hasn't got the ring of it about him, and his ship's a hell afloat."

"How do you know that?" said Money Marks.

"Because a pal of mine sailed with him, worse luck. He just made one voyage, and then he cried quits—and no fool either, seeing as how he'd had his belly full of it."

"Perhaps, you are prejudiced against him?"

"Not I!—ask any man in the place."

"Well, ask them."

"I say, mates!" cried the sailor, "what do you think of Captain Monkhouse and the *Ocean Queen*?"

A deep groan arose, and hisses were audible above the tumult.

"We can't all be prejudiced," continued the sailor.

"No—of course not."

"And there are men here who are badly in want of a ship, and wouldn't have a halfpenny to spend if it wasn't for the crimps, and they wont sail under Mr. Monkhouse, and small blame to them, say I."

"Thank you for your information," said Money Marks, "what will you have to drink?"

"Well, as you're so pressing I wont say no to a drop of rum."

Shortly afterwards Cuffy and his master left the place and hunted about without finding any ship which was in want of hands; owing to the severity of the blockade, ships were scarce and sailors numerous.

On the morning of the next day Money Marks proposed that they should keep their appointment with the captain, and go on board.

"If you do not like it," he said, "we can always leave the ship; she does not sail for a week and they will not want us to join at once."

"Rather stay on shore, Massa Marks."

"Oh! nonsense; let us go and see and judge for ourselves. It wont do to remain long here, because of the scarcity of money—our supply will soon be exhausted and then what are we to do? We want a ship and I do not think we can do better than sail with Captain Monkhouse, in the *Ocean Queen*."

"Very well, massa; you know best," replied Cuffy, who with the usual docility of a negro, was perfectly ready to agree with anything his master decided upon.

The two men went down to the quay and hired a boat to take them to the *Ocean Queen*, which was lying exactly where the captain described her to be. She appeared to have been moved in the night outside the bar, as if in readiness for immediate sailing.

The man whom they had engaged to row them was an old salt, such as may frequently be met with in American ports. He was a thorough-going Yankee, believed in the Union, could not make up his mind to believe in Secession, never bothered himself much about politics, and hated the English like poison, which is always a characteristic of low-born Americans.

He remembered the fight between the *Shannon* and the *Chesapeake*, and would spin you the yarn any day and any number of times in a day, if you would ease his utterance with a glass of grog.

"Going to the *Hocean Queen*, sir?" he exclaimed.

"Yes, that's the ticket," replied Money Marks.

"Got any friends aboard, sir?"

"No; I am only acquainted with the captain."

"Ah! he's a bright perticklar star, he is."

"Do you know him?" asked Money Marks, feeling a little curious and wishing if possible to drag some information out of the old sailor respecting the captain under whom he was going to sail.

"I've known Jimmy Monkhouse this eighteen year, sir, off and on," replied the sailor; "and he's what I call a tarnation rum card. It takes a chap some time, it does, to get round Jimmy Monkhouse, I'm blessed if it don't, but when he does open a cove's eyes, lor, don't he stare."

"You don't seem to give the captain of the *Ocean Queen* a very good character."

"I ain't said nothing agin him, have I?" inquired the sailor, in a hasty voice, as if he was alarmed at some slip of the tongue.

"Well, you haven't said anything in his favour."

CUFFY FINDS THE STONE HARDER THAN HIS HEAD.

"I don't care as long as I ain't said nothing, 'cos Jimmy Monkhouse ain't the man to be put out without letting of you feel as you mustn't take no liberties with him."

"Is he such a determined man as that?"

"He is and no mistake, guv'nor; Jimmy would just swamp the universe sooner nor not have his own way; he'd go in for etarnal smash, he would, rather than be bested. He says he means to run for the Presidency of the United States, he does, when he's made his fortune."

"How is he going to do that?"

"I'm mum."

"Can't you speak?"

"I've 'ollered loud enough, urreddy."

"But to me——"

"Who are you more'n any one else?"

"Well, you're a funny fellow."

"That's what my mother allers said of me when I wouldn't be weaned on nothing but sponge-cakes and gin."

"What's your name?"

"What's yourn?"

"Money Marks."

"Mine's Cyrus Blast."

"What are you?"

"What be you?"

"A sailor."

"Ditto."

"Are you attached to a ship?"

"Are you?"

"I'm going to join the *Ocean Queen*."

"Jine the *Queen!*" echoed Cyrus Blast, in a tone of intense surprise. "Well I'm jiggered! Blow me tight! That's a licker! Do you know what you're agwine to jine?"

"No."

"Shall I tell you?"

"If you please."

Cyrus Blast lowered his voice to a whisper as if afraid that the winds would hear what he had to say and run away with the intelligence to the four corners of the earth, if the earth, which is popularly supposed to be round, can be said to have corners.

"Did you ever hear of a hell afloat?"

"Yes, but——"

"Don't you interrupt me. You did?"

"Yes."

"Well then, you're agwine to one."

"You're joking."

"Am I?"

"You must be."

"No, I musn't; there ain't no must about it."

"Do you mean——"

"That'll do; you'll see presently."

"If that's the case," said Money Marks, looking alarmed, "the best thing we can do is to go back again."

"Yes, Massa Marks," interposed Cuffy, "let's make tracks."

"I don't care what you do," said Cyrus Blast; "you look a likely young fellow, and I shouldn't wish to see you mix with the scum of the earth, and go on board a vessel, to whose sides you have been lured by false pretences."

"By George!" exclaimed Money Marks: "the ship's close to us—we are almost under her sides. That to the left is the *Ocean Queen*; I can see her name on the stern."

"So it is," said Cyrus Blast; "but it ain't too late now—you can go back or go on, as you like. I ain't saying this 'cos I's got a spite agin Jim Monkhouse, not I."

"I know that."

"It's merely out of regard for you, young man."

"Thank you; you are entitled to my gratitude, and I'm sure you have it."

"Which will you do, go on or go back? Make haste and choose."

Money Marks fixed his regards for a moment or two upon the *Ocean Queen* before replying. She was a black piratical-looking vessel, hull down in the water. Her appearance was not calculated to reassure the timid mariner; on the contrary, it inspired Money Marks with so much involuntary dread that he shuddered visibly, as if fearing he knew not what.

The sides of the vessel were pierced with holes, through which the brass muzzles of guns protruded. There were five guns on each side, and a large swivel in the bows with which the captain would be able to rake an enemy with great advantage.

"Well, guv'nor, have you made your mind up?" inquired Cyrus Blast.

"Yes," replied Money Marks, laconically.

"What's it to be, cut and run?"

"That's it."

"Right you are."

Cuffy's face broke into smiles which denoted how pleased he was with the decision that his master had come to.

"That seems to please you, nig," exclaimed Cyrus Blast.

"Yes, that's the 'coon for my tree," replied Cuffy.

A man had been standing on the deck of the *Ocean Queen*, for some time watching the oncoming boat through the help of a powerful telescope.

This man was Monkhouse.

He had not failed to recognise the two men with whom he had spoken in the spirit store the day before.

His usually severe countenance wore a smile of satisfaction, triumph, and pleasure.

He called his first lieutenant to his side, and exclaimed—

"Look."

The lieutenant gazed at the boat, and said—

"New hands."

"They are."

"That will just complete our complement."

"It will."

The lieutenant was named Demon Magos, and was in disposition a perfect fury; his cruelty to the men under his command was notorious and unprecedented; but more of this man's character presently.

Cyrus Blast turned the boat round with some difficulty, and proceeded to scull back to shore.

This manœuvre was instantly remarked by Captain Monkhouse, who cried—

"Do you see that? eh, what's the meaning of such strange conduct?"

Demon Magos looked steadily at the gradually receding craft, and said—

"They smell a rat."

"Ha! do they so? we will teach them something. It shall be a musk rat they smell. Bring a shotted gun on deck; meanwhile I'll hail them."

Demon Magos departed on his errand, and the captain exclaimed in a stentorian voice, and bellowing through his hands, which he had raised and placed close to his mouth—

"Boat ahoy!"

No answer.

"Ahoy, there, I say!"

Still no answer.

"Boat ahoy! Heave to."

Still there was no answer, although the words were distinctly audible to those in the boat.

"Jimmy Monkhouse is going it," said Cyrus Blast.

"He can't hurt us."

This was Money Marks' idea.

"Can't he? wait a bit; you ain't out of the wood yet, my hearty, although you may be presently; you don't know Cappen Monkhouse so well as I do, and I can tell you one thing."

"What's that?"

"If we don't obey his summons, do what he tells us, and heave to, we may look out for squalls."

Money Marks and Cuffy looked blankly at one another, while Cyrus Blast sculled away from the fatal ship with all the energy of which he was capable, but he could not make much way against the tide, which was flowing out of the harbour.

"Stand to, there," again vociferated the captain, who held in his hands a gun, which Demon Magos had brought him.

No reply.

"Stand to, or by heaven, I fire."

Cyrus Blast continued his exertions with undiminished vigour.

Captain Monkhouse handed the weapon to Demon Magos, saying—

"Do you fire, my hand trembles with rage."

"Shall I kill?" inquired Demon Magos, with a bloodthirsty look.

"No, over their heads; you have the second barrel, and besides, we can lower a boat and overtake them, if all else fails."

Demon Magos did not trouble himself to take aim; he lifted the gun to his shoulder in a careless manner, and drawing the trigger, watched the dismay of the inmates of the boat, as the missile flew by them, and ploughed up the water, a little in their front.

With a vigorous stroke Cyrus Blast turned the boat's head and heaved to.

"What are you doing?" indignantly cried Money Marks.

"A 'eaving to."

"What for?"

"Cos he tells us to."

"But I want to escape."

"Can't help that."

"Yes you can."

"Tell you I can't. Guess I know Jimmy Monkhouse a tarnation sight better nor you do; he only fired that journey to fret us, next time he shoots he'll send a bullet at once on us, and let daylight in, which ain't good for this child's complaint."

"No—nor dis child's either," chimed in the swarthy negro.

"If you wont row to shore, I'll see if I can't make you," cried Money Marks, with the light of frenzied determination flashing from his eyes.

"You, boy! who are you talking to?" replied Cyrus Blast, contemptuously.

"To you."

"Then hold you jaw, 'cos it ain't no good your threatening me. I'm an old sailor, and chaff don't do me no good; I'm apt to get riled, and when my wool's rose, I'm dangerous."

Money Marks saw that he was comparatively helpless, and that he could do nothing to extricate himself from the unpleasant position in which he found himself.

"You should ha' thought of all this afore you comed aboard the *Hocean Queen*," continued Cyrus Blast, "if you'd taken the trouble to make inquiries, anyone one would have told you the crackter of the vessel, but you was so hot after a berth, I expect, that you couldn't do nothing."

Money Marks sat still, and resigned himself to his fate; he would very much have preferred gaining the shore to going on board the *Ocean Queen*, but as he could not do the former he became a philosopher, and hoped that no harm would result from his becoming the involuntary guest of Captain Monkhouse, who was evidently a different sort of man from what Marks had in unsuspicious innocence imagined him to be.

CHAPTER X.

THE HELL AFLOAT.

CAPTAIN MONKHOUSE noticed with satisfaction that the runaways had diligently obeyed his instructions to heave to.

Turning to Demon Magos, he said—

"Keep your persuader to your shoulder, so that they may see that you are in earnest; they have done as I wish, and now I must make them come aboard."

"Boat, ahoy!" he exclaimed.

"Sir," replied Cyrus Blast.

"Pull up to my ship."

"Ay, ay, sir."

Cyrus Blast pulled with a will, the boat made way, and in about ten minutes from the firing of the gun, which Monkhouse had playfully called his "persuader," the boat was alongside.

"Make your boat fast to the chains," said the captain, "and all three of you come aboard."

"You don't want me, cappen?" said Cyrus Blast.

"You'll have a glass of grog."

"Well, I don't mind if I do, along with my mates."

"Step on board, then; and you nigger chap show us how spry you can be."

Money Marks was the first to ascend, followed by the boatman; Cuffy came last.

"Well, my fine fellows," said Captain Monkhouse, as they were all three standing in a row before him, "what made you take a sudden dislike to the service, and 'bout ship?"

"Well, cappen, it was this way," replied Cyrus Blast, who took upon himself the office of spokesman: "These gentlemen who are standing by me had been and forgot their kits, and they thought it was never no good going aboard without their kits, so we turned back."

"That's a clever excuse, but it will do. So long as you're on board, I don't care. And now, my old salt, what will you have to drink?"

"What have you got, sir?"

"Everything—sherry, port, grog: which will you have?"

"Well, sir, I don't mind a glass of sherry and a topper of port, while the grog's getting ready."

Monkhouse laughed, and gave orders that the demand of the sailor should be obeyed to the letter, and that the hospitality of the ship should be extended to Money Marks and the negro.

Cyrus Blast kept on looking about him suspiciously, as if he expected some foul play every moment.

Money Marks and Cuffy stood by the captain, who conversed in a friendly tone with them, asking them many questions about a sailor's life, which they did not find it at all difficult to answer.

"Have you been long on the sea?" he said.

"Not a long time."

"Do you like a sailor's life?"

"Yes, if I sail with a good captain, nice officers, and an agreeable crew."

"In what capacity did you sail during your last voyage?"

"Captain's secretary."

"What did that oblige you to do?"

"Write the captain's letters, read to him when he was idle and lazy, talk to him, amuse him, and tell him stories and anecdotes, drink his wine and smoke his cigars, and have the use of his cabin."

"You had a good berth of it then," said Monkhouse, with a smile.

"I always reckoned so."

"And I don't think you were far wrong."

"No, sir."

"Do you expect the same berth on board my ship?"

"I shouldn't object to it."

"No, I should think not. But I don't imagine that I shall be able to oblige you—we want hands, and you will have to work before the mast."

"I didn't agree to that," said Money Marks.

"Possibly not," replied the captain, who turning to Cuffy said—

"Now, nig, what are you up to?"

"Cookin', massa."

"We've got a cook; what else can you do?"

"Work in fo'castle, massa, wid other sailors."

"That'll do. We'll make your black hide sweat, or we'll know the reason why."

During this conversation Demon Magos had been below; he emerged from the hidden depths of the ship, and appeared upon the top of the companion ladder with something heavy and round, which he with difficulty supported with both hands.

He approached the side of the ship with it, and leant over the part of the sea in which the sailor's boat was lying.

Cyrus Blast caught sight of him in a moment, and rushed forward, but before he could reach the lieutenant, that worthy had dropped something over the side.

It was an immense shot.

There was a dull thud, a crash, and a tremendous hole appeared in the bottom of the boat.

It was ruined for ever.

The water began to pour in a stream, and the boat was rapidly sinking.

"You d—— villain!" cried Cyrus Blast; "curse you!"

As he spoke he struck him a severe blow in the face, which the lieutenant returned, and a battle began.

"Do you want any help?" asked the captain.

"Not I," replied Demon Magos, who slipped his hand into his pocket, and put something on his knuckles.

The next moment Cyrus Blast fell to the deck with one half of his face smashed and battered in an awful manner.

Demon Magos had armed himself with one of those terrible weapons called a knuckle-duster, which is made of a band of iron with rings for the fingers to fit in on one side, while on the other is a row of sharp spikes.

He struck the boatman with great violence, and tore the flesh from his face in a dreadful way.

Cyrus Blast was insensible and bleeding profusely.

Demon Magos looked around him with a revengeful glance, and said—

"That's discipline; that's how we do it on board the *Ocean Queen*."

"Away with him; let the doctor see him," said Captain Monkhouse. "And Mr. Magos."

"Sir."

"See that the men raise the anchor immediately; we sail in an hour."

"Ay, ay, sir."

Money Marks was more astonished than ever.

Cuffy did not attempt to disguise his terror.

Money Marks was not a man who hesitated long when it was necessary that a decisive course of action should be assumed; indeed his decision of character recommended him to all those who were acquainted with him. He saw that it was essentially a time for action, and he did not spend much time in rumination. Going up to the captain, he exclaimed, touching his tarpaulin hat respectfully as he spoke—

"Will you, please sir, give me some work to do, for I hate being idle; perhaps I can help the men to raise the anchor?"

Monkhouse appeared agreeably surprised at the decided change which had taken place in Money Marks' demeanour. The fact was that Marks saw it would be useless to rebel. The fate which had overtaken the unfortunate boatman who, unluckily for himself, had undertaken to row them to the mysterious ship, of whose crew he was now a recognised member, was a sufficient warning to him of what would infallibly befal himself and Cuffy, should they have the hardihood to resist what appeared to be, for a time at least, their inevitable destiny.

He did not, in his heart, like either the captain or the ship, but he was of opinion that he was safely entrapped, and that to get back to Wilmington would be an impossibility.

Both Monkhouse and Demon Magos seemed lawless and determined characters, who would feel little compunction in shedding human blood, should it answer their purpose to do so.

He resolved to attempt to escape at the first port they touched at. They could not keep him always on board, and he would endeavour to inspire confidence in their minds by good conduct and cheerful behaviour.

That this was a sensible resolution on his part, nobody can doubt.

"You can lend a hand, my good fellow, anywhere for the present," said Monkhouse.

"Make myself generally useful, sir?"

"Yes, that's about the size of it."

"Excuse me, sir, but——"

"But what?"

"You wont be offended?"

"No; speak out."

"The negro once saved my life, and I look upon him as a faithful servant—he will do anything for me."

"Well!"

"I merely wanted to ask, sir, that he might be let down easy."

"Oh, never mind the nigger," replied Captain Monkhouse, "he'll find his level. Don't you talk too much about the nigger, or else the men will think you're nothing better than a mean white yourself."

"But——"

"Listen to me, sir!" said Monkhouse, sternly. "I have had a man tied to the capstan for less than that, and flogged till his back was like a piece of liver."

Money Marks' face flushed indignantly, which the captain was not slow to remark.

"Ah! the blood flies to your cheeks, does it, at the idea! well, we can soon let a little out for you, if you are troublesome. You leave the nigger to himself. Let him slide, and if anybody tries to see which is the toughest—a nigger's hide or a well-made boot, take my advice, and don't interfere. Cave in, or else you'll get hotly handled yourself!"

"Very well, sir," replied Money Marks, who saw that his only chance of being at all comfortable was to stand by himself, do whatever duty he was called upon to perform, gain the captain's good will, and be charitable by stealth, if at all.

Cuffy telegraphed a thankful glance to his master, which showed that he appreciated the effort which had been made on his behalf, and he, too, resolved to be humble, and follow his master's wise example in everything.

"This is indeed a hell afloat," muttered Money Marks, as he moved slowly towards the fore part of the vessel.

"Eh! what's that you're saying?" cried a voice at his elbow.

He looked up, and recognised Demon Magos, the cowardly wretch who had stricken Cyrus Blast to the deck with that frightful instrument—a knuckle-duster.

"Nothing, sir," he replied.

"Oh, yes it was!—don't tell me lies."

"I beg your pardon, but——"

"I tell you I heard you, and we never allow murmuring on board our ship."

"Whatever I said was not intended for your ears!" said Money Marks, a little angrily.

"Oh, indeed! Then that is intended for your ears," replied Demon Magos, hitting him a severe blow on the side of the head with his open palm.

Money Marks was naturally choleric, and this insult was more than he could bear. He found it impossible to help venting it, and even with the fear of the knuckle-duster before his eyes, he clenched his fist, and struck the lieutenant very much as Cyrus Blast had done.

He did more execution.

The blow took effect upon the brute's upper lip, and cut it completely in two.

With a howl of furious rage, Demon Magos prepared to retaliate.

Money Marks saw him feeling in his pocket for his knuckle-duster, and he determined that his face should not be crushed and disfigured for life, if he had the power to help it. So he took up a knife, which like most seafaring men he carried at his belt, and, rapidly opening it, held it up in self-defence.

Demon Magos was so blinded with rage, that he did not notice the knife, and as he rushed to the attack the blade struck him, and penetrated his side, entering just below the fifth rib, but not proceeding far. A loud cry, more like a despairing wail than anything else, arose from Demon Magos, bringing the captain on the scene.

Monkhouse comprehended everything in a moment.

The lieutenant lying on the deck, supporting himself on his left elbow, raining curses and denunciations on his antagonist, the blood pouring from his wounds profusely the while.

Money Marks standing with the blood-stained knife in his hand, his face flushed, and his breath coming irregularly.

This all went to tell the tale.

"Hang him! hang him!" cried Demon Magos.

"Certainly not—you are too handy with your fists," replied the captain. "This will do you good, and cool your courage."

Demon Magos scowled, but said nothing more.

Some sailors approached and took him below, where his wound was dressed and attended to by the ship's surgeon.

Turning to Money Marks, the captain said—

"Don't suppose for a moment that because I have reprimanded my lieutenant that you are going to escape; I must and will enforce discipline. Instead of taking the law into your own hands, you should have come to me, and I would have seen justice done you."

"He assaulted me," said Money Marks.

"Possibly, but you must remember that he is your superior officer." Turning to an old sailor who stood hard by, he said—"Sling a rope!"

"Where, sir?"

"Over the davits."

"Ay, ay, sir."

A rope was quickly slung, and the captain gave some instructions to his second mate, who was a little deformed fellow, known amongst the crew as Devilskin, though his real name was De Morgan.

Money Marks stood trembling, more with anger than with fear, and awaited his fate, of which he was not destined to remain long in ignorance.

Were they about to hang him?

He could not tell.

Devilskin was a man with a big head—a preposterously big head—no neck to speak of, round shoulders, almost open to the reproach of humpbackedness, long elfin arms, and fat stumpy legs.

He was an ungainly creature.

Devilskin gave orders that the rope should be fastened round Money Marks' shoulders, which was accordingly done with great promptitude.

He was then launched over the side, and soused into the sea, in which he remained until he was half suffocated. Then Devilskin exclaimed—

"Haul up."

Money Marks came to the deck dripping wet, and looking very foolish and uncomfortable. He tried to say, "curse you all," but before the words were half out of his mouth down he went a second time.

This innocent amusement lasted nearly a quarter of an hour, and only ceased when it was evident that if it did not the man would die.

Now Captain Monkhouse did not want him to die, because he intended to make use of him, and the worst use you can put a man to is to kill him.

He was pulled up, and placed on the deck, where he gasped for breath; then he was untied and taken below, where stimulants were given him.

For the rest of the day he remained in his berth and ruminated over what had happened to him: he vowed to have revenge upon Demon Magos, who was a man he regarded with the utmost abhorrence; he looked upon him as the author of the misfortune which had befallen him and he swore that he would never rest until his vengeance was full and complete.

He bitterly regretted ever having been so foolish as to ship on board the *Ocean Queen*, which he could see easily enough was a hell afloat; he had his doubts and fears that it was something worse.

The next day Demon Magos was pronounced out of danger, and the doctor said that he would be able to get about again, and resume his duty in a fortnight. This was cheering news for Magos, who sent for the captain, who attended him in the infirmary of the ship, and inquired after his health.

"I am going on well, as you may have heard," replied Demon Magos; "but I cannot rest contented until I know that Marks is punished."

"He has been punished already," replied Monkhouse, quietly.

"Ah!" cried the wounded man, whose eyes sparkled with gratified malignity.

"I did not allow an hour to elapse before I impressed

upon his ardent nature that discipline was always enforced on board my ship."

"In what way was he punished?"

"We dropped him over the side, and only left off when it was considered dangerous to go on."

"Bah!" said Demon Magos, "that is worse than nothing."

"What do you wish?"

"I have served you well."

"You have."

"I am the most faithful officer you have."

"I believe so."

"Then gratify my whim in this instance."

"What is it?"

"Let Money Marks be flogged."

"If you wish it, certainly," replied Monkhouse."

"I will have my bed carried on deck so that I may witness the spectacle, which will be so pleasing to me that I am persuaded I shall recover much sooner than I otherwise should do; let everything be got in readiness at once. Let me sentence him."

"It shall be as you wish. I thought that the fellow had been sufficiently punished."

"What! for stabbing me?"

"As you think differently, I will make no opposition," replied Captain Monkhouse, who went away to give orders for the event which was about to take place.

The vessel had set sail the day before, and was sailing before a fair wind, which promised soon to take her to her destination, wherever that might be, only the officers knew what port they were bound to; the men were all blindly ignorant.

Money Marks had emerged from his berth early in the morning, feeling none the worse for his sea-bath; he had been placed in a watch and was doing duty.

The men with whom he conversed seemed to be a discontented set of fellows, but they were afraid to speak openly and give utterance to their real sentiments for fear of punishment, as the officers were always walking up and down the deck, prying into this hole and corner and then into that, as if they were spying, and endeavouring to collect materials for a charge of insubordination.

The officers, too, appeared to be in a perpetual dread of revolt, for they were always armed to the teeth; they never thought of going about without carrying with them at least two revolvers, one bowie knife, a loaded life-preserver, or life-destroyer, as the case might be, and a rattan with which to enforce their commands upon the wretched sailors, who wished themselves in purgatory, sooner than where they were.

The crew for the most part had been, from what Money Marks could see, entrapped like himself on board the ship; and they were proportionately indignant at being the victims of specious lies and clever artifices.

At about half-past eleven, Money Marks was leaning over the bulwarks, and watching the ripple of the dark blue sea, wishing that he was back again in Wapping with Mr. Samkin, and drawing beer for the sailor customers of the "Pint of Porter."

Suddenly Devilskin came behind him and touching him lightly on the shoulder, exclaimed with an elfin chuckle—

"You're wanted."

"Wanted?"

"Yes."

"What for?"

"You'll know presently."

"Why not now?"

"Because it ain't for me to tell you."

"Who wants me?"

"Cappen," replied Devilskin.

"Where is he?"

"Follow me and you'll see."

Money Marks followed Devilskin aft, and the captain said to him—

"Marks."

"Yes, sir."

"The offence you committed yesterday is a very serious one. The punishment you have already received is only part of what you will have to undergo. In ten minutes' time all hands will be piped on deck, and you will be flogged."

At this announcement Money Marks felt sick and ill, and reeled against the hammock nettings; recovering himself by a great effort, he went up to the captain, and said—

"I hope you will reconsider your resolve, sir. If you carry out your intention it will only make me mutinous and discontented. At present——"

"Ah! do you threaten me?"

"No, sir, not at all. I merely say that I am willing to serve you well and faithfully at present."

"It will be my fault," said the captain, with a sneer, "if you do not do so at all other times."

Money Marks turned away, seeing that to remonstrate with the captain was worse than useless, but he swore in his heart of hearts that so sure as the cruel lash descended upon and ploughed up his back into hideous furrows, he would have a terrible revenge.

He swore an awful oath—he swore by the God that made him, by the mother that bore him, by the soul which lived in his body, that he would *wash out the unjust deed with blood!*

Presently the captain's myrmidons seized him and carried him to the middle of the ship. When he was amidships, they stripped him and bound him so that he was unable to extricate himself.

Demon Magos came on deck as he said he would. He could not—like he that was sick of the palsy—take up his bed and walk, but he had himself carried on deck, and ill as he was, he said to the boatswain and his mates—

"Give him four dozen, and mind it is well laid on, bo'sun, or your own back shall suffer for it."

Money Marks bore his punishment bravely, but ere it was finished he was insensible, and the doctor ordered him to be taken down or he would infallibly die.

When Demon Magos saw that he was baulked of his prey, his rage knew no bounds; he urged the boatswain to go on, declaring that the man was shamming, and that it was a dodge and an artifice to excite sympathy and get off the infliction of the ten or twelve lashes which yet remained as his due.

The captain had confidence in the doctor, and ordered that Money Marks should be placed under medical care.

The negro, Cuffy, witnessed all this, and grated his pearly white teeth together. He did not make any sign, because his good sterling common sense informed him that to do so would be imprudent in the extreme, and probably expose him to the same fate as that which had befallen his unlucky master.

Cuffy shuddered as he saw the bloody and mangled back of Money Marks, and wished it had been in his power to prevent the occurrence of such a catastrophe.

He came to the conclusion that as long as Demon Magos lived, their would be no peace for either himself or Money Marks, and he was not far wrong.

He made up his mind that night to slay the man who had been mainly instrumental in bringing about the indelible disgrace which Money Marks had lately undergone.

CHAPTER XI.

A BLOODY DEED.

DEVILSKIN thought it perfectly fair and legitimate to amuse himself as much as he liked with a negro.

Cuffy being the only one on board, he did his best to extract some fun out of him. He had him down on the evening of the day of Money Marks' disgrace, in the gunroom, and said to him—

"Guess they were a long time ablacking of you, Sambo."

"Comed nat'ral, massa," said Cuffy, with a broad grin that threatened to part his head asunder.

"Oh, it did, eh? Comed nat'ral like grunting to a pig?"

"That's it, massa."

"Bring us a brush, and let's see if I can get a polish on yer."

"Calc'late that'll be rather difficult, massa."

"Off with you. Bring a brush, and mind it's a hard one."

Cuffy departed on his errand, well knowing what would happen to him, for he was well acquainted with Devilskin's cruel nature, and it wasn't the first time that Cuffy had been "polished" by a white man.

He chose the softest brush he could find, and gave it to Devilskin, who took hold of one of the black's arms, and, spitting on it, proceeded to rub the brush up and down upon the unprotected flesh—just for all the world as if it had been an inanimate thing, such as a boot, a coat, or a hat.

The pain to Cuffy was intense, as may be imagined.

"Guess this blacking ain't no good," said Devilskin.

"Oh! oh!" cried Cuffy.

"Hurt you?"

"Yes, massa, him hurt orful bad!" said Cuffy, from whose arm the blood was trickling slowly.

"Go 'long!" replied Devilskin, "it don't hurt; it's only your artfulness."

"No it tain't, indeed, massa."

"Can you split a cheese with your woolly head?"

"Have done that trick, massa. Do it once, do it twice—as the saying is."

"Steward!"

"Yes, sir."

"Bring us in a couple of cheeses."

"Yes, sir."

A rapid sign, which was unperceived by Cuffy, passed between the steward and Devilskin.

Cuffy was about to be made the victim of an atrocious plot. It was a favourite scheme with white men to tell negroes to split cheeses with a butt of their heads, and when they did actually split a real cheese *to substitute a millstone in its stead!*

This was infamous enough in all conscience, but Devilskin knew very well that it took a great deal to break the head of a negro, which is popularly supposed to be as thick as two brick walls, the side of an iron-clad, a yard of solid rock, and a lump of cast-iron put together.

Seriously, the only vulnerable part of a negro is his shin—give a thorough-bred woolly-headed negro a good kick on the shin, and he will howl like a bull-calf for mercy.

Achilles was only vulnerable in his heel, and the negro bears this resemblance to the ancient hero, that he is only to be badly hurt about his lowest extremities.

The steward returned with a cheese, which he put on its end on the ground. It was firmly fixed by two heavy pieces of lead placed on each side of it.

Then he went away to bring the millstone.

Cuffy was unsuspicious of the trick which was to be played upon him—he smiled, baring his gums, and showing his teeth.

Then he stooped down, bending himself almost double, and rushed forward with great force, striking the cheese in the centre with the crown of his head, and breaking it in three pieces.

"Bravo! well done!" cried Devilskin.

His applause was echoed by the rest of the inmates of the gun-room.

"Here, steward!" continued the second lieutenant, "bring the negro some grog—mix it stiff. He's done the trick well, and deserves encouragement."

The steward obeyed these instructions to the letter: he made the grog of two-thirds rum, one-third water, and handed it to Cuffy, who bowed to the company, pulled his wool in token of respect, and drank the strong and powerful mixture without winking.

"The nigger can take his grog," said Devilskin.

"Yes, massa, Cuffy know how to put de rum away, tho' it ain't offen he gits the chance of puttin' hisself outside suthin."

"Are you ready for t'other un, nig'?"

"Yes, massa."

"Set it up, steward!"

The steward proceeded to do so, although he could not help feeling some compassion for the poor fellow—the thickness of whose skull was to be tested in so severe a manner. He felt sorry for him, and although like most white men born in the South, he did not think much of the negroes, he determined to save him if he could.

A word would put him on his guard.

But how was that one word to be uttered without the knowledge of the officers?

If they were to hear it, their indignation would be very great, and they would infallibly vent their spite and disappointment upon him.

"Shall I give the nigger another drain, sir?" he said.

"Hasn't he had enough?" replied Devilskin.

"Make him hit harder, sir."

"Very well—fire his black blood for him."

"Trust me, sir."

When he presented the second glass of rum to Cuffy, he contrived to whisper the monosyllable—

"*Stone!*"

Cuffy at once understood him, and resolved to take pre-

cautions accordingly. He had all along wondered what made the officers of the *Ocean Queen* so civil to him, and he now saw the reason of their unwonted affability.

To decline to run at the stone would be hazardous; the safest course which he could pursue was to strike the stone ostensibly with great force, and to fall back as if stunned.

In a word, to play a part.

He stood with conscious pride, rejoicing in the strength with which a beneficent nature had endowed him, naked to the waist, with the muscles standing out on his skin. Though black he was a splendid and a magnificent specimen of humanity.

"Now then, nigger, don't waste no time!" exclaimed Devilskin, who was anxious for the negro's discomfiture.

Cuffy ran with head depressed at the stone as he had done at the cheese, pretended to strike it with great force, and then recoiling, fell back as if stunned and senseless.

A roar of triumph and exultation was heard—a hoarse roar which, as it arose, swelled into a positive tumult, as if the officers in the gun-room had performed an achievement of which they ought to be proud.

Not a word of sympathy or commiseration was bestowed upon Cuffy, not a syllable of pity was thrown away upon him, though they believed him to be lying in a state of insensibility upon the ground.

"Ha, ha!" laughed Devilskin; "the nigger got more than he bargained for that journey."

"Yes," said another; "it'll be a Yankee caution to him another time. It's a trick, and no mistake. Oh, I dearly love besting of niggers."

"Yes, you're right. I hate nigs; darn the black cusses."

For fully half-an-hour Cuffy lay on his back, not thinking it prudent to rise; when he did so, he put on a dazed look, and slunk from the room like a whipped hound with his tail beneath his legs. Much laughter was expended, and many coarse jokes were made at the poor fellow's expense.

Cuffy's nature was not a violent one; he was seldom inclined to deeds of violence unless he was provoked beyond the power of human endurance; but when he was alone in the darkness of the 'tween decks, he gnashed his teeth together, and vowed to be terribly revenged on everyone in the ship, for he thought them all his enemies.

His immediate task, however, was to kill Demon Magos. The lieutenant lay in his hammock, which was swung in his own cabin.

Of this fact the negro was fully aware.

He resolved when the lights were out to steal into the cabin, draw his knife from his girdle, and plunge it up to the haft in Demon Magos's bosom.

Until dark he brooded over his project, until it became a settled conviction with him that it was fated by Heaven that the lieutenant should die by his hand.

The man whose position on board the ship assimilated in its duties to that of master-at-arms on board a larger vessel, had scarcely seen all the lights out, before Cuffy stole from his berth, and went on tip-toe to the lieutenant's cabin.

Demon Magos slept.

A small lamp shed a sickly light upon surrounding objects, flashing its rays upon a looking-glass, which evidenced that the possessor of the cabin was somewhat of a dandy—Jack, as a rule, not being much given to gimcracks and Parisian kickshaws.

The negro looked very horrid in the dim light; his eyes were like two live coals, and seemed like stars shining through a black and murky firmament.

Demon Magos was all unconscious of the great peril which menaced him; he apparently slept the sound sleep of innocence, though God only knew how many black and awful crimes his soul was answerable for, how many murders he was guilty of, and how many times he had transgressed almost every one of those laws which were given to the children of Israel amidst the thunders of Sinai.

He slept.

In a short time he was destined to sleep in the fell embrace of death.

Cuffy hardly dared to breathe, lest the movement might awake his victim and frustrate his attempt at assassination.

He advanced on tip-toe, and stood by the bedside of Demon Magos.

It was a terrible moment.

One movement, one cry, one inarticulate exclamation, might arouse attention and baffle the murderer.

The swarthy negro looked like an avenging fiend; and

yet he did not profess to avenge his own wrongs, he was simply honouring his master—that earthly master in whose fortunes he had interested himself, and to whom he had attached himself.

He considered Money Marks ill-treated and ill-used, and he thought the bad treatment he had met with imperatively called for retribution. He was not avenging his own wrong, but one with which he had identified himself.

The blade of the knife, uplifted in the air, flashed in the lamplight.

The flash was momentary, for the next instant the deadly weapon descended and pierced the breast of the sleeping man.

There was a groan, subdued but audible.

A gurgle in the throat succeeded, a spasmodic tremor convulsed the frame, and Demon Magos was a corpse.

Oh! what a multitude of injuries was avenged in that one stroke!—what an infinity of crime! The avenging angel must have shuddered as his eye ran along the lengthened list of unrepented sins.

Cuffy wiped the bloody knife when he had withdrawn it from the wound from which the sanguinary stream welled swiftly, wiped it upon the dead man's garments, and having obliterated all traces of the ruby fluid upon the blade retraced his steps, and sought his own berth.

He had just gained the entrance to the cabin when some one carrying a lantern in his hand stopped him.

"Who are you?" exclaimed a voice which Cuffy instantly recognised as Devilskin's.

"Cuffy, massa."

"What are you doing about the ship at this hour of the night?"

"Been to the infirmary, massa."

"What for?"

"Get something for my head."

"Are you sure you're not telling me a lie?" said Devilskin.

"Sartain sure, massa."

"I'll prove you."

"How?"

"Come along with me."

"Where to?"

"Don't ask no questions, if you don't want your head broke."

"All right, massa. Cuffy wont speak—Cuffy wants to turn in. Dis child's considerable knocked up."

"Not yet; come with me to the infirmary."

"Go to bed first, massa—go to th' infirmary to-morrow morning."

"You refuse?" demanded Devilskin, angrily.

Cuffy saw that to refuse would be fraught with great peril, so he said—

"No, massa; Cuffy thought massa joking."

"Not I."

When the infirmary was reached Devilskin called for the surgeon. The infirmary was a narrow hole or bunk, which was not worthy of the name with which it was dignified, but it held a dozen or more berths, and the wounded and the sick were kept apart from the others, which was not altogether a negative advantage.

The surgeon had gone upstairs to report to the captain; only his assistant was in the cabin.

"Stop you here," said Devilskin to Cuffy.

"Yes, massa."

"I shall be back directly."

Devilskin looked about him, and exclaimed—

"Mr. Miles——"

"Yes, sir," replied the surgeon's assistant.

"Look to this nigger, if you please, and if he attempts to run probe him with a lancet or any other weapon you happen to have handy."

"Certainly, Mr. Morgan."

Devilskin, on receiving this reply, went away, leaving Cuffy within whispering distance of Money Marks' bed.

The faithful fellow found himself in an unpleasant predicament. He had told Devilskin a lie, and the chances were a thousand to one that he would in a short time be detected and exposed.

Nothing more would be thought of the matter until the murder of Demon Magos was discovered, then there would be a hue and cry, and a general consternation. Devilskin would give what information he was possessed of, and consequently Cuffy would be implicated.

The evidence was certainly very strong against him. He had been seen prowling about at night after the lights had been extinguished. When questioned as to where he had been he had told a lie. What was the inference?—simply that he was afraid to speak the truth, and that he was guilty of a vile assassination, and the perpetrator of a cruel and barbarous murder, which was the more aggravated owing to the fact of the deceased man being wounded, and incapable of acting in his own defence.

Insubordination is always severely punished on board ship. If so, what would the penalty of murder be?

Death!

This was the issue which stared Cuffy in the face, and which made him flinch a little.

Finding that he had a few minutes to spare until the return of the second lieutenant, and not finding the contemplation of strangulation at the yard-arm a pleasant amusement, Cuffy determined to say a few words to Money Marks.

"How you do, Money Marks?" he said, when he had approached the berth sufficiently near to be able to speak without fear of interruption.

"Is that you, Cuffy?"

"Yes, massa."

"How did you get here?"

"Brought here."

"Indeed."

"How you feel now?"

"I feel like a wild beast. I could strangle every man on board the vessel. I feel like a demon from Hades."

"Um! Cuffy feel de same."

"You!"

"Yes."

"Why should you be revengeful? My wounds are stiffening, and I have been disgraced; but you can have no grievance to complain of."

"Yes, I have, massa."

"Tell me what," said Money Marks.

"First ob all, I take up your quarrel, Massa Marks."

"My quarrel?"

"Yes; with Demon Magos."

"Curses on him."

"It no good cursing him," said Cuffy, gravely.

"Why not?"

"Becos him gone where de bad niggers go, massa."

"Dead is he?"

"He is so."

"I am sorry for that," said Money Marks, in a tone of deep regret; "I did not mean to kill him—it was unintentional. I very much regret having killed him, though he deserved his fate."

"You did not kill him, Massa Marks," said Cuffy.

"Not kill him?"

"No."

"What do you mean?"

The negro bent down until his mouth was close to the ear of his listener, and said, in a whisper—

"Cuffy kill him."

"You?" cried Money Marks, in terror-laden accents.

"Yes."

"I hope and trust you will not have involved yourself in any unpleasantness. Does any one suspect that you are the culprit?"

"One does."

"Who?"

"Massa Devilskin."

"That is bad."

"He brought me here."

"Is the event known all over the ship?"

"Not yet; him only just knifed."

"What induced you to commit the crime?"

"'Cos he your enemy, Massa Marks," said Cuffy, with a look of intense devotion.

"For me?"

"All for you."

"You are a faithful fellow," replied Money Marks, while the tears sprang to his eyes at this mark of affection on the part of the negro.

"You blame me, massa?" pursued Cuffy.

"Not at all; only I am sorry you took such extreme measures to vindicate my honour. You were hasty and precipitate; you might have waited until we touched at some port where you would have had a much better opportunity, and have done the deed with much less risk."

Cuffy hung down his head, and replied—

"I have my pride, massa, and I not like to see you beaten. You my master—I give myself to you, and I look after you. Just now you say you could strangle every man on board de ship, why you change so—be lion one minute and change to lamb the next ? Why not be lion always, Massa Marks, and jump up some night, get men on your side, kill all officers, and take ship yourself ?"

Take ship yourself.

These words rang in Money Marks' ears for a long time afterwards, but he had not time just then to inwardly digest it, so he said—

"I hope most sincerely that nothing will happen to you."

Just at this juncture, Devilskin returned with the surgeon, who was a stout good-natured looking man, about fifty years of age.

He sat himself down on an empty medicine-chest, and said—

"Well, Mr. Morgan, what can I do for you ?"

"Nothing in your line, just at present : I only wanted to ask you a question or two."

"A hundred, if you please."

"Thank you."

"Fire away," said the surgeon.

"In the first place, do you see that nigger ?"

"He's big enough."

"Do you see him ?"

"Yes."

"Have you seen him before, this evening ?"

"I saw him yesterday."

"That ain't what I mean—was he here just now ?"

"Not to my knowledge. Ask Mr. Miles ; I have been away for a short time."

The assistant denied having seen Cuffy, and it was clearly established that he had told a lie.

"Look you here, you black cuss," exclaimed Devilskin. "You're bowled out ; you've been and pitched a lie into me, and I'll take it out of your tarnation hide, I will, to-morrow. Go back to your bunk now, but, so help me, Sambo, you'll know it at day-break."

Cuffy went away, glad to escape so easily, and hoping that the next day would bring some unforeseen accident prominently forward so as to exculpate him.

"What's he been up to ?" said the surgeon.

"Lord knows. Stealin', I suppose."

"Ah ! there's no trusting the niggers ; they're all thieves."

"Yes, sir," replied Devilskin, "they are thieves all up their blessed backs."

Cuffy did not sleep much that night, but towards morning he happened to fall into an uneasy doze—he was too anxious for the events of the morrow to arrive, to enjoy a good night's rest.

CHAPTER XII.

CONDEMNED TO DEATH.

THE chances were very much against Cuffy's acquittal. An accident had betrayed him and in all likelihood the whole truth would, with the turning out of the first morning watch, be discovered. The poor fellow was as benighted as any dusky-skinned African in his native wilds as far as religion went ; he did not know that he had been guilty of a cowardly and unpardonable act, all he wished to do was to avenge the affront and indignity put upon his master, and in order to do that he had plunged the deadly knife up to the very hilt in his adversary's breast.

Money Marks' spirit burned for revenge, but when Cuffy told him of the awful vengeance he had taken, he could not help wishing that the black had stopped short of murder.

That was the one crime, to the commission of which he could not bring his mind to submit.

He felt that by being cruelly and wantonly flogged he had been degraded, and that he had lost his manhood's dignity, and when the thought came across his mind he was almost reconciled to what had happened.

The fairy-like figure of his much-loved Viola often flashed across his memory in a dream, and he fancied he saw her standing before him and weeping bitter, scalding tears, entreating him to come to her rescue for she was in great and immediate peril.

He dismissed all this mysterious warning from his mind as if it had been the result of a hideous nightmare or the fevered imagination of a throbbing brain.

After all Cuffy was not much worse than himself—the black had killed a man in cold blood, while he had slain Captain Arlee in the heat of the moment.

To murder a white man, when the murderer is a negro, is always a terrible crime, and one punishable by death.

Money Marks knew this, and he trembled for his faithful servitor's safety.

Although his wounds were still stiff and painful, he got up as soon as day broke to see if he could not befriend Cuffy if any great danger menaced him.

It was with great difficulty that he contrived to dress himself, but when he had accomplished this feat to his satisfaction, he sauntered up on deck, touched his cap, and reported himself to the mate who was on duty.

Devilskin happened to be standing by, and he exclaimed—

"About again so soon ?"

"Don't like to be idle, sir."

"Where's that lazy nigger-friend of yours ?"

"In his berth, I suppose, sir."

"Well, just be good enough to wool him out ; we've got a bone to pick, and it may as well be picked now."

Money Marks was about to obey this command when a lad who held the somewhat undignified post of cabin-boy on board the *Ocean Queen*, ran up the hatchway and stopped opposite the second lieutenant, gasping for breath.

This boy was called Boosey, owing to a wonderful propensity, in one so young, for ardent spirits of all sorts. The inclination seemed to be in the blood, for those who knew him well said that his father had died raving mad through drink, and that his mother was insensibly drunk when he was born.

He would, like a thief in the night, break through anything and steal whatever spirituous compound he could lay his hands upon.

Boosey generally contrived to be half his time more or less drunk.

He was very much excited—his eyes were starting from their sockets, and he appeared to have seen, heard, or felt something that had evidently disturbed his mental serenity.

"Well, Boosey ; what is it ?"

"Oh, sir ! oh ! oh ! oh !" replied Boosey.

"Have you seen the ghost of a rum bottle ?"

"Oh, sir ! oh !——"

"Can't you speak ?"

"Oh ! oh !——"

"Stash that. If you've lost your tongue we must see if we can't find it for you."

He raised his hand and gave him a slap on the face with his open palm, which had the effect of completely sobering Master Boosey, who said in a thick, husky voice—

"I've seen him, sir."

"Seen who ?"

"Mr. Magos."

"Demon Magos ?"

"Yes, sir."

"What of him ?"

"He's dead."

"Eh ! did you say dead ? Has he died of his wound ? Nay, then, this will be a hanging matter."

And he turned round glaringly at Money Marks, who felt sick and ill, dreading some new calamity.

"It isn't that wound, sir," said Boosey ; "he's been struck again."

"Impossible !"

"I see the hole, sir, and all the blood a pouring out."

"I must investigate this. Lead the way," said Devilskin, who followed the boy into Demon Magos' cabin, upon a bed in which, the first mate's cold and rigid body was lying. He had gone to his last account, and was then in the presence of his Maker.

"There has been foul work here," exclaimed Devilskin : "by my life I will swear there has been foul work."

He raised the sheet and the counterpane and looked at the awful gaping wound, around which a mass of clotted blood was clinging, and he then let it fall with a curse, for there were two wounds, around one of which the bandages of the surgeon were still lying securely.

There could be no moral doubt that a brutal and cowardly murder had been committed.

Going up the hatchway again, he approached Money Marks, and said—

"Demon Magos is dead. I have my suspicions. Consider

MONEY MARKS PLACED UNDER ARREST.

yourself under arrest. I shall rouse the captain presently, and then if you are not summarily tried and executed for this diabolical deed, you will be instantly placed in irons."

Money Marks bowed his head. He knew that he was innocent, but he would not betray Cuffy who had jeopardized his own life for the express purpose of avenging a wrong done to, and a slight put upon his master.

This was noble generosity. This was courageous self-denial. In fact it was an utter abnegation and annihilation of self.

He went down to the large cabin, in which he in conjunction with several other men slept. Most of them were dressing themselves, as it would soon be their turn to undertake the duty of watching the ship. These men were not a bit better affected towards the captain of the ship and his officers than was Money Marks himself, and they commiserated him, and bewailed the harsh treatment he had met with owing to the malignant spite of Demon Magos.

"What cheer, mate?" said a man called Tom Castaway.

"Bad enough. The first mate's dead."

"Well, it's a judgment upon him," replied Tom Castaway.

His eyes, in conjunction with those of the other men in the cabin, twinkled with delight; for Magos had made himself thoroughly unpopular with every one in the ship, and they were all glad to hear of the removal for ever of a man who was a cruel bully, and a detestable tyrant.

Money Marks went up to Tom Castaway, and said in a whisper—

"It is a pity you fellows don't make me captain of the vessel. We would take a cruise on our own account, and show you a little sport."

"We would be glad to sail under some one different to what we've got now," replied Tom Castaway.

"Why not combine and do it?"

"That'd be mutiny."

"Never mind what it would be."

"We should be strung up to the yardarm."

"Not you. Do the thing well, and no one would know anything about it, until a ball went crashing through the captain's skull and those of his myrmidons."

"You speak boldly," said Tom Castaway.

"Ay, and I mean boldly."

"Well, there's nothing like pluck," replied Tom Castaway. "You and I'll talk about this again. I'm pretty well known to all the crew, and they'll follow me anywhere. Not one of them is satisfied with the present state of things, but I say——"

"What?"

"Do you know what sort of a ship you're sailing in?"

"Know?"

"Yes."

"Of course."

"What?"

"A merchantman."

"Not a bit of it."

"Well, what is the *Ocean Queen*?"

"*A Slaver!*" replied Tom Castaway, between his teeth.

"God bless me!" exclaimed Money Marks, profoundly astonished. "Are you certain of the truth of what you allege?"

"Perfectly certain. We go to some place in Africa, of which I do not know the name; there we exchange our cargo of fantastic goods for a ship-load of slaves, and sail for Cuba, at which island we dispose of our living freight, and our officers make a large profit."

"Who told you this?"

"No one; but I am an old stager, and know the tricks of the trade."

"We have been infamously duped."

"There can be no doubt of that."

Money Marks wrung the old salt's hand, and sat down upon the edge of his hammock. The pain of his wounds, the reflection that he had been flogged like a slave, that he had been robbed of Viola, or what was as bad, that he had been compelled to leave Charleston and his beloved behind, that he was on board a slaver, and that everything was unsatisfactory and disagreeable, almost maddened him.

He became furious, and his repugnance to the shedding of human blood was not half or a quarter so great as it had been some short time before.

The demon of ambition had laid siege to his soul. It had circumvallated it, and, like an insidious insect, impregnated it with quickening eggs. He felt himself wronged, and he wanted to raise himself from a subordinate position to that of a governing man. This it was not easy to do, except it was done by a hop, skip, and a jump. If he worked for years and years before the mast, he might never become a commander. If he slaved and toiled all his lifetime, he might never succeed in getting a vessel of his own, but if he made a bold venture, and raised a mutinous spirit amongst the crew of the *Ocean Queen*, he might kill all the officers, and induce the men to elect him captain of the ship.

All this was wild, rash, and speculative, but it contained the germs of something great, on the old principle of nothing venture nothing have.

Some hours elapsed, during which Money Marks had full time and leisure to think over his ambitious schemes.

At the end of which time he was sent for. A file of marines did not come to fetch him, as on board a man-of-war, but it so happened that Tom Castaway was the messenger, and he contented himself with saying—

"Look out for squalls, mate. The captain wants you."

"Wants me!"

"Yes."

"Very well; I am ready."

Money Marks knew that something serious was about to occur. In all probability, Devilskin had come to the conclusion that he was the murderer of his friend and companion, Demon Magos; and he had gone to the captain with that belief, and prejudiced his mind to such an extent, that a belief in Marks' guilt was a foregone conclusion.

In reality this was the case. Devilskin, in the excitement of this new occurrence, had forgotten all about the negro Cuffy. It seemed clear to him that Money Marks had killed Demon Magos.

They had never been good friends, and he had endeavoured to stab Magos; for which offence he had been publicly disgraced, and flogged in the presence of the whole crew.

This being the case, what was more probable than that Money Marks should attack his enemy, and endeavour to revenge his injuries by taking blood?

There was, on the other hand, this consideration to be looked at, and it was not altogether a circumstance to be overlooked and treated with contemptuous neglect.

Money Marks had been in the infirmary, and under the doctor's charge—very likely was it that the functionary in question would be ready to swear that Marks had not left his berth for a moment, and if the doctor himself could not swear to that effect, it was very evident that his assistant could do so; because the latter had been in the bunk all the time, and would have been able to see any attempt at moving made by Money Marks.

When he reached the deck, he found the entire crew assembled on the forecastle, while the captain, surrounded by his officers, stood on the poop, or afterpart of the vessel.

The captain looked severely at Money Marks, and said—

"I have sent for you because one of the officers of the *Ocean Queen* has been foully murdered. Need I say that I allude to my esteemed friend, Demon Magos. He was stabbed in his sleep. No one but you had any motive for getting rid of the unhappy man, therefore we have in solemn council come to the conclusion that you are the culprit. What have you to say in your defence?"

"Simply this, Mr. Monkhouse, that I am innocent of the deed you impute to me. I did not kill Mr. Magos, nor had I any desire to do so."

"What evidence have you to adduce in your defence?"

"I was ill at the time and in the infirmary, which I did not leave for a moment from the time of my entering it until daybreak this morning."

"Call the assistant surgeon," said Mr. Monkhouse.

That young gentleman was duly called and said, that as he was asleep the best part of that eventful evening he would rather not give any opinion upon a subject which was at once solemn and of great importance to the one accused.

"Your own witness fails you," said Captain Monkhouse; "I have no doubt myself of your guilt and I shall at once order your execution."

"I am innocent," replied Money Marks.

"Your asseveration to that effect is useless. I believe you guilty, and my sentence is that you be hanged by the neck at the yardarm until you are dead."

As this decision was heard there was a murmur of applause amongst the officers; they saw in it a guarantee that their own lives would be held sacred, and they were rejoiced in consequence.

Money Marks raised his voice, and said in an angry tone—

"You are guilty of a crime, for I can call God to witness that I am as innocent of the crime for which I am condemned as the child unborn, and not only innocent in fact but innocent in deed. You will have to give a solemn account of this *murder*, for it is nothing else, when the breath leaves your body and you are arraigned like the rest of frail mortality before the throne of grace."

"Let him be taken away," replied the captain, without noticing Money Marks' adjuration; "And give him a quarter-of-an-hour to make his peace with heaven."

As this decree went forth an unusual commotion was noticeable amongst the crew, and some one appeared to be pushing his way aft by main force.

CHAPTER XIII.

A STRANGE SAIL.

MONEY MARKS gave himself up as lost. His death seemed imminent. For the nonce he became a philosopher, and tried to laugh at death.

"What does it matter?" he said to himself, "after all it is but a small matter of strangulation. Who cares for me? Who am I? Nobody knows. Perhaps the child of shame. I have no father or mother to lament my untimely loss, or to shudder when they hear that I have died a shameful and a violent death. It may be that it is better I should die as I am. It is impossible to say what misfortunes and what hardships I escape by an early decease."

While he was reasoning in this cynical and fallacious manner, Cuffy had succeeded in pushing his way to the front. He approached Captain Monkhouse, and said—

"Beg pardon, massa."

"What do you want?"

"Say a few words to massa."

"This is not the time."

"Too late afterwards, massa."

"Come again."

"Must speak now."

"What do you mean?"

"Massa Marks not do dis thing, sir."

"Who then?"

"Cuffy did it."

"You?" cried Monkhouse, in astonishment.

"Iss, massa," replied Cuffy, looking very solemn and very woebegone.

"Yours is an extraordinary statement; do you know what will happen to you if it is found that what you have stated is strictly true and matter of fact?"

"Suppose, massa, hang."

"Yes, that is just what I shall do. Do you still persist in saying that you killed Demon Magos?"

"It all true, massa; Cuffy did it."

"Can you prove it?"

"Massa Morgan saw me come from de cabin," said Cuffy.

Devilskin stepped forward and said—

"That is perfectly true. I did not witness the commission of the deed, but I saw the negro stealing back to his cabin when all the lights were out."

"Ha!" cried the captain, "that gives colour to his story."

"Foolish fellow," exclaimed Money Marks, "I would have saved you; why not have held your tongue?"

"No, Massa," replied Cuffy, seizing his young master's hand, and kissing it devotedly. "Your life worth more than mine. Cuffy understand fetish, and it tell him that young massa's life very valuable one."

"I am sorry that your love for me should have got you into this trouble."

"It no matter," said Cuffy, "we all die once; what matter when we die? no one miss Cuffy."

"Yes, yes, you are mistaken. I shall miss you—miss you deeply—and would give worlds had I the power to save you."

"That you have not," interposed Captain Monkhouse, "your life is saved; the negro by his terrible explanation and confession has saved your neck from the halter only to put his own within the fatal embrace. Go forward, sir, and join the rest of the crew, while justice takes its course."

Money Marks grasped Cuffy's hand, and wrung it warmly; he was too much agitated to speak a single word, but this mute action was wonderfully expressive, and Cuffy looked up gratefully, bidding his master a silent adieu.

Money Marks then walked slowly forward, and sat down in the bows near the anchor, hiding his face in his hands, so that he might not witness the dismal spectacle that was about to be enacted.

The revulsion in feeling was very great. He had made up his mind that he was to be strangled, and he had by the exercise of a fictitious but efficacious philosophy resigned himself to his fate.

When the jaws of death, the portals of the tomb, the darkness of eternal night yawned before him, he had shuddered, but contented himself with thinking—hoping—trusting that there was a life to come and that new scenes would open to his view, new scenes, more bright, more lovely, more ethereal, than any that the mind of man, imaginative though it is, had ever dreamt of.

Oh, the comfort that this thought and this reflection was to him in the midst of his agony, when he firmly believed that his last hours on earth were numbered.

Words fail me when I endeavour to convey to the mind of the reader the great consolation he derived from the active intervention of this comforting creed.

Tom Castaway was selected as the executioner of the negro. He did not much like the task, and Devilskin volunteered to lend him some assistance, which was cheerfully accepted.

A long rope was slung over the yard-arm, a noose was formed, and three men were selected to help Castaway in his repulsive task.

The negro was allowed some few minutes to say his prayers, but he did not appear to be in the humour for praying, or else he was unacquainted with those formulas with which civilized nations propitiate the Deity—or that particular heartfelt form of prayer which is peculiar to none but familiar to all alike.

Devilskin, with a disgusting officiousness, placed the noose around the black's neck, and with considerable harshness pulled it tight, half throttling the poor fellow in the endeavour.

"Is all ready?" asked the captain.

"Yes, all is ready."

"Haul up, then."

Suddenly the three men, with Tom Castaway leading them, pulled with all their might at the rope, and poor Cuffy was soon swinging and dangling in mid air.

At this critical juncture, the man on the look-out at the mast-head sang out—

"Strange sail to leeward!"

"Where away?" said the captain.

"North north-east."

"Lower the nigger," cried Mr. Monkhouse.

Tom Castaway was not slow in obeying this injunction; he let Cuffy down with a run, and when he came to the deck gasping and choking in a manner awful and sickening to witness, said—

"Come, messmate, wake up; there aint no harm done."

Cuffy was not nearly dead, but the rope had strangled him until it had raised a huge lump in his throat and half choked him.

"Take him below," said the captain; "the sentence can be carried out to-morrow."

"Ay, ay, sir," responded Tom Castaway, who assisted gleefully in carrying the negro below.

Money Marks heard an unusual commotion, and looked up, fully expecting to see the body of his faithful attendant swinging in mid-air.

But he was agreeably mistaken.

Cuffy was carried past him, and he went below in order to be able to render the first offices of affection to one whom he regarded as a friend.

In the meantime, the captain and De Morgan were engaged in an angry altercation.

"Why did you order the black to be taken down?" exclaimed Devilskin.

"By what right do you question me?"

"I have an interest in the ship."

"She is not your venture."

"No, I admit that. But if officers are to be stabbed in their beds simply because they have made themselves obnoxious to the crew by doing their duty, I, for one, would rather ever so much be put on shore on a desert island and take my luck."

"The negro will be punished to-morrow."

"Why postpone his execution?" persisted Devilskin.

"Because it would look bad, and damn us in the eyes of those on board the vessel which is bearing down upon us if they saw us hanging a fellow-creature. We have no right to take away life, and their telescopes would no doubt inform them of all that is taking place on board our ship."

"You frighten yourself without a cause."

"Not I," replied Monkhouse. "I know very well what I am about; I do not want to be schooled by you. I am captain of this vessel, and if you do not at once admit that fact by going below and confining yourself to your cabin, I shall undertake to prove it to you in a manner more forcible than pleasant."

"You have lost the assistance of Magos through treachery or revenge, be careful that you do not lose me through other causes."

"Men of my stamp can stand alone," replied Monkhouse.

Devilskin cast a malignant look upon the captain, and went away grumbling.

He had never been devoted to Monkhouse in the faithful way that Demon Magos had—he was more ambitious, and he felt that he should like to have the supreme power.

The slight which the captain had put upon him made him more than ever desirous to achieve this object, and he determined to lose no time in intriguing to accomplish that end.

He thought that Money Marks would be extremely likely to aid and abet him in his mutinous ideas, and he sought him out for the purpose of putting a few questions to him, with a view of ascertaining what his real opinions were, and whether he was likely to join in any enterprise such as he contemplated.

Money Marks and Cuffy were together; the latter wore chains upon his hands, arms, and legs; this was doubtless to prevent him from attempting an escape. He was not pardoned; the captain had simply respited him for his own credit sake, and in all probability the sentence which had been hastily passed upon him would be as hastily carried out on the succeeding day.

Devilskin beckoned Money Marks to him, and said—

"Do you wish to save your friend?"

"What friend?"

"The nigger."

"I would do anything in the world to accomplish that object. It is shocking to think that he must be hurried into eternity. He has not the ideas of right and wrong that we entertain, and therefore he is not so culpable; first of all civilize your negro, and then execute him for not obeying the laws of civilized society."

"There is much truth in what you say, but Captain Monkhouse is not likely to allow any considerations of that sort to weigh with him; unless some energetic action is taken, the negro will infallibly die."

"What do you mean by energetic action?" said Money Marks, eyeing his companion narrowly.

He could not divest his mind of the suspicion that De Morgan was acting the part of a spy; he had never been on friendly terms with the men, and Marks himself had not received a civil word or look from him since he had been on board the ship.

"How shall I explain myself?" replied Devilskin; "suppose I put a suppositionary case; shall I say that there was once upon a time a ship in which several men sailed, none of whom were treated well, and none of whom liked their officers."

"Well!"

"During the voyage several acts of cruelty and oppression occurred, which only served to exasperate the men, and inflame their already disordered minds."

Money Marks began to comprehend the drift of the lieutenant, but he held his peace, wisely refusing to commit himself to any decided opinion, or expression of opinion, until he heard all that Devilskin had to say.

"The state of things on board the said ship," continued De Morgan, "became so intolerable at last, that the men could bear it no longer."

"What did they do?" queried Money Marks.

"They rose up in open rebellion—in other words, they mutinied—killed the captain, and took possession of the vessel."

"That was a crime."

"Undoubtedly, but one that was justified by the events which had taken place."

"Why do you tell me this story?"

"In order that you may deduce a meaning from it."

"Do you suggest that we should go and do likewise?"

"What do you think? Are you satisfied with your position? Have you been treated well? Are you happy or as contented as you hoped to be?"

"Before I answer those questions," said Money Marks, "I should like to know what your motive in asking them is: I am apt to be distrustful of people with whom I am not well acquainted, and you may be seeking my destruction for all I know. I have experienced the temper of the captain, and I have no particular wish that my back should receive a repetition of the scoring it had inflicted upon it."

Lowering his voice, Devilskin said—

"I would help you to avenge all this; instead of being punished, you should be in a position to punish. I will no longer disguise my meaning—I propose to seize the ship. Having organized a small and trustworthy band upon whom we can rely, all the officers shall be killed, and their bodies thrown into the sea; I will be captain, and you shall be my first lieutenant. Come, what do you say to that?"

"The prospect is enticing enough, but the programme is rather difficult of execution."

"Do you think so? You have only to give your consent," replied Devilskin, in a persuasive voice, "and I can manage the rest. I have no doubt you know whom among the common sailors to address. Discontented minds are sympathetic; what do you say?"

"Simply that I do not know whether to trust you or not," answered Money Marks. "What would become of me if you were to tell the captain of what you had mooted to me, and that I had acquiesced in your scheme? What would

happen to me? Why, I should without doubt be hung in chains, and such a fate is very horrible."

Devilskin drew a pistol from his belt, and gave it to Money Marks, saying—

"Take that—it is loaded—place it in your pocket, and if I play you false, send a bullet through my heart. If you know that you are betrayed, and condemned to death, you may also know that no further punishment can await you for occasioning my death."

"Very well," replied Money Marks, grasping the pistol, "I accept your terms, and now I will give you my answer."

He spoke in a low voice, and Devilskin bent forward to listen to him.

"I will take no active part in the slaughter of the officers, but I will help you if it so happens that you are in need of assistance, and I will co-operate with you afterwards."

"Very well—with that answer I must rest satisfied. I have great reason to complain of Monkhouse's treatment to me, and I am determined to resent it in a manner little anticipated by him; but before I commence hostilities, it is necessary that I should make friends, and sound the opinions of those on board, so that I may know what support I am to expect in the event of a conflict occurring."

Before anything more could be said, all hands were piped on deck. The strange sail had been overhauling the *Ocean Queen* with great rapidity. She proved to be a British schooner, and lowering a boat, evinced a disposition to board the ship, in order to see what she was, and where she was bound for.

Monkhouse had put his vessel about as soon as he perceived the British vessel, so that instead of sailing to the coast of Africa, where he intended to take in a cargo of slaves, he appeared to be making for the Gulf of Mexico.

The officer in command of the boat quickly boarded the *Ocean Queen*, and advanced to the captain, saying—

"What ship is this?"

"*Ocean Queen*, from New York, bound for the Bahama Islands."

"You are strangely out of your course."

"We have met with bad weather, but hope to reach San Salvador in a fortnight."

"Possibly you will. What is your cargo?"

"Miscellaneous—Yankee notions, and that sort of thing."

"Produce your papers."

The captain produced some forged papers, at which the British officer glanced in a casual manner, and afterwards requested to be conducted below. This demand was, for a wonder, complied with, and the 'tween-decks was fully searched, without the slightest sign of a slave being discoverable. The officer expressed his satisfaction, and apologized for the minuteness of his search, saying—

"There are so many slavers about, that it is impossible in these seas to tell who is honest and who is not."

"Don't apologize," said Captain Monkhouse, "when next we meet I hope you will remember me, and be able to discriminate."

"I hope so, too. Good-day."

Monkhouse bowed; the lieutenant slipped down the ship's side with the agility of a cat, and, jumping into the boat, was speedily being rowed to his own vessel.

The captain continued his course until dark, when he veered round, and pursued his way to the coast of Africa.

He was bound for an obscure port, named Carteras, which was only known to a few of those infamous adventurers who deal in human flesh, and traffic in their fellow-men as if they were oxen or sheep.

Carteras was the principal port of the kingdom of Bootan, a petty principality, the natives of which were excessively warlike and ferocious. They were the terror of all the surrounding tribes, upon whom they frequently made war with the avowed intention of taking prisoners to sell as slaves to the traders, who came with their vessels to buy men.

The very name of the Cumbagees, as the natives of Bootan were called, was quite sufficient to cause a panic for miles along the coast, and for many miles inland.

Not only did the slavers get men from the Cumbagees, but also gold-dust and elephant-tusks, which gave them fine ivory, and for which they supplied nothing but the most trumpery articles, such as beads, knives, pieces of glass, gaudy, but inexpensive clothing, cloth of a bright and vivid hue, and other knicknacks, the value of which would not have been estimated at much in the British town of Birmingham.

Money Marks had another interview that night with Devilskin, and the latter promised to exert his influence, and get Cuffy reprieved. He kept his word. Seeking an interview with the captain, he talked so energetically, and so represented things to him, that he consented to spare Cuffy's life.

The following was the most potent argument with Monkhouse—

"He is a fine stalwart negro. What's the good of killing him? When we get in our cargo of slaves put the manacles on him, and shove him along with the rest. That is true wisdom; that is our best policy. You punish the scoundrel, and you make money by him as well, when you get to Cuba."

"You are right," replied Captain Monkhouse, "let the rascal be well watched, and let his execution be postponed. Do not let him know that he is pardoned. I would rather that the penalty he has incurred should be kept hanging over him."

"Very well," said Devilskin, who left the cabin to tell the good news to Money Marks, who was anxiously awaiting his arrival.

CHAPTER XIV.
CARTERAS, THE SLAVE-MART.

THE old sailor whom Demon Magos had so shamefully ill-treated on his first arrival on board the ship had gradually recovered from the effects of the terrible blow he had received.

The iron-made knuckleduster had done its work, though, in so efficient a manner that he was likely to carry the scar with him to the day of his death.

Money Marks was glad to see old Cyrus Blast about again. He spoke to him, and congratulated him heartily upon his recovery, and found in him an apt pupil whenever he mentioned the subject of a rising and a mutiny which had for its object the murder of the captain, who, if not so cruel as his officers, was at all events so weak as to fall into their way of thinking and agree to anything inhuman that it pleased their monstrous inventions to suggest.

When an opportunity offered, Money Marks sought Devilskin, and said—

"If you will take my advice, you will wait until we are in harbour before any attempt is made upon the captain. Discipline will then be relaxed, and we can do very much as we like."

"The same thing has occurred to me," replied Devilskin. "I have made several of these voyages, and my experience teaches me this—viz., that the captain and his officers always go on shore first, leaving the ship in charge of one officer. They do this in order that they may visit the king and enjoy his hospitality."

"That will assist us very much."

"Of course it will. I shall volunteer, owing to a pretended sick-headache, to take charge of the ship; and no sooner has the boat left the ship's side than, with a rifle, I shall begin to fire at the crew. It will not be difficult to shoot the half dozen men she will contain. The seamen who row her I shall respect, as their lives ought to be held sacred."

"There I agree with you," replied Money Marks; "and I shall be very happy to adopt your views."

The conversation ended then, but Devilskin was in earnest. He did not think that Money Marks was half or a quarter so ambitious as he really was; he looked upon him as a quiet, passive tool—a humble instrument to be made use of—a link between the common able-bodied seamen and himself; and he did not apprehend any mischief from a quarter where it was in reality hatching.

Money Marks, in conjunction with Cuffy, Cyrus Blast, and Tom Castaway, was very active. These four were the very backbone, the very soul of the mutinous movement; and they sounded the men, gaining many over to their side, and reassuring the rest.

When the ship sailed into the bay of Carteras the little town, consisting of strangely constructed edifices, rejoicing more in bamboo than in brick, was dimly visible.

The *Ocean Queen* was not well armed, but she could boast of four guns; one of which was duly shotted and fired to impress the King of the Cumbagees, who, like all monarchs of savage nations, was impressed by outward display and noisy show.

Devilskin simulated illness, as he had already arranged, and he was left in charge of the vessel. The captain, with the third mate, the steward, the boatswain, and sundry other functionaries who enjoyed his confidence and constituted his body-guard, got into the yawl, and were rowed towards the shore by four seamen, of whom Cyrus Blast was one.

Devilskin had taken care to load a dozen long-range rifles, which he had obtained from the armoury; and directly the boat had left the ship's side, and progressed a few yards, he took up one, handed it to Money Marks, giving another to Tom Castaway, and taking one himself.

"I will fire first," he said. "You, Marks, follow me, taking care to cover your man; and Castaway must follow you."

He raised his rifle to his shoulder directly he had done speaking, and, pulling the trigger, fired. It appeared as if he was not desirous of killing the captain, for his bullet struck the steward, who sprang forward, pressed his hand to his side and fell overboard, dyeing the waves with his blood.

Possibly he felt some compunction in attacking one who had for a long time been his friend, adviser, and companion.

The utmost consternation was excited in the boat at this fatal discharge of firearms. Mr. Monkhouse, who, whatever his faults were, was not destitute of courage, stood up in the boat, and levelled his revolver at De Morgan. The shot was an unerring one, for it struck the second mate on the arm, shattering the bone, and causing him the greatest agony.

His rifle dropped to the ground.

Monkhouse was overjoyed at the success of his shot. He thought fondly that he had by his energetic conduct broken the back of the mutiny; but in this sanguine belief he was mistaken.

He urged the boatmen, by word and gesture, to row back to the ship with all the strength they were capable of exerting.

Cyrus Blast endeavoured to retard their progress in a retrograde direction, by catching crabs and throwing impediments in the way, which the captain perceiving, he levelled his pistol at the man's head and blew his brains out.

Poor Cyrus Blast fell back dead—dead as a stone.

It was an awful moment for all parties. Human blood was then not thought worth much more than salt water.

The bulk of the crew hung back, taking no side in particular, contenting themselves with watching the course of events; which, in point of fact, was the wisest course they could pursue.

Devilskin leant against the mainmast, and his arm hung powerless by his side; but he stimulated Money Marks to exertion in a noisy manner.

"Fire!" he cried. "Fire quickly, or all is lost! Fire, and kill Monkhouse, or he will shoot you down like dogs!"

Money Marks did not need this incentive; he had been "drawing a bead" upon the captain for some seconds.

He had not fired because he wished to make sure of his mark.

Having secured what he thought a good aim, he pulled the trigger.

There was a flash, a puff of smoke, a loud report, but the captain did not fall; he had hastily changed his position, and all Money Marks' care was thrown away. The work remained to be done.

"Fire!" cried Devilskin to Tom Castaway; "and you, Marks, take another rifle. I am useless, or by —— the fellow should not baffle us thus."

"Confusion!" muttered Money Marks between his teeth.

He stooped down and picked up a rifle which was undischarged. This time he took no aim. It was dangerous to do so. He flung the rifle to his shoulder as if he was going to snap a cap.

Tom Castaway and he fired at the same moment.

It was impossible to say which of them sent the captain his death-billet.

He fell.

The other officers begged with loud voices that their lives might be spared, but Devilskin urged Money Marks to shoot them.

"They cannot be trusted," he said. "Kill them—kill them all!"

A few shots, well directed, sufficed to do that; and the boat was rowed back to the ship's side with only three inmates. They were the three seamen.

Devilskin was captain of the vessel; and although he was

bleeding copiously from his wound, he called the men round him, and said—

"My men, I have thought it my duty to take the violent course I have this day taken, in conjunction with some of yourselves. You have been badly treated and unjustly entrapped, but your tyrant and your oppressors are dead. They have expiated their crimes with their lives and with their blood. I assume the command of the vessel, and I expect you all to render me such submission and obedience as I am entitled to as your captain."

"We don't want you for a captain," said a voice in the crowd of seamen.

"Who spoke then?" demanded Devilskin, fiercely.

"Never mind who," was the reply; "we wont have you."

"Choose your own captain," said Devilskin.

"We mean to."

"Who will you have?"

"Money Marks," was the unanimous reply.

"Yes, yes; Money Marks—Money Marks!" cried the men.

"A new broom sweeps clean," said one man; "and you're a darned old one."

"Ha! ha!" laughed the crowd.

Devilskin was foaming with rage. He was intensely disappointed; but what could he do? Unfortunately he was wounded. Had it not been so, he would probably have endeavoured to assert his authority and independence.

Cuffy glided up to Money Marks in the midst of the tumult, and whispered in his ear—

"You leave Massa Devilskin to me, and I will soon show what to do wid him. He bad man and much offend Cuffy. Devilskin and Massa Marks not live in the same ship. You be captain, Massa Marks, and give Massa Devilskin to me."

"Very well," replied Money Marks, who began to see his way to supreme authority through the death of Devilskin, in addition to the deaths which had already taken place.

He was surprised to find himself so popular with the crew. But they looked upon him as one unjustly treated—as a martyr—and they were disposed to follow any leader who had the sanctity of oppression about him.

Cuffy approached Devilskin with a knife in his hand, which he flourished in his face, saying—

"Ah, Massa Devilskin, how you do? Not quite so well for seeing Cuffy, hey!"

"Go away, you black cuss!"

"Not yet."

"I'm sorry I didn't have you hanged."

"Ha! ha! You see dis knife, Massa Devilskin?"

"Well, what of it?"

"It the knife that kill Massa Demon Magos."

"Indeed!"

"Yes, and it the knife which will kill you."

"Me!" said Devilskin, in terror-laden accents.

He turned pale—ashy pale—and his lips quivered, while his limbs trembled.

"Marks! Marks!" he exclaimed.

Money Marks affected not to hear him.

Cuffy gave utterance to another fiendish laugh, and then he plunged his knife in De Morgan's side.

The wretched man fell with a groan to the ground.

He expired instantly.

The negro had done his work well.

With the utmost coolness Cuffy took hold of the man, still struggling in the convulsive throes of death, and carried him to the side of the vessel, ready to throw over, saying—

"Ha! ha! more food for de fishes. Sharks will have him bellyfuls."

The crew looked on in placid wonderment, inclined to accept any sort of government that might be inflicted on them, so long as it improved their individual comfort, and did not interfere with their personal safety.

As Money Marks had been one of the principal ringleaders of this revolt, the men appeared to be anxious to make him their captain, and elect him to the sovereign command. They were none of them ambitious of holding a dangerous post—all they wanted was plunder, and that they did not at all times find it easy to acquire.

They elected Money Marks their leader by acclamation, and Cuffy smiled grimly as he looked around him and saw that all his enemies were dead. Where was the captain?—the first and second mate?—where Demon Magos?—where Devilskin?

Dead—all dead.

It was indeed a scene of slaughter, but the captain had provoked it—and so had his officers, by the thoughtless way in which they had slighted the men, ill-treated them, and used them cruelly without the slightest provocation.

Money Marks spoke a few words to Cuffy, who disappeared, presently returning with a pail of water and a mop, with which he cleansed the deck from the foul stain of blood, and, removing the dead body, threw it overboard with a curse instead of a funeral oration, or a prayer for those who have gone to the land of spirits.

In fact, Cuffy was unacquainted with prayer; he had been brought up in a savage state, and was filled with savage instincts, which all the softening influences of the civilization of which he had been the fosterchild, had failed to drive away and eradicate.

Money Marks beckoned Tom Castaway to his side, and said—

"The men seem a little sullen and undetermined; do they not?"

"Yes," replied Tom, "and I'll tell you the reason why. It's this way, sir. They are waiting for you to speak. Give 'em an allowance of rum, and then you'll see a change."

Money Marks knew that Jack likes his grog, and he strongly approved of the suggestion. He felt a little faint and in want of a stimulant himself; for he had passed through great excitement, and the sight of the blood which had been shed in the late murderous contest had sickened him.

"Go at once to the spirit-store," he replied, "and serve out a double allowance to each man. When they are in a good humour, I will say a few words to them."

"That's right, sir; make it short and pithy. The men like a speech, but they don't understand too much jawing-tackle."

Tom Castaway did not lose a moment in obeying the instructions that were given him. No discipline had as yet been established, and he feared that if the men were not met half way, they would take the law into their own hands, and help themselves. This act of insubordination would have been fatal to the new rule—more bloodshed must have taken place, and it would have been impossible to tell how the affair might have ended.

The rum was served out to the men, who evinced every symptom of the liveliest gratification, and became instantly amicable and jocular.

As the sun dissipates the clouds, and drives away noxious damps and vapours, so did the liberal present of spirit drive away their gloom and ill-temper.

Money Marks stepped forward and made a speech, in which he said—

"My men, I need not dwell upon what has taken place – it is undoubtedly sad, but I do not for a moment question that your verdict will be—'Serve them right!'"

A voice exclaimed—

"So it is!"

"It is not with the past, but with the present that we have to deal. The ship is in our hands. I have been asked to assume the command, but before I do so, I want to know if such an assumption is perfectly agreeable to yourselves? Does it meet with your approbation? Is there one dissentient voice amongst you? Will you—I put the question to you frankly and openly—will you have me? Do you want me for your captain?"

He paused, and awaited the reply of the men with some anxiety.

They one and all said that they would have him, and that it was their wish to sail under him. This declaration was expressive enough, and he proceeded, while a gratified look of ambition realized passed over his countenance.

"There is one more thing for you to do, and that is, to elect your officers. I want my men to be thoroughly contented. Now I venture to propose that Tom Castaway be my first mate; the second and third mates shall be nominated and elected by yourselves, as also the remaining officers of the ship. I want you to be contented. There shall not be a single cause of complaint amongst you, as long as it is in my power to avoid it. I am thoroughly in earnest in what I say, but, mind you, if when we are settled again, my authority, or that of my officers, is called in question, I shall not be slow to punish the offender."

"What flag do you mean to sail under?" exclaimed an old salt.

"That is a fair question to ask," replied Money Marks, "and I will not hesitate to answer it. Of course you all know the late captain's reason for coming to Carteras?"

"Yes, yes."

"It was with the openly avowed object of collecting slaves with which to run to Cuba. Now I have a strong objection to do anything of the sort. I do not care about trafficking in negroes, rather let us take a bolder course and hoist the black flag."

The countenances of the men assumed a startled expression as they heard this bold proposal. The black flag was a phrase of ominous meaning which was not to be mistaken. It meant piracy, and that is a hanging matter.

Seeing that there was some hesitation amongst the crew, Money Marks continued—

"There is at present, as you all know, a terrible war waging between the Northern and Southern sections of the once United States of America. Let us sail under the Confederate flag, and plunder Northern or Federal merchantmen; and not neglect any other favours, that luck, in a good-natured way, may throw into our hands."

There was a laugh at this.

"If any of you wish to leave the vessel, and will express the same to me at the first civilized port we touch at, he shall have his instant discharge. We will go ashore here and take in a cargo of gold dust and ivory, with palm-oil, and whatever else the natives may have to dispose of; and do a little legitimate trading before we act bravely, and throw down the gauntlet to the world."

Money Marks paused ere he added—

"Every man on board this vessel shall have a fair share of the profits of our ventures. If we make a hundred pounds, I will take for my share ten per cent.: the rest shall be equally divided amongst you. Is that fair? Is that generous? Does that meet with your approbation? why, in a short time, you will all be rich enough to buy a vessel of your own."

This promise pleased the men and they cheered vociferously.

Money Marks went below with Cuffy, leaving Tom Castaway with the men to arrange about the election of the officers, and to settle other minor details.

"What a change!" soliloquised Money Marks, "a short time ago I was a barman in Ratcliff Highway; now I am, what shall I say? a bold buccaneer, a pirate. Oh! Viola, Viola, I trust I have not forfeited your love; were you mine all my hopes would be realized."

CHAPTER XV

KING OF THE CUMBAGEES.

IN a short time all elements of discord vanished from the ship. Money Marks' authority was recognised, and by a strange combination of circumstances he found himself a Highwayman of the Seas.

His great ally was Cuffy, and after him Tom Castaway. Cuffy wore a red scarf, and carried a long, murderous-looking knife in his hand or in his girdle at all times. It was difficult to tell his reason for this, but probably he had seen so much bloodshed lately, that he dreaded a repetition of scenes that had terrified him.

He had himself escaped from the jaws of death.

The crew were much more contented than they had been for a long time. There was no tyranny, no punishment, a liberal allowance of grog and provisions, and although the discipline was good it was not severe and vexatious.

Money Marks ordered a boat's crew to row himself, Cuffy, and Tom Castaway to the shore. The natives had not ventured near the ship although they could be discovered hovering about in canoes at a respectful distance.

It was subsequently explained that these people were in the act of rowing towards the *Ocean Queen* when the firing at the captain's boat took place, and this so frightened them, they thinking that a similar fate might await them, that they refused to come any further until some one from the strange mysterious sail came to re-assure them.

Money Marks had dressed himself in the captain's clothes, and carried several arms with him. The boat was laden with a few little knicknacks, with which it was purposed to conciliate the King of the Cumbagees.

This monarch was named Procul-ny-watti, and was a man

of about forty years of age, friendly in his intercourse with foreigners, but said to be treacherous and unreliable in the highest degree.

Many stories were current among seamen of the bad conduct of Procul-ny-watti; and it was whispered beneath the breath, that in the dungeons beneath the king's summer palace more than one Englishman was confined.

Money Marks was smoking a cigar, and conversing amicably with Cuffy.

Tom Castaway held the rudder lines, and looked after the boat's course.

Cuffy's face wore a proud, almost exultant look, as he said—

"Dis chile can tell you something, Massa Marks."

"What is it, Cuffy?"

"Never tell no one before, but now I feel free, and approach my native land——"

"Your native land!"

"Yes, Massa Marks; me native of Africa."

"I always thought you were born in the southern states."

"Me live there long time, but me born in Africa, and sold as slave. That's how me come to Charleston."

He looked steadily at the advancing shore, and then said in a tone of deep emotion—

"There was war. Mother, father great folks; father mighty warrior. His house full of skulls, more skulls than anyone else. We fought with the Cumbagees; they beat; all killed and sold; me sold, but now I come back I feel proud because my father great warrior."

"How long ago is that, Cuffy," enquired Money Marks.

"Oh! it some years, many years; too many to count."

"Can you speak the Cumbagee language?"

"Speak it well."

"That is fortunate, for you can be our interpreter."

Many boats came out to meet them, and the natives appeared to be very friendly. Cuffy said they were great thieves, and kept them off with a boat-hook. He declared that they would take anything they could lay their hands on.

The natives led the way to the shore, and conducted the strangers to a harbour by an intricate passage of about a quarter of a mile in length, and at one place not two hundred yards wide.

Here they found themselves in a circular basin upwards of half a mile across, with deep water, and completely sheltered from all winds.

On its western shore they saw a large and beautiful village, almost hid amongst trees, with a high wooded range behind it, stretching to the south.

The eastern shore was low, and laid out in fields, with a few huts here and there. At first sight, this basin or harbour did not appear to have any outlet, except by the one they had examined. But on rowing to its upper or southern side, they were surprised to find that it was joined by a narrow channel to another harbour still larger, and, if possible, more beautiful than the first, for here the land was high on both sides and richly wooded from top to bottom.

Proceeding onwards through this basin and still conducted by the friendly Cumbagees, they came to another outlet not above a hundred yards wide, formed by cliffs rising abruptly out of the water to the height of a hundred feet.

Both sides being covered with trees which nearly met overhead, the space below was rendered cool and pleasant.

The depth of water in the lake varied, it was conjectured from four to six fathoms. They rowed directly across and landed at the southern side at the foot of a wooded range of hills; they soon came to the city or village, the houses of which were made of wattled rattans connected by a light, open bamboo roof. The cottages were for the most part thatched and enveloped in creepers, encircled by a rattan fence at two or three yards distance.

In a yard was a number of goats, and it was singular that the inside of the cottages was black and dirty, owing to there being only a small hole in the wall to admit light and air and allow the smoke to escape.

The chiefs wore little case-knives in the folds of their robes, and the lower classes carried larger knives. The natives were small in stature, and watched nervously while Tom Castaway loaded a musket; it was pointed over their heads, and when it was discharged some of them fell on their faces as if they had been shot, but almost immediately got up and looking at one another burst into a timorous laugh.

A cartridge was given to one man who was nearly blowing himself up with it by putting it in the bowl of his lighted pipe, no doubt thinking that it was something to smoke. Cuffy only knocked it away just in time.

The negro asked the natives for some water in their own tongue, and they gave it cheerfully, evidently much surprised at finding him acquainted with their language.

They made no objection to Money Marks going into the village, in the principal house of which the king lived; for the present that was closed, as the monarch of the Cumbagees thought it derogatory to his dignity to show himself all at once to the strangers.

In the offices to which he was admitted was a stable, in which were two handsome bay ponies; there was also a well-stocked pigsty and a poultry-house.

In another quarter stood a mill for husking corn, consisting of a grooved solid cylinder of wood fitted neatly into a hollow cylinder, the sides of which were also grooved; near this lay a hand flour-mill and several baskets of cotton. In another part of the court was a granary, erected on posts about six feet above the ground, having billets of firewood piled below it. At another place, under a tree in the village, he saw a blacksmith's anvil fixed in a block; the forge was of masonry, having an air hole, but the bellows was wanting.

In the centre of the village stood a building like a temple, surrounded by a stone wall. It was filled with elegant vases of different shapes and sizes, closed up and ranged in rows on the floor; the verandah encircling the building being also covered with vases. According to the account of the natives, the remains of the dead are deposited in these jars. Round the building, bamboo poles were placed so as to lean against the thatched roof, having notches cut in them, to which bundles of flowers were hung, some fresh, others decayed, apparently funereal offerings; but their exact import he was not able to learn. The elegant shape of the vases, and the tasteful way in which they were arranged, with the flowers hanging all round, gave to this cemetery an air of cheerfulness, which we are in the habit of thinking unsuitable to a depository of the dead.

A chief came out of the king's house; he was an old man, and carried a green bough in his hand. He advanced to Money Marks and presented him with the bough.

Money Marks took it with a respectful inclination of the head, and reaching out his hand tore down a similar bough and presented it to the old chief in return.

This appeared to gratify him very much. He then took Money Marks and his party over the king's garden, in which sugar canes were growing. Cuffy admired the crop, but they did not take much notice of him, thinking he was the slave of the white man; when Marks also admired it, he ordered some canes to be pulled up by the roots and given to him, in return for which favour he received a few buttons cut off Tom Castaway's jacket, whereat he rejoiced very much.

As the walls of the houses were made of wattled cane, they looked more like large baskets than dwelling-houses. Rude pictures and carved woodwork figures were hanging on the walls, along with inscriptions in unknown characters.

The chief was curious to know whether the brig was coming into the harbour, and Cuffy replied in the negative by Money Marks's orders.

The weather became a little fresh; there was no sign of rain, but the wind rose and a heavy swell rolled in towards the shore. The weather, in fact, threatened to be squally, and Tom Castaway congratulated Money Marks on having made the shore, as he had noticed several coral reefs as he steered the boat to the harbour in the first lake.

Everyone was anxious now to see the king, but they were told his majesty was dressing and would not be visible until he had completed his *toilette*. There was nothing to be done but to wait patiently, and they tried to amuse themselves as best they could.

A range of hills of a semicircular form embraces the village, and limits its extent: at most places it is steep, but at the point where the north end joins the harbour there is an overhanging cliff about eighty feet high, the upper part of which projects considerably beyond the base. At eight or ten yards from the ground on this inclined face, a long horizontal gallery has been hewn out of the solid rock: it communicates with a number of small square excavations

still deeper in the rock, for the reception of the vases containing the bones of the dead.

The trees and creepers on the edge of this precipice hung down so low as to meet the tops of those which grew on the plain; thus a screen of leaves and branches was formed which threw the gallery into deep shade: everything at this beautiful spot being perfectly still and silent, the scene was exceedingly solemn and imposing. It took the party, indeed, somewhat by surprise, for nothing in its external appearance had indicated the purpose to which the place was appropriated; and on passing along they happened to discover an opening amongst the trees and brushwood, and resolving to see what it led to, entered by a narrow path winding through the grove. The liveliness of the scenery without, and the various amusements of the day, had put them all into high spirits; but the unexpected and sacred gloom of the scene in which they suddenly found themselves had an instantaneous effect in repressing the mirth of the whole party, who marched out again like so many people from the cave of Trophonius!

Tom Castaway had taken care to bring several bottles of spirits with him, and being of a mischievous disposition, he determined to make the old chief tipsy. Cuffy told him that the chief's name was Loochoo, and it was soon evident that he was not altogether unacquainted with the virtues of brandy.

"Why, bless my eyes!" exclaimed Tom Castaway: "the old gentleman's a regular soaker. Don't he take kindly to his liquor?"

The party had selected a quiet spot in which to regale themselves during the time that they would have to wait before the king of the Cumbagees made his appearance. It was richly wooded and Loochoo did not meet with a hearty response when he invited Tom Castaway to come out in the sunshine and dance.

"Give the old gentleman a drop more drink, nigger," he exclaimed to Cuffy, "and tell him it's rather too warm for dancing, although I shouldn't mind seeing him do a little of the light fantastic toe business; I'm too delicate a craft to stand such a breeze as that."

Loochoo began to abuse Tom when his refusal was made known to him, but a tumbler full of brandy appeased him.

"What's the old gentleman a-saying?" asked Tom.

"He says you're no good," replied Cuffy, "and he'll have your head."

"Will he!" cried Tom, clapping his hand to his neck; "not he, by G——. I can take his broadsides as quietly as the rock of Gibraltar."

"I must confess," said Money Marks, with a laugh, "that it is too hot for violent exercise. Cats object to being skinned in the hot weather for fear they may take cold, and the wind would be too warm when the sun goes down."

Loochoo all at once ceased his exertions, and, standing still, put himself in a singular position, with the right arm extended and the left foot drawn back; then he lifted up his voice and sang, in a loud tone, the following lines:—

"Ty'wack koo, tawshoo, shee kackoofing,
Chaw ung, itchee shaw, shooha neebooroo;
Ting shee, you byee, chee taroo shoo ninnee
Nooboo cadsee meesee carra shaw jeeroo
Shing coodee sackee oochee noo shing."

Cuffy was unable to translate and make sense of them, though he said it was a scrap of a jovial drinking song and full of praises of wine and the god of wine.

Loochoo asked for some more brandy, which was refused him. He had already drunk more than three parts of a bottle; the effect of which was soon apparent upon him, for he fell forwards on his face, and lay on the ground as insensible as a stone.

At this unfortunate juncture there was a loud cry, indicating that the king was coming.

All eyes were turned in his direction.

King Procul-ny-watti was a tall man, of prodigious stature. We were afterwards informed that the office of king was not hereditary, but that when the monarch died it was customary to elect another, and probably Procul was chosen because of his great size.

He was richly but fantastically dressed.

His eyes fell instantly upon Loochoo, but he bowed to Marks and gesticulated for fully the space of a minute.

By his side hung a ship's cutlass. He drew it flashing from the scabbard, and, advancing to Loochoo, stood over

MONEY MARKS ATTACKS CAPTAIN ARLEE.

him; then raising the sabre he severed the unlucky courtier's head from his body at a single stroke.

Money Marks would have interfered and saved Loochoo's life had he been able to divine the king's intention.

The whole thing was so sudden that he and those with him were unable to do anything.

When the king had taken vengeance on Loochoo he beckoned the party towards the village, and was much pleased when Cuffy addressed him in his own language. A conversation ensued between them, which Cuffy interpreted in this way:—

"The king," he said to Money Marks, "wants you to come to his principal temple, where he has provided refreshments. There he will talk about slaves and gold-dust, and regulate the principles of trade. He will lead the way and we are to follow him."

Money Marks nodded his head.

First walked the king, behind him Marks, by Marks' side the interpreter, the rest of the whites, the chiefs, and the crowd of Cumbagees following. In ten minutes 'time they reached the place in which the banqueting-hall, as it may be called, was situated.

It was an oblong inclosure, sixty yards by forty, surrounded by a wall twelve feet high, rather well-built with squared blocks of coral: the entrance was by a large gate on the south side, from which there extended raised gravel walks, bordered by clipped hedges, the intermediate spaces being laid out in beds, like a garden. A temple occupied one corner of the inclosure, and was completely shaded by a grove of fine trees, which also overhung the inclosing wall. In that part of the garden directly opposite to the gate, at the upper end of the walk, there stood a smaller temple, nearly hid by the branches of several large banyan-trees; and before it, at the distance of ten or twelve paces, a square awkward-looking building, with a raised terrace round it. The great temple first spoken of was divided by means of shifting partitions into four apartments; it had a verandah running all round, with a row of carved wooden pillars on its outer ed-e to support the roof, which extended considerably beyond the columns. The floor of the verandah was two feet from the ground; the roof sloping and covered with handsome tiles, those forming the eaves being ornamented with flowers and various figures in relief; there were also several out-houses, and a kitchen communicating with them and with the temple by covered passages. In one of the inner apartments, at the upper end, there was a small recess containing a green shrub, in a high narrow flowerpot, having an inscription on a tablet hanging above it on the wall.

On another side of the same room, there hung the picture of a man rescuing a bird from the paws of a cat; the bird seemed to have been just taken from a cage, which was tumbling over, with two other birds fluttering about in the inside: it was merely a sketch, but was executed in a spirited manner. In one of the back apartments we found three gilt images, eighteen inches high, with a flower in a vase before them. The roof of the temple within was ten feet high; and all the cornices, pillars, and other wooden parts of the building were neatly carved into flowers and fantastic figures of various animals.

The ground immediately round it was divided into a number of small beds, planted with different shrubs and flowers; and on a pedestal of artificial rock, in one of the walks close to it, a clay vessel of an elegant form, full of water, with a wooden ladle swimming on the top.

On a frame near one of the outhouses, hung a large bell three feet high, of an elegant shape, resembling a long beehive; the sides were two inches thick and richly ornamented, and its tone uncommonly fine.

Everyone was much entertained by these evidences of taste and skill on the part of the Cumbagees.

The repast provided for the whites was of its kind excellent. It would be tedious to describe it here in detail; let it suffice to say that fowls were cooked in every conceivable way, that rice was made the most of, and that numberless animals good for food, but of the names of which the strangers were ignorant, had been killed for the feast.

There was also a strong, but rather harsh sort of wine upon the table. This was made by the Cumbagees and did them great credit.

When the feast—for so it deserves to be called—was over, cigars made in a rude way, and not nearly so perfect in shape as European ones, but much superior in flavour, were distributed, and Money Marks was told by Cuffy that the king would be glad if they would walk in the garden, which was well-wooded, and of considerable dimensions, at the back of the temple.

This proposition was very acceptable to the whites, because the hot air in the Temple was not dissipated and cooled by means of punkahs or other devices.

The king thinking it derogatory to his dignity to walk with the white men, thought it best to remain behind and take his siesta in the sacred walls. He delegated some chiefs to go with the party, and Money Marks, much struck with the intelligent face of one called Bowka, told Cuffy to invite him to accompany them.

He did so with alacrity.

They had not gone far before they came to a grove of cinnamon-trees, in the midst of which was a peculiar structure.

It was the hull of a ship; about that there could be no question, for on it was written in large letters "The *Fair Margaret*, of London."

The ship had probably been wrecked on the coast or driven into the harbour of Carteras; but that the structure they saw was part of a British vessel it was impossible to doubt.

The ship's hull had been reared up in a peculiar manner, and served for the dwelling of a fakir or holy man, not exactly a great high priest, but a man whose sanctity was much revered, and whose opinion was highly valued, and whose judgment was always consulted when the monarch thought it incumbent on him to go to war.

The hermit was a fanatic of the worst description; he had not for many years cut his nails or his hair, he was old, and he had when young clenched his left hand, and kept it clenched so that the finger nails ran into the flesh and made their exit through the back of his hand.

When only sixteen he had been famous for travelling nearly two thousand miles, and measuring every inch and yard of earth with his body as he went.

This devotee was called Nar.

The sight of the remains of a British vessel excited Money Marks' curiosity, and he told Cuffy to inquire what the meaning of it was, and how it had got there.

At the same time the various tales he had heard about British seamen being held captive flooded his memory, and he experienced a sensation of dread and anger when he thought that possibly some of his countrymen might be immured in dungeons or held as slaves in the dominions of Procul-ny-watti, the half-civilized king of the Cumbagees.

He told Cuffy to put a few questions to Bowka, which he was not slow in doing.

An earnest conversation took place between them.

After which Cuffy came to Money Marks, who was curiously regarding the fanatic, Nar, the latter having emerged from his obscurity and confronted the strangers.

"Well, Cuffy," exclaimed Money Marks, "what does he say ?"

Cuffy beckoned the captain on one side before replying.

CHAPTER XVI.

THE "FAIR MARGARET" OF LONDON.

WHEN Money Marks had retreated to a spot which was sheltered by the spreading branches of a banyan-tree, he exclaimed—

"Did you get the information I am in want of from Bowka?"

Cuffy nodded his head, and replied—

"Yes, Massa Marks, it am all right."

"What did he say ?"

"Him say that the ship was wrecked."

"In the harbour ?"

"No, down the shore."

"Along the coast, I suppose you mean ?"

"That what mean, Massa Marks. Well, I ask what become of crew, and he shake him head."

"You were not satisfied with that ?"

"Not me !" replied Cuffy.

"What did you do ?"

"Questioned him again."

"With what result ?"

"This he say : 'Seven men saved.' "

"Seven ?"

"Yes."

"What became of them ?"

"That he would not tell me; all I could get out of him, Massa Marks, was, 'King know.' "

"The king knows, eh ?"

"Yes, Massa Marks."

"That," said Money Marks, "is as much as to say that King Procul—what's his name?—knows more about these seven men than he chooses to tell?"

"P'raps they dead."

"I am inclined to think not."

"How it possible to tell?" said Cuffy.

"By dint of diligent inquiry, which I feel it is our imperative duty to make," replied Money Marks; "if we were not backed by the power, and the guns of the brig in the harbour, we might be treated in the same way. Do you not remember the natives asking us if we intended to bring the vessel nearer the shore ? I believe them to be thoroughly bad people, and treacherous to a degree. Do you think that these seven Englishmen of whom he speaks are really in existence, and in captivity ?"

"I do," answered Cuffy.

"In that case we must not leave the place until we have rescued them; but it is better to be cautious and circumspect. We must endeavour by art and strategy to find out where these seven men are confined, and if we liberate them they will make an important addition to our crew."

"They will, Massa Marks. Leave Cuffy to find out all about them; he know how to do it, and he has some advice to give."

"What is it?"

"First of all, gain the confidence of the Cumbagees."

"Why they seem to be an insignificant people !"

"Not they, massa," replied Cuffy; "you not see all *here*. They have a place further in the country, where they keep their warriors. Bowka told me they had five hundred fighting men."

"That cannot be true."

"I don't know, massa; p'raps not. The barracoons, or places where they keep the slaves, are in the country, and so is the summer-palace of the king."

"Indeed!"

"So I advise, Mas' Marks, that we invite the king and his chiefs to dinner on board the brig, and——"

He hesitated.

"What!" demanded Money Marks.

Cuffy lowered his voice, bent down his head, and said in a soft tone, which was inaudible to anyone but his listener—

"*Keep them there!*"

Money Marks started back in astonishment at the audacity of this proposal.

To keep the king and his principal men on board the vessel was an admirable method of obtaining the release of the Englishmen who had been on board the *Fair Margaret*, supposing that there were some of them in captivity. The idea showed that Cuffy was not devoid of intelligence. Money Marks was disposed to adopt his suggestion, but, before doing so, he called Tom Castaway to his side. Tom was drinking some of the wine already mentioned, and holding up a glassful in his hand, he exclaimed to Bowka, in a loud voice—

"Here's fortune, guvnor!"

Bowka smiled and bowed, and seemed pleased at what he presumed was a great compliment, and Tom approached Marks.

"Well, Master Marks, what's the next move afoot?"

Money Marks looked severely at him, and said in reply to this rude remark—

"You are getting drunk, Castaway, and I warn you that the consequences will be serious if you go much farther. I am captain of the *Ocean Queen*, and I allow no familiarity from you, or anyone else, when we are amongst strangers. Do you understand that?"

"If you are captain, who made you so?" replied Tom.

"Another remark like that, and I knock your brains out on the spot!" cried Money Marks, his eyes flashing, and his whole frame quivering.

"You make a friend of the nigger," said Tom.

"I make a friend of nobody to the prejudice of others. If I did, it is no business of yours; I choose my friends as I like. Am I obliged to ask you or anyone else?"

"A white man's as good as a nigger any day."

At this reply Money Marks was so incensed, that he clenched his fist and was about to dash Tom Castaway to the earth, when Cuffy interposed and stayed his wrath. Tom slunk away to the root of a tree and laid down. He had not been in a recumbent position long before he went to sleep, and snored loudly.

"Leave him alone, massa," said Cuffy; "when he come to he will be sober, and then him apol'gise."

"If he does not I will make an example of him."

"You take my word he will do so."

"It will be best for him to do so," replied Money Marks, turning on his heel.

He was sorry that any difference should have taken place between himself and Tom Castaway, for he was really a good fellow at heart, and had done a good deal to secure him in the position he thus held as captain of the *Ocean Queen*.

But it was absolutely necessary that every attempt at insubordination should be promptly suppressed. He was the commander of a lawless set of men—lawless, because he had made them so. He had transformed them from common able-bodied seamen into pirates, and devourers of harmless merchantmen.

Such fellows required to be ruled with a rod of iron; if he relaxed his discipline for a moment he would lose all power over them, and they would be his masters.

Tom Castaway slept for two hours, during which time Money Marks walked about and conversed with the different chiefs with whom he came in contact, and by Cuffy's aid managed to pick up a good deal of information about various matters.

When Tom awoke he remembered a little of what happened, and he was sorry for having offended the captain.

Cuffy came to him, and said—

"You had better go to Money Marks, and tell him you're sorry, or it will be squally weather, as de sailors say."

"What did I do, mate?" enquired Tom.

"Called him everything. You were drunk. Go and say so and he will forgive you."

This advice was too good to be disregarded; and Tom at once sought Money Marks, to whom he made an awkward bow, and exclaimed—

"Beg pardon, I'm sure, sir; but I was a little on, and didn't know what I was saying an hour ago. I hope you'll look over it, and say no more about it."

"Since you have apologized I consent to do so," replied Money Marks, "but I cannot help saying that you behaved very badly and that you deserve punishment."

"Not this time, sir."

"Well, let it be a warning to you; for by the God that made me, if you or any man under my command attempts to use the slightest familiarity with me, I will shoot him down as I would a dog."

Tom winced.

"Do you hear me? I would shoot him as I would a dog," continued Money Marks. "I am not going to be made a milk-and-water captain having no control over his men; my control shall be absolute and uncontradicted. Do you hear that?"

"All right, sir," replied Tom; "it's the last time I'll put anything in my belly to steal away my brains. You're my captain, and as such I will respect you, whatever flag we sail under."

"That is enough," said Money Marks, putting a pistol he had been handling in a restless manner in his pocket; "go to the boats and call them together, and hold them in readiness to return to the vessel in half an hour."

"Ay, ay, sir," replied Tom Castaway, touching his hat.

When he was gone Money Marks said to Cuffy—

"Keep your eye on that man; I distrust him."

"Me too, massa," replied Cuffy.

The negro drew his knife from his girdle and holding it up in the light, grinned a ghastly grin, which, rightly interpreted, meant a great deal.

Money Marks invited the king to dinner on board the ship, and begged that his principal officers might be permitted to accompany him.

To this proposition King Procul-ny-watti made no objection; he expressed his entire willingness that the invitation should be accepted, and promised to come the next day at one o'clock. A few questions were asked about the traffic in slaves, and Marks replied that all he wanted was ivory and gold dust, with any other natural products of the country they had to dispose of.

After this dialogue was over Money Marks and his party took their leave.

The result of their visit was duly promulgated to the crew, and the men were promised a holiday on shore after the royal visit.

At the appointed time the king and his friends arrived, and were shown all over the vessel. They showed themselves to be observant, and to be possessed of a good deal of curiosity.

The party consisted of twelve, which seemed to be a mystical number with them. It included the king, who was treated with the utmost veneration and respect by all with whom he was accompanied.

They looked over everything with great attention, taking particular notice of globes, books, and mirrors; nevertheless they stood in need of some encouragement to induce them to come forward, being restrained by a well-bred self-denial from hastily gratifying their curiosity, lest it might be thought obtrusive by those to whom its objects were not new. Their dress was singularly graceful; it consisted of a loose flowing robe, with very wide sleeves, and tied round the middle by a broad rich belt or girdle of wrought silk; a yellow cylindrical cap, and a neat straw sandal, over a short cotton boot or stocking. Two of the chiefs wore light yellow robes, the other dark blue streaked with white, all made with cotton. Their caps were flat at top, and appeared to be formed by winding a broad band diagonally round a frame or cylinder, in such a manner, that at each turn a small portion of the last fold should be visible above in front, and below at the hinder part. The sandals were held on the feet by a stiff straw band passing over the instep, and joining the sandal near the heel; this band was connected with the forepart of the sandal by a slight string, drawn between the great toe and that next to it, the stocking being made with a division, like the finger of a glove, to receive the great toe. They all carried fans which they stuck in their girdles when not in use; each person had also a short tobacco pipe in a small bag hanging along with the pouch at the waist. During all this morning, the whole space between the ships and the shore was covered with canoes, each containing about ten persons. The scene was exceedingly lively; for, as few of the parties who came to look at the ships remained long, the canoes were continually passing backwards and forwards, and the numbers which came in this way must have been immense. They seemed highly gratified with being allowed to go wherever they pleased, nor was this licence ever abused. The manners of these people, even of the very lowest classes, were particularly good; their curiosity was certainly great, but it never made them rudely inquisitive; their language sounded very musical, and in most cases it was easy of pronunciation.

A loose flowing dress is naturally so graceful that even the lowest boatmen at this place had a picturesque appearance. Their hair, which was observed to be invariably of a glossy black, was shaved off the crown of the head; but this bare place was effectually concealed by their mode of dressing the hair in a close knot over it. Their beards and mustachios had been allowed to grow, and were kept neat and smooth. When they had seen everything, the Cumbagees were asked into a large cabin where dinner had been provided for them.

Captain Monkhouse was sufficiently fond of wine to have laid in a good supply of champagne, moselle, port, and sherry, with other light wines.

Those of course, Money Marks had appropriated to his own use, and had brought out to do honour to the chiefs. When the covers were removed they became silent, and looked on either hand for directions how to proceed. On being helped to soup, they did not stir till they saw the crew take spoons, in the management of which they really showed but little awkwardness. The knife and fork gave them more trouble, but they set seriously about acquiring a knowledge of their use, and in a short time, found no difficulty in helping themselves as we did. They ate of everything; using a great deal of salt, with the fineness and whiteness of which they were much pleased. A tart, however, being put upon the table, they all objected at first to touch it; they would not say why; they were at length prevailed upon to taste it, which they had no sooner done, than they exclaimed that it was "massa! massa!" (good! good!) It was made of Scotch marmalade; and Bowka, in recommending it to his friends, told them that it was "injássa, amása," (bitter, sweet), a union which does not appear to obtain in Cumbagee cookery. They drank wine, but said they feared it would make them tipsy; upon which they were taught to mix it with water, which was evidently new to them, for they relished it so much in this form, that they were in a fair way of running unconsciously into the very excess they had apprehended. As soon as the cloth was removed, they rose, and went to walk about the ship; on a wish being expressed to accompany them they entreated everyone to keep their seats.

During this dinner, though it was probably the first they had ever seen in the European style, these people not only betrayed no awkwardness, but adopted our customs, such as drinking wine with each other, so readily, that the English were frequently at a loss to determine whether they had but just learned these customs, or whether their own usages in these cases were actually similar to those of Europe.

The time at last came for the Cumbagees to be tired of the hospitality which had been extended to them, and to wish to go home.

The king considered it beneath his dignity to hold a conversation with Cuffy, and he delegated the duty to Bowka, who performed it in a very satisfactory manner.

When Bowka proposed to take leave, Cuffy told him in polite language, that it would be necessary for his party and himself, to stay on board for two days, and he extenuated the harshness of this measure by stating that such was the custom of the country from which the *Ocean Queen* had sailed.

The indignation of the Cumbagees at this declaration was prodigious.

Some of them took knives and other weapons from their girdles, but a superior power overawed them; and they felt compelled to acquiesce in this measure, however unpalatable it was to them.

Money Marks felt it prudent to keep all boats off; and he ordered that those which approached too near should be fired upon.

He also ordered that the brig should stand nearer in shore.

The king and his officers were entertained in a princely manner, and had nothing to complain of. Cuffy and Bowka became great friends, and were talking together over some rum-and-water, for more than two hours.

At midnight, Cuffy sought Money Marks' cabin; he was engaged in conversation with the boatswain, whose name was Karslake; he was an intelligent man, but sadly deficient in the science of navigation. Marks had contrived to learn the art of navigation; and was fully competent by the aid of the books he found in Captain Monkhouse's library, to steer the ship, and guide her to any part of the globe.

As Cuffy entered he was giving the boatswain a dissertation on tides, for he wished to make all his officers efficient, so that no accidents might happen—and all of them were glad to learn.

Money Marks soon saw that Cuffy wanted to speak to him, and he dismissed Karslake.

"Well, Cuffy, what is it?" he exclaimed.

"Got news for massa," replied Cuffy.

"News!"

"Yes."

"Of what description?"

"Been talking to Bowka."

"About what?"

"The *Fair Margaret* of London."

"Ah! and what did he say?"

"Not much at first, but a good supply of rum soon loosen his tongue."

"Did he reveal anything?"

"Everything, Mass' Marks," replied Cuffy, looking very important, and very proud of being the proprietor of the news he was about to communicate.

"Lose no time and tell me," said Money Marks.

"He tell me, massa, that the *Fair Margaret* was wrecked, and that all but seven drowned. They are slaves in the summer palace up the country, and work like negroes all day and all the year round."

"You are sure he spoke the truth?"

"Certain sure."

"They shall be rescued, and that before many hours have passed over their heads," exclaimed Money Marks.

He paced the cabin with long strides, and stopping suddenly, dismissed Cuffy until the morning.

CHAPTER XVII.

THE RESCUE.

THE surprise of the chiefs was excessive when it was notified to them that they must stay on board the vessel; but as has been stated they thought the most prudent course they could adopt would be to acquiesce without making a disturbance, which could not result favourably to themselves.

The object of this compulsory measure they could only guess at. The wily nature of the natives made them believe that some ill was intended them; for they had had intercourse with whites before, and they had never found it to be one of their customs to keep visitors on board ship for any length of time.

They were well treated; having plenty to eat and drink given them, and being allowed to wander about the ship, though they were well guarded by strong hands and watchful eyes.

Escape was impossible.

Early the next morning Money Marks selected a crew of twenty men, with which he manned the launch and put to sea. It was a lovely day and the men were in high spirits, both at the idea of going on shore, and also at the prospect of rescuing some imprisoned fellow creatures; for the object of the expedition was well known to them, having been bruited abroad by Cuffy, acting under the orders of Money Marks.

They were all well armed.

When King Procul-ny-watti saw this warlike party leave the ship, every doubt which had lingered in his mind as to the object of his own and his companions' detention vanished, and he knew that some hostile demonstration was about to be made into the heart of his territory.

He foamed at the mouth, and showed every symptom of violent anger, and so did his courtiers, but their irate gesticulations only excited the laughter of the guard, who did not for a moment relax their watchfulness.

The boat as it neared the land gradually receded from view; when it reached the shore it was met by an old chief who had been left in command during his majesty's absence.

This aged dignitary fully believed that King Procul was being honoured with a passage back to his dominions, and that he should see his royal master in the launch.

His surprise at being disappointed was most intense.

Cuffy was delegated to speak to him, having in the first instance received his instructions from Money Marks.

"Tell him," exclaimed the latter, "that the king has expressed a wish for the liberation of his white prisoners."

"Yes," replied Cuffy.

"And that his majesty is waiting on board the *Ocean Queen* until our party returns with the captives."

"Anything else?"

"Tell him also that it is his majesty's pleasure that he should accompany us and show us whereabouts the prisoners are confined."

Cuffy nodded his woolly head, and immediately jumped on shore to hold a palaver with the old chief. Their conversation was of some length, lasting nearly half an hour. The chief appeared from his manner to have his doubts as to the truth of Cuffy's statement, and he glared savagely with his lack-lustre eyes at the English and Americans, whom he evidently considered the hereditary enemies of his race.

At length Cuffy left him, and returned to the boat.

"Well," cried Money Marks, eagerly, "what does he say?"

"Him not believe a word of what I stated," replied Cuffy.

"The old infidel!"

"Not a word, massa, and him further say there are no prisoners."

"None!"

"No; and him say him not going to take us to Summer Palace. If we want to go, take ourselves."

"You can make nothing of him?"

"No, massa; nothing."

"Very well, we must leave him, and act independently."

One of the most striking points in Money Marks' character was his energetic decision. His mind was always clear and comprehensive; and he was ever ready to form an opinion and act upon it without any vacillation.

He told the men to land, which they at once did, forming themselves into a double line. Three men he left in charge of the boat, ordering them to row a good way from the land, so as to guard against surprise and also to have the protection of the ship's guns. They were to hold themselves in readiness to row in when they heard a given signal, which was the firing of three shots in quick succession.

Several natives were hanging about the skirts of what may not inaptly be called, the invading army. Two of these were captured by Money Marks' direction, and bound together. Pistols were levelled at their heads, and Cuffy was entrusted to tell them that if they did not instantly lead the way—without any deviation from the direct path—to the king's Summer Palace, where it was reasonably supposed the prisoners were confined, they would have their brains blown out upon the spot.

They listened to this declaration with an oriental stolidity, and replied in the negative. All that Cuffy could elicit from them was *No kamo*, which meant "I cannot." Cuffy assured them that he was in earnest; and opposed as Money Marks was to bloodshed, he felt constrained to sacrifice one, if not both of the men, in order to terrify others into compliance.

Taking a pistol from his girdle, he advanced to Cuffy's side.

The eyes of all the men, natives and Europeans, were fixed upon him.

In a loud voice he told Cuffy to state that a life would be taken if the men hesitated any longer.

They heard the fell decree, but did not pay any heed to it; whereupon Money Marks deliberately levelled his weapon at the native nearest him, and blew his brains out.

The man fell to the ground stone dead, dragging the companion to whom he was chained after him.

The surviving one was bespattered with blood and brains, and so startled at the awfully sudden fate that had overtaken his friend, that he exclaimed to Cuffy that he was perfectly ready and willing to conduct the entire force to the Summer Palace.

Forming themselves into lines four deep, the sailors marched, conducted by Money Marks, with Cuffy and the native Cumbagee, while the rearguard was composed of Tom Castaway and another.

By dint of questioning, it was elicited that ten miles would have to be traversed before the palace was reached, and the men on passing a fountain filled their canteens to guard against thirst on the way.

The little force was followed at a respectful distance by a crowd of black men of various ranks, who were anxious to see what was about to ensue. They offered no violence to the invaders, although, being numerically superior, it would not have been surprising if they had attempted to do so; but it appeared to Money Marks that they were disorganized, and knew not how to act in the absence of the king and the other chiefs, by whom they were accustomed to be led and guided.

The body politic was there, but it wanted a head. It was found on arriving at the Summer Palace, that the king had what may be called a standing army, but its strength had been greatly exaggerated—instead of five hundred men, there were not more than fifty trained to arms, and these were studiously concealed from the notice of foreigners who touched at the Port of Carteras.

It is true that on an emergency the entire able-bodied part of the community could join the ranks, and probably did so to a great extent whenever a slave-hunting expedition was organized.

The Summer Palace was a spacious building of no great altitude, though it covered a vast extent of ground. It had no claim to architectural excellence, though it was in some places finished with great care, and even with artistic effect.

Of course innumerable courts might be seen filled with choice flowers and shrubs, amongst the branches of which lurked melodious birds; fountains, too, gurgled up and cooled the air; all the luxuries of tropical life, except ice, might be found in various parts of the king's Summer Palace.

As the English and Americans advanced a shrill noise was heard. It proceeded from a curiously carved reed, held to the mouth of a sentinel. Its sound was not unlike that of a trumpet.

It was evidently a signal.

The standing army of King Procul came flocking from their quarters, and were soon drawn up in martial array.

They were armed with spears and knives, firearms they had none, nor did they seem fully to understand the terrible use to which the latter might be put.

Cuffy and Money Marks boldly stepped forward. Their example was followed by two of the enemy, who did not seem indisposed to hold a conference, and see what the reason of the invasion might be.

They were told that the invaders were desirous of obtaining the release of certain white men held as prisoners by the Cumbagees, and that if they were given up, the invaders would retire; if not, they would be forcibly taken from the palace, and that place burnt to the ground.

The chief appeared much surprised at this.

It was further stated to them that the king and his principal officers were captives on board ship, and would not be surrendered until the survivors of the crew of the *Fair Margaret* were given up.

This latter statement was most fully corroborated by some of the stragglers who had followed the sailors from the village, and who mingled with the soldiery, giving them all the news.

After a consultation had taken place the two chiefs retired to talk to their friends before making any reply.

Money Marks and Cuffy, following their example, withdrew to the leading column of their own men.

A high palisade had been erected all round the palace; this was formed of tall bamboos placed closely together, and cut into sharp spikes at the top, so as to form an effectual barricade.

The Cumbagee warriors had emerged into the open plain through a gate of large size, also constructed of bamboo, but the stakes were much wider apart, and admitted of the hurling of spears through the interstices.

The chiefs consulted together for some time, and then it was apparent that they had determined to defend the place, for they retired in good order and with remarkable rapidity through the gate, forming in line behind it, with their spears poised and their shields held before their kneeling bodies.

One man of gigantic stature, however, remained behind.

He was quite a Goliath of Gath, for he stood at least seven and a half feet high, and was of great strength. His shield was an enormous piece of wood, and his spear was like a huge lance heavily weighted with an iron head at the front.

This monster bellowed out something at the top of his voice, which appeared to be a challenge.

Not certain whether it was so or not, Money Marks applied to Cuffy, who said—

"Him great big beast, Massa Marks, and him say, 'Come out and fight me. Let your captain come and fight with me, and when I kill him let some one else come fight me, and so will I kill you all.'"

Money Marks on hearing this addressed his man, saying—

"I will accept the fellow's challenge, and astonish him a little."

There was a loud cheer at this, and Money Marks was regarded favourably by the on-looking and admiring crew.

Money Marks was simply provided with a pistol, a Minié rifle, and a cutlass. He held the Minié rifle in his hand as he advanced to meet the Cumbagee champion.

The only danger the Englishman ran of being defeated by the native was in the quick throwing of the spear, which was a weapon difficult to avoid. So heavy looked this spear, that Money Marks rightly judged that it would be extremely difficult to project it any great distance, therefore he wisely refrained from going too near the Philistine.

The giant appeared enraged at this, and beckoned to him to come nearer, but Money Marks moved off in a side direction, drawing the other after him.

It was known that some of the African tribes poisoned the tips of their spears, but it was not generally believed that the Cumbagees had recourse to this pernicious and cowardly custom.

Money Marks was perfectly certain that if his aim was true, the bullet of his rifle would penetrate the shield of his antagonist and kill him upon the spot, but he did not wish to take an advantage of him, and he determined to allow him to throw his spear before he fired.

The Cumbagee advanced to Money Marks, who stood still.

As soon as he did this, the giant also stopped, and poising his spear by the side of his head for a moment, hurled it with inconceivable force.

Money Marks had been watching him, and he no sooner saw the spear leave the champion's hand than he fell forward on his face.

The spear passed harmlessly over his head.

His *ruse* had been perfectly successful.

A cheer arose from the sailors when they saw that their captain was unhurt.

Money Marks sprang to his feet in a moment, placed the rifle in rest, and took a steady aim.

The Cumbagee, finding his attempt to transfix his enemy with the spear was unsuccessful and abortive, uttered a howl of rage, and drawing his knife rushed forward to engage in mortal combat. He evidently thought that the rifle Money Marks held in his hand was a spear, and holding up his shield, he laughed at its tiny dimensions.

Money Marks pulled the trigger, and the result was not long doubtful.

The bullet went crashing through the woodwork of the shield, and sank deeply into the Cumbagee's lungs.

He fell with a crash to the earth, which seemed to groan and tremble under the infliction.

The contest had been eagerly watched by both parties, and a hoarse roar of rage ascended from the Cumbagees, who threw open the gate as if they were determined to make a sortie and rescue the body of their champion, whom they did not consider dead.

Money Marks retreated to his men, ordered them to form into a double line, the first rank kneeling.

Each sailor was armed with an improved rifle.

The Cumbagees advanced, and as they did so Money Marks gave the word to the front rank to fire.

They did so, and six men of the Cumbagees fell to the ground. A panic seized them, and they ran helter-skelter back to their entrenchments, but ere they could reach their shelter, the second rank received a command to fire, and this time seven of their number fell mortally wounded.

The sailors reloaded, and Money Marks gave the order to advance in close column. So terrified were the natives, that they had omitted to throw their spears at the advancing column; the fatal action of the rifles was so terror-inspiring that they were frightfully alarmed, and retreated as best they could.

When the whites were seen advancing, a man emerged from the palisades, and carried a white flag in his hand. It was evident that he was a messenger to negociate peace. He had an interview with Cuffy, and told him that no further resistance would be offered, and that the little party might do as they chose; all he begged for was mercy to be accorded to those who were survivors of the late massacre.

Money Marks acceded to these terms with pleasure. He directed his men to keep close together, and to have their firearms in readiness for immediate use, for were they to neglect salutary precautions, there was little doubt that the treacherous natives would take any advantage of them that might be thrown in their way.

He halted the men at the entrance to the palace, and said that he gave them full permission to pillage the palace of all gold, jewels, and other valuables they might find; but that if any wanton mischief was done the offender should be severely punished.

He also forbad the use of intoxicating liquors, and the men were so pleased with permission to loot that they readily agreed to the stipulations imposed upon them.

Money Marks through Cuffy told the surviving Cumbagees that any attempt at retaliation would be punished by death, and he warned them not to molest one of his men, or so much as to touch a hair of his head.

The party was met by an old chief in the principal court of the palace. He was at dinner, and a really sumptuous affair it was; he had three or four different sorts of fish, several joints of meat, and innumerable *entrées*, or side dishes, plenty of wine and rice in various shapes.

Money Marks thought this dinner the fair spoil of war, and told his men to sit down in companies of ten at a time and regale themselves, so that half dined while the other half watched.

The old chief was told to go on with his dinner, but he could not be prevailed upon to do so.

His only answer consisted in pointing to the new comers and making signs of eating, and then drawing his hand across his throat, by which it was understood that it might be all very well for the whites to talk of eating, but for his part eating was of little moment if he was to lose his head.

The sailors laughed at this, for they had no notion that his apprehensions were well-grounded, though it was evident that the old man thought the king would execute him for allowing foreigners to enter the walls of the palace.

A crowd of people employed and living in the palace assembled around the sailors, and the old man seeing that the presence of the people was not agreeable to the whites, told some soldiers to disperse them; this they did in a moment by pelting them with stones.

When the sailors had gratified their appetites and washed down their dinner with a fair allowance of wine, they were ordered to move, and an attendant in the palace was pressed into Money Marks' service and told to lead the way to the place in which the white prisoners were confined.

He did so reluctantly at first, but with more alacrity when he was pricked on and urged to greater exertion by the aid of the point of a bayonet.

Money Marks and his party were conducted into the very centre of the vast building called the palace, which did not appear to be one homogeneous design, but simply a congeries of buildings put together and added to the original block at various times and afterwards surrounded by the bamboo fence.

The interior had the appearance of being older than the other part, which gave support to the theory which has just been advanced.

In a round space surrounded by canes, and sheltered from the sun by reeds was a mill for grinding corn. This was turned by means of a long pole, to which were strapped the seven Englishmen, of whom Money Marks and his party were in search.

It was their daily task to grind a certain amount of corn, and they were given the husks and the straw to lie upon.

It was a life of awful and of hopeless labour, and taskmasters stood by with long thonged whips to make them work harder by the application of corporal punishment, if they allowed their exertions to flag for a moment.

Money Marks' blood so boiled at the sight of this, that when one driver struck a white as he entered the place, he drew a pistol from his belt and shot him dead.

The surprise of the English, who were instantly liberated, may be easily imagined. They wept, laughed, danced, and sang, and seemed never to tire of shaking their countrymen by the hand.

They were supplied with food, drink, and arms, and assisted to pillage the palace.

In answer to questions put to them they said that they were the only captives in the country, except the black slaves, that they had been working as they were found for more than six years, and had given up all hope of rescue: they had wished to die.

A rich booty was found in the palace, and every man returned from it loaded to excess with pure gold and other valuable things.

CHAPTER XVIII.

IN SEARCH OF VIOLA.

THE party succeeded in reaching the ship without any further conflict with the natives. The English who had been rescued were only too glad to join the ship's crew, and the king together with his courtiers were allowed to depart in peace.

But before they were liberated, Money Marks extracted a good supply of fresh water, meat, and vegetables from the natives, who had cause to regret the visit of the *Ocean Queen.*

The ship had some difficulty in getting away, for on going to the westward she fell among coral reefs and islands which are extremely dangerous.

The examination of a coral reef during the different stages of a tide is peculiarly interesting. When the tide has left it for some time it becomes dry and appears to be a compact rock exceedingly hard and rugged, but as the tide rises and the waves begin to wash over it, the coral worms protrude themselves from holes which were before invisible. These animals are of great variety of shapes and sizes, and in such prodigious numbers, that, in a short time, the whole surface of the rock appears to be alive and in motion.

The most common worm is in the form of a star, with arms from four to six inches long, which are moved about with a rapid motion in all directions, probably to catch food.

Others are so sluggish, that they may be mistaken for pieces of the rock, and are generally of a dark colour, and from four to five inches long, and two or three round.

When coral is broken, about high-water mark, it is a solid hard stone, but if any part of it be detached at a spot which the tide reaches every day, it is found to be full of worms of different lengths and colours, some being as fine as a thread and several feet long, of a bright yellow, and sometimes of a blue colour; others resemble snails, and some are not unlike lobsters in shape, but soft, and not above two inches long.

The growth of coral appears to cease when the worm is no longer exposed to the washing of the sea.

Thus a reef rises in the form of a cauliflower, till its top has gained the level of the highest tides, above which the worm has no power to advance, and the reef of course no longer extends itself upwards. The other parts, in succession, reach the surface, and there stop, forming in time a level field with steep sides all round. The reef, however, continually increases, and being prevented from going higher, extends itself laterally in all directions.

But this growth being as rapid at the upper edge as it is lower down, the steepness of the face of the reef is still preserved.

These are the circumstances which render coral reefs so dangerous in navigation; for, in the first place, they are seldom seen above the water; and, in the next, their sides are so steep, that a ship's bows may strike against the rock before any change of soundings has given warning of the danger.

Money Marks contrived to steer the ship with such skill that he avoided a wreck upon the reefs, and determined to go back to the South American coast.

The fact was, he wished to see Viola, and to offer her his hand and heart; as long as he was ignorant of her fate, he could not be happy, and he told the crew that he should go into Charleston as a blockade-runner, having first taken in a cargo such as would be agreeable to the Confederates at a port like Nassau.

The crew were satisfied with Money Marks, and made no objection to his proposal, though they would much rather have sailed in a different and safer direction and under a less hazardous flag.

They were not their own masters, however, and they considered it dangerous to express a decided opinion, because Money Marks had more than once evidenced a disposition to put down any attempt at grumbling and incipient mutiny with a high hand.

After all, seamen are to a great extent similar to school-boys, and must be treated in the same strict manner in which every good and successful schoolmaster treats boys.

Tom Castaway had not made any overt act of rebellion to constituted authority, but Cuffy declared that he had watched him, and detected him in many little speeches and remarks calculated to destroy the confidence of the men in their captain.

Money Marks, however, was a man with a large mind; and he did not think it was worth his while to take any notice of these secretly muttered expressions of discontent. He watched Tom Castaway narrowly, and endeavoured by many acts of kindness to gain his good will.

Owing to a reverse the Federal fleet had lately met with, running the blockade was not so difficult an affair as it was when Money Marks first essayed that hazardous undertaking.

His part of the treasure taken from the summer palace of King Procul-ny-watti amounted to a large sum, and he felt no compunction in appropriating the money belonging to Captain Monkhouse, which he found on board the *Ocean Queen;* consequently he was able to carry a considerable cargo into Charleston, and assume the character of a merchantman, but his good luck threw him in the way of a Federal ship, which he overhauled, plundered, and then allowed to go on her way.

He was welcomed at Charleston with acclamation. This doomed city was gradually acquiring all the appearance of extreme desolation. Many houses were in ruins, many more were deserted by their former inhabitants, and in some of the principal thoroughfares weeds were growing breast-high.

Yet the Confederacy did not despair of ultimate success. Money Marks cared little about the success of either party. All he wished to satisfy himself about was the fate of Viola. If he could only succeed in finding her, he felt he should be happy. Oh! much more happy than he had ever been in the whole of his existence.

Leaving Tom Castaway in command of the ship he took Cuffy with him; and entering the city sought the house of Mr. Dalgren, in which Viola Cathcart was living on the day of his departure through the swamps for Wilmington.

Money Marks had during the last few months become more manly in appearance; his beard, whiskers, and moustache had grown, giving him a more mature look, and the sun had bronzed his face, and hands, and neck.

Walking quickly, he soon arrived at Mr. Dalgren's house.

Judge of his surprise and dismay when he found that it was a heap of ghastly ruins.

He fairly reeled against the brick-work, unable, for the moment, to support the force of this blow, which was so sudden—so awfully sudden—and so unexpected.

The enemy must have shelled the city with more than their usual bitterness, and a great catastrophe had taken place. What had happened to Mr. Dalgren? What to Viola?

Was he dead? were they both dead?

He could not bring himself to believe in so melancholy an event; he hoped most fervently that his Viola lived and would yet find consolation for all her misfortunes in his arms.

Oh! the rapture of their meeting. The bare thought of it deprived him of breath.

He was not a coward; far from it.

Nevertheless, the thought that Viola might be dead agitated him, as if he had been struck with a sudden palsy.

Some one passed by.

Money Marks took two steps—two long hasty strides—and stopped him.

"What do you want?" said the stranger.

"Are you acquainted with Charleston?"

"I ought to be, considering I was raised here."

"Good. This I believe was Mr. Dalgren's house?"

He pointed to the ruined mass with his finger, as he spoke.

"It was."

"What has become of Mr. Dalgren?"

"He is dead."

"Dead! did you say?"

"It is too true."

"Then my worst fears are realized."

"Was he your friend?" demanded the stranger, casting a kindly glance upon the young man.

He was evidently moved by his palpable distress.

His face was convulsed with grief, and his hands trembled nervously; while his lips quivered like those of a girl who had sobbed herself into an hysterical state.

"I knew him but slightly."

"Yet you are strangely moved."

"I am."

"And why?"

"There was one beneath his roof in whom I—I took the greatest interest."

"Ah!" said the stranger, with a smile of peculiar meaning, "I perceive."

"Can you inform me," exclaimed Money Marks, "whether all within the house perished?"

"I can, for I am familiar with all the circumstances," replied the stranger; "I live close by here, and happening to be passing by the house at the identical time of the catastrophe, you may rely upon what I am going to tell you as being correct."

"Yes, yes," said Money Marks, impatiently.

This long preface, when he wished to know the truth—wished to know whether his darling Viola was alive or dead, was wearing him out.

"The mansion was struck by a shell, which created great havoc. Mr. Dalgren, who was walking in his garden, was killed on the spot, but the servants, and a young lady," here the stranger smiled again, "who was staying in the house, were saved."

"Indeed!"

"Yes."

"Thank God!" said Money Marks, piously.

There was a pause.

"Where is she—the—the young lady?" asked Money Marks.

An immense weight was taken off his mind; he cared for nothing now that he knew she lived.

"She was taken to my house," replied the stranger.

"To your house!—Viola in your house?" exclaimed Money Marks, in an ecstacy of joy. "Oh, blessings on you for that declaration! Thank you! thank you! a thousand times over. Give me your hand, dear sir. Let me grasp it with heartfelt gratitude."

Money Marks in his enthusiasm grasped the old man's hand, and shook it violently. As soon as he was able, the man withdrew his hand, and said, with a sad smile—

"Your congratulations are premature."

"What!"

The wretched look that pervaded Money Marks' face when this announcement was made was dreadful to look at.

"She came to my house, but she was soon afterwards taken away."

"By whom?" demanded Money Marks, fiercely.

"By a gentleman calling himself Captain Arlee."

"That name again—Arlee! Impossible!"

"Why so?"

"He was dead."

"You are mistaken."

"But I saw——"

"What?"

"No matter—proceed," said Money Marks, controlling himself by a violent effort. "An attempt was made to assassinate Captain Arlee, but providentially that attempt was frustrated, for though badly wounded he escaped with his life."

"Curses on the unskilful hand that dealt the blow!"

"Why do you say that?"

"I like him as I like poison. He has wronged me," replied Money Marks. "But tell me, did Viola—Miss Cathcart—go willingly with Captain Arlee?"

"Frankly, she did not."

"And you—did you stand by and see her dragged from your house?"

"I was but a friend of Mr. Dalgren's."

"What of that?"

"I gave her hospitality gladly, and would have done so up to this time, if Captain Arlee had not been her uncle."

"Ha! ha!" laughed Money Marks, almost maniacally.

"And had a prior claim over her."

"Ha! ha!"

"As she was an orphan—her father having died at sea—or I should not have let her go."

Laying his hand upon the stranger's shoulder, he said, in a hoarse whisper—

"You have been the dupe of a scoundrel, sir! for as God is my witness, I swear that Arlee was in no way whatever related to Miss Cathcart."

"Can that be true?"

"If it were not, I should not have made the asseveration. How long is it since the young lady left your house?"

"Not more than a fortnight."

"That is a short time; perhaps it is not now too late to rescue her. Heaven give me wings and speed me!" said Money Marks.

The stranger regarded some one coming up the street, looking at him in a curious manner.

He started.

Placing his hand on Money Marks' arm, he said—

"Look! look!"

"Where?"

"Before you."

Money Marks did so, and saw Captain Arlee.

This man who had been snatched from the jaws of death by a miracle, was dressed in the height of fashion. His ship had gone on a homeward voyage without him, and he was daily expecting its return. The Confederate Government had supplied him liberally with money, and since his release from the hospital he had been enjoying life in a manner peculiarly agreeable to a vain and conceited man—which he was, in spite of certain sterling qualities in the shape of courage and patriotism possessed by him.

He did not know Money Marks, and the most prudent course the latter could have adopted would have been to stand still—allow him to pass, and have followed him at a distance.

If he had not been too angry to have recourse to that plan, he would have tracked him to wherever Viola was confined.

Cuffy, with his clever instinct, saw that this was the best mode of procedure, and he said—

"No talk, Massa Marks—let him be. Cuffy follow trail, like bloodhound, and soon get Missy Viola away."

"No, no; I *must* speak."

"Better not, mass——"

Before Cuffy could complete his sentence, Money Marks had dashed up to the unsuspecting captain of the *Swamp Snake*, and catching him by the throat, exclaimed—

"Wretch! where is Viola?"

"Loosen your hold of my throat, and possibly I may be able to answer your inquiry," Arlee managed to gasp.

Money Marks relaxed his grasp without altogether quitting his hold.

Captain Arlee held a cane in his right hand—raising this weapon, he brought it suddenly down with great violence upon Money Marks' arm.

The blow for a time paralyzed him, and he was forced to let go his hold.

Captain Arlee drew a pistol—a revolver—from his coat-pocket.

In times of war, which are always perilous, it is the custom of all men to go armed.

"Now," he said, "I can talk to you. Keep off, and tell me who you are?"

"Where is Miss Cathcart?" cried Money Marks, who was almost inarticulate with rage.

"I have got to learn what that is to you."

"A matter of moment."

"Who are you?"

"Money Marks."

"What! are you the villain who attempted to murder me?

DEATH OF BOB CANNON.

It is strange that I should wait so long for the vengeance I had promised myself, and that it should come at last."

"Where is Viola?" said Money Marks.

"Where you will never find her."

"Every drop of blood in your body shall be shed before I will give up the search."

Captain Arlee raised his pistol to a level with his shoulder, and was about to pull the trigger, when Cuffy, who had been carefully watching his movements, dashed up his arm, and the bullet flew harmlessly over Marks' head, lodging in a wall hard by.

"Foiled!" he exclaimed.

"You are in my power now," said Money Marks, "but I will spare your life on condition that you will tell me where Miss Cathcart is?"

As he spoke a second bullet whistled past Money Marks' head.

Cuffy had omitted to notice the fact of the pistol's being a revolver.

But now that he saw it, he snatched the weapon from the captain's hand, and defied him to fire again.

He did not attempt to run away until there was a cry of—

"The patrol! The patrol is coming!"

The soldiers had been attracted by the noise of the firing.

Captain Arlee took to his heels and ran away, before his enemies could follow him.

Money Marks and Cuffy were about to follow his example, when the stranger whispered in his ear—

"Arlee lives in the Seventh Avenue, number fifteen; I hope the address may be of use to you."

The next minute he was gone.

Cuffy drew Money Marks down a by-street, and when they considered themselves safe from pursuit he stopped, and looking at Arlee's pistol, said philosophically—

"Well, dis chile's got something; not 'tall bad pistol."

Money Marks contented himself with repeating, "Fifteen,

Seventh Avenue; fifteen, Seventh Avenue," as if the address pleased him.

No doubt it did.

For was it not a clue to the whereabouts of Viola?

CHAPTER XIX.

IN CAPTIVITY.

VIOLA CATHCART had remained at Mr. Dalgren's, wondering what had become of Money Marks, and hoping that he would re-appear soon.

She did not know for some time that Captain Arlee had been wounded by Money Marks, for the former was so much injured that he was taken to a military hospital, where he lay for nearly two months before he could give an intelligible version of what had happened to him.

Then he made no secret of Money Marks having been the author of the calamity which had overtaken him.

He had taken her away from the house of the gentleman who had sheltered her after Mr. Dalgren's death, but she had quitted that hospitable mansion unwillingly and with regret.

It is needless to say that Captain Arlee made love to her. She disliked this, as the death of her revered father was so recent as to make it indecent for her to love anyone whatever. She had even prevented herself from looking upon Money Marks as anything than a brother.

She came to hate and detest Arlee, and did not hesitate to tell him so.

In times of civil war deeds of violence and lawlessness are much more prevalent than in times of peace; and why?

Because they are less likely to be detected and punished; wickedness, comparatively speaking, may be committed with impunity.

Captain Arlee knew this, and he determined to leave no means untried, no stone unturned, so that he might gain Viola's love, and if he could not gain her love, he would gain her hand.

He was one of those men who believe that if it is possible to gain the hand of a woman in marriage, love will quickly follow. But in this belief he was mistaken.

Nevertheless, he determined to do what he could to make Viola love him, though the means he adopted with that end in view were very strange. First he cajoled her, then he threatened; but she was alike indifferent to his promises and fair words, his threats and his menaces.

Finding that she was obdurate, and that no amount of kindness and blandishments had any effect upon her, he sought her in the garden of the house to which he had brought her, and in which, by the kindness of a relative, he was staying.

She was very pale and sad. She sat on a rustic seat beneath the spreading branches of a leafy tree; her thoughts were preoccupied—she heard and saw no one.

Mr. Arlee stole softly behind her, and listened angrily to some words which fell from her lips.

She softly murmured, like the rippling of a pellucid brook—

"Oh, why—why does he linger on the road? why does he not come to my assistance, and bear me far away from the hateful thraldom to which I am compelled to submit? If he only knew how I longed for his dear society, he would not leave me where I am. But perhaps he is the victim of wicked wiles and cruel plots even as I myself am. Oh, my dearly beloved, come, come, come."

As she spoke, she extended her arms as if to receive some imaginary friend—some phantom, some ideal conception.

Captain Arlee bent gently forward.

The girl's arms closed around his frame.

When she felt something tangible she looked up, uttering a startled scream.

Then she shrank away from him as if he had been a viper, or something leprous and unclean.

"So—so, my little darling," exclaimed Captain Arlee, with a laugh, "you caught the wrong man in your embrace."

Arlee knew whom she was apostrophizing well enough. Who else could it be, if not Money Marks?

She burst into tears.

"Am I ever to be persecuted by you?"

"I do not persecute you. Be my wife, and you shall be mistress of all I have."

"Never."

"Then thank your own senseless folly for whatever may happen to you."

"Permit me to leave this house. I do not wish to eat your bread, or trespass any longer on your hospitality."

"What would you do?" inquired Captain Arlee, fixing keen, lynx-like glance upon her.

"What would I do?" she repeated, with all the energy of the fiery Southern blood which burned in her veins; "I would work, ay, work my fingers to the bone."

"You shall go," said Captain Arlee.

"Go?"

"Yes, on one condition."

"Ah!" she said, sadly; "there is a condition."

"Marry me; go from this house as my bride, and then the winds of Heaven shall not be more free than yourself."

"You have already received my answer."

"You are obdurate."

"I am."

"In that case I shall not allow you the liberty you have already enjoyed—I shall place you in close captivity."

"That will not subdue me."

"We shall see."

"You had better beware," she cried, rising to her feet and stretching out her right hand with the air of a Cassandra. "I am not one to be trifled with, but I am in your power at present. Yet I predict that in a brief space one will return and claim me—one before whom your coward frame will tremble and your coward heart quail."

"Your prediction is worthless."

"You may think differently."

"Were he of whom you speak to return, I would have a gallows as high as that of Haman erected, upon which he should hang, for he broke the laws in attempting to take *my* life, in return for which it shall be my business to see that the law, which is impartial, shall take *his* life."

"If you are a patriot, as you say you are; if you love your country as you boast," said Viola, her lip—that well-cut, beautifully-chiselled lip, of the possession of which Hebe might have been justly proud—curling with contemptuous scorn as she spoke; "why do you not go on the battle-field, and fight for her liberation from the yoke the North is seeking to impose upon it? Does fear keep you on land to make war upon a helpless, harmless woman? If so, for shame; let the blush of cowardice mantle your cheek. But, oh! were I a man, I would rush to arms when the first trumpet-call sounded, sooner than see my brethren dead and dying while I remained in silken dalliance."

"I am no coward, Miss Cathcart," responded Captain Arlee, "as any man in this unhappy city would tell you. Only yesterday my name was mentioned with cheers in every fortress we hold in the harbour, for I took temporary command of the troops in Fort Sumter, and as the Confederate flag was shot away three times in succession by the Yankee guns, I ascended to the summit amidst a storm of shot and shell and replaced it."

He drew himself up proudly as he spoke.

"If you were as brave as Hector and as handsome as Apollo, I would never consent to be your wife," replied Viola.

"I have sworn that you shall—yes, I have sworn by G——, that you shall be mine."

"If that is true, you have taken the name of the Almighty Creator in vain."

She rose to go.

"Stop a moment."

She paid no heed to this command.

"Stay, Miss Cathcart; one moment, I beg of you."

As his tone was more courteous, she consented to do as he wished.

"What do you want with me?" she inquired.

"Do not drive me to extremities; you will regret having done so when it is too late."

"Your threats do not, and shall not deter me."

"Why not allow the memory of the young man you prefer to love sink into oblivion? You will be happy with me—happier than you ever were before."

"That is not my opinion."

Viola would not wait to hear another word from Captain Arlee; she considered that to do so would be to waste time in a useless discussion.

Viola did not retire to the house; she continued to walk about the garden in an absent manner, but at the expiration of half-an-hour, an old woman approached her.

Viola did not recollect having seen this old woman before. She was a hideous old hag, having a countenance wrinkled and ugly, the expression of which was singularly repulsive.

This old woman was a creature of Captain Arlee's; she was known as Old Post. Up to the time of the outbreak of the civil war, she had kept a whipping-house for the correction of female slaves.

If a master or mistress in Charleston was dissatisfied with the conduct of a female slave belonging to them, they would send her to Old Post's with a note, requesting that so many lashes might be administered.

Old Post received the money and carefully executed the sentences herself, sending the unfortunate slaves home crying and bleeding, to the satisfaction of their inhuman masters.

Old Post was the woman whom Captain Arlee had selected to govern Viola Cathcart, and as his object was coercion it must be confessed that he could not have made a better selection.

When the war broke out and the slaves ran away and became demoralized, Old Post's occupation was nearly gone.

She was glad to accept any offer, no matter what, as her life was in danger. Several female slaves, whom she had flagellated, had openly sworn to burn her whipping-house to the ground and to hang her to a rafter.

When Captain Arlee made her an offer and asked her to come and look after a young lady, who was disobedient and would not listen to reason, she gladly accepted his offer, which was the more enticing as it gave her a house to live in, that is to say, apartments in a house, and took her away from the malice and vengeance of the slaves. She swore that she would compel Viola to do as the captain wished, if he would give her absolute control over the girl.

This he did as a matter of course.

Old Post thought her new employment the best she could have secured, because it was congenial to her feelings and she entered on it with an indescribable zest and enjoyment.

If Viola had not refused to do as Mr. Arlee requested her on that afternoon, Old Post's services would not have been required; but finding that the girl was obdurate, the captain had given a signal to the harridan who was in waiting, the result of which was her appearance before Miss Cathcart in the garden.

Viola shuddered when her eyes fell upon Old Post. She scarcely knew why, but she dreaded her. Moving on one side, she endeavoured to avoid her; but Old Post pertinaciously followed in her footsteps, until she reached a conservatory, into which the hag pursued her.

This hot-house was filled not with exotics as we call them, not altogether with such flowers as we English prize, but with many hardy European plants; nevertheless, with those that were indigenous to the soil it presented a striking and beautiful appearance.

Turning abruptly round, Viola exclaimed in an angry voice—

"Who are you, and why do you intrude yourself upon my presence?"

"Ah, my dear," replied Old Post, in a harsh and rusty voice, which she in vain endeavoured to render pleasing: "you will know me well enough, I hope, before long."

"Know you?"

"Yes, deary; I'm sure I shall be as good as a mother to you."

"What do you mean?" demanded Viola, aghast.

"Just this, deary; you and I will have a great deal to say to one another presently; and the more civil and respectful you are to me the better it will be for you."

Poor Viola was quite at a loss to understand the meaning of this speech.

"Pray have the goodness to explain yourself," she said.

"Don't be frightened, my dear," said Old Post; "don't flutter your pretty wings against the bars all for nothing."

"Against what bars?"

"Prison bars."

"What have they to do with me?"

"You're going to prison."

"For what?"

"Disobeying Captain Arlee's orders."

"Are you in earnest?"

"Old Post never jokes, deary, except when she has a lot of money give her," replied the hag.

"Do you mean to tell me that I am your prisoner? that Captain Arlee has appointed you my guardian, or rather let me say my gaoler?"

"Yes, deary! that's the identical ticket for soup. What a thing it is to have to do with clever people. Lord a' mussey, what a lot o' time it saves!"

"I refuse to submit to your authority."

"Do you?"

"Yes, most decidedly."

"Aint it odd they allus says that," exclaimed Old Post; raising her bleared eyes to Heaven's glorious canopy.

"Who are you alluding to?"

"Those as I has had under my charge."

"Poor unfortunates!"

"Not they; there never was a happier lot in the world, nor the sun never set on a happier half-dozen."

"Set on them! Do you mean that they died?"

"They did so, ducky, but it wasn't my fault; but come along, it is tea-time, and I want a cup of something."

"Come with you?"

"Yes, ducky."

"Not for worlds."

"Then I shall have to make you. Gals like you is always stubborn, but I brings them round."

"You may boast your skill, but I will defy you."

"Not for long, deary, not for long; what d'ye think I was before the war?"

"How should I know?"

"You needn't jump into the stirrups over your ignorance. It costs nothing to be civil. I kept a whipping-house for women; and they might be ever so independent when their masters and missises sent them to me, but when they left they were civil enough. I made them sing small, but they sang big first; and if you give me any trouble I'll find a means of taking it out of you."

"I tell you once for all," replied Viola, "that I do not recognize your authority."

"Oh! but you'll have to."

"That remains an open question."

"Come along; we've got our own apartments give us."

"You may go as soon as you like; but I resolutely refuse to move—with you at least. Mr. Arlee has no right to dispose of me in this illegal way. It is against the law of the land."

"Law! my dear. Bless your innocent heart; there isn't much law now-a-days. It's all war, not law. You'll have to make a very great noise before anyone will take the trouble to come and help you; and I've got little things such as gags, deary, and the like, which will make you hold your tongue."

"Go away," cried Viola, in a passion.

"Not without you, ducky."

"You will have to."

"I think not; at all events, we'll have a tussle for it."

As she spoke Old Post drew some polished glittering handcuffs from her pocket, and advanced to Viola, who had no idea that the old wretch was in earnest when she threatened personal violence.

So shocked and surprised was she that she did not even struggle, but passively allowed the cuffs to be placed on her wrists.

Having committed this fatal error, it was too late to endeavour to retrace it. All she could do was to submit to the terms of the conqueror.

"How do you feel now, ducky darling?" inquired the old hag, with mock sympathy. "Not quite so fine, eh?"

"What do you intend to do with me?" said Viola, gasping for breath, and dreading some new indignity every moment.

"You will know presently; we shan't hurt you, if you're quiet and civil."

"But explain why you treat me thus."

"Don't you know?—well, that's strange, too. I'm only going to shut you up as long as you're obstrepolus, when you're quiet you'll be let go, but you must agree to marry the captain."

"Never—never—never!" said Viola, resolutely.

"Very well, my dear; I hope you'll stick to that till one of us dies, 'cos I think I've got a good place, and it'll last as long as you holds out, which I hope it may be till the day of my death, when I'm lying stiff and stark, and cold on the stones."

"You must be a wicked old woman."

"So the parson said, my dear, when he came for a twopenny poor-rate which I wouldn't pay, saying I'd applied the money to my own use, as I was poor and wanted it."

Old Post wasted no further time; having rendered her captive incapable of further exertion, she seized her by the arm and dragged her roughly along the garden towards the house.

"'Oller," she said; "why don't you 'oller? I should like to hear you. It will show you that it is no good—nobody will hear you."

Viola felt inclined to try the effect of a tiny scream, but she refrained from doing so as she was afraid Old Post's words would be only too true if put to the test.

Instead of entering the house in the usual way, the harridan entered by a side door near the entrance to the street, and ascending a flight of steps, up which she compelled Viola, her unwilling captive, to follow her, she walked into a set of apartments which had been specially set aside for her own use and that of Viola.

The rooms were neither spacious nor lofty—they seemed to be the very worst that the whole house could supply, and the furniture was not only scant but of the worst description.

Viola sank into a chair, saying—

"Take these off."

She held up the manacles which galled her wrists.

"Not till I see how you behave yourself."

"Oh! for Heaven's sake rid me of these fetters!"

"No, my dear, not just now; later in the evening I may."

Viola burst into tears, and sobbed as if her heart would break.

"That's right, ducky," said Old Post; "cry a good 'un—it wont hurt. It's like letting the steam off, and you'll settle down and be all right presently."

In the evening Old Post took the fetters from Viola's wrists, and tossing an old cotton dress towards her, said—

"Put that on."

"That!"

The girl recoiled with horror at the idea of arraying herself in such a plebeian garment.

"Yes."

"What for?"

"You'll know, time enough. Put it on, I say."

"Suppose I refuse."

Old Post held up a small riding-whip in a threatening manner, and said—

"You'll precious soon have this across your shoulders."

"You dare not!"

"Dare not! What's to prevent me?—who's the strongest? you or I?—who can clench a fist tightest, and hit hardest? Dare not! that's a pretty story."

Viola saw that to resist this old hag would be fruitless, so she complied with her demand, unfastening her own rich silk dress and allowing it to sink upon the floor, as she did so Old Post crept noiselessly behind her and struck her sharply with the whip across her naked shoulders.

Viola screamed aloud, and writhed with the pain of the blow.

"Ha! ha!" laughed Old Post; "that's only to show you what it can do. That wasn't very nice, eh? How would you like a few dozen, and you tied up to the wall and not able to help yourself? I'm your missus, and it's as well for you to know it at once, so that you don't get yourself into trouble—you'll have to obey me. Put that dress on, and that cap on your head."

She tossed her a common servant's cap, and an apron.

Viola attired herself in this menial garb, and sat down upon a chair, bursting into tears as she did so.

"Stop that snivelling," said Old Post.

"I can't."

"You must."

Viola started, for the whip was held up threateningly.

Checking her tears, and repressing her miserable thoughts she said—

"I wish you would give me a cup of tea."

"I was just thinking that I shouldn't mind a cup of tea," said Old Post; "it is just the time for it, and with a little Dutch cream, such as I have in the cupboard, it will be very nice."

"Will you make me some?—I shall be very thankful to you," said Viola.

"Make you some?"

"Yes."

"Me make you some?"

"Why not?"

"That's a good 'un—that's what I call fun," cried Old Post, with a roar of laughter. "No, my little beauty, not if I know it; I don't wait upon you."

"What then?"

"You'll have to wait upon me—you're my servant."

"Servant!" repeated Viola, in dismay.

"Yes, to be sure—what else did I dress you for? Come, wake up, and go to that cupboard and get out the tea things, and spread the cloth, and lay the things on the tray, and put the kettle on—you will find all the things you want in that little kitchen at the back. Look spry!—it wont do to be idle. Cut the bread-and-butter thin—I likes it thin. Or stop, I wont have bread-and-butter to-night, I'll have a round of toast; don't you burn it, or I'll skin you."

Viola's soul was ready to sink within her at this coarse language. Poor, delicate Viola! gently nurtured Viola! ladylike, wellborn Viola, accustomed as she had been to every luxury from her infancy—surrounded with slaves who were at all times ready to do her slightest bidding—was horrified to think that she was, by a sudden turn of fortune's wheel, the handmaid of the desperately wicked old wretch whom Captain Arlee had suborned to do his repulsive bidding.

But that she was so there could be no doubt, and it was equally certain that if she refused to do as she was told, she would be cruelly beaten.

Rather anything than the stinging lashes of the degrading whip.

So she set about her task with alacrity, if not with willingness, and consoled herself with the thought that she might possibly be able to escape.

Escape.

Yes, that was the glorious thought—the almost sublime hope that upheld her in the midst of her misery and her misfortunes.

She went to the kitchen, filled the kettle, put it on the fire, made the tea, toasted the bread, and was about to sit down and partake of a cup of the cheering beverage when Old Post cried, angrily—

"Who told you to sit down?"

"No one."

"Stand up, then."

"I thought——"

"Never mind what you thought."

"I'm very sorry."

"You'll be more sorry if you put my monkey up, and give me the hump; you'll be a good deal more sorry then, I can tell you. Now, then, look alive; move, or——"

"Please don't hit me," cried Viola, in an agony of apprehension.

"You behave yourself, then."

"What shall I do?"

"Stand behind my chair as a servant should, and when I want anything be ready to hand it to me."

Viola obeyed her mistress's instructions to the letter, and avoided the administration of condign punishment with which she was repeatedly threatened. At length she was permitted to take some refreshment.

This scene is a fair specimen of her daily life for some time.

Captain Arlee made repeated applications to her for submission, but she steadfastly refused to grant him the slightest concession.

Old Post grew fat on luxurious fare, and liked her place very much, which is not surprising seeing that all she had to do was to muddle herself with strong drink, and if she wanted to vent her spite upon anyone, she could always attack Viola with her tongue and whip, and satisfy her bad, vindictive spirit.

Old Post was so vigilant that Viola could find no chance of escaping.

This was how affairs stood when Money Marks made his appearance in Charleston.

———

CHAPTER XX.

VIOLA'S ESCAPE.—SEVENTH AVENUE, NO. 15.

THAT was the talisman that haunted Money Marks' imagination until nightfall.

Until that time, he did not think it prudent to make any attempt to rescue Viola.

How he would have flown to her on the wings of love had he known how her poor heart was bleeding!—how the imprisoned bird was beating its bruised wings against the bars of its cage, and panting for liberty!

Captain Arlee was fully aware that he had been guilty of a mean and despicable action in shutting Viola Cathcart up, and delivering her into Old Post's hands.

But he being a soldier and a sailor, thought that if all things were fair in war, so all stratagems were fair in love.

There are many who hold the same opinion.

He thought that he deserved credit for not having had recourse to any overt act of violence to Viola. He did not know that Old Post was in the habit of whipping the poor girl whenever she offended her, and treating her at all times with the cruel indifference with which she would have treated a dog, had such an animal been sufficiently unfortunate to fall into her power.

He only saw Viola once a week, and although she had once complained of Old Post's treatment, she had met with no redress—the only answer she received being—

"If you are harshly treated, and find your captivity irksome, you have no one but yourself to thank for it. Agree to my wishes, consent to love me and be my wife, to honour me as your lord and master, and I will at once fling open the doors of your prison—refuse, and you must be content to endure your imprisonment until you become docile."

If Viola had been ever so much inclined to complain again, Old Post's ill-treatment after her attempt to excite compassion in Captain Arlee's breast, would have deterred her from so doing.

Money Marks held a conference with Cuffy when the sun went down, and they were sitting together in an insignificant eating-house, whither they had resorted for quiet and repose.

"What you think best be done, Massa Marks?" said Cuffy.

"I have been thinking that Captain Arlee—curses on him! I can hardly pronounce his name with patience—will not take any extra precautions against us," replied Money Marks; "because he is not likely to guess that we know where he lives."

"He may leave Charleston," suggested the black.

"Ha! that thought never struck me."

"Him sailor, Massa Marks."

"So he is."

"Then why not his ship take him off, and Missy Viola, too?"

"Very true."

"Go down to docks and see what ship there, and if know Cappen Arlee."

"By all means, and if not——"

"If not, go to cappen's house, and ask for him. See him in his drawing-room, fight him, and then take Missy Viola away."

"I think that is good advice, but——"

He broke off abruptly, and his face flushed deeply, as if he dreaded something.

"What?"

"If she is his wife? Good God! my heart would break. If he has harmed her, I will kill him."

"Ha! ha! he difficult to kill. You try kill him once, Massa Marks, and you no do it. Him like cat; him got seven lives," said Cuffy.

"He shall not escape me a second time, I'll take care of that," said Money Marks, bitterly.

He went with Cuffy in the direction of the wharves, which did not present the animated appearance that once characterized them. They were nearly deserted; a few sailors lounged about here and there, and one or two blockade-runners were to be discerned in various places, but it was easy to see that war had set its mark upon the fair city of the South, and that its grandeur had gone from it—its glory had departed.

A ship with a low-sweeping outline arrested Money Marks' attention. By the bustle on board of her, she appeared to have recently arrived.

"I think I know that ship!" he exclaimed.

"Yes, massa, I know dat ship somewhere," replied Cuffy.

"Ha!" cried Money Marks, as a name written on a streaming pennon caught his eye.

Cuffy looked up inquiringly.

"It is the *Swamp Snake!*"

"Cappen Arlee's vessel?"

"Yes."

"Him am just 'rived then."

"I don't think she has been long in harbour. What a strange occurrence! It is well that I acted upon your suggestion, or we should have been in ignorance of this important fact; for when I landed the *Swamp Snake* was certainly not in harbour."

"No, massa, that am true enuff."

Suddenly a heavy hand fell upon Money Marks' shoulder, and a voice exclaimed—

"Aha, my hearty! how are you? Dash my daylights! and it's like old times to clap a peeper on you."

Money Marks recognised a familiar voice, and turning round with great delight, looked upon Bob Cannon.

A meeting of this sort was peculiarly agreeable to Money Marks, for Bob Cannon was one of his oldest and best friends, and he knew that the rough and ready sailor possessed as true a heart as ever beat behind a jersey, and that he was much attached to him, so he said in a pleased tone of voice—

"What, Bob! is it you?"

"It's me, safe enough; but where have you been?"

"To Africa."

"When?"

Money Marks smiled.

"What did you go there for?"

"To see the King of the Cumbagees."

"Who's he?"

"A great swell in his own dominions. We are great friends."

"Friends! you and the king friends? Come now, draw it mild to an old friend who isn't a marine, and who has heard a few toughish yarns in his time."

"I'm telling you the truth."

"Then I should like to know what a lie is?" cried Bob Cannon, indignantly. "I suppose you deserted from the ship, and have been hidden by the crimps ever since? That's about the size of it, and now you're afraid to show your nose farther than you can draw it in again."

"It doesn't look like it," replied Money Marks, good-temperedly. "But we were talking about the king."

"Oh, bother the king!"

"That's just what I said when he stopped two days on board my ship. I couldn't get rid of him."

"Your ship!"

"Yes, my friend; why not?"

"Well, that's a good 'un, that is," said Bob Cannon, with a loud laugh.

The negro was much amused at this scene, and grinned from ear to ear, opening his prodigiously big mouth, and showing his pearly teeth which were as white as ivory.

"I'll tell you what," continued Bob Cannon, "I swallowed the gnat, but I can't swallow the camel."

"My ship—that is, the ship of which I am captain—is riding at anchor in the harbour," said Money Marks. "If you like to join, say so, and I will take you on board with me."

"If you mean, will I sail in the same ship with you, and cut my present companions, I reply, I will; but if you must have your joke, have it—only don't let's quarrel over it. Drop it, for I can feel my wool beginning to rise, and the best thing we can do is to go and have a friendly glass together. What do you say?"

"With all my heart," said Money Marks. "We will not talk about a matter that seems to puzzle you, but you shall soon have an opportunity of judging for yourself."

"That's right."

"Seeing's believing."

"Yes, and when I see, why I'll believe—that's all."

The three men went into a wine and spirit store, and called for some sparkling Micawber wine, which when nicely iced is not very inferior to champagne. After many questions had been asked and answered on either side, Money Marks told Bob Cannon that Viola Cathcart was in Mr. Arlee's power, and that it was his firm resolve to rescue her from the intolerable thraldom in which she was placed. It was possible that some resistance would be offered, and so powerful a coadjutor as Bob Cannon was not to be despised.

"The fact is, Bob," said Money Marks, "that I love this girl, and would go through fire and water for her, and I believe she returns my passion and hates Captain Arlee, who is a villain and a scoundrel to treat her as he does, and take the liberties he ventures to take with a young and un-suspecting girl. I have reason to believe that he has made her a prisoner, and keeps her confined against her will. What can be more odious and more tyrannical than that?"

Bob Cannon rubbed his forehead with the back of his hand, as if he were trying to recollect something, and the working machinery of his brain was not so bright as it should be, and stood in need of polishing up a little.

"Tell you what it is," he said: "I heard on board the *Snake* this morning that we shouldn't stop two days in Charleston, and I think there is some truth in it, for the crew and the niggers are unloading the cargo as fast as it is possible for them to do so; but that isn't what I wanted to say; it's this—the steward said in my hearing that the captain was coming on board to-morrow morning, and that a state cabin was to be fitted up for a lady."

"A lady!" echoed Money Marks.

"Yes, sir."

"Can that mean that now Captain Arlee is recovered he resumes command of the ship, and intends to take Viola with him on his next voyage—it must be so; my prophetic soul tells me that it is so, and if that is the case, the sooner we commence operations to thwart him and rescue Viola, the better will be our chance of success."

In spite of Money Marks' anxiety, it was necessary that they should wait for nightfall, because under the shelter of the darkness they could better impose upon Captain Arlee.

This was Money Marks' plan—

Bob Cannon was to call at Captain Arlee's house, and say that he had just come from the *Swamp Snake*, and wished to speak to him; Money Marks and Cuffy would be behind and prepared to attack the captain at the right moment.

The night soon came.

All were ready for action, and like brave men eager and panting for the fray.

Money Marks' heart throbbed faster than he liked to confess.

They entered the avenue in which Captain Arlee lived, but they had not gone far before a fly drove by, from which proceeded an agonized scream.

This cry thrilled Money Marks to his heart's core.

"Was that the voice of Viola?" he exclaimed; "or did some pleasing delusion mock me?"

"Ha, ha!" laughed Cuffy; "Massa Marks him very funny, him think it all Missy Viola."

"But I tell you I heard her voice."

"Where?" demanded Bob Cannon.

"In that fly."

"Impossible."

"It was not a piercing scream, but it was full of agony, and I thought stifled before it had quite died away with a natural cadence."

"You must be mistaken."

"I trust I am; for if I am not, Captain Arlee has taken the alarm, and carried away the bird, so that we shall find the cage empty."

"Are you sure you are not on a false scent?" inquired Bob Cannon.

"Not I."

"Well, if we come across 'em, we'll take 'em on the broad-side, rake them fore, aft, and ahead, whilst they shan't have a ha'porth of starn way, and no room to tack."

"I will be quits with Captain Arlee some day," said Money Marks, bitterly.

"So I would."

"His vessel's only a privateer."

"That's all; but the dirtier the hole the more comfortable the toad."

"That's not her in the fly, you may take your oath of that, and if it is we'll find her, so don't you fret, sir. We'll teach Cappen Arlee something: we'll teach him the use of ratline, and how to box the compass in real arnest. Shall we go on now, sir, or slew ourselves to an anchor and take in ballast?"

"Of what kind?"

"I've got a locker, sir, that has always a shot in it, and I fancy it's a drop of rum at this moment. Taste it, sir; it's righteous; it's the proper sort. Take a taste, sir; you look pale enough, though you may feel as serene as a man-o'-war in mill-stream."

Money Marks did not refuse the offer, but took a good pull at the rum bottle, feeling considerably refreshed after-wards.

"Now, sir, have a quid out of my 'bacca box, what Sall Turoun give me."

"No, no, not now. We must attend to business," replied Money Marks, hastily. "This is fifteen, consequently we have arrived at Captain Arlee's. Do you, Bob, ring at the bell; we are your companions, and will await you in the hall. When you are alone with Arlee, cry out 'Yo, ho!' and we'll be with you."

"Sing out 'Yo, ho!'"

"Yes."

"All right, I'll do it; there isn't a thing in the world I wouldn't do for a friend and a woman, and when the two are shoved into one, why the mixture's as irresistible as Honeydew or Old Virginia."

Bob Cannon gave a hearty pull at the bell, while his com-panions fell a little into the shade.

A servant appeared and said—

"What's your business?"

"Cappen in, if you please?"

"He is, but he's busy. Who are you, and what do you want with him?"

"I belong to the *Swamp Snake*, and have come with a message."

"From whom?"

"That, my little dear, is a secret," replied Bob, with a smile; "perhaps you'll want to know the message next, but that's only for the captain's own ears, so perhaps you'll scud along and let him know Bob Cannon wishes to speak to him."

The girl left the door open, and Money Marks with Cuffy entered. She was gone a few minutes; when she returned she told Bob that he might walk into the dining-room, where Captain Arlee was sipping his wine after dinner; he did not refuse to avail himself of the permission given him, and entered the room where Captain Arlee was.

It was an anxious moment for Money Marks, who was awaiting the signal upon which he would rush into the room and attack Arlee with all the violence that his animosity to that gentleman had engendered.

What passed between Captain Arlee and Bob Cannon was never known. The reason why will shortly be seen. Their interview may have been stormy, it may have been pacific, but it is impossible to say.

Five minutes elapsed.

Five long weary minutes, such as at times appear to be the essence of a lifetime, the epitome of a century.

Suddenly Bob Cannon's voice rang out shrilly and clearly like a clarion, and the words agreed upon flew towards Money Marks on the wings of the wind.

"Yo, ho!" he heard, "yo, ho! my hearties, yo, ho!"

Without losing a moment he ran to the room from which the sound emanated, and which he had seen Bob Cannon enter.

Captain Arlee was on his legs, holding a pistol in his hand; that the weapon was loaded there neither was nor could be any doubt.

Bob Cannon was retreating to the door; it appeared as if the captain had threatened him with immediate death, for he was pale and his lips trembled a little.

Money Marks, when he entered the room, happened to be exactly behind Bob Cannon.

At the sight of Money Marks, the irascible captain's wrath culminated, and he pulled the trigger of his pistol, crying—

"Thank God! at last the chance has come; I can rid myself of one scoundrel at least."

There was a flash and a report, the room was filled with smoke, but the deadly bullet did not strike Money Marks; it hit Bob Cannon in the chest, perforating his back and injuring his spine in its passage.

Money Marks, finding himself unhurt and that his life was in danger, drew his own revolver and fired two shots in quick succession at Captain Arlee, who uttered a cry of pain.

His right arm hung powerless by his side, and his pistol fell from his grasp with a loud noise upon the floor.

Money Marks' shot had broken his sword-arm.

The smoke was very dense, and it was difficult to see what really had happened, but Captain Arlee saw one thing.

And that was that he was outnumbered.

So he thought the best thing he could do was to make his retreat as fast as he could. It being very hot, the window of the room was open.

He made towards it.

With one bound he sprang through the casement and landed safely in the street, down which he ran with almost incredible speed.

When the smoke cleared off, Money Marks peered into every part of the room, without finding the slightest trace of Captain Arlee.

He heaped curses and imprecations upon his head, but stopped in the midst, for a dismal sight met his gaze.

As dismal a spectacle as he had ever looked upon during the whole course of his life.

Bob Cannon lay on his back on the rich Turkey carpet, with which the floor was covered. His head was supported by Cuffy, who looked reverently upon the face of the *dying* man.

For he was dying.

Money Marks rushed forward, and falling on his knees, gazed with tearful eyes upon his friend, who had by a fatal shot met his death. It was very clear that Captain Arlee had intended the bullet which struck Cannon to pierce Money Marks' heart, but it was not the will of Heaven that he should at that time succumb to the malice and wickedness of his enemies.

The blood was oozing slowly from poor Bob Cannon's mouth, and the ruby fluid also welled up from a deep wound in his chest.

His breathing was heavy and laboured; he drew each respiration with the utmost difficulty, and appeared to be suffering great pain.

"Are you much hurt, Bob?" exclaimed Money Marks.

"Yes, my boy," replied Bob Cannon, huskily.

"Don't say that."

"It's no good disguising it."

"But——"

"No, no; my route's come, and I'm bound to go. Every bullet has its billet, and that one of Captain Arlee's has found its."

"Curse him! by——"

"Don't, don't," said Bob Cannon, softly.

He held up his hand reprovingly as Money Marks' impatient exclamation fell upon his ears.

"I can't help it, Bob; that man Arlee has been the curse of my life. He first took me to sea, he robbed me of my love and made me what I am. If I ask Heaven to curse him, it is not without reason."

"Softly, sir, softly," replied Bob Cannon, as well as the failing powers of nature would let him. "I feel that I am dying. I'm going afore my God, and I haven't many minutes to live. I don't want no doctoring fellow to tell me that. Well, Mr. Marks, isn't it an awful moment now? I'm with you trying to collect my thoughts, and bring to mind a prayer, such as my mother taught me. It's years ago," he continued, "but I can remember it as if it was yesterday; the old woman used to sit me on her knee, and teach me to say my prayers. There was 'Our Father,' that was the Lord's Prayer, and I used to say that oftenest. We sailors are a rough lot, and don't think much of praying, except when we're on a reef or in a thunderstorm, and then we find our marrowbones, and so we do when we are dying."

He paused in order to regain breath.

"Forgive him," he went on, "forgive him as I do, and let all animosity sink into the grave. I am dying, and when you come to the same pass you will understand my feeling."

"I doubt it."

"Forgive him."

"I cannot."

"I ask you."

"Forgive the man who has injured me in every possible way, and who by his last act has robbed me of one of my best friends? Oh, no, you know not what you ask," replied Money Marks.

Bob Cannon's frame was convulsed, a gush of blood more violent than any of the preceding ones took place, and he fell back, a corpse, with the broken word, the expressive syllable on his lips—

"For—for——"

Forgive him, he would have said, but ere he could speak the gracious word, his breath had fled.

"Is he dead?" inquired Money Marks, with tearful accents.

"Yes, Massa Marks, him dead, wuss luck," replied Cuffy.

The young man grasped his hand with the force of affection, and remained absorbed for a time with manly grief.

The black was not so much affected: he liked Bob Cannon, but not so much as his master did. To Money Marks Bob Cannon was a link which bound him to the past. He recalled Ratcliff Highway and many a scene that had passed and gone for ever.

For a time Marks forgot the object which brought him to the house, and all was misery and despair.

Suddenly Cuffy touched his master upon the shoulder, saying—

"Massa Marks,"

He started.

"Well?" he said.

"You forget."

"What?"

"Missy Viola."

"You are right."

"It all dam fine, Massa Marks, to think of poor sailor, but you no love sailor man like you love Missy Viola; p'raps she want your help at this very moment, and not get it, 'cos you grieve over Bob Cannon. Poor Bob! him dead; massa, you no bring him back to life, so why you sit still and waste time."

Money Marks, thus adjured, sprang to his feet, but taking a melancholy look at Bob Cannon's stiffening body, said—

"There lies as good a fellow, and as fast a friend as ever man could wish to have."

Turning his eyes up to Heaven piously, he added—

"God rest his soul!"

Such was the sailor's simple prayer. Such was the tribute he paid to the dead.

All honour to our sailors; if they are a rough set of men they are sterling and honest. They are the backbone and the heart of the country, and as such we ought to be proud of them—all honour to them. May they have few storms, and less wrecks. "A life on the ocean wave" is all very well when the idea is mooted in a drawing-room, or sung in a concert-room—but the reality! There it is that poor Jack gets the romance knocked out of him. When the winds blow, and the waves run mountains high, and the lightnings flash, heralding the roaring of the awful thunder, and all nature—marine nature—is convulsed. Then Jack, honest, sterling Jack knows that the Almighty liveth, and that His wrath is terrible—too terrible to be withstood.

With a last reverent glance at the still warm body of honest old Bob Cannon, Money Marks ran from the room, followed by Cuffy. The former held a loaded revolver in his hand, the latter was armed with a thick stick loaded with lead, and capable of making a hole in a man's skull big enough to let the daylight in.

Money Marks' revolver had seven barrels; two had been discharged. There were five left, consequently he had the disposal of as many lives.

Every room in the house was searched, but no one was found except a number of servants who were half-terrified at the events which were taking place, for they had heard the firing, and were afraid that blood had been shed.

"Where is the young lady who was confined here?" exclaimed Money Marks, addressing one.

"She is gone, sir," replied the man, in a tremulous voice.

"Gone?"

"Yes."

"Where?"

"I think on board Mr. Arlee's ship, sir."

"How do you know this?"

"Well, sir, if you'll put your gun down, and promise not to shoot me, I'll tell you all I know."

"Do so; I will not harm you."

This declaration re-assured the man, and he did not hesitate to make Money Marks acquainted with all the circumstances which had come to his knowledge.

"I knew that Miss Viola, as she was called, was confined here, sir," he began; "because servants have eyes and can't help seeing, and they have mouths, and sometimes nothing better to do than to talk. Well, Miss Viola, it was said, would not marry the captain, and would have nothing to say to him, so he got hold of an old woman who was the biggest wretch in this city, and put the young lady under her charge so that she might not escape, and so that captivity might soften her spirit and incline her to obey his commands, and fall in with his views. But all was no good; she would not have anything to say to him, and to-day the young lady got away from Old Post."

"Who is she?"

"The woman in charge of her, sir."

"Yes; go on."

"And got into the garden and was climbing over the wall, when Old Post ran after her and brought her back."

"Infamous!" ejaculated Money Marks.

"The captain then ordered her to dress herself, and she was taken away in a fly."

"Whither?"

"To the ship, I think, sir; Captain Arlee sails to-morrow morning early, for we are to shut up the house, and have had our board-wages given us."

"That is proof presumptive, at all events. Where is this Old Post?"

"Upstairs in her room."

"I did not see her, and I have been all over the house."

"She may be drunk, as usual," suggested the man.

He volunteered to lead the way and to unearth the infamous old wretch if she was to be found, and he succeeded so well, that Money Marks was presently standing by her. She was drinking brandy out of a bottle, putting the neck in her mouth and taking deep draughts of the fiery spirit.

Cuffy was about to rush forward and say something, but Money Marks restrained him. The black stood still, his eyes flashing and his lips quivering, as if he was deeply agitated.

"So you are the person that had charge of Miss Viola?" exclaimed Money Marks.

"Yes, sir," was the reply, in a dubious tone of voice, as if Old Post did not know how to take the remark; questioning whether he was a friend or a foe.

"I hope you treated her as rigorously as you could."

"That I did, sir."

"Then you deserve to be rewarded. But you are sure you were as severe with her as possible?"

"Why, sir, look here," replied Old Post, holding up her whip; "she felt that nearly every day of her life while she was under my charge."

Money Marks' blood boiled.

Old Post went on glibly; now that the shackles were taken off her tongue, she did not mind what she said, for she felt assured that she was talking to a friend, and one who hated Viola, and was glad to hear that she had been placed under harsh discipline.

She blunderingly fell into a very skilful trap that Money Marks had set for her.

"Why, sir," she went on, taking another suck at the bottle as she spoke, "the poor devil couldn't call her life her own. She had a miserable time of it; 'stead of my waiting upon her, she was my servant, and had to do my bidding, or else I knew the reason why. She used to stand behind my chair at meals and wait upon me, and wash-up, and do the bed-rooms, and get up at six, and even when she did her best, I larruped her as I would a nigger."

"Very well," said Money Marks, bitterly; "you have betrayed yourself."

"What, sir?"

"Out of your own mouth has come your condemnation."

Old Post looked blankly at Money Marks, as if she feared something, but did not altogether understand his meaning.

"I say that you have condemned yourself, and I shall proceed to pass sentence upon you."

"For what?"

"For having brutally ill-treated a young lady whom I love better than my life."

"I never did, sir. She was treated better than a queen. It's all lies."

"In that case you have told them."

"Don't believe it, sir. I never said a word, or did a thing that anybody could take hold of," said Old Post, in an agony of terror. "The gal's gone, sir, and if she were here she'd say so too, and tell you I was her best friend, or I'd—" she checked herself in time, though the words "skin her" were on her lips, and said, "I'd prove it before her."

"You are a determined old hypocrite," replied Money Marks, "and I am resolved to make an example of you."

"Of me!"

"Yes, of you. Cuffy!"

"Yes, massa."

"Get a coil of rope."

"Or right, massa," said Cuffy, with a grin. "You give her to me to do with her as I like. Cuffy and Old Post have met before."

"When?"

"She one devil, Massa Marks. Once she keep a whipping-house for nigs, and she was there when my master sent me there, and Cuffy's back ached for a month, so Cuffy not forget her. Oh, no! Cuff remember Old Post. Give her to Cuff, massa."

"Very well, do as you like with her."

Old Post on hearing this threw down her brandy-bottle, and fell at Money Marks' feet, crying out in a most abject voice—

"Mercy! mercy! For the love of Jehoveh in heaven, have mercy upon a poor woman who never did you any harm in thought, word, or deed!"

"If you have not harmed me, you have one whom I love," replied Money Marks. "But I will not bandy words with you. Cuffy, do what you like with the old hag, and make haste about it—for we have little time to lose."

The negro, fortunately or unfortunately—if Old Post's interests are taken into consideration—had a long coil of rope in his pocket. It was quite large enough for his purpose, and he flung it over a stout hook which protruded from the wall, and, with great dexterity, made a noose at one end.

Old Post was in an agony of terror, and fell on her knees, calling on man and God to save her from her impending fate, but neither seemed inclined to stretch out a helping hand to her.

"Come here!" cried Cuffy, as he roughly laid hold of her, and adjusted a rope round her neck.

Her screams at this were frightful, and might have been heard some distance off; but her noisy declamation did not avail her, for Money Marks was terribly enraged at the idea of Viola—his beloved Viola—having been subjected to the old hag's ill-treatment, for, by her own confession, Old Post admitted that Viola was her servant, and that she had cruelly whipped her every day. This was quite enough to induce Money Marks to give her over to Cuffy, and allow the negro to do as he pleased with the wicked mass of iniquity.

In spite of Old Post's screams and struggles, Cuffy succeeded in placing the noose over her neck, and while he held it tight, nearly throttling her in his endeavour, he said—

"Ha! ha! Old Post, me got you at last. Many poor nigs you make bleed, now Cuff make you sing small. Say your prayers, cos in ten seconds it am all over."

He waited ten seconds, and then he threw all his weight into the end of the rope, and pulled it down, causing Old Post to be jerked up with a violence that choked her, and made her eyes roll fearfully, while her limbs swayed about convulsively.

Fastening the end of the rope to a bar of the fireplace, Cuffy said—

"Let her hang there, massa—it wont hurt her; she soon be dead. And now we go and look for Missy Viola."

"Yes, that is good advice," replied Money Marks.

And leaving Old Post strung up like so much carrion, they departed together, and left the room.

CHAPTER XXI.

THE CHASE.

WHEN Money Marks reached his ship, he summoned Tom Castaway, and ordered that a good look-out should be kept, lest the *Swamp Snake* should pass them in the night, which, however, was not at all favourable for any enterprise of that sort, as the stars shone out brightly, and the crescent moon illuminated the water, and all upon it.

Money Marks paced the deck with an impatient step. The officer of the watch looked towards him as he passed, but did not receive any comment or welcome. The men remained at their post silently, or conversing in whispers; for their commander was gloomy, and it was considered dangerous to take liberties with him when in a disturbed state of mind.

The young man, whom fate had transformed from a harmless adventurer into a highwayman of the seas, looked up at the coerulean vault of heaven, and wondered whether he should ever find a home upon the surface of one of those bright stars which scintillated so prettily.

These speculations did not last long, for a cloud which had obscured the moon during the last half-hour rolled away, and Money Marks looked towards the place where

THE MUTINY ON BOARD THE "SWAMP SNAKE."

the *Swamp Snake* ought to have been lying, but he was unable to see her.

She had vanished—disappeared; gone no one knew whither; flitted away like a child of mist.

Money Marks struck his forehead with his open palm, and uttered a deep groan. He had intended to fire into the *Snake*, and board her as she passed him in the morning. As his vessel was not a steamer, he could not hope to overtake her and fight on the open seas—he had relied solely upon being in the mouth of the harbour, and being able, owing to that circumstance, to board the ship and capture her. The *Snake* would have been a rich and desirable prize. In her he could have done much, and he was severely disappointed at the disaster which had befallen him.

There was, however, no help for it.

He had lost not only his intended prize, but also Viola. Heaven alone knew whither the ship commanded by Captain Arlee was going, and what would be the ultimate fate of Miss Cathcart.

She would certainly be exposed to the ill-treatment and unchivalrous behaviour—at times amounting to tyranny and persecution—of Captain Arlee, who, by putting her under the command of Old Post, had proved what he was capable of.

Sullenly Money Marks paced the deck until the grey dawn of morning appeared.

A sound aroused him.

What was it?

The echo of heavy guns, the noise of firing in the offing.

He could not repress a feeling of exultation, for he hoped most sincerely that his foe had met with the enemy, and received a check from the Federal cruisers which would send him back to Charleston in a disastrous condition.

Oh! how fervently he hoped this. How his heart leaped within him as this idea, lightning-like, passed through his brain, but unlike the electrical fluid, lingered there until it took firm hold of his hopes and his imagination!

Nor was he mistaken.

Precisely what he conjectured and what he hoped for had taken place.

Captain Arlee had raised his anchor early in the evening, and during a temporary gloom had crept out of the harbour unperceived by Money Marks, but not unnoticed by the enemy, who fired upon him, and an action of a severe nature took place.

At first Captain Arlee had only one vessel to contend against, but the noise of the firing brought a cloud of warships and notably some two or three monitors about his ears.

He blamed himself for essaying to leave the harbour of the beleaguered city on a bright night. He would not have done so if he had not thought Money Marks to be on his track, but this suspicion made him bold and reckless; he knew the power of love, and dreaded that it would stimulate Money Marks to great exertion. He would do anything sooner than lose Viola.

Arlee was compelled at length to withdraw from the contest; his vessel was not badly injured, but had he stayed much longer exposed to the enemy's fire there is little doubt that the ship would have been riddled with cannon balls, for the Federals burned the magnesium light, which illuminated the entire horizon, and enabled them to take aim with an accuracy which was in its effect truly surprising.

Reluctantly Captain Arlee ordered his engines to be reversed, and put back into Charleston.

Money Marks was tired and worn out for want of sleep, but he would not go below; he had a sort of presentiment, a sort of prophetic feeling, that the *Swamp Snake* was compelled to return, and he waited for her.

At nine o'clock in the morning the partially shattered hull of the *Snake* appeared on the horizon. She steamed along gaily enough, which showed that whatever else was the matter with her, her machinery was all right and her stock of coals good.

When he satisfied himself that Captain Arlee's vessel was really steaming back to the harbour, Money Marks called the whole of his crew on deck, and intimated to them in a brief speech that he wished to attack the *Snake* and capture her if possible.

His principal argument was that the *Snake* was a better vessel than the *Ocean Queen*, because it was fitted up as a steamer, and therefore much better for piratical purposes.

The crew responded heartily to this appeal, and said they were quite ready to undertake the arduous task of endeavouring to capture the vessel commanded by Captain Arlee.

Money Marks' plan for so doing was simply this.

To attempt to run down the *Snake* would be absurd and ineffectual, but to fire into her as she entered the harbour, and to board her with a couple of boats' crews almost simultaneously would be an excellent scheme, for the men under Money Marks' command were brave, determined fellows, and considerably more numerous than those of the blockade-runner.

Ships intended to run the blockade carry as few men as possible, relying not upon numerical strength, but solely upon speed and skill in navigation.

Money Marks lowered two boats, filled them with armed men, who held themselves in readiness to attack. There was some danger that the forts on Morris Island might depress the muzzles of their guns and fire upon Money Marks and his men when they saw what was going on, but the latter relied upon the rapidity of his motions, and the sudden way in which everything was to be managed.

When the sun began to acquire power, it exhausted the moisture from the air, and created a dense fog, which like a misty curtain obscured the horizon.

This sort of fog was a very common occurrence in those regions, and essentially transitory in its nature. It might last half-an-hour or even an hour, but it could not by any possibility last until the middle of the day.'

The *Swamp Snake* could not help passing within fifty yards of the *Ocean Queen*, and when the engines were heard, the boats put off and made for the devoted vessel, which they reached without any difficulty. At the same time the *Queen* launched forth a volley of shot and shell, which had the effect of bringing the *Snake* to a standstill.

Money Marks and Cuffy were the first on board the ship. The swarthy, sunburnt sailors with their cutlasses in their mouths, tightly held between their teeth, with their pistols in their belts, climbed the sides of the vessel like so many cats.

A terrific hand to hand combat took place, but it was not of long duration.

The crew of the *Swamp Snake* were outnumbered by at least two to one, and finding their cause hopeless, escaped by their boats.

The fog was so dense that it was difficult to tell what was going on.

Those men who remained on board submitted without a murmur.

Money Marks was master of the ship.

But had he gained all that he wanted?

That was a question that remained to be solved, but fortunately it was not very difficult of solution.

"Cuffy," cried Money Marks.

The faithful black was at his side in a moment.

"Come with me to the cabins. Quick, quick! Some devilish device may be at work to defeat us. If you see Arlee, shoot him down as ruthlessly as you would a dog."

"Yes, massa," said Cuffy, flourishing a smoking pistol in one hand and a bloody cutlass in the other.

CHAPTER XXII.

THE MUTINY.

EVERY cabin in the ship was diligently searched, but not the slightest trace or sign of Viola Cathcart or Captain Arlee could be discovered.

"They must have escaped in the boats," exclaimed Cuffy.

"Then, what were you doing to allow them?" said Money Marks, turning fiercely upon Cuffy.

"Me fight with cutlass, massa," replied the negro, hanging his head, while his eyes gleamed with a revengeful pride.

"Is there a curse of God upon my endeavours to rescue Viola?" cried Money Marks, in a tone of agony.

"No, massa, it not de cuss o' God," said Cuffy, "it am de luck of de thing—de fortun' of war, and all that; nex' time you be more fort'nit."

"I hope so; but these continual disappointments sour my spirit and wear me out. I know not what to do."

"Sall Cuffy tell massa?"

"Well?"

"Persevere. Never mind what dey say or what dey do, stick to 'em, Massa Marks, and when chance come, then kill Cappen Arlee."

Money Marks kissed the blade of his sword with almost religious fervour, and took a terrible oath, that should Captain Arlee's life ever be in his hands, he would not spare it—that no power on earth should induce him to spare it. And yet the time was to come when that life he had solemnly sworn to take was in his power, but he heroically forbore to take it.

This, however, is anticipating.

While he was speaking a bright light burst over Sumter, and a huge shell came thundering along, passing happily over the deck of the *Snake*.

"Ha!" cried Money Marks, "what I dreaded has come to pass; Arlee has gained the fort, and they are firing at us. Fortunately the fog is too dense to enable them to see our exact whereabouts. We must move at once."

He rushed on deck, and found his men collected in excited groups.

To the officers he gave such directions as seemed fit to him. The engines of the *Snake* were at once reversed, and in ten minutes time the *Ocean Queen* was made fast by a hawser to the steamer, and was being towed out of the harbour.

To have stayed in the harbour would have been suicidal infatuation, for there was no doubt whatever that Captain Arlee had gained the forts, and had told the officers commanding them of what had occurred, and that they would endeavour to do all in their power to sink Money Marks, and destroy him and all his crew as soon as the fog lifted.

They evidently looked upon the capture of the *Snake* as a sharp Yankee trick—a Federal *ruse*, and they were annoyed accordingly.

Their hostility was pretty well evidenced by the number of heavy shell and shot which continued to be discharged at random.

As yet none had hit the vessel, though several had gone dangerously near.

Money Marks gave his orders with rapidity, and the *Snake*

was soon under full pressure of steam and towing the *Ocean Queen* out of the harbour.

The fog luckily continued.

Money Marks had a chart of the coast, and instead of making for the sea, he hugged the land until he found a small creek which afforded a desirable anchorage.

When the horizon cleared, the blockading fleet was out of sight. The sea was quite smooth, and the scene was lively in the extreme. The shore was well cultivated, a fact easily ascertainable in spite of the rapid passage of the ships.

The navigation was rather uncertain, and sometimes dangerous, and caused Money Marks considerable anxiety.

It was fortunate that he was equal to the duties of the occasion, for at four o'clock in the afternoon the tide suddenly shifted, and carried the vessels towards a reef of rocks, but the engines being reversed immediately, the danger was avoided.

If Money Marks had thought fit to abandon Viola to her fate, he could have stood out to sea, and there would have been no hazard of running upon rocks; but he would not leave her to the mercy of Captain Arlee, and he resolved to run the vessels into the first creek he came to, and make a land journey to Charleston, and see if he could not succeed in carrying her off.

This was a speculative venture, in the fullest sense of the word. Possibly the crew might have felt inclined to be mutinous if he had not found something for them to do in his absence; as it was, Tom Castaway took upon himself to make some remarks which were unpalatable to his captain.

It was Money Marks' custom to call the men on deck, and speak to them collectively whenever he had any special object in view, and on this occasion he summoned them as usual.

The men did not look very contented, and it was noticeable that several of them conversed together in a low murmuring tone.

"My men," exclaimed Money Marks, "we have made an excellent prize; the value of the steamer we are now in greatly exceeds the value of the slaver we took forcible possession of when lying off the coast of Africa. It is necessary that we should stop some time in a convenient place to transfer everything we may want from the *Ocean Queen* to the *Swamp Snake*, which I propose hereafter shall be called the *Captain Kidd*, in honour of that illustrious individual, whom we must regard as our prototype. I have a little matter of business to transact on shore, and during the two days I shall allow you to move your property and whatever else it may be desirable to move from the sailing vessel while I shall be absent. When you have finished your task, scuttle the *Queen*, and allow her to sink, so that no trace of her may remain."

Tom Castaway stepped forward, and folding his arms, exclaimed—

"I wish to say a few words, sir."

"Certainly; say what you like."

"Well, it's just this—I don't like the way things are going on; the men are not satisfied; they've got grievances."

"Indeed! Let them state their grievances, and I will endeavour to give them some redress," replied Money Marks, turning slightly pale.

"Better out with it at once, mates, eh?" said Tom Castaway.

"Yes, yes," replied two or three voices in close proximity to him.

The remainder of the crew appeared to be neutral, or to be waiting for the result of the contest which was about to ensue. They were wise in their generation, and wished to see which way the wind blew, so that they might join the winning side—a praiseworthy resolve, and one which it would have been better for discontented Tom had he adopted.

"We want a new captain," exclaimed Tom Castaway, with an insolent air of defiance.

"A new captain, eh!" repeated Money Marks quietly.

"Yes, and we mean to have one."

"Are you aware that what you have said is rank mutiny?"

"Never mind what it is; we want a new captain. We don't care about a man whose beard's no better than a bit of fluff."

"Is that your only objection to me?" said Money Marks, with a laugh.

"No; we've got others—we don't want to hurt you, but when you go ashore stop there, and try your luck elsewhere."

Money Marks waited to hear no more; he sprang forward with a bound, seized Tom Castaway by the collar, and sent him reeling along the deck by the force of an energetic push.

While he was rolling and staggering, and in vain trying to grasp something to steady himself, Money Marks aimed a revolver at him, and shot him through the head.

He threw up his arms despairingly, uttered a doleful cry, and was a corpse.

Holding the still smoking weapon in his hand, Money Marks exclaimed—

"Is anyone else discontented with my rule? I have an excellent specific for dissatisfaction; I have cured one very bad case, and I daresay I can cure another, or as many as you like."

No one replied.

"Why should you be dissatisfied with me?" continued Money Marks; "I have done all I can for you. Have I not given you a better ship? and have I not placed money in your way? and have I not innumerable schemes for enriching you in the future? To be sure I have. If you were to get rid of me, you would be killing your golden goose. What does my youth matter? what my juvenile appearance? I have a head," he said, touching his forehead, "I have a head which is capable of divining many grand schemes which will enrich all of you. I firmly believe that the man who lies a corpse before you is the only one who thinks he has a cause of complaint against me; I believe he is the *only* malcontent. If I am right, tell me so."

"You are, you are; it was all Tom's doings," and similar exclamations arose on all sides.

"You are satisfied?"

"Yes, yes."

"Then I will put this little persuader in my pocket," said Money Marks, stowing away his revolver. "But let me warn you that if I find or hear of any rebellion against my constituted authority, I shall take the same energetic means of repressing it as I did a few minutes ago. I advise you all most fully to understand that."

During this scene—this altercation—this tragedy, the officers of the ship had remained by Money Marks' side with their swords drawn, prepared to defend him to the last should any attempt be made by the crew collectively upon his life.

Turning to this little band of heroes, this collection of trustworthy friends, Money Marks shook them individually by the hand, and thanked them in the most cordial terms for the support they had shown themselves prepared to render him, in the event of such support being necessary.

"In your hands and in your charge I leave the ship," he said; "I am convinced that I cannot leave her in better hands. I shall not be absent long, but should unanticipated circumstances compel me to linger longer than I intended in this country, wait for me as near in shore as you conceive compatible with your safety, and be prepared to sail at a moment's notice."

Having given these instructions, he attired himself in a suitable costume, and summoning Cuffy to his side, was rowed ashore in the ship's boat.

The spot at which Money Marks chose to land was a wild looking part of the coast, sparsely inhabited. When they landed, they perceived some women engaged in husking rice in a mortar with a wooden beater; men and boys were seen carrying loads on a wooden frame hooked to the shoulders.

In a square wooden platform near the village, a number of women and children were employed winnowing corn, by pouring it from a height, so that the husks blew away. Fishing-nets were spread to dry on most of the houses.

One house in the little village upon which Money Marks had intruded his presence, arrested his attention in particular, and he, in conjunction with Cuffy, took the liberty of examining it.

Before the door, on a neat, clean, level space, enclosed by a bridge covered with a sweet-scented white flower, they found several heaps of corn and straw, and several of the wooden mortars in which the rice is pounded; also a number of vessels, some filled with water, and others with rice. Cooking utensils were lying about, and a number of fishing lines coiled neatly in baskets; and split fish, spread out to dry on the top of little corn ricks, on one side of the court. The inside of the house was dark and uncomfortable; the mud floor was very uneven; the walls were black with soot, and everything looked dirty. On the left of the entrance, two large metal boilers, twenty inches deep, were sunk in brick-work, the upper part being about a foot above the floor. The fire-place was between the boilers, and on the hot embers lay three split fish. On the wall opposite to the fire were shelves, having a number of cups, basins, and cooking utensils, principally of coarse stoneware, and some few of a sort of bell-metal. The number of inhabitants in one house must have been considerable, if we can form an estimate from the quantity of their dishes and vessels. There were three neat small pieces of furniture on one of the shelves, the use of which was dubious; they were made of wood, elegantly carved and varnished, with a round top, about a foot in diameter, and four legs a foot and a half long. The roof was well constructed, the rafters being mortised into the ends of the horizontal beams, and braced to the middle by a perpendicular beam or king-post.

Over the rafters was a net-work of rods, to which the thatch was tied.

There was no chimney to this house, and only one window, made of slender bars of wood, forming square spaces three inches by two, covered by a thin, semi-transparent paper, defended by the roof, which extends so far beyond the wall as to shelter it not only from the rain but from the sun.

Most of the houses had a sort of raised verandah under the eaves, about a foot or more above the ground, extending from the door on either hand to the end of the house; these places were neatly levelled, and afforded a cool seat.

The walls of the houses were from six to eight feet high, and from fourteen to twenty feet long; the top of the roof being about fourteen.

The walls were of stone and mud; the doors, of which there were two, moved on the bar, which formed one of its sides; this bar was somewhat longer than the door, and so contrived as to work in a hole in the beam above, and in another in a stone below. On opening this was found a bare bank of earth as high as the house, at the distance of three feet from the walls, and a hedge rising still higher on the top; this effectually excluded all light from that quarter.

Having completed this minute survey of the house, Money Marks was glad to see an old man approach him. Of him he inquired the distance to Charleston, and the road.

He was told, with the utmost courtesy, in reply, that the city was distant twenty miles, and that if they would pay for it they could have a carriage drawn by two horses to take them there.

With this offer Money Marks at once closed, and the carriage was brought out of the primitive place in which it was kept.

CHAPTER XXIII.

A CATASTROPHE.

CUFFY drove, and it required all the perseverance and strength of the negro to make the wretched cattle go at a decent pace; he had to stand up in the chaise and drag at the reins, and ply the whip with an energy foreign to his real nature to make the thick-skinned horses move at all.

By dint of great and praiseworthy industry they reached Charleston, and put up at a small *auberge*, or inn, in the outskirts.

This was called the "Plantation Nigger," and had for a sign a black with curly hair of the wool species, something like a black sheep who has used the "incomparable oil Macassar" for a length of time.

At this place they put up their carriage and horses, and by liberal payment procured some dresses which effectually disguised them.

When Money Marks was ready he looked in vain for Cuffy, whom he at length discovered standing before a glass.

"What are you doing?" he said.

"Cuff am artful nig; him chalk him face."

"What for?"

"'Cos his hat cover his wool, and then him be taken for white man."

"It is lucky the sun's gone down," said Money Marks; "or else your pictorial decoration would soon disappear."

In order to reach Captain Arlee's house they had about two miles to walk. This distance they traversed cheerfully, and without loss of time.

Money Marks had left orders that the horses were not to be unharnessed, but to be fed well, and to be kept in readiness for any emergency.

The sun was just sinking below the verge of the horizon, bathing the sky in a flood of golden splendour, when the two men entered the avenue in which Captain Arlee lived.

Cuffy had provided himself at the "Plantation Nigger" with a basket filled with pine-apples, and with this on his head, followed by Money Marks, he descended the area of the captain's house, and said to a servant who came to answer his summons that he had brought the fruit by the captain's express order.

This stratagem sufficed to gain them an entrance to the mansion, and one or two maid-servants came forward to have a look at a fruit of which they were particularly fond.

"Is the captain better, my dear?" inquired Money Marks of a blooming maiden, with rosy cheeks, and full lips denoting her half-and-half origin.

"He's still bad with his broken arm," was the reply; "we all thought he was going to sea for good yesterday, but he came back this morning."

"And his young lady with him?"

"Yes; he's brought her, but what there is to see in her I can't think. She's not my style of beauty."

"Where is she now?" asked Money Marks.

"Upstairs, by herself."

"No one with her?"

"No; Old Post, who looked after her formerly, hanged herself, or somebody hanged her, I don't know which. It was a good riddance of bad rubbish; and, for my part, if a gentleman can't make a girl marry him he ought to let her go and marry whoever she wants to."

"So I think, my little creole."

This answer was scarcely out of Money Marks' lips before Cuffy touched him on the shoulder, and said—

"Let us go, massa, I hear the sound of footsteps."

"Where?"

"In the street."

"What of that?"

"I fear something."

"What can you fear? I am not to be deterred from my set purpose; I will go through fire and water to save Viola—follow me. We will rush upstairs and see if she be still in the tyrant's power."

The servants fell back, and Money Marks dashed up the stairs, followed closely by Cuffy. Marks made for the suite of apartments he had formerly visited, in the hope of finding Viola, but in which he had simply discovered Old Post.

The door leading into these rooms was locked.

This slender precaution availed nothing to a determined man.

With one vigorous kick, Money Marks forced the door open, and was astounded at the scene which was presented to his view.

Viola—his own loved Viola—was sitting in a half-fainting attitude upon a chair.

Captain Arlee was upon his knees at her side, and entreating her in audible tones, which trembled with emotion, to hear his prayer, and grant it.

She was, however, obdurate, as she always had been, and it was clear from her manner that she would give worlds to be released from the persecution to which she was subjected by a man whom she detested.

Money Marks's unexpected appearance created as much consternation as if a bombshell had fallen amongst them.

Captain Arlee sprang to his feet, coloured, and gnawed his nether lip impatiently. His right arm was bound up, and surrounded by surgical strappings.

Viola looked up, recognised Money Marks in an instant, and uttered a pleased scream.

"Leave this room instantly!" cried Money Marks, addressing Captain Arlee.

"Why?" was the answer, made in an angry tone.

"Because I bid you."

He hesitated.

Money Marks and Viola were in one another's arms. Oh, the rapture of that meeting! Words are inadequate to describe one-tenth part of the joy which was experienced by the lovers. Lips fondly met lips, and heart beat passionately against heart.

Captain Arlee was enraged beyond measure, and would have done something vindictive if Money Marks had not made a sign to Cuffy, who advanced to the gallant captain, and, without the least ceremony, bundled him neck-and-crop out of the room.

This was a horrible indignity to Captain Arlee, but with his disabled arm it was totally out of his power to help himself. He was compelled to submit to the harsh treatment, which was ten times more galling because it was experienced at the hands of a black man—of a negro—one of the despised—the hated—the trampled under foot—the inferior—the despicable, whom we in England look upon as a man and a brother. The hand of God fashioned black and white alike, and we who are liberal and large-minded do not care about a trifling distinction of colour, which is more the fault of a hot sun than of the man himself.

Cuffy kept guard outside the door, and left the lovers together, which was an act of delicacy for which he deserved credit.

"Oh, Viola!" cried Money Marks; "this is, indeed, happiness. Forgive me if I speak with a freedom which I have no right to arrogate to myself, but we have long been separated; and although I have done much to succour you, you have suffered deeply. Yet that suffering has not been the fault, or the result of any neglect or dereliction of duty on my part."

"Oh, no! I am sure of that," replied Viola, with tearful eyes; "but you are right when you say that I have suffered. At times I thought, in my despair, that death itself would be preferable, but hope buoyed me up, and I did not succumb to the seductive feeling which bid me take my own life, and fly in the face of my Creator."

"Thank Heaven that it was so. Will you tell me that you have thought of me?—if not with the ardour with which I have regarded you, at least with a kindly feeling."

Viola hung down her head, and said in a low tone, while a scarlet blush suffused her head, neck, and shoulders—

"I have done more than that."

"More!"

"Yes."

"Pray enlighten me."

"Do not think me unmaidenly."

"I think you so?"

She whispered in a low tone—

"I remembered you with thoughts of love."

"Oh, thanks, thanks, for that declaration!" cried Money Marks, clasping his hands, and regarding her with the evidence of the most ardent affection. "Thanks for that blessed assurance!—you have made me intensely happy, and I cannot find words with which to show my gratitude to you my dear, dear, darling Viola."

She allowed her head to sink upon his bosom with confiding trust.

The moment before, she had been defying Captain Arlee with all the vehemence of which her nature was capable. A change had come over the spirit of her dream. The reaction had set in, and she burst into tears.

A scuffle was heard outside; the shouts of men were audible, and the tramp of soldiers, as it seemed, might be distinguished on the stairs.

The door was burst open, and Cuffy rushed in followed by several people.

"Fly, massa, fly!" he cried, levelling his revolver at the invaders.

But the caution came too late. Whither could he fly? he was surrounded and escape was cut off. Now he saw the mistake of which he had been guilty, in permitting Captain Arlee to go away with his life; had he shot him down as he would have shot a dog, he could not have summoned soldiers to his aid, and Money Marks would not have been placed in such a hazardous position.

He was at all times prepared to sell his life dearly, but he did not see the utility of fighting with such tremendous odds of ten to one.

It occurred to him that his best course would be to temporize with those who had evidently come to arrest him, and to conciliate them, if possible, with moderate behaviour.

"Arrest him," cried Captain Arlee, pointing to Money Marks, "arrest him; he is a traitor to the Commonwealth. Arrest him, and place him irons."

Cuffy was about to offer a desperate resistance, but his master checked him.

When Viola could master her emotion sufficiently to speak, she, clinging passionately to her lover the while, exclaimed, in tremulous accents—

"What would you do? You cannot have the heart to part us after so long a separation."

"I do my duty," said Captain Arlee; "and these men whom I have brought hither, must do theirs."

"You will not be so cruel."

Arlee crossed over to where she was standing, and said—

"Love me, and I spare his life."

"Love you?"

"Yes."

"I cannot."

"Then he dies."

"Oh, save him!"

"I will on the condition I have named to you."

"What does he say?" cried Money Marks, interposing.

"He will save you if I promise to—to love him," replied Viola, bashfully.

"The villain! Tell him you loathe him, scorn him, hate him, and will never, never give him a word of encouragement."

"I can honestly say so, for I do hate, detest, and loathe him."

"Say you so? Then, soldiers, seize your prisoner."

The men waited no longer, but approaching Money Marks and Cuffy, took them both in custody, and marched them from the room.

Viola fainted away, and did not hear the last words of Money Marks, which were—

"Cheer up, my Viola; although dark clouds may environ us, we shall have a bright future; or if death should cut short our earthly career, let us hope for a bright hereafter."

The prisoners were taken to a rudely-constructed guardhouse without the town, to await the court-martial, which would try them on the morrow upon some charge that Captain Arlee was ready to prefer against them.

His enemies were in his power. How he rejoiced and chuckled over that consummation!—he thought no more of the pain of his broken arm, of the innumerable accidents that had befallen him, of the loss of his vessel: all—all was avenged in the fact of Money Marks' capture.

CHAPTER XXIV.
FREEDOM.

THE captives were treated much alike by the soldiers, who thought it their duty to ill-treat both black and white, and to drag them along in the manner most convenient to them.

They were imprisoned in a close, stifling shed, in which there was little air and still less light. War had made these men brutal, and they had usurped the functions of the police. A cup of water would have been a God-send to Money Marks, and he determined to ask the soldier who was on guard outside the shed in which he was confined.

Cuffy was sitting in a corner, with his mouth bleeding from a severe blow he had received in his passage through the streets.

It was clear that they were regarded with suspicion, and the fact of their being well-guarded was undoubted, because they could hear the interminable footsteps of their guard as he walked up and down in front of the house or shed.

Going to the door, Money Marks knocked with his knuckles against it.

"What do you want?" said a gruff voice.

"A cup of water."

"Got no water for fellows like you."

"I shall die of thirst."

"Die, then," responded the fellow, brutally.

Now that soldier four years back, was not the unbending ruffian that he then was—hard-hearted, unfeeling, uncharitable, unsympathetic. He had been a farmer working for his father, but the cannon thundered against Sumter, and fierce alarms of war resounded through the land; he, fired with martial ardour, did not wait to be conscripted but enlisted at once. After a time his whole nature became changed; the milk of human kindness curdled and turned to gall—he was a standing example of fierce, relentless warfare.

"What am I confined for?" asked Money Marks through the door.

"For being a pirate and an abolitionist."

"Oh!"

This threw a new light upon Money Marks' meditations; he was almost at a loss to know what charge Captain Arlee would trump up against him. To say that he was an abolitionist was undoubtedly clever, and would do him a deal of injury with his judges. He had expected that he would be styled a pirate, on account of his attack upon the Confederate steamer, *Swamp Snake*, but he chuckled when he thought that his captors had not the least inkling of his being in reality a pirate.

Captain Arlee had caused Money Marks to be taken to the eastern extremity of the suburbs of Charleston, because the captain commanding that solitary outpost was an intimate friend of his, and he knew that he could get Money Marks tried by a drum-head court-martial, condemned, and shot without much difficulty.

Had he on the other hand delivered him to the municipal authorities, there would have been some delay; Marks would have been able to secure the services of counsel, and perhaps escape after all.

Rather anything than this contingency.

The largest part of the Confederate force was concentrated at the north-western part of the city, which was threatened by Federal General Gilmore. At the eastern side little was going on, and Arlee thought he should have it all his own way.

Money Marks gave himself up for lost; he sat down on the ground, and folding his hands over his knees, bowed down his head, and gave way to an intense melancholy.

"What you melancholy for, Massa Marks?" inquired Cuffy.

"How can I be otherwise?"

"It will be all right presently."

"Yes, when we have half-a-dozen bullets in us."

"Oh, no, you not going to be kill yet, massa," said Cuffy, cheerfully.

"That is more than you can tell; for my part, I think affairs look as dismal as they well can."

"They not very lively," Cuffy was forced candidly to admit.

A loud noise was heard outside the door, which was thrown violently open, and Captain Arlee accompanied by his friend, Loyd G. Bannister, commanding battery No. 3, entered.

"Are those the rascals of which you told me?" said Bannister.

"They are."

Bannister walked over to Cuffy, and gave him a kick in the ribs, saying—

"Get up."

The negro got up, and so did Money Marks, to avoid a similar insult.

"So you are an abolitionist," he said to Cuffy.

"Yes, massa; bobolishun's all de go, and these are fine times for poor nigs."

"You scoundrel! Do you dare to speak to me in that familiar way?"

"Massa, him speak to me."

"What of that?"

"Tar and feather him," cried Captain Arlee.

"Ha, ha! a good idea."

"Tar and feathers," said some one outside.

And immediately several men ran off to procure the necessary articles for that interesting ceremony.

Money Marks stepped forward.

"Whatever your spite and ill-will against me may be," he exclaimed, "at least be generous."

"In what way?" asked Arlee, frigidly.

"What harm has this poor negro done you?"

"He is in the same boat with you."

"He is my servant, if that is what you mean."

"I mean nothing of the sort."

"What do you mean, then?"

"You are conspirators together."

Money Marks laughed.

"Conspirators?" he said.

"Yes."

"Against what or whom?"

"The Confederacy; you are also a pirate, and a brigand, and an abolitionist."

"A weighty list of accusations, certainly," replied Money Marks; "but I do not think I should have much difficulty in proving the falsity of the charges against me."

"That is mere bravado."

"Certainly not; it is the truth."

"You will have an opportunity of justifying yourself, my good fellow," exclaimed Loyd G. Bannister, "when you are tried."

"By whom?" demanded Money Marks, proudly.

"By me."

"You?"

"Yes."

"I demand that I be tried by an authorized tribunal; I am a British subject, and I request that the services of the British consul be allowed me, or that I may be permitted to correspond with him."

"Your request cannot be granted."

"And why, I should like to know?"

"It is in my discretion to grant such a request."

"Excuse me, but I deny that *in toto*. I request, sir, that the charges against me may be deposed and sworn to, that they may be put in writing, and that information of the fact may be given to the British consul, if there is one at Charleston."

"That is wisely put in," said Loyd G. Bannister.

"What?"

"If there is one."

"Are British subjects, then, deprived of consular assistance?"

"I have every reason to believe so, but anyhow I should not allow you to communicate with your consul, were there such a person in existence."

"Pray why not?"

"I do not choose to bandy words with men like you," said Loyd G. Bannister.

"At least give me an answer."

"I do as I like; I am responsible to no one but my commanding officer, and he has entire confidence in me. To-morrow you will be tried, and if condemned, shot without an hour's delay."

"I beg to enter my most decided protest against——"

"One word more, sir, and I have you shot without trial."

Money Marks held his tongue; his condition was so thoroughly forlorn and helpless that he did not know what to do. He could not escape, because he was manacled, although he would cheerfully have made the attempt had it been possible.

The lawless soldiers under Bannister's command had hailed the idea of tar and feathers with the utmost satisfaction; it was charming to them to think that they would be permitted to torture a fellow creature, and they brought a barrel of tar, and feathers in abundance.

"Here are the materials, captain," said a sergeant coming forward.

"Where?"

"Outside, sir."

"Take the nigger out, and get a rail to ride him on."

"Yes, sir," replied the sergeant, with a grin.

The negro was taken outside, and the dungeon closed once more on Money Marks, who was horrified at the idea of Cuffy being so violently ill-treated.

To be tarred and feathered is anything but a joke, and to be ridden on a rail afterwards may be productive of laughter and amusement to the on-looker, but it is undoubtedly painful in the extreme to the sufferer. Tar, as is well known, sticks to the skin with great pertinacity; if ever so small a piece adheres to the finger, it is with the utmost difficulty got off, and then only with the aid of lard, hot water, and pumicestone; fancy, then, the effect of having the *whole body* smeared with the noxious compound, and thick layers of feathers stuck all over it. What can be more unpleasant?

Nothing.

Emphatically and absolutely nothing.

This, however, was to be Cuffy's fate.

"I don't care about the nigger," said Captain Arlee to his friend; "you may do what you like with him, but the other man is a desperate criminal, and must be shot."

"I suppose what he said about being a British subject and all that was so much bunkum?"

"All bunkum, my dear sir; he is a Yankee, a thorough-going Yank; I have known him some time, and can vouch for the truth of what I say."

"Well, he shall be summarily disposed of, I'll take care of that; but let him bide till we have had our fun out with the nigger. I hate and abominate niggers, and always did, and I'm not going to turn silly in my old age and show them any indulgence."

"Nor would I. Do as you like with him."

"Trust me. Hartopp."

"Yes, sir," replied the sergeant who had been chiefly instrumental in providing the tar and feathers.

"Materials all ready?"

"At your service, sir."

"Nigger!"

Cuffy looked up.

"Strip."

Cuffy did so, knowing very well that all opposition on his part would be useless, and he endeavoured by a show of alacrity to win the goodwill of his captors.

In less than five minutes he was stripped to the skin.

"Lie on your belly," cried Hartopp, coarsely.

He did so.

And with a brush Hartopp smeared him from top to toe with tar—thick viscous tar. Throwing the brush aside, he plunged his hand into a bag of feathers and went on with his singular if not repulsive task.

When Cuffy was covered with feathers from head to foot, he presented a most ludicrous spectacle, and all those in battery No. 3 laughed most heartily.

"Go it, ye cripples," cried Hartopp; "crutches are cheap."

Turning to the negro, he added—

"'Bolish the feathers, nigger, if you want to abolish anything."

"Where's the rail?" said Captain Loyd G. Bannister.

"Here, sir."

"Put him on."

Cuffy was placed upon the rail, and holding on with his hands as well as he could, was dragged about all over the battery with the greatest demonstrations of joy, amidst screams of delight and shouts of satisfaction.

When the procession reached the extreme limit of the battery No. 3, Cuffy was set down for a brief space while the men regaled themselves upon spirits and other things which they had a mind to.

The black had been watching his opportunity, and now that it had arrived he was sensible enough not to neglect it.

With a stealthy gliding motion, closely allied to that of a snake, he slipped away from his brutal captors, and ran with all his strength in the direction of the road he had that morning traversed in Money Marks' company.

Cuffy presented a strange sight. Actæon changed into a stag, and chased by his own hounds could not have presented a stranger. The feathers stuck to him as if he were of the bird tribe, and they had grown by the force of nature out of his skin.

He was as white as a goose from head to foot.

He passed many in his swift flight, but he dashed onwards like a flash of lightning, or a thunderbolt, and gave them no time to comment upon the strange figure he cut.

Cuffy's object was to make for the vessel, rouse the crew, and bring a large body of armed men to battery No. 3, so that they could make an attack, and rescue their commander from the cruel death Captain Loyd G. Bannister had threatened him, and which it was positive Captain Arlee would insist upon having carried out.

Cuffy ran with the most praiseworthy perseverance and endurance until he reached the little bay in which the ship was lying.

Losing no time, he made the signals which had been agreed upon, and a boat was instantly lowered.

This pulled to the land, and the first lieutenant—formerly second, but first since Tom Castaway's sudden death—jumped ashore.

His name was Sampson Hercules, and well he deserved the appellation, for he was a prodigiously strong, stalwart, and powerful man, of almost gigantic size, standing at least six feet four in his boots and stockings.

He went by the nickname of the dwarf, on the *lucus a non* principle, and was an honest, straightforward, good-natured fellow as you could expect a highwayman of the seas to be.

The appearance presented by Cuffy was so ludicrous, that Sampson put his hands to his sides and laughed so heartily that his huge frame trembled again.

His cachinnations rang through the air, and found an echo in the surrounding cliffs.

The sailors also laughed, and for some little time Cuffy was unable to get an hearing.

"Well, my young and intelligent black," said Sampson Hercules, who it may be mentioned in passing, was an Englishman, "what's the meaning of all this, and where's the captain?"

"Up a tree, Massa Herc'les."

"Like the colonel's 'coon, eh?"

"Yes, massa."

"Tell us all about it."

"We go to the rebels, and they cotch us."

"Is the captain in the hands of the Confeds?"

"'Iss," replied Cuffy.

"That's bad."

"And they serve me like this."

The second lieutenant was in the boat, and he being an Irishman of the name of Pat Doolan, could not refrain from chiming in—

"The cuss of Crummle on them," he said, winking his eye at the sailors.

One thing is worthy of remark here, and that is that although discipline in a certain manner was insisted upon and enforced on board the piratical vessel, the officers and men were always hail-fellow-well-met with one another, and they evidently considered themselves all on a level, which is not surprising, seeing that Money Marks had had recourse to manhood suffrage, and allowed the men who sailed under him to elect their own officers, of which permission they had availed themselves to put in office Sampson Hercules and Pat Doolan, two of the best natured and jolliest fellows in the entire crew.

They both were attached to Money Marks, whom they considered a man of talent, and one who would do everything to conduce to the interests of the whole community.

Nor were they mistaken.

When they heard that Money Marks was taken prisoner, and that he was in the hands of the enemy, they were much concerned, and so were the boat's crew, for the pirate without Marks would have been like a tail without a head—a dismembered and useless body.

"It's this way, Mr. Doolan," said Cuffy, "the cappen, God bless him, and me was cotched and put into a little hole of a prison in battery No. 3, at the extreme east of Charleston. Well, they tarred and feathered me——"

"Ha, ha!" shouted Pat Doolan; "shure, and it's enough to make a cat laugh."

"Ha, ha!" laughed Sampson.

"Ha, ha!" laughed the crew.

For some minutes so great was the merriment excited by Cuffy's disaster, that the negro could not get a hearing, and was obliged to desist.

At last the mirth of the pirates subsided, and Hercules said—

"Go on, nigger, we're ready to hear you."

"They rode me on a rail," continued Cuffy, "and when they'd had 'nough sport they set me down, and 'gan to liquor up: seein' a chance, I gave 'em leg bail, thinking I'd run to de ship, and get you to come up to batt'ry No. 3, and reskew de capt'n. What you say to old Cuff's plan?"

"Is Money Marks condemned to death?" inquired Hercules.

"Yes, Massa Hercules, him condemn'd safe 'nuff."

"By whom?"

"Cappen Arlee; him cap'n of ship we now in, one we tuk t'other day; that's why he's goin' to be shot."

"How long will it take you to get that tar and those feathers off?"

"That work ob time, sar."

"But we can't do without you."

"'Cos why, Massa Herc'les?"

"We want you to show us the way."

"De way! oh yes, to be sure; dis nig never thought ob dat."

"Can't you throw a long cloak over your body?"

"'Iss, Cuff can do dat."

"Very well, the boat shall go back to the ship and get you one. Pat."

"Yes, lafftenant," replied Doolan.

"We mustn't desert the captain."

"Desart him, is it? no, by Jabers, more power to his elbow."

"The only thing I can think of is to take say thirty men."

"Thirty, yes."

"That will leave enough to guard the ship in case of any surprise; then we will follow the nigger and make an attack upon the battery, before they are aware of our intention."

"Beware of our intintion, yes," said Pat Doolan, who had a way of interrupting everybody when they were speaking, and repeating their own words.

"Don't interrupt me when I'm speaking."

"Interrupt ye when ye're spaking, is it ? shure, and my father's son would be the last who'd do it."

"So you see," Sampson Hercules went on, "we can rescue Money Marks and bring him back safely."

"Right you are. That's your sort. Hurreo! Go it, ye cripples; Stickers will discount yer bill," shouted Pat Doolan.

"You had better wait here with the nigger, Pat."

"And why ?"

"Because if I take him on board like this, the men will all go into fits, and it would be bad for their health; do you see that ?"

"I'll stay, don't flurry your fat, I'll stay all right," replied Doolan.

When the boat had taken its departure again, Doolan looked at Cuffy with an exquisitely comical countenance.

"Come, nig, turn your starn round, and let's sarvey you all over, so that I can make a good chart of you fore and aft in my mind's eye. Och, by the piper that played before Moses, shure and wouldn't a dhog roar."

In a short time the boat returned with a number of men fully armed to the teeth, and went back to bring some more.

Half-an-hour had not elapsed since Cuffy's arrival, and yet the little army was fully equipped and organized.

Cuffy, wrapped in a long cloak of a whitey-brown colour that descended to his feet, was not the strange and eccentric object he had been a short time before.

Notwithstanding the serious work upon which the men were bent, a smothered laugh would break out whenever their thoughts recurred to Cuffy and his tar and feathers.

CHAPTER XXV.

CONDEMNED TO DEATH.

As Money Marks saw no more of Cuffy, he was forced to come to the conclusion, though much against his will, that his captors had wreaked their vengeance upon the black, and killed him in some brutal manner congenial to their depraved tastes and fancies.

"So," he muttered to himself, "they have sent his soul to the land of spirits, and I shall be the next victim. Well, the sooner the better; nothing can be worse than this torturing suspense, though I could have wished to live for Viola's sake."

A hoarse discordant laugh startled him.

Looking up, he perceived through the dim light afforded by the fantail-window, which ventilated his dungeon, the long and stalwart frame of Captain Arlee.

"You are afraid of death, eh ?" inquired Arlee, with a cutting, sneering laugh, as he drew the ample folds of his military cloak around his shoulders.

"Who ever said so, lies!" responded Money Marks, proudly, and rising as well as his fetters would permit him.

"This is bravado when the halter is round your neck, choking you with its strangling coil; when your tongue lolls out of your mouth; your blood rushes to the brain; your eyeballs start from their sockets!"

"Why, then, if I can sufficiently collect my faculties, I shall pray God to receive my soul," replied Money Marks, calmly.

The simple and unostentatious piety perceptible in this answer should have rebuked Captain Arlee, but he merely laughed another Mephistophelian laugh, and exclaimed—

"You are young."

"Yes."

"And life has its charms for those who are young."

"Well."

"There are passions which sway the youthful mind—such as hatred, revenge, love."

Money Marks moved uneasily.

"Ha! have I touched a tender chord at last ?"

"Inhuman scoundrel, leave me! Let me die in peace! Do not insult and mock my last hours!" cried Money Marks, who foamed at the mouth with rage.

"I came here to gloat over your misery," said Captain Arlee, "and I shall not leave at your dictation. I shall stay here until I am surfeited."

"Wretch! a time may come when 'twill be my turn."

"It must be beyond the grave then."

"Oh, well! but you—you would not dare to taunt me thus."

"I have a message for you."

"A message ?"

"Yes."

"From where ?"

"My Viola."

"Your—your Viola!"

"Yes, she is mine. She has consented to be my wife."

"It is false! By Heaven I swear it!"

"You cannot know the truth or falsity of what I say; for you have no means of ascertaining the fact, except by your own cleverness at guessing."

"The message!" cried Money Marks. "What was the message ?"

"Would you hear it ?" said Arlee, in a tantalising manner.

"At once. Every word that falls from her dear lips is as precious as my own life-blood. What was her message ? Tell it me quick, or I burst my bonds by a furious effort, and strangle you where you stand!"

"That, I am afraid, would puzzle you."

"The message!"

"It was this——"

"I am listening."

"She said—are you attending to me ?"

Money Marks made a gesture of impatience.

He was listening with the utmost attention, and extremely annoyed at the prosy way in which the captain delivered himself of the message, which had by Viola been entrusted to his care.

"She said," continued Captain Arlee, slowly and solemnly, "that she hoped you might die easily."

"Hell-hound!" shrieked Money Marks, who perceived that he had been duped, and that the captain had been playing with him as a cat plays with a mouse, and trifling with his most tender feelings.

"Oh," he added, "for half a minute of freedom !"

He struggled frightfully to get loose; he exerted himself to the utmost. Arlee's mocking laughter maddened him.

The veins upon his forehead were swollen almost to bursting; they stood out like cords, and were full of inflamed dark-coloured blood.

Suddenly there was a snap, a shout, a cry, as of a wild beast tasting blood for the first time, and Money Marks was free.

At first, Captain Arlee could not believe the evidence of his senses, but when the terrible and overwhelming fact made itself clear to his sluggish comprehension, he started back with an affrighted shout, and endeavoured to gain the door.

His movements were quick and agile.

But his efforts were in vain.

Nemesis in the shape of Money Marks was upon him. He had provoked the dog until he had broken his chain, and he must pay the dreadful penalty of his cowardly conduct.

With a sob of joy and gratified revenge, Marks sprang upon him.

The captain felt a couple of hands grasp his throat, tighten around it, and, with a feeble groan, he fell tottering to the ground.

It was a critical moment in the life of Captain Arlee.

The battle was turned with a vengeance, and he who had lately been the cruel, insulting tormentor, was now the victim at the mercy of a relentless conqueror.

In sober truth, it seemed as if the days on earth of Captain Arlee were numbered.

The glass containing the sands of his life was on end, and the golden grains were running through with a velocity that was truly awful in their rapidity.

He had, in mocking jest, but recently spoken in graphic language of the horrors of strangulation.

He had described to Money Marks, in the most vivid terms, the shocking spectacle of a hanging man—of one condemned to die upon the gallows.

There was the black and swollen tongue—out-lolling from the mouth—the starting eyeballs, and the black cord-like veins upon the forehead.

These now were his; for Money Marks' hands were clenched in a vice-like grip around his throat, and his life did not appear worth a minute's purchase.

Yet help was at hand.

Unexpected succour was advancing, for it was not

MONEY MARKS ATTEMPTS THE LIFE OF CAPTAIN ARLEE.

Heaven's good pleasure that the bad man should die then, with all his unrepented sins upon his soul.

The flight of his spirit to another world was checked; it had began to prepare for its heavenward flight, but a whisper made it fold anew its glossy pinions, and await the Creator's own good time.

The patrol fancied he heard a sound inside the prisoner's dungeon, which was indicative of a struggle.

Nor was he mistaken, as the reader knows.

Pushing open the door, he admitted a flood of light which enabled him to see that Captain Arlee was on the ground, and that Money Marks was bending over him.

There was not a moment to be lost.

Money Marks' murderous intention could be read in his flashing eyes, his quivering frame.

Clubbing his musket, the sentry dealt Money Marks a slight blow upon the head, which was not sufficient to break his skull, although it had the effect of stunning him, and causing him to roll over like a helpless log.

Captain Arlee was saved.

Yet was he too weak and feeble to move.

The soldier dragged him into the open air, and allowed the cool breeze to fan his disfigured features.

"Just in time," muttered the patrol; "a minute later, and all would have been over. This service ought to be a pound or two in my pocket; for I have saved his life."

Captain Loyd G. Bannister was communicated with, and he was speedily upon the spot.

"What is the meaning of this disturbance?" he inquired.

"Been a fight, sir."

"Whose body is this lying on the ground?"

"Captain Arlee."

"Indeed! Water here! Make haste! Call the surgeon! Let him be blooded instantly!"

This was a precautionary measure which it was wise in the extreme to adopt. The surgeon made an incision in his left arm, and allowed the hot and streaming purple blood to fall upon the ground.

When he had let out enough, he bound up the arm with a piece of linen rag, and had the satisfaction of seeing his patient open his eyes, and return to his senses.

As soon as he was conscious, he asked, in a weak tone of voice, for some water, which was given him.

Then he said—

"Hang him! Let the prisoner die—*at once!*"

"At once!" repeated Captain Loyd G. Bannister.

"Yes, yes," replied the prostrate man, eagerly.

"He has not been tried."

"I will hold you harmless."

"I daresay; but you forget I am not under your orders. I am only amenable to the commander-in-chief, as I myself am the officer commanding in this district. I cannot reconcile it with the conscientious discharge of my duties to hang the man until I have tried him, and given him the benefit of a doubt, if there be one in his favour. I am sorry to disagree with you, but——"

"Say no more," cried Captain Arlee. "I recognise the difficulty in which you are placed, and bow before your cogent reasoning."

"What shall I do to please you?"

"Order a drum-head court-martial at once."

"Willingly."

"I can give my evidence as I lie here. Perhaps you have some wine or spirits in the guard-house—if so, may I beg the favour of a stimulant?"

"You shall have one," replied Loyd G. Barrister, who despatched one of his men for the required cordial.

Money Marks was still, in a state of stupor, and knew not that by Captain Arlee's determined and malignant hostility his hours on earth were drawing to a close.

Captain Arlee drank a tumbler of wine at a draught, and it seemed to supply the place of that blood which he had lately lost.

A soldier, by his desire, propped him up with a few lumps of turf, which served the purpose of pillows, and he was prepared to give his evidence against the man whom he hated beyond all others.

A drum was placed upon the ground, and as it was then dark—that is to say, as dark as a full moon and a clear sky, studded with burning glowing stars would permit the evening to be—several torches tied to long poles, which were fixed in the earth, were lighted.

They spitted and sputtered, and cast a lurid glare upon the romantic scene.

Captain Loyd G. Bannister sat upon the remains of a broken gun-carriage, and all those men in the battery who could be spared from their posts were ordered to stand around the space of ground enclosed by the flaring torches, so as to be a guard of honour, more than a guard for defensive purposes.

A little drummer-boy stood within the enclosure, and rattled away on the parchment at a signal from the colour-sergeant.

Two men went for Money Marks, and finding him insensible, knew not how to act.

The colour-sergeant was applied to in this dilemna, and he, too, was puzzled.

It seemed advisable under the peculiar circumstances of the case, to go to his commander and ask his guiding counsel.

"What is it, sergeant?"

"Man's insensible, sir."

"Let the surgeon attend him, and tell him to use what measures he thinks fit in his discretion to restore the prisoner to consciousness."

"Yes, sir."

The colour-sergeant returned to the dungeon, which was hard by, with the doctor, who was smoking a cigar.

"What's the matter with the fellow?" he inquired.

"Sentry, sir, touched him lightly on the head with the but-end of his musket."

"Oh! stunned is he? I'll bring him to."

"Very well, sir. Do you want anything?"

"Give me your bayonet."

He was supplied with a bayonet, and holding it up critically, felt the sharpness of the point, with which he was apparently satisfied, for he nodded his head, and, falling on his knees, began his operations.

Money Marks was in a state of extreme prostration, rather than in a deadly swoon. A little cold water sprinkled on his face would have revived him in a moment, but that was not accorded him—the surgeon in whose tender hands he was had a sharper and crueller method of restoring people to consciousness, and he was determined to use his skill in the present instance.

He deliberately ran the point of the bayonet with great force into the calf of the insensible man's leg.

Money Marks, roused by the pain, sprang into a sitting posture, with a cry of agony, wrung involuntarily from him by the severity of the torture to which he was ruthlessly subjected.

"Found your tongue, eh?"

Money Marks looked about him with a bewildered expression.

"Where am I?" he asked.

"In H—ll, my boy, and what do you think of your new quarters? You have just been hanged, you know," was the coarse reply which the surgeon thought fit to make.

"Hanged!" repeated Money Marks, mistily.

"Yes, to be sure. Now then, you young Satanos, wake up there, and bring a few dry pine faggots to roast our new guest."

"Water! water!" said Money Marks.

"We don't keep it on the premises," replied the surgeon, with a laugh.

Money Marks in a few minutes recovered sufficiently to know where he was, and what had happened. He was very faint and ill.

"Give the poor devil a little Bourbon," said the surgeon.

This was a sort of whisky, so-called from being manufactured principally in Bourbon County, Kentucky.

They gave the prisoner a horn-mug full of the fiery spirit.

He drank it to the dregs.

The powerful stimulant had an extraordinary effect upon him, and, in a few minutes, made him, if not quite intoxicated, certainly light-headed.

In this sad state he was led out of the prison, and taken between two soldiers to the place selected for the holding of the drum-head court martial.

Directly he appeared, Loyd G. Bannister read the article of war constituting the court-martial, and this formality disposed of, he called upon the prisoner to plead.

"Are you guilty or not guilty?"

"Before I reply to that question," replied Money Marks, in an unsteady voice, "I demand the written accusations and charges to be brought against me."

He was perfectly right in demanding this, and Captain Bannister made no opposition to the demand, although Mr. Arlee was sadly annoyed at the delay.

He was longing to feast his greedy eyes upon the inanimate form of his enemy as it dangled cold and lifeless from a gallows.

"Captain Arlee, what do you allege against the prisoner?"

"First, that he is an enemy of the Confederate States."

This was written down.

"Secondly, that he is a Federal spy."

"Yes."

"Thirdly, that he has been guilty of piracy upon the high seas, and that he captured, illegally and piratically, the ship of which I was formerly captain, when she was peaceably steaming into Charleston harbour."

"Is that all?" asked Mr. Bannister, laying down his pen.

"It is; and enough too to hang him and a dozen more," he muttered beneath his breath.

"You hear the charges against you, prisoner," said Loyd G. Bannister; "what reply do you make? You are now in possession of the ear of the court and may say whatever you have a wish to say. I will only urge upon you the necessity of being as brief as you can, and of keeping as close to the point as you are able."

"I dispute the authority by virtue of which this court is constituted, and I refuse to admit its jurisdiction, and I also most distinctly refuse to plead," said Money Marks, emboldened by the liquor he had imbibed.

"On what grounds?"

"Because I am a British subject."

"Ha, ha!" laughed Captain Arlee, "that excuse will not avail you, my good fellow."

"Nevertheless, it is true."

"And I, who am well known as a man of honour and veracity, declare the contrary, for I have no doubt whatever that you are little better than a Yankee spy."

"It is false; I am, as I say, a British subject, and I demand the assistance of my consul."

"The excuse is not legitimate; and I, as president of this court, rule that it cannot avail you," said Captain Loyd G. Bannister.

"Then you will be my murderers," said Money Marks, lifting his eyes solemnly to Heaven.

"That is our own risk; we think differently. If you have no more to say I shall proceed to pass sentence upon you."

"I deny the legality of the court, and I enter my most solemn protest against your murderous proceedings."

"Have you anything further to say, prisoner?"

Money Marks folded his arms resolutely across his breast, and looked disdainfully at those who were about to promulgate his death-warrant.

"The charges I consider fully proven, for the prisoner has not attempted to deny what has been alleged against him," said Captain Bannister. "There is another thing which would in my eyes be quite sufficient to justify sentence of death being passed against him, and that is his audacity in daring to raise his slaughtering hand against a gentleman holding the commission of the Confederate States, with intent to murder him."

"I wish I had," interposed Money Marks, with a maniacal laugh.

"Silence!"

"Taking everything into consideration, and seeing that there is not one extenuating circumstance which can go in mitigation of punishment, I shall proceed to pass the sentence of the court upon the prisoner."

There was a death-like silence, which lasted for half a minute.

Captain Arlee's eyes twinkled with gratified malignity.

The torches flared and glittered and cast their ghost-like light upon the scene, which was picturesque and interesting in spite of the iniquitous work which was going on.

"The sentence of the court upon you, Money Marks," said the president, "is that you be taken without the battery, and there hung by the neck to the first tree, until you are dead."

This sentence startled Money Marks, who was horrified at the idea of being hanged. To be shot would have been a less ignoble way of losing his life.

"I have one favour to ask," he said.

"What is it? If it be in my power and consistent with my position and my duties to grant it, I will do so."

"Let me be shot. I cannot bear the idea of being hanged like a dog; you may at least grant me this poor favour."

Captain Loyd G. Bannister was about to comply with this request, when Arlee caught him by the arm in a nervous and excited grip, and pulled him towards him, saying in an anxious whisper—

"No, no; shooting is the death of an honourable man and a soldier. Don't listen to him; let such a scoundrel as he be hanged by the neck with the thickest rope in the battery."

"I cannot grant your request," said Bannister, in a cold, hard voice.

"I am sorry I condescended to ask so slight a favour," replied Money Marks, loftily.

"Let the prisoner be taken away and executed in half-an-hour's time in accordance with the terms of the sentence which this honourable court has imposed upon him."

Money Marks was accordingly taken away, bound, and placed in a corner of an earthwork.

"Come, my fine fellow, settle your feathers before you take your long flight," said the sergeant; "and if you have anything to do in the way of prayers, do it quick, for we've no parson to help you along, and time's short."

"Sergeant," said Money Marks.

"Well, my lad?"

"I want a word with you."

"Two if you like."

"There is a lady in Charleston, who is in Captain Arlee's power. Contrive to see her, and say that I died with her name on my lips, and with a prayer for her welfare in my heart. Tell her, sergeant, that I loved her as I firmly believe man never loved woman before, and that I am her's in Heaven as I have been her's on earth."

"It may be you wont go there," said the sergeant.

"Go where?"

"To Heaven."

"Why not?"

"If you have done all they say you have, you're not likely to get the celestial ticket."

"Ah! you have life before you, and you may have your joke. I am to be cut off in the flower of my youth, and I have no joking in me now; but I do not think I was presumptuous in saying that I would think of Viola in Heaven, for my path hitherto has not been deeply sin-stained, and I truly repent me of those sins which I may have committed in the rashness and folly of youth."

"You want me to go to this lady."

"Yes."

"What do you say her name is?"

"Miss Cathcart—Viola Cathcart."

"And tell her you died loving her."

"If you will be so kind."

"Oh, yes; I'll do it safe enough. My mother used to say it was unlucky to refuse a dying man anything, and so I believe it is. I'll do it for you; don't you fret."

"Sergeant," said Money Marks.

"Well, what now?"

He pointed to a small ring which he wore on his little finger. It was made of plain gold with a small diamond sparkling in the centre.

"Take this to her with my fondest love; bid her think of me whenever she sees the ring."

"I will, I will," replied the rough sergeant, who was affected to tears by the speech he had just heard, so simple and moving was Money Marks' tone and manner.

He brushed a tear from his eye with the back of his hand, muttering—

"Sam Collins, what's the matter with you? are you turning silly in your old age? This wont do, Sam."

He then went away, leaving Money Marks for ten minutes to his own reflections.

The unfortunate young man, whose intense devotion to the woman he loved had made him rush into the hands of his enemies, was incapable of deep thought or serious reflection; his mind was a mass of chaotic ideas, and his brain was in a whirl.

In ten minutes he was to die!

Ten minutes only had to elapse before his soul was violently hurled into the fathomless gulf of eternity.

Awful reflection! awful thought!

No wonder his cheek blanched, and his countenance fell.

CHAPTER XXVI.

AT THE FOOT OF THE GALLOWS.

But a short time elapsed before the sergeant again made his appearance and intimated in a few rough words that the time had arrived for the thread of his life to be cut.

Money Marks rose silently and followed his conductor to a small plantation some dozen and a half yards from the battery.

The sergeant and his prisoner were accompanied by a file of six men, not to guard against an attack or a rescue, for they never dreamt of the possibility of such a thing, but for the sake of appearances, and to see that the sentence which had been passed upon the prisoner was duly carried out.

Captain Arlee made a desperate effort to walk as far as the spot appointed for the execution, but he was so exhausted from the effects of the severe handling he had received from Money Marks, that after he had progressed a few paces, he staggered and fell.

A soldier was standing by, and he at once ran to his assistance.

"Why the devil, sir, did you allow me to fall?" said Arlee. "I shall report you to your superior officer, and have you punished."

"What for, sir?"

"Don't question me. Help me along; I want to see the ruffian who was just now tried by court-martial executed. Lead me to the place."

The man offered Captain Arlee his arm, but even with that support he was unable to go on; his legs tottered and gave way beneath him.

"Stand up, sir," said the man, with a grin.

He was not under Arlee's command, and he thought he could afford to have his joke.

"Curse your impudence. I'll make you smart for this, my good fellow," cried Captain Arlee, passionately.

"Beg pardon, I'm sure, sir; only said 'stand up,'" replied the man, apologetically.

"Hold your tongue."

"Certainly, sir."

"Get a litter; I must—I will see this man hanged."

"A litter, sir?"

"Yes."

"Haven't one, but I daresay a hurdle will do. Have a hurdle, sir?"

"Yes, yes, anything I can lie on; make haste or he will have been turned off, and all will be over."

"Shan't be a minute, sir."

The soldier went away at that species of jog-trot, which in military parlance is called the double, and in a short time he returned with a hurdle, which had been used in the erection of fascines and earthworks.

Laying it on the ground, he lifted upon it the body of Captain Arlee, who was half-fainting and only sustained by the hope of seeing his enemy hanged.

Then arose a new difficulty; the burden was too heavy for one man unaided to carry, and he stopped short.

"Well, my good fellow, what are you waiting for?" said Captain Arlee.

"Too heavy, sir."

"What's too heavy?"

"You are."

"Get some one else, then."

"All on duty, sir."

"Go and find some one," vociferated Arlee, whose pallor changed to an angry purple as he grew warm with rage.

The soldier went to another part of the battery and found a man who was able to help him. The two took up the hurdle and carried it without the battery.

Money Marks was at the foot of the gallows.

The rope was round his neck.

He had said his last prayer.

The rope had been slung over the projecting branch of a tree, and the process of strangling a man was ready to be commenced.

"Stop! stop!" cried Captain Arlee, anxiously.

"What is it, sir?" said the sergeant, who was the executioner, loosing the rope around Money Marks' neck.

"Stop till I can come up. Stop, stop! I want to see it all."

"Very well, sir."

Captain Arlee had by this timely exclamation reprieved his enemy for a few minutes. The hurdle was carried up close to the foot of the hastily-extemporised gallows, and laid upon the green sward.

"Prop me up," said Arlee.

One of the men did so.

"Ha! ha!" laughed Arlee. "Look at me, Money Marks, I have come to see you hanged—to see you die—and gloat over your struggles and mortuary convulsions—do you hear that? Look at me. I, your enemy, am here; and I want you to know it, so that the knowledge of my proximity may embitter your last moments. Have you forgotten that Viola is mine—mine—MINE?"

As he said this his voice rose gradually higher and higher, culminating at last in a shrill treble.

Money Marks cast a glance of compassionate pity upon him. He seemed to be at peace with all men, and to feel neither vindictiveness nor malignity.

Yet those who watched his countenance narrowly might have remarked a twinge of exquisite anguish and most acute pain convulse his features when the captain alluded to Viola and said that she was his.

The exertion of speaking was too much for Captain Arlee; his head fell back, and his eyes closed.

He had swooned.

"Two men here," cried the sergeant.

Two men came at his call.

"Lay hold of the rope, and when I say pull, haul him up."

"Right, sir."

A few seconds elapsed.

Money Marks looked at the blue sky, and cast an imploring glance, which seemed to penetrate its fleecy depths and ask the prevailing genius of the clouds for sympathy and help.

"Pull," cried the sergeant.

The men had scarcely taughtened the rope, however—Money Marks had scarcely began to choke and gurgle and gasp for breath, when two shots came from the thicket, and laid the executioners low.

Fancying that an attack was being made by the enemy in force, the sergeant ordered his four remaining men to retreat to the shelter of the battery, which they immediately did without the least delay.

Indeed, so anxious were they to gain its shelter, that they did not stand upon the order of their going; the consequence of which was that they left Money Marks to his fate, which turned out to be a much pleasanter one than they had intended for him.

Fortunately his own men had arrived, under Cuffy's guidance, just in time to save him from a violent and ignominious death.

Running forward, Cuffy seized his master by the arm, and drew him into the middle of the little band of heroes, by whom he was instantly surrounded.

Then the retreat began.

Great merriment was excited owing to Cuffy's having lost his coat; and many a joke was made about the negro having appeared in his true colours, and having shown the "white feather."

Money Marks recovered his serenity, and although awfully shocked at the imminency of the danger through which he had passed, was forced to join in the hearty cachinnation which resounded on all sides.

Cuffy was as good-humoured as any of them; and seeing that there was no help for it, submitted with a good grace to the ridicule with which he was overwhelmed, and marched along with an air of conscious dignity, as if fully aware that he was somebody of distinction—at all events an object of notoriety—and consequently the observed of all observers.

In the hurry of the moment Money Marks did not think of Captain Arlee, who was afterwards taken into the battery by the soldiers, who at first thought the enemy was concealed in the neighbourhood and intended to make an attack in force upon their position! but when some hours elapsed, and no more shots were fired, they ventured to send out a party to reconnoitre, who brought back Captain Arlee and the two dead soldiers, and reported that the country round was entirely free from men.

Money Marks soon recovered from his fright, but it was some time before Cuffy could get rid of the tar and feathers with which he had been so carefully covered.

By a plentiful application of lard and hot water the feathers were eventually got rid of, and he looked more like a human being again.

The vessel was reached in safety, and Money Marks was forced to continue his cruise much against his will; had he been able to use his own discretion, and have his own way, he would have remained in the neighbourhood of Charleston until he heard some tidings of Viola, and was able to rescue her and make her his wife.

But it was clear that the temper of his men would not tolerate this measure; they were eager for action and tired of an idle life, so that all he could do was to acquiesce with as good a grace as possible and lead them onwards.

CHAPTER XXVII.

THE PHANTOM SHIP.

MONEY MARKS now gave himself up to his fate, and threw off the faintest semblance of disguise. He had assumed a piratical career, and he determined to gain the reputation which he felt assured would shortly accrue to him.

They sailed some miles before they met with any craft which they cared about overhauling; but at length they met with a merchantman, which turned out a great prize.

It had been to California with a cargo of spices and other delicate goods, and was bringing to Havanna a number of cases of bullion.

The crew were unarmed, for they had not anticipated an attack upon the great and pathless waste of ocean; highwaymen of the seas, in their opinion, being things of the past and gentlemen to read of in romances which chronicle the life of Paul Jones and Captain Kidd.

It was considerably against Money Marks' will to injure the crew of the vessel, but self-preservation compelled him to put his merciful feelings on one side and treat them as prudence dictated.

The crew, fifteen in number, were bound round the eyes with a handkerchief or convenient piece of bunting. Their hands were fastened securely behind their backs, and they were made to walk the plank.

That is to say, a plank was put over the ship's side and the unhappy men were told to walk along it.

They, never suspecting the infamous cruelty of which they were to be the victims, obeyed the mandate of their conquerors and walked, not knowing that they were wandering towards a watery grave.

But so it was.

A despairing wail and a dull splash heralded their death, and was their only epitaph.

When this mournful scene was over the ill-fated ship was scuttled and permitted to sink, and the pirate pursued her iniquitous way.

It is best at all times to have a hero who is good and virtuous, but it is well known that a great proportion of the world is desperately wicked, and it is as well sometimes to portray the deeds of the ungodly, so that the rising generation may by their fate be deterred from emulating an example which can only be fraught with extreme mortification and condign punishment in the end.

Money Marks was led almost insensibly into a career of crime; he was to a certain extent the child of fate and the victim of circumstances.

Yet it is to be regretted that he was not sufficiently high-principled to battle against the temptations with which his path was beset, and so defeat the machinations of the arch-fiend, who is ever wandering over the surface of the earth seeking whom he may devour.

All we have to do, as a faithful chronicler of this extraordinary young man's singular career, is to record faithfully what befel him, and how he sped in the matter of his love for the unfortunate but always lovely Miss Viola Cathcart.

Poor lady! hers was indeed a sorrowful life, and one not at all enchanting to the eye of a young and beautiful girl.

The sailors found themselves in possession of a large sum of money when the booty was divided amongst them, and they clamorously sought their commander, and, in a manner, insisted, that they should be allowed to touch at some port, and spend the money which they had earned.

Money Marks refrained from giving them a decided answer, telling them that he would think the matter over, and let them know his decision in a short time.

Going to his cabin, he sent for Hercules and Pat Doolan, and conferred with them.

They were of opinion that the wisest and most sensible thing he could do would be to acquiesce in the crew's request.

"You see, it's this way with them, captain," exclaimed Sampson Hercules, "they're not what you may call regular sailors, subject to the Articles of War, and all that. They're true salts to the backbone, of course; but we're all leading a risky sort of life, and now they've got about fifty pounds apiece, they want to go ashore and see a bit of life."

"Yes, I can see that is their motive," said Money Marks.

"Jack never can keep his money, and what I say, cap, is, let 'em go and spend it, and when it's all gone they'll think of the jolly spree they've had, and be all the more anxious to get another haul."

"Do you think there is any chance of any of them informing against us?"

"Not I."

"You know them better than I do; let me have the benefit of your advice—I ask it frankly."

"I don't think there ever sailed under the black flag a truer-hearted set of fellows," replied Hercules.

"Or any other flag," interposed Pat Doolan; "sure, and they are altogether like a hive of bees glued to one another with new honey."

"Are you both sure of this?"

"Troth yes, captain, darlint."

"And you, Sampson?"

"I agree with Pat; the crew are true blue, all of them, and I would not mind trusting them with my life to-morrow."

"That is good," said Money Marks. "Your united assurances have decided me in letting them have their own way; they shall be allowed three days in which to get drunk and spend their money."

"Three!" said Hercules, deprecatingly.

"Yes; is it not enough?"

"Give 'em six, and sail on Sunday."

"Very well. I thought a sailor could spend any amount of money in a given time."

"So he can," replied Hercules, "but I don't want them to be driven. When they've spent their money, which will be long before the six days have elapsed, they will come on board, and wish for the engines to be moving and the sails to be set."

"Talking of engines reminds me that we are getting short of coals."

"Then we can kill two birds with one stone," replied Hercules; "we can coal and oblige the men."

"What port are we near?"

"As well as I can make out, captain, we are on the coast of Africa."

Money Marks went to his bureau, and looking at some of his books, began with pen and ink to take the ship's reckoning.

"We are within fifty miles of Buenos Ayres," he exclaimed, "shall we put in there?"

"Rather hot and dirty, but a first chop place, cap," answered Hercules.

"Very well, then; be it so. Go to the men and tell them that we are going to steam into Ayres at once, and that I have consented to give them a week there, bar Sunday."

"Yes, sir."

"And Hercules."

"Sir."

"Tell them also that they must work well afterwards."

"Divil doubt them but they will," chimed in Pat, with a sagacious shake of the head.

"You, Pat, had better take the helm for a time, and change the ship's course three points to the south-eastward."

"Ay, ay, sir. Three points, is it?"

"Three."

The two lieutenants went away, and soon afterwards a tremendous cheer rang through the vessel; it was the spontaneous outburst of the crew, who were overjoyed at the idea of having a good fling in a town, while they had plenty of money in their pockets.

That evening the sun went down fiery red in the heavens. The old sailors shook their heads and prophesied a storm, but those who had less experience on the bosom of the fickle ocean laughed at the predictions of those whom they called the croakers, and said that before the storm came upon them —if any storm was coming at all—they would be in harbour and enjoying themselves in defiance of boisterous and tempestuous weather.

At eleven o'clock at night the wind whistled ominously through the cordage, and seemed to talk to the sailors in a mysterious tongue. They could not understand these wind utterances, but as the waves began to hiss and boil, no one could deny that the elements were about to battle.

The night was as dark as pitch; thick, heavy, rapidly drifting clouds obscured the sometimes luminous surface of the horizon, except when the moon, faint, pale, watery, broke through them, and threw a few sickly flashes of intermittent light upon the heaving, seething waters.

Oh, grand is a battle of the elements, when viewed from the deck of a vessel tempest-tossed upon the bosom of the trackless sea.

Splendid indeed is the combat, truly magnificent the horrid fight.

The din of the crashing thunder, the heavy pelting of the rain—tropical in its volume and its violence—falling with a hiss into the water, the rapid flashes of the blinding lightning, with its dangerous fork which has deprived many a man of his dearly prized vision.

Money Marks was always to the fore in times of danger; he never shrank from the performance of the most arduous duty, and this quality endeared him to his men, and was their admiration quite as much as his unvaried good humour and general kindness of behaviour to one and all.

He gave his orders through a speaking-trumpet, and the ship was put well before the wind, the engines were worked at quarter power, and the vessel rode before the blast with bare poles.

Pat Doolan was standing by the captain's side, Sampson Hercules being a good helmsman, and moreover the strongest man in the ship, was steering.

Suddenly a lurid flash of lightning lit up the surrounding objects with a momentary splendour.

What was Money Marks' surprise to perceive a ship bearing down upon him with incredible swiftness.

She was of an ancient build, and square-rigged, yet she had all sails flying—even the studding-sails were set.

She burnt no light.

It seemed to Money Marks that a bad look-out was kept, though he could plainly distinguish several shadowy forms upon the deck.

Turning round with great quickness and equal presence of mind, he shouted to the man at the helm—

"Hard-a-port."

"Ay, ay, sir," was the response only faintly heard in the rush of the wind.

"Ship on the larboard bow."

"Port she is, sir."

Money Marks trembled from head to foot. It seemed impossible that his ship could avoid being run into by the approaching vessel.

The ensuing few minutes were the most anxious of his life.

But no; all was safe—the danger was avoided. There was no shock, no crash, no bulwarks staved in, no foundering.

"Whist, captain," said Pat Doolan, in a terrified whisper.

The Irishman was very superstitious, and fancying something supernatural about the appearance of the strange ship, thought, in the exaggeration of his imagination, that he smelt sulphur.

"What is it?" replied Money Marks.

"It was an awful moment any way."

"Why?"

"It was no mortial vessel."

"What then?"

"That we've so often heard of."

"What do you mean?"

"Vanderdecken's flying craft."

"The flying Dutchman?"

"Yes, the phantom ship. Whist, whist, captain darlint, and don't be saying nothing against it."

"Silence, you fool," cried Money Marks, clutching him angrily by the arm.

"Oh, yes, I'll be silent; but it's all as thrue as Brian Boru, and that big bosthoon of a giant what——"

"Hold your tongue, I say," repeated Money Marks, in a still more exalted tone; "and not one word to the crew of what you have seen, or what your superstitious fears bid you suspect."

"No, no."

"Do you understand me?"

"Is it undherstand, you—you mane?"

"Yes."

"Troth, an' it's me father's son——"

"Listen to me. If the crew fancy they have seen the famous phantom-ship of which Philip Vanderdecken was commander, they will be discontented."

There was another flash of lightning, which, as before, illumined the ocean.

Eagerly Money Marks strained his eyes in every direction, but the mysterious craft was nowhere to be seen.

She had altogether disappeared.

Pat Doolan slunk away, muttering—

"Sorra a one of us will be alive to-morrow. Oh, Lord! oh, Lord!"

The phantom-ship had vanished. Whither had she gone? Money Marks was perplexed, and well he might be.

To see distinctly with your own eyes—eyes that are not in the habit of deceiving you—a ship bearing down upon you in full sail—and how she could live in such a sea with such a press of canvas was not the least remarkable circumstance about the affair—was very wonderful.

Wonderful, in point of fact, is not the word for that species of astonishment which took possession of the captain of the pirate.

He was completely overwhelmed, for he could not treat the occurrence as an optical delusion, it being seen by another besides himself, and perhaps by many others, though of this fact he was not as yet fully advised.

It happened, unfortunately, that the crew, who were for the most part on deck, had witnessed the apparition—for such they took it to be.

Everyone knows how superstitious sailors are, and how they are always affected by anything which partakes of the supernatural. They conversed with one another in whispers, shook their heads gloomily, and predicted all sorts of calamities and misfortunes of which they were to be the victims.

The storm continued with unabated fury during the whole of that night and part of the next day.

Money Marks now found the use of that knowledge which he had acquired on board the *Swamp Snake*, during his first voyage, for it enabled him without any difficulty to manœuvre the vessel, and make her ride out the storm.

He was not driven a single inch out of his reckoning, and when the afternoon arrived and the storm abated he was sailing direct for Buenos Ayres before a steady wind and engines that were propelling the ship at the rate of ten miles an hour.

When the tempest subsided, and the crew found that no accident had happened to them they regained their serenity, and some of them tried to laugh at the phantom-ship which had met them in the storm of the night before.

The laugh, however, with which they favoured their companions was an unhealthy, somewhat unnatural laugh, which jarred and grated upon the ear, making the listener think that the other did not mean it, and was not in earnest, but simply playing a part.

There was one man whose name was Croker. He was Croker by name, and croaker by nature; for he always looked on the black side, and did what he could to frighten and discourage his comrades.

Croker did not neglect the opportunity which the appearance of the phantom ship gave him, of indulging in his favourite pastime. He declared that he had sailed in many ships, and had been to every country on the face of the globe, and the result of his experience was, that whenever Vanderdecken's craft showed itself in a tempest, the ship to which the spectacle was vouchsafed was sure to go to the bottom!

"That ship," he said, emphatically, "is doomed, mates, just as much as if she had lost her A 1 at Lloyd's, and was sent to the breakers to be broken up."

Finding that Croker was unsettling the minds of the men Money Marks sent for him, and remonstrated with him upon his conduct, but he found that the most persuasive arguments were of no avail, to shake Croker's faith in the apparition.

"I have sent for you, Croker," said Money Marks, "to ask you, why you are so silly as to fill the men's minds with a lot of trash. I should have thought that a man of your sense and experience knew better than to believe in phantom ships."

"It ain't ships, sir."

"What then?"

"*The* Phantom Ship. There is but one, and that belongs to Vanderdecken! Didn't I see the Dutchman last night standing on the deck, with his trumpet in one hand and his right hand pointing to the bottom of the sea? To be sure I did. It was all just as I saw it before, now, more than ten years ago."

"Saw it before?"

"Yes, sir."

"Where?"

"Not in these latitudes."

"Pray let me hear about that. But, Croker——"

"Sir."

"Don't be pitching any of your long yarns into me: you are not in the forecastle now."

"Ay, ay, sir. I wont pitch you no yarns; what I shall tell you is as true as gospel. We was off the coast of Corea, an arkypellago they call it. Mebbe you've heard of it?"

"I have seen it on the maps, though I have never been there."

"Right, sir: it's in the China Seas, and the islands lay as thick together as clusters of grapes, so you may think it is no easy matter to steer through them."

"I should think not."

"Well, sir, we did with great care, and one night we got near a mountain which was a volcano, and it began emptying as hard as it could, sending out smoke and stones as thick as hail.

"Two of our men were killed by smoking hot stones falling on them."

"Indeed."

"In the midst of this we saw the Flying Dutchman scudding along as no mortal ever went, and she passed over all the rocks without being damaged in the least.

"Really; that is wonderful," said Money Marks, mockingly.

"The rocks, sir, if you understand me, seemed to go right

through her. You may laugh, but if it isn't true I wish I may drop down dead."

"True or not true—and I don't for a moment doubt your veracity," said Money Marks, "I must beg of you, Croker, not to upset the minds of the crew with silly stories."

"Saving your presence, they're not silly," replied Croker, doggedly.

"Never mind whether they are or not; my orders to you are to hold your tongue, and say no more about it."

"Very well, sir; I didn't do it with any bad intention."

"Of course not. I did not accuse you of that. Go back to the men, and tell them we shall run into port in four hours' time: the land is visible through a glass at present."

Croker went away with his news; a loud hurrah broke the stillness of the sultry air and the men soon forgot the phantom ship in their joy at the near prospect of being able to land and enjoy themselves after their own fashion with their ill-gotten money.

CHAPTER XXVIII.

A WEIRD PREDICTION.

BUENOS AYRES is an ancient city though it cannot boast of the highest antiquity. Its trade is tolerably large, and would be larger were it not for the unhealthy nature of the climate, which prevents Europeans from settling there.

Money Marks left some men in charge of the ship; the others were permitted to go on shore, he knew that he could trust them, and felt persuaded that for their own sakes they would not prolong their stay on shore beyond the time he had allowed them.

There were just hands enough on board the vessel to prevent any outrage being committed upon her by any hostile craft.

Money Marks left Pat Doolan in command, and went on shore with Sampson Hercules. They put up at a small inn or caravansery outside the town.

It was built upon a portion of an ancient road consisting entirely of firmly embedded pebbles which having never been broken up, stand alone like the fragment of an elevated causeway.

Near the inn was a shrine, in which dwelt an aged female, noted for her sanctity. Many ignorant persons made pilgrimages to the hermitage, and the saint was in the habit of giving her blessing to some and her curse to others, but to all and of all she would prophesy, if sufficiently well paid for doing so.

The sides of the road leading to the shrine had gradually been lowered by numerous pilgrims, who for years have sought the pebbles to preserve as relics.

A wide arch-like excavation, produced by the same superstitious industry, had given it the resemblance of a dismantled bridge.

Through this aperture it was considered an act of devotion to pass; and people at all hours might be seen performing the ceremony with all due solemnity, rubbing their shoulders against the pebbly sides, while they repeated certain prayers and formulas with great earnestness.

Money Marks and Hercules were idle, and wished to see all the sights which a rather dull city could afford them, and as the cave or hermitage of the old lady was close at hand, they resolved to pay her a visit, and consult their oracle.

They accordingly waited until the heat of the day was past, and then sought the secluded spot in which the hermitage was built.

The place was a prison of the most extraordinary kind.

The woman had caused a small tomb-like structure to be built, when she was only two and twenty years of age. She had entered it, and made the bricklayers wall her up with the strongest masonry; a little window at the top admitted light and air, and a hole in the wall permitted the recluse to utter her weird predictions to those without.

Through this hole the contributions of the admirers of the saint were dropped; and the saint declared that she should accumulate an immense sum, so that when she died, the dwelling in which she lived might be her sepulchre, and the money the people would find inside was to be devoted to the building of a church of magnificent proportions, to be erected on the site and over the tomb in which her bones rested.

For more than forty years the strange woman had lived in that awful tomb.

Away from the world, from all she loved, from the smiling face of nature, and the communion of her fellow-creatures, cut off from social intercourse and buried alive.

It was a terrible fate!

People who were fond of legendary lore said they had heard that Sister Therese, as she was called, had in days gone by been a lovely young woman, with long flowing golden hair, a soft skin, a loving disposition which beamed out of soft, blue, dove-like eyes.

If that were the case, it was pity the authorities allowed her to immolate herself as she had done. Yet her singular sacrifice redounded to the fame of the town, and many people from the surrounding districts came trooping in to pay their vows, and show their devotion to the chaste and sanctified sister Therese.

But there were others equally well versed in legendary lore who declared, in an equally solemn manner, that Therese was not chaste—that there was a spot upon her 'scutcheon, and that remorse had driven her to expiate, by a life of prayer, the one great sin of her youth.

These people were generally looked upon as base calumniators, but they stuck to their story nevertheless.

They spoke of a handsome man who had professed love to Therese, and who gained the confidence of a weak loving and affectionate girl only to break his vows, and shatter the fond, confiding heart which had, in a moment of foolish infatuation, placed itself in his power for good or evil.

He exercised his power for evil—cast away the loving heart, and left its owner desolate and forlorn, to pine for the days that had gone, and to long in vain for her lost honour.

Every one believed that Therese had the power of prophecy; it was a gift, they said, accorded to her in return for the life of piety which she had led for so many years.

When Money Marks and his companion Sampson Hercules reached the tomb, they had to wait a short time—until two pilgrims, who had preceded them, had been disposed of by the saint.

At last, it was Money Marks' turn, and he went laughingly to the little orifice, and, putting in a gold coin as his votive offering, said, in a low voice—

"They say you have the gift of prophecy?"

"They told you the truth," replied a harsh voice, from within.

"Can you prophesy as to my future?"

"I can."

"What am I?"

"A sailor."

"Ha! you know that."

Money Marks was surprised at this declaration, for he was not aware that the saint could see him, except in a very cursory manner, and that only through the narrow and circumscribed aperture through which the conversation was conducted and carried on.

"I can tell you more than that," continued the same harsh hollow voice.

"You can?"

"Yes."

"Speak."

"Your calling is more hazardous than that of a sailor usually is."

"Strange!" muttered Money Marks to himself. "Can this woman have the gift of second sight? What else can you tell me?"

"More than you would like to hear."

"Fear not that I shall be moved. I am able and willing to hear all that you have to say."

"You speak with the levity of a young man, and though puzzled at my powers of divination, you deride what you cannot understand."

"Have the kindness to say what you know about my future?"

"I will mention one or two circumstances which intimately concern you, and which are about to happen shortly," replied the hermit.

"I am ready," said Money Marks.

"More at present I will not tell you, but if you should have reason to believe in my prophetic powers, you can seek me again, and I will then further raise the veil of the future for you."

There was nothing jocular about Money Marks' manner now.

He had imbibed a respect for the saint, and waited wonderingly, almost tremblingly, for what she might say next.

"You had a vision forty-eight hours ago," she said, in a weird-wild tone of voice. "My spirit was on the waters, and I also saw it. How the storm raged and crashed! The phantom-ship——"

"Good God!" ejaculated Money Marks, involuntarily.

"What is the matter?" inquired Sampson Hercules, coming forward.

"Nothing! nothing! Stand back!" said Money Marks, waving him off with outstretched hand.

The first lieutenant fell back.

"The phantom-ship," resumed the saint, the thread of whose discourse had been broken by Money Marks' hasty exclamation, "bore down upon the pirate."

"It did."

"And then it vanished."

"Yes."

"That vision prognosticates misfortune and calamity."

"Alas!" said Money Marks, feeling that the strange and mystic being within the vault was speaking truth.

"But out of that shall come good."

"How good!"

"You love."

"Incredible! Nothing is concealed from you!"

"Time and space are nought to me, when the mystic cloud envelopes me," replied the saint.

"Proceed."

"You love, I say."

"I do."

"But a short time will elapse before you will meet her."

"You say this in all sincerity?"

"Yes."

"She will be in want of your assistance."

"And I—shall I render it her."

"You will; at the same time, your enemy will be in your power."

"My enemy!"

"You have but one, and you will spare his life."

"Never, never, never!" he cried, in a loud tone. "Until now, I have placed implicit credence in your predictions, but I venture to deny the truth of what you have just stated, because I hate my enemy with such utter desperation, that were he in my power I should slay him with as little compunction as I should place my foot upon a worm."

"Nevertheless, you will find the truth to be as I have stated it," said the priestess, quietly.

"What else have you to tell me? Pardon me for my rude interruption."

"More! much more could I tell you, but——"

"I conjure you to answer me one!—only one question."

"Name it."

"Shall I die in my bed?"

"You will not," replied the oracle, in slow and solemn tones.

"That is as much as to say I shall die a violent death?"

"It is."

"Grant me one more question?"

"Well?"

"My parents—my unknown mother and father—shall I ever see them, and call them by their names?"

"I can answer no more questions at present," replied Sister Therese.

"I beg of you!"

"No prayers or intercessions will move me. When you have proved the truth of what I told you to-day, you may seek me again."

"Many thanks for the revelations you have made," said Money Marks. "I will, as you tell me, call upon you the next time I touch at this port."

He slipped another piece of gold through the aperture, and was about to take his departure, when the voice of the recluse sounded ominously, saying—

"Stop."

He stopped abruptly, and turning back, said—

"Have you aught else to say to me?"

"A few words of warning."

"Warning!"

"Yes."

"I listen."

"Danger lurks in the air of Buenos Ayres."

"Where? In what way? Explain," cried Money Marks, hurriedly.

But though he waited some time at the aperture, no answer was given him by the mysterious lady.

With a heavy heart, he left the oracular tomb, and taking his friend's arm, walked down the causeway in the direction of the town.

"What did she say to you?" inquired Sampson Hercules.

"A great deal."

"I wanted to have had my fortune told, but you hurried me away so quickly."

"Another time," replied Money Marks.

"Oh, yes; I know that there's time enough. What did she say to you?"

"Many things."

"Did you get your money's worth?"

"Yes, and more than it's worth," answered Money Marks gloomily.

"In that case I shall try my luck."

"Will you?"

"Yes."

"Take my advice."

"What's that?"

"Don't."

"And why not?"

"I'll tell you; I heard nothing that was good and gratifying."

"P'r'aps it's all lies," said Hercules, holding out his hand menacingly.

"It may be, for what I know, but *I don't think so*," replied Money Marks, thoughtfully.

After this the conversation flagged, and the two men walked on in silence until they reached the main streets of the town.

The weather was hot, and a sailor on shore is always more or less fond of drinking. Hercules proposed to his captain that they should recruit the wasted energies of the inner man.

No objection being made to this proposition, a *restaurant* was entered, and the pirates began to regale themselves on some iced liquors, while they smoked cigars made of very good tobacco.

Their manner was indolent, and they both wished to enjoy their dignified ease.

On the opposite side of the table at which they were sitting were three nautical men—that fact was easily perceptible from their garb. They were conversing eagerly together, though the greater part of the conversation was managed by two who appeared to have authority over the third.

The latter only spoke now and then, and when his interference seemed to be called for. The two already alluded to appeared to be gentlemen, their demeanour and general bearing being conducive to the support of that supposition.

CHAPTER XXIX.

H.M.S. "LOWFLYER."

MONEY MARKS was in what is commonly called a brown study. Sampson Hercules had gone to sleep over his Manilla cigar, its soporific properties having completely overpowered him.

Marks, although not intending to do so, was unable to help listening to the conversation of the men opposite to him.

They talked with the less reserve because Money Marks' eyes were shut, and it appeared to them that he, like his companion, had gone to sleep.

It may be as well to observe that the three men were officers on board Her Majesty's ship *Lowflyer*, which vessel had been put in commission by the Lords of the Admiralty, and sent to the Cape station and thereabouts to put a stop to the pernicious system of slavery which had obtained very much lately.

These three men will play an important part in this history, and it may be as well to describe them here.

Captain Stockwell was a man of about fifty years of age; he had been a disappointed man; having no interest, he did not get a ship until he was appointed to the *Lowflyer*, and then he determined to do his duty like a man, make a name for himself in the glorious annals of his country, and exterminate all slavers and pirates from off the face of the seas.

Mr. Stafford, his first lieutenant, first cousin and great friend, was twenty years younger, shrewd, ambitious, and daring.

BENBOW GIVES INFORMATION REGARDING THE PIRATE.

Benbow, the third man, was the boatswain of the *Lowflyer*, a hardworking, steady fellow, and taken about when on shore with the captain, as the latter's servant more than in any other capacity.

Benbow, unlike his splendid namesake, had the use of both his legs, and was almost as fine a specimen of humanity as Sampson Hercules himself, only he lacked a couple of inches of Hercules' stature, which was certainly as mighty as that of the far-famed Goliah of Gath.

Captain Stockwell and Stafford were engaged in an animated conversation, as has already been stated.

"I differ with you altogether," said Stockwell.

"But you have not weighed my arguments thoroughly," responded Stafford.

"I have, indeed."

"Allow me to repeat them."

"If you please," replied Captain Stockwell, carelessly.

"Well, then, in the first place, I am not at all satisfied with the appearance of the vessel."

"What is there unusual in it?"

"She is not a vessel of war apparently."

"Perhaps a merchantman?"

"No."

"Why not?"

"She is not laden; I can prove that assertion, because I can guess a vessel's tonnage as soon as I row round her; but she floats high in the water, having nothing but necessary ballast on board."

"What else?"

"She has hoisted the flag of the Federal States of America."

"What of that?" demanded Captain Stockwell.

"Simply this: I have noticed the crew while on shore, and they do not seem to me to be genuine Yankees; besides that, what ship will you find which permits so many of its men to go on shore at a time as this one? Almost all the men are allowed to land, and the money they spend is immense in its amount."

"How do you know this?"

"From my own observations; if you doubt the accuracy of my statements appeal to Benbow."

"Well, Benbow," said Captain Stockwell, "what have you to say?"

"It's all true, captain," replied the boatswain; "and I must say I don't like the lot at all: the way they goes on isn't the proper sort of way."

"Indeed! Well, Stafford, taking all you say for granted, what is the practical result of your observations? What does it all come to in £ s. d., as they say in the City?"

"I have scarcely made my mind up yet."

"Do you think she is a slaver?"

"Possibly," replied Stafford.

"You say that hesitatingly. What is your real opinion?"

"It is a singular one."

"Never mind."

"If I am wrong you will all laugh at me."

"Not I, for one."

"Well, if you will promise to treat my fantastic idea with tolerance, I will tell you what has occurred to me."

"Do so," replied Captain Stockwell, bending forward and listening attentively.

Money Marks almost held his breath, so great was his anxiety to know what was about to be uttered by the first lieutenant of H.M.S. *Lowflyer*.

He felt certain that his ship was the one in question and the one they were talking about, and his fear was that they suspected her to be a piratical craft.

"I think," said Lieutenant Stafford, "that she's a pirate."

"Ha, ha!" laughed Captain Stockwell.

"Ha, ha!" laughed Benbow, the bo'sun.

"What are you laughing at?" said Stafford, indignantly.

"At you. Why, who ever now-a-days heard of a pirate? The idea is absurd."

"Why so?"

"When highwaymen of the road went out of fashion, through a habit society had of hanging them at Tyburn, so did highwaymen of the seas. Ha, ha! what a funny notion!"

Money Marks had heard quite enough; he did not know who the men were whose conversation he had overheard, but he was positive that his ship was suspected by the acute Lieutenant Stafford.

He was not exactly alarmed, although he was a little frightened at the consequences.

Waking up with a simulated start, he touched his friend on the arm, and having awoke him, together they left the coffee-house.

"You have had a good sleep, haven't you?" said Money Marks, when they reached the street.

"Pretty tol-lol," replied Sampson Hercules, stretching his huge frame, and throwing about his arms so that he knocked off the hat of an inoffensive passer-by.

"What are you up to, eh?" cried the indignant—and justly indignant passenger.

"Only throwing my fins about like a big fish out of water," replied Hercules, with equanimity.

The passenger picked up his hat, clenched his fists, took three steps forward, and then hesitated, the size of his antagonist being so gigantic and out of the common, that for fear of a broken head he hesitated to attack him.

"Good night, my little shrimp," cried Hercules, with a loud laugh that sounded like a shout.

"Why don't you keep your arms to yourself, you overgrown monstrosity?" said Money Marks, jocularly.

"Don't know," replied the other, carelessly.

"Do you want a row?"

"Shouldn't object to a bit of Donnybrook, if it should come."

"What is the use of making a disturbance, just when we want to avoid notoriety?"

"No use that I see of."

"Why do it, then?"

"Oh! I don't know; we can't help our nature, captain, and it's mine to crow louder than other folks."

"But about your sleep."

"Well, what of it?"

"You slept soundly enough."

"Like a top."

"You didn't hear anything?"

"Not a breath of wind."

"That's a pity," said Money Marks, philosophically.

"Why?"

"Because there was something going on which would have interested you."

"Was there, though?"

"Yes."

"And what was that?"

"Two officers of some ship in the harbour——"

"There's only one to-day."

"What's the name of her?"

"The *Lowflyer*, one of Her Britannic Majesty's slave cruisers."

"Then the men I am speaking about belonged to that craft."

"What did they say?"

"That there was a ship in the port which they could not make out."

"Our ship!" cried Hercules, in a tone of astonishment.

"I suppose so."

"That's funny."

"It's worse than that."

"Worse?"

"Yes."

"How?"

"In this way. They came to the conclusion that our vessel was a pirate."

"Like their d—— impudence too," said Hercules, angrily.

"Such is the fact."

"Can they do us any harm?"

"Not that I know of, except they follow us about. I knew that something unpleasant was about to happen."

"You did?"

"Certainly. Sister Therese told me so; she said, 'Beware of Buenos Ayres—danger lurks in the air.'"

"Well, that's odd anyhow."

"So I thought."

"She said that, did she?"

"In the precise words which I have related to you."

"What do you mean to do, captain?" inquired Hercules.

"Nothing."

"That's funny, isn't it?"

"What would you have me do?" replied Money Marks. "These men, who are both shrewd and sagacious, suspect something. In point of fact they have hit upon the truth. If I were to run away in a hurry, they would have fresh fuel thrown upon their suspicions; and would probably sail after, and overhaul us."

"If they do, they will find nothing; we have our papers ready."

"Forged!"

"What of that; who's to prove it?"

Money Marks was silent.

"If they overhauled us to-morrow, I shouldn't care," continued Sampson Hercules; "they may do it as soon as they like for me."

"It is better to avoid anything of the sort," replied Money Marks. "You must go about, and be amongst the men, so that no agent from the *Lowflyer* tampers with their honesty. Pat Doolan will want to go ashore, and I will go back to the ship, and take the command."

"You're one of the right sort, captain," said Hercules, enthusiastically.

"At the expiration of the six days you and Doolan," added Money Marks, "must see every man, drunk or sober, on board."

"Ay, ay."

"Can I rely upon you?"

"Can you?"

"Yes."

"Did I ever fail you?"

"Never!"

"Then, by G——, I never will," cried Hercules.

Money Marks grasped the hand Hercules extended to him, and pressed it heartily.

He did not sacrifice much, in saying that he would go on board, and liberate Pat Doolan, because he loved Viola so passionately, that he found the greatest consolation in thinking of her.

The prediction of Sister Therese had implanted new hopes in his breast, and he felt confident that he should speedily behold her.

With what intense rapture he hugged this thought to his breast.

If he could only see Viola and make sure of Viola's love,

he determined to abandon a life of maritime brigandage and a career of crime on the instant.

With Viola for his wife, he felt capable of being able to live upon a few pounds a month, and to work for his living.

Hercules kept his promise, and looked after the men in the strictest manner. There were no black sheep among them. The crew of the pirate had been carefully weeded, and the result was a collection of brave fellows who were true to the backbone.

They liked Money Marks all the better when they heard that he had consented to make a sacrifice for their interests; and in a sailor's eyes, no sacrifice can be so great as consenting to remain on board, when a man can go ashore.

Money Marks got on very well in his solitude; he thought incessantly of Viola; passed a great part of his time, in his cabin, writing verses to her.

At last the six days elapsed, and the crew to a man returned on board. At least, so thought Money Marks, but when the roll was called on deck, before the weighing of the anchor, it was discovered that one man of the name of Cogan was absent.

In vain he repeated "Cogan." There was no answer.

He beckoned Hercules to his side.

"Where is Cogan?" he inquired.

"I do not know," was the reply, "I saw him a couple of hours ago."

"Well, he is not here, and we must sail without him."

The fact was, that Cogan had been picked up by Lieutenant Stafford, of H.M.S. *Lowflyer*, and had been induced by specious promises to tell all he knew about the pirate, and to take temporary service aboard Her Britannic Majesty's vessel.

This at present was unknown to Money Marks and his associates.

When the anchor of the pirate was raised, and the engines began to move, it was remarkable that the *Lowflyer* also made every symptom of leaving Buenos Ayres, and she followed the pirate closely for many miles. The *Lowflyer* and the pirate were pretty equally matched; there was not a great amount of difference between them. Perhaps the British cruiser carried heavier guns, but that remained to be seen.

Money Marks was afraid of his opponent; and being a prudent commander, he always avoided a fight from which there was nothing to gain and much to be lost.

He ran his vessel at full speed in the direction of the Canaries, but he could not get rid of the *Lowflyer*, which dogged his heels, with a pertinacity worthy of a good cause.

CHAPTER XXX.

THE WRECK.

THE day drew to a close, the sun sank in the heavens. In poetical language,

> "A summer's day was drawing to its close;
> The busy hum of insect life arose,
> And lowed the cattle as they homeward sped,
> Cropping the grass."

Though this description is not very appropriate when the sun goes down upon the ocean.

The sun was like a ball of fire—huge, lustrous, resplendent.

> "The lofty sky with golden splendour flushed,
> As from the glowing orb the magic lustre gushed."

Of course it would have been madness in Money Marks to risk an engagement with one of Her Majesty's ships of war.

The frigate carried more guns and was well manned. The only thing that the captain of the pirate could do with any credit to himself was to give the frigate leg-bail, and that he did in a clever manner. When darkness came on, the queen's vessel was not more than a couple of miles astern of the pirate, and had daylight continued much longer, the former would inevitably have overhauled the latter.

When the frigate saw her prey escaping her she made desperate efforts to overtake her, but without success.

Her most strenuous efforts could do no more than bring her within firing distance.

Charging one of the heavy guns with ball the *Lowflyer* sent a shot after the pirate.

It was at the first glance an unjustifiable act, but Captain Stockwell was acting upon information which he could not doubt was correct.

It will be remembered by the intelligent reader that a man was missing from Money Marks' vessel.

His name was Cogan.

This fellow was a double-faced scoundrel.

He had deserted from the pirate with the express intention of joining the queen's ship, and selling his information to Captain Stockwell.

He was received with kindness and taken on board at once.

When Captain Stockwell was satisfied that the piratical vessel had left port, he pursued her with the intention of overhauling her papers, and taking prisoners of the crew, who would upon the evidence of Cogan be convicted and condemned to death as pirates.

Money Mark had always treated the wretch with the greatest kindness.

Yet his idea of gratitude was, for an uncertain reward to weave a rope for his former benefactor's neck.

Before the captain fired the shot after the pirate he questioned Cogan in the presence of his principal officers.

"You are sure," he said, "that you have been telling us the truth?"

"If I have told you a lie, I wish I may——"

"Don't swear, my good fellow," interrupted the captain, sternly.

"Very well, sir."

"Oaths will not render your testimony more valuable."

"No, sir."

"And I do not allow my quarter-deck to be defiled by blasphemous exclamations."

"Quite right, sir."

"You say that you are certain of the truth of what you told me?"

"Quite certain," replied Cogan.

"Namely, that the vessel which we are pursuing is a pirate?"

"I sailed aboard of her, sir, and ought to know."

"That is true."

Turning to his officers, Captain Stockwell said—

"Shall I be justified in sending a shot after the pirate with a view of bringing her to?"

"Most undoubtedly," was the unanimous reply.

The gun was loaded, the shot was fired, but without a very damaging result. Another shot and another succeeded in quick succession.

Darkness came on, and those on board the frigate were prevented from continuing the action and from discovering what harm they had inflicted upon the chase.

It was suspected that she had been injured in some way, but no one could speak with certainty about the matter.

Everyone anxiously waited for morning.

We must now return to the pirate.

Just as evening was drawing on Money Marks and Cuffy were walking together on the deck.

Marks had made a confidant of Cuffy of late, and had entrusted him with all his plans for the future.

He found the black very faithful, highly intelligent, and devoted to his interests, which is saying a great deal.

The crew of the pirate were dangerous people to deal with, and Money Marks had some difficulty in managing them.

They claimed the right of every month electing their own officers, and he dared not gainsay them.

That day they had exercised their privilege of universal suffrage, and elected some new officers in the place of the old ones.

This system was not altogether satisfactory to Money Marks, but he was unable to help himself.

After all it did not much matter who were the executants of his will as long as they obeyed his orders and did as he told them.

The new lieutenants were Jasper Main, a Yankee; Harry Canning, an Englishman; and Charley Fox, ditto.

The first was an insolent, swaggering, blustering, drinking, chewing, swearing American.

The second was a hardworking sailor.

The third was a wily, cunning, ambitious man, to whom

Money Marks at once took a dislike. He feared him as a possible rival, and regarded him with great jealousy.

"The frigate follows us pertinaciously," said Money Marks.

"Yes, massa; him got some information," replied Cuffy.

"How?"

"That's just what dis nig done know, wuss luck."

"It would never follow us like this if the captain did not suspect something."

"Never."

"Ha! do you see that?"

"What?"

"The puff of smoke—the flash; there is the report, and we are lucky if we are not struck."

"Oh, golly!" said Cuffy; "it am gettin' hot."

The shot fortunately fell short of its mark, and sank, hissing, into the sea.

"Thank God!" cried Money Marks.

"Ha! ha!" cried Charley Fox, with his peculiar chuckle; "that gentleman wanted legs."

"Wings, you mean," said Jasper Main.

"A little more powder would have done it, and we should have had a hole in our bulwarks," interrupted Money Marks.

"Dat am it," replied Cuffy.

"Well, it is fortunate for us that darkness is coming on; we shall soon escape them. It would be folly to fight them, for there is nothing to be gained even if we beat them, which is doubtful," said Money Marks.

Everyone was now on deck, and Money Marks passed the word to the engineers to make the engines revolve at their greatest possible speed.

They did this by placing the most inflammable materials upon the fires, which heated the furnaces to an alarming extent.

This manœuvre had the desired effect of taking the pirate out of range.

When darkness enveloped the vessel she had not been struck once by the queen's ship.

She showed no light, as such a course would have been the height of imprudence, and fraught with immense peril.

"So we got out ob dat well, Massa Marks," said Cuffy to the captain as he still paced the deck anxiously.

"Yes," replied Money Marks, absently.

"What you tink about, Massa Marks?" inquired Cuffy.

"A great many things."

"What in perticklar?"

"About Viola."

"Missy Viola?"

"Yes. An old fortune-teller at Buenos Ayres prophesied that we should meet again."

"Missy Viola very pretty girl," said Cuffy, profoundly; "make nice wife for any man."

"She is in Arlee's power—that is what drives me frantic," replied Money Marks, passionately.

"If she love you——"

"If! She does love me—I know it."

"Well, if she does, Massa Marks, she wont marry Massa Arlee."

"I wish I could think so."

Cuffy was called away to attend to some business which fell within his especial province, and the conversation was brought to a close.

The ship made her way for some days and saw nothing more of the *Lowflyer*, which had lost sight of the pirate during the night.

On the evening of the sixth day a terrible storm arose. It bore a great resemblance to the tempest during which the crew of the pirate saw the phantom ship.

Towards midnight the storm increased in intensity.

Money Marks, as usual in cases of danger, was on deck. The three lieutenants were grouped round him, and Cuffy was not far off; he always made a point of being as near his master as he could, so that he might protect him in the hour of danger, and ever keep the eyes of vigilance fixed upon him.

The lightning was terrific, and the thunder roared as it can only roar in tropical regions.

The rain descended in torrents, and perpendicularly.

It was an awful night.

Suddenly there was a crash, followed by a strong smell of brimstone.

Fearful cries arose and rent the air.

"What has happened?" cried Money Marks to Charley Fox, who was nearest to him.

"The ship is struck by lightning I fear," was the reply.

"Struck?"

"Alas! yes."

"Where?"

"The mainmast has gone by the board."

Seizing a speaking-trumpet, Money Marks walked to the hatchway leading to the engines, and cried, in the voice of a stentor—

"Stop the engines!—put out the fires!—let the ship take her own course!"

Then he went to the middle of the deck and said, in the same commanding tone of voice—

"Cut away the mast—all hands to work!"

This was a necessary order, for the mast, which had been rived and splintered by the flash of lightning, was hampered by other cords and rigging and could not get clear.

It was clearly of no use now, and the best thing that could be done was to let it drift away.

The men worked with a will, and the useless mast was soon floating upon the surface of the tempestuous ocean like a log, as it was.

Surely nothing can be more awful than a storm at sea; in the dead of night, too, accompanied with thunder and lightning.

When the men had accomplished their task, they were sent below again, because heavy seas washed over the vessel now and then, which if precautions were not taken, might have the effect of taking off a few of the crew.

"Hallo!" suddenly exclaimed Charley Fox.

He was standing by the side of Money Marks, and peering out into the black waste of heaving waters, which, at least three or four times a minute, were lit up and illuminated by the very vivid lightning which was almost blinding in its intensity.

"What is it?" inquired Money Marks.

He wondered what could be the cause of the man's wonderment.

Charley Fox was not usually excitable. Quite the contrary. If he was subject to emotional fits, he usually contrived to keep them below the surface.

"There! did you not see it?"

"See what?"

"It."

"What the devil do you mean by 'it?'" demanded Money Marks.

His curiosity was piqued and he was provoked into losing his temper.

"The ship."

"A ship! Where?"

"On the larboard bow."

"Impossible."

"I say it is not," vociferated Charley Fox. "I tell you I saw a ship with all her sails set bearing down upon us, and if God does not work a miracle in our favour we must be sent to the bottom."

"A ship with her sails set on such a night as this?" said Money Marks, with an incredulous smile.

"Yes."

"You must be dreaming."

"You will soon see whether I am dreaming or no."

"I say it is impossible," resumed Money Marks; "the wind would blow the canvas to rags."

Another flash illumined the horizon.

Charley Fox exclaimed triumphantly—

"Look now; am I right or wrong?"

Money Marks looked and saw—what?

Something that made the blood leave his cheeks and his heart beat faster.

It was not a new sight, for he had seen it before, but there was something mysterious and awful about it.

A ship with all her sails set, even her top-gallant and studding-sails, was, as the third lieutenant had truly said, bearing down upon them with all the speed and velocity with which the wind was capable of carrying her.

Charley Fox fell on his knees and began to mumble a half-forgotten prayer.

The remainder of those on deck remained petrified to the boards and stupefied with fear.

"The *Flying Dutchman!*" exclaimed Money Marks; "it is that fatal craft, by all that's wonderful."

He did not fear a collision, such as his officers dreaded;

that he knew was impossible. The phantom vessel was a thing of air—there was nothing tangible about her; therefore she could not strike any vessel and send her to the bottom.

Money Marks was, unlike most sailors, not at all superstitious; he laughed at the fears of those by whom he was surrounded; but this second apparition of the *Dutchman* was certainly very remarkable, to say the least of it.

What did it mean?

What did it portend?

He could not say.

It was a common belief amongst seamen that the apparition of the craft of Philip Vanderdecken was a sure forerunner of catastrophe and wreck and speedy ruin.

There were well-authenticated instances of an appearance of the phantom ship being followed by a wreck and the loss of all hands.

Money Marks contented himself with hoping that it might not turn out so in this instance.

When the lightning next flashed, the ship was gone; it had vanished into thin air and the pirate was unhurt.

"Miraculous!" exclaimed Charley Fox, springing to his feet and peering into the darkness.

The storm continued during the night.

None of the officers dreamt of turning in; they paced the deck thoughtfully, speaking occasionally. Now and then Money Marks would descend into his cabin to take the reckoning and see in what part of the ocean they were.

When the crew heard of the appearance of the phantom ship they were sullen and discontented; their grumbling was audible, and one and all anticipated a catastrophe.

At half-past four in the morning, Money Marks descended again into his cabin, and stayed there some time.

Cuffy was in the habit of standing outside the cabin door. Just as a sentry stands on guard outside the cabin door of a captain in the Royal Navy.

At the expiration of half-an-hour Money Marks exclaimed—

"Cuffy."

The negro was by his side in a second.

"Yes, massa." he replied.

"Go on deck and tell Mr. Main I shall feel obliged if he will have the goodness to step down here."

Cuffy departed upon his errand, and in a short time Jasper Main entered the cabin.

"Well, cappen; what's the move, now?" he inquired.

"It is a serious matter."

"Serious?"

"Yes."

"How?"

"I am out of my reckoning."

"Can't you cast it?"

"I have been trying for some time, but in vain," replied Money Marks.

"That's bad, tarnation bad," said Jasper Main, squirting a shower of tobacco juice upon the floor.

"What had better be done?"

"There is no one but you on board who knows anything about nautical astronomy, and finding a ship's course. I don't know what we can do. Stop a bit; let's consider.

"Take your time."

"S'pose we send for Charley Fox and Canning."

"Do so."

Cuffy was called in and told to summon the two lieutenants, which he did.

A few words made them acquainted with the state of the case.

"My instruments are out of order," Money Marks said; "and I know no more where we are than a baby, though I rather think we must be somewhere in the region of the Caribbean Sea."

"Is the navigation dangerous?" inquired Canning, who was a practical man.

"Very."

"How do you know that?"

"Because I have been told so by my books."

"What makes the danger?"

"The number of the islands with which the sea abounds—also the coral reefs, which are of such quick growth that it is absolutely impossible to mark them in any chart."

"Have you a chart of the Caribbean Sea?" continued Canning.

"I have, but it is useless, as I cannot determine our position."

"Of what are you afraid?" queried Charley Fox.

"I am afraid of nothing but losing the lives of my men," replied Money Marks. "For myself, I fear nothing."

"You are brave."

"I ever was so."

"Are the islands inhabited?" asked Jasper Main.

"They are chiefly inhabited, though, in some cases, sparsely."

"By whom?"

"The Caribs."

"Ah!" exclaimed Canning.

"Why do you say ah?" inquired Money Marks.

"Because I have heard that the Caribs are man-eaters."

"Cannibals?"

"Yes."

"I never heard that," replied Money Marks, "and I trust your information is not correct."

"It seems to me," said Jasper Main, "that we are up an almighty tall tree."

"It is a nice and lively look out to suppose that we have a chance of being roasted and eaten," said Charley Fox.

"We are not on land yet," remarked Canning, "and perhaps we shall fall in with some ship soon, which will be of some use and assistance to us."

The council of four separated without having settled anything. Canning's advice was the most sensible. It was to this effect. Let us go slowly on, exercising the greatest care, until we meet with something to guide us. We are well provisioned, and the men are tolerably contented.

The officers laid down in their berths to snatch a few hours' rest, but Money Marks was watchful, thoughtful, and vigilant as ever.

CHAPTER XXXI.

THE SEA-SERPENT.

THE storm did not abate in the morning, as had been expected; it continued to rage with great violence.

The position of the ship was critical; for breakers were seen on all sides, which led to the belief that rocks abounded.

The sailors were much dissatisfied, but they were powerless to do anything to help themselves.

All were in a quandary, and the only thing to do was to get out of it as well as possible.

At length the storm went down. The sea was smooth. The wind vanished, and the ship was becalmed. Soundings were taken, and it was found that the water was prodigiously deep.

So deep in fact as to be almost unfathomable.

When the sun shone once more and the water was calm, and the ship rode smoothly, the sailors forgot their openly expressed discontent. The spirits of every one rose, and Money Marks ordered a double allowance of grog to be served out, which command was obeyed by Cuffy with no niggard hand.

A small island was sighted, and at the unanimous request of the crew, Money Marks ordered the engines to be worked, and the ship to be steered in that direction.

The men quickly cleared away the wreck of the mainmast, and stepped another mast; so that the ship was in good-sailing order.

Money Marks knew the value of coals in such a region as he found himself, and he determined to trust to the sailing properties of his vessel, while he remained in the unknown seas in which he found himself, and save his fuel until it was absolutely necessary.

This was a wise resolve.

He had only a small supply of coal, and he did not like to be extravagant with it.

A man stood in the chains, with a lead in his hand, carefully taking soundings. The island seemed to be well-wooded, though not of large extent.

It did not appear that it was inhabited.

The ship was well underweigh, and working slowly—certainly not more than three miles an hour.

This precautionary measure was taken because it was impossible to tell when a rock might be met with, and when it would be necessary to reverse the engines to prevent a hole being staved in the bottom.

Seeing that the navigation was dangerous, Money Marks called Canning to him, and said—

"As we are ignorant of the coast and as I conclude that almost all these islands are of coral formation, I think it strongly advisable to lower a boat, which shall pioneer the way, and so relieve the ship from the danger she is in at present."

"Lower a boat !" said Canning.

"Yes. Do you disapprove of the plan ?"

"Not at all."

"Well, then, have the yawl lowered, and tell off twelve men to man her."

"Yes."

"Then take the command yourself."

"In person ?"

"Exactly. Keep a dozen yards or so in advance of the ship, and report when you see rocks ahead. Endeavour to discover some good bay or harbour, and let me know."

"Very well."

"I shall be standing in the bows, and you can communicate with me verbally."

Canning touched his hat, and proceeded to execute the commands given him. He had the boat lowered, told off the men for service in her, and soon shot ahead.

He was not long in discovering a passage.

It was exceedingly narrow, and the least deviation from the direct course brought the ship close to the rocks.

Money Marks took the helm himself, and was regulated in steering by two marks on the land, lying in the same straight line with the centre of the passage.

Of course every sailor knows that it is necessary to keep these together.

Money Marks, after a time, feeling tired, relinquished the guidance of the ship, and Charley Fox, at his request, took the helm.

Now Charley Fox was a sailor, but not an educated one. He did not know that such nicety was required when sailing in a narrow channel.

The marks were allowed to separate, by which error they found themselves, in a minute or two, within three yards of a coral reef—the rugged tops of which were distinctly visible two or three feet below the surface, whilst at the same moment the leadsman, at the other end of the ship, sounded in nine fathoms.

This early proof of the danger of navigating amongst coral, by teaching the necessity of extreme caution, was of great importance to all the officers on board the pirate in their future operations.

Money Marks was very indignant with Charley Fox.

Rushing up to him, he violently took the helm out of his hands, saying—

"Stand on one side."

"Why ?"

"You are ignorant of the first principles of seamanship."

"Who says so ?" demanded Fox angrily.

"I do. You are perfectly worthless; it was not your fault that the ship was not a wreck just now."

"I don't believe you know much more about it than I do," replied Charley Fox.

"If you show the slightest sign of insubordination," exclaimed Money Marks, firmly, "I will have you instantly placed in irons."

"You will ?"

"Yes; and you shall be tried by court-martial."

"I doubt whether the court would convict," said Charley Fox, with a sneer.

Jasper Main was the officer of the watch; to him Money Marks spoke.

"Mr. Main."

"Sir."

"Place Mr. Fox under arrest."

Mr. Main did not hesitate; he knew the determined character of Money Marks, and was not particularly fond of the third lieutenant, who, however, was popular with the crew.

He advanced to him for the express purpose of placing him in durance, when Fox, who saw how things were going against him, reversed his tactics, and taking off his hat to Money Marks, said—

"I beg your pardon, sir; the words which escaped me just now were spoken thoughtlessly, and I hope you will give me permission to recal them."

Money Marks regarded him steadily for a small space.

"You apologise ?" he said.

"I do, sir."

"Mr. Main."

"Sir."

"You are a witness to Mr. Fox's apology."

"I am, sir."

"You are aware of my reason for rebuking him ?"

"Yes."

"I apprehend you coincide in it ?"

"Most fully."

"That will do."

Jasper Main went away and resumed his duty.

"I pardon you, Mr. Fox," said Money Marks, "but I really must beg that you will not favour me with a repetition of the scandalous conduct you have exhibited to-day."

Charley Fox bowed and walked away. The reproof was public; it had no doubt been heard by the chief part of the crew, and Money Marks' triumph was complete.

He again took command of the vessel, and much to his satisfaction found that the channel led into a deep bight or bay, in which was an excellent shelter for ships.

As the coast was unknown, it was not considered advisable to carry the brig too close in.

The ship was brought to a standstill, and the boat was despatched to reconnoitre. Canning returned, saying that he had found very good anchorage, and shortly afterwards the steamer went in.

The bay that they anchored in was of large extent and apparently of great depth. No signs of sharks could be seen, though it was believed that the dangerous creature known as the ground-shark was lurking in his hiding-place.

Money Marks gave one half his crew permission to go on shore and explore the island, promising the remainder that they should go the next day.

This was only fair; the ship could not be deserted, and no one could complain at the old rule of "turn and turn about."

Money Marks left the ship in charge of Canning, who was, in point of fact, both in work and experience, the best officer he had.

Then he took Cuffy with him and landed, in order to make some observations in person.

The vegetation was very luxuriant; all those wonderful trees which are to be met with in the tropics were to be found in the island in great profusion.

The only wonder was how they got there, for there could be no doubt that the island was the direct result of the industry of those indefatigable little insects or worms who manufacture the coral.

Money Marks, after a walk along the shore, sat down under a palm-tree which was covered at the top with cocoa-nuts.

The peculiarity of the cocoa-nut palm is that it goes up into the air to a great height, and is destitute of branches or other garniture until the top is reached, and this is bushy and covered with fruit.

The nuts are too high to be brought down by a stone or a piece of wood, and the trunk of the tree is too smooth to be climbed, so that the cocoa-nuts hang temptingly above the thirsty wayfarer's head, but too securely placed to enable him to get at them.

"I feel very thirsty," said Money Marks.

"Why not drink then ?" replied Cuffy.

"Drink what ?"

"Milk."

"Milk ?"

"Yes."

"Where is it to be procured ?" said Money Marks, with a laugh. "Milk is a very nice thing, but you forget, my good fellow, that we are not in civilized latitudes, and I don't suppose a cow was ever heard or dreamt of in these parts."

"I don't mean cow's milk; cocoa-nut milk," replied Cuffy.

"It is all very well to talk of cocoa-nuts, but how are we to get them ?"

"Cuff know."

"Do you ?"

"Yes."

"You are a clever fellow then."

"Shall Cuff show Massa Marks how him get coke-nut ?"

"If you like."

"Massa see those things jumping about ?"

"Where ?"

"On the tops of de trees."

"Yes; what are they ?"

"Dem monkeys."

"Monkeys?"

"Yes."

"What good are they to you?"

"Massa see d'reckly," replied Cuffy.

The negro sat down on the ground, and putting his hands to his mouth, made a most unearthly noise, which was heard by the monkeys up above.

The simeous tribe appeared to disapprove most strongly of this novel serenade.

They set up a dismal howl, which, if nothing else, was responsive.

At this Cuffy redoubled his exertions, and made the air resonant with his shouts.

At last the monkeys got so enraged that they tore off the cocoa-nuts and literally pelted Cuffy with them.

Now was the time for the black to exhibit his skill: he rose to his feet and dodged the nuts with great cleverness.

Money Marks had, in obedience to his directions, removed himself out of range, and watched the amusing spectacle with continued cachinnations and great hilarity.

Presently Cuffy approached his master loaded with ripe cocoa-nuts, which he rolled in a heap at his feet, saying—

"Dere massa. Drink; plenty milk dere."

"Open one for me."

Cuffy soon accomplished this task, and Money Marks found himself much refreshed by the copious draughts of the cocoa-nut milk which he took.

When the cocoa-nuts were drained of their fluid contents, they attacked the solids and made an excellent meal of the hard part which lines the inside of the shell.

When they reached the coast they found most of the men sitting down in such shady places as they could find, tired of their ramble, and anxious to get back to the ship.

Cuffy had brought as many nuts as he could carry, and these he gave away to his personal friends.

The ship's boat came at a signal to meet the party, and took some on board. It went away with its cargo as a first instalment.

It had not gone far before a loud shout from those on board aroused the attention of those on land.

All strained their eyes in one direction.

Jasper Main was in charge of the boat, and Money Marks, addressing him, and making a speaking-trumpet of his two hands, said—

"What's the matter?"

"A big snake," replied Jasper Main.

"A what?"

"Darned if I don't think it's the sea-serpent."

"The SEA-SERPENT!" exclaimed all those on shore, almost breathless with curiosity and excitement.

"Yes, I calc'late it's that very identical party."

"Look! look!" cried some one on shore.

The monster had at first only shown his head above water, but now he raised his whole body.

It was a monster in every way resembling what is commonly called the sea-serpent. Its size and length were prodigious; its girth was that of a large elm-tree, while its length was ninety yards, if it was an inch.

Probably it was a deep-sea snake which had been in some way disturbed by the storm of the preceding night, and driven in shore to take refuge from the rage of the elements.

Its head and jaws were snake-like, resembling those of the python more than those of the eel.

Its neck was ornamented with a long shaggy mane, like that of a horse, and its body seemed to float on the top of the water, undulating softly, as it moved with some celerity towards the narrow channel through which the pirate had entered the bay.

"Oh, golly!" cried Cuffy; "he am somet'... 'ke a fish; reckon him good fried."

"You are right; it is the sea-serpent," ex... ... Money Marks.

"No doubt about that; what shall I do?" responded Jasper Main.

"When you are within speaking distance of the ship tell Canning to fire a gun at him, loaded with grape and canister."

"Ay, ay, sir."

"Do not risk the consequences of a shot yourself."

"No, sir."

"The beast might turn round upon you, and do you all a mischief."

"All right, sir," replied Jasper Main.

The ship was riding placidly at anchor, and the boat would be within hail in five minutes.

The sea-serpent did not take any notice of the boat. It appeared to have been asleep, and to have just awoken. It was very leisurely making its way out to sea.

When Jasper Main was near enough, he shouted—

"Ship ahoy!"

"Ahoy!" replied Canning.

"Look ahead for the sea-serpent."

"For what?" asked Canning.

He thought some joke was about to be perpetrated upon him.

"The sea-serpent."

"Oh, no! That wont do."

"It's true."

"Yes; and so are mermaids."

"I tell you he's close to us."

"Is he?"

"He is, on my honour."

"It wont do, my boy."

"Bring a glass to bear then, and you'll be satisfied."

Canning took up a telescope, and was soon convinced that his brother officer was speaking the truth.

If the reptile was not the sea-serpent, it bore a marvellous resemblance to it. He had always had his own ideas about the sea-serpent, and he thought that possibly there was a deep-sea snake—an exaggerated species of conger eel—which rarely came to the surface.

Of course we are necessarily ignorant of the inmates of the water which lies nearest the bottom of the ocean. It may be inhabited by many strange creatures, but we cannot prove the fact.

"Are you satisfied now?" inquired Main.

"Yes; I am."

"The captain's orders are to load a gun with grape and canister, and to fire upon the snake."

"Fire upon it?"

"Yes."

"Very well; you had better get out of the way of the lash of its tail."

"We'll take care of that."

Canning ordered the pivot-gun to be loaded nearly up to the muzzle, and being no mean gunner himself, he determined to fire the gun.

In the meantime the anxiety of all was intense; the snake did not hurry himself in the least. He, at all events, apprehended no danger—perhaps he had never seen a vessel of war before, and did not imagine that there was anything to be apprehended from it.

The boat's crew pulled away from the snake, so as to avoid any rough usage should it be injured by the discharge of the gun.

"I'll tell you what——" exclaimed Charley Fox, who had placed himself on friendly terms with Money Marks again.

"Eh?" said Money Marks.

"Why, it's my opinion the beast can carry a sight of shot in his belly without being much hurt."

"You think he can."

"I've no doubt about it; Main may be a good shot—I believe he is; but if he puts a bag of grape and canister into the snake, he'll dive and take it out to sea with him."

"If the shot is well directed it ought to cut him in half."

"A chain shot might; but maybe he hasn't thought of that."

Bang! went the gun.

Boom! boom! went the echo.

"He's fired—he's fired!" resounded on all sides.

"What damage has he done the snake?" inquired Money Marks.

"Look—look! he's gone under!" replied Charley Fox.

So, indeed, he had. The shot was as well directed as it could be, and there was little doubt that a large quantity of the charge had penetrated the snake's body.

With a peculiar snort, followed by a still more peculiar cry, the reptile began to lash the water with its tail, causing quite a storm and commotion in the bay.

It did not give Canning another chance to shoot at it, for it glided along beneath the surface.

It was evidently severely wounded, because the water was stained with blood for some distance; but, to the disappointment of all, it got off with its life, and sank into the coral caves of unfathomed ocean, where some finny doctor probably healed its hurts.

"I'm uncommonly sorry the beggar got off," said Jasper Main to Canning, when he reached the deck.

"So am I," replied Canning.

"I calc'late Barnum and the New York chaps would have given a few thousand dollars for the carcase."

"That they would."

The boat shortly afterwards returned to the shore, and took in another boat's load, almost immediately setting out on the homeward voyage.

When they were midway between the ship and the shore the water burst into foam on both sides of them; something struck the bottom of the boat with great violence, and sent it flying into the air.

Those of the sailors who knew anything about the whale fishery, and had been to Greenland, thought that they were struck by a whale.

They were mistaken.

There were others who dreaded something worse than that.

These were correct in their surmises.

The fact was that the sea-serpent had risen again, either to take air or because the pain of his wound distracted him.

He had struck the boat, possibly inadvertently, but with a force and precision that was undeniable.

The utmost terror and consternation took possession of everybody when this catastrophe was fully understood.

Canning had the swivel loaded, and would have been delighted to have fired again at the monster, but he was afraid to do so, lest the shot might strike some one of the crew floating in the water.

It was an anxious moment.

If the snake was embued with cannibalistic tendencies, and was gifted with a voracious appetite, there is no saying what he might not have done in the way of decimating the crew of the pirate.

Fortunately he was contented with the mischief he had done, glared around him with his fishy lack-lustre eyes, and sinking rapidly was seen no more.

Canning lowered another boat with as much rapidity as circumstances would admit of, and he was ably seconded by the men, who were frantic in their endeavours to save their friends and comrades.

In time every one was rescued, and those on shore were conveyed back to the vessel.

Everyone talked about the snake, which was a very singular creature, and the first that any of them had seen. Afterwards, however, they saw several small serpents basking in the sun, but never so magnificent a specimen as the one they had wounded, but did not, unhappily, succeed in killing.

I say unhappily, not from any ill-will to the reptile, but in the interests of science. For if a specimen of the sea-serpent could be brought home by some enterprising mariner, a new field would be open to scientific men. The gorilla, which has for so long a time held a foremost place in our museums and our lectures, would sink into insignificance, and the sea-serpent would became an acknowledged fact for men to wonder at and speculate over.

CHAPTER XXXII.

ON THE ISLAND.

THE pirate did not stay long in the bay. A spring of water was looked for, and in vain—there was none to be met with. Indeed it would have been an extraordinary thing to have met with one on a coral island.

Still, the stock of water on board the pirate was running lamentably low, and it was clear that the supply must be replenished before long.

Money Marks accordingly resolved to run slowly along the islands with which the sea was studded, until he found one inhabited.

Where there were inhabitants, it followed as a matter of course that there must be fresh water, for no human being can live upon brackish or salt water.

After a week's sailing an island was sighted upon the shore of which some black men were seen.

Canoes were also to be distinguished by the aid of a powerful glass, but when the frigate was discovered by the natives, they, one and all, rowed rapidly to the shore and pulled their canoes upon the beach.

Money Marks did not think it prudent to go on shore until certain negotiations had been commenced.

He had heard of poisoned arrows, and ambuscades, and as he valued the lives of his men highly he did not like to jeopardize them.

An anchorage was discovered, and here the ship was brought to a standstill, Money Marks resolving to wait a day or two to see if any canoes put off from the land to reconnoitre and see what the business of the strangers was in that locality.

As they were prevented from going on shore, Money Marks gave Canning permission to examine a reef, which formed the north side of the anchorage.

He found a field of coral, about half-a-mile square, dry at low water, with the surf breaking very high on the outer edge, which lay exposed from the waves to the north.

The surface of the rock was everywhere worn into small holes, which being left full of water as the tide goes out, were occupied by a number of beautiful blue fish.

Canning found the coral exceedingly hard, and though at many places it stuck upwards in sharp points, it required a hammer of considerable weight to break it, and in a short time it entirely defaced the hammer.

While Canning was thinking about the wonderful industry of the tiny insects who had made the rock, he was favoured with a striking proof of the inconvenience to which he was likely to be exposed, for the tide rose suddenly and fairly washed him off.

The next day a canoe put off from the shore.

It contained three men, one of whom appeared to be a chief or commanding person, and the others were in all probability his dependants.

He brought some fresh fish, some of which were red and some blue, and seemed highly pleased when Money Marks by signs expressed his gratitude for the present.

By him a formal message was sent to the chiefs or king commanding the tribe, saying that the ship was in want of fresh water, and a request was made that the boats might go on shore with the casks for the purpose of procuring that very great necessary of life.

The chief seemed perfectly to understand Money Marks' meaning, and went away giving him to understand that he would do his best.

In a short time after this message had been delivered, quite a number of canoes came alongside with large tubs of water.

This was a strong proof of their address in telling the pirates that they were wishful of preventing all attempts at landing.

In the afternoon of that day an elderly gentleman, one evidently who had authority, paid the ship a visit, and was received by Money Marks with great cordiality.

His appearance and manner being greatly in his favour, Money Marks paid him every attention in his power.

His wish was to be permitted to go all over the ship at his leisure. It was granted, and in this way he examined everything on board with the greatest minuteness and curiosity.

He employed himself for six hours in examining the upper deck and never left anything until he thoroughly understood its use.

He next went into the cabin, where he was a long time examining books and furniture.

He would not accept anything valuable, but was grateful for samples of rope, canvas, and cloth.

He completed his examination of the ship that day, though there is no doubt he would have protracted his survey, had he thought permission would have been given him.

The sailors were pleased with him and his reverend appearance, very readily assisting him in his inquiries.

The next day, not having received permission to land, but thinking that the natives of the island were inclined to be friendly, Money Marks resolved to risk the chance of landing.

The crew was divided into two sections, one remaining to guard the vessel against any attack from the natives should they evince a hostile spirit, the other going on shore with Money Marks.

The reef which has recently been spoken of was reached by the boats in an hour, but as it was low water, the coral was left nearly bare for a considerable way out, and as this reef lay betwixt the ship and the island, the large boats could not get near the beach.

MONEY MARKS; OR, THE HIGHWAYMAN OF THE SEAS. No. 11. Price 1d.—GEORGE VICKERS, Angel Court, Strand, London.

MARKS PROTECTS THE NATIVE WOMAN.

To go round and make a long circuit would have been very tedious.

In this dilemma Money Marks took forcible possession of a canoe, which was lying at anchor, and in several trips all the party landed.

The first object which met their gaze on the shore was a hut. Before it were about a dozen people, who stood looking at them till they landed, and then ran away, leaving their tobacco pipes, pouches, and various other things, on the ground about the hut, in which was a pot of boiled sweet potatoes and several jars of water.

Money Marks in vain tried to allay the apprehensions of the natives by waving to them. It being breakfast time, the party sat down to a hasty meal, which they had hardly done when an old man came and prostrated himself before Money Marks, apparently in great alarm.

A glass of rum was the only thing which reassured him and induced him to stand on his legs. When his confidence was gradually gained, he informed Money Marks, as well as

he could by signs and gestures, that his canoe had been taken and when the coxswain was told to restore it, the old man's happiness knew no bounds.

They then gave him some buttons and some pieces of bread and meat, with all of which he was much pleased.

Soon afterwards some chiefs, accompanied by a vast crowd, came down and told Money Marks that he and his men might walk about the beach as long as they pleased, but that any attempt to penetrate the interior would be resented.

The day, however, was excessively hot, and the sand on the beach deep, so that walking in it was anything but pleasant. They soon got tired of their walk, and told the chiefs as well as they could that they were surprised at so cold a reception, and that it was extremely disagreeable to walk along the beach and be exposed to the sun at such an hour.

The remonstrances of Money Marks were not productive of much effect, for when he objected particularly to the heat, they showed him to a sort of cave in the rock, where they put down a mat, and wished him to drink tea in the shade, since he objected to the sun.

This, of course, could not be submitted to, and Money Marks told them that his object in landing was to walk about under the trees in order to recover his health, impaired by a long residence on board ship.

The chiefs tried all their eloquence in dumb show to persuade Money Marks that he was better in the cave, but all to no good; he was determined to explore the island, and he gave them to understand that he should use force, if need be.

Several of the men wore gold earrings, and gold bracelets and rings, which excited the sailors' cupidity. The objections made by the natives to the pirates penetrating the interior led them to think that a vast treasure was concealed in the city.

They even went so far as to talk and whisper among themselves, saying that the streets were paved with gold, and that they would find diamonds as big as pigeons' eggs.

By this way of talking and reasoning they so inflamed their imaginations that nothing would do but that they must go and sack the city, kill the natives, and possess themselves of the imaginary treasure which they had conjured into existence.

The chiefs finding that Money Marks determined to penetrate into the interior, at last, and with reluctance, gave their consent to his going to the top of a hill; but they took the precaution of sending a couple of runners on before, probably to give warning to any women who might be in that direction.

About half-way up the road, which winded along a steep fall, they came to a neatly-built well, supplied by a stream which ran along a curved watercourse.

Near it were three or four rudely-carved stones, about a foot long and four inches across, with a small quantity of rice laid upon each.

"Cuffy!" exclaimed Money Marks.

"Yes, massa."

"What are those stones for and that rice?"

"That's religion, massa."

"What do you mean?"

"De God ob de Well."

"Oh! I see. The rice is placed there to propitiate the guardian deity of the well."

"Iss, massa, dat it," replied Cuffy, with a sagacious look, which seemed to say, "I know all about it."

The side of the hill was cut into horizontal, irregular terraces, cultivated with much care and irrigated by means of ditches leading from the well.

On gaining the brow of the hill the chiefs stopped; but as Money Marks saw a shady grove within a few yards of the summit, he begged them to proceed.

After a short deliberation they consented.

By gaining that eminence a view of an extensive valley, more beautiful than anything they had yet seen, was given them.

In the valley was a congeries of huts, forming the nucleus of a large town; in the centre of which towered a big house, which one and all supposed to be the king's palace.

The sun was shining upon it, and gave it the appearance of burnished copper or pure gold. The sailors immediately supposed that it was built of gold, and their impatience to go and explore it became greater every minute.

Some questions were put to the chiefs, but they answered in an evasive manner, and showed symptoms of the greatest distress.

Money Marks remained under the trees for an hour smoking a pipe; some of the sailors had burning-glasses with them, and they amused the natives very much by lighting their pipes by the aid of the glasses.

One old gentleman pretended to know more than the others, and, suspecting some trick, held out his hand that it might be exposed to the focus.

He was soon undeceived, to the great amusement of every one.

Cuffy and Money Marks were talking together, when the negro said—

"Massa Fox no friend of yours."

"Why not?"

"You scold him and kick up row."

"Yes, I know; but he apologized."

"He hate you."

"Not he."

"Cuffy heard him talk."

"What about?"

"Him say he like to have de ship himself—he would do all sorts of tings with it."

"Ha!" cried Money Marks, "did he say that?"

"He did, massa."

"Who did he say it to?"

"Jasper Main."

"How did he take the communication?"

"He shake him head——"

"Yes?"

"And he say no."

"Oh! he refused to help him in his treasonable and traitorous designs?"

"Yes, him refuse. Then he go to Massa Canning——"

"Well?"

"And talk to him."

"What did he say?"

"He shake him head too, and say it no go."

"That is good. I would have staked my life on Canning's honour."

"After that, Massa Fox go back to Massa Main and talk long talk with him."

"A second time?"

"Yes."

"Go on."

"And Massa Main, him say him tink about it."

"So, there is treachery in the camp? Will the men follow Fox, think you?"

"Um. It diff'kult to say," replied Cuffy, reflectively.

"You are a faithful fellow, Cuffy," Money Marks said, with some feeling.

"Do anyting for massa," replied the black; "poor nig die for massa."

"I hope I shall never call upon you for so severe a sacrifice as that; but you must keep your eyes and ears open, and give me news of this conspiracy. I will nip it in the bud."

"Dat am de way to do it."

"I do not fear anything from Charley Fox."

"Him nobody."

"The men, I think, are attached to me."

"Yes, massa, dey like you."

"That is consolatory. Now, run away; we must not be seen talking together long; conspirators are always suspicious."

Hardly had Cuffy gone away with a cunning smile upon his sagacious countenance, than Charley Fox approached Money Marks.

The young pirate did not know whether some overt act of insubordination was not going to take place.

In order to be on his guard, he put his hand in his pocket and grasped a pistol, which he always carried with him, and held it ready for action at a moment's notice.

"The men have deputed me, captain, to come to you and have a few words."

"What about?"

"Just this," replied Charley Fox, taking his pipe from his mouth; "we haven't done much lately."

"In what way?"

"Why, our own particular."

"Piratically, you mean?"

"Exactly."

"Are they discontented?" queried Money Marks, a little anxiously.

"No; I can't say that."

"We have been out of luck lately; but it does not follow that we shall always be so."

"The men think they are in luck now," replied Charley Fox.

"Oh! I'm glad to hear it."

"Are you?"

"Yes; but as your meaning is a little obscure, perhaps you will be good enough to throw some light upon the subject."

"Certainly. The men seem to be of one mind, and they have made me their spokesman."

"You said that before," cried Money Marks, impatiently.

"I am coming to the point now, captain, but I never could do it without a bit of circumlocution."

"Well."

"The men have taken it into their heads, that these nigger chaps on the island have got a lot of gold and precious stones."

"What makes them think so?"

"Because they wear gold bands round their wrists and ankles, and have rings made of gold."

"What do they want to do?"

"They want to go to the city and take what they can find."

"Suppose the natives offer any resistance," said Money Marks.

"Why, in that case they will have bad luck," replied Charley Fox.

"Do you know that you are advocating a marauding expedition?"

"I know that; but we are by profession pirates, and we should be the last to stick at trifles. There is some swag to be got at here, and I don't at all see why the men shouldn't have it."

"Your opinion has nothing to do with the matter."

"Hasn't it? I maintain that as one of the superior officers of the vessel I have a right to express my opinion."

"Indeed!"

"You will never succeed in keeping up the discipline of a man-of-war on board such a vessel as your own."

"I may be of a different opinion," replied Money Marks, with dignity.

His hands itched to knock the fellow down, but he controlled his temper, and resisted the temptation. Many things and circumstances combined to prove to him that such a course would be injudicious and inadvisable.

"If you do not like to lead the men, I will take charge of the expedition, captain," said Charley Fox, artfully feeling his way.

He would have liked nothing better than to head the marauding party, because it would have endeared him to the men, and have given him a hold over their affections.

Since they had become pirates they were frightfully demoralised, and ready to do anything their evil passions suggested to them.

It was hardly possible that the natives would submit to be pillaged, and to have their homes ransacked and rifled, and, in all probability, their woman-kind insulted, without struggling for their hearths and homes.

Money Marks was fully alive to this contingency. Of course the sailors with their fire-arms and cutlasses must be victorious in the end.

Still it was extremely probable that some of his crew would lose their lives. If they were led by Charley Fox, he knew that the man would gain an increase of influence with the crew, so he determined to lead them himself.

It was against his will that he came to this conclusion, because he felt that a great and useless massacre of the natives would take place; and for his part, he doubted whether the sacking of the town would give any adequate reward.

When the sailors were excited, as they soon would be, when one or two of them had been killed by the natives, there would be no holding them.

They would kill, and sack, and burn, like so many demons!

"Tell the men," he said, "that I grant their request, though I am afraid they will be disappointed."

"All right," replied Charley Fox.

"Add that I will lead them in person."

"You!"

"Yes."

"I thought you had given me permission to do so," said Charley Fox, with a crestfallen air.

"Not at all."

"I shall relieve you from a painful and dangerous duty."

"Have I ever shrank from encountering peril or fatigue?"

"No."

"Why then do you insult me, by supposing that I shall do so now?"

Charley Fox made no answer. He was discouraged and beaten, whereat he displayed the chagrin he felt.

CHAPTER XXXIII.

THE SACKING OF THE TOWN.

CHARLEY Fox was walking away when Money Marks called after him, exclaiming—

"Stay."

He turned round.

"I will speak to the men myself."

"You will?" said Fox.

"Yes; lead me to them."

The men were grouped under the trees, smoking and drinking some cold grog which they had brought with them. Several were standing together and talking in an animated manner.

They were instantly silent when Money Marks made his appearance, and looked anxiously at him.

"My men," he exclaimed in a loud voice, "your request has been faithfully transmitted to me by Mr. Fox, and I grant it."

A tremendous burst of cheering took place, and so pleased were the men that they laughed and shook one another by the hand.

"I must ask silence for a brief space," Money Marks resumed, "for I wish to make a few remarks to you."

"That's right, silence all; hold your noise, lads," exclaimed somebody.

Once more there was a dead silence, and Money Marks said—

"It will be advisable, I think, to send for more men from the ship, because the natives will probably make a determined resistance. You are all of you armed?"

"Yes, yes; we have twenty rounds of ball cartridge and our cutlasses."

"Very well; the natives have but their spears and their bows and arrows, and the result of the conflict that is about to ensue cannot be doubtful."

"Not it."

"I could wish that you had not entertained the idea. I have my reasons."

"What are they?"

"Never mind. Since you have set your hearts on it, and I have given you permission, to moralize would be worse than useless."

"So it would."

"All I will impose upon you is to be moderate in the hour of triumph."

"We will."

"And if the result of your expedition should not be what you anticipate, do not blame me, for I was not the organiser of it, neither do I approve of it."

"We wont blame you," said the men.

"On that understanding I consent to take the command. Mr. Fox."

"Sir," replied Fox, touching his hat.

"Go at once to the ship and bring with you half the men on board, choosing them by lot."

"Yes, sir."

"Also bring an additional supply of ammunition."

"Certainly, sir."

"My lads, how are you off for grog?"

"Not over well, captain."

"Bring two gallons of rum with you, Mr. Fox."

"I will not forget."

"Don't let the grass grow under your feet, for it will be as well to make the attack to-day, when the heat of the sun goes off."

"Exactly."

Charley Fox set off on his journey, which was not of an arduous nature; and the sailors during his absence discussed the chances of the coming raid.

An expedition, with plunder for its avowed object, was just the thing to stimulate them. Money Marks discouraged the expedition, because he doubted the existence of the plunder.

The natives certainly wore a few gold ornaments, but because they did so, it did not follow that they had a store of gold, silver, and precious stones piled up in some secret warehouse or treasure-house.

Cuffy came to Money Marks, and said—

"Dey all dam fool."

"What for?"

"Going to fight Ingun."

"So I think."

"De natives been talking, and some word I know."

"You understand their language?"

"No, not all; but here and there word I can make out."

"Indeed!"

"Yes."

"What do they say?" asked Money Marks.

"Dey suspeck someting."

"Do they?"

"And dey say dey will fight de whiteskins."

"What are their weapons ?"

"Only de bow and de spear."

"Are their arrows poisoned ?"

"No; tink not."

"I am glad to hear that. Are they rich ?"

"No ; poor as de church mouse."

"But they have gold ornaments, and the chances are they have gold utensils."

"P'raps."

It was clear that Cuffy did not believe in the fabulous wealth of the natives, with which idea the sailors were impregnated,

"Who put the idea in their heads?" inquired Money Marks.

"Massa Fox."

"I suspected as much."

"I heard him say to sailors, ' Go to de village and kill de niggers. Dey have lots of money and gold. It will all be yours.' "

"He said so ?"

"Yes, and he told dem dat if de captain—dat you—would not go, he would lead them on to wealth and victory."

"The scoundrel !"

"He be one dam scoundrel," replied Cuffy.

"For my part, I would rather not go, but I must," said Money Marks, in an abstracted manner. "I have no option. In this case, the men lead me; to disappoint them would be dangerous, and, after all," he added, in a wild, reckless laugh, "what is the harm of shedding a few bucketsful of black blood—the blood of semi, if not complete savages ? I have embarked in a career of crime, and one life more or less is of no particular value. What if we slay a couple of score of human beings, they will not be missed, and their place will be soon supplied."

"Dat de way to talk ?" said Cuffy, who was always much impressed by a speech or a soliloquy.

Money Marks believed that he was to a certain extent the child of destiny, yet he would have prevented the massacre of the Indians if he could have done so. He had chosen a career of blood, and he would not shrink from shedding blood.

At length Charley Fox returned from the ship with the men he had been sent for, and the little army organized themselves into two companies.

It was observed that the natives had retired to their city. Whether they had entrenchments there or not, it was impossible to say.

Probably not.

As well as a glass enabled the officers to make out, the houses, which were rather numerous, were surrounded by stockades, that is to say, a high hedge of bamboo had been erected in order to guard against a possible attack.

Rum was given to the sailors, which made them more reckless and intemperate than they were before.

There was, in truth, but a poor chance for the natives.

Money Marks put himself at the head of the first column, and Charley Fox followed as leader of the second. They marched down the hill, with their hands upon their muskets, ready for action. A walk of four miles was before them. This was not a very arduous undertaking, as the sun had partially gone down. A cool breeze had arisen, and the heat was not nearly so great as it had been.

The city when neared was found to be surrounded by a stockade of bamboo, eight feet in height—not a single native was to be seen outside the gates, which were kept sedulously closed.

Seeing that their further progress was impeded, Money Marks held a council with his officers.

"What shall we do ?" he said to Fox.

"I should advise setting fire to the bamboo," replied Charley Fox.

"Setting fire to it ?"

"Most decidedly."

"No do dat !" exclaimed Cuffy.

"Why not ?" asked Charley Fox, angrily.

"Cos Cuffy know why."

"It would be better for you if you held your tongue," said Charley Fox.

"Let him speak !" cried Money Marks, interposing the weight of his authority.

"I don't like it."

"Like what ?"

"Why, being interrupted and dictated to by a rascally nigger."

"I will not have him spoken of in that way !" retorted Money Marks, his eyes flashing. "He is my servant, and, what is more, my friend, and I listen to his advice. He has been a native of a wild country, and he knows the plans and subterfuges that wild tribes have recourse to."

"Well, let him say what he has to say quickly, and not keep us here all day," said Charley Fox.

"This intemperate language shall be punished, sir, in the proper place, and at the proper time," said Money Marks.

"Do it now."

"No, not now."

"Why not ?"

"Because neither time nor place are suitable."

"Well, I aint going to wait for any nigger's advice. I'm going to set fire to those palisades. Come on, my lads ! who'll follow ?" exclaimed Charley Fox.

Money Marks drew his revolver from his pocket, as if he intended to fire at Fox and kill him, but Cuffy laid his hand upon his arm, in order to restrain his palpable intention.

"Why do you do that ?" he cried.

"Cuffy know why."

"Take your hand away."

"What for you want to draw pistol ?"

"To shoot that scurrilous mutineer !"

"No shoot."

"Why not ?"

"Becos he not live long."

"How do you know that ?" queried Money Marks.

"Massa, see those holes ?"

"Where ? In the bamboos ?"

"Yes."

"They shoot through there."

"Shoot what ?"

"Spears and arrows."

Charley Fox found three followers. The other sailors prudently held back until Money Marks gave them the word; for they had more confidence in him than in the rash and blustering lieutenant.

Charley Fox took a small bag of gunpowder from one of the men, and, affixing a slow match to it, lighted it, and ran to the roughly-made palisades.

A cloud of arrows flew around him, of which two stuck in his flesh, wounding him, but not mortally. Brave enough was he. He pushed on, and succeeded in hanging the bag on a projecting piece of wood. Then his task was done.

He endeavoured to retreat, but in vain—a fresh shower of arrows was discharged at him by the enraged natives, and he fell with a feathered shaft quivering in his heart to rise no more.

When the sailors saw that their comrade was dead, they grew furious. Fierce gestures followed fiercer exclamations, and Money Marks had to exert all his influence to restrain them from rushing madly towards the stockade.

"Wait," he cried, "wait until the powder-bag has exploded, then a breach will be made and you will be able to avenge the sad and melancholy death of the lieutenant."

"Death to the blacks ! Death to the blacks !" arose on all sides in savage tones.

The natives uttered the most demoniacal yells; they did not imagine for a moment that Charley Fox's last act was to undo them all. They rather thought that the death of the Englishman had deterred the others from approaching, and they restrung their bows and fitted fresh arrows to the strings in anticipation of another attack and speedy conquest.

The minutes flew slowly by amidst deep curses, fearful threats, deep lamentations, and gnashing of teeth.

Suddenly there was a loud explosion.

A large mass of the stockade was blown to atoms and hurled high in the air. Many of the natives who were crouching behind the stakes were horribly mangled, and fell back dead and mutilated in the arms of their astonished comrades.

A breach was made, and now was the opportunity of the attacking party.

Money Marks formed his men into a double line and ordered the first line to pour in a volley, which they did.

The natives, who had no idea of firearms, fell like corn before the sickle of the reaper, yet they would not give way. They thought that Heaven was warring against them and that they were the victims of magic. Still they stood in the breach and continued to discharge their clouds of arrows.

Money Marks' grand aim was to preserve the lives of his men. Charley Fox had fallen bravely, but his death was the natural and to be expected result of his rashness.

Although Marks admired him for his courage, he did not regret him; he did not feel his loss, for there was one turbulent and unruly spirit the less amongst his crew.

When the pieces of the first line of sailors were discharged, Money Marks ordered them to fall back, and the second line to advance and fire while the first reloaded.

The arrows of the natives, owing to the distance of the attacking party, did little damage; a few men were struck, but not hurt much.

Money Marks himself received an arrow in the left arm, which he carelessly plucked out and threw away, binding a handkerchief round his wound.

At the second discharge, which was well delivered, the native ranks were awfully thinned, and desperately brave as they were, the chiefs saw that it was impossible for them to hold the breach; they therefore retired helter-skelter as best they could.

A loud cheer arose from the English, in which Money Marks did not join, for he felt that the whole affair was nothing better than a sickening slaughter and an inhuman butchery.

To interpose between the natives and his men would have been useless; to raise the voice of mercy and toleration was in vain, for the men were half mad.

They pointed to the dead body of Charley Fox, and gave way to the most sanguinary threats against man, woman and child.

He made them all load their pieces, and then putting himself at the head of them, gave the word to advance. This command was promptly complied with, and the sailors rushed forward to the attack in serried ranks; only a few stragglers offered any resistance, and they were shot down like so many wild animals.

The chiefs with the more valiant of the survivors had taken refuge in the king's palace, in which dwelling they intended to perish in defending the person of their revered and well-beloved sovereign.

The sailors stepped in the breach to rifle the bodies of their enemies of the golden ornaments with which they were decorated, and presented a most undignified spectacle as they did so.

If the natives had then been able to take advantage of their preoccupation, they would have done some execution, but the poor fellows were trembling for their safety and mourning over the bodies of those who had fallen.

More than ten minutes were taken up before the plunder was appropriated. All the men of high degree were lavishly adorned with gold ornaments, and the sailors smiled with gratification as they felt their pockets weighed down with the precious metal.

It was a melancholy sight to see the scantily-clad bodies of the natives with large gaping wounds, through which the blood was flowing; but the pirates thought of nothing except revenge for the murder of their comrade.

Some of them were smarting from wounds inflicted by the arrows, and plunder and revenge was the war-cry of the ruthless invaders, crueller than whom was never Goth or Vandal.

Those houses which were nearest to the palisades were given to the flames, and all was destruction, rapine, and robbery.

The women and children stood gazing sorrowfully on the destruction of their dwellings. A sailor attempted to kiss one of the women, and she ran shrieking towards Money Marks for protection.

The appeal was irresistible. She had a child at the breast, and as she held the little innocent up she spoke some pathetic words in her own language, the drift and meaning of which it was impossible to misinterpret.

She was asking for mercy and protection.

Raising his arm, Money Marks exclaimed, in a voice of thunder—

"Plunder as much as you like, my lads; it is our trade, but leave the women alone. The man who insults a woman, or outrages her modesty, shall die by my hand. He shall, by Heaven!"

Some of the men cheered his speech, the others lowered and looked sullen.

"Another thing," cried Money Marks, "I wish to impress upon you, and that is, *keep together*. If you become separated, your lives will most probably be the forfeit of your rashness; *together* you are irresistible."

The women were for the most part unmolested after this proclamation, as it may be called, but there were a few ruffians who secretly disobeyed the commands of their captain; fortunately, these instances were isolated and few and far between.

All the houses up to the king's palace were in flames; the women and children and aged people took refuge in the furthermost part of the town, and there filled the air with their screams and frantic lamentations.

The palace was quickly surrounded; it was made of reeds and bamboo like the other houses. Such a material was highly inflammable, and blazed with great fierceness. Several volleys were fired into the palace, but without doing much apparent damage.

Suddenly a white-headed old man appeared at the gate; he walked with the assistance of a stick. There was an air of majesty about him; no doubt he was the king. A sailor raised his matchlock and was about to fire upon him, but Money Marks indignantly knocked up the muzzle, crying—

"Coward! cannot you respect grey hairs? besides, the man is defenceless; out upon you for a cur!"

The fellow fell back a pace or two, abashed and mortified.

Money Marks called Cuffy, and said—

"Do you think you can make out enough of his language to distinguish what he is saying?"

"Yes, massa; pick out a few words and soon tell you what him mean."

Cuffy walked to meet the old man, and was soon observed to be in close conversation with him. This interview lasted five minutes, at the end of which time the black returned, and Money Marks eagerly asked him the result of his interview.

The officers and some of the men crowded round the negro.

"Him say," exclaimed Cuffy, "why you come here and kill my people with your heaven-fire? why you burn my town? we do noting to you to provoke you. Tell me why you do this. If want kill me, kill, but no kill all my people, and burn all houses."

"Tell him," said Money Marks, "that we want all the gold he has in the place, and all the golden ornaments which his people are wearing."

Turning to the men, he added—

"I think, my lads, that will do. If he gives us all the gold they have we may safely promise the king that we will withdraw without doing any further mischief."

There were one or two murmurs, but this proposition was generally applauded, so Money Marks said—

"Tell the king this, and add that we will withdraw when he has complied with our demands."

Cuffy did so. The old king, whose heart was nearly broken, was only too glad to comply with the request, and in a short time five sacks full of gold ornaments were brought out and laid down for the sailors to appropriate.

When the booty was in their possession, the sailors were too anxious to get back to the ship to examine it to continue their devastations, and, quieted by Money Marks, they commenced an orderly retreat, taking with them the body of Charley Fox, to which they intended to give decent sepulture on the morrow.

He was the only one of the whole crew who had perished.

The treasure was found on examination to be very valuable. The gold was good, and though the ornaments were roughly and rudely made, and the designs crude, they were of great weight and solidity.

Thus ended a disgraceful passage in Money Marks' life, but one which he was in a measure powerless to prevent.

CHAPTER XXXIV.

THE WRECK.

As the marauding party went back to the ship, the wailing of the women for their dead was affecting in the extreme, and rang in the ears of many for a long time afterwards.

The life of a pirate is, however, so eventful, and so full of change, that it is difficult to dwell upon any one subject for a long time together.

Blood is continually flowing, and one horror is quickly followed by another. Money Marks had no conscience to speak about; when he began his infamous career he threw character, reputation, future, conscience, all overboard.

The crew were not so callous as to wish to remain on or near the island, and they petitioned Money Marks for an immediate move.

He complied with this request. The anchor was raised, and the ship making her way through the dangerous navigation with as much speed as was consistent with watchfulness and care, soon left the blood-stained island behind.

But her dangers were only just beginning; perhaps a retributive justice was following her, for a terrible calamity overtook her and all on board.

It was a lovely morning, and all the men were in high spirits. The air was as calm as it could be; the sea like a mill-pond—not a ripple disturbed the surface of the water, which for all the world resembled glass.

Suddenly one of those terrible gales peculiar to the tropics, called sometimes monsoons, sometimes typhoons, arose, and everything was convulsed in a moment.

The rigging was blown to tatters, and the sails were torn to shreds.

The ship was driven before the gale, and rendered completely unmanageable.

She was at the mercy of the waves.

And it was little mercy that they showed—the mercy that the sailors meted out to the savages was the mercy that the elements gave them.

A huge wave dashed the rudder to pieces, and when the vessel had no steerage-way her condition was desperate indeed.

Then the men remembered the *Flying Dutchman*, and thought of what the double apparition had portended.

Canning was no grumbler, no fatalist, no superstitious chatterer, but he came aft to Money Marks and said—

"We had better get all ready for a wreck, sir."

"A wreck?"

"Yes."

"Why so?"

"Because a wreck is inevitable."

"I am surprised that you, Canning, should fall into the popular error," said Money Marks.

"I fall into no error, sir—I simply draw my own conclusions."

"They deceive you."

"I do not think so."

"You of course think that the apparition of the *Flying Dutchman* forebodes misfortune."

"Undoubtedly."

"What is that, if not rank and gross superstition? If you think that it would be advisable to make certain preparations, I give you my permission to do so."

"I am essentially a prudent man, sir."

"Very well, you are the officer of the watch; do as you think fit."

"We shall be wrecked, sir, as sure as fate," continued Canning.

"I hope not, I'm sure. Nothing would please me more than to find you a false prophet, though I am forced to confess that there is some truth in your statement; you have some ground for your assertion."

At this moment the look-out man reported that he saw breakers ahead and land on the leeward bow.

"Ha!" cried Money Marks; "this is serious. I had thought that we were going out to sea."

"What did I tell you?" said Canning, with a grave smile.

The wind—terrible, irresistible, undeviating—obliged the vessel to near the land.

A wreck was only a question of time. The sailors secured their treasure around them as well as they could, and made every preparation for a catastrophe.

The sea was going mountains high, and the ship was carried along from the surface of one wave to another with great velocity.

Suddenly it shifted a little, or else a current caught the vessel, for she was drawn away from the breakers and sent flying towards the land.

At half-past eleven the storm arose, at one the pirate was within a quarter of a mile from land—a doomed ship.

The land was low and ugly, and the ship was driven by the force of a huge wave high and dry upon the sand.

This was very remarkable, for she was altogether uninjured with the exception of the damage the storm had done

to her rigging, so that the wreck was of a very peculiar description.

The tempest subsided very much as it had risen, and the pirate was left some three hundred yards on land away from the margin of the ocean.

Everything and everybody on board of her were much shaken, as may be supposed; but all were soon walking about the shore congratulating themselves upon a wreck of such a wonderful kind.

Money Marks and Canning kept order as well as they could amongst the men, who were inclined to plunge into excesses.

"Let them have a run," said Canning; "it will do them good and keep them quiet."

Accordingly Money Marks gave them an allowance of grog and some tobacco, telling them to go and explore the island.

This they did with great alacrity.

"If this is your wreck," said Money Marks, with a smile, "it is not such a terrible affair after all."

"It is miraculous."

"So I think."

"Only there is one objection to the theory of a miracle."

"What is that?"

"Heaven would never work one in our favour," replied Canning.

"I can explain our escape satisfactorily, I think."

"I shall be glad to hear your explanation, for I am fairly puzzled," said Canning.

"Those who are born to be ——, h'm! I don't like to pronounce the word——"

"Hanged."

"Yes, that is it. Those who are born to be hanged will never be drowned."

"Ha! ha!" laughed Canning; "that is not so bad."

"The ship, as far as I can see, is not materially injured in any way," said Money Marks.

"Not at all."

"Where are we, think you?"

"I cannot pretend to say."

"In my opinion, we are on one of those numerous islands with which the Pacific abounds."

"It is, I conclude, uninhabited."

"How shall we get off?" inquired Harry Canning.

"In the simplest way in the world."

"All great ideas are simple."

"We must make the men work and cut a canal."

"Ah! I see."

"Through the sand."

"To be sure."

"Did you not think of that?"

"No."

"I am surprised at that."

"I am no genius."

"When we have our canal," continued Money Marks, "we will let the water in and she will float."

"That's it—that's the way to do it."

"You had better tell the ship's carpenter to set to work over a new rudder; and now there is a chance of doing it, let the vessel's sides be cleared of barnacles and all other foulness. It will improve her speed half a knot."

The men cheerfully fell in with the views of their commander; but they would not work until they had enjoyed a three days' holiday, during which they amused themselves after their own peculiar customs.

On the morning of the fourth day, when the men were settling down to their work, a cyclone, similar to that which drove Money Marks on the island, arose; and thinking it would be a grand sight, he took Cuffy with him, and ascended the sides of a steep hill in order to get a good view of the raging wind out at sea.

"Well, Cuffy, old friend, what do you think of our numerous adventures?" said Money Marks, in a kindly tone.

"Like it very well, Massa Marks."

"That is right. What do you think of this storm?"

"It am grand."

Marks took up his spyglass, and swept the horizon with it far and wide.

He saw nothing.

"I can see nothing!" he exclaimed. "I have often heard you boast of the keenness of your sight; take the glass and see what you can make out."

The negro did so.

He started.

"What do you see?" inquired Money Marks.

"You see noting, sar?"

"No."

"That odd."

"Why?"

"Cuffy see someting."

"Where?"

"At sea."

"What is it?"

"A ship."

"Really?"

"Yes; and it coming dis way."

Money Marks snatched the glass from his hand, and took another long and searching look. The negro was in the right. A ship was being driven as the pirate had been driven towards the island.

She was, however, beating against a ridge of rocks, and there seemed to be little hope for her.

"She will be wrecked," said Cuffy.

"Alas! yes," replied Money Marks. "We had better go to the beach and see what good we can do to the poor wretches on board."

"May save some lives," said Cuffy.

"I am sure I hope so."

They descended the hill rapidly, made the crew of the pirate acquainted with what was about to happen, and going to the beach with ropes, awaited the sequel.

On came the devoted vessel. She was not obedient to the helm; and those on board appeared to be unable to exercise the least control over her.

On she came, steadily drifting to her fate.

Within a few yards of the land she struck.

Oh, the shrieks that arose—the despairing death-cries—the awful wails—the terrible spasmodic shrieks!

Several heads were seen floating on the water, then they sank. Two people were washed on shore and taken to the pirate vessel to be carefully tended.

It was a man and a woman.

Money Marks did not look at them. He contented himself with commanding that they should be cared for, and then went on with his humane work of rescuing the ship-wrecked from the devouring waves.

But those two solitary ones were all that the sea would give up alive.

All the rest perished!

CHAPTER XXXV.

A STRANGE MEETING.

"WHAT a shocking affair!" Money Marks exclaimed, addressing Canning.

"Ay, it is indeed, sir."

"We, you see, are not the only ones in misfortune."

"No; a sailor's life is ups and downs—here to-day and gone to-morrow. No wonder Jack-tars like to be jolly when they are on shore. The poor devils never know when they will be there again. With a sweetheart in every port, the ocean is nevertheless their bride."

"And one that frequently engulfs them in a fatal embrace."

"Yes, 'tis so."

"Are you sure that all, save those two, have perished?"

"I am afraid there is little doubt of it, sir," replied Canning.

"Have you made careful inquiries?" said Money Marks.

"I have, sir. The dead bodies are being washed on the sands along with barrels of meat, hencoops, and tins of biscuits. We shall have to dig a deep trench to hold all the dead."

"And no one to read a funeral service?"

"Say, 'God rest them!'"

"Would the prayer avail coming from us?" said Money Marks.

Canning was silent. He hung down his head, and memories of his former days seemed to flit across his memory. There had been a time when he was pure and spotless, but the purity had gone; and many a crime had stained his immaculate character, as his conscience painfully reminded him.

"What countryman is the stranded vessel?" inquired

Money Marks, changing the subject, which was not a remarkably pleasant one.

"American, from what I can learn, sir."

"Indeed!"

"Yes."

"North or South?"

"Well, there's the difficulty."

"How?"

"There is a mystery somewhere."

"What is your own opinion?"

"I think——"

"Well."

"That she is a Confederate cruiser."

"If so, why should the survivors endeavour to conceal their nationality?" inquired Money Marks.

"For a very plain reason, sir."

"What is that?"

"They do not know who we are," replied Canning.

"Ah! I perceive your meaning. What are the rescued people like?"

"The man is evidently the captain of the vessel. I can tell that by the gold lace on his coat, and his manner. He was the last to leave the ship, and did his duty like a man."

"And the woman?"

"Lady——"

"Well, well, you know my meaning."

"She is exquisitely beautiful. I do not know that I ever saw a fairer creature in my life."

"You are enthusiastic."

"The theme is one to raise one's enthusiasm."

"Think you she is the captain's wife?" said Money Marks.

"That I cannot pretend to determine."

"You must have an opinion, one way or another."

"Indeed, I have not."

"That is strange!"

"Here comes Main—he has but lately left the ship, and is probably desirous of making a report!" exclaimed Canning.

Jasper Main advanced with a slouching gait, peculiar to him, and approached Money Marks, to whom he touched his hat in a respectful manner.

"Well, Main, what is the best news with you?" Money Marks said.

"If you please, sir, I have just come from the vessel, and wish to report about the survivors."

"What of them?"

"They are Confederates."

"Are they so?"

"Yes, and their vessel was far-famed as a cruiser. It is a sad loss. They were driven by a storm into unknown latitudes, and were as much puzzled as ourselves as to where they were."

"Are they man and wife?"

"No."

"How do you know?"

"From what I have seen and heard."

"And that is——"

"The woman or lady—for she is, I should say, perfectly ladylike, both by birth and education—has a great dislike for the man. Her dislike amounts to perfect horror at times, yet she feels under an obligation to him; for when the ship went to pieces, he undoubtedly saved her life at the risk of his own."

"I suppose that is so," replied Money Marks, reflectively.

"The gentleman has sent word that now he finds himself sufficiently recovered, he would be glad to see you," resumed Jasper Main.

"Me?"

"Yes, sir."

"Tell him that I will wait upon him in half an hour's time."

"Half an hour?"

"Yes, and be sure that he has the best of everything that the ship affords."

"Certainly."

Jasper Main went away, and Money Marks, taking Canning's arm, walked slowly back to the ship, around which a number of men were hard at work. Some were employed in digging the canal which was to liberate the sand-bound vessel, and enable her to cleave the sea once more with her wonted speed.

Others, again, were at work at her bottom, scraping the

copper free from parasitical molluscs. Every one was busy, and cheerfully busy. Songs arose on all sides, and all appeared to be happy and contented.

Money Marks climbed on board by springing into the chains, and having reached the deck, inquired if the captain of the wrecked vessel was visible, for, if so, he would be happy to give him an interview.

The answer returned was to the effect that the captain—whose name no one appeared to know—was waiting in a cabin which had been placed at his disposal.

Accordingly Money Marks went below, and walked into the cabin, fully determined to sympathise with a brave man who had fallen a victim to disastrous circumstances, over which he could possibly have no control.

Why, then, did he start back? press his hands to his eyes as if to reassure himself that he was not dreaming?

Why did he grow pale and red by turns?

Why did he at last utter a cry of joy, and exclaim—

"Fate, fate, fate! Fate is indeed all-powerful."

The captain of the unfortunate vessel was equally affected.

He uttered no cry of joy; he did not appear agreeably surprised. The only cry he uttered was one of dismay—of fear—of despair!

Why was Money Marks so excited at a casual meeting in a desert island?

This is the reason.

The man who stood before him was—

Captain Arlee!

Arlee, his inveterate enemy! Arlee, his foe for years! The determined man who had sworn to have his blood, and had been baffled only by a miracle. The man who had ravished Viola from his arms, and swore that she should never be his, stood before him!

Money Marks was not long in recovering his equanimity. It was now his turn to triumph, and he did not neglect the opportunity.

The young pirate was mortal; all mortals are frail; he could not resist the temptation of torturing his enemy.

"So, Captain Arlee, we meet once more," he exclaimed, with a smile of ironical fierceness.

"Yes," replied the Confederate, who could also be proud when there was occasion for his pride, "we meet again."

"I always cherished a hope that this hour would arrive," continued Money Marks, "and now that it has arrived, I could die to-morrow without a murmur."

Arlee was trembling violently; his agitation was so excessive that the words that escaped his lips left them tremulously.

"You will be generous in the hour of triumph?" he said.

"Generous. *I* generous to *you!*"

"The truly brave are always so."

"That is as much as to say that you are a coward."

"Why?"

"Because it was little generosity you showed me in *your* hour of triumph."

"Let the past be forgotten."

"Never, never, so help me God, never!" cried Money Marks.

"Do not you call upon God," said Arlee, with a sneer.

Money Marks' demeanour had goaded him into bitterness, because that demeanour was so hopelessly merciless.

"Why should you invoke Him more than myself?"

"Because whatever I may be, and whatever my officers may be, I never have done what you have been guilty of."

Money Marks looked upon the boldness of demeanour exhibited by the Confederate captain as the insolence of despair.

And so in a great measure it was.

"What do you know about me?" he said.

"I know this," returned Arlee, fearlessly—"you are a pirate; a bloodthirsty ruffian, who ought to be swinging at your yardarm!"

"Take care that such a fate as that you describe is not awaiting you," said Money Marks, with emphasis.

"Ha, you threaten me with death?"

"I do."

"Where, then, is your boasted generosity?" said Arlee, turning as white and pale as any ghost.

"I never vaunted my generosity; I never boasted its possession; whatever milk of human kindness there may be in my composition is all turned to gall and bitter wormwood so far as you are concerned."

Arlee's pallor increased.

But a day had elapsed since he was the proud captain of a noble ship; and now, what was he? Lo! a transformation had taken place. Fickle Dame Fortune waved her wand and he was a prisoner; sentence of death had been virtually passed upon him—his hours on earth were numbered.

It was indeed a change.

His heart no longer bounded with hope and beat wildly with a mad joy as he revelled in a sense of ecstatic triumph.

All that was changed.

Money Marks could not help thinking of the fortune-teller he had met with in Buenos Ayres.

The weird prediction of Sister Therese floated through his brain. This strange woman had declared that he would soon meet with his inveterate enemy, and he had so met with him. She had added that he would spare his life, and that he would see Viola.

Viola, his soul's idol!

This part of the prophecy he laughed to scorn. What was more unlikely than for him to have news of Viola, who was thousands of miles away, perhaps in a prison, perhaps dead; who could tell?

Was it likely that he should spare his life, now that he was cast unexpectedly in his power? No; he had hungered for this man's blood, and his thirst would not be quenched by aught else.

"You and I, Arlee, are determined enemies," exclaimed Money Marks. "I was lately in your power, and you did all you could to kill me; I escaped from your machinations by a miracle."

"You did," was the calm reply.

"Now you are in my power, and I have too much revenge to gratify, too much malignant feeling to appease to permit you to go away scot-free."

"I expected no more."

"And yet you asked for mercy!"

"Who would not?"

"It is an additional triumph for me that you should have condescended to plead for my clemency. You are humbled and abject, you have begged your life at my hands."

"I have."

"You have pleaded in plaintive tones."

"That is true enough."

"It is a confession of weakness."

"I pleaded for my life, because life is sweet and it is hard to die."

"You have asked your life at my hands, and I refuse to give it you," said Money Marks, whose features scintillated with a fiendish glow of pleasure. "Do you hear me?" he continued; "I, Money Marks—I, the pirate—the bloodthirsty ruffian, who, as you say, ought to swing at his own yard-arm, tell you that you must surely die."

Captain Arlee bowed his head.

"You are resigned to your fate?"

"I bow to the irresistible force of circumstances."

"Have you any request to make?"

"You are relentless?"

"Inflexible as a stone," replied Money Marks, through his clenched teeth.

"How long have I to live?"

"In two hours you die."

"I would ask one poor favour."

"What's that?"

"Let me die like a gentleman."

"No."

"No? Are you in earnest?"

"Sternly so."

"Shoot me with your own hand."

"Again, no."

"What will you do with me, then?"

"You shall die the death of a dog; the commonest man in my crew shall place the cord round your neck, and you shall dangle in the air like a malefactor."

Captain Arlee became shockingly convulsed; his features were contracted, his face blackened, and his eyes started from their sockets as if he already felt all the agonies of suffocation. Money Marks gloated over his misery, and seemed to enjoy keenly every sign of distress exhibited by the unfortunate captain of the Confederate cruiser.

"Curses on you!" cried Arlee, when he had sufficiently recovered from the paroxysm of rage into which he had been plunged, to be able to speak—"curses on you for a hard-

CUFFY STOPS THE WAY.

hearted cur! Oh! would to God that I were armed; but stay, nature has given me nerve and muscular power. I will essay a struggle. Beware! Look to yourself, for by Heaven the devil is roused within me, and there will be blood spilled."

These ferocious words had scarcely escaped Captain Arlee's lips before he sprang forward with a cry resembling that of a wild beast when goaded to madness by the spears and arrows of his cruel pursuers.

His intention was undoubtedly to make so furious an onslaught upon the pirate, as to be able to bear him to the ground and strangle him before a sound could be uttered or help obtained.

Money Marks's eagle eye and quick comprehension had, however, taken everything in at a glance; he saw what was happening and was prepared. The muzzle of a pistol gleamed in the obscure light of the cabin, which was here and there illuminated by a ray of sunlight streaming, or rather creeping, in through a half-opened port-hole.

When Arlee saw the pistol presented at his head, he stopped short; not through fear, however. His feeling was the reverse of that. A flash of pleasure illuminated his countenance, and he fell on his knees, saying—

"Heaven, I thank thee for this one blessing."

He thought that he had by his determined action provoked Money Marks into shooting him in self-defence, and that he had thus escaped, or rather cheated, the cord and the hangman.

In this belief he was, however, mistaken.

Money Marks had not the slightest intention of killing him by a shot from a pistol; he knew that the heart of the proud Confederate would be inexpressibly wrung by a public execution. He intended to keep him standing on the deck, with the rope round his neck, while he taunted him and sneered at him.

Captain Arlee shut his eyes, his lips moved as if he were uttering his last prayer; he fully expected death to overtake him every second.

Money Marks raised his pistol and reversed it after lowering the trigger.

The click of the trigger roused Arlee, who opened his eyes, only to receive a stunning blow on the head from the butt end of the pistol.

He uttered a frightful cry and endeavoured in vain to rise to his feet.

Money Marks dealt him another blow, and the wretched man was soon lying in a pool of blood on the floor.

"He will lie there until I want him," muttered Money Marks, "and now to make preparations for his execution; I must on deck. By the way," he added, in the same tone as his thoughts flew from one subject to another, "I wonder who the woman is that Arlee took such an interest in and saved from the wreck; some vagrant flame, I presume. Still if she pleases him she may please me. There will be no treason or infidelity to Viola in my speaking to this mysterious beauty."

He took a few strides across the cabin in the direction of the door.

Suddenly he stopped.

Loud knocking was heard.

The door was pushed violently open from without.

A woman entered, and Money Marks was confronted with —with whom?

CHAPTER XXXVI.

THE POWER OF LOVE.

THE last chapter ended with a pertinent question—Money Marks was confronted with some one.

With whom?

With *Viola?*

Yes. His astonished eyes informed him of the fact—his startled ears told him that his dearly-loved Viola stood before him, and was speaking to him in tremulous accents, as she exclaimed—

"Oh, Heaven, you have killed him !"

"Viola !" said Money Marks, in a deep, thrilling voice.

He was hardly able to believe the evidence of his senses.

This, then, was the mysterious beauty about whom Jasper Main had raved, and whom he had declared to be one of the most radiant creatures with whom he was acquainted.

Money Marks's exclamation made Viola conscious of whose presence she was in. Her surprise equalled, if not surpassed, his.

For fully a minute they stood gazing at one another, incapable of speech and action.

Then Viola darted forward, and threw herself into Money Marks's arms. She fell with a sob and sigh upon his manly bosom and wept.

He gently repulsed her—not driving her away from him, but simply holding her at arm's length with one hand whilst he pointed to Captain Arlee with the other, saying, with as much sternness as he could command and compress into his features—

"That man is not dead, Viola; I struck him to the earth in self-defence. He is simply stunned, if the intelligence is gratifying to you."

"To me—gratifying to me !" repeated Viola.

"Before I return your caress," said Money Marks, "I must demand an explanation from you."

"From me?"

"Yes."

"Of what kind?"

"You were on board the same ship as Captain Arlee, my foe, my enemy. Do I exaggerate when I say my curse? Tell me in what capacity you sailed with him; tell me—I will believe you—I will take your word. All your companions are drowned. The sea is the repository of their secrets, and the waves are as silent as a sepulchre."

"You suspect me of infidelity to you," said Viola, with dignity.

"I suspect nothing. I merely put a question to you, to which I expect an answer. It is not asking much."

"You are wrong to suspect me," said Viola, laying her hand upon his arm and looking up in his face with her eloquent blue eyes.

Had she been false to all her vows he could have forgiven her when he looked into their liquid depths.

"Speak !"

"I will, my own. If I did not immediately explain what seemed mysterious and obscure, you must attribute it to my delight at seeing you again and to the confusion which that delight produced. You do not know, my own, how I have longed for and looked forward to this day—this blissful day —this happy hour ! I knew it would come—I felt certain of that, and yet the happiness seemed too great. When I saw you so unexpectedly just now all the blood left my veins and rushed into my heart : I felt as if I should drop to the earth, and I could not talk to you."

Money Marks gave vent to a deep sigh.

"Yes, my own, I was overcome with happiness; for I have ever cherished your dear memory in my heart. You have been my idol, and I know that you are worthy of my idolatry, because you are so good and pure."

The pirate winced at this.

It was clear that Viola did not know what he was; she was ignorant of the infamous trade he was carrying on, and he cursed the hour in which he embarked in it.

A terrible thought occurred to him.

Suppose that some malignant reptile, some enemy, some snake in the grass, being well acquainted with Viola's purity and innocence of mind were to go behind his back and reveal the truth in all its naked hideousness, telling her that he was no better than a pirate—an ocean robber—a highwayman of the seas; what would the consequence be?

He dared not think.

Would she not recoil in affright from his blood-stained hands? would she not shudder to think that he was so young and so depraved—and, worse than all, would she not give him his *congé*, bid him a long adieu, and leave him for ever and ever?

He trembled when he thought of this, to him, awful contingency.

What would he do without Viola's love? It was all that his inner self or mortal being had to live upon.

That gone, the little good that yet remained in him would go also, and he would become a demon incarnate.

"You are well aware," continued Viola, "that Mr. Arlee held me a captive in his house."

"I am."

"When he received a ship from the Confederate authorities at Charleston he immediately placed me on board, but without consulting my wishes or gaining my permission."

"That I can readily believe," said Money Marks, with a bitter smile.

"Oh, how he pressed me to be his wife ! What promises he made, which were to be my reward in the event of my complying with his desires; but no, my own, I was ever faithful to your memory. If you are poor, you are good; you have a noble profession, and I am convinced my trust has not been misplaced."

"You are good," "a noble profession;" these phrases jarred Money Marks's ears. He saw on what a sandy foundation his hope of an alliance with Viola rested. He saw how insecure his position was, and he wished that he was anything but what he was.

Nobility in piracy ! Well, there might be; but there is seldom much nobility in a hanging matter. Yet a halo of grandeur hangs about a great criminal, even as Satan—the fallen angel—the grand creation of Milton, stands so prominently and not altogether repulsively in "Paradise Lost."

If his character had any "good" in it, he had for some time been doing himself an injustice, for he placed his light under a bushel.

Viola's voice once more sounded through the room, and broke the spell of his meditations.

"Are you listening to me, my own?" she said; "you look abstracted."

"Yes; I am listening," he replied, rather sullenly.

He was not angry with her, but he was inclined to quarrel with his fate.

"Arlee," Viola went on, "told the crew that I was his cousin, and a passenger to some remote port. By the crew, and by the officers, who I am sorry to hear are drowned, I was treated with the greatest kindness, and it is a matter of regret with me that they should not have met with a better fate. Captain Arlee, however, was an exception to the general good treatment I received; he was for ever persecuting me, and being a man of a violent and intemperate disposition I was always fearful of some ill-usage—nor was I wrong in my anticipations. A few days before the storm, which drove us out of our reckoning, occurred, he swore to me, with the most awful oaths, that if I did not marry him at the next port at which we touched he would be fearfully revenged, and further that he would take measures more severe than any he had yet adopted to compel me. What was I to do? I protested in vain, and told him that nothing would ever induce me to become his wife; at which he grew exceedingly angry, and reproached me in no measured terms. I retaliated, and told him that he was the constructive murderer of my father. We had an angry interview, and he went away declaring that I should be his wife or die within less than a month."

"The scoundrel!" interposed Money Marks between his teeth.

"Oh! how I prayed for your help, your guidance, your assistance—oh! how I implored Heaven to send you to my rescue in the long and weary watches of the night, when I passed unutterably miserable and lonely hours, sleepless and solitary."

"My poor darling!" said Money Marks, commiserating her wretchedness.

"I have much cause to hate Arlee."

"You have; but set your mind at rest."

"About what?"

"His tyranny in the future, if by any chance you should be separated from me."

She caught hold of his arm clingingly, and said in tearful accents, as she looked at him confidingly—

"I must never, never be separated again from you."

"I trust we shall not be parted."

"But what of Arlee?"

"He must die!"

"Die?" repeated Viola, terrified.

"Most certainly."

"And why?"

"Because he is a wretch, and has more than once nearly successfully compassed my death. It is not safe for me to allow him to be at large. It is good for me that he should die; therefore I must kill him."

"Oh! don't kill him!" cried Viola, clasping her hands in a supplicating manner.

"You ask me not to kill him—you ask me to spare Arlee. The age of wonders will never cease. Has he not grossly outraged your virginal feeling, and your maidenly instincts?—and yet you say spare Arlee. Has he not been your enemy with as much determination as he has been mine? He is to all intents and purposes my murderer, for it was not his fault that I was not shot in the lines before Charleston, and yet you say spare Arlee."

"Yes; I reiterate my request."

"Can it be possible, Viola, that this man has inspired you with affection?" demanded Money Marks, almost angrily.

"No; yet he has a claim upon me."

"How?"

"Are you ignorant of the fact that he saved my life?"

"I have heard so."

"Well; do I not owe him a life?"

"I cannot see that you do."

"You will not hear me?"

"Let me talk about something else; I am too pleased to see you to wish to dwell upon unpleasant matters."

"Pleased to see me!—and yet you deny me the trifling favour I ask at your hands."

"Trifling!" said Money Marks, scornfully.

"Pardon me; I may have made use of an improper expression—no one's life can be a trifling matter."

"He tried to take mine."

"That is no reason why you should act revengefully. Do you not remember that One who is mightier than man has said, 'Vengeance is mine?'"

"A sermon never issued from prettier lips," said Money Marks, with a smile of doubtful appreciation.

"Return good for evil—give him his life, because he gave me mine."

"He saved you for his own selfish purposes."

"I grant that, because my knowledge of the man's character will not allow me to deny it; still he saved me. Are you not grateful to his strong and protecting arms, my own? Had it not been for him I should not be standing by your side at this moment."

Money Marks was perplexed; he saw the cogency of Viola's reasoning—yet he had steadfastly made up his mind that Captain Arlee should die. He did not wish to hurt Viola's feelings by telling her so in so many words, but he wished to make an evasive answer—postpone the conversa-

tion for an hour or two—induce her to closet herself in her cabin, and while she was absent string him up to the yard-arm, where he would soon dangle like so much carrion.

Just at this juncture Captain Arlee began to recover his senses, and moved uneasily.

"See! see!" cried Viola, "he moves."

Touching a hand-bell which stood on the table, Money Marks waited, knowing that the sound would summon Cuffy.

CHAPTER XXXVII.

THE PREDICTION FULFILLED.

In less than a minute the black entered the cabin, and looked curiously around him. He recognised Miss Cathcart at a glance, and making an obsequious bow, touched his wool in token of respect.

Captain Arlee's face was turned from him, therefore he did not know him until a few minutes later.

"Glad to see you back to de massa, Missy Viola!" exclaimed Cuffy, taking advantage of that freedom which his master permitted him to use.

He was an old friend and a privileged person, as well as a faithful servant and devoted adherent.

"You drop from de clouds, Missy Viola?" he continued.

"No, no. You will know all shortly. Let this man be taken to the infirmary."

"Yes, massa."

Going nearer to him, Money Marks took occasion to say in a whisper—

"Guard him well."

Cuffy nodded his head, and taking Arlee in his arms, prepared to carry him to the "sick bay," or infirmary of the ship.

"Tell the doctor to be careful with him," said Viola, in a peremptory tone, which she always adopted when speaking to a negro.

She was a thorough Southerner, and had, before the war, been accustomed to command great numbers of slaves. However faithful a black might be, she considered him an inferior animal, and treated him accordingly.

Her creed was a hard one, but it was the one in which she had been brought up, and she was not altogether answerable for the prejudices which she had imbibed almost with her mother's milk.

Cuffy uttered a cry of joy when his eyes fell upon Captain Arlee's features. Looking at his master, he saw no responsive glance, so he said nothing, but quietly pursued his way with his burden.

"Will you retire to your cabin?" said Money Marks to Viola. "I am sure you must be fatigued, and in a warm latitude like this a siesta in the latter part of the day is almost indispensable."

"Thank you for your kind consideration," replied Viola, "I will lie down for an hour. Pray let the steward rap at my door at the expiration of that time."

"He shall do so."

Money Marks saw Viola to her cabin, and, as he left her, respectfully raised her hand to his lips, imprinting a kiss thereon, whereat she blushed, and went hastily into her own apartment.

Money Marks called Canning to his side, and gave him instructions relative to Arlee's intended execution. He wished the affair to be managed without much publicity.

When Viola entered her cabin, she threw herself on her knees, and poured out her soul in prayer. She felt very grateful to Heaven for all its mercies—not the least of which was her restoration to Money Marks, after whom her soul had panted fiercely. Arlee had played the part of a tyrant of the most repulsive sort whenever he had any control over her, but she did her best to forgive him, and flattered herself that she had so worked upon Money Marks's better nature as to induce him to spare his enemy.

When she had brought her prayers to an end, she opened that good and precious book which has aptly been called the Book of Life, and which had been her friend and companion all through her solitary wanderings, and read some of the sweetest and most touching passages, which were singularly applicable to her state of life.

Suddenly, she heard a great noise, as of some one trampling heavily on the deck overhead.

A terrible suspicion took possession of her. Could it be

possible that Money Marks had broken his half-pledged word, or was about to break it, and that Arlee was in momentary danger of losing his life?

She was a resolute woman, and her determination was soon taken.

Going to the door of the cabin, she opened it, intending to ascend to the deck by the hatchway, and interpose the weight of her authority, so as to prevent the commission of a crime which she rightly supposed was about to be perpetrated.

A black man, however, barred her exit.

This was Cuffy.

"Let me pass!" she said.

"No, Missy Viola."

"You will not?"

"It am against orders."

"Whose orders?"

"Captain Marks'."

"I am sure you are wrong," said Viola. "Go to your master and say that Miss Cathcart wishes to go on deck. He will, I feel confident, give you the required permission without delay."

"No, missy, him not do that. Cuffy just left him, and he say, 'No let Missy Viola go on deck.'"

"Is this true?"

"As de Bible!" responded Cuffy.

"Alas! then my suspicions are true, and likely to be realized. Let me pass, I conjure you. I will make you handsome presents."

"I want nothing."

"Are you sure?"

"I do my duty."

"Stand on one side. I will pass. I am not to be dictated to in this way!" vociferated Viola, who was becoming frantically angry, and desperately anxious.

It was a passion with her to save Arlee's life, not because she loved or even cared for him, but he had snatched her from the jaws of death when they were yawning to receive her, and she was grateful for the service.

Cuffy presented an impenetrable front, and would not move one way or the other.

Rushing back into her cabin, Viola snatched up a small silver-handled, sharp-bladed knife, and holding it up menacingly, exclaimed—

"Let me pass or some evil may befall you; I am not to be further restrained."

"What missy going to do?" cried the astonished black.

"Stab you!"

"Me?"

"Yes, if you do not permit me to pass."

Cuffy scarcely knew what to do. He was certain that Money Marks would not like to see the least violence used towards Viola, and yet it was important that she should remain down below.

And why?

Because Captain Arlee was in five minutes to be hanged like a dog by the neck, until he was dead!

The tables were turned now with a vengeance. The day of retaliation had arrived, and the once proud Confederate was humbled in the dust.

"You must no go, Miss Viola," he said. "Cuffy your friend, and he tell you so."

"Why?"

"'Cos someting goin' on up there."

"What? speak!"

"Only Cappen Arlee; him gwine to be hanged."

"Is it so? Then I must go. Stand on one side, or look to yourself. I would not do you an injury, but at this moment I am hardly mistress of myself, and not responsible for my actions."

The blade of the knife gleamed in the air, and wishing to keep a whole skin Cuffy moved slightly on one side.

Viola darted past him with inconceivable velocity, and was on deck before he could recover from his surprise.

What a sight met her startled gaze!

A small group of men were discernible aft. The centre of this group was Captain Arlee, around whose neck was noosed a strong cord, the other end of which was thrown over a beam of wood, or more strictly speaking a spar.

Four men had the end of the rope in their hands, and were only waiting for orders to jerk the miserable captive into mid-air, where he would swing an insensible mass, dead and disgraced.

Money Marks was talking to his victim.

She stood petrified for a brief space.

During this space she heard the pirate exclaim—

"Let one last drop of bitterness fill your cup to the brim. Viola is below. Viola is mine. She has told me that she loves me more than ever; die with this fact ringing in your ears. Die with the full consciousness that what I say is the truth. Viola is mine."

Arlee made no answer; his head drooped a little, and his eyes were moist.

"Have you anything to say?" continued Money Marks.

"A few words," replied the Confederate, in a low voice.

"What are they?"

"Be kind to her. We both loved her. I loved her as much as yourself. Be kind to her."

Money Marks was touched by the sincerity of this request, and replied in the affirmative.

"Now then, men," he cried, "are you ready?"

"Yes, sir."

"Pull!"

"No, no, no!" cried Viola, with a loud shriek, springing forward, and slashing away at the hands of the men who had in obedience to their orders jerked the body in the air.

Her efforts were maniacal.

The men finding that the small knife was as sharp and as keen as a razor, and that their hands were becoming terribly gashed, let the body run down to the deck with speed.

Then they stood ruefully regarding their maimed hands.

Arlee was saved by a miracle!

He fell on his back, and lay panting and struggling. The blood had rushed to his face, to his head, to his brain.

Although he had been let down unexpectedly, the rope was still tight round his neck, and he was strangling!

When Viola's quick eye perceived this she fell on her knees beside his body, and with her own delicate hands undid the hard cord which, by the tightness of its folds, would soon have made a corpse of him.

Money Marks folded his arms, and looked sternly.

When Viola flung the rope with a dull noise upon the deck, he made a motion to the sailors bidding them take the rope away and retire for the present.

This dumb order they executed silently, but with dispatch.

The pirate's brow was clouded, and his evil passions were at work.

Cuffy had ascended, and his master beckoned him to him.

"Why were my orders disobeyed?" he said.

"I couldn't help it, massa. De Lord knows that it wasn't Cuffy's fault."

"Conduct this lady to her cabin."

"No. I will not go until——"

"You will not go?" said Money Marks, with a smile.

"I said so."

"Do you know who you are talking to? Have you forgotten that I am the captain of this vessel? Has that fact escaped your memory? If so it is but proper that I should remind you of it."

"I cannot," repeated Viola; "in saving Captain Arlee's life I have done my duty as a Christian. God knows that I did so from no feeling of personal attachment to the man."

"Go," replied Money Marks.

"I will not until you promise me on your sacred word of honour that you will not proceed with Captain Arlee's execution."

"I make no promise."

"Give him his life. Tell me that you give it to him, and I will go away in peace and contented, because I know you will keep your word."

"The man has wronged me."

"I have done you no wrong; grant me my poor petition."

"He deserves death."

"That may be so."

"He showed me no mercy."

"All the more reason why you should exhibit your clemency."

Arlee woke up while Money Marks was hesitating.

He sat upon the deck, and stared wildly around him. It was evident that he failed to recall his scattered senses.

"Where—where am I? because I feel as if I had just awaked from a terrible dream! A hideous night-mare! The rope was round my neck, the executioners stood by me, the cord tightened, there was a rush of blood to my head, then I fell against some hard substance, as if I were striking against the sides of the bottomless pit! Is this another land? Am I disembodied or still in the flesh? Oh! speak, speak, you that are around me. Tell me, are—are ye fiends or something human?"

"You live," replied Money Marks.

This voice recalled Arlee to himself.

"Ah! I see it all now. I was not wrong, for you are a fiend! Is this respite—this calling back the spirit to a world it thought it had quitted for ever, an instance of your devilish ingenuity and diabolical cunning?"

Money Marks pointed to Viola.

"You must thank that lady for your deliverance."

"Viola!"

"Yes."

"Do I indeed owe my life to you?"

"I endeavoured to return the life you saved for me," she replied earnestly.

"Heaven pour its choicest blessings on your head for your kind generosity," cried Arlee, with passionate feeling.

"Mr. Marks!" exclaimed Viola.

How the "mister" jarred and grated in his ears.

"At your service," he replied.

"The fortune of war has once, if not more than once, placed you in Captain Arlee's power."

"It has."

"It may do so again."

"Knowing that fortune—whether of war or otherwise—is proverbially fickle, I wished to put it out of its power; if Captain Arlee, in whom you seem to take a great interest, were dead, fortune never could put me in his power. Do you follow me? do you see the force of my argument?"

"Yes, I do; but I daresay Captain Arlee will promise that he will exert himself on your behalf if ever you should require his influence."

"Is it a promise on which I could rely?"

"Will you spare his life if he gives it you?"

"A gentleman's word may always be relied upon," said Arlee faintly, but with dignity.

Money Marks saw that he should be obliged to comply with Viola's oft-repeated request, unless he wished her to think him vindictive and bloodthirsty, and he determined to yield the point with the best grace he could, and with as much advantage to himself.

"Will Captain Arlee promise that if ever I should be in want of his assistance he will grant it me, providing I at this moment agree to spare his life, and land him at the first port my ship touches at?" said Money Marks.

Arlee eagerly caught at this proposition.

"Yes," he said; "I agree to that, and I promise on the word and honour of a gentleman, holding the commission of the Confederated States of South America, that I will do my best to serve Mr. Marks, should he ever be in a position to demand my aid."

"You promise that?"

"Most distinctly."

"Then I give you your life, Captain Arlee, which I considered forfeited by the attempt you made to kill me some little time back in the lines before Charleston."

"It is a bargain?"

"Certainly," replied Money Marks.

And this was how Money Marks gave his life to Captain Arlee—a step he could not help taking, and which he thought ill-advised and injudicious. In his opinion, he would have to regret his action in the matter before many years had rolled over his head; for, although an old saying, it is very hard to kill an enemy with kindness.

Captain Arlee was so unwell, and so shocked through what he had undergone, that he was obliged to be put under the surgeon's care.

Viola retired to her cabin, and Money Marks descended the side of the ship, and watched his men at work.

They were making great progress, and the vessel promised to be afloat again in less than a week.

As he was walking up and down upon the sand he thought of Sister Therese and her prediction.

"Well," he said to himself, "this is indeed wonderful; I had totally forgotten that she had made such a prediction, yet it now comes home to me. She declared that I should spare Arlee, and, strange to say, she spoke the truth."

The prediction was fulfilled.

CHAPTER XXXVIII.
THE SNAKE MOVES IN THE GRASS.

CAPTAIN ARLEE might have been very grateful to Money Marks, but at all events he did not show his gratitude in any way. He was content to keep it under a bushel and let people guess at its existence.

He was always walking about the deck in a stealthy, cat-like manner, which was indicative of anything but good faith.

Viola avoided him now that she was satisfied his life was safe; she knew that any exhibition of friendship on her part towards the Confederate would be distasteful to Money Marks, and most likely misinterpreted.

At last the ship was floated, and the pirates did all they could to get out of the strange locality in which they were. For a long time they were unsuccessful in their endeavours, but after a time they once more got into the regular track, and sailed with their minds at ease.

One day Money Marks was walking on deck with Viola.

Captain Arlee was standing at some distance with his arms folded, and gazing with ill-disguised hatred at the happy pair.

It required no supernatural prescience to enable him to see that Money Marks was whispering words of love to her—to her whom he loved with all his heart, for whom he had risked and suffered much, and for whom he was prepared to suffer more.

"My darling, my own!" exclaimed Money Marks; "I cannot find words to express the joy I feel at once more being united with you in thought and feeling."

"And I too am happy," was the softly uttered reply, "I am very happy; can I say more?"

"Oh, yes!"

She blushed.

"Will you consent to be mine, Viola? my wife, my dearly beloved, my adored, the angel of my heart, the idol of my soul, the——"

"Oh! you must stop, you must indeed," she exclaimed, with downcast face.

"May I not lay bare my inmost thoughts?"

"I would rather not; at least, not now. Speak to me about yourself; the time will come when you may talk to me as you are desirous of doing, but not immediately."

"Your father has been dead some time; do you still grieve for him?"

"Oh, yes! I shall ever grieve for him; it was cruel of you to remind me of him—very cruel."

Her tears were half-inclined to flow, but she checked them as well as she was able.

"Pardon me."

There was a pause.

"I could wish that you were anything else but a sailor," Viola at length exclaimed, breaking the silence.

"And why, my little one?"

"Because it is an uncertain life. I have lost a father—the sea robbed me of him, and—and——"

She hesitated.

"What would you say?"

"It would be very dreadful if it robbed me of a husband also."

Money Marks blessed her for that remark, for it indicated that at some future time she was not unwilling to become his wife.

His wife!

Oh! the ecstatic bliss that happy word gave him; what exquisite delight it afforded him! She would then stand in the most sacred relation of human life to him, and what could be more charming, more delightful, or more joy-giving?

Nothing, absolutely nothing.

"May I hope that you will be mine some day?" said Money Marks; "may I hope it, dear, dearest Viola?"

"You may," she replied, in a tone a little above a whisper.

"Thank you a thousand times for that blest assurance!" he said, rapturously.

"Will you live on shore, and settle down in some place where we can live in pastoral simplicity?" she continued, a flash of hopeful joy breaking through her tear-blotted eyes, as the sun breaks through the clouds after a shower of rain.

"Is that your dream?"

"Oh, yes!"

"I would do anything to please you, dear Viola; therefore

I am ready to make a greater sacrifice than any the adoption of that course would entail upon me."

"You will give up the sea, give up your ship, your companions, the life of your choice—give them all up, my own, and for *me*. Oh! this is good, generous, kind of you."

At this juncture Jasper Main approached the captain, and looking curiously at Viola, said—

"Can I speak to you, sir ?"

"Certainly."

Again Jasper looked at Viola.

This time Money Marks interpreted his glance, and this is how he read it.

"Let her go away ; I want to talk to you on a little matter of business, which it will be best for her not to hear."

So turning to Viola, Money Marks said—

"Will you excuse me ? my lieutenant wishes to speak about some technical matter of business, which I do not think will interest you."

Viola bowed and walked away, but she did not go to where Captain Arlee was sitting disconsolately. He would have given the world for a kind word or a look from her, or even the chance of a little conversation with her. But she passed him on the way to her cabin without appearing to take the least notice of him.

When she reached the sanctity of her own apartment she took pen and ink and occupied herself with making entries in her diary. In this book she was accustomed to chronicle all sorts of ideas; everything that happened to her was put down with her comments thereon. It was a repertory of the curious, and of the beautiful.

We must leave her for some time and return to the deck, where events of moment are about to take place.

Captain Arlee judged from the appearance of unwonted excitement that something unusual was about to take place, but what that something was he could not tell.

So he watched and waited.

Money Marks had no sooner rid himself of Viola, than he turned sharply to his first lieutenant, and said—

"Now, Main, what is it ?"

"The lookout man, sir, reports a ship bearing down towards us north by west."

"What sort of a ship ?"

"A merchantman, by the cut of her jib."

Money Marks said nothing.

"The men seem to think that she will be a prize, sir," continued Jasper Main ; "the news has already spread like wildfire through the ship, and one and all are looking forward to a little legitimate work. For my part I must confess that I am not at all sorry our period of forced inaction is over."

Still Money Marks said nothing.

"Shall I order the ship's guns to be shotted, sir, and the engines worked at double speed ?"

"No, I—I think not," replied Money Marks.

"Excuse me, sir," said Jasper Main, with a stare of sheer amazement, "but I must speak my mind. Here is a ship which will probably turn out a rich prize, and yet you say, 'Do nothing.' The men will be very discontented ; they have always hitherto found you a brave, able, accomplished, and fearless commander. What will they say if you decline to help them to some prize-money, which will be highly acceptable when they enter port ?"

"I do not care for the men."

"It is best to be popular," said Jasper Main, without appearing to notice the half sneer which accompanied the contemptuous speech of his leader.

"What is popularity to me ?"

"May I speak plainly to you, sir ?"

"Yes."

"If you do not fight and capture this ship there will be a mutiny amongst the crew."

Money Marks started.

"For making that remark I ought to order you under arrest."

"It was a friendly remark."

For fully a minute Money Marks was wrapped in thought. Then he placed his hand upon Jasper Main's shoulder, and said—

"Perhaps you are right. I would rather avoid this encounter, because," he lowered his voice, "a lady is on board whom I—I love. I need not make a mystery of the matter, for I suppose it is pretty generally known on board."

Jasper Main nodded affirmatively.

"She does not know what we are or what I am, and I would wish to keep her in ignorance. She has thwarted me once to-day, and——"

"What more easy than to keep her in her cabin ? Let her be well guarded, and then all danger will be at an end ; she is not to know what has been done. I sympathize with you, but I frankly tell you that you will lose your prestige and injure yourself with the crew if you allow this merchantman to go by without robbing her. Who is to tell ? Who is to speak of what has been done, when the crew of the vessel have walked the plank, and the vessel itself has gone to the bottom of the ocean ?"

"There is truth in what you are saying; you are right," said Money Marks, hurriedly. "I thank you. Go at once and give the orders of which you spoke; let the ship be steered for the merchantman, let the engines work at increased speed, have the arsenal thrown open, and let the men be well armed ; have the guns loaded with grape and canister ; serve out a treble allowance of grog to each man. Quick ! let no time be lost."

Jasper Main lifted his hand to his cap, and went away on his errand.

Money Marks spoke with feverish eagerness. When the lieutenant had gone, he called for Cuffy, who was not long in making his appearance.

"What you want, massa ?" he demanded.

"You did not serve me well just now."

"Not my fault, massa ; poor Cuff done his best."

"Prove your penitence by doing better this time. I want you to go and keep watch over Miss Viola Cathcart ; on no account let her leave her chamber. Do you fully understand ?"

"Cuff am afraid to touch Missy Viola."

"In this case you may use manual violence if you cannot prevail in any other way—I give you permission. But whatever you do, do not allow the lady to know what is going on on deck."

"What am it, massa ?"

"We attack a merchantman presently, and there will be bloody work."

"I see, massa. Cuff will do as he is told ; Missy Viola shall not go on deck. No fear this time."

The negro went away, and Money Marks gave orders to the crew and saw that everything was being got in readiness.

Captain Arlee, with a shrewdness peculiar to him, took in every word which was uttered by the seamen, and began to have a suspicion of what was going on.

Canning passed him, and he questioned him. But Canning was one of the uncommunicative order of men ; he was, in vulgar parlance, "a dry old stick," and did not care about opening his mouth to fill other people's.

"What's all this preparation for ?" exclaimed Captain Arlee.

"Don't know," was the laconic reply.

"You don't know ?"

"Didn't I say so ?"

"Yet you are one of the superior officers."

"Who told you so ?"

"Never mind ; I know it," retorted Captain Arlee, warmly.

"What is your knowledge to me ?"

"Will you reply to my query ?"

"If you don't know, I'm not going to tell you."

"I asked you a civil question, my good fellow, and I expected a civil answer," exclaimed Captain Arlee.

"You didn't get it then," replied Canning, with a grin.

"Your insolence ought to be punished."

"It's a pity you don't punish it then."

"Take care I don't attempt ; you would never forget my rough handling."

"Never ?"

"Not till the day of your death. Why cannot you reply to my question ? What is about to happen ?"

"How should I know ?"

"If you don't know, who does ?"

"The captain."

"Will you tell me ?"

"Don't be curious," said Canning.

"What's that to you ?"

"Remember Lot's wife."

"What of her ?"

"She was turned into salt, but you stand in no danger of that, because you are not worth your salt."

With this parting shot, which enraged Arlee beyond the power of utterance, Canning took his departure, and was speedily lost sight of amongst a crowd of men.

Stifling his rage as best he could, he made a further scrutiny, and found that a vessel was approaching. He saw the guns loaded, and he saw that a different flag from that floating from the masthead was ready to be hoisted at a moment's notice.

And what colour was that flag?

"Black!"

Yes; the insignium of the freebooters, of the highwaymen and robbers of the seas, was about to be run up to the peak, but not before the flag of Old England had lured the unsuspecting trader to her destruction.

He came to the conclusion that the highwaymen of the seas were about to give "a taste of their quality," and pursue their bloody trade before his eyes.

What was he to do? He was to all intents and purposes a passenger on board. He could not openly object to what he suspected was going to happen, but he could inwardly determine to remain in his cabin and take no part in the fracas either one way or the other.

He accordingly went to Money Marks, and said—

"I presume I have your permission to retire below."

"Certainly," replied the pirate chief, politely.

"Ah!" said Arlee to himself, as he descended the stairs. "If Viola only knew of this! By the Lord, I have an idea! I will communicate the fact to her. If she only knows Money Marks to be a pirate, she will never love him; her heart is too pure and innocent; she will leave him for ever. Her religion will compel her to do so, and then she may be *mine*. Oh, happy, rapturous thought! Mine! mine! mine!"

The snake was beginning to move in the grass.

CHAPTER XXXIX.

WALKING THE PLANK.

THE ship which hove in sight was, as had been correctly surmised by Jasper Main, a merchantman.

She was perfectly unarmed, for her nation being at war with no one, she thought she had no need of a convoy.

She belonged to English owners, and the British flag flying at the masthead of the pirate made her believe that she had fallen in with a friend.

She took in sail and hove-to. Money Marks ordered a boat to be lowered, and manned with two dozen of his best men armed to the teeth.

He took the command of the boat himself, and had it rowed quickly to the vessel. The captain, an aged man, was standing on deck, and welcomed him with cordiality; he was a native of Scotland, and his barque, the *Caledonian*, was bound for the Clyde.

"Heaven be blessed, my friend," he exclaimed, "that you have met us; we will sail a little way in consort, and you shall taste my wine? What sort of weather have you met with?"

"Rather rough."

"Ah! so have we. It has been dreadful; still, thank heaven, we have not suffered much."

"Have you a valuable cargo?"

"To tell truth, we have more specie than cargo; we have a consignment of bullion for Messrs. Frennedy and Co., of Glasgow."

"Indeed!"

"And where do you hail from?"

"Port of Liverpool, bound for Valparaiso."

"Ah, I ken the town varra weel," replied the Scotchman. "You do?"

"Yes. What countryman are you?"

"English," replied Money Marks.

"And you sail under that flag."

"No."

"Ah! I thought not. There is something about you which told me you were Yankee built," said the old Scotchman, rubbing his hands, and thinking himself very clever.

"I do not sail under the American flag either," replied Money Marks.

"Confed?" enquired the captain of the *Caledonian*, confidently.

"Wrong again."

"Eh? What the devil are you?" cried the Scotchman suspiciously.

"Look at my mast-head," said Money Marks.

As he spoke he turned round, and fired his pistol in the air. This was a signal. The black flag was run up immediately, and the British ensign fell fluttering to the deck.

The captain of the *Caledonian* fell back in mute surprise. He could not believe the evidence of his senses, which were strangely startled. The black flag was to him a thing of the past; he would as soon have thought of meeting a highwayman upon Hampstead or Hounslow Heaths as of encountering a pirate upon the high seas.

"Do you see it?" enquired Money Marks.

"Yes," replied the captain, with a half-articulate gasp.

"Seeing then is believing, or it will have to be in your case."

"Are you a—a—a——?"

"Pirate! why don't you say what you mean, old man?"

"Aweel, aweel; that's what I meant."

"I am!"

"I thought there were no pirates now-a-days."

"Then you thought wrong."

"What do you want of us?"

"More than you are prepared to give, perhaps; let all your gold be brought on deck."

"What if we resist?" said the Scotchman, thinking that his crew were a match for the crew of the piratical boat.

Money Marks at this semi-defiant threat waved his hand, and the swarthy evil-looking fellows he had brought with him threw back their cloaks, and revealed the arsenal of daggers, pistols, and swords, with which they were armed.

The ferocious aspect of these men proved to the captain of the *Caledonian* that there was nothing for him but to submit. Perhaps submission might bring leniency and pardon in its train, and the pirates would be satisfied with plunder and induced to give them their lives, and leave them their ship.

Such, however, was far from Money Marks's intention. He would gladly have spared the men and the ship had he been able to do so with safety; but if he allowed a ship after being plundered to go into port, she would give notice of the robbery, describe his ship and his crew, and so set cruisers upon his track, which would infallibly in the end capture him.

The crime of piracy brought other crimes in its wake, as will be seen presently.

The crew of the merchantman, thirty in number, receiving no orders from their captain to defend the ship, suffered themselves to be made prisoners, and were bound by the pirates, who seemed to take a ferocious pleasure in their work.

A supply of linen was taken out of the hold, and this was torn into strips, with which the crew of the ill-fated ship, who were all doomed to die, were blindfolded!

It seems a frightful and an awful thing that so many men were to die in cold blood. To be butchered like cattle, incapable of resistance!

The cries for mercy! The appeals to the better feelings of the pirates were dreadful to hear, and yet affecting in the extreme to a sensitive mind.

By Money Marks's express command a large plank was brought and placed on deck; one end of it was allowed to rest on a wide deal table, the centre part was on the wooden side of the ship, and the extreme end protruded over the sea; a small ladder was arranged by the side of the table so that the prisoners could reach the table by this means, and then—Heaven help them!

The captured men, of course, were apprehensive of some violence, but they did not guess what was really going to happen to them, nor did the pirates choose to enlighten them.

Some of the captives clasped their hands together and prayed in the most fervent manner, others trembled and looked aghast.

Money Marks hurried the cruel business on. He did not wish it to be prolonged more than was absolutely necessary. He was himself sickened and disgusted beyond measure.

Jasper Main having arranged everything, caught hold of the captain's arm, and said—

"Come along, sir; follow me."

"Where? where?" cried the wretched man.

"To see the captain; perhaps he will give you your liberty."

"Do you think so? Is there any chance of that?" enquired the old man, eagerly.

He believed the shameful fiction of the first lieutenant of the pirate.

"I think there is," replied Jasper Main. "But step out; we must not keep him waiting."

"No, no—certainly not. If you tell me the way to go, I will step out as well as I am able. It is a pity you put this rag over my eyes."

"Never mind that. It won't make much difference presently."

The old man mounted the table, and stepped on the plank as he had been directed. He fully believed that he was going to the captain, and he hoped that the result of his interview might be favourable to himself and the interests of his crew.

Jasper Main no sooner saw him on the plank, than he told him to walk straight on. As he gave this direction, he turned to those who were standing near, and, putting his tongue in his cheek, favoured them with a wicked wink.

It was as much as the pirates thus favoured could do to refrain from giving way to a loud burst of laughter.

Prudence, however, restrained them.

Had they laughed, the old captain would have had his suspicions aroused—would probably have stopped short, and the anticipated sport of the pirates would have been baulked.

The captain walked briskly along the plank—suddenly he came to the end of it, fell forward, tried in vain to throw out his arms, uttered a doleful cry, and was presently immersed in the pitiless water, which knew no more how to spare than did the pirates themselves.

As the old man was bound, of course he could do nothing to save himself. He sank in deep water, but bounded to the surface again before insensibility, attending upon suffocation, set in.

The bandage had been washed off his eyes, and he turned his face towards those on the deck of the ship—upon it was an expression full of agony, full of reproach, horror, rage, fear, tinged with despair.

Ha! what is that? What is that smooth and oddly-shaped thing darting with wonderful velocity through the water; its fins are rapidly moving, its belly is white.

It is the marine monster—the terror of the sea—the shark!

The old man utters a sharp cry of pain. The expression of agony on his face intensifies; he is drawn under, and disappears.

A crimson stain pervades the place where he floated momentarily. No sooner has it made its appearance, than the sea seems to be alive with sharks. They have snuffed blood afar off, and are hastening to the rich banquet Money Marks is preparing for them.

The death of the captain, so far from being a propitiatory sacrifice, was only the preliminary and forerunner of more murder. The men who were passively awaiting their fate with him, eyes bandaged, and their arms bound, were marched up to the table, and from thence to the plank in quick succession.

Splash followed splash, shriek succeeded shriek, and in less than half an hour the entire crew of the merchantman, without one exception, had been made to walk the plank, and had become the prey of the voracious sharks; some of which were so gorged with their disgusting meal, that they floated lazily on the surface of the water, unable to move or feast any further.

When Money Marks saw that the men were all dead, and that not one could ever reach a port to tell the tale to an earthly tribunal, he gave orders that the specie should be taken on board his own vessel, and that the merchantman should be sunk.

He preferred to sink the vessel for this reason. If he blew it up, the attention of some other vessel accidentally cruising in those latitudes might be drawn to the fact, and if they were gifted with ordinary intelligence, they might form their own opinion on the matter, which would be prejudicial to Money Marks, who was desirous above all things of having his sins hidden from the public gaze—known only to those who were embarked with him in the same nefarious trade.

A hole was scuttled in the ship's bottom, and the water began to rush in with great force. The cargo was valuable, but it was of no use to the pirates. They had no room in their own ship for it, and they could not take it to any port, so they allowed it to sink to the bottom of the sea, where so much valuable merchandize has been lost.

*   *   *   *   *   *

While this horrible tragedy was being enacted on board the merchantman, Captain Arlee was cunningly improving his opportunity. He sought Viola, but was refused admittance to her cabin by Cuffy.

"I wish to see Miss Cathcart!" exclaimed Arlee.

"Can't be done, massa."

"Why not? I only want a few minutes' conversation with her."

"'Gainst de massa's orders."

"Come, I'll give you a dollar if——"

"Not for thousand dollars!" replied the negro, decisively.

"You need not go away," said Captain Arlee. "Stay where you are. The door of the cabin shall be left open, and if you wish it, you can come close enough to hear what we talk about. The subject matter of our discourse will not be treason. We are not going to organize a plan of escape. Your master may possibly wish to keep Miss Cathcart in her cabin, but he did not mean you to keep her from her friends."

"Don't know dat."

"She is not a prisoner."

"Well, no; not exactly."

"Just have the goodness to open the door then."

After some further debating, Cuffy hesitatingly knocked at the door.

"What is it?" demanded Viola, from within.

"Massa Arlee, miss."

"I can see nobody."

"Dere," cried Cuffy, triumphantly, "de young lady will not see anybody."

Approaching the door, Captain Arlee rapped with his knuckles, and exclaimed—

"I was in hopes, Miss Cathcart, that you would have granted me a few minutes' conversation."

"Since you are so persistent, sir," was the reply, "I must perforce admit you, though I feel so unwell as to feel a need of rest."

"I will not detain you long. Many thanks for your compliance with my request, which I regret I should have urged so persistently."

Viola opened the door, and Captain Arlee entered. The door was left open, so that Cuffy could keep an eye upon his captive, but although he did his best to overhear what Captain Arlee was saying to Miss Cathcart, he was unable to do so, as they conversed in a low tone, evidently with a view of outwitting him.

"Do not be offended, once and ever, dear Miss Cathcart," exclaimed Captain Arlee, tenderly, casting an impassioned glance upon the girl, young, lovely, radiant, upon whom he had set his affections long, long ago, never faltering or swerving.

Viola looked up deprecatingly.

"Be not alarmed," he resumed; "I am not going to talk to you of love; I know that you have given away your hand and your heart."

"You know it?" she asked in some surprise.

"Alas! yes; would to Heaven that I did not."

"Do you blame me for following the bent of my inclination—for bowing my head to fate, and submitting to what I feel must be?"

"No; far from it. I do not come to blame you, but to warn you."

He spoke very gravely, and his face wore a severe look.

"To warn me!" repeated Viola, in surprise.

"Yes. You stand in need of advice and guidance. I love you, therefore I am your friend, and though you reject me and prefer another for your partner through life, I will not desert you; I will give you the benefit of my knowledge and my experience."

Viola made an inclination of the head, as if she wished to intimate that she was perfectly ready to be enlightened about any subject.

"Do you know who the man is that you are going to marry?"

"Strictly speaking, he may not be a gentleman, though, on the other hand, he may, because his birth is shrouded in mystery. I know him to be a gallant sailor, and an honourable young man."

"You *know* this?"

"I do."

"Permit me to contradict you. Money Marks is neither a gallant sailor nor an honourable young man."

"How dare you asperse his character and calumniate him?" cried Viola, with flashing eyes.

AN UNEXPECTED ENCOUNTER WITH THE WILD MAN OF THE WOODS.

"I am not in the habit of aspersing any one," returned Arlee, quietly.

"What can you say about Money Marks?"

"I say that he is not what you describe him to be."

"What is he, then?"

"A pirate!"

"A what?"

"A pirate."

Having delivered himself of this shot, Arlee threw himself back in his chair, and watched the effect of his communication upon Viola.

It was quick, unmistakeable, decisive. At first she turned ghastly pale, then she appeared to be about to faint, but this passing off, she sat still and gasped for breath.

Arlee smiled grimly.

It was his hour of triumph.

———

CHAPTER XL.

WHAT VIOLA DID.

Money Marks a pirate!

This communication fell like a thunder-bolt upon Viola. She was completely overcome and prostrated with grief to think that she should have loved a man so utterly unworthy of her priceless affection.

Thank God, she was not yet married to him. There was time to retrieve her error; she had not committed herself beyond the power of redemption.

That was one consolation.

Captain Arlee happened to cast his eyes in the direction of the port-hole, which served the purpose of a window, and he saw what was going on on board the merchantman, which was lying-to within a short distance of the pirate.

Money Marks' figure was at all times commanding, and he could be seen standing upon the deck. Arlee singled him out at a glance. The drowning of the prisoners was about to commence.

Presently the old captain walked the plank and was eaten by the shark; the despairing wail he uttered fell faintly upon Viola's ears and roused her.

Starting up, she exclaimed, in a hurried, hasty voice—

" What proof have you of the truth of what you advance ? You cannot expect me to credit your unsupported assertion, since you have so great an interest in prejudicing me against Money Marks."

" You mistake me," replied Arlee; " I have no interest such as that you describe; you may fancy so, but I assure you that you have formed an erroneous estimate of my character. There was a time when I could have made you my wife with pride and pleasure, but now the dream is over."

" Give me proof," persisted Viola.

Captain Arlee took a small telescope from his pocket, and handing it to Viola, said—

" Look at that ship yonder."

" To what purpose ?"

" Look."

She took the glass and watched the ship for some time: her hand trembled, and she became paler than before.

" Oh, what does it mean ?" she said, in a quivering voice; " why are those blindfolded men falling one by one into the sea ? Some awful tragedy is going on; explain to me—and yet it speaks for itself—it requires no explanation."

" Money Marks has just captured that vessel, and that is the way in which he disposes of the crew. You are witnessing a most horrible butchery."

Dropping the glass, Viola covered her face with her hands and wept bitterly.

" Do you believe me now ?" said Arlee, with fiendish malignity sparkling from his eyes.

" Alas ! yes."

" I have one favour to beg of you."

" Name it."

" Do not mention your discovery to Money Marks until I have landed at the first port we touch at."

" Why do you ask this of me ?"

" Because his hatred and revenge will be so great as to prompt him to kill me. You have saved my life once; renew the obligation under which I am to you—make me eternally your debtor."

" I will."

" May I rely upon the honourable preservation of your word ?"

" Most certainly you may."

Captain Arlee was satisfied with this promise, and went away. He knew that his life would not be safe if she were to tell Money Marks that he had undermined her respect and love for him.

How sweet was the revenge he had taken ! Viola was a high-spirited girl as well as a very religious one, and the chances were that she would rather submit to anything sooner than give her hand to a man who followed the disgraceful and infamous occupation which was associated with Money Marks' name, and with which she had that day identified him.

Arlee had sown his seed well: there was little doubt that it would soon bring forth good fruit.

Everything went on as usual for two days. Viola was more melancholy than usual, and confined herself to the privacy of her cabin as much as she was able.

On the evening of the third day Money Marks discovered that he was in the neighbourhood of a port. Before he liberated Arlee he pledged him to secrecy, and made him take a weighty oath that he would not betray him in any way, either by word or deed.

Then he ran the ship into port and gave the Confederate captain his liberty, wondering when he should see him again. They were both on the threshold of fate, and Money Marks was on the eve of many and great adventures.

The pirate stayed one day in this port for the purpose of taking in supplies of a trivial nature. No sooner had Viola satisfied herself that Captain Arlee was in safety, than she sought an interview with Money Marks, which was readily accorded her.

The young pirate was seated at a table in his gorgeously-furnished cabin; a little negro-boy was swinging a punkah, in order to keep the air moving and create a draught, while Cuffy was employed in sprinkling the floor with iced water to keep the place cool.

The heat was intense. It was the hottest part of the year, and the ship was in a tropical climate. Money Marks was master of his ship and of great wealth. He was fond of luxury, and he did not neglect any opportunity of indulging his almost oriental tastes.

On the table were wines and cigars. Marks was smoking as fine an Havannah as never paid duty. Occasionally he quaffed a deep draught of some iced wine, which was a favourite with him. His occupation was reading—and what was the book upon which his vagrant fancy had fixed itself upon, butterfly-like, for half-an-hour's light reading ?

The true life and adventures of Captain Kidd.

One paragraph especially arrested his attention; it was to this effect:—

" It is well known that on one occasion when Kidd—gallant, glorious, and immortal—was hotly chased by the British cruisers, he had vast treasure on board. Kidd was not the man to part with his gold without a struggle. He fought, but seeing there was every chance of his being worsted in the fight, he set his sails, and, in technical language, cut and run. Having baffled his pursuer, he was still afraid to venture out of his hiding-place, which some say was on the coast of Corea, and others, again, declare to be more southward in the China seas. The times were troublous with Kidd then, and his end was approaching, though he knew it not. He had been a great star, and his name had been in the ascendant for a long time. It was, however, on the wane. Thinking that it would be the height of imprudence to carry so much valuable property about with him, he is reported to have landed in the middle of the night upon a small island, in the sand of which he concealed an immense sum, which would make the finder thereof richer than many Jews of reputed wealth. Kidd never saw his gold again, for soon afterwards he was captured by his enemies, and this is all that is known about the vast treasure—the thought of which makes the mouth water."

He had just finished reading this paragraph when Viola sought admittance to his cabin. Laying down his book, and taking the cigar from his mouth, he advanced to meet her, wearing a smile upon his lips, and evincing every demonstration of delight.

Viola was sad, still, repellent, almost nun-like in her manner. There was an air of conventual discipline about her, but it was the result of the heavy sadness which had fallen upon her. Her love had met with a severe check, and resulted in ruin.

Her idol had fallen down from its lofty niche, and had been shattered to atoms.

" I am glad you have come," said Money Marks, gaily, forgetting all about the pirate and his buried treasure, under the influence of a new excitement.

" You will soon be sorry," replied Viola.

" Sorry ?"

" Yes."

" Why ?"

" I wish to go on land."

" Ah !" replied Money Marks, gaily, " so do I wish you to go on land. You are not the close prisoner you suspect you are. I have bought a marriage license, and I have arranged that we shall be married before the ship sails. What do you think of that, my pretty Viola ?"

Viola gasped for breath, turned all colours of the rainbow, and staggered to a seat.

This was what she would have ardently longed for some short time back, before Captain Arlee made his communication, and proved, beyond the power of contradiction, that Money Marks was leading a course of life which rendered him altogether unworthy of her love.

It might break her heart to part with the loved one, but her religion would never allow her to marry a man who was doing wrong, as the young pirate undoubtedly was.

Money Marks attributed her agitation to natural emotion, and congratulated himself, thinking that he was on the point of making himself happy in the loving smiles of his Viola.

How greatly he was mistaken !

At length, Viola conquered her emotion by the exercise of an heroic effort, and nerved herself to the accomplishment of the arduous task she had undertaken.

" I can never be your wife !" she said, in a low tone, and keeping her eyes fixed upon the ground.

Money Marks started, as if a serpent had stung him.

" You cannot ?" he cried.

" No."

She shook her head gravely, solemnly.

"Will you tell me why you cannot be my wife, Miss Cathcart?" he exclaimed, severely.

"Because you are what you are."

"Ah!"

Again he started—this time more markedly than before.

"And what have my enemies told you I am?"

"My eyes have told me."

"Well, what have your eyes told you?"

"That you are not what I took you to be. I pledged you my love and my truth when I thought that you were worthy of so great a trust. I find myself mistaken, and I revoke my promise."

"So that is consistent with your idea of honour?"

"Oh, yes!"

Money Marks' lips quivered and trembled, but as Viola was calm, he forced upon himself a bastard sort of quietude, which deceived nobody but himself.

The two spectators of this singular scene, Cuffy, and the negro-boy swinging the punkah, were too well trained to take any notice, or to interfere in any way, not even by showing that they understood the meaning of what was going on.

The negro-boy continued to swing the punkah. Cuffy went on cooling the room by sprinkling iced water over the carpet.

"Will you be a little more explicit, Miss Cathcart?" said Money Marks. "I feel as if I were in the position of a criminal. You have allowed your eyes to bear witness against me—I will not say false witness——"

"You cannot!" she cried, hastily.

"You have judged me," he continued, without heeding her emphatic and somewhat rude interruption.

"I have."

"At least then I have a right to demand the evidence against me."

"You may do so."

"And will you comply with my request, which you own is reasonable?"

"Most certainly."

"That is well."

"What is it you want to know?"

"On what ground do you condemn me?"

"I saw the fate of those poor wretches who were taken prisoners by you. I saw them drowned in the most barbarous manner. When shall I get the horrid sight out of my eyes? I see them now! I hear their shrieks and their cries for mercy! Oh, Heaven!"

She paused, and covered her face with her hands; the painful reminiscence was too much for her.

"Arlee has done this," said Money Marks; "I presume you wish to leave me, in order that you may join him in the town."

"As I hope for mercy in the life to come, I swear most solemnly that I have never, even in my dreams, contemplated the shadow of such a thing," cried Viola, solemnly.

Money Marks laughed bitterly.

"What am I to understand you wish?" he asked.

"I wish to be permitted to land."

"And then?"

"Then, oh! then death would be very, very welcome!"

She clasped her hands and turned her eyes towards the ceiling, as if invoking the aid of Heaven, and the kind interference of the destroying angel.

Money Marks' heart was touched. His pride of manner vanished, and falling on his knees by her side, he exclaimed in a penitent voice—

"Oh! Viola, I am awfully miserable: can I help my fate? I wish I had never been born. Oh! Viola, forgive me. I—I——"

Viola turned her expressive eyes full upon Money Marks. They were full of tears which every now and then rolled down her cheeks, and fell in large blots upon the ground.

"Will you quit the life you are leading?" she asked. "Will you be virtuous and good; will you by a probation of two years spent in works of godliness prove to me that your soul is redeemed, and that you are again in the fold, and no longer a lost sheep? will you do this?"

Money Marks was sorely tried by this home question, which was put to him in so straightforward a manner that there was no possibility of avoiding it. It wrung his heart. At one moment he felt inclined to throw everything to the winds, and to trust to fortune for to-morrow's dinner. A

terrible struggle raged in his mind. She did not press him for an answer.

On the contrary, she would have allowed him an hour or more to thoroughly revolve the momentous point in his mind.

Her lips moved: she was offering up a prayer for the conversion of her backsliding lover.

"Viola," he said.

"Well."

Her heart thumped against her ribs, and she could scarcely articulate.

"You ask too much," he replied.

"Then your protestations are worthless," she replied, frigidly.

"I would do much to please you."

"Much! you should do all. Love is not genuine unless it is self-sacrificing."

"Is your love not called upon to make a sacrifice?" he asked, reproachfully.

"Not at the expense of my conscience."

"You are obdurate. I regret the fact but I am powerless to alter it. I embarked in my present career against my wish and inclination, but now I am wedded to it, and am not inclined to be divorced from it. I take a pride in it and venture to predict that when a few years have passed over my head I shall be generally known as Money Marks the Pirate and Highwayman of the Seas. That will be famous."

"Say rather infamous," cried Viola; "you may fancy such notoriety fame, I, on the contrary, look upon its acquisition as a calamity, for it gives you a passport to the bottomless pit."

"You ask my permission to go on shore; have you forgotten that I am the master of this vessel, and that no one leaves it, without it is my will that they should do so?"

"But it is your will," said Viola, surprised; "you surely cannot wish to detain me?"

"Arlee did so."

"He is different from you."

"How different?"

She was puzzled how to reply. Before she knew Money Marks to be a pirate, she had thought him incomparably Arlee's superior, looking upon the latter as a ruffian and a man who had no consideration for women.

"You cannot answer me. I am a pirate and he is—well, I will not say anything about him behind his back," exclaimed Money Marks, who had enjoyed her embarrassment. "Arlee kept you on board his ship, and resorted to every artifice with which he was familiar to induce you to marry him, and did not succeed after all; perhaps I may be more successful if I were to adopt his tactics."

"You cannot be in earnest; but if you are, your threats will not influence me in the least; when I was in the power and under the thraldom of Captain Arlee, my love for you, and a hope that we might meet soon in a happy re-union sustained me, now I should have but little to——"

"Little! Is your vaunted religion nothing?"

"It might be powerless to prevent me from sinking under my grief, if I were exposed to constant ill-treatment at your hands."

Money Marks had already risen to his feet, and he walked impatiently up and down the cabin.

"You are completely in my power," he said, "I can do as I please with you; there is no one here to gainsay me, or to thwart my will."

"You will spare me! I know you will when I appeal to your love," she said.

"Where is your love?"

"Vanished."

"Then why should not mine vanish also?"

"Excuse me. I made use of an incorrect term. It has not vanished, but recent events have placed it under a cloud. It exists, but a heavy weight is bearing it down and crushing it into the lowermost chambers of my heart. Oh! the misery it causes me. When I appeal to you I feel I am appealing to a man of gentlemanly instincts."

"Was not that the case with Arlee?"

"It was not."

"And yet you will not marry me? Yet you persist in your mad determination to leave me. Oh! Viola, you are ruining your happiness and my own for ever by espousing a silly idea: be practical, be worldly, be——"

"No, no, no," she said, firmly, "I must do my duty, whatever come of it. I must do my duty. Should a blighted existence and a broken heart be my lot on earth, I must look forward to a heavenly reward which will compensate me for all that I have undergone or shall have to undergo."

"Supposing I were to grant your request," Money Marks said, "and were to let you go wherever you liked, should I not have a right to demand what your plans are, and where you intend going? You have no money, no home, and no friends. How then can you subsist? It is this reflection which makes me think that you purpose going to Arlee, who will give you protection. This idea is enough to madden me, for mark me well, Viola, dearly as I love you, and highly as I cherish you, I would rather see you in your grave—ay, I would rather slay you where you stand with my own hand, than know that you were the wife, or still worse, the mistress of that man."

"You are determined to wrong me and do me injustice," replied Viola; "I will tell you my intention and you shall see me execute it. I intend to go to the first convent I find in the town; convents are refuges for the bruised in spirit and wounded in heart—I will take the veil."

"No, no; that would be an irrevocable step."

"I wish it to be so."

"You will drive me to desperation."

"Why should I do so? I am determined to enter a convent and take the vows if you will not leave off your evil ways and live a life of probation on shore for two years. At the end of that time, if your spirit is really chastened and your soul purified, I shall be glad to reconsider my determination."

Money Marks shook his head sadly.

"I cannot do what you ask," he said; "but I will prove my love for you by granting your request. Go, Viola; go and immure yourself in the cloisters of a convent as you propose—the time will come when you will bitterly repent having done so. May my image ever rise between you and the altar at which you kneel, may my name rise to the tip of your tongue when you ought to be thinking of a more holy person—in a word, may your life be one long regret—yet, let me recall that wish, it is too harsh, far too harsh. 'Twas my passion, not my love dictated it. Be happy, and God in Heaven bless you."

Viola wept.

Going to her, he said—

"One kiss; let us seal our separation with a kiss."

She made no resistance, and stooping down he imprinted a hot feverish kiss upon her burning brow.

CHAPTER XLI.

THE DIE IS CAST.

THAT afternoon Money Marks accompanied Viola to the gates of a convent. She had an interview with the Lady Superior, and afterwards told Money Marks that she had arranged everything, and that for the future she should, after taking the veil, be the bride of Heaven.

Suddenly an idea struck Money Marks. He took leave of Viola with every evidence of regret and sorrow of the most violent description.

But instead of going away he lingered in the courtyard of the conventual establishment, saw her taken away from his longing gaze in the grasp of two sisters of mercy clad in long, black, sepulchral-looking garments, and then appealing to the porter at the gate, requested a personal interview with the abbess, which was granted him.

Entering the convent, he was brought to a standstill at a low iron grating, through which a voice which once was musical and now was sweet, said—

"What do you want, and what brings you hither, stranger?"

"I want the lady abbess, and to her I will tell my business," responded Money Marks.

"Wait here," said the voice.

He waited: presently a door revolved on its hinges and he was confronted by a hooded nun, who told him to follow her along a narrow passage which led to an apartment in which the abbess was sitting.

Having ushered him into the apartment, the nun fell on her knees near the door and began to count her beads as if oblivious of everything around her.

"What is your pleasure, sir?" exclaimed the abbess.

Money Marks pointed to the kneeling nun, and said—

"Can she be trusted?"

"With your life; she is my confidential attendant."

"Indeed; then I will proceed without fear. I should not like what I am about to say to be overheard, but your reply has reassured me."

The abbess bowed.

"A young lady in whom I am much interested has just entered these walls."

"She has."

"Her intention is to take the veil."

"It is most praiseworthy."

"She will repent some day."

"God forbid!" exclaimed the abbess, raising her hands on high, religiously.

"We will not argue the point," answered Money Marks, "for we are sure not to agree. I wish to ask a favour of you—it is this: let the young lady remain an inmate of the convent for some time, say for two years, until I return; but until you see me again do not on any account let her proceed to the grand consummation of taking the vows; let her be what I think you call a lay-sister, or novice."

"In what way is this to be done without sin, or why should it be done?" inquired the abbess, raising her eyes, suspiciously.

"I will tell you. Viola—that is her name—would be my wife on certain conditions which I am unwilling now to accede to; in two years' time the case may be different. I do not wish her to take irrevocable vows which she may not break. The convent of St. Ursula is, they tell me, poor; forgive me if I am wrongly instructed."

"Alas! it is too true; we are afflicted by Heaven, but we have hope," said the abbess, meekly.

"Would a thousand pounds——"

"A fortune; it would be a fortune to us, and relieve us of our debts."

"Very well; that is the point at which I wanted to arrive. You are in need of money; Viola is poor; she will not bring you a halfpenny, and will only be an additional burden on the convent."

"We must not study wealth; our charity is broad."

"That may be, but you must not forget that it is necessary to have money in order to live."

"That may be."

"Heaven provides," said Money Marks; "that is well known by those who have faith. Now I will make you an offer."

"Do so."

"Keep Viola here for two years; do not permit her to take the vows, and I will give you a thousand pounds now and the same sum when I return. Is that agreeable to you?"

The abbess made no immediate reply; she appeared to be debating the matter in her mind and to be unable to come to a decision.

"I will consult Father Azellio, and let you know by early dawn to-morrow morning."

"Who is Father Azellio?"

"A worthy monk; confessor to the convent of Saint Ursula."

"Very well. Let him come to the ship which lies off the Custom House Quay and ask for Captain Marks. I will have the money in readiness for him, and I shall trust to the faithful fulfilment of your word."

"Do I understand you rightly when I think that if at the expiration of two years from to-day you do not appear, I shall be at liberty to induce Sister—Viola did you say?"

"Yes."

"Sister Viola to take whatever vows may seem fit to me?"

"That is placing a constrained construction upon my words; but let it pass. If I do not return within two years you may do what you like."

"That is agreed?"

"It is."

The abbess bowed; the nun ceased telling her beads, rose from her knees, and led the way out of the apartment. Money Marks returned to his ship, and awaited the coming of Father Azellio.

If he could prevail upon the abbess to prevent Viola from taking the vows until a certain time, Money Marks thought he should have made enough money to enable him to live comfortably for the rest of his life and to quit the hazardous work in which he and his daring crew were then engaged.

He did not always wish to go about with a noose round his neck, as it were. He wanted to enjoy the world and life while he was young, and he knew that he could not enjoy it without money.

At daybreak the next morning, a little boat put off from the shore. It contained one man, who wore a cowl, and was dressed like a monk of some severe Franciscan order; his feet were bare, and his garments of the scantiest and coarsest kind.

This was Father Azellio.

Money Marks was expecting him, and had risen early so that he might not be kept waiting.

The monk would not enter the ship; he sent word that Money Marks must come into his boat. This the pirate readily did, and Money Marks was soon side by side with the strange being who was to give him the answer of the Lady Superior of the Ursuline Convent.

"Do I address Captain Marks?" said Father Azellio.

"You do."

"My son, the abbess bids me say that your terms are accepted. You shall have the satisfaction of knowing that Sister Viola is not to be irrevocably the bride of Heaven until two years have flown over her head."

Money Marks, on hearing this, made a sign to Cuffy, who went into the captain's cabin, and brought therefrom, one by one, four bags, each of which contained two hundred and fifty pounds.

These bags of gold were lowered into the boat.

"There," said Money Marks, "there is your gold."

"It is a gift to Heaven, my son."

"That may be, only I don't exactly see it in that light," replied Money Marks. "You have made a promise, father; mind that you keep it, or——"

"The servants of Heaven never lie!"

"It will be the worse for them if they do. This is a small port, there are no troops in the town, and a handful of determined men could raze the Convent of St. Ursula to the ground with the greatest ease."

The monk smiled.

"Rest assured that I will do it, holy father, if I am trifled with. So beware! Keep faith with me and you shall reap great advantages; trifle with me, and take the consequences, which I swear by the hilt of my sword, will be most disastrous."

Father Azellio assured Money Marks, in the most emphatic terms, that he had nothing to apprehend. The interview was over, and the little boat with its precious cargo put back to land.

Half-an-hour afterwards the anchor of the pirate was raised, and she was scudding over the waves with great velocity.

The die was cast.

Money Marks and Viola were separated. Heaven only knew if ever they might meet again. It was tolerably certain that Viola would not take the irrevocable vows which would doom her to a life in a convent till the day of her death, until the two years, for which Money Marks had stipulated, had elapsed.

He did not mind her being an inmate of the convent, for that circumstance would be to him an excellent guarantee that Captain Arlee would not be able to wrest her from her spiritual protectors, and place her once more in his power; than which a greater misfortune could not happen.

He felt more savage and ferocious, more merciless and cruel, than he had done before. Viola had always been his guiding star, and now that she had cast him from her in disgust, as if he had been something leprous and unclean, he was more hardened and callous than he otherwise would have been.

His fate was to plunder, burn, destroy, and kill.

Nor did he flinch from the repulsive task.

CHAPTER XLII.

THE OLD MAN OF THE DESERT ISLAND.

THE pirate made a very lucrative journey of about a month in the obscure part of the Pacific Ocean. He overhauled several merchantmen, and acquired a great deal of plunder.

On one occasion a ship ventured to show fight, and an action of some severity took place, during which several men on board the pirate were wounded, and two killed.

When the obstinate ship was captured, a dreadful retaliation was taken; for all the people on board, including two women, were put to the sword.

It happened one day that the pirates found themselves running short of water.

They were not in the vicinity of any port, but some islands were marked on the chart, and distinguished by the ominous word "desert."

They came within view of one of these, and Money Marks, ordering the ship to lay to, had a boat lowered. This was manned by a dozen men, who were steered by Jasper Main. Money Marks sat by the side of his lieutenant, allowing him to grasp the tiller.

The island was approached by a broad expanse of sea, which shoaled gradually as the shore was neared. It seemed well-wooded, and the vegetation was, as is usual in the tropics, luxuriant. It was a wonder that the vagrant foot of man, ever-wandering and erratic, had not been set upon it—but so it was.

The map-makers called it a desert island, but its deserted condition was no reason why water should not be found thereon. There might be springs of sparkling fresh water—at any rate, when water was so scarce on board the ship, it was worth the venture.

When the island was reached, Money Marks told six men to stay with the boat, ordering the rest to go in twos in various directions, but to be back in the boat before dark. If they discovered water, they were to return instantly, so that the casks and butts might be filled without delay, and on their way to the tanks in the ship.

Jasper Main and Money Marks went together. The vegetation was, in some places, so dense, that it was necessary to cut a way with a hatchet, which Jasper Main handled with the practised ability of one who had been a backwoodsman in the early part of his career.

No snakes were to be seen, nor wild animals of any description — birds, however, were numerous, and when Money Marks saw one that peculiarly arrested his attention, by the brilliancy of its plumage, he raised his gun to his shoulder, and fired.

The shot took effect in its wing, and it fluttered dismally to the summit of a tall tree, and then alighted, uttering a forlorn shriek, by way of protest, to such a novel mode of attack.

The sound of the shot reverberated through the surrounding country, and startled a hundred birds from their resting-places. Probably it was the first shot they had heard fired since the day they were hatched.

Suddenly Money Marks, who had relieved his lieutenant from the pioneer business, saw what appeared to be a path. Either some one had been in the habit of walking about that particular spot for some time, or else wild beasts had made a run of it.

But they had seen no wild beasts.

Here, then, was a mystery.

"Here, Main!" cried Money Marks, "what do you think of this?"

"It looks like a path."

"To my thinking it is one."

"In that case, the island is inhabited."

"I don't know. It might be a wild beast."

"Shall we follow it?" inquired Jasper Main.

"Shall we!—of course. Why should we not? Neither you or I are so enamoured of our lives as to be afraid of an adventure."

"Not I!" returned Jasper Main, with a wild laugh. "I was disgusted with the world long ago. The only things I care about are wine and women."

"Bravo! that is a favourite sentiment of mine. Cock your pistols, and follow me."

It never occurred to Money Marks that there might be a number of black men on the island. He knew that if that were the case the circumstance would be noticed on the authentic Government chart, by the aid of which he steered his course.

His idea was that some tiger or lion had made the path his own, but he looked in vain for what in lion-hunting countries is called the "spohr," that is, the footmark.

After going half a mile, Money Marks debouched upon an open space, in the centre of which was a spring; its waters welled up as pure as crystal.

"Here we are at last," cried Money Marks.

"A spring," ejaculated Jasper Main.

"Yes; I suppose wild animals come here; that would

account for the path, more especially as it seemed to me to commence in the jungle."

"Ah, but look higher up."

"Well!"

"Do you not see a continuation of it?"

"You are right, it is continued."

"Shall we follow it up?"

"No."

"I am curious."

"So am I. You said ' we.'"

"Well, what of it?"

"This—both of us cannot be spared. This is probably the only spring on the island. Our men will get into mischief if they have nothing to do; go back to the boat, and show them the way to the spring."

"But the path," said Jasper Main, anxiously.

"I will follow that up, never fear."

Seeing that his leader was determined, Main also saw that there was nothing for him but to obey; he accordingly slung his axe over his shoulder, and set off on the backward track.

Money Marks went to the spring, and bending down, took a deep draught of the water, which was deliciously sweet and fresh.

He turned to go, after having done so, but he stopped, started, changed colour, and remained stationary.

What was it that had so startled him?

What was the cause of his excessive agitation?

He had seen the print of a man's foot in the mud around the margin of the spring.

Thinking that he might by some possibility be mistaken, he looked again, and this time with more care and caution. But no! there it was—the mark of a man's naked foot as plainly defined as was that of the savage which so startled Robinson Crusoe on the island of Juan Fernandez.

He looked round in all directions, but could see no further trace of the inhabitation of the island. That one man at least lived there, he could not doubt, He determined to pursue the path, and see if he could not make a discovery which would do him credit.

The overhanging brushwood did not deter him : he followed the path, and when he could not walk upright he crawled on all fours.

In this way he in an hour had gone a mile, such was the difficulty of locomotion.

Whiz !

Something went past him with a strange hissing noise.

What could it be?

A second time the noise was heard, and a piece of wood stuck in the ground at his feet.

It was an arrow—a glance sufficed to show him this. The island was then inhabited, but by one only, or there would have been a flight of arrows; possibly there might be other inhabitants in other places.

It was a dangerous situation.

He did not know what to do. To retreat with precipitation was very averse to his inclination.

He decided to advance.

This he did with a shout, brandishing a cutlass, and flourishing a pistol. Emerging from the bushes which had hitherto partially concealed him, he found himself in a small open space, which had evidently been cleared by the hand of man.

But there was no one to be seen, nor was there any house, or cave, or wigwam. The grass had in some places been so much trampled upon as to become bare.

While he was searching for some trace of the person who had fired the arrow at him, a third arrow went past him, in unpleasant proximity to his head.

This time he looked up instead of looking down.

A figure appeared about half way up a large tree, whose girth was more surprising than its height.

It held a bow in its hand, and would have let go the cord had not Money Marks, with great presence of mind, fired his pistol in the air.

No sooner did the man see that the stranger was armed than he disappeared. The tree was hollow, and he had fallen of his own accord into its depths : it was his home—his abiding place—his cave.

Money Marks had not time to observe the man very closely : he could see that he was dressed in a very primitive fashion, somewhat resembling that of Adam after he had eaten the apple, for his principal garment seemed to be made of several large thick leaves strung together in anything but an artistic manner.

These were evidently employed more as a protection against the heat of the sun than for the sake of decency.

When the man, who was hairy, rough, and savage-like, had vanished, Money Marks stood still, waiting for his reappearance, and thinking what it would be best for him to do.

While thus engaged, he saw a large baboon striding from branch to branch, with the evident intention of following the man into the cave.

This creature had a very intelligent face, and appeared to regard Money Marks with every feeling of hostility and hatred, as if he either knew or felt intuitively that he was an enemy.

From a feeling of wanton mischief rather than one of inherent cruelty, Money Marks raised his pistol to a level with his shoulder, and fired.

The baboon, which was of the size of a small gorilla, uttered a terrible cry. The ball had struck it in the chest. It put its paw to the wound, and endeavoured in vain to stanch the blood, which, in spite of its efforts, trickled slowly to the ground, where it formed into a black pool.

Then it gave utterance to a series of cries very much resembling words; these were evidently addressed to the being who had gone into the hollow of the tree.

Before he could make his appearance, however, the poor beast tottered frightfully, and throwing up its paws, fell with a crash to the ground.

The inmate of the cave seemed to throw fear on one side when this catastrophe was made evident to him ; he appeared on the summit of the wall of the hollow, and peered over. The dismal spectacle of the dying ape—evidently the friend and companion of his solitude—affected him deeply.

Without the slightest hesitation, though he might, for aught he knew, be incurring instant death, he glided rapidly to the earth, and running towards the baboon, threw himself on his knees by his side, while the tears fell in countless numbers from his eyes.

Money Marks was exceedingly loath to kill the old man, but he was fearful that if he allowed him to live his rage and despair at the death of his favourite would be so great as to compel him to endeavour to do his destroyer all the harm that lay in his power.

Nor was he wrong in his conjecture.

When the first frantic rush of grief was over, the old man sprang to his feet and glared fiercely around him.

He was looking for the slayer of the ape.

Raising his bow to his shoulder, he fitted an arrow to the string, and was about to fire.

It was a critical time for Money Marks, because it amounted simply to this : either he must kill the old man, or the old man would infallibly kill him.

Money Marks never fired a shot in his life with greater reluctance than he fired on the present occasion.

He never felt so much like committing murder.

He was almost inclined to run the risk and take his chance, letting the old man fire at him. That, however, would have been chivalric folly. To kill the old man was one of the painful necessities that his position forced upon him, so he submitted to his fate, though not without a murmur.

The trigger was pulled, the leaden messenger of death flew through the air and struck the old man in the chest.

He uttered a cry, threw up his arms, and fell by the side of the dead baboon. Money Marks allowed his gun to fall to the ground, and rushed forward to see if he could render any assistance to his victim.

He found the blood steadily welling up from a severe wound in the neighbourhood of the right lung. It was clear that he could not live long. The old man was sensible. He spoke in a low tone to Money Marks, but he did so with difficulty ; for he was every now and then nearly choked by a gush of blood into the thorax.

"I—I forgive you," he said. "I have lived in peace with all men for many years, and I will not die at enmity with you because you have sent me to the shades a few years before my time."

"I acted in self-defence," replied Money Marks. "Believe me, I never regretted any action so much in my life as——"

"Say no more—time is precious. I shall not live long, and I want to say something to you which you will find of importance."

"To me?"

"Yes, but first tell me how you came here?"

"We were cruising in these seas, and were in want of fresh water, which I fancied I could get on this island."

"You were not wrecked then?"

"No," replied Money Marks, laconically.

He wondered what the old man had to communicate to him which was of such importance, and he was desirous of economising the time, so that he might not die before he spoke.

"I came to this island ten years ago," he said, "with a purpose. I caused myself to be landed here."

"Why? What was your purpose?"

"You shall hear. I have been a sailor all my life—when young, I was the friend and associate of Prettyman Parker."

"The pirate?"

"The same."

"I have heard of him," replied Money Marks, "and respected him as a brave and bold man."

"I saw him hung, my boy—saw his body swinging on the gallows, and the brutal populace heaping all sorts of opprobrious epithets upon the dead man's memory. It nearly broke my heart. I saw him and spoke to him in prison, and he made me the depository of a secret which I will now reveal to you. Listen. Come nearer."

Money Marks fell on his knees, and bent over the old man, who resumed.

"We had touched on this island during a cruise, when we were hotly pursued by a British vessel. Thinking capture probable, Prettyman Parker landed all his treasure, which was of great value—the specie alone amounting to upwards of a hundred thousand pounds."

"Indeed!"

"I knew that he hid the treasure somewhere, and so did the crew—but where, we were never able to find out."

"None of you?"

"None of us."

"Proceed."

"Just before he died, Prettyman Parker told me to go to this island, and look in the long range of caverns, some of which are subaqueous and some subterranean, and there I should find the hidden treasure."

"But where? In what part? Have you no more explicit directions to give me?"

The old man did not appear to hear this passionate appeal which was made in an agony of apprehension, lest death should intervene before the promised revelation was made."

"I did not intend to tell you," said the old man, "for you incensed me, by killing the companion of my solitude; but since you have been equally kind, or unkind to me, I will not die with the secret locked up in my breast."

"Where is the treasure? Have you found it?"

"I have not," was the reply, "though for ten years I have never allowed a day to elapse without looking for it."

Money Marks jumped up with a shout of disgust. He thought the old man had been trifling with him, and that he had been made the credulous victim of his pleasantry.

"Why excite my hopes," he said, "by speaking to me of a colossal fortune which was within my grasp, if I could trust to your description?"

"Peace," said the old man, solemnly. "I am dying, and dying men do not lie. They are about to go before their Creator, and they dare not trifle with the truth, or with their souls."

"Pardon me."

"I do."

"I was hasty."

"You are forgiven. I will hand the secret to you, as it was delivered to me by Prettyman Parker. *I know that the treasure exists*, because I was here when he placed it in the caverns. He said in prison, while the bell was tolling for his execution, 'When you enter the caverns from the seashore, turn to the left—keep to the left for upwards of half a mile—then you will come to a spacious chamber, in the centre of which is an aperture: down this you must go; then you will come to a passage, which always seemed to me to go under the sea, follow it up—for in a small vault at the end of this I have placed the treasure.' "

"He said that?"

"He did."

"And have you followed his directions?"

"To the letter—as far as I have been able."

"Then how do you account for your non-success?"

"I am at a loss to account for it."

"Think you that his mind at such an awful moment was feverish and perturbed, and that he was carried away by his inventive faculties?"

"No. I blame myself more than his instructions."

"How far have you penetrated?"

"I never could get beyond the spacious chamber he described."

"In that case you have been unable to find the aperture which was to lead you to the passage under the sea?" said Money Marks.

"You are correct in your supposition; I have not. All my efforts and endeavours to find it have been unavailable, and latterly I have had great difficulties to contend against. When I first came to the island I thought I should only stay six months, and I commissioned a ship to call and take me off. It called five different times, and would have called a dozen times more, had I been able to pay its captain; but my stock of money was soon exhausted, and I could not find the treasure to replenish my exhausted exchequer. When the ship called, it left me supplies of all sorts; but when it discontinued its visits to the island, I soon found myself without oil or candles, which were essential to——"

He broke off abruptly.

Money Marks thought he was dying, but it was not so.

"Did you hear anything?" he said.

"No," replied Money Marks.

"Ah! possibly I was mistaken; though I could have sworn I heard a footstep in the brushwood. Having lived here so long has made my sense of hearing preternaturally acute."

"You must have fancied it."

"Your companions——"

"Are on board, or——"

"What?"

"Going to the spring for water. They cannot be near here. What did you do for lights when your oil was gone?"

"I had to kill what birds and animals I could, in order to get their fat, which I melted down. I hope you may be more successful than I was. Oh, Life! I liked you not while you lasted, and yet I am sorry to give you up. Vain is ambition. Hope, but a lying phantom. Good-bye, my friend. Bury me beside the ape. He was my friend in life; let him lie beside me in death. I forgive you. Pray, pray for my so—so—my soul!"

These were the last words which escaped his lips.

The next moment the blood rushed in a torrent to his lips, a tremor convulsed his frame, and he was dead. His eyes glazed, his lips quivered, his cheeks blanched.

All was over.

Money Marks sat down upon the ground completely overcome. The strange meeting—the wonderful and almost incredible revelation about the treasure puzzled him extremely.

What was he to believe? Was the old man a maniacal castaway who had lived a Robinson Crusoe sort of existence, with an ape as his man Friday, until his mind gave way and he fancied himself the friend and former companion of Prettyman Parker, the celebrated pirate who was hung in America for his misdeeds?

It might be so.

Money Marks resolved to test the truth of the story, and to go himself to the caverns, whither he would proceed at once.

The ship should cast anchor, and the men have permission to go on shore and roam about the island with fowling-pieces, seeing what they could find to shoot. It would be a change and a holiday for them, which there was little doubt they would appreciate.

He always endeavoured beyond everything else to keep his men in a good temper, and to make them contented. If they had a grievance to complain of he proceeded to redress it at once to the best of his ability, for he knew that his tenure of power was slender and precarious amongst such a set of hardened ruffians as he was making them.

Turning his back upon the old man, over whose face he had reverently placed some grass, he set off on the homeward track; but he was not aware of one thing.

This one thing, however, was of the greatest moment to him, and of the utmost importance to his interests.

The whole of his conversation had been overheard by some one.

Every word that fell from the old man's lips had penetrated deeply into the ears of one who was playing the spy upon them.

Jasper Main had come back to the spring quickly, thinking to assist Money Marks in his expedition up the narrow path. He had met a man from the ship, near the spring, and he despatched him with Money Marks' orders.

When he heard about the treasure he resolved to try if he could not discover it, and dispose of Money Marks in the awful solitude of the primeval caverns, after which he felt assured that he could easily prevail upon the crew to make him the captain of the pirate.

Money Marks went back to the ship without suspecting for a moment that Jasper Main was his enemy, and that he was determined to do all he could to injure him.

CHAPTER XLIII.

THE COMMENCEMENT OF THE SEARCH FOR THE HIDDEN TREASURE.

WHEN the crew were told that they might go on shore, and that the ship was to remain off the island for a few days they were rejoiced at the freedom it gave them, though they were at a loss to guess why their commander chose to be so generous and obliging.

Not so Jasper Main.

He knew well enough the motive which actuated Money Marks in making the order; and he smiled in his sleeve as he thought of the probable triumph he was about to achieve.

Why should he not have the money, the jewels, and the vast wealth which Prettyman Parker had stored up in the caverns under the sea?—those submarine chambers which had but once been exposed to the eye of man.

Money Marks called Cuffy to him. The negro advanced smilingly—Cuffy always appeared to be in a good temper. It took a great deal to put him out and disturb his equanimity.

"Iss, massa," he said when he entered the captain's cabin.

"I want you, Cuffy, to come on shore with me," began Money Marks. "Take a spade with you, a couple of lamps full of oil, some brandy, and some biscuits, with a little salt beef; also sling a canteen of water over your shoulder."

Cuffy knew that to ask his commander any questions would only anger him; his duty was not to question but to obey, and he did obey the commands which were given to him with his usual alacrity.

In ten minutes' time he made his appearance fully equipped; a boat was lowered, and Money Marks and Cuffy were rowed on shore, whither a number of the crew had preceded them. The water was being brought on board with rapidity. Jasper Main, however, was nowhere to be seen.

"Where is Mr. Main?" said Money Marks, addressing Tony Lucas, an officer in command.

"I don't know, sir."

"He had not my permission to absent himself; tell him that he must attend more strictly to his duty."

"Yes, sir."

"For the present, I supersede him, and place you in command of the vessel during my absence. Do you understand?"

"Perfectly."

"If Mr. Main should return place him under arrest, and send him on board."

"I will, sir."

"Execute my commands faithfully and fearlessly."

"Yes, sir," replied Tony Lucas, with a smile of proud satisfaction upon his lips. He fancied he already saw his superior officer disgraced, and himself in his place.

Having made his arrangements, and wondering much what had become of Jasper Main, Money Marks began his walk, followed at a respectful distance by Cuffy.

His first object was to bury the old man, of whose name he was in ignorance, but whose murderer he really was.

When he reached the spring, he stopped and spoke to the men at work, telling them that the sooner they finished their work and filled the water-tanks, the sooner they would be able to enjoy the liberty he had given them.

Passing on he quickly arrived at the spot where the old man and his ape were lying side by side in death; he pointed them out to Cuffy, and said—

"Bury them."

"Man and monkey togeder?" asked Cuffy.

"Yes. It was his request."

At this Cuffy set to work, and speedily dug a hole which was large enough to contain the bodies, which, with his master's assistance, he placed in the trench.

Money Marks occupied himself with making a rough and rugged cross, which, when the grave was filled up he placed on the top so as to mark the spot.

Then Money Marks called Cuffy to his side; and told him as briefly as he could how he had met the old man, and what he had bequeathed him as a legacy. Cuffy's eyes sparkled at the idea of getting so much wealth, not because he wanted it, or cared about it himself, but because he wished Money Marks, the master of his choice and his adoption, to be independent, and to quit a life which was dangerous, and at the same time difficult to pursue.

"Get plenty money, massa," he said, "and marry Missy Viola; that de way to be happy."

Money Marks sighed as if that was indeed his dream of happiness.

Would he ever realise it?

The future alone could tell!

The caverns they were about to explore were of immense size and extent. The entrance to them was narrow and not easily discovered, although by dint of diligent scrutiny Money Marks at length found it out.

The rocks rose precipitously to a great height, and the sea rolled peacefully some little distance from their base.

"This must be the entrance," said Money Marks, as they saw a narrow opening; "light your lamps."

"What dis, massa?" said Cuffy.

He pointed to something that looked remarkably like a human foot.

"I suppose that must be the print of the old man's foot; it can be no one else's," answered Money Marks.

If they had thought fit to examine it more closely, they would have discovered that that footmark was made by some one who had nails in his boots: now the old man had no nails because he had no boots; so the impression must have been made by some one belonging to the pirate.

Money Marks took a lighted lamp, and gave the other to Cuffy, saying—

"Open your brandy bottle; we shall want something to keep our spirits up."

He drank a deep draught of the fiery liquid, afterwards permitting Cuffy to do the same.

"Dis good stuff, massa," said the black, rubbing his stomach with the palm of his hand, "Dere is no mistake 'bout dis. It right enough. D—— good liquor, massa."

"Warms you, eh?"

Cuffy grinned all over his face.

"Keep close to me; that is, about a foot behind me."

"Let me go first, massa. Send the old nig fust."

"Why?"

"'Cos something might happen to massa, and his life vallyble. Poor old nig no account. Nobody miss him."

"You are wrong there, Cuffy, I should miss you," said Money Marks, who was touched by the devotion shown to him by the black.

Cuffy's eyes were moist. Money Marks was the only individual in the whole world that he cared for; he had attached himself to him exclusively, he was his master. He had given himself to him, and had Money Marks taken him to a slave-auction at New Orleans or elsewhere and there sold him the faithful fellow would not have murmured.

"No, Cuffy," he continued, "you shall not expose yourself to unnecessary danger for me. This is my adventure and the risk is mine, therefore, I will run it."

After this Cuffy ceased to make any objection.

"Keep close to me; have your pistol cocked, and hold your lamp up so as to shew a good light."

Having given these instructions he plunged into the darkness of the caverns, and found himself in a passage which went right and left of the entrance.

Remembering the instructions which the old man had given him Money Marks turned to the left and walking slowly and cautiously, reached the vaulted chamber in something over ten minutes and under a quarter-of-an-hour. It was a spacious room, but of such vast size that it was impossible to see across it. It was like a couple of St. Paul's Cathedrals knocked into one.

To find out the aperture which led to the place in which the treasure was stored seemed a Herculean task.

THE PIRATE CHIEF AT THE MERCY OF THE ENEMY.

No wonder the old man had been ten years at it, and was unable to succeed!

Money Marks' heart sank within him because his enterprise seemed so hopeless.

He resolved to walk across the place and then round it, and then across again so as to see the nature of the flooring; but in so doing he took care to exercise twice as much caution because he might pitch upon the aperture unawares, and fall headlong, which would be putting an unpleasant termination to his illustrious career.

"Shall I follow you, massa?" said Cuffy.

"Yes; I think it would be unwise to separate."

"Very well," answered Cuffy.

Money Marks had not gone far before some heavy body hurled itself upon him.

He felt fingers at his throat and was borne towards the ground. A terrible struggle took place.

Money Marks did not know whether he was fighting with man or demon, but what he did know was that he was battling for dear life.

Cuffy held up the light but did not interfere, as it was difficult and dangerous to do so.

He could see two dark forms struggling together, but which was his master he was unable to say.

Money Marks gradually recovered from the frightful shock which had been given to his nerves, and as he did so he regained possession of his strength, which had temporarily quitted him.

Then he exerted himself heroically, and proved himself superior to the situation and to his adversary, for he twined his long arms around his waist and compressed his ribs until he heard the bones crack, then he took him up and held him for a moment aloft.

The next instant he was flying through the air with considerable velocity, for Money Marks had hurled him from him with all his strength.

Cuffy shook him by the hand and patted him on the back and wept and laughed by turns.

It was an awful conflict.

But what had he fought with?

If a man, what man?

Was the place peopled with ghosts and goblins, and were they enraged at the idea of any one trespassing upon their territory?

Money Marks hastily swallowed some brandy, and then he exclaimed—

"Give me your lamp and follow me."

His own had been shattered when he was first borne to the ground.

His object, of course, was to go to the body he had cast from him, and see what manner of man or devil his assailant was.

He walked to the spot at which he calculated he ought to find him, but he was unable to see the slightest trace of anything or anybody.

This was very perplexing and mysterious.

What could have become of him? Was he spirited away? Had he wings with which he could go wherever he liked, and so escape his enemies?

Suddenly Money Marks came upon an aperture, a hole, a hollow—call it what you will.

He uttered a cry of surprise and joy as he did so.

Apparently the body had fallen down it, for little stones and dust rolled down as if the sides had lately been disturbed.

"I have it," cried Money Marks ; "I can guess how it has happened. Prettyman Parker forgot to tell the old man that he had covered up the mouth of the aperture, and that is how it was so difficult to discover its whereabouts."

Cuffy nodded approval of this suggestion.

"But an accident has solved the problem of years, a pure accident—or shall I say fate, for there are those who declare that everything happens by design and predestination. It may be so; our intellects are too small and too finite to allow us to prove the contrary, but it is clear that when I hurled the body from me, it fell upon the rubbish with which Prettyman Parker had hidden the hole which conducted to his treasure; the force with which it fell made the covering give way, and it has fallen through."

He called his antagonist "it," because he did not know what other fitting appellation to bestow upon it.

Cuffy held the light over the hole, which was about three feet by two and a half, and exclaimed—

"I see, massa, deep down there, something black; him a man—him stunned."

"How deep do you think it is?"

"Me tink 'bout four foot."

"Get out of the way."

Cuffy stood on one side.

Money Marks took a hasty look, and then lowered himself into the hole. The height was about what Cuffy had guessed it to be, and he alighted without any difficulty or danger upon something soft and yielding, which he afterwards discovered to be the pit of a man's stomach.

Cuffy was by his side in a moment, and holding the light, the glimmer of which fell upon a man's pallid features, without saying a word Money Marks recognised one of his own men.

And that one was *Jasper Main!*

"Massa Main!" cried Cuffy. "By de powers 'bove, dat odd! How him come in here, and why for he attack you? It am all dam rummy odd."

He shook his head sagaciously.

"What you do now, massa—you kill him?" asked Cuffy.

"No; if he is not dead already, I will do nothing to accelerate his decease, though the scoundrel deserves it well enough."

"Better kill him, massa; he your enemy, and you may be sure he will do you some harm one of dese days."

"No; bind him so that if he comes to before our return, he may not escape. I will put him in irons and punish him when we get back to the ship; his life, however, I will not wantonly take, although he had forfeited it twice over."

That they had found the way to the treasure neither of them for a moment doubted, and Cuffy was as pleased as his master, who it must be confessed was overjoyed and satisfied beyond measure.

He would be able to give up his piratical life if he had only one-tenth of the wealth of which the old man had

spoken, and which he fully expected to find in a short time.

He would be a millionaire!

CHAPTER XLIV.

THE TREASURE.

CUFFY, like most seafaring men, usually had a coil of rope in his pocket, and he was not long on the present occasion in producing sufficient yarn to fasten Jasper Main's legs and make a prisoner of him.

Money Marks, by putting this and that together, came to the conclusion—which was correct—that his first lieutenant must have come after him instead of staying at the spring, and overhearing the old man's account of the treasure, allowed his mind to be so inflamed with ambition and greed for wealth that he had intended to kill his commander, possess himself of the treasure, and so become captain of the pirate and the terror of the seas.

He had not much time at his disposal for thinking just at present; he was too much excited at the idea of getting possession of Prettyman Parker's treasure to be able to reason calmly about anything.

The passage they now found themselves in was spacious, and from the absence of anything like pure air, seemed to be under the sea and deprived of all kinds of ventilation, except what it derived from the huge hall, from which the explorers and treasure-seekers had just emerged.

Although breathing was difficult, Money Marks pushed boldly on at a sort of jog trot, closely followed by Cuffy.

They obeyed the old man's instructions to the letter with the most favourable result, for in a short time they found the treasure of which he had spoken and of the existence of which they had once doubted.

There it was before their eyes placed in a small nook or cranny. The gold was in canvas bags, which had partly rotted away in one or two instances, allowing the bright metal to fall out in a shower. The jewels and precious stones were in caskets and boxes, which Money Marks had not time to open, for the atmosphere was so heavy and oppressive that he was only too anxious to get back again to the seashore.

His lungs seemed to be impeded in their actions by impalpable dust, perhaps the dust of ages.

"Load yourself with as much as you can carry; we shall have to make several journeys before we convey the whole of this treasure on board ship," he said to Cuffy.

Thinking that what breath he had in his lungs was precious and not to be wasted in an extravagant manner, the black preserved a discreet silence, contenting himself with obeying the order he had received.

Money Marks took a number of jewel cases which he placed in his pockets. Having appropriated all that they could conveniently carry, they started for home with every feeling of the most agreeable satisfaction.

Money Marks was almost deliriously joyous. To be the possessor of so much money in such an unexpected manner was wonderful—more wonderful than anything he had ever read of, even in the "Arabian Nights," and other brilliant works of Oriental fiction.

When he reached the aperture through which he had to ascend he found Jasper Main had recovered himself and was able to talk.

"You are a fine fellow," said Money Marks, tauntingly, giving him a contemptuous kick in the ribs as he spoke; "you are a fine fellow to steal a march upon me in this way, and to endeavour to kill me in the dark; what would you say if I were to leave you here to perish of thirst and starvation?"

Jasper Main groaned, not so much at the pain of his hurts, and that was not inconsiderable, but at the reflection which occurred to him that he had lost all chance of getting the treasure, and that he had been badly defeated in every way.

This was not a gratifying reflection by any means, and no one can wonder that he gnashed his teeth and was ready to tear out his hair by handfuls.

"You would not be inhuman enough to do that," he said deprecatingly, in reply to Money Marks' exclamation.

"Why not?"

"Because it would be barbarous."

"Is it a bit more barbarous than your attempt to murder me? Certainly not. Cuffy."

" Yes, massa."

" Make the cords a little faster; pull them together so that the scoundrel cannot escape."

This to Cuffy was a congenial task, and so he considered it. The bonds were made tighter, and Jasper Main groaned.

" What are you going to do with me?" he said, in an agonized voice.

" Leave you here to die," was the solemn reply.

" No, no—for Heaven's sake no! anything but that."

" I have said it."

" Knock me on the head; put me out of my misery at once."

" That is exactly what I do not wish to do," responded Money Marks, sedately, but in a tone of resolution.

" It is worse to die like this than to be shot at once. The misery is in feeling that death is inevitable—that death is creeping and crawling upon you gradually—you can feel him coming, see him, touch him, shake hands with the grim tyrant. *That* is the real pang, and misery, and sting of death. Oh, spare me that! kill me at once."

" I tell you no."

" Spare my life; you have ever been generous, and good, and kind. Spare me! I will be the humblest of your slaves; that negro by your side is not more submissive than I will be."

" He is no slave of mine; he is my friend and companion; I esteem him, while I loathe and hate you for your infamous treachery."

" Have some mercy."

" None."

" Think, oh, think, what may be your own fate; you may stand in need of mercy from Heaven and from man, and how can you expect to receive any if you have shown none?"

" The future has no terrors for me," replied Money Marks; " I live in the present. If I were to recal the past I should go mad: if I were to speculate upon the chances of the future I should die of despair and apprehension. I repeat that I live in the present."

" You will not save me?"

" No."

" Then may the heaviest curse that Heaven has in its all-powerful hand descend upon your head before long."

" Curses return to those who give vent to them," replied Money Marks, who with Cuffy's help got through the aperture, and stood in the immense chamber with his treasure by his side.

Jasper Main uttered a despairing wail which sounded dismally in the cavernous recesses of that wonderful network of caves.

Money Marks and Cuffy pursued their way until they reached the sea-shore, then they paused to gain breath and take some refreshment, of which they stood very much in need.

" You mean to leave him dere, Massa Marks?"

" Leave who?"

" Mas' Main."

" No."

" Then why you tell him so?"

" To frighten and punish him."

" Better shoot him when go back."

" No. I told you I meant to spare his life, and I see no reason at present to change my mind. He shall live, be the consequences what they may."

" You, massa, of course best judge of what you do," said the negro, " so Cuffy say no more."

Money Marks was highly elated. His spirits had risen very high—unusually high, for his temperament was generally saturnine rather than merry, and he felt communicative.

" We shall go back to the vaults and get the rest of the treasure, Cuffy," he exclaimed, " and during the last trip we will release Jasper Main. I will keep my eye upon him when on board ship, for I know him to be a desperate fellow; he may command the pirate after awhile, if the men will have him."

" Command de pirate?" said Cuffy, in amazement.

" Yes."

" And what you do?"

" I shall retire in his favour."

" What you mean by that?"

" Simply this: I shall be rich enough to live on my own resources, and I will leave off a piratical life, which is anything but pleasant and agreeable, to say nothing about the great risk one has to run, and I will settle down on shore."

" Will you take me with you?" asked Cuffy, whose face elongated at the bare idea of a separation.

" Why you may be sure I will; have I not always promised to make what return lay in my power for your long-continued devotion?"

" Yes, dat true enuf."

" Then make your mind perfectly easy upon that point; what I promise I fulfil. You shall still be the companion of my fortunes. I am not afraid of your making any base use of your knowledge of my former life, because I know I can trust you."

" Ole Cuff die for massa, can't say more," replied the negro.

" I believe that. You are the best friend I have—in fact the only friend; you shall go with me. We will live very differently to the way in which we are now living. I have done some harm, and I will endeavour to atone for my misdeeds by living a life full of charity and goodwill towards all men."

They placed the treasure in Money Marks' private cabin, in which was a bureau containing some secret drawers, which were made the receptacles of the precious stones and the gold.

After that they had some dinner, for they were in want of food. The heat of the day had passed, and they sallied forth again in the cool of the evening; six journeys sufficed to enable them to remove the treasure. It was dark when they had finished their task, but darkness in a happy clime like that in which they were is not the funereal affair that it is in more northern countries.

The moon played over the waters in a gladsome manner, and it was as light as day, and much more pleasant, because the ferociously hot sun had gone down.

Money Marks paused the last time at the spot where Jasper Main was lying.

The unfortunate wretch was tortured with the most awful thirst which consumed him; his tongue lolled out of his mouth, and was black and swollen; he was incapable of speech or motion.

Cuffy, at his master's request, gave him a horn full of brandy and water; and what nectar and ambrosia are to the gods, was that brandy and water to Jasper Main.

It saved his life—there could be no two opinions about that.

When he was a little better, the cords which bound him were cut, and he was, comparatively speaking, a free man.

Looking around him with the most profound astonishment, he said—

" Is it a dream, or am I really unbound?"

" You are unbound, for I have spared your life."

The shock of this unanticipated intelligence had such an effect upon Jasper Main that he staggered against the wall and fell down insensible.

The revulsion of feeling was too much for him.

He thought when his cords were cut that Money Marks had relented and taken pity on him to a certain extent, and that he intended to shoot him and put him out of his wretchedness, treating him very much as one treats a lame dog.

Cuffy placed him on his back and carried him to the open air. A little salt water sprinkled on his face revived him, and he stood up.

" Brandy," he said, in a hoarse voice.

They gave him a moderate supply of the liquor he required, but he did not thank them. At Money Marks he cast a dark malignant scowl, and put on a sullen air, which showed that his mind was filled with low revengeful feelings, and that he was not in the least grateful for the clemency which had been extended to him.

" I shall count upon your gratitude, Main," said Money Marks.

" For what?" was the surly reply.

" For allowing you to live."

" You may count upon what you like."

" Is that as much as to say that you have no gratitude n your rascally composition?"

" Perhaps it is."

" If you do not talk a little more civilly to me   pistol you where you stand."

" A very courageous act, too, considering that I am un-armed," replied Jasper Main.

"What is to prevent me?"

"Nothing. It is just the sort of thing I should expect from you."

"You are insolent."

"I was born so!"

"You had better be civil."

"You had better make me."

"How would you like to pass the rest of your days on this desert island?"

"Oh! I should not care; another has done it before, and I don't see why I should not follow his example. You will not produce any good effect upon me by threats. I am desperate! I don't care for anything or anybody."

"Do you care for that, you insulting scoundrel?" cried Money Marks, firing a pistol over his head to alarm him.

Jasper Main turned calmly round, unbuttoned his coat, and exposing his breast, said—

"There if you wish to kill me, fire! I am not afraid of you!"

Going closer to him Money Marks hissed in his ear—

"Are you afraid of *Death?*"

"Are you?"

"That is no answer to my question."

"It is the only one you will get."

"I am sorry I spared your life," said Money Marks, hardly knowing what to make of the man's odd manner.

"Take back your gift then," said Jasper Main. "Here I am, man alive! Fire away! Murder me! I am unarmed! You are a pirate, and have no reputation to lose; or, if you have a reputation you will only lose it by showing mercy. Why should you not commit murder in cold blood? I shan't hurt you! Fire!"

Cuffy looked at Money Marks and touched his forehead significantly.

The negro was right in his surmise; the brandy, acting on an empty stomach and an excited brain, had produced intoxication!

Jasper Main was as tipsy as a lord after a cock-fight.

CHAPTER XLV.

THE MUTINY.

WHEN Jasper Main became sober, after a night's rest, he saw that he had been guilty of great folly in defying his commander as he had done. His only chance of success in an intellectual combat with him was to be very discreet; to simulate penitence, and to work in the dark, like a mole.

So he apologized to Money Marks, thanked him for his noble generosity and undeserved kindness, vowed eternal gratitude for his favours, and declared himself the most devoted of his adherents.

Money Marks was unfortunately thrown off his guard by this clever simulation of sentiments which the first lieutenant was far from feeling.

When the men had tired themselves by running about the island, when two had been bitten by snakes, and one had died of a sunstroke, the ship heaved her anchor and proceeded on her voyage.

Main was set at liberty, and reinstated in his former position, much to his satisfaction and delight.

By Cuffy's advice Money Marks selected the most precious of the diamonds he had found among Prettyman Parker's treasure, and fastened them in a belt which he wore round his waist, so that if a storm occurred in which they were wrecked, they would not be deprived of the means of sustenance.

This precaution was a very salutary one as will eventually be seen.

Such perfect confidence had Marks in the negro that he made him a belt similar to his own which he stocked full of precious stones, and gave him to wear, and to hold in trust for him.

Jasper Main knew that Money Marks had the treasure on board, and his mouth watered with cupidity as he thought of it: and the more he allowed his mind to dwell upon it, the more he resolved by hook or by crook that it should be his.

The boatswain was a man of the name of Cook. He was a jolly, jovial fellow, and much beloved by the crew, to whom he was uniformly kind.

Cook was a personal friend of Main's, and the latter made up his mind to propose the seizure of the ship to him, and to take him into his confidence.

Cook was tall and brawny. The *beau ideal* of a wrestler; like Charles in "As You Like It." His strength was prodigious, and he was as much respected for its possession as he was for his numerous good qualities.

Main invited Cook to take a glass of grog in his cabin, and took advantage of the opportunity to sound him, and see if he were inclined to share in a mutiny, the object of which would be the seizure of the pirate, and either the death or the safe bestowal of Money Marks.

He did not wish to kill Money Marks, because he had spared his life when it was justly forfeited. All he wanted was the treasure, and the command of the vessel.

If he could once achieve these two objects, he would be perfectly satisfied, for he intended to touch at the first port, land, and make off with his treasure, leaving the ship's crew in the lurch, and thrown upon their own resources.

"You and I have known one another, and sailed together for some time now, Cook," he exclaimed, filling his companion's glass, and raising his own to his lips directly afterwards.

Cook nodded his head, and puffed out a cloud of smoke which floated lazily towards the ceiling.

"Now, I have an idea."

"You have?"

"Yes."

"That's something unusual, isn't it?"

And Cook's hoarse laugh sounded hollowly through the cabin.

"Ha! ha! you're fond of your joke, but never mind. I can stand chaff as well as anyone going."

"Well, what's your idea?"

"It is just this—but——"

"What?"

"I should like you to promise me one thing."

"All right."

"If you feel that you can be with me, hand and glove, will you swear that you will keep my secret, and not reveal any word I say to the captain?"

"Not I. Do you think I am a chattering magpie? what do you take me for?" replied Cook, heartily.

"You swear?"

"Ay, on anything, or by anything you like."

"That's your sort," said Jasper Main, gleefully; "now I can go a-head."

"So do," said Cook, charging his pipe anew.

"I suppose you don't know why we stopped on the desert island?"

"No, I don't, without it was for you to get drunk."

Again there was a hoarse laugh, and again Jasper Main joined in the merriment against himself.

"That's not the reason," he said, "but I'll tell you."

"Very well."

"We stopped there to enable the captain to get possession of a treasure."

"A what?"

"A treasure."

"Go along with you," said Cook, increduously. "There was no treasure there, I'll be sworn. What sort of one was it?"

"Gold and jewels."

"Are you in earnest?"

"I never was more so in my life. I will explain to you, and the matter will then be easier to comprehend. Money Marks obtained information—never mind how—that the famous pirate, Prettyman Parker, who was executed some years ago, had concealed a treasure in some caverns on this island. This happened to be the fact, and Marks has found the money and the jewels, which are worth an immense sum, Probably there is no less than a quarter of a million of property and coin on board this vessel."

"You don't say so!"

"I do though."

"And we are not to have any of it?"

"Not a halfpenny!"

"That's what I call unfair."

"So do I. That is just what I say. We ought to share the treasure, as we usually share the booty we take from ships we destroy."

"He means to smouch it all himself."

"Every rap."

"If your little game is to stop that performance, I'm with you."

"Say you that?"

"Do I say it? Yes, and mean it, too. I have always stuck up for the governor because I considered him a good sort, but when he tries on such tricks as the one you have let daylight into, why it's about time that we put a stop to it. What do you propose to do?"

Jasper Main lowered his voice to a whisper before he replied—

"I propose that you and I——"

"Me?"

"Yes, you are a valuable ally. You can influence the crew, and lead them like a flock of sheep."

"You are right there," said Cook, stroking his beard in a manner that denoted satisfaction.

"Very well, you and I must undermine the minds of the crew, and take possession of the ship."

"We can do it!"

"Of course we can. Well, let us grant, for the sake of argument, that the ship is in our possession, we will kill Money Marks?"

"No, no," said Cook, "I wont agree to that. No killing the captain. All we want is the treasure."

"But he must not continue captain of the ship after we have mutinied against him."

"Why not?"

"Because he would have no authority over the men."

"Who is to be captain then?"

"Oh! I don't know. Put it to the vote. Let the men choose their own captain—that will be the way to do it."

"I suppose you want to be skipper yourself?"

"Me? Not I. I don't want the worry and the trouble of it. Oh, no! I would rather see you captain. You are a practical man, and would make an excellent commander."

"I flatter myself I should," answered Cook, whose vanity was tickled.

"We would put Money Marks in a boat with that darned black cuss, and give them some arms and provisions, and let them take their luck."

"Why not land them somewhere?"

"At some port?"

"Yes."

"What would be the good of that?"

"Why a great deal."

"I don't see it. If we landed them at any port, they would infallibly trump up some story, and tell the authorities we were pirates, which would have the effect of starting a lot of cruisers after us, and it would be too hot to be pleasant."

"Ah! there is much truth in what you say."

"Will you be with me?"

"To the death!"

"Give me your hand upon it?"

"I will."

They shook hands cordially.

"We must be cautious," said Cook.

"I am aware of that fact. Money Marks is strong and determined. He does not value a man's life very highly."

"That is precisely why I advocate caution."

"Do you go amongst the men and sound them," said Jasper Main. "Let me know the result of your labours daily; I will do the same. When you think all things are ready, say so, and we will draw the sword."

"And throw the scabbard away."

"Precisely so."

After a little further conversation the two men separated. Cook was ambitious of becoming captain of the vessel, and he fell readily into Main's plans. Although the latter intended to reserve that honour for himself, he also resolved to have the major part of the treasure.

His plans were well laid, but he did not choose to reveal them all at once—if at all—to Cook, who was more his tool than his accomplice and coadjutor.

Money Marks never so much as dreamt that a plot was in existence against his authority, his liberty, and his treasure.

He had all along suspected that Jasper Main would endeavour to penetrate to his cabin, and find out of what the treasure consisted—so, as a precautionary measure, he placed the gold in small sacks, and wrote with a pen on the outside: "Swan-shot," "Dust-shot," and so on.

He could not label it "Biscuit," or anything of that sort, because of its weight. He thought no one would suspect the *ruse*.

Nor did they.

The sacks were placed on the floor, as if they were almost worthless; and no one thought anything of them—not even Jasper Main.

Money Marks took it into his head to cruise northwards, in the direction of the Hudson's Bay Company's territory, and, on the way, the pirate picked up several merchantmen, all of whom were robbed and scuttled—the men being either blown up in the ship, or made to walk the plank.

Money Marks had no mercy upon them. He seemed to have become more thoroughly hardened and merciless since Viola had left him and gone into the convent.

In three weeks the plans of Main and Cook were all matured, and they only waited an opportunity for the outbreak.

The men who were in the secret of what was going to happen, mustered strongly on deck, and began to talk loudly, and smoke in defiance of rules and regulations.

Money Marks happening to come up unexpectedly, a little awed the mutineers, but upon receiving signals of encouragement from Jasper Main and the boatswain, they recommenced, and showed more insubordination than they had done before.

Marks, as a matter of course, ordered them below.

Not a man attempted to move. Rank mutiny had commenced. Money Marks clenched his teeth and turned pale.

"Do you men hear when you are spoken to?" he exclaimed.

"Yes, we hear fast enough," was the reply from one man, who fearlessly constituted himself the ringleader.

"Then why do you not go below when I tell you?"

"Because we don't choose to."

"Mr. Cook!"

"Sir!"

"What is the meaning of this conduct?"

"I must refer you to Mr. Main, sir, as being my superior officer."

"Answer the question. I put it to you, and from you I expect a reply."

"Then you expect more than you will get, that is all I can say."

"What do you mean?"

"What I say."

"You are insolent."

"That may be," returned Cook, coolly.

Jasper Main stepped impudently forward, with a short pipe in his mouth, his hands in his pockets, and his hat set jauntily on one side of his head.

"The fact is, captain, the men are dissatisfied."

"With me?"

"Yes."

"Why are they dissatisfied?" asked Money Marks, calmly.

"You have a vast treasure on board, and you have not offered to share it with us, as we consider you ought to have done."

"Anything else?"

"More than you will like, perhaps. If we do not get the money, we shall help ourselves to it."

"Indeed!"

"You may sneer, but we are in earnest."

"Try it, that's all—try it," said Money Marks.

Jasper Main was perplexed at the calmly-defiant manner of the young pirate. He was about to give the word which would cause a dozen men to spring upon him, when the lookout-man reported a sail in sight.

Money Marks immediately raised his telescope to his eye, and took a long and steady gaze at the approaching ship.

Suddenly he lowered his glass, and said—

"This is no time, my men, for playing at mutineers. I recognise the ship in the distance. She is one we have cause to fear and dread; for she is no other than H. M. S. *Lowflyer*, from which we escaped so providentially on a former occasion. There is nothing before us but a fight. We may, if we are determined, beat her off. If we do not fight, she will overhaul us, and you know as well as I do the consequences of that."

The crew looked incredulous. They thought it a clever plan of their captain to divert their minds into another channel, and make them think of something else.

"The money I have in my possession," he continued—"and I do not deny its existence—is fairly my own, yet, if you think you are entitled to a part of it, you may have it."

There was a slight attempt at a cheer when this was said, but a judicious frown from Main, and a deprecatory wave of the hand from Cook, effectually put it down.

All who had glasses began to reconnoitre the ship, which was making good speed, and coming up with them rapidly.

When they were at Sierra Leone the crew had enjoyed an excellent opportunity of observing the *Lowflyer*, and there were those amongst them that fancied they recognised the British cruiser. They would rather have discovered any other ship, for it was tolerably clear and certain that the vessel was after the pirate.

"The governor is right," cried Cook, to Jasper Main.

"I am inclined to think so, too," was the reply.

"There will be bloody work presently."

"I don't doubt it."

"For my part," continued Cook, "I would cut and run; for there is no money and little honour to be gained by a battle such as the one we are going to fight."

"Fight we must. The infernal ship is too close upon us. We cannot escape. It is better to die the sword in hand, than to tamely surrender and be strung up to the gallows."

"It will be hot in an hour or so," said Cook, significantly. "I think we had better postpone our mutiny until after the action. Let the captain lead us to victory. He is a devil to fight, and tolerably lucky."

With great reluctance, Jasper Main agreed to this, and cursed the *Lowflyer* vehemently in his heart, for interfering in his affairs at a time when the interference was not needed.

The British vessel did not leave them long in suspense as to her intentions. When within firing distance she discharged a gun, the shot from which fell a little short of the pirate.

Seeing that the danger was imminent, the men returned to their duty, and Money Marks, forgetting their misconduct in the excitement of the moment, took command of the ship, determined to pull her through in a glorious manner if possible, or else to die in the endeavour.

CHAPTER XLVI.

THE FIGHT BETWEEN THE PIRATE AND THE BRITISH SLOOP OF WAR.

THE proper and legitimate occupation of her Britannic Majesty's ship *Lowflyer*, was to look after and capture slavers, but she had received express instructions to follow and capture the audacious pirate which had of late become the scourge of the seas.

Although the pirates thought that they had effectually killed all their captives, they were mistaken in certain instances—where men had escaped in the most miraculous way, and, when on shore again, related what had happened to them with all the gusto and exaggeration of men upon whom the shadow of death has fallen, and who have passed through a terrible adventure.

The indignation that the pirate excited throughout Europe and America was prodigious, and a reward had been offered for the apprehension of Money Marks, while the *Lowflyer* was specially commissioned to go in pursuit of her.

Captain Stockwell and Lieutenant Stafford of the *Lowflyer* were in raptures when they sighted the craft of which they had been so long in search.

They were pretty equally manned; and the pirate had the advantage in one respect, which was that it had a swivel-gun amidships, with which it could do great and rapid execution.

Both were steamers. The *Lowflyer* being able to do half a knot an hour more than the pirate.

Money Marks ordered the men to their guns; favoured them with an energetic speech; pointed out the horrors of capture, and recommended death on deck to hanging in chains on land.

The men bared their brawny arms, and clenched their teeth. They were going to fight a battle which was displeasing to them, but, as a matter of necessity, they resolved to do their best.

Money Marks kept two bodies of men in reserve, one was to go into the rigging, well armed with Minié rifles, and practise sharpshooting when the two ships were close together. The second was to hold itself in readiness for boarding.

Every man had sixty rounds of ammunition given him; all the revolvers were breech-loaders; Cook served the swivel. Jasper Main and Money Marks were to head the boarders, should their services be required.

But the boarders and the sharpshooters were kept out of sight and harm's way until their services were required.

Bang!—boom!—bang!

The action had commenced. The *Lowflyer* had fired a second shot, to which the pirate replied by a broadside.

Cook worked the swivel with effect, and the shots told.

After half-an-hour's brisk firing, during which both ships were about equally injured, and neither had gained any material advantage, Captain Stockwell thought fit to close, which he did with great promptitude, endeavouring to run into the pirate and take her amidships.

Money Marks' quick eye perceived this, and he gave instructions to his engineers which caused them to veer round sharply, so that the ships glided close by one another.

Grappling irons were thrown out which caused them to touch.

Then the sharpshooters swarmed up the rigging like so many monkeys, and having taken positions allotted to them beforehand began to pour a deadly fire on to the enemy's deck.

At this moment the black flag was run up to the peak.

Money Marks' original intention had been to throw his men on board the British vessel and take her by storm, but he thought it would be better to let his sharpshooters do their work, and allow the English to board him or not as they pleased.

Captain Stockwell had no option but to board. He had discharged his broadside point blank at the pirate, and had received him simultaneously. When fired at so short a range frightful execution was of course done.

The mangled and mutilated bodies of men were lying about the 'tween-decks in frightful quantities.

The horrors of war—more especially its practical terrors—were being experienced, for the carnage was terrific.

The swivel was still worked by Cook, who cast clouds of grape and canister at the *Lowflyer*, which did prodigious execution.

Sword in hand and ably seconded by Lieutenant Stafford, Captain Stockwell led the way on to the enemy's decks. Then came the tug of war.

Money Marks fought with great skill and bravery.

Cuffy followed him like a shadow; he was with him wherever he went, and more than once saved him from receiving a mortal blow.

Captain Stockwell saw by the uniform that Marks wore that he was a person of distinction on board and probably the captain of the pirate.

He literally cut and hewed his way through a mass of men to cross swords with him. Money Marks was not in the least anxious to disappoint him.

They met.

Both were accomplished swordsmen, and the practice they made was excellent; they appeared to be armed at all points.

Achilles was vulnerable in his heel.

These men were vulnerable nowhere.

Ha! his foot slips—he falls! A pool of blood has treacherously refused to support his footsteps, and Money Marks is at the mercy of Captain Stockwell.

The Englishman's sword was at his throat in an instant.

The next moment he would have been carrion and food for sharks.

But a bullet fired by an unerring hand entered his skull.

No cry escaped him; he was stone dead, and fell forward heavily upon his face.

Rising to his feet, Money Marks looked about for his deliverer, and saw Cuffy with a smoking pistol in his hand which had evidently recently been discharged.

The negro was grinning with delight.

His master shook him cordially by the hand to prove to him that he appreciated the service he had done him.

When their captain fell, the man-of-war's men thought it high time to beat a retreat, which they did with as much dignity as they could. They were beaten; they had suffered severely, and the gallantry of the pirates had been crowned with success.

The command devolved upon Lieutenant Stafford, who ordered the ships to be unlocked, and stood away to sea, still continuing the action with his big guns.

The pirates were too pleased to get rid of so dangerous an antagonist to follow her. They made a show of going on with the battle, but it was nothing more than a show, for they turned tail and steamed away, as well as the disabled state of their engines would permit them.

The pirate had lost at least one-half of his men in killed and wounded; the decks were like slaughter-houses.

Money Marks looked around him, and saw with regret that his enemies Cook and Jasper Main were alive, though the former had been shot in the arm, and the latter slightly wounded in the foot with a splinter.

The dead were thrown overboard, but, to his credit be it said, Money Marks ordered the wounded who belonged to the *Lowflyer* to be carefully tended and cared for, as if they had been his own men.

The sun went down upon a scene of bloodshed.

CHAPTER XLVII.

ADRIFT.

THINKING that his gallantry had appeased the dissatisfied spirit of his men, Money Marks went into his cabin, and after lying awake some time, ruminating upon the events which had lately taken place, he fell asleep.

His enemies were, however, sleepless. They went from dormitory to dormitory and spoke to the survivors of the battle, endeavouring to make them believe that Money Marks was alone responsible for the slaughter which that day had witnessed.

Unfortunately they succeeded.

When any disastrous event happens, those who are sufferers by it are usually too glad to find a scapegoat upon whom they may vent their rage and disappointment.

Many were wounded, and all had lost friends and companions. They would in any other cause have gained great glory, for they had behaved gallantly; as it was, they gained nothing.

The entire affair was an unmitigated calamity, which they, right or wrong, thought that a prudent commander would have avoided.

They were impregnated with discontent, and when Cook and Jasper Main came round and made them specious and flattering promises, giving them an extra allowance of spirits, and telling them they should do as they liked in future, they lent a willing ear to the delusive nonsense, and declared that they would sacrifice Money Marks, and that the two conspirators might do what they would with him.

Nothing further was needed; the two men could go to work without any apprehension of being interfered with.

"Well," said Jasper Main, "I think we have succeeded tolerably well."

"And I agree with you," replied Cook, rubbing his hands.

"The men are with us."

"Thoroughly."

"Still, I don't like to trust them to a greater extent than I can help. Let them have as much as they can drink; if they all get drunk what matter? they will be harmless then."

"What do you think will be the best way of capturing Money Marks?"

"He is a desperate fellow, and we must do nothing rashly," said Jasper Main, who was both cautious and cunning.

"Why not pounce upon him while he is asleep?"

"That was my own idea. He must be asleep now. Let us bind him and the nigger, and put them in a boat and cast them adrift before the men are about. The watch I can rely on."

"Oh, yes; we may make ourselves easy about them."

"Very well; we cannot have a better plan of action. Are we agreed upon it?"

Cook cordially concurred, and the thing was definitively settled. A boat was amply provisioned; bread, meat, and water was put in it, together with firearms, powder and shot; a sail and a mast was given them, and the two men thought they had behaved in a most charitable manner.

At three in the morning Jasper Main, accompanied by Cook, stole gently into Money Marks' cabin, and found him sleeping soundly.

Before he could imagine what was going to happen to him, he was securely bound, and he only awoke when the tightness of the cords created an amount of physical pain which he could not withstand.

"What is it?" he cried, springing up.

A glance sufficed to show him what had happened. He ground his teeth together with impotent rage. He was in the power of his enemies. His first impulse was to cry out, but he checked that when he saw the gleaming barrel of a pistol presented at his head by Jasper Main, who exclaimed—

"If you utter one word I will blow your brains out. No one can save you—no one, in point of fact, will raise a hand to save you. Take my word for it, you are completely in my power."

"You viper—you wretch! were I unbound, you would scarcely dare to speak to me in that way," said Money Marks.

"You are our prisoner," replied Jasper Main, "and it is useless to comment upon the fact."

"What do you intend doing with me?"

"I will tell you; a boat is prepared, into which you will be placed; it is amply provisioned, so that you will not perish of starvation, a sail is also at your service. You can make for the mainland, which I doubt not you will reach, if the weather is favourable."

"And if not?"

"Why that is a contingency with which I have not bothered my head," returned Main, carelessly.

"Am I to be cast adrift by myself?"

"No."

"Who will be my companion?"

"The negro."

"Cuffy?"

"Yes."

"You are an infamous scoundrel," said Money Marks, indignantly.

"Possibly I may be; I have been told so before."

"Not without reason."

"That is your opinion; you may be right; we will not stop to argue the point."

"I spared your life."

"And I return the compliment by sparing yours. What more do you want?"

"This is infamous."

"I have no doubt you think so, but your opinion is not infallible. Get up and dress yourself; I will unfasten the cords; make but the slightest attempt to escape, and——"

He tapped the butt of his pistol significantly.

"The crew will rally round me."

"Do not flatter yourself about that fact; I happen to know them better than you do; they are devoted to Cook and myself, besides which they are all at this moment drunk."

"All?"

"Without exception. Come, make haste."

Money Marks groaned in anguish of spirit, but he got up and dressed himself as he was told to do. He was allowed to wear his belt, for Jasper Main did not guess that it contained much valuable property. This was one source of consolation to Money Marks in the midst of his great and overwhelming trouble.

"Perhaps it is all for the best," he said to himself, as he was dressing. "I have enough in this belt to maintain me well and in affluence for life. If Cuffy succeeds in getting his part of the treasure into the boat, we shall be better off than I expected. We may reach the mainland; I rather think the chances are in our favour. If we do, I shall have quitted a course of life of which I am tired, and all danger of being captured and hanged as a pirate will be obviated. Viola, too, will claim more of my attention; I can try to fulfil the conditions upon which she has promised to become my wife. I must put the best face I can upon the matter, and thank my stars that the ruffians have not decided to kill me outright. I might have known that no reliance was to be placed on such fellows as I have had to command. Play with edge tools and you are sure to cut yourself. The man who sups with the devil should have a long spoon."

When Money Marks was ready, Jasper Main put himself by his side and marched him up the companion-ladder. The ship was standing nearly still; she carried no sail, and the engines were stopped, while the sea was as calm and placid as a mill-pond.

Money Marks was told to enter the boat which was riding placidly alongside, and he did so.

"Stay there," said Jasper Main. "Don't attempt to move or cry out. Cook is going for the negro, and I shall watch you during his absence."

"Do not alarm yourself," said Money Marks; "I am only too glad to get away from your society."

"Let those laugh who win. I have won at present, and you laugh on the wrong side of your face, I think."

"We may meet again."

"I hope not; I have no desire, I am sure, to meet you."

"No, I don't suppose you have. When one man has wronged another he is always afraid to meet him."

"Talk about something more practical," said Jasper Main, biting his lip. "Is there anything you want?"

"You are becoming generous all at once. There is one thing I should like to have—one thing I regret not having taken when it was in my power."

"My life I suppose you mean?"

"I do."

"That is beyond you now."

"I will beg one favour of you."

"Name it."

"In my cabin you will see half-a-dozen or more bags of shot of different sizes, let me have them, and some powder. I cannot have too much ammunition. Who knows but that I may be cast amongst savages."

"Very well; Cook shall get them for you when he returns," replied Jasper Main.

Money Marks smiled inwardly. It was evident that his enemy did not for a moment suppose the bags of shot were Eldorados on a small scale, and that they contained an immense amount of gold in all coinages.

Cook in the meantime had gone to Cuffy's cabin. The negro had laid down hastily in his clothes, thinking he might be wanted in a hurry in the night by his master.

Several sailors were sleeping in bunks and hammocks near him, though many bunks were empty, their former occupants having been killed in the late battle.

Cook flashed his lantern in the black's face, and Cuffy awoke.

"Am de sun rose so early?" he said, half asleep and half awake.

"Wake up you nigger," cried Cook.

"What de rumpus, massa?" queried Cuffy, rubbing his eyes.

"Your master wants you."

"Where?"

"On deck."

"Tell him I'm a coming."

Thinking that this was a genuine exclamation, and that Money Marks really did want him, Cuffy hastened on deck, and was ordered into the boat. His consternation knew no bounds; his eyes rolled fearfully, and he was inclined to drop down in a fit, produced by sheer amazement.

"Jump into the boat, nigger," cried Cook, "unless you want to be pricked with a bayonet."

It actually was necessary for Cook to galvanize him into life by running the point of a bayonet into his leg before he would move.

Cuffy fell into the boat "all of a heap," as the saying is, and lay at the bottom, completely nonplussed.

"Good-bye, Marks," cried Jasper Main; "I'm a Yankee, you know, and I rather calc'late I've done a 'cute trick to-day. I hope we shall meet again. I should be sorry to lose sight of so promising a young man."

Money Marks was enraged at his banter, and said—

"If we do meet again it will not do one of us much good."

"Ha! ha! that remains to be seen. If you should see any ice on your travels, tell the polar bears we are coming."

With this pitiful and sorry joke Jasper Main turned away and ordered the engineers to put on the steam.

They obeyed this order, and the pirate speedily sailed out of sight.

It was almost incredible to Money Marks that so great a change of fortune should have taken place in so short a space of time. An hour ago he was the trusted and popular commander of a large ship. Now what was he? An outcast, at the mercy of the waves and the wind. Probably it was his fate to die of starvation or of thirst. All dooms that were horrible occurred to him in succession.

He was very miserable.

The lamp in the stern of the pirate soon faded away, but it was not missed by the castaways, for the morning light was gradually increasing in intensity, and day had broken.

Money Marks was not so much stunned and overcome as Cuffy; the black was completely prostrated, and sobbed and cried at the bottom of the boat like an infant. Marks did not attempt to disturb him for some time; he resigned himself to his fate with the stolidity of a philosopher, and walked up and down the boat looking at the things Jasper Main had thought fit to give him wherewith to soothe the misery of his long voyage. Meat and biscuit abounded: there were three kegs of water, several bottles of wine, about the same number of spirits, in all nearly five dozen; a piece of canvas to make an awning, a mast, a sail, oars, a rudder and strings, some books taken at random from the shelves in his cabin, firearms, shot, and powder, together with caps in plenty.

One thing, however, was wanting.

There was no compass.

This was a serious misfortune, because Money Marks could no more tell in what direction he was sailing than the child unborn.

He had been liberally provided with everything, and could not accuse Jasper Main of inhuman cruelty; his provisions would last six weeks, perhaps more if they were judiciously used.

On searching further he found some fishing tackle and a small stove for cooking, with a supply of coals and wood in the bows, evidently put there by the thoughtfulness of Cook.

If a storm arose all these precautions would be useless; for the little boat, though not exactly a cockle-shell, would infallibly go under in a high sea.

A storm! The very idea made Money Marks blanch with terror. And why?

Because it foreboded death.

If he had good weather and tolerable luck, the chances were he would reach the mainland without much suffering.

"If;" how much depended upon that apparently trifling monosyllable.

CHAPTER XLVIII.

THE FROZEN SEA.

THINKING that Cuffy had had quite enough time to recover himself, Money Marks gave him a gentle reminder by way of a kick in the ribs.

The black turned over on his side, and said, with a moan—

"Oh, Massa Marks, is dis all true? are we by ourselves on de bosom of the wide, wide sea?"

"Look about you and judge for yourself."

Cuffy sprang to his feet.

"Oh, de wretches!" he cried; "dis chile be one wid them some fine day or oder. A fine ting to turn us out of our beds and our ship in the dead of night."

"They have not treated us so badly after all."

"How's dat?"

"I have my belt with the precious stones, and I presume you have yours."

"Iss, have dat," replied Cuffy, putting his hand to his waist.

"Look at those bags."

"Which?"

"Marked 'shot.'"

"Iss, massa."

"Those are full of gold, and I got them by a remarkable subterfuge, telling Jasper Main—the scoundrel—that they contained shot. Ha! ha! a good joke. If we succeed in landing we shall have nothing to regret. My only fear is that we are drifting towards the Arctic regions, and shall soon be in the neighbourhood of the Frozen Ocean. Do you not mark how cold it has become?"

"Me felt the cold very much lately," replied Cuffy, with a slight shiver.

"Ha!" said Money Marks, "there is something else I had not noticed—a little bag of tobacco, some pipes, and a couple of boxes of matches. Come, they have not treated us so badly after all."

"Wish I was on board, massa," said Cuffy, with an ill-suppressed whine. "Cuss dat tresher; if it not be for de tresher Massa Main never take it into his head to treat us like dis."

MARKS AND THE DIAMOND MERCHANT.

"I don't know that. Very likely he had been revolving the idea in his mind for a long time: it is impossible to say."

"Bad job—very bad job."

"If you talk like that, Cuffy, I shall begin to wish that they had not put you in the boat with me. I never thought you were a coward before."

"Not a coward, massa; but poor nigger feel all-overish."

"Dismiss your fears; whatever happens to you will happen to me also. We are literally in the same boat. It is a calamity, I admit, and we run a fearful risk; but what cannot be cured must be endured. I do not despair, why should you?"

Cuffy was reassured by the bold and courageous language made use of by his master; he dismissed his terror, and bustled about the boat, having become quite another man.

Money Marks, wishing to keep up the spirits of himself and his companion, opened a bottle of wine and lighted a pipe. Cuffy drank a tumbler of sparkling Catawba, an

American vintage not at all to be despised, and felt much refreshed.

After that he raised the mast and set the sail to a fine breeze, which was blowing from the south-west.

Money Marks took up a line, and having baited it, indulged in the sport of fishing, determining to take matters as easily as he could and to make light of his misfortunes.

"It seems to me," he said, "that it is a toss up whether we die or live. If we die there is an end of us, and we shall not be gainers of a negative advantage, because we shall quit a stormy world and throw all our troubles off our shoulders; that is something gained. If we live, I for one shall have to congratulate myself; I shall have quitted a dangerous mode of life, in which there was very little to attract me save its adventurous character; I will atone for the past by living the life that Viola has prescribed as a stipulation before she consents to forgive me. When married I will devote my existence to finding out who my mother and father are—or were, should they not be in the land of the living. I shall not have to work, for the money I have about me is amply sufficient to enable me to live in luxury."

"Dat will do, Massa Marks," said Cuffy, with a grin.

"Were you listening to me?"

"Couldn't help."

"Never mind; I knew not that I spoke aloud, but you are my friend, and there is no reason why you should not know my secret thoughts."

They were obliged to let the boat go with the wind. At length they found themselves in the vortex of a current, which was, as Money Marks feared, gradually drifting them towards the North Pole.

He could do nothing to prevent this consummation.

The current was probably a branch of the Gulf Stream; it was an unpleasant contingency, but such as it was he was obliged to accept it.

A week passed. The cold became greater, but as their clothes had been given them, the castaways did not suffer on this account; they had met with no bad weather, had had plenty to eat and drink, and up to the present time nothing had troubled them but their anxiety, which was, as may naturally be supposed, intense.

On the evening of the eleventh day the air became very cold, the sky was overcast, no stars, no moon could be seen.

Money Marks looked anxiously around, and said to Cuffy, who was shivering beneath the covering of three coats—

"I fear we shall have a snow-storm; there is every appearance of it."

"Dat true," said Cuffy, whose spirits were sinking as far below zero as the mercury in the thermometer.

"We are drifting to the frozen ocean; in another two days we may expect to find ourselves in the midst of snow and ice."

As he spoke, a thick shower of flakes descended, and the air became full of them. The feathery molecules settled upon everything, and the prospect before the castaways was truly discouraging.

Money Marks gave some spirits to Cuffy and took some himself; then they made the best bed they could, and lying side by side went off to sleep. The black man was the white man's brother; there was no invidious distinction on the ground of colour.

The boat drifted a considerable distance during the night.

When day broke a strange sight met the eyes of Money Marks and his faithful companion. The cold had increased at least ten degrees. The boat stood still, and when they looked around for a reason for this strange phenomenon, they were electrified at what they saw.

And this was what they saw—

The entire sea as far as their vision stretched *was a mass of ice!*

The water had suddenly congealed, as is the case in those seas, and all was a blank, desolate expanse of snow and ice.

Here and there were blocks of snow and pillars of ice; nothing could be more wild and bleak and dreary. They were in danger of being frost-bitten, so that it may be imagined the cold was excessive.

There was very little hope for them; the severe season of the year had just set in, and the chances were it would last six months out of the twelve.

"Gracious Heaven!" cried Money Marks. "Is there nothing before us? have we nothing to hope for? is everything to be the same to-morrow as to-day, and to-day as yesterday? nothing but silence and despair? always this sepulchre of ice under a winding-sheet of snow? no ray of sunshine on these eternal icebergs? no succour to hope for? Oh, my God! it is awful."

"Oh-h-h!" said Cuffy, shivering and clapping his hands to keep his fingers warm. "There is some difference between this and Ole Virginny."

"So I should think."

"Never mind, massa."

"It is easy to say that; what shall we do?"

"Someting turn up."

"Nothing but snow and grizzly bear, I expect, with here and there a seal."

"Never mind," again said Cuffy.

He had in his turn become comforter.

"It come all right some day."

"That is more than you can tell," replied Money Marks, despondingly.

"If we stuck in the ice, it's no matter—we manage to live; this ice will join other ice, and other ice must join shore. Why not travel over ice and reach de shore and kill plenty of bears on de way? that's what Cuffy say."

"H'm!" said Money Marks, reflectively.

"It's no use letting one's spirits go down."

"I don't suppose that is of much use, so we had better drink some spirits to keep them up. Then we will build a hut of snow, in which to live while we stay here and mature our plans. Thank goodness, those villains gave us a good supply of provisions; what should we have done without them?"

The situation was an unpleasant one, but both Money Marks and the negro had been in one more embarrassing. There was nothing so very terrible in their position that they should sink under the ill treatment and desertion of Jasper Main; if they could for a space go into winter quarters, and either wait until the ice broke up and the sea was once more at their service, or else journey over the ice towards those regions where the Esquimaux live, they would have nothing to fear.

Marks had an idea that Esquimaux would be found at a distance of some two hundred miles to the north-west of them, and he was right, which showed the value of the geography he had taken the opportunity of learning in his spare moments.

He determined to go into winter quarters for a time and deliberate as to what was the best to be done. Accordingly he, with Cuffy's assistance, began to mould the pliant snow to his will, and in the course of the day—which was of very short duration, the best part of the twenty-four hours being passed in comparative darkness—a hut of tolerable size arose, which did credit to its architect and builder. In this they placed all their stores, for they were fearful of leaving them in the boat, which was wedged into the ice, and where the stores were at the mercy of the first wild animal that chose to take a fancy to them.

In the polar regions there are no insurance offices either for life or property, so that voyagers in those remote and dismal regions are obliged to be more careful than they otherwise would be.

The hut was warmer than those unacquainted with such a structure would have supposed. But they found that they had made a mistake in not erecting the house upon the boat; if they had constituted the boat the foundation of the structure it would have been warmer, drier, and more comfortable.

Seeing this they soon changed their quarters and repeated their work. They were startled and delighted by the appearance of the celebrated northern lights; Cuffy was especially pleased with the aurora borealis, whenever he could see one of the magnificent specimens with which they were occasionally favoured.

Wild animals seemed scarce; seals were to be met with, but it was difficult to catch them, although a shot was now and then obtainable before they could dart into the holes in the ice made by themselves, the result of their own indefatigable industry. These holes gave them air, without which they could not have existed for any length of time.

Marks discouraged Cuffy when he wished to fire at a seal, because, although their ammunition was not then getting short, it would infallibly do so shortly, if they were to expend it in a reckless manner.

When their temporary home was arranged to their satisfaction, Money Marks proposed that they should make an excursion in search of bears, to which proposition Cuffy did not demur; he would have followed Money Marks everywhere. Snow-storms were of constant occurrence, so that they could not reckon with any certainty upon finding their way home by their footsteps. If there was no fall of snow to obliterate their tracks, they could easily find the road back to the hut, which a quarter of a mile off it was impossible to see, because it was of the same colour as the widespread hideous carpet which lay all around in prodigal profusion.

Marks was naturally anxious, under these circumstances, not to go very far away lest they should become benighted, and unable to retrace their steps to the hut, to lose which would be the greatest calamity that could happen to them, and which would probably result in death.

The blast was bitterly cold, keen and freezing, the vast expanse of snow dazzled their eyes, and made them devise a covering, which after the manner of spectacles protected and preserved them from becoming stone-blind, as is often the case in these latitudes.

After rolling a block of ice against the narrow inlet which served them for a door, the arctic voyagers started on their excursion. They were well armed, and protected from the weather by such wraps as the pirates had given them when they turned them adrift. They carrried spirits, meat, and biscuits with them, and were in high spirits at the idea of chasing a large bear and killing it.

In order to find his way back again Money Marks stopped at every hundred yards, and with Cuffy's help, made a large mound of snow, which would show above everything even if a severe snow-storm set in.

"What a strange eventful life mine has been as far as it has gone," said Money Marks, who was inclined to moralize; "I never knew my father and mother, though I have a presentiment that I shall see them some day or other; and by the iron force of irresistible circumstances, I have been obliged to do deeds that would make my parents blush for the criminal excesses of their offspring."

He was wrong in attributing what he had done to the force of circumstances. No amount of fortuitous occurrences, however weighty and overwhelming, ought to influence a good man for evil; but a little self-delusion is pleasing at times, and Money Marks, like the rest of us, now and then indulged in the self-deluding process.

He fancied himself the child of fate, thinking he had no power over his own actions, but that he was obliged to work out a predestined course!

"What dat big ting dere?" suddenly cried Cuffy.

"Where?"

"To de left. Oh! golly, what eyes him have."

Money Marks turned his eyes in the direction indicated by Cuffy, and saw a bear of considerable size, sitting on its haunches, and looking curiously at the intruders upon his privacy.

A fine, stately, patriarchal-looking old bear it was, with a grave, sage face like a polar Solon. Probably he had never seen a white man before, and if so it is equally certain that he never saw a black one. Cuffy's colour did not seem to please him at all. Money Marks was white, and he did not seem to regard him with so much anger as he did the negro, towards whom he advanced slowly, as if he wished to see what manner of man he was.

"Him coming, Massa Marks, him coming," exclaimed Cuffy; "what I do? pull the shoot gun?"

"Yes. When he is near enough, you fire first; if you should not succeed in disabling him, I shall be able to support your shot. Aim at his heart. I believe they are difficult things to shoot, and I have heard that they will fight to the last gasp and extremity, if they have cubs in the vicinity."

He had no time to say more, as the bear sat upon its hind legs, and delivered itself of a great roar, which found an echo in the surrounding icebergs.

With one peculiarity of the polar bear Money Marks was unhappily unfamiliar. It is their custom to travel in bands, and although one solitary bear may often be met with, the rest of the band are not far away. When an old bear goes out hunting for seal, he will select a hole which seems to have been lately made, and he will sit by the side of the cavity for any length of time until the unwary seal ascends from the ocean, is immediately captured, killed and eaten.

No sooner was the unearthly shriek of the polar bear heard, than the distant air seemed alive with sounds of a similar description, which reverberated dismally amongst the masses of driven snow, and the huge, unwieldy, yet picturesque blocks of ice.

"Don't fire, Cuffy, for your life don't fire!" said Money Marks, hoarse with excitement. "Don't fire! the place is full of bears, we shall be torn to pieces."

His admonition came too late, for Cuffy had pulled the trigger, and the bear had received a bullet, in what may be called the pit of his stomach. Now this was excessively disagreeable to him, for he had but lately devoured a whole seal, and he did not relish the sort of digestive pill which the black had given him.

Money Marks' exclamation only had the effect of making Cuffy nervous, causing him to aim lower than he intended.

When the bear found that he was hit he uttered another shriek, more prolonged and more unearthly than the first. There was more of pain and rage mingled with astonishment

in the latter. The animal placed his paw to the hurt, just as a Christain might put his hand to a wound, and withdrew it covered with blood, at which he looked in a perplexed manner for a few seconds; putting out his tongue he licked it, and feeling convinced that Cuffy had done him, or endeavoured to do him, a mortal injury, he gave vent to a third cry, and darting forward, would have thrown himself upon Cuffy to take summary vengeance for his unprovoked assault, had not Money Marks fired two barrels of his revolver into his head.

The bear dropped instantly and without a groan.

Money Marks did not consider it safe to stay and skin the creature, though he would have been glad to do so, as the skin would have been of great service to him whilst he dwelt in the land of snow and ice.

"Run, Cuffy," he cried, "we cannot afford to wait until the whole herd is down upon us; we can kill one or even half-a-dozen, but a score would be too many for us. If bear doesn't eat bear we will return for that gentleman's skin, and have it, too."

A few descending snow-flakes warned them that they had to expect a storm. Their tracks were discernible, and they experienced no difficulty in retracing the mile they had travelled from home.

"Hallo!" cried Money Marks, looking at the hut, "what has moved the ice away?"

The block of ice had been pushed away from the aperture and something had apparently gone in; it was impossible to say what.

"Dere is someting inside; we have visitor come to leave his card on the new comers," said Cuffy, with a laugh.

"We must find out who or what it is. But it is a dangerous thing to do; I should not like to enter the hut, and I will not subject you to anything I would not do myself. Suppose we pull a part of the wall down, it is easily built up again?"

Cuffy cordially approved of this plan, and taking his knife from his girdle, he began to cut a square hole about three feet from the ground.

Marks rolled the block of ice to the entrance again, and stood by with his loaded revolver, in case Cuffy should want any assistance.

After ten minutes had been cut to waste, some energetic hacking and hewing sufficed to drive about two feet square of frozen snow into the interior of the house.

It fell with a crash!

There was a subdued growl.

Presently a white nose was protruded through the hole, this was followed by a head, which Marks saw in a moment belonged to a bear, who had taken possession of their cabin during their absence.

"Ha! ha!" he laughed; "we didn't know that when we came back we should find a man in possession!"

"Ha! ha!" laughed Cuffy.

The bear growled.

"You might as well be civil over it, old fellow, if you are in possession," said Money Marks.

"Shoot, massa," said Cuffy, "him been at de beef and biscuit; we have none left if he go on like that; him skin make nice fur mat, and him flesh be nice change from salt junk."

Aiming at the beast's eye, which was flashing with angry and indignant glances upon him, Money Marks fired.

The ball crashed through the skull, and the animal fell back dead as a stone. He was dragged out and skinned at once; for had they allowed the body to stiffen, which it would soon have done in so cold a climate, they would have found it impossible to have removed the skin at all.

The flesh was cut up and placed in a secure corner, while the skin was hung up to dry. Then Cuffy lighted a fire and proceeded to boil some slices of flesh in a tin pannikin.

"It is fortunate we placed the lump of ice against the door," said Money Marks; "had we neglected to do so, we should have been in ignorance of the bear having effected an entry, and one of us would have fallen a victim to his deadly hug, which would have been frightful. Life here with a companion is bad enough, but life alone would be intolerable."

The bear's flesh was a little rich and oily, but it was tender; and both of the men liked it much better than the fare upon which they had for so long a time been subsisting.

After this adventure they did not stir out much, for fear

of drawing the flock of bears upon them. One journey they made to discover the carcase of the bear they had left in the snow, but they could find no trace of it.

Consequently they came to the conclusion that it had been devoured by its fellows, and that the remnants of the skin were buried beneath the snow, which had fallen heavily in the night.

CHAPTER XLIX.

THE CASTAWAYS JOURNEY TO THE NORTH-WEST, AND ARE IN DANGER OF PERISHING BY THE WAY.

IN about a month's time Money Marks grew tired of the horrible monotony of the region in which his lot was cast. The occasional shooting of a polar bear was the only excitement which fell to his lot, and to a man of his active temperament and energetic disposition this sort of existence was intolerable.

He wanted to be up and doing; he wanted to see if he could not work his way across the ice to some settlement. If he could only strike the Esquimaux country he would be satisfied, because he could from there work his way to the Hudson's Bay territory, and by crossing that vast country, arrive in the United States, where he could turn his jewels into gold and make some practical use of the riches of Prettyman Parker.

The bags of gold he would be compelled to leave behind him; they were too heavy to be dragged through the snow; he must abandon them; there was nothing else for it.

He was consoled for this loss by thinking that he and Cuffy had together a quantity of valuable jewels, worth in the aggregate nearly a couple of hundred thousand pounds, which was fortune enough for any man.

One very chilly morning Cuffy and himself were sitting in the snow-hut smoking their pipes. The snow was descending in clouds outside, and the howl and tear of the wind were painful to hear.

Inside the hut all was comparatively snug and comfortable. It was dark, of course; but Cuffy had, like his master, become habituated to the darkness, and could like a mole almost see his way about. He knew every corner of the hut, knew where everything was stowed away, and could tell where Money Marks was from the sound of his voice.

"I am getting confoundedly tired of this, Cuffy," exclaimed Money Marks.

"So'm I, massa," responded Cuffy; "but what we do?"

"I'll tell you. Strike our camp and go to the north-west."

"That dam dangerous," replied Cuffy, with a doubtful shake of the head.

"Why?"

"It long journey; don't know where may lead us; p'raps noting to eat—only snow to drink; perish of cold. No, no, dis de place, massa; warm, snug, plenty to eat and drink, plenty bear; when ice break up den boat free, and we sail away once more."

"That is a very pretty picture; but I am afraid that if the sea were free to-morrow the currents would never let us get back to a civilized country, and the chances are we should be overwhelmed in a storm or crushed by an iceberg."

"All dat berry true," said Cuffy, who could make no pertinent reply to these remarks.

"If by enduring eight months of this sort of life we get afloat on the ocean, only to know that our death is certain, had we not better essay the passage of the ice and trust to Providence?"

"Berry well; when you go, massa, I go to," said Cuffy, with that species of sublime faith and confidence in his master which he always exhibited.

"That is agreed upon. Let us strike our camp to-morrow morning. I can steer my way by the stars, which shine as brightly here as they do in Europe. We will stake our all upon a single throw. Who knows but that in less than six months we shall be in a civilized country?"

This idea, so boldly broached and so bravely taken up, was at once acted upon. They made two packs or knapsacks, in which they put as much food as they could carry, and they also provided themselves with ammunition.

It grieved them beyond measure to leave so much that was valuable behind in the boat to become the prey of the waves; but it could not be helped.

Thinking that they would like some fresh meat before

they started, they sallied forth to look for bear, and were fortunate enough to find their prey nearer home than they expected.

They sighted an old female bear, who, from her motionless and expectant attitude, they guessed was waiting at the hole of a seal for the creature to appear.

Nor were they mistaken.

Standing still for a minute, they had the satisfaction of seeing the seal emerge from his hole. He took no notice of the motionless white mass before him, thinking from its immobility that it was a lump of snow.

Then his enemy pounced upon him. One blow of her paw laid the seal senseless at her feet, but she did not live long to enjoy her triumph; a bullet from Money Marks' unerring pistol, followed by another in quick succession, laid her low, and seal and bear lay side by side in death.

Cuffy drew his knife, and at once proceeded to cut up the bear. He had scarcely commenced before he heard a strange bleating sound to the right of him.

"Hush!" he exclaimed.

Money Marks listened.

"She has whelps," he said; "they miss their dam, and are bleating for her. Be on your guard, lest the sire be somewhere near."

"Yes, massa."

"I have an idea, Cuffy," continued Money Marks.

"What dat?"

"Let us capture the cubs."

"What de use ob dat?"

"Never you mind; you'll find out some day, if you live long enough."

Cuffy left off cutting up the she bear and rose to his feet.

The cubs were placed behind a mound of snow, which the bear had scraped together with her paws to protect them against the inclemency of the weather and the merciless severity of the wintry blast.

They were not so young as Money Marks had supposed them to be. On the contrary, they were fine lusty young fellows, with some strength though not much sagacity. They ran away when they saw the strangers. When Cuffy perceived this he went back to where the bear's skin was lying, and threw it over his shoulders; then he armed himself with some pieces of meat, which he threw towards the young bears, and they ate them all, unconscious of the startling fact that they were devouring the flesh of that mother whose absence they were wondering at and whose loss they had to deplore.

Thinking that the creature advancing on all-fours, covered with a skin such as they had been accustomed to, was their mother, they permitted Cuffy to approach them, and he succeeded in capturing the biggest one, which he collared round the neck and held as he would a dog or a puppy.

This he handed to Money Marks, who tied some cord round its nose to muzzle it, afterwards tying its fore legs together. When the other was caught it was treated in the same manner. The cubs did not appear to be at all vicious; they were more timid than anything else.

When their legs were untied the rope was put round their necks, and they suffered themselves to be dragged along with praiseworthy patience.

When they reached the hut Cuffy said—

"Now, what you do with them, Massa Marks?"

"Turn them into beasts of burden. What is to prevent us from making a sledge which these animals can convey? We can always feed them as long as we can shoot a seal or a bear; they devoured their own mother, and I don't suppose they will be very particular about making a meal upon any of their relations."

"No, s'pose not," said Cuffy, with a grin.

The idea of making a sledge for the young cubs to draw was really a brilliant one; it obviated the necessity of leaving their stores behind, and it enabled them to take some if not all of the gold.

The snow was frozen hard, as to its surface, so that the feet did not sink in at every step, which was a great advantage.

The sledge was of course made out of the timbers of the boat, which was broken up for the purpose. It was rudely put together, but it answered their purpose, and they did not care about elegance or workmanlike finish.

A harness was made out of ropes—some bearskin being wrapped round the collar to prevent the hemp from chafing the necks of the cubs.

The journey to the North-West was of course postponed for a short time, until the sledge was completed. It held all they wanted it with ease, but the gold was found to be too heavy for the strength of the cubs, and they had to abandon it after all.

"Perhaps it is better that we should leave it," said Money Marks.

Cuffy was tossing the last bag on to the snow with a sigh. Looking up inquiringly, he said—

"Why, massa?"

"Because it would only excite the cupidity of those whom we may meet in our travels. Men will shed blood for gold, and, in point of fact, do anything."

"Oh, golly! what a lot of bacca him buy," said Cuffy, who did not like parting with the money.

Cuffy guided one cub with a string, walking on one side; and Money Marks imitated his example on the other. They walked with their rifles cocked, and were on the *qui vive* for the slightest sign of an enemy.

Little did they think, when they started so joyously, that they were undertaking a tremendous task, and one of which they would get weary long before it was accomplished.

They intended to journey twelve hours every day, and to camp during the next twelve, which was a wise and salutary arrangement.

To erect a snow-house at every stoppage would have been too great a labour. They had several bearskins—some of which they wore on their shoulders, some of which were placed on the top of the sledge to cover over the stores. These they stretched every night over some timbers they took from the boat, and made a comfortable house; as they filled up the crevices and interstices with snow, so as to keep the wind out.

After tramping for some time in the snow and wind, they became very gloomy and cogitative, like Napoleon's army when it retreated from Moscow.

To Money Marks' mind there was something overwhelmingly grand, and yet stupendously awful, in being on the wide expanse of frozen water—on a vast prairie, as it were, of ice and snow.

There was ice to the right of them, ice to the left of them, ice in front of them, and ice behind them. It stretched for almost incalculable distances on each side, and, in one instance, went to the impenetrable region of eternal snow.

Eternal snow!

How sublime and yet how terrible! Should Money Marks miscalculate, and allow his footsteps to betray him into that dread region into which Sir John Franklin and his followers penetrated but to die!—where Bellot found an early grave, and where many brave men have travelled to sleep their last long sleep! Why, if he should so miscalculate, there would be nothing for him and his simple-minded companion to do but to leave their bones there.

Literally, they would leave their bodies there; for in the region of eternal snow there is no such thing as corruption. No sooner is your blood cold than it congeals—it becomes ice—your flesh is frozen also; then, in death, you preserve the image of what you were in life, just as much as if you had passed through the skilful hands of a clever embalmer.

Should Money Marks go thither he must bid adieu for ever to Viola—bid adieu to all his dreams of happiness and atonement.

This vast and awful solitude which I have endeavoured, though feebly, to bring before the mind's eye of the reader, had an extraordinary effect upon Money Marks.

For a long time he had been callous as to the truth of revealed religion, but the effect of his sojourn on the ice was to make him think deeply on many great problems with the following result:—

He acknowledged the majesty of the great Creator, for he was convinced by the stupendous character of His works. The endless snow, the vast accumulation of ice, the gigantic ice-bergs, caught and held still in a firm embrace, frowning upon him majestically like aqueous mountains, brought him on his knees.

He said that he had been leading a vile and odious life, and he was willing to atone for so doing, and he wished to make all the reparation that laid in his power.

If he got back to Europe, he inwardly declared that he would seek Viola out in her conventual retreat, promise her to live a life of which she and her spiritual advisers could approve, and, when his term of probation was at an end, he

would claim her as his bride, and in her gracious and holy society, devote himself to such works as might propitiate offended Heaven.

So impressed was he with the wickedness and worthlessness of the life he had been leading, that he looked upon the treatment he had received from Jasper Main as a well-merited punishment for his sins.

Such was the power of solitude and deep thought.

He often thought that he was never destined to escape from the field of ice on which he was. Perhaps it was his fate to perish of cold and starvation. It was a fearful death, and he struggled against the conviction which, when he was low-spirited, would gain ground upon him.

Bears were plentiful on the route, and they subsisted almost entirely upon their flesh, in order to save their slender stock of provisions. This was wise and prudent; they also took care of their limited number of bottles of spirits, but at length this supply became exhausted, as did their tobacco, and they felt this deprivation most keenly.

For six months they tramped with more energy than could be expected from men in their forlorn, desperate and almost hopeless condition. Their troubles were further increased by the death of one of the cubs, and as the other was not strong enough to draw the sledge, they had to abandon that useful appendage.

But this coming at the time it did, did not matter so much as it would have done at the outset of their march; for they had consumed nearly all their provisions, and were in a bad strait.

Money Marks saw that they were in evil case, and his spirits fell—misfortunes were fast overtaking them. The end of their career seemed to be arriving.

Cuffy did not value his life very highly—he thought a great deal more of his master than he did of himself. He would cheerfully have laid down upon the ice, and have given up the ghost, if he could by so doing have prevailed upon some good fairy to waft his master to kindlier shores, where the elements do not cruelly compeer together to take away men's lives.

For two days the voyagers were without provisions, and Money Marks was unable to see the slightest trace of a bear, or even a seal. He thought their doom was sealed. They lay down exhausted at the base of a small iceberg, wrapped themselves in their furs, and tried to snatch a few hours' sleep, which would refresh them, and enable them to go after food with increased zeal in the morning.

They were in a most desponding state.

"I am sadly afraid that it is all over with us, Cuffy," said Money Marks.

"Never dead til de breff gone, massa."

"I know that. Well, let us go to sleep, and hope for better luck in the morning."

Their eyes had not been closed in slumber for more than an hour before they were awoke by a horrible rumbling.

Each started to his feet, and gazed horror-stricken around him.

And what a sight met their gaze!

Oh, God! it was enough to appal the heart of the strongest man.

The ice all around them was cracking and breaking up into small patches, which the excited waves tossed up and down in a tumultuous manner.

With a hysterical sob, Money Marks fell on his knees, and cried in an agonized voice—

"All is over! Viola, farewell! farewell for ever!"

Cuffy lay on his face immoveable with terror.

The iceberg, with a few square yards of ice attached to it, began to move in obedience to the action of the wind, which was blowing from the south-west.

It was the action of the warm wind which had caused the break-up of the ice, and heralded the approach of the brief and unsatisfactory arctic summer.

Peril was succeeding peril.

CHAPTER L.

THE MAWGAWKEE TRIBE OF ESQUIMAUX.

THE iceberg did not topple over, as Money Marks expected it would, nor did it come in contact with one of its own species.

It held its own, and pursued its way with a lofty disdain for everything and everybody.

When Cuffy found that there was no immediate danger, and that he was not to be buried beneath the engulphing waves, he raised up his head, and then sat up—to stand upright was not altogether safe, for the berg gave alarming lurches, now and then, which were enough to upset anyone's equilibrium upon so slippery a surface as ice.

"We not dead yet, massa," said Cuffy.

Money Marks had been absorbed in private but heartfelt emotion.

"I am afraid," he said, divorcing himself from his thoughts, "that our doom is only postponed, my good friend."

"Oh, no! we be all right presently."

Money Marks shook his head; he could not agree with this hopeful opinion. The sickly rays of an infant moon glimmered faintly on the scene, sufficing to reveal a tithe of the horrors that surrounded them.

A polar bear that had been surprised by the ice, as had been the voyagers, had taken refuge on the very iceberg which carried the illustrious person of Money Marks.

When our hero saw this, his hopes revived; because if he were fortunate enough to succeed in killing the creature, he could contrive in his half-famished state to eat its flesh raw, and he would then be saved from an awful death—that of starvation.

His hand was weak, and his strength much diminished, but he contrived to hold the pistol.

His aim was true, for the bear threw up its paws, and then fell forward upon its face. It was dead. Cuffy found strength and skill enough to cut it up, and when he had done so, both Money Marks and himself ate the raw and reeking flesh ravenously.

This to those who are nursed in the lap of luxury may seem a proceeding worthy only of a savage, but those who have experienced the pangs of hunger know that when famine takes possession of a man delicacy leaves him.

They appeased their hunger, and then they crammed handfuls of snow into their mouths to quench their thirst. The rice they could not eat, because it was salt.

The time passed on, a weary night they had, which, in its turn, was succeeded by a weary day. The flesh of the bear so exhilarated Cuffy that, by dint of cutting holes in the ice, he managed to climb to the top of the berg.

Having ensconced himself in this elevated position, he kept a good look-out ahead, and towards evening reported land in sight.

The wind was blowing the berg in a direct line for the shore, so that the chances were a hundred to one that it was cast upon the sands and wrecked.

The cry of land in such a desolate region did not re-assure Money Marks to any great extent. He fancied that he was somewhere near Labrador, and he knew well what a sparsely-populated part it was, and how inclement and inhospitable its shores are.

He fancied that the island which the negro saw might be a second Spitzbergen ; a land upon which the foot of man is never set ; a patch of country which nourishes nothing but trees and reindeer. Better the bottom of the sea than a home in such a place.

The berg drifted rapidly towards the shore, and to avoid being hurled violently upon the beach, upon which the surf was rolling, Cuffy descended from his look-out station, and sat quietly by Money Marks' side.

The catastrophe came sooner than they expected it ; the berg rolled over on its side, struck the shore violently, and the two men were precipitated into the icy water, through which they swam until they reached land, upon which they mounted.

So exhausted were they that, wet as they were, they sank upon the land, and went to sleep. They must have slept for some hours—when they awoke, their clothes were dry and their limbs stiff. The water about them was hanging in icicles, and everything was frozen.

Money Marks was the first to awake. He endeavoured to get up, but found that he was unable to do so.

"I suppose that is the effect of sleeping in anything wet," he muttered, thinking that his limbs were stiff.

But when he came to look about him he found that his hands and feet were securely bound with something resembling cat-gut, but which was in reality the intestine of the reindeer. Turning to Cuffy, he exclaimed—

"Cuffy."

The negro awoke at the sound of his voice—he too was bound.

"What is the meaning of this?" said Money Marks. "Here am I hampered and tied like a chicken going to market, and you seem to me to be in the same condition."

"It proof of one ting, massa," said Cuffy, rubbing his eyes with the knuckles of his fingers.

"What is that?"

"The island, or whatever it is, is not uninhabited, and dat some ting. Some people's made us prisoners."

"I expect you are not far wrong," replied Money Marks. "If that is the case let us be thankful. We must have landed in close proximity to a tribe of Esquimaux. All we can do is to remain passive until they return. Probably a hunter found us sleeping here, and being unable to attack us, or to take us home singlehanded, he has gone to his village for reinforcements, having taken the precaution to bind us before so doing."

"Dat it ; dat de ticket, massa," responded Cuffy.

Marks was not at all wrong in his conjecture. A man belonging to the tribe called Mawgawkee, one of the most powerful of the Esquimaux, had been out hunting for seal; during his peregrinations he had met with the two men, and had hampered them as described.

In about an hour after their awakening he returned with a number of his tribe, who, without saying anything, proceeded to unfasten their legs and take the prisoners to the village, which was distant a couple of miles from the seashore. It was built in a hollow ; which, while it kept the wind from them, exposed them to heavy deluges of snow, which they were obliged to take away almost as fast as it fell, for fear of being smothered.

The Mawgawkees looked upon Cuffy as something wonderful ; they had never seen either a white or a black man in their lives, and they wondered how many colours there were in men. They themselves were of a deep olive tint and extremely oleaginous, which was the result of their living upon oil, in a great measure, when the ice prevented their catching fish. Their hair was long and black and straight ; they seemed good-natured to a degree.

They took Money Marks and Cuffy to the village, and the chief had them for his servants. They were especially anxious to know how they came into those regions ; but as Marks did not know a word of Esquimaux, and the chief, whose name was Quampau, did not understand a syllable of English, communication under the circumstances was slightly difficult.

The chief determined to teach Money Marks Esquimaux. It was too much trouble for so exalted a personage as himself to attempt to learn English. In three months' time Money Marks had made such progress that he was able to speak the language very tolerably ; and he ingratiated himself with the king by saying that he was a sailor who had been wrecked, and that Cuffy was his servant, also by the numerous tales and anecdotes he could tell, and the descriptions he could give of foreign countries, of which King Quampau had never so much as dreamt in his wildest and most ungovernable state of nightmare.

Money Marks asked, in return for all his information, if the king had ever seen a European. He replied in the negative, saying—

"Until I saw you I never saw a white man, though I have been told that some Esquimaux living more to the north-west have seen several."

Money Marks took this reply to refer to Sir John Franklin and his expedition.

He wanted to go away from the settlement, but the Esquimaux would not allow him to do so. He was useful to them ; he taught them many things which went far to civilize them, and they did not wish to part with him. The king told him so plainly, and said that if he did not marry some Mawgawkee woman and settle down amongst them for life, he would put him to death.

Money Marks appealed to the various chiefs, but they were all of the king's opinion. They liked him too well to part with him. Such is the disastrous effect of becoming popular. To save his life, Money Marks married the best-looking Mawgawkee that he could discover ; but as the women were all ugly, according to the opinions of a European, he did not feel at all flattered by the lady's acceptance of his offer.

He held several conferences with Cuffy, and the result of

their deliberations was that they would pretend to be resigned to their lot, but that they would in reality get all the information as to the Hudson Bay route from their entertainers, and when a fitting opportunity arrived make use of it.

If Money Marks had chosen he might have been a king amongst the Esquimaux, but his ambition was of a different description and lay in a different direction; he did not wish to be Triton amongst minnows, but a Triton amongst Tritons.

They sojourned six months with the Esquimaux, and at the end of that time they found a means of escaping. Many perils and hardships did they suffer by the way, but at length they reached the outskirts of civilization; for this great mercy they were humbly thankful. Suffering, and a release from it, begets thankfulness.

* * * * *

Money Marks and his attendant friend, companion, devoted adherent—what you will—arrived in New York exactly fourteen months after their expulsion from the pirate by Jasper Main and Cook the boatswain.

CHAPTER LI.

THE DIAMOND MERCHANT.

It was late in the day in mid-winter, and darkness was coming on apace, when two men—travel-stained, footsore and weary, dressed in rags, and those of the most preposterous description—entered the palatial city of New York.

One of them, a white, spoke earnestly for a few minutes to his companion, who was a black, and then entered a pawnbroker's shop.

It was one of those grand, almost colossal shops, in which gas is the prevailing feature, while gold, jewels and silver predominated in the background.

The shabbily attired young man, whose costume was certainly not the correct thing for Broadway, entered a box, and placed a small gem upon the counter. After waiting a short time the assistant in the shop come up to him and said, in a sharp, jerky voice—

"What can I do for you?"

"How much will you lend me upon this jewel?" replied the young man.

The assistant took up the gem and examined it from a dozen different points of view.

"Diamond!" he said, laconically.

"Yes."

"How much do you want for it?"

"Five pounds."

"Give you three, then."

"I must have more than that."

"Not a halfpenny from this establishment."

"Then I'll try another."

"You are perfectly at liberty to do that."

"Is that all you will lend?"

"Every halfpenny."

"Are you sure?"

"Quite. Will you take three ten?"

"Yes."

"Then why didn't you say so at first? It's such buffers as you that give us all the trouble; you don't know your own minds."

Money Marks, for it was he, made no answer.

"Here's the money," said the assistant. "But I say——"

"What?"

"What name shall I put on the ticket, and where do you live? Now I come to look at you, you don't seem to be up to diamonds."

"You should never go by people's appearance, my good fellow," replied Money Marks. "I and my pal have tramped across country from San Francisco, and we have worked in the mines in Brazil. That's where this stone came from."

"Oh! it's good water enough; I have no fault to find with it."

"That's a comfort."

"What did you say your name was?"

"Name of Blissett."

"What address?"

"Haven't got any."

"Haven't got any?" repeated the assistant, suspiciously.

"No."

"What do you mean?"

"What I say."

"But look here——"

"Well?"

"You must live somewhere, you know."

"Of course."

"I can't make you out."

"You don't take the trouble," replied Money Marks.

"I think I ought to send for a policeman and let him investigate this case."

"Send for a dozen if you like, or if you don't think that enough send for a score."

"I'll tell you what I'll do; I'll send for the master, and he may do what he likes."

"Very well; send for him," said Money Marks, quietly.

The assistant sent word, through another clerk, that the master of the shop was wanted, not liking to lose sight of Money Marks, thinking that he might improve the opportunity, and run away.

The proprietor of the pawn-shop was a Jew of the name of Ben Israel. He was a tall handsome-looking man, with an open countenance, but he wore a shrewd look upon his face which showed that he was "wide awake," and a man of the world.

"What is it?" he said, addressing his assistant.

"Gentleman wants to pawn a diamond, sir."

"Very well. He could not have come to a better place; am I not a diamond merchant?"

"Yes, sir."

"Very well; what does he want for his jewel?"

"Five pounds."

"Let me see it."

It was handed to him. Ben Israel took it up, eyed it narrowly, and looked at it through a microscope, then he tested it in a way only known to himself and others in the trade.

"Give him five pounds," he exclaimed, when he had ended his examination.

The assistant approached his master, and whispered in his ear, but what he said did not appear to be altogether intelligible, for Ben Israel vociferated—

"What?"

"I don't think he's respectable," replied the clerk, still in a whisper.

"Why?" was the laconic inquiry.

"He don't look it, sir."

"Nonsense!" replied Ben Israel.

Turning to Money Marks, he said—

"Be good enough to step into my private room, sir."

"With pleasure."

Marks followed the diamond merchant into his private room, which was at the back of the shop, and taking a seat in obedience to an openly expressed command, prepared, to the best of his ability, to answer the questions which he surmised would be put to him.

"Pardon me for asking you a few questions?" said Ben Israel.

"Certainly."

Money Marks looked round, and saw a short, stoutly-built man, sitting in an arm-chair, reading a book.

"Your friend, I presume, is in your confidence?" he said.

"Ah! my brother," replied Ben Israel; "pardon me for not introducing you to one another, but really Sol is so small that I am apt to overlook him."

Sol looked as if he would much have preferred to be overlooked. He was not a man who courted notoriety; he shunned society, so he said; and was never so happy as when he was reading. In fact, he became absorbed in whatever study he fixed his mind upon.

When Money Marks heard this he looked suspiciously at Sol, thinking that he was either a pretentious humbug, or else a very deep designing scoundrel.

Having come to this conclusion, he came to another, and that was not to say more in his presence than he could help. He scarcely knew why, but he had an antipathy against him.

"That is a fine jewel, sir, and cheap at five pounds," exclaimed Ben Israel.

"I am aware of that. I intend to redeem it," replied Money Marks, "or I should have demanded more money for it."

"Have you any more of them?"

"Why do you ask?"

"In the way of business."

"Does that mean that you are in a position to buy more, supposing I have them to sell?"

"It does. Did I not say distinctly that I was a diamond merchant? if so, is it not my trade to buy jewels of price, whenever they fall in my way?"

"Of course; but if I were to sell some of my jewels I should demand their market value."

"Which I am prepared to give you."

"In that case, we can trade together."

"With one preliminary."

"And that is?"

"This: I should like to know who you are, where you live, and, if you do not think my curiosity impertinent, I should not object to being told where you obtained your jewels?"

"I shall have great pleasure in answering your questions," replied Money Marks. "In the first place, I am a Californian miner, my name is Blissett, I have worked in the diamond mines of Brazil. I have no address here, because I only arrived in New York an hour ago; being in want of money, I naturally wished to pawn something of value that I had about me. I shall be very glad if you will recommend me a lodging; if you can, you will know my address."

"My brother, then, will be glad to take you in. He does not receive boarders as a rule, but he has more bedrooms than he wants, and he can let you one."

"I have a friend."

"Well, you will want two bedrooms instead of one."

"That, however, can be arranged afterwards; with regard to the jewels."

"But my lodging?"

"Oh! go to an hotel to-night."

"Very well."

"How many jewels do you wish to dispose of?"

"A great number."

"To-night?"

"No. I would rather wait till you have made inquiries about me, and satisfied yourself that your assistant was mistaken when he mistrusted me. Recommend me an hotel, lend me five pounds on the stone I tendered you, and you shall see me in the morning."

"Very well; I have no objection to that course. Go to the Astor House. I will, with your permission, breakfast with you to-morrow."

"Thank you, no," replied Money Marks, with quiet dignity; "I am not sufficiently well acquainted with you as yet."

Ben Israel bowed.

"Well," he said, "if my society is displeasing to you, let it be so; at what time shall I see you to-morrow?"

"I will call upon you here between eleven and twelve."

"And bring your jewels with you?"

"Certainly."

Ben Israel wished him good night. Solomon sprang up, and said in a thick voice, with a nasal twang, indicative of his nationality—

"Perhaps the gentleman will accept of my escort as far as the hotel?"

Money Marks hesitated.

Ben Israel looked approvingly at his brother, as if he would say—"that's right; that is just what I wished you to do. Find out who he is; let's know all about him."

"Thank you," replied Money Marks, "I cheerfully accept your offer, and shall be glad to be guided by you."

They left the house together; outside they were joined by Cuffy, whom Marks introduced as his servant. Solomon suggested that Money Marks should call at a tailor's shop, and purchase some clothes ready-made, as his appearance at a grand hotel, in such a costume as he was then attired, would attract a considerable amount of suspicion.

"That occurred to me," replied Money Marks; "perhaps, as my stock of money just now is so slender, I had better go to the first cheap lodging-house we come to, and take up my quarters there. I have slept in odd places, during the last twelve months, I can assure you."

"I have no doubt; see here; will not this do for you?"

Solomon Israel stopped before an old-fashioned house, which advertised in black letters upon its windows that "chops, steaks, and good beds," might be obtained on the premises.

Money Marks was pleased with the place, and went inside, and ordered a homely but substantial supper; sat down with Cuffy in the coffee-room; asked Solomon to have some whiskey, which he did not refuse; and glanced over the papers, such as the *Herald*, the *Times*, and the *World*, saying incidentally—

"What a time it is since I indulged in the luxury of reading a newspaper!"

"I was not aware that California was destitute of newspapers," remarked Solomon, with a keen penetrating look.

"Who said it was?"

"You told me you came from San Francisco; if so, you must have seen papers."

"Oh! to be sure," replied Money Marks, "but you must know that I was too busy to look at a paper."

"Diamond hunting, I suppose?"

"I really don't see how the nature of my occupation can interest you," replied Money Marks, boldly.

"Only curiosity, my dear sir," said Solomon, hastily, seeing he had gone too far, and was likely to offend Money Marks, *alias* Mr. Blissett. "May I have the pleasure of seeing you at my brother's to-morrow?"

"Your brother is master of his own house."

"Ah! quite so; well, good night. I must run away. You will be tolerably comfortable here. Nothing else I can do for you?"

"No; much obliged. Good-night."

They shook hands and parted. The coffee-house was quiet and respectable; the travellers wanted nothing more. They were tired and much in need of rest, for they had enjoyed little since they quitted the Esquimaux village, and sought the Hudson's Bay Territory.

The next day Money Marks took some of the largest of the diamonds out of his belt, and placing them on some wool, in a box he had bought for the purpose, leaving Cuffy at the coffee-house, sought Ben Israel, the diamond merchant.

The old Jew was much struck and impressed by the beauty and worth of the stones. He took them up in his hands and examined them a hundred times. Solomon was there, and he assisted his brother with his opinion and his critical acumen.

During this minute investigation Money Marks sat perfectly still, and looked from one to the other as occasion called.

"These are certainly fine stones, Mr. Blissett," said Ben Israel; "the truth in a case of this sort cannot be denied. I presume you are a judge of precious stones?"

This was artfully thrown out as a feeler to discover whether Money Marks had any knowledge of the value of his diamonds. The Jew would have been pleased to buy hatful at—his own price.

"I am sufficiently acquainted with the value of jewels to know what I want for each of the diamonds I have brought you."

"That is it—that is what I wished to know. When a man who wants to sell knows his price, and fixes it, a deal of trouble, I calculate, is saved to the buyer."

"Exactly."

"Now, what do you think this is worth?" continued Ben Israel, holding up a diamond about the size of a hedge-sparrow's egg.

"For that?"

"Yes."

"Twenty thousand dollars," replied Money Marks.

"Ha, ha!" laughed the Jew; "that is a good joke—an excellent joke; twenty thousand fiddlesticks, my dear sir. Ha, ha! how funny you are! I could scarcely with justice to myself say half that."

"I am very sure that you will not have it for half," replied Money Marks, resolutely; "if you will not have it, there are plenty of dealers in this city who would think it cheap at the price I have named for it."

"Well, well, to oblige you——"

"I don't wish to be under any obligation."

"Well, well; don't be so hasty. On consideration of your letting me have the rest of the stones cheaper——"

"I never said so."

"No, that's true enough; but you mustn't be hard upon me—you must not, indeed. The war has injured trade, so that money is very scarce."

"So are diamonds."

"Ha, ha!" laughed Ben Israel, who saw that he had a

CUFFY MAKES USE OF HIS LIFE PRESERVER.

shrewd fellow to deal with; "you are like a fretful porcupine, armed at all points with an answer for everybody. You should be a counsellor, my dear sir, and practise pleading in the courts. Well, well; to business, to business. Let us split the difference and say fifteen thousand dollars."

"Twenty."

"Sixteen?"

"Twenty," reiterated Money Marks, with great firmness.

"'Pon honour, stranger, you're too hard upon old Ben Israel," said that worthy. "I can't afford to give such a price; it aint likely. Come, be reasonable. Nobody buys diamonds now-a-days; they are a drug in the market. I might keep this lot on my hands for years, and where's the interest of my money all that time?"

Money Marks knew very well that he was stating the reverse of the truth, for the war, which was then just over, had caused numerous individuals who were formerly in a low position in life, to amass large fortunes by contracts and other means. These men in most cases had wives and daughters who, like all people who acquire riches unexpectedly, made their husbands and fathers live in grand style. They would have carriages, horses, opera boxes, diamonds, and the like, and cared not what they paid for it. So far from gold or money being scarce, it was plentiful at a low percentage, and was daily flowing into the market through channels which had for four years been blocked up.

Ben Israel had no fear of not selling the diamonds, but it was part of his nature to chaffer and haggle for some time before he concluded his bargain. He would never buy anything without a wrangle of at least ten minutes' duration.

At length he agreed to give Money Marks the price he asked, and a sum approximating to their value was given for the remainder of the stones. Some hours had been consumed in bargaining, and more than one bottle of wine imbibed, but Money Marks went away with nearly fifty thousand pounds in his pocket—the net proceeds of about a quarter of his stock of diamonds. He placed this in the hands of an agent who was well known as a trustworthy man, and who agreed to give eight per cent. for the use of the money.

In a short time Money Marks sold the remainder of his jewels and those of Cuffy, retaining a few in case of accident. These few he always carried about with him. He found himself the possessor of a very handsome income and a magnificent fortune, so that he came to bless the memory of Prettyman Parker.

His next object was to go after Viola, but he had gone through so much suffering and so many perils, that he could not all at once tear himself away from the delights of the capital.

He determined to enjoy himself to the best of his ability for a month or six weeks, and then he would go to the convent in which Viola was immured.

He remembered that the year which he had stipulated for with Father Azellio had expired. There was a possibility that Viola had been induced, if not compelled to take the veil; if such turned out to be the case, he thought that his vast wealth would enable him to buy her a dispensation which would restore her to the external world once more.

CHAPTER LII.

THE DIAMOND MERCHANT'S DAUGHTER.

SOLOMON BEN ISRAEL played the spy upon Money Marks with his accustomed sagacity, but his inquiries were singularly barren of any result; he could discover absolutely nothing against him or about him.

He found Cuffy as close and reticent as the tomb; not a syllable of information could he extract from him. Yet Solomon Ben Israel did not altogether like Mr. Blissett; he was suspicious, but could find no peg upon which to hang his suspicions.

Perhaps he had been so long in the detective department of the police force that he had acquired a habit of suspecting everybody.

Money Marks did not object to be on friendly terms with Solomon; he wanted some one to show him what places of interest there were in the city, to take him about and help eat his dinners. All this Solomon did with pleasure and alacrity. If he wanted a small sum of money, his friend's purse was always at his service, but though he watched and waited, Solomon could not induce Money Marks to betray himself or speak of his former career. He tried to intoxicate him, but without success; Marks was too wary a fox to fall into so shallow a trap as that, and he proved to Mr. Solomon Ben Israel that while he could drink his wine with anyone, he always knew when he had had enough.

He lived in excellent style at the first hotel in New York; his horses were faultless, and his carriage a miracle of the coachmaker's art. He was a frequent visitor at Ben Israel's, who could give a dinner as well as any one, and he did not mind entertaining Money Marks, since he made nearly twice as much out of his diamonds as he gave for them.

The intelligent reader will perceive that the wily and cashy Jew could well afford to be generous in the matter of an occasional dinner. It was also a pleasure to him to entertain any one who did not want a dinner, and who was able to return his compliment. If his guest had been a poor man, to whom a dinner was a charity, he would politely have dismissed him with a baked potato and a glass of water.

On one of these occasions Marks saw at the dinner-table a very lovely girl, dark as the night, but possessing those classic features which are at all times so striking and fascinating; her manner was at once elegant and ladylike.

No one would have believed that she was Ben Israel's daughter—but so it was.

Her name was Rebecca.

She had been to the most fashionable ladies' seminary in the vicinity of New York. It was in this school that she received a finished education; her father had spared no pains, and he had not spared his money to make her highly accomplished.

In this praiseworthy endeavour it must be admitted that he had succeeded. Rebecca could play, sing, speak several foreign languages fluently, and was, in a word, a well-educated young lady.

She was Ben Israel's only daughter, and he loved her as the apple of his eye. Her mother was dead, and all the love

that Ben Israel had cherished for her was transferred to her child, with all the additional love that he could spare from his money.

He did not confine her in the close atmosphere of the city, he had invested several thousand pounds in the purchase of an estate on the banks of the Hudson—that charming river, which once seen is never forgotten, so lovely is the scenery that surrounds its picturesque banks.

She lived in this sylvan, and one may almost say suburban retreat, with her aunt, who loved her with the affection of a mother, and cared for her with the utmost solicitude and tenderness.

Occasionally she came up to town to see her father, who, however, always made a point of going to his country-seat on Saturday afternoon, staying there until the following Monday.

This was the happiest period of the old Jew money-lender's life.

He did not care much for his sister, who had undertaken the care of Rebecca; he did not care for his brother Solomon, except when he was useful to him. Solomon and he had begun life together with the same amount of capital, and the same chances. Solomon had not succeeded, and was nothing better than an *employé* of the police department, but he was shrewd and clever, nevertheless. He had not his brother's aptitude and application for business, so he followed the bent of his inclination, and became a detective.

Money Marks was very much struck with Rebecca Ben Israel, but he did not love her; his affection was centred upon his absent Viola, whom he idolized. Her harsh treatment of him he forgave, because his sense of right and wrong told him that he was to blame, and that she had very properly rejected him when she knew that he was unworthy of her love.

He induced Ben Israel to take him to his country-seat on the banks of the Hudson, and he passed his time very agreeably in Rebecca's society.

Money Marks had grown into a handsome young man—he was nearly five-and-twenty. He wore whiskers, but no beard; his hair always curled a little naturally; and his auburn locks hung over his forehead in wavy clusters. He was tall, and stout in proportion; his figure was good, his manner gentlemanly, and his air that of a man who knows the world, who has suffered a great deal, and been purified by suffering.

Ben Israel had never taken any of his friends to his country-house. Rebecca was only seventeen, and he thought her too young to marry; nor did he wish her to espouse any one beneath her in position. He would have consulted her happiness above all things, but he thought her so good, so lovely, and so accomplished, that she ought to make a marriage that would reflect credit upon her choice and upon the family.

He intended to bring her out, and get her introductions to good families in another year, but until then he preferred keeping his little rosebud in his garden, protecting it from the sun, which would cause it to unfold and bloom prematurely, were he not to guard it sedulously.

Ben Israel saw that there was a chance of securing Money Marks as a son-in-law, and he determined not to neglect it; for a man with two-hundred thousand pounds, or about eight-hundred thousand dollars, was well worth catching.

He consulted his brother Solomon about the matter, but Solomon shook his head, saying—

"There is something about the man which I will be positive is not altogether 'square.' I am watching him as a cat does a mouse. Leave me to it, I may find out something by-and-by. There is no hurry, is there?"

"I'll tell you one thing, Sol," said Ben Israel.

"What is that?"

"The girl's fond of him."

"Fond of him?"

"Yes."

"How do you know?"

"I'll take my testament-oath of it."

"I don't believe Beck would be so silly."

"In affairs of the heart, conduct is thrown to the winds. The action of love is sudden and spontaneous. Our sister agrees with me that Rebecca has conceived a violent passion for this young diamond-hunter, and if I knew more about him, I should not object to him for a son-in-law—always provided he will settle some of his money upon his wife."

"H'm," said Solomon, thoughtfully, "so that is how the wind blows, eh? Leave it to me. I will redouble my exertions, and perhaps something will come of it."

With this reply Ben Israel was forced to be content, and he left the matter in his brother's hands.

His suspicions were well-founded. Rebecca had fallen in love with Money Marks.

The poor unsophisticated girl never dreamt that the man to whom she had, unasked, given her heart, was the slave of another. She scarcely knew herself what love meant—all she knew was that she derived the greatest pleasure from Money Marks' society, and that when he went back to the City, a cloud of desolation fell upon the horizon of her daily existence, and made her miserable until his return.

CHAPTER LIII.

MONEY MARKS ATTENDS A BALL GIVEN BY THE FIRE-BRIGADE.

A GRAND ball was advertised, to which the public were to be admitted by paying a large sum. It was given by the members of the Volunteer Fire Brigade, and it was supposed that it would be a very great success. Ben Israel determined to take his daughter to this ball. It was the first she had ever seen, and he anticipated great enjoyment for her. Money Marks was informed of the would-be-projected arrangement, and of course he signified his intention of being present. The Jew hinted to him that his daughter would be proud of dancing the first set of quadrilles with him, to which Marks replied that he should be much flattered.

Already had he been two months and a little more in what is called the Empire City of the West. He had thought little of Viola—his course of dissipation pleased him, and he was loth to quit a scene from which he derived so much enjoyment.

Cuffy, however, could not forget Viola, and the duty that Money Marks had prescribed for himself. He did not like the gaiety into which they had plunged—had he been acquainted with ancient history, he would have thought of Hannibal and the city of Capua, in which the great general halted with his soldiers, instead of prosecuting his victories with vigour, with this result, that the army became enervated through excessive indulgence in unwonted pleasures, and fell an easy prey to their enemies when next they met them in the field.

The negro saw that Money Marks was attracting a great deal more attention on all sides than was consistent with prudence; he was endangering his safety, and courting innumerable perils. He should at once have gone to Viola, have claimed her, and, having complied with her terms, married her, and have gone to Europe, where he could have taken up his abode where he was not known, and where there was little chance of his ever being recognised as Money Marks, the sanguinary pirate.

He looked so gentle, and withal so merciful, that few would have supposed he could have headed the band of miscreants who had committed so many atrocities, and who were still burning the vessels of all the maritime nations on the face of the earth, whenever such vessels came in their way.

"I am going to the ball on Wednesday, Cuffy," said Money Marks, one morning when the negro brought him the daily papers.

"De ball, massa?"

"Yes."

Cuffy shook his head.

"What's the matter with you now?"

"It one tousand pities, massa."

"What is?"

"You forget Missy Viola."

Money Marks made a gesture of impatience.

"I do not forget her," he said.

"Then why not go to her?"

"I intend to."

"This year, next year, or t'other year after," said Cuffy, with a grim of reproval and scepticism.

"Oh! there is plenty of time."

"What dat you say amongst de snow and ice, massa?"

"Things are altered now, and I think differently. I have suffered a great deal, and it is only fair and reasonable that I should enjoy the wealth that my friend Prettyman Parker was kind enough to bequeath me. If you would like to go to this ball, you can go."

"Will they admit black men?"

"Oh, yes! everything is changed; and black is as good as white."

"By golly! dat fine change anyhow, massa."

"That is as it ought to be. If every black man is as good as you are, Cuffy," replied Money Marks, feelingly, "the abolition of slavery is a grand accomplishment, and one of which the Yankees ought to be proud."

Money Marks was right. Cuffy was allowed to enter the ball-room; but he was twenty times in an hour mistaken for one of the waiters, and requested to get something for the white people. He had sense enough not to assert his independence, replying that he would do as he was asked; but he walked away, and those who accosted him never saw him again.

Money Marks danced with Rebecca, who was the belle of her circle. She was not the belle of the room, for the fair girls were more admired than the dark ones; for fair hair has for some time been more fashionable than black. The girl was in high spirits, and seemed to enjoy everything immensely. Money Marks could not help thinking that Rebecca was very pretty and engaging, but she could not compare to Viola. The latter was queenly in her beauty, and he loved her more when he contrasted her with others.

Rebecca Ben Israel tried to fascinate Money Marks, but she did not succeed as well as she expected. He paid her every attention, but he did not make love to her. The ball was a brilliant one. There were nearly a thousand people present; and, although they were not the best people in New York, they were a fashionable assemblage.

When the dance was over, Money Marks promenaded the room with his partner. He was talking vivaciously to Rebecca, and making his way to the refreshment-room, where he wished to get some champagne, when he saw a face that made all the blood in his veins stand still.

He trembled in every limb, and was agitated by a thousand different questions.

If he could believe the evidence of his senses, *he saw Captain Arlee.*

Arlee, his enemy, the man who hated and detested him above all things, who knew what a life he had been living, and who could by his own single and unaided testimony place the rope of the hangman around his neck.

Why had he not taken Cuffy's advice? Why had he not left the city and gone whither duty and Viola called him? What evil fate induced him to go to the ball?

Yes, he was not mistaken; Arlee was in the ball-room. He no longer wore the uniform of a Confederate soldier. How had he contrived to receive a pardon for his rebellious practices now that the war was over?

In the following way. His brother was high in office in Washington. He had at the outbreak of the war taken the winning side, and he was now reaping the fruits of his fidelity. His influence was sufficiently great to enable him to save his brother's life and to place him in office.

Captain Arlee now served another government, and was an inspector of military police.

He was also a friend of Solomon Ben Israel.

It was an exciting moment for Money Marks. If Arlee recognised him, his life would not be worth a month's purchase. The papers would be supplied with a sensation heading—"Capture of Money Marks, the bloodthirsty Pirate and terrible Highwayman of the Seas;" the result of which capture would be hanging. As Money Marks had abandoned the profession, he did not wish to suffer the pains and penalties he had incurred, thinking that by becoming a respectable and prominent member of society he had condoned his crimes.

Rebecca felt him tremble, and on looking at him was almost frightened to see how awfully pale his face was.

"You are not well," she said.

"Well!" replied Money Marks, in an abstracted manner.

"I say you are not well, I fear."

"Oh, yes; quite well."

"But so pale."

"'Tis a passing giddiness."

"Some wine will perhaps restore you."

"Perhaps. The heat is great."

"Ah! yes, the heat and the fatigue of dancing may have caused a passing faintness," said Rebecca.

Money Marks was as white as any sheet. He went to

the refreshment-room with Rebecca, and called for some champagne. The girl sipped a little out of a wine-glass; Marks drank it thirstily in tumblers.

It seemed to inspire him with fresh courage, and to give him a strength which he had formerly wanted.

Arlee up to the present time had not perceived him. Money Marks continued to drink wine in large quantities, and to cast nervous glances over his shoulder to see if his arch foe was coming in his direction.

During one of these hasty and rapid glances he had the mortification of seeing Arlee approach. He was with some one. Who could it be? They come a little nearer. Yes—no—it cannot be.

"Solomon Ben Israel," said Money Marks to himself. "Are they then acquainted? Solomon with Arlee—wonderful!"

The two men were in evening dress and walking arm in arm, and conversing in the most friendly manner. They were both on duty. Solomon was looking out for thieves and criminals; Arlee was on the watch for political offenders.

They approached the buffet at which Money Marks was standing with Rebecca. Solomon gave him a nod, saying to his niece—

"How do, Beck?"

She replied with a smile.

"Come away; the dancing is about to recommence," whispered Money Marks, fearing to speak aloud, lest his voice might more than his face betray him to Captain Arlee.

Rebecca was nothing loth to do this. She drank up some wine that remained in her glass, and placed her arm upon her partner's. As they were walking away, Money Marks heard Solomon Ben Israel say—

"My sister, sir; fine girl, eh?"

"Very fine. Who's the man with her? I didn't see him."

"Mr. Blissett. Lots of coin; but nobody knows who he is."

"Indeed! Turn this way. He must round this corner. So—that is it—ah!——"

This exclamation was caused by his seeing Money Marks' profile. He started forward and took another look; then he walked rapidly down the room, suddenly stopped, reversed his walk, and met Money Marks face to face.

The latter appeared not to see him; he held his head up disdainfully and walked on as if a dozen Captain Arlees were of no consequence whatever to him.

But his heart was filled with despair and dismay.

Arlee returned to his companion with a chuckle.

"Well," said Solomon.

"I know your friend," replied Arlee.

"You do?"

"Yes."

"Are you sure?"

"Perfectly; and a pretty beauty he is."

"I thought so—I said so—I told old Ben so," cried Solomon Ben Israel, with every symptom of the wildest glee.

"You were not far out, then."

"Who is he?"

"You shall know some day."

"But now——"

"No, not now. I will tell you all when the time comes; but I must think over the matter and reflect how to act."

"Very well," said Solomon, looking much crest-fallen.

"Will you answer some questions?"

"With pleasure. Fire away."

As it happened, Cuffy was standing by. He as well as Money Marks had recognised Arlee, though the latter failed to recognise him. It was a favourite saying of Arlee's that "the black cusses were all so damnedly alike, there was no telling one from t'other. They had the same wool, the same skin, the same splay feet and ugly hands, the same blubber lips and squashed noses, and the same pig's ears and oleaginous appearance."

Cuffy thought that he might glean something from their conversation which would be of use to him or to his master, nor was he mistaken.

"How long has this Mr. Blissett been in New York?"

"This 'Mr. Blissett,'" repeated Solomon. "Do you mean to insinuate that his name is not Blissett?"

"Never mind what I insinuate; I say nothing. How long has he been here?"

"About ten weeks."

"Not more?"

"No; he came to my brother Ben's shop with a diamond, and said he had a lot to sell. Ben bought 'em, and, truth to tell, made a good thing out of the transaction; for precious stones are at a premium in this country. He would not mind another lot like it."

"I suppose he had no money till he got some from your brother?"

"Not a halfpenny."

"Did he bring a nigger fellow with him?"

"Yes."

"A black, ugly, twopenn'orth of man's flesh?"

"That's him."

Cuffy could not be said to have got red in the face, but the blackness of his face intensified, and the facial region seemed more shining than usual. He, a free negro, to be called "a black, ugly, twopenn'orth of man's flesh!" He had a good mind to resent the insult, but for various reasons he remained silent.

"A precious pair of worthies they are, too," said Arlee. "I've met them before to-day; but I certainly did not expect to meet them here to-day."

"Tell me something about them, will you?—do now," said Solomon, who was as anxious as a woman, and dying with anxiety.

"All in good time."

"Give me an inkling, then. It will be a triumph for me. I always told Ben I didn't like the fellow. I thought there was some secret history about him which he wouldn't care to have raked up. Ben thinks a great deal of him, and wants him to marry Beck."

"Your niece?"

"Yes."

"Does the man—what did you say he called himself?"

"Blissett."

"Ay, Blissett. Does he seem to like the match?"

"I don't think he does much; I have not seen any indication of such a thing."

"That is very intelligible to me, for I happen to know that his affections are placed elsewhere."

"You do?"

"Certainly."

"The scoundrel! Oh, Ben shall hear of this. I wont have Beck trifled with, not I. Mr. Blissett will find he has gone a little too far, if he does not pay very particular attention to his conduct. What do you think of a breach of promise?"

"Absurd; you have nothing to go upon."

"Ah, well!" said Solomon, "brother Ben has a long head, and he will pursue that course which in his wisdom he thinks best."

"Of course."

"But I say——"

"Well?"

"Can the criminal law touch this man? Can it seize him?" said Solomon, extending his fingers, and clutching at the hair with them as if he had hold of some imaginary victim.

Arlee smiled sardonically.

"Answer me that one question," resisted Solomon.

"It can," replied Arlee.

"That's fine; that's something like. Now I've a nice tale to go to Ben with. I say——"

"What now?"

"Do you mean to put the law in force, or what's your little game?"

"Cela depend;" which, being interpreted, means that depends upon circumstances.

"Can't you give me an answer?"

"Not now."

"Did he recognise you, think you?" asked Solomon Ben Israel.

"I cannot say. I am inclined to think not," replied Arlee, thoughtfully.

"If he did recognise you, the best thing you can do is to put the law in force at once, or else he may escape you."

"I'll forgive him if he does."

"A sharp, shrewd, cunning fellow, such as I know him to be, would take the hint in less than no time. If he has recognised you, take my word for it he will be miles away from New York to-morrow morning."

"There is truth in that."

"Of course there is."

"What shall I do?"

"Have you sufficient information to enable me to make an arrest?"

"Ample," returned Captain Arlee, confidently.

"Perhaps he'd give something handsome to us to let him go?"

"No doubt of that."

"Suppose we could sink fifty thousand dollars apiece, it wouldn't be a bad night's work," said Solomon, with a cunning twinkle of the eye.

"Not at all."

"For my part, I never put a man in prison so long as he can afford to pay for his release. I am like Peachum in the 'Beggar's Opera;' money's the only thing worth caring about. I am uncommonly glad you have made this discovery; it has probably saved poor Beck a deal of trouble and suffering."

"You advise making the arrest to-night?"

"I do."

"As he is leaving the ball-room?"

"Why not? That will be as good a time as any other."

"To be sure it will," replied Arlee.

"Shall we dispense with the formality of a warrant?"

"Yes; I can get one if you think it desirable," replied Solomon. "We should, however, have to specify the offence, state the name of the culprit, and all the rest of it, which would spoil our plans. A warrant is all very well when you wish to lodge a man in gaol; but when we want, as we do to-night, to reap a plentiful harvest out of the fears we are going to sow in his breast, we can do better without than with a warrant."

"Quite so."

"If he is unruly and will not fall in with our views, we can lodge him in the station-house—say he was drunk and disorderly—he will think he is accused of the crime of which you know him to be guilty; and when he finds that he is in safe custody he will be prepared to do anything to obtain his release—at least, that is my idea; and all will turn out as I say, unless I am much mistaken. Do you go and guard the stairs," added Solomon, after a slight pause. "Let no one see you. Keep in the background; but be sure he does not pass you. I will dodge him about the room, and in about an hour's time I will communicate with you and let you know how affairs are progressing."

"Very well, that is agreed," said Captain Arlee.

"Another glass before we part."

"A bumper, to drink success to our enterprise."

The wine was imbibed, and the conspirators separated to pursue the tasks that they had allotted themselves.

Cuffy in the meantime glided off in search of Money Marks.

CHAPTER LIV.

THE HIGHWAYMAN OF THE SEAS IS IN DANGER.

CAPTAIN ARLEE was inclined to be merciful to Money Marks for two reasons.

The first was that he had sworn, if his life was spared, to return the compliment by exerting himself to save Money Marks, if ever he should have an opportunity of doing so.

The second was that the fortune of war had robbed him of the greater part of his fortune, and a few thousand pounds would be a very acceptable addition to his income, if he could get them.

Nothing would have pleased him more than to give Money Marks in charge, and to aver and prove that he was a pirate; but if he did so, he would lose the contemplated sum of money, and also prove himself unworthy the name of a gentleman and a man of honour.

These were weighty considerations.

Cuffy, poor fellow, was very much alarmed for Money Marks' safety. He thought a crisis in his history had occurred, and he was right.

He had no difficulty in finding him; he was at the orchestra-end of the ball-room, talking to Rebecca and her father Ben Israel. Solomon was lurking behind a pillar, like a snake in the grass. He was evidently on the look-out. If Money Marks had attempted to escape by the windows, Solomon would at once pounce upon him, and frustrate his intention.

"Want to speak to you, massa, if please," exclaimed Cuffy.

The black took in the situation at a glance. He saw Money Marks was uneasy and wished to get away. He saw that Ben Israel was happy, joyous, and unsuspecting. He saw that Rebecca was slightly troubled, as if unable to understand the alteration in her partner's manner, and his abstraction. He saw Solomon lurking in his hiding-place, and he cursed him for a rascally Jew.

"Excuse me one moment, Miss Ben Israel," said Money Marks.

Rebecca smiled an assent.

Ben Israel himself began to talk to his daughter, who sat down on a sofa by his side.

"What is it?" said Money Marks, sharply.

"Suffing of importance," replied Cuffy.

"Well, make haste. I am put out, and have no time to lose."

"Have you seen anyone?"

"Yes."

"Massa Arlee?"

Again Money Marks said—

"Yes?"

"He can see you"

"Are you sure of that?"

"Quite, massa. Him talk to Massa Sol Ben Israel, and they arrange everything."

"What?"

"Tell you presently; tell all by-un-bye."

"Make haste, if you do not want to madden me."

"They want to capture you."

"Ha! do they say so?"

"They did. Cuff was standing by—old nig know his way about—and so he dam well listen."

"What was the result of your eaves-dropping?"

"Just this. Massa Arlee and Massa Solomon want to take you in charge. They no warrant, and don't mean to get any."

"That is important."

"They will lock you up on a charge of drunkenness and assault. You not to know dis den—they say give us many thousand dollars and you shall go. They think you give de money, and den they let you go."

"Where are they?"

"Massa Arlee on the stairs, Massa Solomon behind that pillar; him watch all you do."

"I am much obliged to you, Cuffy; had it not been for your sagacity I should, in all probability, have fallen into the trap."

"Ha! ha! trust old Cuff. Him artful nig; him know him book."

"Wait here, as if in attendance on me."

"Very well, massa."

Cuffy retired to a discreet distance, and Money Marks went back to Ben Israel. He felt that a crisis in his life was approaching—strange to relate, his spirits rose, and made him equal to the occasion. He felt bold and defiant, and resolved to show Captain Arlee that he was not to be caught in a trap like a timid mouse.

"A delightful evening!" he exclaimed to Ben Israel. "I don't know when I have enjoyed myself so much."

"You have got over your faintness, then?" replied Ben Israel.

"Oh, yes! it was only a temporary uneasiness. It does not distress me now."

"That is right. Do you dance again?"

"I am afraid to trespass too far on Miss Ben Israel's kindness."

"Not at all. She is young; and all young people like dancing."

"Perhaps a walk in the conservatory would be more to her mind?"

"I am passionately fond of flowers!" said Rebecca.

"Come, then, let us see whether moonlight improves the petals of a geranium."

"Will you wait here, father?"

"Yes, my child."

Money Marks walked away with Rebecca hanging on his arm. They traversed the whole length of the ball-room, and came to the conservatory, which did not contain many people, as a dance was going on, and most of the company were engaged in dancing.

The conservatory was a large room in itself. It contained a large quantity of handsome flowers in full bloom. Money Marks was not, externally, in the least agitated or anxious—he made love to Rebecca in the most transparent manner, and she, poor silly child, was transported into the seventh heaven with happiness, thinking every loving look, every fondly-breathed sigh, a genuine sign of love.

Solomon of course followed him, and was so impressed by the levity of Money Marks' manner, that he thought he could not have seen Arlee, and that he was as unsuspicious of danger as a dove.

This caused him to relax his diligence a little. He did not hide behind pillars and people, and crawl into nooks and angles, as he had done before; he acted more boldly, kept Money Marks in sight, but still mingled with the throng.

At length Marks took Rebecca back to her father, suggesting that to dance with her too much in one evening would be indicative of bad taste.

"Bad taste!" exclaimed Ben Israel, bluntly, "what do I care about bad taste? The girl came here to enjoy herself, and so did I. Let her do it in her own fashion."

"We must conform to custom to a certain extent."

"I don't know that. If you don't want to dance with my daughter, say so. I'll be bound she can find as good a partner as you in the room; and if she couldn't, it wouldn't break her heart."

Money Marks coloured at this, and said—

"Indeed you mistake my meaning."

Ben Israel grew furious; he thought that Money Marks was purposely insulting him. This enraged him beyond measure, but Marks fortunately allayed his anger by saying—

"If Miss Israel will allow me the honour, I shall be proud to dance with her."

Rebecca bowed stiffly. She too thought that Money Marks had intended to slight her.

She placed his arm in hers, and they walked away together. Money Marks felt that it was incumbent upon him to speak to Rebecca and make his peace with her. He wished to enlist her sympathies in his cause, and to demand her help and assistance to escape, if he could contrive to do so.

"You are very silent," she said, as she noticed that he was absorbed in contemplation. "Have I unconsciously done anything to offend you?"

"Nothing whatever, but something has happened which distresses me very much. I will make you the recipient of my confidence. I will, in a word, throw myself upon your generosity."

Rebecca started at the vehemence with which her partner spoke, and at the strange expression which pervaded his features.

"Speak!" she said, "I am listening."

He drew her into the shelter of an alcove, and then, in a voice which was really agitated, said—

"Some years ago, when I was much younger than I am now, I had the misfortune to kill a man in a duel—he offended me in the grossest manner, and it appeared to me that nothing but blood would wash out the insult. You are aware that to kill a man in a duel is an offence of a serious nature—the authorities have ever since been on the look-out for me, and I am apprehensive this evening of arrest."

"What can I do for you?" asked Rebecca, who thought him a persecuted man, and sympathised with him.

"Much, if you will," replied Money Marks. "Cover me with your figure while I turn my face to the wall, and do not be alarmed if you see a change in me."

The girl did as she was requested, and Money Marks took some useful aids to a disguise from a small parcel which Cuffy had slipped into his hand a short time before. A wig made of black curly hair, bushy whiskers of the same colour, and a fierce-looking moustache, completely changed his appearance; so great, indeed, was the change that Rebecca scarcely knew him again.

She uttered a slight cry, and then said—

"You are indeed changed. I should not have known you."

"That is a testimony to my skill," replied Money Marks, with a smile; "when we reach your father, you must say that I have left you, and that you are much annoyed with me. Do you understand?"

"Perfectly, but who shall I say you are?"

"Say I am a gentleman who was introduced to you by your brother. I shall leave you with your father and make my escape."

"Shall I see you no more?" Rebecca asked, with an affectation of sadness.

Money Marks sighed. Had he never met Viola, he might

have been happy, as the husband of the beautiful young Jewess: he saw that he had made an impression upon her, and he regretted he was unable to return her affection, which was pure and artless.

"For a day or two, or perhaps longer," he answered, "I shall be away: during my absence I shall endeavour to compromise this matter which now drives me from you; when that is settled I will return and pay you a visit at your charming villa on the banks of the Hudson."

She sighed with a softness allied to that of a fairy when she mourns over the absence of the dew-drops absorbed by the heat of the morning sun !

CHAPTER LV.

THE ATTEMPT TO ESCAPE—HOW IT SUCCEEDED, AND HOW CUFFY ASSISTED HIS MASTER AT A CRITICAL PERIOD.

BEN ISRAEL stared curiously at the partner with whom his daughter was walking, and upon whose arm she hung so confidingly.

Who could he be? where had she picked him up, and what had become of Money Marks?

These were questions he asked with weary repetition, but without being able to arrive at any satisfactory solution.

"Where is Mr. Blissett?" he asked fiercely.

It must be borne in mind that Blissett was the name by which Money Marks was known to him.

"He has left me," replied Rebecca, blushing deeply.

"Left you, has he? This is intolerable; by my life, such insolence must be punished; and who is this gentleman?"

"A friend of my brother's; Solomon introduced him a short while back."

"I did not know Solomon was in the room."

"Oh, yes."

"Whereabouts is he? I would fain speak with him."

"You will find him near the refreshment counter, I think."

Money Marks took advantage of this conversation between father and daughter to make his escape. He bowed very politely to Rebecca, and making an inclination of the head to Ben Israel, walked slowly away. He met Cuffy on the landing, on the top of the stairs, that led to the entrance hall. The negro did not know him. In a rough voice, Money Marks exclaimed—

"You black fellow, go and call me a car."

"Dis nig can't go," was the reply.

Coming nearer Marks whispered—

"Where is Arlee?"

The black started, but with great self-possession took his cue from his master's demeanour, and replied—

"Him on stairs with Massa Solomon; they look out for you."

"Very well; follow me in five minutes. I shall wait at the corner of the street for you."

Cuffy nodded, and Marks walked on; his heart palpitated with unusual violence. Twelve months ago he would not have cared so much for arrest. Now he had everything to lose, now next to nothing. Now he was the possessor of a large fortune which it would be most galling to lose in the moment of triumph.

He blamed himself for deserting Viola. If he had not lingered in the American capital, flirting with the beautiful and accomplished Jewess, the danger which menaced him would never have threatened. He had only himself to thank for his present desperate position.

Captain Arlee and Solomon Ben Israel were standing together and conversing in a low tone.

Suddenly Money Marks recollected that he wore two rings of price upon his fingers. Solomon Ben Israel had often admired them, and praised their beautiful water. The cunning Jew would be sure to notice and recognise the stones, if he did not the individual whom they embellished.

With a rapid movement the pirate thrust his hands into his pockets, hoping that he was in time, but the quick eyes of Solomon had noticed the glittering stones.

"Here he is !" he cried, in an eager and excited voice.

"Where?" asked Arlee.

"There! Why no, that isn't him, and yet——"

"What?"

"I'll take my oath on the Books of Moses that I saw his rings."

"You must have been dreaming."

"No, I wasn't," answered Solomon, surlily, "I tell you I saw his rings."

"Fancy; nothing but fancy. The pirate's fair, that man is as dark as night."

"Nevertheless, I tell you I am positive."

"Oh! very well; if you are so sure about it, you had better go and speak to the man. I daresay he will not refuse to show you his rings."

"All right. You stop there, while I run after him," replied Solomon Ben Israel, scampering down the stairs, the bottom of which Money Marks in fear and trembling had reached; he was as yet unable to congratulate himself upon his escape, though he began to think that he had surmounted the principal danger.

"I beg your pardon, sir," said Solomon, out of breath with his exertions.

Money Marks started, and turned pale. He knew that voice well! Was he discovered? Was his career about to be cut short, after all? Alas! it would appear so. He was equal to the occasion. Putting on a careless air, he said, in a disguised voice—

"What is it, my good man?"

"If you please, would you mind showing me the rings you have upon your fingers? I am a diamond merchant and a fancier of precious stones, so that you may easily understand that I take the greatest interest in a good gem, whenever I see one."

"Very possibly," replied Money Marks, "but that is no reason why I should display my jewels to every pocket-picking fellow who wishes to impose upon me."

"I am no pocket-picking fellow, nor do I wish to impose upon you. I have another motive beyond those I have assigned, for wishing to look at the rings on your fingers. I have seen similar ones upon the fingers of a friend of mine, and I rather suspect that he has been plundered by you or your accomplices."

The pirate lost no time in drawing his hand from his pocket, and dashing his clenched fist in the Jew's face. Solomon saw the diamonds in a different way to that he had intended, he also felt them.

The crushing blow felled him to the ground, but he contrived to cry out for assistance; with a few bounds, like those of a spring-bok or an antelope, Captain Arlee was by his side and in pursuit of Money Marks, whom he overtook in a doorway.

Many people were leaving the ball-room, and the hall was full of well-dressed ladies and gentlemen waiting for their carriages. The confusion was very great. Some thought Marks was a swell mobsman, all took him for a thief. Arlee collared him, and succeeded in throwing him on his back, by giving him what is known among policemen as the "elbow chuck;" that is to say, he caught hold of his elbow with his thumb and fingers and contrived to jerk his arm upwards, almost dislocating it at the shoulder. In the struggle Marks' wig fell off, and when he rose up in custody, he had only one whisker, and half a moustache.

Arlee laughed savagely as he contemplated the ludicrous spectacle which his captive presented. Solomon had recovered himself and he at once joined Arlee, saying—

"Capital! You have succeeded admirably. It is our man, after all. It was lucky I had an eye for precious stones."

"That idea was worth a Jew's eye to us."

"Don't be personal."

"I must have my joke. I feel hilarious at having made this capture."

"Let me remove him at once, I don't wish to excite more attention than I can help," replied Solomon Ben Israel, in a whisper, "you know my reason."

"I do; where shall we take him?"

"Put him in a fly, and I will tell you."

They roughly dragged Money Marks through the gaping crowd. The pirate was too securely held to be able to make any attempt at escape which was likely to be attended with success; so he submitted, and went quietly.

A fly was procured into which Money Marks was pushed, his captors sitting, one by his side and the other opposite him. Solomon instructed the man to drive to a small watch-house over which he had complete control, it was in an obscure part of the city, and seldom visited by the heads of the police.

As the fly drove off, a black man emerged from the friendly angle of a wall, in which he had been hiding, and jumped up behind the fly.

This was Cuffy.

The faithful fellow had witnessed the attack upon and capture of his master, but he did not interfere, because he was fully aware that any interference on his part would be worse than useless; he bided his time, hoping that he would be of service subsequently.

The fly dashed over the stones at a good pace, which made the windows rattle to such an extent that conversation was impossible. Captain Arlee put his lips to Money Marks' ear, and said—

"My turn has arrived again. There are strange ups and downs in life, you see."

Money Marks made no answer; he was too much enraged to speak. He could have torn Arlee's heart from his breast, and have tossed it to the street curs, upon which to make a noon-day meal.

The watch-house was made of slender materials, principally wood; it had been originally a shanty, and was seldom used for the detention of prisoners. This was the place to which the pirate was conveyed. He was placed in a miserable compartment, badly ventilated and worse lighted; the rain penetrated through the roof in one or two places where the tiles were loose, and made little puddles upon the muddy floor, which was composed entirely of mother earth

A chair was provided for the prisoner, and a rushlight candle stuck upon a nail in the wall cast a fitful glimmer upon the cell and its surroundings.

Cuffy saw his master taken in here, and watched Solomon Ben Israel and Captain Arlee follow him; he crouched down under the eaves and waited, knowing that it would be of no use whatever to attempt a rescue until the captors emerged from the watch-house.

Arlee and Solomon Ben Israel followed Money Marks into the cell; they had no handcuffs with them, so that they confined the prisoner's hands with a piece of stout cord, tying them behind his back with a force and tightness that caused him great pain.

Solomon leant against the wall, while Arlee stood before Marks, and addressed him, saying—

"You are in our power; we can have you executed as a pirate, but we are willing to extend our clemency to you—that is to say, upon certain conditions."

"And those are?" inquired Marks, looking up proudly.

"That you give us a hundred thousand pounds—that will be fifty thousand for Solomon Ben Israel, and fifty for myself."

"I haven't the power," cried Marks, with a laugh; "you think I am made of money, just because I have spent a few pounds since I have been in New York."

"I know for a fact that you have as much as twice the sum that we demand," exclaimed Solomon Ben Israel, who had hitherto abstained from making any remark.

"And how do you know it?"

"I know it because I am in my brother's confidence, and you cannot deny that he purchased your jewels and gave you in hard sterling cash nearly a quarter of a million of money for them. Contradict me with any truth, if you can."

"That is true enough," said Marks; "but there is one fact of which you are in ignorance."

"Indeed!"

"I have employed the major portion of that money in paying old standing debts, and I should now be puzzled to put my hands on ten thousand pounds."

"Ha, ha!" laughed Solomon. "That may be all very well, but it will not do for us: we have met foxes before, and understand their way of doubling upon us, do you see that? We know you have the money, and, unless you agree to give us what we ask, we shall be under the painful necessity of handing you over to the hangman, who will make short work of you, and there will then be one bloodthirsty pirate the less in the world."

Money Marks contented himself with saying—

"I have no money, and even if I had I should not think of giving either of you a halfpenny."

"In that case, the law must take its course."

"Not so."

"Eh! what do you say?"

"This—I demand my life from Captain Arlee; when I spared his at the intercession of a lady who shall now be nameless, he promised—he *swore* upon his honour that should I ever be in his power he would return the compliment, and spare mine. The time has arrived—I make the appeal—let him redeem his word."

Arlee shook his head.

"You shake your head; what do you mean?"

"I have not the power with which you invest me," replied Captain Arlee.

"And why not?"

"You forget I have a companion."

"Who is he?"

"Mr. Ben Israel."

"Well, what of that? Is he not under your orders?"

"No; unfortunately, I am under his."

"And you mean——"

"That I am impotent to release you."

"This is a subterfuge worthy of the man who could invent and stoop to it," cried Money Marks in a fury.

"As you are not in a yielding frame just now, and as you will probably be in a more reasonable state of mind to-morrow, I shall leave you to your own reflections. You know my terms—death, or liberty for one hundred thousand pounds. Good-night. By dawn of day we will be with you."

Money Marks sullenly bowed his head, and the next instant was alone.

When Arlee and Solomon emerged from the guard-house they were followed by Cuffy, who overheard the remarks they made.

"Do you think he told the truth when he said he had no money?" exclaimed Arlee.

"The truth! certainly not. It was a most absurd invention; he has plenty of money. Perhaps he has it concealed somewhere: I know it was in a bank, but he may have drawn the bulk of it out when he felt apprehensive of detection."

"Possibly. Shall we get it from him?"

"I have no doubt of it. We will try him again in the morning," answered Solomon Ben Israel.

Cuffy was armed with what is known as a life-preserver, though the name is a bad one, for it is as often as not a death-giver and life-destroyer as the reverse.

It occurred to him that in the darkness he might successfully assault both of his master's enemies; at all events, he was determined to try it.

Going behind them he raised his bludgeon and struck first Solomon Ben Israel, who fell like an ox with his skull broken.

Arlee, alarmed, terrified, I may almost say stupified, at the suddenness of the attack, was incapable of motion; he put his hands before his face, as if to ward off an attack from some invisible foe. The next instant he was lying beside Solomon Ben Israel. So expeditious and so clever had Cuffy been, that not a cry had been uttered; the police, if police there were in the vicinity, were not aroused by the utterance of a groan.

The black was not satisfied with having broken the heads of his master's enemies; he had not forgotten the training he received on board the pirate, for he fell on his knees beside the bodies and hammered at their skulls as if desirous of braining them.

It is certain that two minutes afterwards he left them for dead, with the blood running from their wounds in streams.

When he had, as he thought, killed Arlee and Ben Israel, he walked rapidly away, making peculiar signs with his hands, and talking "fetish" to himself.

In a short time loud cries were heard, and a policeman's rattle was observed waking the echoes far and near. The desperate attack upon two U.S. citizens had been discovered, yet Cuffy would not run; he thought that to run would betray him, so he walked quietly back to the watch-house, to do other and more serviceable work to his beloved master.

CHAPTER LVI.

CUFFY ENABLES MONEY MARKS TO ESCAPE, AND MASTER AND MAN VISIT THE SEAPORT TOWN OF VAN NOORDEN, WHERE EXCITING EVENTS BEFALL THEM.

IT is not too much to say that Cuffy would willingly have at any moment laid down his life for Money Marks, to whom he was devotedly attached.

He had run a great risk in attacking the two men whom he had left weltering in their blood, in an obscure street in New York, yet he had rendered his master invaluable service.

The police fortunately found the wounded men before they had bled to death, and took them to the nearest hospital, where their hurts were carefully attended to. Solomon Ben Israel was pronounced in great danger; he had experienced concussion of the brain. Captain Arlee was not so seriously injured, though he was insensible, and the doctors said it might be days before his depositions could be taken, and weeks before he could go about again and resume the ordinary business of his daily life.

Consequently, neither he nor Ben Israel could follow up the advantage they had gained by incarcerating the pirate. They had him safely enough, but they could not proceed against him or take further steps to gain possession of the hundred thousand pounds about which they were so covetous.

Such are the extraordinary changes and reverses that are to be met with in every-day life.

Cuffy went back to the watch-house, and rolled about in a most extraordinary and suspicious manner. Was he intoxicated, or was he pretending to be so? most assuredly the latter.

Dash—smash.

Up he went against the ricketty wooden door of the watch-house; the fastenings creaked and threatened to part asunder. Then he fell down in the mud and began to groan and curse inarticulately.

Presently out came the guard, who was, when disturbed, enjoying a sweet slumber on a bundle of straw; he rubbed his eyes and flashed his lantern on all sides.

At last he espied Cuffy.

His eyes flashed, and he poured out a volley of curses.

"Get up, you darned black drunken cuss, get up du; if you don't, I'll make small pumpkins of you. Get up, you darned ugly copperhead, du."

He enforced his command by the application of a vigorous kick, which had the effect of causing Cuffy to turn over in the mud, and that was all.

"They says down my way 'as drunk as a nigger,' and I'm blessed if you aint, and no mistake, hoss. Wall, I'll lock you up, becos of your disturbin' my rest. I wish all hated niggers jest 'arf as much as I do, and I'm blessed if there'd be any of the greasy cusses in creation."

Setting his lantern down on the step, he seized Cuffy by the collar of his coat and dragged him into the guardhouse.

Cuffy all this time acted his part admirably. He pretended to be drunk, and kept up the deception with a fidelity and truthfulness that did him infinite credit.

The watchman made sure that he was hopelessly tipsy. He was so much thrown off his guard that he proceeded to shut the door, saying with a chuckle—

"You might have done better than coming here, my fine fellow. I'll bet you didn't know you were knocking up against the guardhouse; did you now? Well, we'll cool your courage, for you shall kick your heels along with that other swell fellow, and in the morning, if you don't get a week from the beak, I'm a Dutchman. You may be fined, but niggers ain't got no frens, and if you've any coin why it's mine, and I'll just take a squint inside of your portmoney."

He stooped down and began to rifle Cuffy's pockets, when to his astonishment that individual's right arm moved steadily upward and clutched his throat with a vice-like grasp!

"Cluck-cluck-gruk-uk-gruck-cluck," went the watchman.

Cuffy renewed his pressure. The man's eyes started from his head, the veins in his forehead swelled, his face blackened, and he was soon insensible with blood oozing from his nose and ears, and his swollen tongue lolling out of his mouth.

"Better make sure," said Cuffy, with a malignant scowl.

Retreating a few steps he dashed quickly and rapidly forward, breaking the man's back with a heavy kick, administered with his ponderous and iron-studded boot.

The man groaned, and closed his eyes for ever!

Having accomplished this tragedy without a blush, Cuffy took the keys from the dead man's girdle, and seizing the lantern, wended his way to the cells.

He came first to that in which Money Marks was confined, and opening the door, found his master sleeping placidly in a chair, with his head and back leaning against the wall.

The negro touched him on the shoulder. He jumped up, crying—

"No surrender! Death sooner than dishonour! I will die sword in hand!"

THE PARTING OF THE PIRATES.

"It is me, massa."

"You, Cuffy? where am I? in prison! Arlee, Ben-Israel, where are they?"

"Dead or dying."

"And you?"

"Cuffy am here to save massa."

"How save me? speak quickly if you do not wish to drive me mad."

Cuffy took a knife from his pocket, and cut the cords which bound his hands.

"There, massa, now you talk cumfitble," he said.

"How is it you are here; are you a prisoner like myself?"

"No, massa, we both free. When you taken away in fly, I follow to this place, and watch til Massa Ben-Israel and Cappen Arlee come out; then I go a'ter them, and when get to a quiet street, I knock 'em both on de head, and leave them for die (i. e. for dead). Den I come back here and sham too much whiskey. Roll up aginst de door, when

Massa Watch come out, and he says, 'you darned ugly drunken black cuss, me get you seven days for spiling my sleep,' and he drag me into the watchuss, but all at once I spring up and catch him by the throat, and den I kick him and break him back, and make more dogs' meat."

Money Marks caught Cuffy by the hand, and shook it heartily, saying—

"You have saved me. You have added one more obligation to the long list of debts I owe you. I will thank you practically some day. Now we must content ourselves with escaping. We will get to Van Noorden, which is the nearest quiet seaport, and then take ship for Africa. Ha! what is that?"

A loud knocking was heard at the door of the watch-house.

Money Marks snatched up the lantern and rushed along the passage, closely followed by Cuffy. The door was shut but not fastened. Marks immediately put up the bar, and so effectually prevented ingress from the other side. This he did noiselessly.

"Open the door, Pawkins!" shouted some one outside. "We've got another gaol-bird for you. Lord bless us! how that fellow Pawkins does sleep. Rattle away again, Jim."

Money Marks was at a loss what to do. The watchman was supposed to be asleep by those without, but if he did not wake up soon, they would regard the fact as suspicious in the extreme, and probably break the door down. Recapture and increased misery stared him in the face. His position was far from enviable.

It suddenly struck him that he might make his escape by some window in the rear.

No sooner was the idea conceived than acted upon.

Bidding Cuffy follow him, he dashed down a passage, at the end of which he discovered a window which was blocked up with two iron-bars. The iron was rusty and old—a few violent efforts sufficed to wrench it away from its resting-place. A cloud of dust arose as Money Marks pulled open the window. There was only a fall of a few feet, which he essayed successfully. The next moment he and Cuffy were free, and standing side by side.

Walking rapidly away they came at length to a place where cars stand. Arousing a sleepy driver, they requested that they might be driven to their hotel, at which they arrived at about four o'clock in the morning.

Neither Cuffy nor Money Marks slept a wink all that night. They ordered a couple of bottles of champagne and some cigars, with which they amused themselves till morning, while they discussed their future plans.

It was arranged that Money Marks should collect all his money the first thing in the morning, and that they should then go to Van Noorden, which was a small sea-port gradually increasing in importance, but at present not much resorted to.

Outward-bound vessels and steamers touched there, so that Marks intended to take a passage, and go from thence to the city in the East, where his beloved Viola was languishing in a convent.

In spite of his external calmness, he could not help thinking that Viola was not in security. Something whispered to him that she was in danger, and stood very much in need of his help. His help should be delayed no longer; he would at once fly to her assistance. The gaieties of New York had kept him dilly-dallying until his eventful career was nearly cut short. He had been guilty of one blunder—no other should be laid to his charge.

The journey to Van Noorden was performed by railway, and in four hours Money Marks and the black arrived there in safety. Marks carried all his vast wealth with him in notes and bonds, but when he arrived at Van Noorden he paid them into an agent's hands, to whom he had letters of introduction, and by his express desire they were transmitted to London, and deposited within the walls of the Bank of England, where the treasure laid at his credit.

Having accomplished this important business, Money Marks went to a clean, comfortable-looking hotel on the parade, facing the sea, and ordered dinner, which was promptly prepared for him. It was low water; the tide had receded, leaving the fishermen's boats high and dry on the golden sand. A few large ships floated securely on the bosom of the water in the artificial harbour. The rigging, the shape, and the cut of one of the latter arrested his attention in a moment. He thought he had seen it before; and so did Cuffy when appealed to. Neither of them could remember where, and as their soup, and salmon, and pheasants came up during the midst of their speculations, they ceased to think about it—devoting themselves to the more serious business of dining.

When Money Marks had taken the edge off his appetite, he called the waiter towards him and said—

"Anything new, Sambo?"

"Yes, massa," replied the woolly-headed waiter, "there are dam big news."

"Well, what is it? Let us have it."

"You see dat ship in harbour, massa?"

"Which one?"

"Dat without flag."

"Yes. That is the very craft I have been looking at for some time. What about her?"

"Him pirate."

"What!" cried both Cuffy and Money Marks, springing to their feet, and exchanging rapid glances with one another.

"Him pirate sure 'nuff, massa. Dat de ship b'longing to Money Marks, de highwayman of de seas. It fought one of our ships, and den two more come up, and Money Marks him beat and give in. Dat for sartain, massa."

"That will do. You can go."

The black went away smiling, much pleased at having been able to give "massa" some news.

Money Marks was fearfully pale, his whole frame trembled, and he said in a low tone—

"That is great news, is it not? Jasper Main is caught in his own toils. He condemned us to a cruel and inhuman death, but judgment and retribution have overtaken him."

"It serves him right," said Cuffy, who felt indignant and revengeful whenever Jasper Main's name was mentioned.

It was Jasper Main who had turned them adrift to perish amidst the awful snow and ice of a polar winter. He had shown no compassion in his hour of triumph, and Cuffy hoped that none would be shown him in his hour of misfortune. What was his surprise then when Money Marks said—

"I must save Main."

"Save him!"

"Why not? he is one of my men. I am no less captain of that vessel than I was a year and a half ago. My name, and not Main's, is famous. That negro just now spoke of me. I must save Main, and do what I can to save those of the crew who have survived the battle. After dinner we will go out, glean information, and make inquiries."

Cuffy heaved a deep sigh.

"And Missy Viola?" he said.

"Oh! the delay of a few days will make no difference one way or the other, as far as she is concerned."

"Much better go on. Dat's what ole nig tink."

"When I want your advice I will ask you for it," replied Money Marks, coldly and sternly; "at present, I can do without it."

Cuffy was abashed, and held his tongue.

On making inquiry, Marks found that the much-dreaded pirate had made so many captures, and done so much mischief of late to the mercantile marine of all countries, that it was deemed absolutely necessary to put a stop to the depredations. Accordingly three of the fleetest U.S. steamers were sent in search of her. When discovered she fought well and bravely, in spite of the overwhelming odds against her. The result of the engagement was that the pirate was captured, and with her Jasper Main, who represented himself as Money Marks, and was held up to popular execration as such, and fifteen of the crew, being all who survived the terrible conflict that had waged for three hours and a quarter. Most of the men preferred death from a gunshot wound, a sword thrust, or sabre cut, to being hanged when taken on shore. Only sixteen survived out of the magnificent complement the pirate had when Money Marks was last on board of her.

Money Marks went to a wardrobe-shop, where all sorts and descriptions of dresses and disguises were sold. Here he bought the dress of a priest, with a wig, beads, &c. In this disguise he wended his way to the prison, and craved admittance, saying that he wished to see if the terrible pirate could not be moved by prayer to confess his sins, as there was no repentance without confession.

The governor of the prison in which Jasper Main was confined, thinking no harm, gave his consent; and the sham priest followed the gaoler down some stairs, and then along a dreary damp passage filled with rats and mildew. At length he stopped before an iron-bound door, and inserted a key in the lock.

In this cell the baffled and defeated pirate, cast for death on the morrow, was confined.

CHAPTER LVII.

JASPER MAIN MEETS WITH A FRIEND.

UPON a miserable pallet within the cell was lying Jasper Main. He was strangely altered from what he used to be. The once gay, proud, dashing fellow, the pride of the mess, and the most gallant in a company of brave men, he was now abject and wretched, disheartened, dispirited, and worn out with mental and physical exertion—a half-healed gash was visible on his forehead. He had been thrown into gaol in precisely the condition in which he was when captured. He had fought in his shirt-sleeves, and the blood-stained garment was still upon him.

The wretch had persisted to the last that he was Money Marks, and his captivity had been more rigorous on that account. He had fallen into a sort of uneasy slumber—starting up, and crying out now and then, as if still fighting a battle, and urging his men on with fierce cries and bitter exclamations.

"Wake up, Mister Pirate! wake up!" cried the gaoler, giving him a by no means tender kick in the ribs.

"What is it?" inquired Jasper Main, waking up and looking sleepily around him.

"Here is a holy and reverend father of God who would speak to you about matters to which you have long been a stranger, I'm thinking."

"I want no priests!"

"That may be, but it's the governor's orders that he is to see and have speech with you—therefore you'd better submit to it, or worse will follow."

By way of giving a decisive answer in the negative, Main threw himself on his pallet once more, and pretended to go off to sleep again.

"I'll leave you with him for half an hour, father, and you must make the best you can of him, though I wouldn't give you much for your best. He is a blood-thirsty scoundrel, who has lived in sin, and will perhaps die in it."

So saying the gaoler went away, leaving Money Marks alone with his old confederate. Marks was desirous of amusing himself with Jasper for a short time. It was evident that at present he firmly believed him to be a priest, so, if he could disguise his voice with success, the deception would still be kept up.

"My son," exclaimed Money Marks, "are you a Catholic?"

"No," growled Jasper Main, "and I don't want any Catholic priests about me; they are no better than the rest of us. I know too much for you."

"I wish to Heaven you knew the jeopardy your soul is in. You are condemned to die to-morrow morning ere the sun rises."

"To-morrow? Nay, that is sudden; I was not told that. I have not yet been tried. Who is your informant?"

"I have but now left the governor, my son; he assures me that the formality of a trial will in your case be dispensed with. In a few hours' time you will surely die: therefore I say make your peace with heaven, for to die in your sin is awful."

Jasper Main sat up and drew his hand across his brow, from which the perspiration was starting in large, beadlike drops. The suddenness of his doom appalled him; he could contemplate death at a distance, but when the horrid monster laid his skeleton hand upon him he drew back terror-stricken, and his coward blood scarce dared to crawl in his coward body.

After a pause, Marks said, in a slow and impressive tone—

"Once more, my son, let me conjure you to unburden your mind, and to make me the recipient of your confidence. I am not actuated by any unworthy motives of despicable curiosity in making this request; I simply study your soul's health. If my presence is still distasteful to you I will leave you; you have but to command me to leave and I go."

"Stay, father, stay," said Jasper Main. "There is much on my mind that I would gladly reveal to you if you think I may thereby gain salvation, even at the eleventh hour."

"Of that be assured. Speak; I listen."

Main crossed his hands and looked at the ground as if collecting his thoughts.

"It would be tedious," he said, "to mention all the atrocities that I have committed on the seas. In many of these acts of violence and of murder I was not the sole responsible agent; I was merely the servant, following the commands of another and bolder spirit than my own."

"Who was this?"

"Money Marks."

"How can that be when they call you Money Marks?"

"They are misled. I call myself Marks, but I am Jasper Main."

"Where, then, is that much-dreaded pirate, my son?"

"Dead; at least, I have every reason to apprehend that such is the case. You must know that I was his first lieutenant, and that I grew jealous of his fame. He had a friend in the person of a powerful negro, whom I hated as much or more than I did his master. Having arranged everything with the crew, I took advantage of a favourable opportunity and seized master and man, putting them, with some pro-

visions and water, into a boat, which I felt persuaded would drift by the force of a current to the Arctic regions, where they would soon perish of the intense cold which eternally reigns in those inhospitable parts."

"You have, I presume, heard or seen nothing of them since?"

"I have not."

"You were guilty of murdering those defenceless men?"

"Alas, yes; but their deaths were nothing compared to the number of men, women, and children I have sent to their last rest since then."

"Have you indeed imbrued your hands so deeply in blood—the blood of your fellow-creatures?"

"I have. I regret that I should be compelled to make the damning confession."

"You say rightly, for it is indeed damning."

"Is there no hope?"

"None—none here, none hereafter."

"Oh! father, are those fitting words to come from your lips?" asked Jasper Main.

"I speak the truth. Hell yawns and gapes for you!" replied the mock priest.

Main threw himself in an agony upon the floor and sobbed like a child. His nerves were unstrung, and he was completely overcome.

"What would you give could you recall the lives you have taken?"

"Much more than I can find words to express. Father, speak to me. Is not your voice changed? Throw back your cowl; let me see your face. I would swear——but no, that is an impossibility; yet throw back your cowl. Nay? then if you will not I must use violence; your face I will see! Do you hear what I say?"

Money Marks had purposely altered the tone of his voice, which irresistibly reminded Jasper Main of his old commander. All at once he cast back his cowl and stood revealed.

"Ha!" cried Jasper Main, catching him by his hand, "does some demon mock me, or does Money Marks stand before me? No, I am not mistaken; it is he, I feel it—feel it here in my heart. And can you forgive me for the base part I acted towards you, or are you come to reproach me for my ingratitude?"

"I have come to do you good, if possible. This disguise was necessary," replied Money Marks. "Forgive me for the part I took just now, and the confession I wormed out of you. It was my whim; and I am, as you know, eccentric at times."

"I have nothing to forgive; it is you——"

"Not a word. I escaped the perils and dangers of the Polar seas—how does not matter. My story will sound better in happier times and in a different place to this. I came to Van Noorden by the purest accident in the world. Directly I heard of the capture of the pirate and your incarceration I resolved to try and save you. I could not leave a comrade in distress—that is contrary to all my training, my inclination, and my antecedents."

"What do you propose?"

"Whatever we do must be done boldly."

"Yes."

"Then I suggest that we seize the warder, who will be here presently to conduct me to the outer air. When we have him safely we will cast him into this dungeon, break his head against the wall, and trust to fortune."

"Nice language to come from the lips of a priest," said Jasper Main, with a laugh.

His spirits were beginning to rise.

As he spoke footsteps sounded in the mouldy corridor, and the rats could be heard scampering away as the warder approached.

"Hush!" said Money Marks; "here comes the gaoler."

"Shall I——"

"No; do you leave him to me. I will take him in hand, because he will be less suspicious of an attack from me."

"That is true."

They waited in silence until the door swung open once more, and the warder appeared lantern in hand. He took up in the other hand the lantern he had left Money Marks, so that both of his hands were filled, much to Marks' satisfaction and delight. The warder was a brawny fellow, who had plenty of fight in him, and could do great things in the way of single combat.

"Time's up, father," he said, in his gruff voice, which was part and parcel of his nature and composition.

"I am aware of it," replied Money Marks, meekly folding his hands before him and casting his eyes down upon the ground. "I could have wished for a longer time, he had much to confess; but I rejoice to say that I leave him in a penitent frame of mind."

"Ah! they always do get penitent when they see they are going to die," replied the gaoler. "I have seen heaps of 'em, and they all draw in their horns when the rope dangles before their eyes; very few die game."

"Lead the way," said Marks to the gaoler, adding to Main, "Peace be with you, my son; I will visit you again to-morrow."

The gaoler led the way; but he had not gone far before Money Marks threw back his cowl and sprang upon him with all the ferocity of a tiger. His long fingers clutched his throat, and he dragged him, kicking and struggling, into the cell, and hurled him head foremost against the moist, slimy, vermin-covered walls with terrific force.

The man was stunned.

This was evident enough, but Jasper Main was not satisfied. All the penitence he had exhibited when he fancied himself in conversation with a priest vanished; he caught hold of the bleeding head and shattered it again and again against the hard bricks till the strong man was little better than a corpse.

Then the two men, upon whose souls so many murders rested, walked away as if nothing had occurred. Main put on the gaoler's cap and jacket, and Marks let his cowl fall over his face once more. They reached the entrance to the prison without meeting anyone, but they found the door locked.

The gaoler had the keys in his girdle, and they had forgotten to bring them.

In this emergency, Marks sent Jasper Main back for them. The seconds passed very slowly until his return, and Money Marks trembled for the success of his daring scheme. At length he returned with the keys; the door was opened and they were in the open air. Going behind a high wall, Marks took off his priest's attire and threw them into an open surface drain, which carried the filth over a piece of waste land. Cuffy met them at an appointed place, but though he was glad—overjoyed, in fact, to see his master, he said nothing to Jasper Main, who scowled upon him, as if brooding over his revenge.

"Where are the men?" queried Money Marks.

"Those who survived the fearful battle we fought against the American cruiser are on board the vessel."

"Under a strong guard."

"I presume they are."

"Can we then take possession of the vessel and rescue them?"

"Impossible."

"Must they be left to their fate?"

"I fear so."

"It goes against the grain with me," said Money Marks, "to desert those who have been my comrades; they claim my sympathy all the more because they are in distress—I am loth to leave them to the gallows."

"So am I. Let us turn into this wine and spirit store; I stand in need of some refreshment."

"I am afraid it will be dangerous; there will be a hue and cry in a short time. If anything is to be done, it must be done quickly; I am in no mood to be in the hands of the police, if you are."

"Indeed I am not."

"In that case, do not be rash."

"So far from wishing to be rash, I will say that I have no will of my own; I am a passive agent in your hands."

"Very well; we will go into this store, take a glass of liquor, and then——"

"Well?"

"I have an idea."

"It is refreshing to hear that," said Jasper Main; "my experience tells me that your ideas are worth listening to."

They entered the store and drank some whiskey, after which, Marks, without saying a word, led the way to the beach, and hired a boat to row them to the harbour.

"I want to have a look at the pirate, boatman," exclaimed Money Marks.

"You can easily do that, sir—there she is."

"That dark-looking craft, hull down in the water?"

"That's the one."

"Pull away, then: I'm out for a day, and mean to enjoy myself."

"So do I," said Jasper Main, crossing his legs.

"Me too," remarked Cuffy, lighting a pipe charged with Old Virginia.

The boatman plied his oars with rapidity, and the little craft shot over the surface of the water in the direction of the *Swamp Snake.*

CHAPTER LVIII.

A GALLANT DEED, AND THE END OF THE "SWAMP SNAKE."

The boat had not gone far before it met three boats laden with sailors, behind them were a dozen boats more, all full of seafaring men in holiday costume.

"What is the meaning of all that?" said Money Marks, addressing the boatman.

"The Northern troops have won a victory, sir," was the reply, "and all the men in harbour who can be spared from their ships, and a good many who can't be spared, are going ashore to shake a loose leg and have their fling."

"Oh, indeed! that is as it should be," replied Money Marks.

This was welcome intelligence to him. At the moment of starting for the pirate, he had no settled plan; he wished to look round her, see how heavily she was manned, in what position she was, and what chance there would be of cutting her out.

When the boat reached the ominous vessel, which always lay low in the water, amply carrying out the idea of the swamp snake, after which she was named, Money Marks found a sleepy sentry leaning on his musket, and wistfully looking after the boats which had gone to the shore. They were going with his comrades, who intended to enjoy themselves, while he, unhappy that he was, must languish where he was—no dancing for him, no fun, no extra allowance of grog. It was enough to drive him out of the possession of his seven senses.

"Captain on board?" said Money Marks, hailing him.

"No, he's not."

"First lieutenant?"

"No."

"Second?"

"No, none of them."

"Then, there's a mate?"

"No, there isn't."

"Who's the officer in command?"

"I am," replied a diminutive little fellow, in a shrill treble, whose head just appeared above the taffrail.

"Who are you?"

"Don't I tell you I'm the officer in command."

"Oh! I beg pardon; I thought you were the ship's monkey."

"I'm a midshipman, sir, and by the stars and stripes under which I serve and sail, if you say that again, or utter any analogous insult, I'll fire a broadside at you and sink you."

"Bravo! I like pluck, and I see you are brave if you're only a little 'un," said Money Marks. "Don't be offended at what I said; we're out pleasuring, and must have our joke."

"What do you want of me?"

"We wished, by your kind permission, to have a peep at the pirate."

"H'm! I don't know about that," said the mid, looking grave.

"We've heard so much about her, that it would be a real disappointment to go away without seeing her. It strikes me that you must be the gentleman they talk about on shore."

"What do they say?" asked the midshipman, complacently stroking the down on his upper lip and trying to persuade himself that he was twirling his moustache.

"They say that a young gentleman boarded the pirate," exclaimed Marks, "and fought like a tiger, and that he is to be rewarded."

"Oh! they say that, do they? well, I did my share of the work, though we are not in the habit of talking about glorious deeds in my family—we leave others to do that."

"Quite right too. Can we come on board?"

"I don't suppose I shall be doing far wrong in giving

you permission; you seem honest, harmless fellows. Step on board."

"Thank you, sir; we're much obliged, I'm sure."

Money Marks, Jasper Main, and Cuffy climbed awkwardly up the chains, as if they were not used to the work.

"It isn't often that you go on board a ship, is it?" he asked.

"Well, no, sir; we have not got your sea legs, you know."

"Ha, ha! I should think not; but I say?"

"What?"

"I didn't bargain for niggers; stow the nigger. Equality and rights of man is all very well, but niggers aint *my* brothers. I say, stow the nigger."

The young man put his fingers to his nose as Cardinal Wolsey might have held his famous pouncet-box when he rode through the streets of London, not over savoury in his days, and pretended to be much disgusted.

"Never mind the nigger this time, sir," said Marks, "he isn't a very big 'un."

"I can't stand the blacks."

"He's only one."

"Well, I'll pass him; but tell him not to come too close to me."

Marks instructed Cuffy to go between the wind and the midshipman's nobility, and the negro nodded sagaciously.

"Got many men on board, sir?" asked Marks.

"No; plague take them, they've almost all gone on shore. There's the sentry on deck and me and three men down below watching the prisoners, and that's all."

"The prisoners; who are they?"

"Why, the captured pirates. What a lot of questions you ask! I can't find time to talk to you."

"I humbly beg your pardon, sir; hope no offence."

"That will do. Jackson!"

The marine walked aft.

"Show these troublesome people over the ship."

"Yes, sir."

The midshipman lay down on an awning and resumed the perusal of a novel, in the midst of which agreeable task he had been interrupted by the arrival of the sight-seeing party.

There were three ships between the pirate and the mouth of the harbour, and more than that number in the rear; most of them were denuded of men, and it was fair to presume that none of them had their furnaces alight. The stokers of the pirate had gone ashore with their mates, and there were only three men downstairs. If Money Marks could only succeed in killing these guards, he would be able to liberate the fifteen prisoners, and the ship was his.

It was a magnificent enterprise, and one worthy of his teeming brain.

The sentry conducted them to the lower deck, where the captured pirates were chained to one another. Pointing them out, he said—

"There is a nice string of gaol birds for you. There's nice hang-dog-looking fellows. Well, they'll soon be carrion, and that's one comfort."

Both Cuffy and Jasper Main looked inquiringly at Money Marks, who said to them, in a low voice—

"You two muzzle our three guards; I will attack our guide and conductor."

They smiled and nodded.

"What's that you're saying?" asked the sentry.

"Only that your nose is too near your mouth."

"You're joking."

"Not I. Shall I try and alter it?"

"It would take you all your time to do that, I'm thinking."

In a moment Money Marks had fitted a knuckle-duster on to his hand, and felled the fellow to the ground with a terrific blow. Seeing that by taking this unfair advantage of his adversary, he had put him out of the combat, he turned round for the purpose of helping his companions, who were fighting bravely with the three men left to guard the prisoners.

By some chance or other their muskets were not loaded. Their bayonets were, however, fixed, and just as Marks arrived with the gun of the man he had attacked and disposed of, Jasper Main fell with the polished blade of a bayonet through his body.

Cuffy with a bowie knife had already slain one man, and was performing prodigies of valour.

Marks' arrival, armed as he was, turned the scale. In a short time four dead men were lying on the deck, and Jasper Main, it was feared, was fast following them to another world.

But little attention could be paid them at such a critical juncture; the keys of the fetters which bound the prisoners to one another, were taken from the person of one of the dead men, and left with Cuffy, who was told to liberate his former companions as quickly as he could.

"Not a word, my lads," said Money Marks to the wonder-stricken prisoners: "I have work to do on deck. As soon as you are free look to Jasper Main's wound, and kindle the engine fires. I will be with you soon."

The magic name of Money Marks had been travelling from mouth to mouth, and they were one and all about to break into a thundering cheer when his remonstrance checked them.

Their good fortune made them mad with joy; they could scarcely believe it.

As Money Marks reached the deck, a puff of white smoke issued from an embrasure in the fortress from which Jasper Main had just escaped. It was followed by a flash of flame and a loud report.

The escape had been detected, and the firing of the gun was an intimation to the military in the town, and the shipping in the harbour, that a prisoner had escaped.

The sea was delightfully calm; not a ripple disturbed the lake-like surface of the placid ocean. The sun's rays, now rather slanting than perpendicular, were fierce and tropical. The fish seemed to be taking a siesta on the top of the water.

"Hallo," said the midshipman, jumping up, "what's that gun for?"

"Prisoner escaped, I suppose," replied Money Marks.

"Indeed. What a jolly row those pirates make downstairs! why don't the fellows keep them quiet?"

"You had better go and see, sir; they appear to be rather unruly."

"Do they? I'll have them cat-o'-nine-tailed in no time, the scoundrels."

The young man walked to the main-hatchway to descend, but he had scarcely placed his foot on the first step, before Money Marks gave him a shove, which sent him reeling and stumbling down the whole length, so that when he reached the bottom the poor little fellow was stunned. Seeing that this was the case, Money Marks contented himself with pushing his senseless body on one side, and rushed forward to his men, who had followed his instructions to the letter. Jasper Main's wound was bound up, and the flow of blood staunched; the fires lighted in the furnaces, and everything looked favourable for an escape.

Inflammable substances were piled upon heaps of dry rosin-rubbed wood, and the water becoming heated the engine soon began to revolve. Slowly the *Swamp Snake* rolled out of the harbour; those ships who could and would at any other time have prevented her egress, were now unable to do so, owing to almost all their best men being away on shore.

One vessel, aptly named the *Wasp*, lying close to the mouth of the harbour, determined to do the best she could, and with this idea firmly planted in the breasts of those on board of her, discharged her broadside at the *Snake*, and sent a quantity of grape and canister into her without doing any harm that deserves chronicling.

After the discharge of this broadside, which was unnoticed by the pirate, great was the commotion on shore; boats put off to ships, and all was confusion worse confounded.

Fortunately for himself, Money Marks had a good start, and could depend upon the sailing qualities of the vessel he commanded; and in a few hours he was out of sight and safe from pursuit.

The midshipman, who had been stunned by the fall, was not much hurt, and Marks, willing to spare his life, put him under a guard.

Jasper Main was not mortally injured, he began to improve after the third day, and in a week was able to walk about and talk.

The crew, as may be imagined, were enthusiastic. They lauded Money Marks to the sky, and made him a greater man than ever. To go back to Van Noorden for a time, we may say that the exploit of Jasper Main's escape, and the subsequent cutting out of the pirate, was all attributed to Marks, and his name became more dreaded, and more terrible than it had ever been before.

On the eighth day from the escape from the harbour of Van Noorden, Jasper Main was lying on a mattrass, under an awning over the deck. It was Sunday. Money Marks was sitting upon a bench by his side. The men were amusing themselves after their own peculiar and eccentric fashion by gambling ; some of them were in possession of large sums of money, and while the stakes were high the excitement was great.

"I am getting much better," said Jasper Main.

"I am glad to hear it, for I wish you no harm, though you treated me badly enough," replied Money Marks.

"Let the past be forgotten."

"It shall, since you wish it."

"You have lately laid me under an obligation I shall never forget."

"I saved your life while you endeavoured to destroy mine," said Money Marks.

"That is true ; but I am prepared, when I recover my health and strength, to sail under your orders, and to obey you implicitly."

Money Marks shook his head.

"You will not trust me ?" said Jasper Main.

"What you propose can never be."

"How ? shall we not sail together ?"

"Never in this world."

"Why ?"

"Because I am resolved to abandon a dangerous occupation."

"Give up the ship ?"

"Yes, more than that."

"You will then let me command ?"

"No."

"What the devil do you mean ?" asked Jasper Main, who was much perplexed.

"I mean this, Jasper Main, that I shall as soon as we sight land blow up this ship. I will not jeopardise the lives of my men any longer. I have much to do on shore."

"Yet your former career will always hang by you. Every one will know you, as the Highwayman of the Seas."

"I must take my chance of that."

"If you are detected, you will as surely be hanged as if you were still the Highwayman of the Seas. Why not die in harness ? do not hang out the coward's ensign, captain. Never say die !"

"No, no : I have made my election."

"It goes against the grain with me."

"That may be."

"I am sorry you've lost your pluck, captain."

"I have lost none ; I am as brave as ever ; but I am tired of a roving life."

"Does your conscience prick you ?" said Main, with a sneer.

"Did yours, when a priest spoke to you in your cell, at Van Noorden ?"

"You have me there. Well, if you have made your decision, I suppose it is useless for me to say anything more."

"Sail on the larboard-bow !" exclaimed the man at the mast-head.

"Where away ?"

"South-east-by-south."

Money Marks raised a glass to his eye, and scrutinized the vessel with great care and anxiety.

"Land a-head !" again shouted the look-out man.

At this announcement the excitement became intense, and when by dint of severe scrutiny Money Marks discovered that the craft within view was no other than the *Lowflyer*, his old enemy, most of the piratical crew gave themselves up for lost.

"What shall you do ?" asked Jasper Main.

"I will tell you," answered Money Marks. "Escape is out of the question ; all we can do is to run the vessel on shore, and blow her up. We have a good start, and shall succeed in getting away from the British cruiser."

"What land are we approaching ?"

"The coast of South America, I fancy. I will go to my cabin and cast the reckoning."

Money Marks spoke to the crew in an encouraging manner, stated the case fairly and plainly to them, and informed them of his plans, which they cordially approved.

The wind blew fresh towards the shore.

So far everything was in their favour.

CHAPTER LIX.

DESTRUCTION OF THE PIRATE—THE HIGHWAYMEN OF THE SEAS SEPARATE, AND MONEY MARKS SETS OUT IN SEARCH OF VIOLA, BUT IS NOT ALTOGETHER SO SUCCESSFUL AS HE COULD WISH.

THE sable wings of night fell upon the pathless ocean, and enveloped all in funereal darkness.

The pirates knew that they were approaching an iron-bound coast, against which they must infallibly dash if they pursued the headlong course that Money Marks prescribed for them.

They were environed with danger on all sides ; there was no liberation for them and no escape. If the hard rocks spared them, H.M.S. *Lowflyer* would not be so tender and so careful ; she would sink their ship and hang their bodies.

The crew gathered in little knots in various parts of the vessel ; utterly dispirited were they and apathetic, not caring much what happened to them. Jasper Main and Money Marks were engaged in close conversation ; they were holding their last conversation, for they were never destined to meet in this world again.

"The moon will be up directly," said Money Marks ; "I have ordered the engines to be stopped until that event happens ; when it does, we can go on ahead again and give the British cruiser the slip."

"Do you not hear the breakers ?" said Jasper Main, placing his hand to his ear to catch the sound better.

"Are we drifting ? has some current caught us ?"

"God forbid !"

"Amen to that," said Money Marks. "I must have light of some sort to drive the ship ashore ; if we go on the rocks in the dark we shall all perish."

The two men looked anxiously at one another.

Well they might, for their lives were in danger.

The rush and roar of the breakers became gradually more and more audible, until the sound was distinctly heard by all on board.

The engines had ceased moving ; the wind, which had been violent enough during the day, had abated considerably. The pirate did not display a shred of canvas to the breeze.

What then caused her to drift into the rocks ?

A subtle and hitherto unknown current which was luring them to their destruction.

To add to the horror of the scene and the peril of the situation, the British vessel discovered the whereabouts of the pirate ; and the discovery was not owing to any superior sagacity on the part of the pursuers ; on the contrary, the pirate was betrayed by the absurdly foolish blunder of one of her own men.

And this is how it was done.

A man wished to light his pipe. Strict orders had been given that no light was to be exhibited ; not even a lantern had been shown ; yet the man, with thick-headed stupidity, lifted a lantern up in the air, bringing it on a level with his head, and leisurely lighted his tobacco with it.

The tiny flame glimmered like a star.

But there were quick and vigilant eyes not far off, which knew that it was no star.

The *Lowflyer* had been for hours patiently on the look-out for the pirate, which she was fully satisfied could not be far distant.

Money Marks no sooner saw the silly action of which the man had been guilty than he rushed up to him, and with an energetic blow dashed the lantern into the hissing sea.

The man turned round in astonishment, for his pipe had followed the lantern.

"What did you do that for ?" he said angrily, thinking that one of his comrades was amusing himself at his expense. "I have done nothing to you."

"Fool !" hissed Money Marks, between his teeth ; "you have betrayed us to the enemy. That light will enable him to see our position."

The man slunk back abashed.

The pirate chief was correct in his conjectures. Scarcely three minutes elapsed after the exhibition of the light before a sharp flash was seen to leeward.

"Down ! down ! for your lives down !" shouted Money Marks, who well knew what that vivid lightning-like flash portended.

And down they all fell ; some hiding behind bulwarks,

some scampering down the hatchways. Marks alone was bold, confident, defiant.

Towering amongst his fellows he stood like Satan amidst his fallen angels, and dared, at it were, the iron missile of death to strike him.

He bore a charmed life.

Crash!

The ship is struck. Two cannon balls, held together by a chain and strong rivets, have torn and ploughed their way through the side, and embedded themselves in the interior, decapitating one man, disembowelling another, and laying open with a terrible gash the skull of a third.

Money Marks was strongly tempted to call his men to quarters, and fight an action with the British vessel. But no, he would not do that; had he rescued those men from gaol only to have them torn to pieces, and battered out of the semblance of humanity by cannon balls?

Going to the stern he took the helm and luffed. The vessel fell off a point or two.

That changed her position.

The next shot from the *Lowflyer* would have to go in search of her.

The noise of the waves breaking on the shore became absolutely deafening; a wreck appeared to be but the work of a few minutes.

The sullen roar of the breakers was also heard by the *Lowflyer*, and she backed her engines, wondering what possessed the mind of the pirate, to induce him to run into such great danger.

All at once the event for which Marks had all along been praying took place. The clouds broke, allowing a gush of argent splendour to descend to the earth; the sea glimmered and glistened as if it was covered with phosphorescent globules.

The moon had risen.

A low black hull about a mile distant denoted the position of the *Lowflyer*, but Money Marks did not pay much attention to her, he gazed in an opposite direction.

The wild and sterile coast before him occupied his mind, for he was looking for a landing place, and fortunately found one.

To the right and to the left rocky cliffs rose perpendicularly, and the sea for ever laved their base, but straight ahead Nature had been kinder, for a small inland bay stretched for a few hundred yards, making a splendid landing place for boats.

In this bay the water was still and quiet as a mill-pond.

"Lower the boats!" shouted Money Marks.

"Ay, ay, sir," was the cheery response.

"And let all prepare to land, for in fifteen minutes the ship will be abandoned."

There were a few sullenly muttered expressions of dissent as this dictum was uttered, for, though the men were in a desperate position, they did not like to leave the old craft in which they had both seen and done much.

There was, however, no help for it, and the men put their kits together, while Jasper Main saw that water and provisions in moderate quantities, together with fire-arms and ammunition, were placed in the boats.

Money Marks placed some men on the upper deck, and told them to work the pivot gun, in order to check the attack of the *Lowflyer*.

This was accordingly done, and the gun was served with admirable precision. The British vessel was checked in its advance, and desultory firing was kept up on both sides without much damage being done to either.

From the position and general appearance of the *Lowflyer*, it seemed to those who were good judges, and ought to know, that she had dropped her anchor, and was prepared to stay in one particular place till morning.

She fancied the pirate entirely in her power, and was prepared to take things easy.

Money Marks suddenly disappeared. Every one missed him, but one man declared that he saw him enter the powder magazine; nor was the man wrong in his conjecture, for Marks emerged from that receptacle of slumbering thunder, with a bucket of gunpowder in each hand, with which he carefully laid a train to a certain spot.

Then he ordered every one on deck; the booming of the guns overhead was heard with a smothered reverberation, and the timbers shook at each fresh discharge.

A slow match was next brought into requisition. Marks placed it in connexion with the train of gunpowder, and

brought it out to a certain distance, so that a good clear ten minutes might elapse before the horrid convulsion took place.

Finding that all was in readiness he ascended the main hatchway, and stood amongst his comrades. They looked at him inquiringly, as if they wished and expected him to make a speech.

This, however, he did not seem disposed to do. There were tears in his eyes; who shall say from whence sprang the emotions which gave them birth? The human heart is a mysterious thing, and difficult of interpretation.

"To the boats! to the boats!" he cried, smothering his agitation, and waving the butt-end of a pistol in the air.

The men crowded into the boats, and, when all were in their proper places, Marks once more descended to the magazine.

In his hand he held a box of matches, and without hesitation set light to the slow-match, which hissed, and fizzed, and spluttered like a little demon as it was.

There was no time to be lost now. Strong arms would have to ply the oar, and make the well-laden boats fly through the water.

A few agile bounds enabled Money Marks to reach the deck, and the next moment he was grasping the tiller of the first boat, while Jasper Main guided the second.

Marks took the lead, and the men who before leaving the ship had had a liberal allowance of rum given them, bent well forward, and made good way.

Their captain's face was anxious. He had two causes of anxiety. One was that the *Lowflyer* might discover the abandonment of the ship, and, by depressing her guns, fire at the boats; the other arose from a fear that the slow-match might burn with more rapidity than he had calculated upon, and so destroy the boats ere they could reach the land.

The former fear was actually realized; for the British cruiser did discover the *ruse* which was being played upon her, and depressing the muzzles of her starboard-guns, sent some angry remonstrances after the flying pirates.

The land was gained upon rapidly. The foremost boat was within three or four hundred yards of the little bay which was so opportunely discovered, when a wild cry, a strange noise arose from behind. One of the shots discharged by the *Lowflyer* had taken effect upon Jasper Main's boat, which was no longer to be seen.

It had vanished from the surface of the water, which a short time before it had ridden like a thing of life.

The shot had shivered and shattered its timbers, and played fearful havoc amongst its crew. Those who survived were struggling in the water, and crying plaintively to their comrades for aid, which they gladly rendered.

The catastrophe was discovered by those who were the cause of it, and a wild shout of exultation arose, which was borne faintly across the water to the desperate men, who gnashed their teeth as they listened.

Those who were not killed by the unlucky shot were drawn on board the other boat, and no time was lost in gaining the shore.

"Where is Mr. Main?" inquired Marks, looking in vain for his lieutenant.

"Dead, sir," replied some one. "I saw him fall."

"Is it so? Then peace be with him!"

This was how Money Marks began to forgive injuries.

"Ha!" cried Money Marks, "the English are lowering their boats. They intend to take possession of the ship: one, two, three. Great Heaven! they will fall into a trap; but it is one that I cannot claim the credit of having laid for them. If the match burns as it should, there will be frightful carnage."

"Him be five minutes—ten minutes little more before reach de ship, massa!" exclaimed Cuffy.

"Very likely."

"You tink de match burn all dat time?"

"Oh, yes! I see no reason why it should not."

"Oh, golly! den dey find it hotter dan in ole Virginny."

And Cuffy laughed till the tears ran down his cheeks. He was pleased at the idea of the enemy being slaughtered wholesale by an unseen foe.

"Give way, my good fellows; for your lives give way!" said Money Marks, who had for some time been doing all he could to stimulate them to greater exertion.

At length they landed, and each man appropriated what belonged to him, and a certain quantity of provisions and fire-arms as well. Retiring to some rocks, they concealed themselves from the enemy's view, while they made a hasty meal and watched the progress of the boats towards the doomed ship.

It was very evident that the English were unsuspicious of the existence of a slow-match which had been ignited, and would shortly blow the ship to atoms; had they had the slightest inkling of this, it is not likely that they would have made so rash an attempt as the one they had in contemplation—namely, to board the pirate and take possession of her in the name of Her Britannic Majesty, Queen Victoria the First.

Money Marks stood in the shade cast by an angle of the rock. His arms were folded, and the expression of his countenance stern, if not forbidding. He was powerless to prevent what he saw must happen, but he considered that he was not morally guilty of the blood which would quickly be shed. He did not light the slow-match with the intention of destroying so many of his fellow-creatures, yet if the truth is told, he was not altogether sorry that the event was about to happen. But a short time had elapsed since a boat filled with his men had been sent to the bottom by a well-directed shot, and why should he pity those who were his enemies?

Why, indeed?

Would they not hang him if they could only lay their itching hands upon him? To be sure they would. Had they not always persecuted him and stood in his way? Of course they had. When he indulged this train of reasoning a grim smile pervaded his countenance, and he awaited the explosion with tremulous anxiety.

The men did not talk much—they, too, were absorbed in the contemplation of the magnitude of the event which would stun their ears with its awful noise.

The boats from the *Lowflyer* seemed to run a race, so eager were they to take possession of their prize. Neither gained much advantage in this harmless contest. One might have boarded sooner than the other, but two minutes did not elapse before, after reaching the side of the pirate, all were on board.

Money Marks could see them swarming up the side like so many monkeys.

A new fear now assailed him.

Was the slow-match too slow for his purpose? Why did not the explosion take place at once? If it was delayed much longer, the boarders would discover and extinguish it.

A very brief interval of great suspense happened. The breathing of the men was hushed, so desirous were they of catching the slightest sound.

At length it came.

First of all there was a vivid flash, and the sky was lit up as if the glorious effulgence of the golden sun had, in defiance of natural laws, risen in the dead of night.

Little specks floated about in this splendid blaze.

They were timbers, pieces of iron-work, men's bodies, limbs torn from the parent trunk, heads with staring lifeless eyes. Oh! 'twas a horrid sight, and yet there was much that was grand about it.

The sound of the explosion travelled quickly, and deafened those whose ears it saluted, and then when the last faint echo faded away all was over. Many and many an unprepared soul had gone to its last account with a heavy weight of sin and guilt upon it.

Money Marks dreaded a terrible revenge from those who were left on board the *Lowflyer*, and he considered it prudent to disband the forces under his command.

A few words sufficed to inform them that he was no longer their leader, and that it was incumbent upon every man to shift for himself. The men were not at all pleased with this announcement, but they could see nothing better before them. If they remained long where they were, capture by the *Lowflyer* would be inevitable.

Money Marks had long ago forgiven the men for being mutinous, and he shook them individually by the hand and then addressed a few words to them collectively:—

"We part," he said, "perhaps never to meet again. I will not say anything to you about the course of life we have all been leading, but I will advise you in future to get your living in a less hazardous manner. I wish you all every success, and if ever we should tumble across one another, we will have a glass of grog and a chat over old times. As well as I can make out, we are on an inhabited shore—but where we shall find shelter, I know no more than a baby: each man must shift for himself. Farewell!"

There was no applause at the end of this speech; the men were too broken down for that. Their only wish was to reach some city and commence a new career. They formed themselves into parties of twos and threes, and went off in separate directions.

Money Marks and Cuffy, as may be expected, cast in their lot together. With some difficulty, they ascended the precipitous sides of the cliff by a winding path, which the rays of the moon revealed to them, and shortly afterwards came to a road—not such a road, however, as is to be met with in England, or in other parts of Europe. It was ill made and out of repair, still it was a road, and of course led somewhere—though where that somewhere was, time alone would show.

They trudged along wearily all that night, and were ready by morning to fall down with fatigue, though they contrived to drag their weary limbs farther.

It was with unlimited joy that soon after daybreak they came to a dwelling erected by the roadside, and found some peasants standing outside the door. Marks made signs to them that he was hungry and thirsty, and they brought him some milk and rudely-made bread. Cuffy was equally fortunate. Not wishing to be taken for a beggar, Marks handed the woman, to whose kindness he was indebted for being able to break his fast, a small American coin.

She took it, turned it over and over in her hand, but evidently had not seen one like it before. It was not the current coin of the country, and it was of no use to her, for she gave it him back again.

It was impossible to derive any information from her, so Marks abandoned the attempt, and started refreshed upon his journey. After walking five or six miles the heat of the sun became intolerable, and he found it absolutely necessary to lie down under the shade of a spreading tree and take a siesta.

This was all the more agreeable to him, as he was nearly exhausted. Cuffy followed his master's example, and they soon forgot their troubles in the arms of Morpheus.

When they awoke the sun had long passed its meridian, and the air, though close, sultry, and oppressive, was not nearly so overpowering as it had been. They sprang to their feet, and looked about them.

"I am in search of Viola," said Money Marks, with a wild laugh; "but it seems to me that H.M.S. *Lowflyer* has made me come to the wrong shore upon which to find her. Well, I have all my life been Fortune's football, and it is useless to complain. Kicked here, kicked there—what matter? It can't last for ever, and will be all the same a hundred years hence."

"What de odds as long as you happy, massa?" chimed in Cuffy.

"Not much, certainly. It is a weary world, though; and I wish I was out of it."

"Ha!" suddenly cried Cuffy, looking up at the branches of a tree over his head.

"What is the matter?" asked Marks, unable to understand the cause of his sable attendant's agitation.

"Take care, massa—you take care; for one damn big cobra be up there."

"Where?"

"Over your head."

"I cannot see it."

"There! there! Now him swing with him tail upon de branch; oh, Gorramighty!"

Money Marks now caught sight of a very large snake belonging to the *cobra di capella* tribe, the bite of which is poisonous and deadly.

The snake contrived at the same time to fix him with his serpentine glance.

After this it was in vain that the pirate attempted to move.

The reptile exercised an irresistible fascination over him, and he was unable to stir hand or foot.

Cuffy, who was not under this influence, shouted loudly to his master, but without effect.

Still the cobra hung on to the bough and glared at his victim with those terrible eyes which cast a spell over the strongest.

THE OLD MAN SAVES CUFFY'S LIFE.

CHAPTER LX.

MONEY MARKS IS IN DANGER, BUT CUFFY MAKES A
SPLENDID SACRIFICE—A NOBLE DEED—THE PIRATE
MAKES THE ACQUAINTANCE OF FRA LUDOVICO.

CUFFY was sufficiently skilled in the habits and customs of
reptiles to know that as soon as the snake thought its victim
was sufficiently under its influence it would dart at him and
bite him so severely with his poison fangs that he must surely
die.

He trembled for the fate of his master, and he had great
cause to do so.

The *cobra di capella* swung itself gracefully backwards
and forwards in the air, never once releasing Marks from the
spell it had cast over him.

Marks himself seemed totally unconscious of what was
going on around him; he was wrapt in some pleasing dream,
and would not have been disturbed in his delightful reverie
for worlds.

Yet he was gazing upon death.

The slightest graze of the skin, the least abrasion would
have been sufficient to cause the eyes to glare, the limbs to
stiffen, the heart to stand still, and the blood to cease to
circulate.

Cuffy saw that his master must surely die if something was
not done immediately to save him from the peril which
threatened him.

He could dart forward and arrest the snake's attention;
but the effort might, and probably would, be fatal to himself.

He had often boasted of his affection for his master, and
had said, in no deceptive spirit, that he would cheerfully lay
down his life for him.

The time to prove those words had now arrived, and should
he hesitate?

If he did hesitate, the hesitation was momentary.

Rushing forward he administered a push to Money Marks,
which sent him reeling many yards away. He was safe thus
far, because the serpent could not follow him. Its rage, how-

ever, was not allayed, only diverted ; and it ran as fiercely in a new channel as it did in the old.

To Cuffy's horrid disgust he darted at him before he could escape, and fixed its fangs in his left arm, cutting through the flesh, and instilling its fatal venom into his blood.

The reptile then dropped down upon the ground, and was making off through the long grass, when Cuffy stepped forward, and putting his foot upon its head crushed and ground it to powder.

He did this fearlessly, because he knew that he was wounded to death, and the creature could do no more than bite him again. It was not the pain of the bite that he cared about, for that is in reality very inconsiderable.

It was the horrible dread of a speedy death that made him tremble in every limb and sink down crying upon the rank, luxuriant grass. Money Marks staggered up to him like one drunk and incapable of understanding what was taking place around him.

He had not yet shaken off the stupor which the snake's intense gaze had steeped his brain in ; he reeled and tottered as if he too had the serpentine virus circulating in his veins.

"Wh—what has happened ?" he contrived at last to gasp.

"I save you from the snake," said Cuffy, with a smile of resignation upon his lips.

"The snake ? Yes, I remember now ; but you—what is the matter with you ?"

"I am dying," answered the black.

"Dying ?"

"Yes, Massa Marks ; de ole nig going home at last."

"You joke."

"No, massa, it no joke. De snake bit de ole nig in the arm, and orready it am as big as two."

Money Marks fell on his knees by the side of Cuffy. He could see it all now—everything was as clear as daylight—the negro was dying, and all through him. Had he not been so devoted he would not now have been in the miserable plight in which he was.

Alas ! that it should be so. Alas ! that he should lose the only friend he had in the world. Now, indeed, he would be desolate. If a cannon-ball had hit the black and stricken him down in the midst of a mighty conflict, he could have borne the shock with more cheerfulness and equanimity ; but to see his friend die from the bite of a snake after escaping so many perils, both by sea and land, was more than he could bear with patience.

"Can I do anything for you ?" asked Money Marks, raising the black's head with the tenderness of a parent.

"No, massa ; de ole nig tank you, but it all over."

"No, no ; do not say that," cried Money Marks, whose voice quivered with emotion. "I wish to God, with all my heart, that I had been bitten by the snake ; but why do I waste time in conversation when something may be done for you ?"

Cuffy shook his head ; Marks seized his arm and stripped the bloody covering from it, and took a glance at the wound which was rapidly assuming an inflamed and angry appearance. Great swelling as high as the elbow had already set in, and Cuffy began to feel faint and exhausted.

Marks had read somewhere or other that the poison of a snake is perfectly harmless and innocuous when taken internally ; it is only when it mixes with the blood that it has a fatal effect.

For instance, a man who would make a slit in a vein and put the virus in the opening, would quickly die ; but the one who took the poison from the snake's fangs and swallowed it, would experience no evil consequences.

Whether this were so or not, he could not say positively, but in order to do Cuffy a supposed good he was willing to make the experiment. Applying his mouth to the wound, he began to suck the blood from it in the hope that he should be able thereby to extract the poison.

He was indefatigable in his exertions, but Cuffy gradually became weaker and weaker, so that Money Marks at length bound up the wound with a piece of rag and waited the course of events with a heavy sorrow at his heart.

He had always hoped to be able to pass the meridian of life in peace and quietness, so that he could in the maturity of age make atonement for the errors of youth ; and he had when indulging in these daydreams pictured Viola his wife and Cuffy his faithful friend.

When the swelling arrived at its height, the black began to groan as if he were suffering great pain.

"Are you in pain ?" inquired Money Marks.

"Yes, much pain."

"And I can do nothing for you ? fate is cruelly unkind—here am I powerless when I would cheerfully cut off my right arm to alleviate your distress, and give my life for yours. Have you never heard of any remedy for the bite of a snake ? Come, old friend, ransack your memory ; is there nothing that will snatch you from the jaws of death ? If there is, and it is to be got, you may depend that I will get it."

"Yes, Massa Marks, dere is one ting, but you will not find it."

"Why not ?"

"You not understand it—I not know it well ; it is a sort of nut which grows upon a tree, and dis tree always somewhere near the place where cobra lives."

"The bane and the antidote together ; that is an odd provision of nature."

"Dat am true. If dat nut could be got, and you put it on de wound, den ole nig not go where de good nigs go."

"Say no more ; I will at least make a search for it," cried Money Marks, springing to his feet and going off in search of the antidote.

He passed the body of the dead snake, which was still twisting and gyrating, for though dead, its muscular action had not ceased. The body of a murderer will quiver on a gibbet long after life has departed from the wretched criminal. Marks gave it a contemptuous kick, which sent it flying on to the road, where it still contorted itself in the dust, moving fantastically about like an eel in a consumption.

Money Marks was aroused by a guttural exclamation, and looking in the direction from which it proceeded, he saw a native.

He was an old man wearing a white linen tunic, not remarkable for its purity at that particular time. He walked along by the aid of a stick, and appeared to be on bad terms with the heat, for he looked tired and worn out.

When he saw the snake he advanced to Money Marks, and pointing to the reptile and then to him, said something in his own language, which was unintelligible to the person to whom it was addressed.

Marks pointed out Cuffy and then indicated the snake by a gesture of the arm. He even ran to fetch it, thinking that the stranger might help him to find the antidote.

The old man walked over to where Cuffy was lying, and comprehending the whole scene in a moment, hobbled away into the brushwood that skirted the road. Marks was at a loss how to interpret this action, but he surmised that he was in quest of something that would be beneficial to the negro's wound.

Nor was he in error.

In an incredibly short space of time the old man came back, and might have been perceived munching something in his mouth. Stooping over Cuffy, he sucked the wound as Marks had done, and then placed some herb or nut that he had chewed upon it. Having done this, he again disappeared to procure a fresh supply, and repeated the operation several times. Cuffy opened his eyes, but was unconscious of what was going on around him—his senses had left him.

For more than an hour did the strange old man attend to Cuffy ; then thinking he had done all that could be done in that place, motioned to Money Marks to assist the black, who was then able to stand. Marks managed to help Cuffy after the old man, who led the way to a small house at no great distance from the fatal spot.

In the house was a bed of straw : upon this Cuffy lay down and was compelled to swallow some medicine that the old man gave him.

Money Marks expressed his gratitude as well as he was able for the old man's kindness, and pressed some gold money upon his acceptance, which he took. That night he lay down by the side of Cuffy, giving him water when he required it and attending to his wants generally.

The next day he talked with the old man by signs and learned that Cuffy was in no danger of dying ; the remedy was applied to his wound just in time. Had it been much later he could not have survived. If the remedy had been applied earlier the black's recovery would have been speedier, for it would now be a matter of some weeks before his blood recovered its healthy tone and he was able to go about with his former mental and bodily strength.

He also gained information to the effect that Buenos Ayres was the nearest town, and could be reached in a day's journey. So when Cuffy became sensible Marks expressed his intention of leaving him to recover his strength while he went on to the city, because his anxiety to gain some intelligence of Viola was so intense.

"De ole nig not gwine to die dis journey after all, Massa Marks," said Cuffy, with a satisfied smile.

"No, thank God! Nothing has given me greater pleasure than your recovery; it is more to me than jewels, gold, or victories."

"More dan Missy Viola?" asked Cuffy.

Money Marks made no answer; he affected not to have heard the question, which was an easy way of escaping from a dilemma.

"I shall go to the city and find out what has become of Viola," said Marks. "and you must wait here until you are better; I will rejoin you in a fortnight's time. Do not think me selfish for wishing to leave you, but I am so much over the time I appointed for returning, that I fear the priests may have coerced her and made her take the veil. Should this be the case, I shall have the utmost difficulty in getting access to her, but I will try at once."

Leaving some money with the old man who had saved the negro's life, he took his departure and walked to Buenos Ayres with a fluttering heart.

He had succeeded in saving a large sum of money from the wreck and his pockets were filled with notes, while he had a belt similar to the one in which he had held his diamonds also well lined with the precious and valuable paper.

When he reached the town he went into an eating and refreshment house near the docks, and, having dined, rested himself before proceeding to the convent where Viola was dwelling.

Now that he was so near the idol and the darling of his heart, he felt that he loved her more than ever; and he blamed himself for having delayed the hour of his arrival so long as he had done. If it were in the power of mortal man to bring her back to a world she had partially quitted he would do it.

He found that many people in the town spoke French and some few English. He had during his travels picked up a smattering of French, and could make himself understood in that language.

When he reached the convent he walked round it, thinking whether it would not be better to make some inquiries before he announced himself. If he were to let them know that he was in the city, and they were practising any treachery upon him or Viola, they would be on their guard immediately and able to thwart him with greater ease.

So he hesitated, and went into a spirit-store, where he drank a glass of brandy, and, half-unconsciously, said aloud—

"If Father Azellio has been trifling with me it were better for him that he had never been born."

"And what has Father Azellio done to you?" inquired a shrill voice at his elbow.

Looking down Money Marks saw a dwarf, having a good-humoured face but a red countenance and a fiery-tipped nose, which indicated that he was addicted to the consumption of spirits.

"I was not aware that I spoke aloud," he said.

"But you did, and I heard you. Having had my curiosity excited I repeat my question—What has Father Azellio done to you that you should speak of him in a threatening manner?"

"First of all, tell me who you are," said Money Marks.

He was aroused at the dwarf's impudence. The little man, who spoke English remarkably well, but had an indifferent accent, tossed off a glass of rum, and replied—

"That is easily done. I am generally known as Fra Ludovico. I was once a priest in full canonicals; but as I liked brandy better than books they unfrocked me, and now I am—what you will. Call me the slave of circumstances and the bottle."

"May I suffer to refill your glass?"

"It is an offer that I accept without reserve or hesitation. Fill, my dear sir; fill to the brim."

The dwarf was candid, whatever else he may have been; and there is at all times a charm about candour, whether you see it in a village maiden or a drunken priest.

It struck Money Marks that he had inadvertently stumbled across just the sort of man he was in search of. He was fond of liquor, and therefore was unscrupulous enough to do almost anything to obtain the means wherewith to purchase it. He had been a priest, and was consequently acquainted

with all their secrets, and knew the ins and outs of the convents as well as ever a father confessor in the town.

He resolved upon cultivating the friendship of Fra Ludovico.

CHAPTER LXI.

THE DWARF LISTENS TO THE PIRATE'S STORY AND AGREES TO HELP HIM TO RECOVER VIOLA—THE CONVENT IS VISITED, AND A TRICK IS PLAYED UPON MONEY MARKS—THE PRIESTS AT LENGTH DEFY HIM.

"Is there any quiet place where we can sit down and talk together?" said Money Marks.

"Yes, there is a room at the back in which some worthy tradesmen of the neighbourhood are drinking their wine; but as you and I are probably the only two people for some distance who can talk English, we shall be undisturbed if secresy is your object," returned Fra Ludovico.

"I did not say so."

"Granted; but you led me to suppose so. However, choose for yourself. I will have a little more brandy, if you are inclined to pay for it."

"Oh, certainly," returned Marks, with a smile; "as much as you like."

"Say you so, then? Landlord, give me a bottle of your best cognac."

This impudence, combined with his cool assurance, was astonishing.

Having received his bottle of brandy, Fra Ludovico led the way into the private room and took a seat at a remote table, where he was joined by his new friend.

"It seems to me," said Fra Ludovico, his face radiant and happy with smiles, "that we shall be good friends. Ha! ha! you must excuse candour; but for the life of me I always say what is in my mind, and that makes me less of a hypocrite than most people."

"Of course."

"You grant me that?"

"I do."

"Then that is a point in my favour. I begin to look upon you as my El Dorado. I have been searching all my life for a goose that will lay me golden eggs, and you are my goose. Own it—confess it—noble stranger, and I am thine for ever!"

"You would sell yourself for brandy?"

"To anyone; to the Prince of Darkness, were he to make the proposal."

"And, supposing that I give you the means of buying more bottles than you can count in half-an-hour, you will, I apprehend, give me the benefit of your services?"

"I will; you have my hand upon that. I am a dwarf—I am a drunkard—I am a disgraced priest, but there is honour in my pocket if there is nothing else; and I will bring an unlimited supply to my assistance in any transaction we may have together. Ah! you are a godsend. My purse is but poorly lined. Being a scholar in my youth has taught me some accomplishments, which I retain, and I pick up my living, not by knocking things down like an auctioneer, but by teaching English to people in the commercial world who trade with London. That is how my day is passed. At night I drink brandy, and spend all I earn; but what does it matter? a jolly life for me under the greenwood tree; that is to say, if there is brandy there, if not I would rather decline the honour."

"Do you find your present state of life more to your taste than mumbling musty Latin on your knees in a convent?"

"Very much so," replied Fra Ludovico. "Now I am my own master. There is

"Never a bell,
With its swagger and swell,
Calling you up with a start of affright,
In the dead of night,
To send you grumbling downstairs
To mumble your prayers."

"Yes, yes, my friend, the clouds of bigotry which obscured my reason have vanished.

"The monks were a little too pious, a little too tame,
And the more is the shame.
'Tis the greatest folly
Not to be jolly;
That's what I think,
Come drink, drink,
Drink and die game."

He had scarcely finished speaking before he crossed himself with mock humility, saying, satirically—

> "From frailty and fall,
> Good Lord, deliver us all."

Then he drank his glass to the dregs and burst out into a loud peal of drunken laughter.

"Come," he cried, "let us take a walk round the convent, maybe we shall hear the voices of the imprisoned nuns chanting some sweet music, for it is vesper time. What do you say—wilt come ?"

"With pleasure," replied Marks.

He hoped that he might hear Viola. Her voice was so imprinted upon his memory that he could recognise and single it out from amidst a full choir.

"What a strange thing is love !" said Fra Ludovico. "I was fool enough once to love a woman, and she jilted me; so now I love all women, and make no invidious distinction amongst the darlings."

"Ah !" sighed Money Marks, looking sentimental and miserable.

"What is the meaning of that sigh ? has the winged god shot his shaft at you and hit the mark ? Come, confess now you are in love."

"Yes, it is so."

"Ha, ha !" laughed Fra Ludovico. "Didn't I guess well ? Now let me question you; I am your father confessor, and I will talk to you as I used to talk to the fair sisters, who always had something to confess about love; a confessor must always put leading questions to a penitent, or he will not get at the besetting sin. Who is the lady, and how long have you loved her ?"

"That is just what I wished to communicate to you," said Money Marks; "so you will find me an excellent penitent. But let us get into the air, the heat of this room stifles me."

"You should have announced your arrival, and the landlord would no doubt have improved his ventilators," said Ludovico, with a laugh.

The dwarf led the way out of the heated, tobacco-impregnated apartment, and they passed into the open air, which was very grateful after the close confinement they had just left.

A cool breeze was blowing. A soft light fell from the starlit sky, and many perfumes deliciously mingled together, borne from the flowers in the convent garden, assailed the senses in an odorous storm.

The tinkling of a guitar was heard from a neighbouring house, but the sound of voices was faintly distinguishable from the convent. This building was of no great height, though it was surrounded by a high wall, the wall being almost as high as the convent itself. It had but two stories; report said that its underground ramifications were very extensive; dungeons abounded, and cells for the silent and separate system — not confined to convict prisons—were numerous. The convent of St. Ursula was conducted on strict principles, and young ladies who were recalcitrant and obstinate were made to understand the meaning of semistarvation diet, solitary confinement, and the sharp sting of a knotted whip.

The convent was nevertheless a popular one with fanatic parents and guardians, and there was seldom less than three hundred women within its walls, a large number requiring some skill to manage.

"Come this way, here, post yourself in this angle of the wall; it has excellent acoustic properties, and you will hear the singing to advantage," said Fra Ludovico.

"Thank you," replied Money Marks. "Are you acquainted with the interior of the convent ?"

"I should think so; I was confessor there once upon a time," answered the dwarf, with a knowing look.

The voices of the nuns were heard to great advantage in the position in which the dwarf had placed Money Marks. There is always something soothing and touching in a woman's voice, and when you listen to a band of devotees chanting hymns and praises to the objects of their perpetual and lifelong adoration, there is something which touches the heart and calls up the moisture to the eyes.

The deep tone of an organ ushered in a Gregorian chant, which was followed by a pathetic solo magnificently sung. Money Marks trembled, for he recognised the voice of Viola; at first it was sad and low, but as she warmed with her subject, and received an accession of what may not be inaptly called celestial fire, she became grander and more inspired; her modulation was perfect and her execution faultless; well might they call her "Queen of the Choir," for she was the most accomplished executant they had within the convent walls.

When it was over, a heavy stillness reigned for a brief space to enable the sisters to pray, which they did with great fervour, for their souls seemed to be purified by the lovely and spiritual music they had just been listening to.

Then the organ pealed forth again, and the whole choir sang—

Nocte Surgentes.
Vigilemus Omnes.

After that there was the *Dominus Vobiscum* of the father, and all was over.

"'Tis she, 'tis she !" cried Money Marks, grasping the dwarf's arm with some violence.

"She ! who do you mean ?" inquired Fra Ludovico, opening his eyes with amazement.

"Viola—my heart's idol—the dream of my youth."

"You don't mean to say you are in love with a nun ?" said the dwarf.

"I have no particular reason to think that she is a nun, but she is an inmate of yonder convent. Listen to me, and you shall understand my story: I was, as I am now, in love with a young lady, who, for causes it is not necessary to explain, wished to go into a convent; I obtained her admission to the convent of St. Ursula, and it was agreed between Father Azellio and myself that she should be a novice for a certain time, and that until that time had expired no attempt should be made to induce her to take the veil."

"Has the stipulated time expired ?"

"I regret to say it has."

"Ah, that is bad."

"I have come to claim this young lady's hand, and to see if I cannot induce her to leave the convent."

"Has she any money ?"

"No. I paid a large sum to Father Azellio to secure his goodwill, but of course that was a free gift and is not hers," replied Money Marks.

"Is she accomplished—can she do anything ?"

"Did you not hear her sing ?"

"What ! the soloist ?"

"Yes."

"Oho ! Why, my dear friend, she is the admired of all admirers; they call her the 'Queen of the Choir,' and they would no more think of letting her go than the strict old abbess would forego the punishing of a refractory nun."

"Is it so ? Has she taken the veil ? Tell me that. You seem to have sources of information at your disposal, and should know."

"She has not," replied Fra Ludovico; "though now I come to tax my memory I think the date of the solemn ceremony is fixed."

"Indeed !"

"And that shortly. Is it not within a month from to-day ?—ay, that it is. It will be a magnificent spectacle, and great preparations are being made for it."

"Is it possible ? Thank God though for one thing, and that is that I have arrived in time."

"For what ?"

"To prevent the sacrifice."

"In what way ?"

"That is for you to decide. Did I not agree to buy your services just now ?"

"You did," said Fra Ludovico; "but I did not then know what sort of work you wanted me to do. It is at all times dangerous to attack Mother Church; I have had a taste of her discipline and revenge once, and my back still aches at the thought of the stripes it has received. I might burn my fingers."

"Are you afraid ?" asked Money Marks, casting a glance of contempt upon him.

"I am. I frankly confess that I am one of the rankest cowards in existence."

"Then you are of little use to me," said Money Marks, with a sigh of disappointment.

"Although my courage is not of the highest order," said Fra Ludovico, "I can screw it to the sticking point if I am well paid for it—like other rogues and clever men, I have my price. I know what I can do, and what I am worth. If you choose to employ me, do so, if not, I daresay I can get as much brandy as I want; I did without you before we met just now, and I daresay I can do the same thing again."

"What is your price?" asked Money Marks.

Fra Ludovico thought for a short time, and then said that he would take a certain sum at once, and the remainder of a fixed sum when the enterprise was ended. If the young lady, as Fra Ludovico called her, was not rescued from the priestly clutches, he was to receive nothing for his services. He went upon the principle of no work no pay, and Money Marks was so satisfied with his offer that he at once accepted it. A long conversation ensued, and it was arranged between them that Money Marks should go to the convent, ask for Father Azellio, who as father confessor was generally there, and make inquiries respecting Viola.

This visit was put off until the following day. At about ten o'clock Money Marks wended his way to the cloister gate of the convent, and ringing a bell, demanded admission to the abode of virginity and prayer, saying that he had business with Father Azellio which was of the utmost importance.

The priest agreed to see him, and he was ushered into a large room, at one end of which hung upon the wall a huge crucifix, the furniture was scanty, but there were seats to sit upon, and at certain times it behoves us to be thankful for small mercies.

The priest "all shaven and shorn" entered the room, making the sign of the cross in the air as if he dreaded an interview with the devil and wished to avert an evil omen.

In some foreign countries the devil is not more hated than a heretic; to be a heretic is to be without the pale of civilization and religion, so intolerant are the Roman Catholics whenever their religion is the dominant one.

Money Marks and the priest spoke in French, the latter opening the conversation with—

"Peace be with thee, my son! What wouldst thou with me?"

"Have you forgotten me, father?" said Money Marks.

"Come hither. Let me gaze upon you; I should know those features, and yet my memory will not serve me."

"I have only to mention the fair-haired lady, the ship, the bargain, the bags of gold I paid to——"

"Hold!" cried the priest, "I have it now. You, my son, have called to inquire after the damsel you call Viola, but who is known to the elect as Sister Speranza."

"I have."

"Perhaps it may have escaped your memory that the time stipulated for by you has escaped. The good sister has decided upon taking the vows; she will not return to the world."

"Will not?" cried Money Marks.

"No, I have said it," returned the priest, decisively.

"You must be mistaken; I will never believe it till I hear it from her own lips."

The priest thought a moment ere he replied.

"It is against our rules to permit one who is soon to become the bride of Heaven to have an interview with any of her old friends, but as you wish it I will strain a point in your favour and the thing shall be done. Wait here, my son, for a brief space, and when I return it will be with the Sister Speranza."

Money Marks bowed, and sitting down upon a roughly-made chair, anxiously awaited the return of the wily priest. If he were permitted to have a short conversation with Viola, he thought that he should be able to rekindle in her breast a desire to return to the world. Could he but succeed in accomplishing this he would be happy. The priests might for a consideration of a monetary nature be inclined to allow their fair and beauteous captive to escape from her cage, but if Viola herself had become enamoured of a life in the cloister she was not her own mistress, and could do nothing.

The sound of footsteps roused him from his reverie. He looked up, sprang to his feet, and saw a thickly-veiled figure ushered in by the priest. It was the figure of a woman about the size and height of Viola. She was dressed in black serge with a piece of rope tied round her waist as a girdle; her hands hung listlessly by her side. Her manner was stony and impassive and she was as frigid as a piece of ice.

"Viola!" ejaculated Money Marks.

"I am here," exclaimed a voice from under the thick black veil—a voice which sounded strange and unfamiliar to the pirate.

"Who are you?" he asked.

"You have called me Viola."

"But you are cold and strange and distant. This is not the way in which I expected to be received by you."

"It is the only way in which she can receive you, my son," replied the priest; "the bride elect of Heaven may not parley with a heretic and an outcast."

Turning to the veiled figure, he added—

"Sister, tell this misguided and impetuous man that you cannot return to the world, that it is your wish to take the irrevocable vows, and you must do so."

"That is the case," said the figure; "nothing will ever induce me to quit these walls, within which I intend to live and die."

Money Marks could not bring himself to believe that he was listening to Viola. He knew that the priests were wily in the extreme, and he fancied that some clever trick was being played on him. With a quick spring he rushed towards the woman and—oh, sacrilege!—oh, horror of horrors!—actually had the audacity to tear the thick veil from her face and fling it indignantly on the ground.

The fraud which was endeavoured to be practised upon him was then discovered.

Instead of a young, lovely, and blooming girl, a wretched wrinkled old hag stood before him, having a yellow face and crow's feet under her eyes.

She glared at him with all the ferocity of a tigress.

Father Azellio was too indignant to be able to speak for a moment.

"Ha, ha!" laughed Money Marks, sarcastically. "So this is Sister Viola, or Speranza as you call her. Ha, ha! an excellent joke, upon my word; she has grown older since she has become an inmate of the convent of St. Ursula. What do you say to this, Father Azellio? can you reconcile it with your conscience? is it consistent with the Christian religion to play a trick upon me, and to make that poor creature a tool in your hands for wicked lying and deception? If this is your religion, or a specimen of it, I cry out upon it."

Black in the face with rage, Father Azellio said, with stifled anger—

"You shall bitterly repent this."

"Oh! do you as a priest think it consistent with your profession to threaten me with revenge? I thought vengeance belonged to one greater than you; you must pardon my simplicity."

The priest beckoned to the abashed nun to retire, which she did, counting her beads and mumbling a prayer.

"Come, come, acknowledge that I had the best of you in that little affair," said Money Marks, in a cheerful tone; "let us be good friends."

"Friends! I friendly with you!" said the priest.

"Yes; why not?"

"Never; sooner would oil and water amalgamate. I know you. The confessional has dragged all her secrets from your Viola; the mighty engines of the Church of Rome have been put in action, and her young and pure mind has been ransacked from top to basement. I know you. There is blood upon your hands; your soul is stained with crimes that will hurl you ten thousand thousand fathoms deep into the unquenchable fire of hell. Wail, wail, and gnash your teeth, for not one drop of water will Abraham give to Dives."

"Not inaptly spoken," said Money Marks, "for I am rich at present—that is to say, I have money in the town," he added, seeing that the priest's eyes sparkled with cupidity.

He thought it better to correct himself, for he was inside the convent walls and in the enemy's camp. There was no saying what power they had at their command or what they might do to him. He had heard of secret torture-chambers and vile engines of torment, which could wrest a cry from the stoutest man. So deeming discretion the better part of valour, he spoke to the priest softly,

"I want not your money," replied Father Azellio.

"You must have need of money; you can always put it to a good use. Say what you will take to let the girl go; I can see that she is averse to prolonging her stay in the convent."

"Why so?"

"If she had been desirous of doing so, you would have allowed her to see me and tell me so with her own lips; I am a man of the world and you cannot hoodwink me."

"I have no inclination to do so, and to prove my sincerity in saying so, I will add that nothing will induce us to part with Sister Speranza. Money, threats, promises—all will be unavailing: she is the property of Heaven, and the grave could not hold her closer than we intend to."

"Are you in earnest?"

"We are."

"Will not a thousand dollars tempt you?" said Money Marks, feeling his way.

"No, nor twenty thousand."

"You shall have thirty thousand."

"It is useless, my son; the die is cast. You will never more look upon the face of Viola. I have nothing more to say. Peace be with you, Amen."

So saying, the priest folded his hands demurely before him and walked out of the room, leaving the pirate to find his way out as best he might.

He had been set at defiance, and he saw that if Viola was to be rescued, a most energetic course must be pursued. There must be no faltering, no hesitation; he must invade the sacred precincts of the convent and carry her off as best he might.

In order to accomplish this desirable end he had recourse to Fra Ludovico, who knew so much about the convent and its inmates that he was an invaluable ally.

When he reached the outer air, Money Marks sat down upon a doorstep and gave himself up to thought.

He had been foiled.

Yet his ill success stimulated him to increased exertion.

CHAPTER LXII.

THE PIRATE OBTAINS ADMISSION TO THE CONVENT—VIOLA IS FOUND IN AN ACCIDENTAL MANNER—SHE IS INSTRUCTED HOW TO ESCAPE—THE IRON ROOM—STRANGE EVENTS HAPPEN.

WHEN a man loves, his passion is generally increased by opposition. It was so with Money Marks. He discovered that he would have to outwit the priests, if he succeeded in inducing Viola to escape. She was no doubt well hidden, and guarded with extreme vigilance.

Upon Fra Ludovico the pirate entirely depended; he made him a handsome present of money, and told him all that had happened, at which the dwarf smiled grimly.

"We shall be successful after all," he said; "I can see my way, but we must proceed with caution. Sancton, the gardener at the convent, is a friend of mine. I can do anything with him; he is old, and easily imposed upon. A little brandy will make Sancton sleep until the convent-bell wakes him at daybreak. At nightfall we will knock at Sancton's door in the wall, and say we have come to spend the evening with him."

"Will he admit us?"

"Not as we are now."

"How then?"

"We must disguise ourselves as nuns. Nothing is easier. We can slip the dresses over our own apparel, so that they can be quickly discarded should the necessity arise. I will make it my business to purchase the dresses, and we will disguise ourselves at the back of the convent wall, where no one is likely to see us. You are tall for a woman, but there are many who equal you in height."

When the evening arrived the confederates met, and having disguised themselves, went to the door in the wall, which gave admittance to poor old Sancton's cottage; they were admitted without demur. The old man hobbled with the aid of his stick, and led the way to his parlour.

Fra Ludovico had brought with him, concealed under his dress, a couple of bottles of brandy. These he placed upon the table, and a carouse began. Old Sancton was not averse to a few glasses, for it was a luxury he only indulged in when his friend the dwarf came to see him, or the Lady Superior, pitying his fast increasing infirmities, was generous enough to give him a glass of something to warm his blood.

The spirit with which the dwarf plied the gardener soon had the desired effect. Sancton's head fell forward upon the deal table, and he was almost directly in a sound slumber, from which it was difficult, if not a matter of utter impossibility, to wake him.

Drinking some brandy himself, and urging Marks to follow his example, Fra Ludovico whispered to him to follow him to the convent. It was now ten o'clock. The night was dark, but the inmates had not all retired to rest. Some

of those who were privileged were walking about in the garden, which was extensive, well wooded, and full of quiet retired walks.

The dwarf knew that many of the nuns and novices who were in favour were permitted to take exercise after dark in the convent garden, the witching hour of night being considered favourable to meditation and religious thought.

He had a faint hope that Viola might be found in the garden, though it was scarcely probable she would be allowed so much latitude when Money Marks was in the city, and she had not yet taken the veil.

In so large a convent all the inmates were not acquainted with one another, so that many nuns passed without a word, or look, or a sign of recognition. This state of things was highly favourable to Money Marks' enterprise; but he wondered at the audacity of the dwarf, who fearlessly led him in every direction, looking by the faint star-light into the face of every nun they met, and telling him to do the same, to see if he could recognise Viola.

They even penetrated to the convent walls, and saw the door at which the nuns passed in and out; but they could not see the object of their search. They did not despair, however, but continued their promenade. The nuns did not look curiously at them, taking them for recluses like themselves, belonging to the same house of compassion.

When they had been twice round the garden and had searched all the bye-paths thoroughly, they approached a grotto, from which voices proceeded. Money Marks grasped his companion's arm, and forced him to stand still.

The soft breeze sobbed and sighed through the branches of the many trees. The patter of feet and the subdued murmur of whispered conversation was at times heard. All was still, quiet, serene.

"At last," whispered Money Marks, "at last we find her we are in search of; she is in there. It is for us to rescue her."

"Hush! for your life, silence."

"Yes, yes; I will be still."

"Let me see who she has with her. We are not far from the garden door. Much may be done by skill and prudence."

This advice of Fra Ludovico was too good not to be acted upon. Money Marks stood in a shadow near the door, and, pretending to count his beads, listened. Viola had but one companion, who had been talking earnestly to her; having finished her argument or exhortation, as the case might be, she said—

"Stay where you are for half-an-hour. Think well over what I have said. When it is time for all to be in the chapel I will come for you."

This was the lady abbess; her rank and position were not betrayed by a gaudy glitter or tinsel splendour. She was dressed as poorly as any of the serge-clad sisters, but the pirate knew her, through having seen her, and heard her voice before.

With the utmost alacrity he moved on one side, causing Fra Ludovico to do the same.

They were not a moment too soon, for the abbess's gown brushed by them; they bowed, and she, without looking at them closely, satisfied with their salutation, passed on.

Ludovico now offered to keep guard while Money Marks made the best of the glorious opportunity with which fate had favoured him.

Marks was only too anxious to do so, and, leaving the dwarf as a sentry at the entrance to the stone-built, creeper-covered grotto, he walked in and sat down by Viola's side. She did not consider the intrusion at all remarkable, for the sisters, feeling themselves fatigued, would often drop in, sit down for a while, and then pursue their way.

But when she heard a voice she knew too well say, in anxious accents, "Viola, my own, my darling, my own for ever!" and felt a hand and an arm steal gently round her waist, and clasp her in a sweet embrace, she uttered a tiny scream, and let her head fall upon his manly bosom.

This act was involuntary; she was so faint that she was unable to help herself, and Money Marks, with an ardour such as only a fond and true lover can feel, rained kisses upon her snowy brow and ruby-coloured lips.

This roused her, and she pushed him gently away from her, not repelling him disdainfully but meekly.

"Can I believe the evidence of my senses; is it indeed you, here, and in this disguise? wonders will never cease."

"Yes, Viola, it is indeed I."

"Are you here with Father Azellio's knowledge and permission?"

"I am not."

"Then you are in danger."

"I care not for that; all I want is to see and love you."

"Why did you not come as you promised? The time you bargained for has gone by, and they wished me to take the veil."

"And you, do you wish it?"

He spoke huskily, for his voice was thick with emotion.

"No. It may be wicked of me to say so, but I don't," replied Viola.

"Thank Heaven for that. I had a suspicion that you were not a party to the plan."

"I fear much that I shall have to submit."

"And why?"

"Am I not in the power of the Saint Ursulines?" she replied, tearfully.

"At present you are, but freedom is within your grasp."

"Oh! no, you are trifling with me."

"As God is my judge, I am not," exclaimed Money Marks, earnestly,

"Oh! explain; tell me what the meaning of your words may be," she cried, for the first time looking in his face, but the light was so dim that she could only discern the luminous glitter of his eyes.

"I have a friend outside this grotto; he has assisted me to enter these gardens, and he will render me further assistance. We came in at the gardener's gate. He is now asleep in an insensible state of intoxication. We need fear nothing from that quarter. Two minutes' walk will bring us to the door: outside we have some clothes for you to attire yourself in, we will then leave the city instantly. What say you to my plan?"

"There is one question which I must ask you, and which I request you to answer truly," said Viola, "before I reply to you."

"What is your question? On my word of honour you shall be answered honestly."

"Have you complied with my condition?"

"In what way?"

"Have you abandoned a career of bloodshed and of crime for the space of one year?"

"I have, Viola. The icy breath of the frozen ocean will bear testimony to the truth of what I say. It was there that I first became penitent. That, however, is a long story. You shall hear it another time. Suffice it to say that I have relinquished the life I was leading. Will you come with me, will you quit the convent, and be my wife?"

There was a momentary hesitation, then she replied in a low tone, which was scarcely audible—

"I will."

"Bless you for that. Bless you a thousand times for that kind and gracious assurance," cried Money Marks, rapturously.

A low whistle from without warned them that some intruder upon their privacy was advancing.

"Some one comes," said Money Marks.

"It is the abbess."

"A hundred abbesses shall not drag me from you," answered Money Marks.

"Pray Heaven she may not penetrate your disguise."

"And why? what could she do? I would——"

"What, have you not forsworn deeds of blood?"

"Pardon me, my nature is impetuous, and I feared to lose you."

"Do you know what would be your fate if discovered here?" said Viola.

"I do not."

"You would be placed in an iron-room, and then kept upon bread and water till the end of your days. In that room there is neither light nor air, save such as comes in from the keyhole. There is a legend in the convent that a man was ten years ago found in these gardens. He was not tried, but at once placed in the iron-room. I will not vouch for the truth of this story, but they say 'tis true—at all events, I will swear that the abbess, who always has the key, goes every morning to the iron-room with a small portion of a loaf of bread and a jug of water."

"Monstrous!" said Money Marks. "It would be only justly turning the tables were she herself placed there."

"Hush!" said Viola, laying her finger upon her lips, "here she comes."

"Where?—yes, 'tis she. I hear a footstep."

The abbess entered the grotto and said—

"Sister Speranza!"

"I am here," was the reply, in a tremulous voice.

"Who have you with you?"

"With me?"

"Yes, methinks I saw another person here."

"One of the sisters, perhaps. I have been absorbed in meditation."

"That is well."

Money Marks during this colloquy had gradually neared the abbess. His purpose was to stifle her cries, bind and gag her. His fingers closed round her throat before she had the slightest inkling of her danger, and a large piece of rag, torn from Marks' dress, was stuffed into her mouth before she had the power to utter a cry—at the same time, her arms were forcibly wrenched round, and fastened behind her back with the same material.

This was not effected without a scuffle, which made Viola aware that something was going on.

While Money Marks was holding the indignant and half-fainting abbess in his arms, Viola exclaimed—

"Oh! what have you done?"

"No harm. She is unhurt."

"She must not be injured."

"She shall not. Where is the iron-room?"

"It adjoins this grotto, and is hid from sight by a clump of trees."

"Quick! lead me to it."

"What would you do?"

"Place this woman where she has put many a victim. Do not hesitate; all depends upon our promptitude."

Thus urged, Viola led the way to the iron-room. Marks informed Fra Ludovico of what had taken place, and he assisted him to drag the struggling abbess to her prison.

The iron-room was a small apartment built entirely of large slabs of iron, and erected in the centre of a group of trees.

So thick were the plates of iron that no sound could escape from within. No furniture of any sort was placed inside; the wretched captive had to make his bed upon the hard floor, which was also of iron.

> "Can such things be,
> And overcome us like a summer cloud,
> Without our special wonder?"

Fumbling in the pocket of the abbess's dress enabled Money Marks to find a thick heavy massive key. This was doubtless the one belonging to the prison-house. When he reached the door he tried it, and found that it fitted the lock exactly. Flinging the door open with a jerk, he looked in and exclaimed—

"If there is anyone there let him come forth!"

This speech he repeated in more than one language, so that he might be understood. What was his surprise when he heard a sepulchral voice exclaim in English—

"Great God! can I believe my senses? Is it an Englishman who speaks to me, after all this long, desolate blank of captivity?"

"It is; and if you are my countryman," said Money Marks, "I am happy to be able to release you."

"Release me!"

"Yes, there is no time to be lost. Do not speak but come forward—if you are not chained."

"Alas! I am confined to the wall by a chain; but if you have the key of this dungeon, you will find a small key attached to it that will undo the padlock."

At length the man was released, and standing outside the iron-room into which the abbess was pushed with rather more violence than was absolutely necessary. The door was relocked, and the little party of fugitives made with all dispatch for the gardener's door.

Old Sancton was still insensibly drunk and incapable of motion. They met with no opposition, and glided through the door in the wall like so many shadowy ghosts.

The man whom Money Marks had rescued from the iron house clung to the dwarf's arm with great tenacity. He had partially lost the use of his limbs, either through fear or long captivity.

Viola leant upon the pirate, for she was agitated almost beyond the power of endurance, her capacity for which was not strong at any time.

The men changed their dresses in a moment by flinging off the nun's apparel, and Viola was assisted to slip a dress over her serge-gown, and she was speedily attired like the peasant-women of the country.

"Now I have so far assisted you," said Fra Ludovico, "I claim my reward. The part I have already taken in this escapade is sufficient to cause me to be put to death, so hazardous is it ; and I cannot risk my life and liberty any further. Pay me and let me go."

"As you like," replied Money Marks, handing him a sum of money, which he took with the utmost alacrity, placing it securely in his pocket.

"*Adios!* ladies and gentlemen," he said, lifting his hat politely; "may Heaven smile upon you, and fickle Fortune turn her wheel in your direction—as my worthy reverend and learned friend, Father Azellio, would say, *Dominus vobiscum.*"

Scarcely had the last words escaped his lips than he vanished, and was lost to sight.

Money Marks saw that he must appeal to his companions to exert their utmost strength, for to remain in the city would be madness.

No hue-and-cry would be raised, because Father Azellio would know better than to allow the scandal to circulate beyond the convent walls. He would, however, employ private and clinical agents, who would permeate the town in all directions, discover them, and bring them prisoners to the convent.

What their fate would be was easily guessed.

The offence of which they had been guilty was always punishable by death.

They had been known to treat an escaped nun and her accomplices with the utmost rigour and unheard-of cruelty.

"I know you are weak and ill, Viola," said Money Marks, "but for your own sake, for my sake, summon all your courage and endurance to your aid, and persevere bravely. There must be no looking back now. The very air is tainted with peril and impregnated with horrible danger. To hesitate is to be lost."

"I am not strong," replied Viola, "but I will do my best."

"That I am positive of. We must not linger."

"And I," said the stranger, "feel stronger and more vigorous at every breath of air I take. Oh, Heaven! what religion is to the soul, this fresh and balmy air is to me."

"Away, away!" said Money Marks. "Cling to me. I am strong, and will give you what aid lies in my power."

Viola seized one arm, while the stranger grasped the other; and thus burdened he led the way out of the city without attracting observation, and took the road which led to the hut in which Cuffy was slowly recovering from the effects of the bite of the snake.

In the meantime, the prolonged absence of the abbess was creating the utmost consternation in the minds of the inmates of the convent.

Father Azellio was at a loss what to think, or how to proceed.

CHAPTER LXIII.

A HALT BY THE ROAD-SIDE—SANCTUARY—PURSUED—A MEETING WITH THE CAPTAIN OF THE ENGLISH BARK "PETRONEL"—HOPE GLEAMS IN THE DISTANCE.

It was a weary journey for the two poor captives whom Money Marks had so bravely and adventurously rescued from a frightful and wearisome imprisonment.

After travelling about five miles they were scarcely capable of dragging one limb before the other.

Money Marks saw that Viola would, in a short time, drop down in the road exhausted; but he urged her on, wishing to go as far on his way as he possibly could. At length the catastrophe arrived. With a low moan she sank upon the ground, saying, in a plaintive voice—

"Forgive me—forgive me. I have done my best, but nature is exhausted."

"Forgive you! for what, my own darling?" said Money Marks, bending over her with tender solicitude.

"I shall delay your journey and frustrate your plans."

"No, no."

"Yes, I know I shall. I am miserably wretched. It seems so easy to walk sometimes; and I would give the world to be able to go a little farther. Hear me, dearest; leave me."

"I would rather perish myself first," said Money Marks, manfully.

"You must do it; I cannot involve you in my capture."

"What!" he cried, "leave you, Viola? Oh, no! As long as I can lift a finger or move a muscle I will never quit your side."

"You are very good—too good; but I must be captured. You and that gentleman (indicating the stranger) may possibly succeed in escaping. Why should we be all captured? Make me the scapegoat—leave me as the propitiatory sacrifice. When a man in a wild country is pursued by wolves, he throws whatever he has with him to them, so that they may growl and snarl over it and give him time to fly from them. Mothers have been known to sacrifice their own babes; why, then, should you hesitate about leaving me?"

"Your death is certain if the priests once succeed in dragging you back to the convent of St. Ursula."

"Kill me, then," she cried, violently. "Slay me where I am! it will be a kindness."

Stooping down, Money Marks raised her in his arms and carried her to an adjoining coppice, where he made her a bed of leaves and dry grass.

"There you can sleep securely, my own," he exclaimed; "we are some distance from the road, and our pursuers, if we have any, will never think of looking for us here. Sleep and recruit your wasted strength. I will watch and guard your life with my own."

She was too tired to speak, but she smiled secretly, and the pirate felt compensated for any little trouble he might have had. He would have gone through fire and water for her; and, to vary the illustration, he would have dashed through burning petroleum. She was his first love, and he felt that were she to die or to be ravished from his arms he could never love again.

Thinking that, under the circumstances, she would not blame him, he stooped over her and kissed her with every demonstration of the most ardent affection.

Her eyes closed as he did so, and she had fallen into a sweet slumber. Marks now turned his attention to the stranger, and bade him lie down, for he thought him in want of sleep.

"Sleep!" he cried. "Ah! you know not what I have suffered, or you would not speak to me of sleep. It is too much pleasure for me to be where I am now to think of sleeping : and look at me, follow my eyes. I am looking—as well as my weakened vision will permit me—I am looking at the stars, at all I can see around me. You forget that for a long and weary time I have been imprisoned."

"For ten years, I was told."

"Not more? To me it seemed a century."

"I can easily understand that ; hopeless captivity is irksome."

"It is more than irksome, sir," said the stranger; "it kills the soul. It is a wonder to me how I contrived to preserve my reason."

"Who are you?" said Money Marks. "Pardon my curiosity, and do not think me impertinent; but I am very anxious to know how you became immured in the iron house."

"You are my deliverer—my earthly Saviour," replied the old man, "and you have a right to my entire confidence."

"I only did for you what I hope any other man worthy of the name would have done."

"Never mind what people would have done," said the stranger; "all that I have to think of is what you did. You restored me to the dear, dear world, for which I panted so ardently. When shut up in that awfully hideous prison I have felt inclined to dash my head against the bars of iron, and end my days there and then ; but a hope of release lingered in my mind. I felt confident that some day I should be free again, and I forebore to take my own life. Yet I was strongly tempted. Only conceive, my dear sir, the awful tortures of ten years' solitary imprisonment, and for no crime of my own."

"What was your offence?"

"In what way did I incur the anger of the St. Ursulines, do you mean?"

"Yes."

"In this way—but I had better begin at the beginning, and then my tale will be clear and comprehensible to you."

"Pray do so," said Money Marks, sitting down upon the bulging-out root of a tree; "but let me beg of you to talk in a low tone, lest any pursuers we may have overhear us. I am not without firearms, and we could make a good stand against any but overpowering numbers. Such has been my

MONEY MARKS OVERCOME BY BITTER REFLECTIONS ABOUT VIOLA.

experience, however, that I would always rather avoid than seek a conflict."

"Exactly my own opinion. We will talk low. Depend upon it I will not betray you, for my own sake. If you have a pistol about you that you can spare, I will thank you a great deal to lend it to me."

"There is one," replied Money Marks; "it is a five-chambered revolver and loaded. Take it; it is yours."

"Many thanks. I will kill five men with it, if attacked; four of my enemies shall fall; and if I see that all hope is fled I will take my own life."

"I hope we shall not be driven to such a strait. Sit down and tell me your story."

The stranger took a seat on some fragrant herbage by the side of the pirate, and Money Marks had an opportunity of examining his face by the aid of the moonbeams, which streamed down in abundance.

The face was pale and cadaverous, a long beard, whiskers, and moustache imparted a wild and savage aspect to him, which was further augmented by the length of his finger-nails and the squalid look of his apparel.

"I am an Englishman, as you may have surmised," said the stranger. "I left England many years ago as captain of the merchant-vessel *Calypso*. My wife and child remained behind; the infant was the only offspring of our marriage lately solemnized. I had engaged with the owners of the vessel to make a long voyage amongst different ports, and I was not to return to England for five or six years. When I returned I could not find my wife. Mutual friends informed me that shortly after my departure she became restless, uneasy, and discontented. The child did not seem to please her; and one day they were surprised at the disappearance of the mother and the infant. What became of them no one knew; their fate was enveloped in the most impenetrable mystery. Enraged beyond measure I sailed again, and put into the port we have just left, arriving there with a large cargo of valuable merchandize. After my wife's desertion of me I began to drink deeply, and frequently took more than was safe for me. I cannot tell you what put the idea in my head, but I conceived the idea of scaling the wall of the convent garden and having a peep at the nuns. By the aid of a ladder I did so, and proceeded to walk about. An alarm was quickly given. I was captured, and without any trial or inquiry placed in the awfully wretched and miserable dungeon in which you providentially found me. Had it not been for you I might have passed the best and last days of my life there. I am not upwards of fifty years of age. There is still a short time left me to enjoy existence, from which I have so long been shut out."

The old man had frequently during his recital fixed his eyes intently on Money Marks' face, which induced the pirate to say—

"You look at me as if I recalled some one to your memory."

"It is so. There is a most marvellous resemblance between you and my wife; you have her features exactly. The colour of the hair and eyes is the same. It is strange how these accidental likenesses are detected."

"My history is a strange one," said Money Marks, in a melancholy tone of voice.

"How so?"

"I am a foundling; I never knew my father or mother; when quite a baby, I was left to the care of strangers."

"That is hard."

"My mother could not have loved me much, for she went into a publichouse in Ratcliff-highway and left me on the counter."

"What was the name of the house?"

"Samkin's, the 'Pint of Porter.'"

"My house—the one I used to frequent in preference to any other," cried the stranger. "Ask them if they know Captain Lancaster, and hear what they will say. They have had pounds of my money."

"I hope you may soon pay them another visit," said Money Marks, cheerfully.

"I have more hope now than I have had for some time; I feel now wildly delirious with joy, and confident of a happy future after all my sufferings. If I could but discover some trace of my poor wife or of my son I should be tolerably contented."

"Is there anything by which you can identify him?" asked Money Marks; "if so, you can advertise in the papers, and may pursue a course which will eventually lead to his discovery."

"Why, yes, he was marked in a peculiar way, now I come to think of it," answered Captain Lancaster. "He had some moles on his forehead."

Walking up to Money Marks, he placed his hand upon his forehead, and said—

"This was the place—just here, and there, and one a little further—eh! what is this?" he cried, with a nervous accent; "God bless me! what is this?"

Money Marks grew pale, and exclaimed—

"What do you mean? Why do you speak so wildly and look so strange?"

"You—you have the marks my infant child had—here, there, and there; you have been cast in the same mould. And my poor Emily's features too! Gracious Heaven! can it be possible that you are my son?"

Money Marks stood still, bewildered; he knew not what to think or what to say.

"Speak," cried Captain Lancaster, still under the influence of strong excitement. "Is there no internal prompting which bids you call me father?"

The pirate made no answer.

"It must be so," continued the captain. "What instrument to save a father is Providence more likely to employ than a son?"

"None," rejoined Money Marks. "If you are my father, I rejoice to think that it should have been my happy fate to rescue you. Calm yourself at present; we will talk the matter over more calmly when we are out of the great danger which at present environs us."

Captain Lancaster, however, could not restrain his feelings; he had firmly persuaded himself that he had found a son, and nothing would turn him from his opinion.

With a hysterical cry he fell forward sobbing upon the pirate's neck, and then wept like a child.

Money Marks did not receive the evidence of his parentage as conclusive, but he submitted to the caresses which were inflicted upon him with the resignation of a martyr.

He was not exactly a fastidious man, but he would have preferred the ceremony postponed until Captain Lancaster had donned fresher and less musty clothing and arrayed himself in somewhat cleaner linen.

Shortly afterwards the two men fell asleep, but woke before daybreak; rousing Viola, who was much refreshed, they pushed on to the cottage, where Cuffy was anxiously expecting Money Marks, and there they found sanctuary.

The black was so much better that he could walk with ease, though he at times experienced a feeling of faintness, which was only removed by a temporary halt and a draught of spirits.

When night fell they agreed to leave the cottage, and guided by the old man, who had cured Cuffy's wound, make the best of their way to the coast, and having arrived at some secluded spot, Captain Lancaster was to go on to the port and make arrangements with some British vessel for conveyance to London, Money Marks furnishing the captain with the money necessary for the purpose.

The party had now received an accession of strength, and consisted of five. Money Marks and Viola went together, Captain Lancaster formed the vanguard, the black, with his friend the old man, brought up the rear.

They were all armed, so that any attack could be well repulsed, and if their arms were not so strong as they might be, their hearts were stout.

The shore was skirted by a dense wood of almost impenetrable thickness; there were, however, paths through the underwood which were known to intelligent natives, hunters, and wild animals.

The old man who had behaved with such kindness to Cuffy had in his younger days been fond of hunting, and he was well acquainted with the paths and intricacies of the forest.

Through these he guided them.

His instinct was unerring and his memory good. To have gone round by the road would have been an act of folly. The paths in the wood were known to other people besides the old man.

Father Azellio soon discovered that Viola as well as the lady abbess was missing; his rage knew no bounds. He fully suspected that Money Marks was the daring author of the audacious outrage. He ran about the convent and its precincts foaming at the mouth, and would have torn his hair, if his head had not been shaven.

The marks of footsteps guided him to the iron house, and having burst the door open, he found the abbess insensible. She was promptly dragged out, restoratives were applied, and then she told her tale, which added fuel to the fire.

Not only had Viola—queen of the choir—been abducted, but the prisoner whom they had jealously guarded for so many years had been snatched from his captivity to unfold a tale which would make the hair of many stand on end with horror and surprise.

A pursuit was at once organized, and Father Azellio, with two acute fellows who knew the country well, set off to find the fugitives and bring them back, or die in the attempt.

They discovered the route they had taken, and found out the place where they slept. This gave them a clue, and they determined to search the wood.

"They must be either captured or killed," cried Father Azellio; "if you succeed in doing either one or the other, the choicest rewards which the Church has it in its power to confer upon you shall be yours."

The men crossed themselves, and vowed that come what might they would do their duty.

It was towards the close of a hot day that Money Marks and his party halted near a bubbling spring, whose softly-welling waters were most grateful to their parched palates.

The hum of innumerable insects and the songs of birds, with the occasional hiss of a gliding serpent, were alone to be heard.

The scene was clothed in all the gorgeous wealth of tropical beauty, and the vegetation, as is usual in those parts, was rank and luxuriant.

The little party were engaged in eating some coarse and indifferent bread which they had brought with them, and being fatigued, were not much inclined for conversation—walking beneath the perpendicular rays of a burning sun being rather inducive of quiet repose than anything else.

Suddenly the brushwood was pushed on one side and footsteps were heard approaching.

Every one started to his feet.

Four revolvers were levelled in the direction of the sound.

Five hearts palpitated as one.

The intruder dauntlessly entered the pleasant glade and seemed surprised at the warlike attitude of those with whom he was confronted.

By his appearance he was an Englishman.

"I am a friend," he cried, "put up your weapons."

"How do we know that?" answered Money Marks, speaking in Spanish, which was the language the intruder had made use of.

"I have been out shooting for my amusement, and knowing this spring, have come for a drink of water. Whoever you are, I mean you no harm."

Money Marks lowered the muzzle of his pistol, and some further conversation took place between himself and the intruder, whom he learnt was the captain of the British vessel, *Petronel*, then in the harbour.

He might be of use to the fugitives.

Hope gleamed in the distance.

CHAPTER LXIV.

THE PURSUIT.

It was refreshing in the extreme to Money Marks to hear that the person with whom the little party had accidentally met was the captain of the English barque *Petronel*.

In a tone of almost nervous anxiety he exclaimed—

"We are also English, and desirous of obtaining a passage to our native land."

"Well, if you have the money to pay for it, I can accommodate you," replied the captain.

"The money! yes, we have a little," Marks said, hesitatingly, not liking to admit that he was well off.

"I shall not want much, but the voyage is long; people eat and drink, and provisions are not to be had for nothing."

"Quite so," returned the pirate; "I see the force of that remark. Then it is a bargain between us that you give us a passage on being paid for it?"

"Yes; how many are there of you?"

"The black, myself, that gentleman—meaning Lancaster—and the lady."

"That makes four."

"Exactly."

"It's a bargain; I'll do it."

"Will you show us the way out of this confounded wood?" said Money Marks; "for I must confess I am lost."

"Oh! I know my way," replied the captain. "I have been here times enough before. We shall be several hours —say four or five—before we reach the port. Take your fill at this spring, for I don't think we shall meet with another. I often wish I was like a camel, and could carry my water supply about with me for several days."

When the party had refreshed themselves, they got up and prepared to proceed on their journey.

It was intimated to the old man, who had treated Cuffy with such kindness, that his further services on guard could be dispensed with, and he took his leave with many demonstrations of affection and regret.

Pushing aside the branches with his hand, he disappeared, but the next instant the report of a gun was heard.

The utmost consternation reigned amongst the fugitives.

They looked blankly at one another and trembled.

All grasped their weapons firmer, and kept their revolvers cocked, in case of an attack in force.

Viola placed her hand to her heart to still its wild tumultuous beating, fearful lest she should faint away with apprehension.

Suddenly the old man rushed through the underwood and stood before them with a gaping wound in his side, from which the blood was welling in a purple stream.

Money Marks ran forward to help him, but ere he could reach him he pointed with his hand in the direction of a tall palm-tree and fell insensible, if not dead, upon the ground.

"What is the meaning of all this?" asked the captain of the *Petronel*. "Are you are all fugitives from justice?—in what way am I to interpret this strange scene?"

Money Marks answered his question, saying—

"I will be candid with you."

"Yes."

"This young lady has escaped from the Ursuline Convent, and I have every reason to suppose that we are pursued."

"A nun, eh?"

"No; she has not yet taken the vows."

"I don't like meddling with religious affairs, young man. It is ticklish work in this country," said the captain of the *Petronel*, dubiously.

"There is little or no danger now," Money Marks urged; "I appeal to you as a fellow-countryman to help us. You cannot call yourself anything but a coward if you allow this lady to be dragged back by the priests, and placed in a convent where they can torture her at their pleasure. Would you have her scourged within an inch of her life, or built up alive in a wall? No—no! you are not the man to do that. Help us to fight for her, and you will not find us ungrateful."

"The work is not to my mind," replied the captain; "but I wont desert a lady in distress. I'll stand by you, and there's my hand on it."

At that moment a gun was discharged in the thicket.

Fortunately for himself Money Marks had just moved forward to grasp the captain's hand, or the bullet would have crashed through his skull.

"Ah!" said the pirate, between his teeth; "this must be put a stop to."

He drew a knife from its sheath, and, holding that in one hand and his revolver in the other, advanced to the thicket. A small patch of bluish smoke was rising above the brushwood. This told him in what direction to fire, and he discharged two barrels in quick succession.

The second shot took effect, for a terrible cry, followed by a dismal howl, was heard. Placing Viola in charge of the black, Money Marks called the captain of the *Petronel* to his side, and together they plunged into the thicket.

They had not gone far before they came to a cleared space of ground, where a singular scene met their gaze. A man, dressed as a priest, was lying on his back, and two men were bending over him. His mouth was full of blood, his eyes fixed in a wild stare, his hands clenched into fists, and his whole appearance denoting that he was not long for this world.

Marks had no difficulty in recognising an enemy in the dying man.

It was Father Azellio—that determined priest who had wrought him so much misery, and who, in following up his victim, had paid the penalty of his rashness and obstinacy with his life.

A ball from the pirate's pistol had entered his lungs, and was fast causing the ruby current to flood his throat and choke him.

When the two men saw that they were surrounded they sprang to their feet, and appeared determined to offer resistance to capture or assault.

One of the most marked traits of Money Marks' character was his decision and quickness of execution. He could see in a moment what it was necessary to do, and he did not hesitate to do it.

To allow the two men to escape would have been an act of little less than sheer madness, for they would have sent more people after them when they returned to the town, so he resolved that he would kill them.

He was not a quarter of a minute in coming to this decision, and raising his revolver to a level with his shoulder he fired at both, killing the two stone dead before they could lift a finger to save themselves.

Going up to their prostrate bodies he assured himself that they were really dead, and giving them a contemptuous kick returned with the captain of the *Petronel* to where Viola was, wishing to alleviate her distress, and assure her that she had nothing to fear.

The girl had been violently agitated, but her dread of recapture had been exceeded by that of Lancaster, who was reduced to such a pitiful state as to be totally unfit for anything but to crawl upon his hands and knees into the brushwood near the spring, thinking to hide himself from the priests and their myrmidons.

"Cheer up, my pet," said Money Marks to Viola.

"Are they gone?" she asked timidly.

"Yes, they are gone," he replied, "they will not trouble us any more. The danger is over."

"Thank Heaven for that."

"There may be other parties, though, for what we know, and I think it will be only prudent to get on board as fast as possible."

"When do you sail, captain?"

"To-morrow morning ; I have made all my arrangements. Being fond of a little wild game shooting, I thought it advisable to have a shot before I went, and to tell you the truth, I wandered farther than I had any intention of doing."

When Lancaster found that he need apprehend no further danger, he got up and recovered his serenity, which had been sadly shaken. It was impossible to bury the bodies, because the ground was hard and the party had no tools to work with. All that could be done was to take several large stones and place them over the four bodies, so as to form some slight barrier against the attacks of wild animals.

This was done, and then all started for the sea. The captain walked with Money Marks, Viola and Mr. Lancaster were together, and Cuffy brought up the rear. All were on their guard, and ready to resist the slightest attempt at stoppage or capture.

All at once an idea struck the captain of the *Petronel*, and he said to Money Marks—

"Will it not be more prudent for you to lie hid in some rocky place by the shore, and let me send a boat to you ?"

"You might forget us altogether, or be unable to send a boat ; perhaps the weather would not permit of such a thing," said Money Marks, fearful that he should lose his passage.

"There is not the least danger of that."

"I would rather risk going into the town ; we shall not arrive there until dark, and the police will not see us or be able to identify us."

"I have myself to look after," exclaimed the captain ; "if you were caught, and I was with you, I should be regarded by the authorities as being as bad as you. Do you see that ?"

"I do," replied Money Marks, gloomily.

"Let me protect myself ; that's all I ask."

"You have a right to do that. We are in your hands ; do what you like to us, but I appeal to your generosity not to desert us."

"I will not—depend upon that."

"Give me your word."

"I do ; I promise you that I will fetch you off. If you descend this pass you will come to the shore. There is, I know, a cavern at the base of the rocks, in which you can conceal yourself until the morning. At about nine o'clock I shall have cleared the harbour, passed the bar, and be about opposite this cavern ; then, I will lower a boat, which shall take you and your friends on board."

"Very well," said Marks, with a sigh and ill-repressed groan, "lead the way to the cavern, and many thanks for your kindness."

The captain did so, and the party began to defile along a rocky pass, which led by circuitous and mazy paths to the sea-shore. The cavern was pointed out to them, and the captain, renewing his promise, left them. Their fate was in his hands, and their anxiety to know what it would be was unbounded.

Money Marks was inclined to believe in the captain of the *Petronel* and trust him, and the encouraging way in which he spoke had the effect of reviving the drooping spirits of his companions,

They began to feel the pangs of hunger, and Marks sallied forth with his gun in order to shoot something. He succeeded in meeting with a couple of birds of gaudy plumage and a squirrel, with which he returned home.

A fire was soon lighted, and the birds cooked in as satisfactory a manner as could be expected. Money Marks could not sleep, he was too restless, but the others contrived to snatch a few hours' rest. The pirate's mind was full of strange, weird thoughts. Should he ever reach England ? Would Viola be his wife ? Would he be able to atone for years of bloodshed by a life of ease and peace, rearing children to fear God like other men, and becoming a respectable member of society ?

This was extremely doubtful.

At about twelve o'clock he had a vision.

He was standing upon the sea-shore gazing out upon the vast expanse of sleeping water, when he fancied he saw something black and horrid rise from the bosom of the slumbering ocean.

It stood before him so that he was enabled to regard it well and steadfastly.

It was a man dressed in black clothes, which fitted him ill. He wore a mask over his face, so that his features were indistinguishable. In his hand he held a rope, which he had formed into a noose.

This dreadful and repulsive figure had scarcely taken up its position a minute before a huge gallows rose by its side.

The hangman, for such it was, threw the rope over the cross beam of the gallows, still holding the noose in his hand.

After that, a second figure made its appearance, and in this Money Marks was astounded to see an exact resemblance of himself.

The hangman placed the rope round the second figure's neck. Innumerable people rose from the sea on all sides : a thousand voices swelling into a hoarse roar, uttered the name of "Money Marks, the Highwayman of the Seas !" Groans and execrations followed, amidst which the effigy was swung up by the hangman, and remained suspended between air and water.

Drawing his hand across his eyes to shut out the horrid phantom, Marks sat down upon a rock, and remained lost in thought and puzzled with hazardous conjectures until the morning dawned, and the moon faded away in the distance before the eclipsing power of the dawning sun.

Was this fearful vision prophetic of his fate ?

He could not tell. All he knew was that he had deserved it.

The sun had scarcely shown his bright face in the glowing heavens, when Money Marks' keen eye distinguished a large ship in the offing.

This he conjectured to be the merchant-vessel commanded by his friend who had promised them a passage.

Nor was he wrong.

The ship lowered a boat, which pulled towards the shore. Money Marks awoke his companions. Viola stood by his side. Her toilet was soon made ; she was compelled to despise and do without the conventionalities of society.

The boat contained the captain himself ; he greeted his friends warmly, and they at once embarked with a feeling of thankfulness which it is difficult to describe.

Money Marks and the captain sat together. The latter exclaimed—

"I thought it best to come in the boat myself."

"Why ?" inquired Marks.

"Because there are strange stories about you afloat in the town, and the men are dissatisfied."

"Indeed !"

"They say a great deal of nonsense."

"What is it ?"

"Amongst other things, that a nun has escaped from the Ursuline Convent."

"Yes, that is true enough."

"And that she has with her a bloodthirsty pirate."

"Ha !" cried Money Marks, starting.

"I assure you I am not romancing," replied the captain. "Of course, I did not believe a word of it."

"Of course not," answered Money Marks, abstractedly.

"Whatever do you think they say ?"

"I can't guess."

"That you are Money Marks."

"Ha ! ha ! a good joke."

"Is it not ?"

"Money Marks, the pirate, eh ? capital."

"They also say that Money Marks may always be known by his familiar friend, a stalwart negro."

"That is odd enough, because there happens to be a negro in our party," remarked Money Marks.

"Yes ; that gives a colour to the assertion."

"But, in my opinion, the report has been circulated by some mischievous monks belonging to the convent who wish to injure us and recapture the nun, which, please Heaven, they never shall do."

"That's right—nothing like determination," said the captain, sympathizingly.

"If you attach any importance to these absurd reports, captain, put us on shore, and let us take our chance."

"No, I will not do that, for I believe you are honest fellows."

"Are you sure ?"

"I am, oddly enough, though they say the vessel belonging to the famous pirate was run ashore on this coast within the month by one of her Majesty's cruisers and blown up."

"Ah !" said Money Marks, as if the item of intelligence was perfectly new to him.

"Well, well ; say no more about it. I thought it right to

tell you, because you might overhear some unpleasant remarks made by the sailors, and be at a loss to interpret them."

"Thank you, I will be on my guard," replied Money Marks.

The ill-feeling of the crew of the merchant vessel towards the new party was unmistakeable.

Flashing eyes, indignant glances, met them everywhere; while hands were laid upon knives with a look that spoke volumes.

Money Marks could not disguise from himself that ere they reached England they had many perils to encounter.

CHAPTER LXV.

A STORM AT SEA—BAD LUCK—THE SAILORS ACT FOR THEMSELVES.

THE old man who had called himself Mr. Lancaster, and discovered a relationship between Money Marks and himself, became more persuaded day by day that such was the case.

He looked upon Marks as his son, and treated him with all the kindness and consideration of a father.

Marks did not altogether return this parental affection. He had been so long without parents that he did not feel the want of them; still he could not help being touched by the old man's newly-awakened love, and behaved as dutifully as he could to him.

Marks was a little disappointed at his father being no better than the captain of a merchant-vessel.

There had been times when, giving way to speculation, he had thought it probable he might find a parent in an earl, or a mother in a duchess.

He had heard and read of such things, and saw no reason why they should not happen to him as well as to other people.

The ship had not been out more than two days before a frightful storm arose, which knocked the ship, as the saying is, all to pieces.

It was with the utmost difficulty that Money Marks could restrain the fear which the conduct of the sailors, after this event, raised in his breast.

They menaced him openly, put down all their bad luck to him, and threatened to throw him overboard.

He laughed at their threats when before Viola, but when in his bunk with Cuffy, a dark shade crossed his face, and he gave himself up to alarm and terror.

It was in vain that the captain strove to allay their savage rage, by declaring that the obnoxious party should be put on shore as soon as a fitting opportunity arrived.

All sorts of bad luck happened to the merchant-vessel.

Men fell overboard; live stock became ill and died; the water ran short; the biscuits were full of weevils; the beef was the briniest junk that ever was made salt.

Of course, the whole of this was set down to Money Marks, whom the sailors believed to be a pirate, and consequently weighted with a curse.

On the ninth day out the sailors sighted an island on the leeward bow. It appeared to be uninhabited, and was little better than a tract of rock and sand.

No sooner had they discovered this, than, without consulting the captain in any way, they dropped anchor, and lowered a boat, much to his astonishment.

Calling Money Marks forward, the chief mate exclaimed—

"Get into that boat."

"What for?"

"Because we don't want any pirates on board our ship."

"My good fellow, you are all of you wrong. I am no pirate, as I can prove to you."

"We know you. Don't be alarmed about that," said the mate: "and we are determined that you and the black shall shift for yourselves on yonder island."

"We shall starve there," cried Money Marks, turning white.

"That's likely enough. We don't care what happens to you so long as we are rid of you."

"Barbarians!"

"Call us what you like, but just be good enough to step into that boat; you will find a pair of oars, and that is all we shall give you; provisions and water are scarce with us, and too good to be wasted on pirates."

Marks shuddered.

He looked in all directions for the captain, but was unable to discover him.

The fact was, he had gone below, to avoid an unpleasant scene. He knew well enough what was going on upon deck, and was sufficiently well acquainted with the character of his men to be satisfied that they would have their way.

If he attempted to interfere his efforts would be unavailing, and he would only lose authority and reputation by preventing, or trying to prevent, the precautionary measures they were taking.

At last Cuffy and Money Marks were bundled into the boat, without provisions, water, ammunition, or anything.

Mr. Lancaster and Viola were spared. The vengeance of the sailors did not overtake them, as their hatred was pointed in another direction.

The old man rushed upon deck just as the anchor was raised, and was astonished beyond measure at seeing his son and the negro drifting along in a boat.

His surprise was intense.

"What have you done?" he cried, frantically stretching out his arms to the boat. "Where is my son, my son? Restore him to me!"

"Your son's all right," replied the first mate, with a smile.

"Why is he there?"

"He aint gone away and forgotten you as some does," continued the mate; "for he left his love, and hoped as how you might meet again in kingdom come."

"Let me join him."

"Well, if you take my advice, you wont. He aint provisioned for a long voyage, and might find you one too many."

Without another word the wretched old man sprang over the side of the ship, and was soon battling it amongst the seething waves.

A cry of wonderment broke from the lips of all. Cuffy, seizing the sculls, pulled towards him.

He was alarmed at what might happen.

It was well known that the sea was infested with sharks, and that to swim in it was dangerous, if not suicidal.

Money Marks was stupefied with grief and apprehension. He sat in the stern of the boat wrapped up in his cloak, looking the picture of misery.

Suddenly there was a loud cry.

An exclamation of horror escaped the lips of the negro.

Mr. Lancaster had been seized by a shark, and the dreadful monster had dragged him below the ensanguined surface—just allowing him sufficient time to utter the awful cry, which had rung in Money Marks' ears, and roused him from his reverie.

And well it might rouse him; that cry was the death-wail of his father.

Swift and terrible retribution!

The pirate had made scores of helpless prisoners walk the plank and fall into the maws of voracious sharks; now the tables were being turned, and he saw the same fate meted out to his own father.

"God is just!" was all he could utter.

Those on board the ship were equally shocked, but it was clear that nothing could be done for the unhappy man who had disappeared: so that the earth knew him no more.

With canvas set and a steady breeze, the gallant ship sailed on her way, and left the outcasts to their own reflections.

CHAPTER LXVI.

BAD WEATHER—THE MERCHANT VESSEL LOSES HER COURSE, AND TAKES A DIRECTION HIGHLY FAVOURABLE TO THE INTERESTS OF MONEY MARKS—A SEAPORT—CHOLERA—DANGER.

THE castaways allowed the boat to drift by means of a current in the direction of the island. Cuffy occasionally gave a stroke or two with an oar, but he, like his master, was too much overcome to be able to work hard, or take any interest in what was likely to become of them.

At length they reached the island, which was apparently of narrow dimensions, and ill calculated to sustain life; for they saw nothing whatever upon it but a few shell-fish attached to the rocks.

It was simply an expanse of rock and sand.

Hauling up the boat, they took shelter from the heat of the sun under a projecting rock, and then ruminated on their forlorn position.

"All my crimes are coming home to me, Cuffy!" exclaimed Money Marks, with dejected air and melancholy voice.

"Very bad men dem sailors," returned the black, who would neither contradict his master nor indorse the statement he had made.

"I cannot blame them. They formed a correct estimate of our character. There is an old saying, that the Devil is known by his hoof. I suppose it is true enough."

"Missy Viola go mad."

"You have mentioned her name," cried Money Marks, "which I dare not do! I drive her from my mind. I must not think of her, or I shall go mad."

"What matter?" replied Cuffy. "Soon die here."

"Death to me will be welcome."

"De ole nig like to live bit longer."

Money Marks fell forward, and buried his face in the sand. His bitter reflections were too much for and totally overcame him.

Cuffy being less sensitive, and having no "Missy Viola" to grieve over, bethought himself of taking stock of the capabilities of the island.

He made a prolonged tour of it, and discovered the molluscs already spoken of. Upon these he feasted, and brought a handful for Marks, who, he doubted not, would want some refreshment when the first outburst of his sorrow was over.

A second journey did not enable him to find any fresh water, and the absence of this indispensable necessary of life caused him considerable anxiety.

To his great delight, however, the sky in the afternoon became overcast, huge clouds collected in all parts of the heavens, and a deluge of rain was the result.

Several natural basins in the rock were filled with it, and Cuffy enjoyed a hearty drink.

Never before in the whole course of his existence had he enjoyed a drink so much as he did that rain-water.

Some shell-fish and a draught of water put fresh life into Money Marks, who changed his mind, and refused to die all at once of love and despair.

We must leave the castaways, whose position was miserably forlorn, to return to the *Petronel*.

When Viola Cathcart discovered that Money Marks had been turned adrift by the indignant sailors, she became very much agitated and sought the captain.

He received her in his cabin, and cast a commiserating glance upon her.

"Why have you permitted this outrage upon humanity?" she exclaimed. "You, as the captain of this ship, should have prevented these blind and silly men from having the blood of two of their fellow-creatures upon them."

"My dear young lady, I could not do anything for them," replied the captain.

"Then you are only nominally the captain of this vessel?"

"It would appear so."

Her lip curled with ineffable scorn.

"The Almighty will punish you all for taking the law into your own hands."

"I was merely a passive agent in the matter. What could I do? The men were violent, and would have their own way."

"Pontius Pilate held himself blameless, but he nevertheless ordered the death of One whom the world worships."

The captain bit his lip.

"You are a weak-minded man," she continued, "and you have done that for which you will be sorry ere many days have passed over your head. Would it not have been better to have left us to take our chance in the forest? Is it not barbarous to bring us on board your ship to separate us, and cause the men to die a cruel death?"

"I had no idea that the men would have behaved as they have done," replied the captain.

"You should have prevented it. And now what do you propose to do?"

"Sail on to our destination?"

"And leave the castaways to perish?"

He made no reply.

"Are you a man, and can you calmly propose such a thing as that?"

"If I attempted to interfere with the men of this vessel, my dear young lady, my life would probably become a forfeit to my indiscretion."

"I cannot believe that."

"Nevertheless it is true."

"My friends must be saved!" she cried imperiously.

"I don't know how it is to be done, miss. If you will suggest any reasonable way to me, I promise you I will listen to and entertain it."

She thought awhile and said—

"Alter the ship's course and put back for them."

"That is out of my power. The men would not let me. I am powerless in their hands."

"You allow them to mutiny and make you a cypher?"

"What else can I do? They are both too numerous and too unanimous for me to contend against them single-handed; in addition to that they have the officers with them to a man."

"Shall I speak to them?" asked Viola.

"You can do as you please about that. I will sanction the adoption of any plan you may induce them to listen to."

Viola's face flushed with hope—she went upstairs expecting to carry all before her. What then was her disappointment when she found that the mate and his ringleading companions would not listen to a word she had to say in favour of Money Marks, against whom they had a deep-rooted aversion.

She besought them with tears in her eyes. She clasped her hands, and strove to bribe them; but they would not hear of returning to take them off the rock.

So she once more sought the solitude of the cabin, and gave way to a flood of bitter burning tears, which trickled down her face in scalding drops.

In the night the elements proved themselves Viola's friend; for the wind rose and the rain fell, the thunder crashed and the lightning flashed, the sea rose mountains high and threatened to engulf the devoted ship.

The very sailors who had been so confident in the day-time now fell on their knees, and gave themselves up for lost.

Many who had not for years breathed the semblance of a prayer, now poured forth hearty aspirations and pleaded for mercy.

Viola walked about fearlessly amongst them; she seemed the spirit of the storm.

When she heard the sailors pleading to offended Heaven for mercy, she exclaimed—

"Mercy! what mercy can you expect? Make atonement for your sins, or you shall have such mercy as you have shown. You dare to talk of mercy while those two men you turned adrift are perishing of starvation on a barren rock. Out upon you! Show your penitence by your deeds."

They listened to her with the utmost attention.

The mate sought her side, and said—

"Do not talk to the men in that way; you will induce them to change their minds."

"Such is my object," she calmly rejoined.

"All this is a judgment on us for having such people on board; it would have been better for us if we had washed our hands of all of you."

Viola saw that she was talking to a vulgar bigot, in whose breast no spark of pity glimmered, and she gave up her attempt of converting him to her opinion, abandoning him in despair.

The storm increased in violence every moment, and the captain and crew became still more terrified.

All at once a terrific wave swept over the ship, carrying with it three men, amongst whom was the first mate, the man who had shown himself so determinedly hostile to Money Marks all throughout.

The groans and shrieks of those who were left behind were painful to hear.

They did not know how soon they might partake of the same fate; to complete their misfortunes a second wave carried away the binnacle, and deprived of their compass they knew not in what direction they were steering.

This was indeed a serious calamity, and as such one and all regarded it.

When morning dawned the storm subsided, and the wretched sailors began to recover their spirits.

The captain of the *Petronel* was sadly embarrassed, for he was out of his reckoning, and could not tell whither his unlucky ship was drifting.

Viola addressed the crew one by one and harangued them whenever opportunity offered, saying that what had happened was nothing more nor less than a judgment upon them for their wickedness and hardness of heart in refusing to listen to the appeals for mercy which their poor prisoners made to them.

They expressed their contrition, and said they should be only too glad to take them on board again, if they knew in what direction they were sailing.

"The fact is," said the captain, "we are entirely out of our reckoning. I really don't know what will become of us if we don't meet with some ship, and follow in her track."

"Cannot you make a new apparatus?"

"To steer by?"

"Yes."

"I fear not. All I can do is to take solar and stellar observations, and steer astronomically."

Suddenly a man on the look-out cried—

"Land a-head."

"Where away?" replied the captain.

"On the leeward bow."

Taking a powerful glass the captain scanned the verge of the horizon, and discovered the land of which the look-out man had spoken.

"Ah! either I am mistaken or——"

He paused and looked again, more keenly than before.

"What?" asked Viola, interested she knew not why.

"That is the desert island," replied the captain, hurriedly. "I see two figures standing on the shore. They tear up their shirts, and make signals to us. Yes, yes. I see them; now they extend their hands, and try to shout to us. They are too weak. One falls down, and is supported by the other. 'Tis they, 'tis they!"

"Thank Heaven!" murmured Viola, who fell back insensible.

The utmost anxiety was manifested amongst the crew to know the whole particulars.

When Viola recovered she made the most of the opportunity and the extraordinary coincidence.

"See!" she exclaimed, in a tragic voice, "see in what a mysterious way Providence works. You endeavoured to kill those two poor men, but it has been decreed otherwise. You sailed away from them, but the wind and the sea have crippled your barque, washed your evil counsellor overboard, and driven you back to the very place where your victims are languishing for help in the agonizing throes of starvation!"

The men hung their heads, and the ship, by the captain's orders, was steered in shore. A boat was lowered and eagerly manned. They rowed to the shore, where they found Money Marks and Cuffy awaiting their arrival.

Marks was nearly exhausted; though strong and wiry, he had not been able to bear up so well as his companion. The black was nearly fainting with fatigue, and immeasurably pleased when he found they were rescued.

But their astonishment was great when they recognised the old faces, and discovered that their saviours of to-day were their destroyers of yesterday.

Ignorant of the storm and what had taken place on board the *Petronel*, this supplied them with materials for a riddle of which Viola gave them a solution.

Money Marks owed his life to Viola; he knew it, and thanked her for her noble exertions in his behalf.

That day they met a vessel, in whose course they sailed, and in five days they arrived at a sea-port, where their ship was laid up in a dry-dock to repair.

Money Marks, Cuffy, and Viola landed. They thanked the captain of the *Petronel* for his kindness; paid him a sum of money to remunerate him for his trouble, and took up their abode at an hotel.

The captain asked them to continue their voyage to England, but they steadily refused, saying that after what had happened they thought it advisable to proceed in another vessel.

The *Petronel* was soon repaired and sailed without them for the port of London. There was no other homeward-bound vessel, so Money Marks was compelled to sojourn in the town until one arrived.

This he did reluctantly, because the cholera was raging, and many people were dying daily, which filled him with dread and apprehension.

It was admitted on all hands that there was great danger.

CHAPTER LXVII.

VIOLA ATTACKED BY CHOLERA—IS SHE DEAD?—SPEEDY BURIAL—THE GRAVEYARD—MONEY MARKS' GRIEF—CUFFY THINKS—HE PAYS THE SEXTON A VISIT—THE GRAVE OPENED.

THE disease which was ravaging the town was true Asiatic cholera of the worst type. Deaths every day were numerous. It seemed that to breathe the atmosphere was to inhale the fatal miasma which carried death with it.

Yet Money Marks braved this in preference to travelling to his native land on board the *Petronel*.

One day they were sitting at an open window in their apartments at the hotel.

When I say "they," I mean the little party consisting of Money Marks, Viola, and Cuffy. The latter would have preferred to have assumed a menial position, and have found his paradise in the kitchen, but Money Marks would not hear of such a thing.

He looked upon Cuffy as a friend, and always treated him with the utmost kindness and consideration. Viola, too, had a great regard for Cuffy, and would not have treated him badly for worlds.

"I wish our ship would arrive," Viola said.

"Are you tired of this town?"

"Oh, yes; I have a longing to reach England. Then we shall be safe."

"Are we not safe here?"

"I fear not."

"What do you dread?"

"In the first place," she replied, "I am apprehensive about you."

"About me?" he repeated, in surprise.

"Yes. We never can tell what may happen. Do not think me a bird of ill omen; it is my love for you which dictates this nervousness."

"I believe that, but you may calm your timidity, dearest; I hope and trust I am far removed from my enemies. I am confident because I feel secure."

"In the second place, I dread the cholera."

"For Heaven's sake don't do that; nothing is so fatally inducive of cholera as fear. To give way to fear is to sign your death warrant."

She attempted to smile in a sickly manner.

"What would you say if I were to tell you that I have had a dream?"

"When?"

"Last night. As I lay in a trance-like sleep I fancied I saw a grim and ghastly skeleton advance towards me—its bony fingers encircled my throat, and my spirit fled beneath the death-giving pressure."

"Horrible!" ejaculated Money Marks, "can it be true?"

"It is, and the dream has weighed me down with a terrible pressure ever since."

"You must be cheerful, my child."

"Alas, I cannot!" she replied, despondingly.

"What cause of alarm have you? Come, cheer up!" he cried, in an inspiriting voice.

"Would that I could do so!"

"Make an effort. You drink no wine. Hand your glass to Cuffy, he will fill it for you."

"When the soul is dark there is nothing like wine to cheer it up," she said, draining the glass Cuffy gave her.

This was meeting Money Marks half way, and he was pleased to see that she did not give way without an effort to raise her drooping spirits.

"I wonder whether we shall ever reach England," said Viola.

"Shall we? Of course we shall."

"Our lives have been very stormy. We must have been born under stormy constellations. What do you think?"

"Possibly," returned Money Marks. "I have led an unquiet life, but that may forbode a peaceful old age."

"It may; God send it to both of us!"

Money Marks drew his chair closer to Viola, and bending forward, whispered in her ear—

"Viola, my own!"

She pressed his hand.

"Listen to me, dearest," he continued.

"I will."

"You have often promised to be my wife."

"I have."

"Why then delay the ceremony? Make me—make yourself—happy at once. What objection is there to such a course?"

She blushed, and turned away her head.

"Be mine, darling. You know I love you."

"That I cannot doubt," she murmured.

"And you may rest assured that I will love you ever fondly."

"Had we not better wait?" she said.

"Have we not waited long enough?"

"It is a great and important step to take; 'twould be madness to take it rashly."

"It would, but we are not lovers of yesterday. We have known one another for years."

"That is true."

"There are priests here," said Money Marks, who was urging his suit pertinaciously.

"There are; but though Christians, they are not Protestants."

"What matter? If we are joined in wedlock by a holy rite what matter whether it be by a follower of Luther, or a disciple of the Pope?"

"You are liberal in your opinions."

"Do not trifle with me, Viola. Grant my prayer. Let us be made man and wife at once, without any further delay."

She hesitated.

"Viola, answer me."

Still no reply.

"Say yes or no, my dearest one," he cried.

Her lips moved, he bent forward to catch the sound, and distinctly heard her utter the monosyllable "yes."

Then he rushed forward and caught her in his arms, imprinting innumerable kisses upon her cheeks and lips.

"Bless you, my only pet," he cried, rapturously, "you have made me happy. This indeed changes all the bitterness of my life into joy. I forget everything, and become oblivious of what I have suffered and gone through when I think of my present happiness."

Her agitation overcame her; with a fond sigh she let her head fall upon his shoulder, and burst into tears.

He comforted and consoled her, and induced her to consent to their marriage being solemnized the next day.

"Let it be as private as possible," she said.

"Certainly; there is no need of pomp and display here."

"I shall not be altogether satisfied with a Catholic priest, so you must not be angry, dearest, if I wish to be married again when we reach England."

"Of course not," replied Money Marks; "you may be married in every parish in the kingdom, if you like."

She smiled.

"What de matter all about, massa?" asked Cuffy.

The black had been an attentive spectator of the preceding scene, and by dint of careful listening had discovered that a marriage had been arranged, but he wished to hear the fact from his master's own lips.

"Just this, my good fellow: Miss Cathcart and I are going to be married."

"Married?"

"Yes."

"Oh, golly! When de event to come off?"

"To-morrow."

"Cuffy go to de church; mustn't leave de ole nig behind," he said, with a solemn shake of the head.

"Oh, no; we couldn't do without you."

"Dat true 'nuff, massa."

Money Marks filled a glass with sparkling wine, and giving it to Cuffy, said—

"Here, take this, and drink the health of the bride elect."

"Oh, and I'll do dat, massa."

He took the glass, and said—

"Here your health, Missy Viola, soon be Missy Marks, and have——"

"No, not Marks; my father's name was Lancaster," said Money Marks, interrupting the garrulous negro.

"Dat your father what de dam shark eat, massa?"

"Yes, you are right; that poor old man, whose life has been a misery, and whose death was a violent one, was my father. I never knew his worth, so that I do not feel his loss, but I am convinced that he was my father, and I mourn his memory."

"Very well, massa. Here's de health of Missy Lancaster, and may she have plenty piccaniny."

Both Money Marks—for we shall still call him so—and Viola blushed up to the temples, but the negro opened his capacious mouth and gave vent to a huge guffaw.

The next day, as had been agreed, the young people were married. The scene was not very impressive, but Money Marks cared not for that; all he wished was to make Viola his wife, and he did so.

They went from the church back to the hotel, scarcely able to realize their new-born happiness.

The people at the hotel had heard of the marriage, and they crowded the entrance to have a look at the newly-married pair. Money Marks was gay and blithesome; Viola was serenely happy, but a sad expression pervaded her lovely countenance.

They went upstairs to their apartments, and sat in their old position near the window. A wandering minstrel, such as they call in Italy an *improvisatore*, heard that a wedding had taken place, and touching his guitar lightly with his fingers, extemporized a song in honour of the newly-married couple.

This effort was highly applauded by the audience which collected near the door, and Money Marks tossed a silver coin to the ingenious musician.

The window was open. The air blew gently into the room, while those within inhaled it freely. All at once a little black speck floated in.

Cuffy saw it and dashed forward, catching it in his hand just as it reached Viola's face.

"What is that, and why——" began Money Marks.

"Dat am de Black Death, Massa Marks," said Cuffy.

"The what?" cried Money Marks, horrified.

"De Black Death."

"And what may that be?"

"It gets into de lungs, and den it all over with you."

"Ha! is it so?"

Viola had not swallowed any particle of the pestilential miasma, the concentrated essence of which had floated in her vicinity, but she fancied she had.

Her dream flashed across her memory, and she became sadly alarmed.

"My dream, my dream!" she cried.

Money Marks turned pale, and looked inquiringly at her.

"The Black Death! he calls it the Black Death," she continued.

"What is the matter?" asked Money Marks, soothingly.

"My dream!"

"Attach no importance to it."

"I must, I must; it is coming true."

"Listen to me, my own—my wife," exclaimed Money Marks.

"No, no; I have inhaled the Black Death, and I shall die."

Money Marks turned yet a shade paler, for he knew that fear would as soon kill his wife as the disease itself. He had once at Sierra Leone seen the people swept off like decayed leaves when the wind blows—King Cholera had made his appearance there and claimed his own.

Where the disease kills one, fear kills half-a-dozen.

All at once Viola became the colour of snow, the blood left her face, and she fell back upon the floor.

"A doctor, a doctor!" cried Money Marks.

"Where shall I find one?"

"A medical man. Ask downstairs, they will tell you."

The door of the room was open, and the loud shouts of Money Marks for a doctor were audible in the corridor.

An English gentleman who happened to be passing heard the cry and stopped.

Cuffy, running out of the room, met him at the door.

"Are you not calling for a doctor?" exclaimed the strange gentleman.

"Yes, massa."

"I am a qualified medical practitioner, and an Englishman. Here is my card."

Cuffy took it.

"You will perceive that my name is Johnson—Dr. Johnson."

"Yes, massa."

"And I shall be happy to render all the assistance in my power."

"Dis way!" cried Cuffy.

He opened the door, and ushered Dr. Johnson into the room.

MONEY MARKS ATTEMPTS TO STRANGLE THE DOCTOR.

Viola was still lying on her back upon the floor. Money Marks was bending over her.

"What is the matter?" inquired the doctor.

"Are you a medical man?" asked Money Marks, springing to his feet.

"I am."

"Thank Heaven! Help was nearer than I supposed."

"Explain the cause of the lady's illness?"

"I fear she is attacked by cholera."

"Ah! that is serious. Stand on one side, and allow me to examine her."

Money Marks did so.

The doctor fell on his knees, and felt Viola's pulse. She struggled now and then spasmodically, as if in pain.

Getting up he shook his head.

"Save my wife, and I am yours for ever."

The doctor sat upon a chair for a little while and thought, then he took from his pocket a small bottle, which contained a white powder of a crystalline description.

"What have you there?" asked Money Marks, wishing to know what remedy was to be given to his wife.

"Strychnine," was the reply.

"Eh! but that is a deadly poison?"

"You are right."

"I cannot allow you to administer such a drug to her."

"In that case, I can be of no service to you."

Dr. Johnson, after saying this, moved towards the door.

"Stay!" cried Money Marks.

"For what purpose?"

"To cure my wife."

"You will not permit me."

"Do what you like; but she must not be poisoned."

"Pish!" cried the doctor. "You are too ready with your conclusions, my dear sir."

"How so?"

"I do not wish to poison your wife. I have no interest to do so, and only wish to stay the ravages of the fell disease which has laid its hand upon her."

"Well, well, do what you like," replied Money Marks.

The doctor once more bent down, and administered a dose of strychnine to Viola, who swallowed it passively.

Dr. Johnson attended to her indefatigably for five hours, at the end of that time he rose, and laying his hand upon Money Marks' shoulder, said—

"Heaven help you, my poor fellow!"

"Why? what?"

"She is dead!"

"Dead? God in heaven!" cried Money Marks, in a voice broken by sobs.

"Alas, it is too true!"

So saying, the doctor slowly left the room.

Money Marks threw himself upon the body of his wife, and sobbed like a child. Cuffy stood by and sympathized in his master's grief.

In vain the black endeavoured to rouse his master. Money Marks was completely stupefied and prostrated with grief.

The night passed. Money Marks wept, but could not sleep. When the morning dawned, two men belonging to the municipality made their appearance, and brought with them a coffin.

In hot countries it is absolutely necessary to bury a body a few hours after death, or else corruption would set in.

They gently roused Money Marks, and pulled him away from the dead body of his wife.

"What do you want with me?" he said, sharply and angrily.

They replied that they had come, by order of the mayor, to put the corpse in the coffin.

"Corpse! what corpse?" he said.

"That one at your feet."

"You lie!" he cried. "She is no corpse; she is my wife."

"That may be, sir, but she is dead."

"What authority have you for that statement?"

"The doctor's certificate duly signed and attested."

"The doctor is a fool. She is not—cannot be dead!"

The official examined the body, which was quite cold, and said—

"There cannot be a doubt of the fact of the woman's death. She is as cold as a stone. What can be clearer? It's our duty to place her in her coffin, and I warn you that it will be useless to make any resistance."

Money Marks fell into a chair with a moan.

He could not realize the fact of his wife's death; it was too much for him.

When he spoke the word "wife" it nearly choked him. She had been his wife so short a time that it was cruel of Fate to treat him so badly, and snatch her away before he had had time to love her.

Dragging the coffin close to the body, the officials took hold of Viola rather roughly, and tore off her dress, and, wrapping her in her petticoats, pushed her into the coffin.

Money Marks was enraged beyond measure at this conduct, and would have attacked the men had not Cuffy restrained him.

Drawing a hammer and some nails from his pocket, one of the men began to nail down the coffin-lid.

Money Marks could not bear this; he rushed forward, and, dealing blows right and left, sent the officials rolling this way and that, and tearing off the coffin-lid with almost superhuman force, uncovered Viola's face, and covered it with kisses.

It was rapture to him to kiss that poor clay-cold face, but exhausted by emotion and his frantic efforts, he sank back as insensible as his lovely bride.

Seeing that their formidable enemy was disposed of, the men returned t their work, and Viola was speedily nailed down

Thinking it best to make hay while the sun shone, and to remove the coffin before Money Marks returned to consciousness, they took up the coffin and carried it to the door, at which a cart was standing.

In this vehicle there were several coffins, all containing dead bodies of people who had died of the cholera—for this terrible pestilence continued its ravages in the town and carried off many citizens daily.

Viola's was thrown upon the others, and the cart drove off.

Cuffy, however, had followed the coffin downstairs, and he drew his knife, as it lay in the cart, and made several slashes and indentations upon the lid and side, so that he could not fail to know it again.

The men made no objection to this; they thought it was some religious custom, intended to pay fit and proper respect to the dead.

The negro had an idea that Viola was not yet dead. Why he should think so it is difficult to say, but he did; and he was determined to follow the cart and see where the coffin was deposited.

After picking up half-a-dozen more bodies, the officials drove to a church-yard, in the neighbourhood of the upper part of the city, and left the cart with its ghastly load in the enclosure.

Then they went away. Their duty was over; they had no more to do.

It was the sexton's part to inter the bodies, and this he usually did as soon as the coffins arrived.

Cuffy had, unobserved by anyone, followed the cart to the cemetery, and seen where it was left. He appeared to be deeply grieved, and put on an appearance calculated to lead people to believe that he had been suddenly bereft of a dear friend, or a kind relation.

He entered the graveyard just as the sexton emerged from his lodge at the gate to look after his charge.

He looked at the cart, and the sexton did the same, the latter exclaiming—

"Not quite so many as usual! that'll make it bad for the body-carpenters. The plague is dying out. Why, there aint above a score and a half, which is considerably under the mark. Well, it'll be better for me."

Turning round he saw Cuffy.

"What do you want?" he asked.

"I just want to have a word with you."

"Make haste then; for my time's valuable."

Cuffy had some money in his pocket; he knew very well that it belonged to his master, but he did not scruple to make use of it, because he felt assured that Money Marks would have spent every farthing he had, if he could thereby do Viola any good.

So he gave the sexton a couple of gold pieces.

The man took them, and after eyeing them inquisitively pocketed them, saying—

"What's this for?"

"I want you to oblige me."

"Do you want a body?"

"I do."

"I thought so. You're some surgical chap, that's about the size of it, isn't it?"

"No. But I nevertheless want a body."

"I don't understand you."

"Listen to me, and you will, Massa Sexton," replied Cuffy. "I rather fancy a lady's been buried before she's dead."

"Ah, that aint at all unlikely. Which coffin is it?"

"At the top somewhere; I've marked it."

"Show it me. By rights all these bodies ought to go into one hole together. I dig one—I and my mates—every morning for the cartload, and there's one ready now. The bodies must go in, but I'll tell you what I'll do."

"What dat?"

"I'll put your coffin at the top, and only a thin coating of mould over it, and if you come at ten o'clock to-night, we'll have it out and examine it."

"Why not now?"

"It can't be done."

"She may be dead by ten."

"Possibly."

"Den do it now, Massa Sexton," urged Cuffy.

"I tell you I can't."

"Gib me de reason."

"This is the reason—there is always a priest or two about at this hour, and if they saw any tampering with the coffins it would be a case of dismissal at once, and good-by to your humble servant."

"Ten o'clock you said, I tink?" said Cuffy.

"That's the time."

"You will let me and my frens see de body?"

"As sure as I am alive."

"I can rely upon you?"

"My oath."

"Don't deceive me."

"May I drop a corpse if I do! No, no; you have paid me to do a certain thing, and, as God is my judge, I'll do it," replied the sexton.

Cuffy went away satisfied, after pointing out the particular coffin he wished placed on the top of the others.

When he returned to the hotel he found Money Marks very ill indeed; he was being held down by three waiters, who were compelled to exert all their strength to restrain him.

Near him stood Dr. Johnson, who had imprudently ventured into the room after Viola had been carried away in her coffin.

"You villain!" Money Marks exclaimed. "Wait till I get at you. You killed my wife—may the pains of hell encompass you, for you killed my wife!"

The doctor had in vain endeavoured to extricate himself from his grasp. Money Marks was fearfully determined; he caught him by the throat and would have strangled him had not the waiters of the hotel rushed forward in the most providential manner and stopped his murderous intention.

"Where is Cuffy?" shouted Money Marks, as the negro entered the room. "Have all deserted me? am I alone in the world? damn them! Prosperity brings friends, but adversity makes one feel a pauper in everything. Let me go, rascals—let me go, if you do not wish me to slay you one and all."

"Alas!" said the landlord of the hotel, "the poor gentleman is going out of his mind. What a pity! The loss of his wife has driven him mad."

"Stand on one side," said Cuffy.

"We dare not," replied the waiters.

"Make room for me; I will speak to him."

They allowed Cuffy to reach Money Marks' head, and kneeling down the negro said—

"Massa Marks."

"Who speaks?"

"I do."

"Cuffy?"

"Yes."

"Where is Viola? give me my wife."

"Dat am all right."

"What mean you?" gasped the unfortunate man.

"I tink she come back to life; I not know for sartin."

"Can it be true?"

"No harm, massa, in try. Get Massa Doc'r to come with us."

"No; he is a scoundrel."

"Indeed, you are mistaken; I have not done you any harm that I am aware of," said Dr. Johnson, stepping forward.

"You killed my wife."

"I deny that altogether. She died from natural causes."

"Then it is to be hoped you never will; if I have the power to prevent your dying in your bed you may rely upon it I will do so."

"Listen to reason."

"I will, but not to you."

"Massa Doc'r not to blame," said Cuffy.

"Why not?" said Money Marks. "Not to blame, indeed, when he killed my wife! The curses of the bottomless pit upon him!"

"I had nothing whatever to do with your wife's death."

"You gave her strychnine."

"Yes."

"That is a deadly poison."

"Yes."

"Then you killed her—you admit it."

"Certainly not; strychnine is a poison, I grant you that—but when administered in small doses it counteracts the particular disease against which its action is directed. In certain cases you must administer one poison to kill another, and then take measures to eradicate the second from the system."

"That may be all very well, but——"

"Massa Marks," interrupted Cuffy.

"Well?"

"Say no more to Massa Doc'r; him right—him be useful."

"In what way?"

"You be quiet, and let me speak."

Money Marks left off struggling; the waiters released him, and he leaned against the wall, and gloomily regarded those who were near him.

Cuffy went to Doctor Johnson, and began to talk to him.

"Me want you, massa, dis evening," he said.

"What for?"

"You come with me to de graveyard."

"What graveyard?"

"Where Missy Viola am buried."

"What then?"

"Why, it strike dis nig dat de missis not dead."

"That's nonsense; if not dead, the officials would not have put her in the coffin."

"Never mind dat, massa; dis nig going to-night, and will open de coffin."

"With what object in view?"

"To bring Missy Viola back to life."

"You can try, of course, if you think it will be satisfactory to your master."

"Oh, yes; it satisfactory to him."

"But what do you want with me?" asked Dr. Johnson.

"Me want you to come because you doc'r, and can tell whether 'live or dead."

"I see what you mean, and if it will be any satisfaction to you, why, I will come."

"Oh, golly! dat good news," said Cuffy, delightedly.

Away he went to Money Marks, and said—

"It am all right, massa; de doc'r say him come to-night at ten o'clock and open de coffin of Missy Viola, and den he bring her back to life."

Money Marks clutched at this chance as a drowning man clutches at a straw.

"Yes, yes," he said, "we will do that. You are my friend, Cuffy; you have saved me from becoming a madman."

Dr. Johnson was a scientific man; he had often heard of cases of trance occurring in hot climates, and he was a little hopeful that he might restore Viola to life; at all events, he resolved to try.

He never travelled without a small galvanic battery, which he had found useful on many occasions and in many ways, and he determined to take it with him to the graveyard, and with it experiment upon Viola.

When night came, three men might have been discovered walking towards the cemetery. Cuffy carried a large box under his arm: it contained a galvanic apparatus.

Money Marks and the doctor had made up their difference, and were walking together, being no longer at variance.

It was a calm, clear night, and both moon and stars emitted a grateful light.

The sexton, expecting his visitors, was standing at the gate. Cuffy advanced and spoke to him; then he admitted the trio.

There was no necessity for a lantern, because the light shed by Nature's lamps was amply sufficient for the invaders of the cemetery.

Occasionally a low cry would break from Money Marks; he would press his hands together, drive back his tears, and stay the fierce, tumultuous beating of his heart.

They reached the grave, which was large and spacious, being at least twelve feet by eight.

The sexton said, in a low tone—

"I hope, gentlemen, you will not be longer about this little business than you can help."

"Oh, no," said the doctor.

"Because my bread depends upon my good conduct; it is against the rules to admit any one in here, and a breach of my instructions to permit a coffin to be broken open."

"You may rely upon our good faith and our discretion," said the doctor.

"Thank you, gentlemen; that is all I wished to say."

Removing a spade from his shoulder the sexton set to work and speedily removed the earth, disclosing a coffin, which Cuffy immediately pounced upon.

It was the one which contained the dead body of Viola.

Money Marks could scarcely breathe, so great was his excitement.

The doctor was cool and cautious.

The negro was hopeful and confident.

CHAPTER LXVIII.

HOPE AND HAPPINESS—THE LATTER IS SHORT-LIVED.

THE exertions of Cuffy and the sexton proved sufficient to drag the heavy coffin to the side of the grave, and from thence it was placed upon the grass.

Taking a screw-driver or chisel and a hammer, the sexton began to open the coffin, which was stoutly nailed down.

It however succumbed to his efforts, which were eventually crowned with success.

Money Marks helped to wrench off the lid, and his joy was great when he once more beheld the dearly-loved features of Viola.

There she lay. Serene and peaceful. It was impossible to believe her dead. She seemed to be asleep.

Money Marks was unable to resist the inclination to throw himself upon the clay-cold body, and kiss the clay-cold lips!

He did so.

His fevered imagination made him fancy that her lips moved responsively to his own, and gave him the nuptial caress of which he had hitherto been deprived.

"Lay her on the grass," said Dr. Johnson, in a commanding voice.

They obeyed his instructions to the letter, and taking the body from the coffin, placed it upon the green sward.

While they were thus engaged, the doctor opened his box and took therefrom his galvanic apparatus, which he arranged in proper order, placing the Leyden jars near the body, and seeing that they were fully charged with electricity, he took two wires and placed them in contact with the girl's body.

Suddenly the girl started up; her eyes opened, her lips moved, and she appeared to be endowed with vitality.

"Ha!" cried Money Marks, "she lives."

"I cannot say that," replied the doctor, as he lessened the force of the electric current.

The body fell back, and resumed its former recumbent position.

Falling upon his knees, and bending over the body, Dr. Johnson placed his mouth to that of Viola, and began to breathe into her, in the hope of being able to inflate her lungs.

This continued for some minutes.

Then he again galvanized her, and with the greatest success: the blood came back to her cheeks, the action of the heart re-commenced, and all knew that she had been in a trance, from which the watchful care of Cuffy and the skill of the doctor had roused her.

Money Marks held her hand in his, and spoke to her. She was unable to reply to him until she was strong enough to recall her scattered senses, and then she sighed deeply.

"My own!" cried Money Marks, "this is indeed happiness. You have been snatched from the jaws of death."

"Is it my husband?" she said.

"It is."

"God bless you!" she murmured, feebly.

Dr. Johnson saw that he had administered a little too much strychnine to his patient, which had produced temporary paralysis of the heart, and suspension of the vital powers.

He did not, however, confess his mistake, but contented himself with the thought that he had corrected his error, and could not, in this particular instance, lay the death of a fellow-creature to his charge.

Although recalled to life, Viola was much too weak to be able to walk to the hotel. She was carried to the gates of the cemetery, and then placed in a carriage which Cuffy fetched from a stable close at hand.

The doctor stayed all night with Viola, and treated her in a most judicious manner, which resulted in her being nearly as well as ever the next day.

Of course she was weak, and required care and nourishment, but she was not the lifeless thing she had been.

Her life had been saved by what was little less than a miracle.

Three days afterwards an English-bound ship touched at the port, and when Money Marks heard of it, he at once secured a passage to London for Viola, Cuffy, and himself.

They found it a comfortable ship to travel in, and made an arrangement with the captain to dine at his table. Mr. Parsons, the captain, was pleased with his company, and paid especial attention to Viola.

One day at dinner he said—

"I have just been taking the reckoning, and I could not help thinking of something that happened to me in these latitudes some years ago."

"Indeed," said Viola; "pray let us hear the story."

"I will relate it with pleasure."

They all placed themselves in an attitude of attention as the captain began.

"I had been sailing in concert with a very old friend of mine, one of the old school; his name was Cathcart."

"What?" cried Viola.

"Cathcart."

"That was my father's name."

"Possibly; it is common enough in Virginia. Well, old Cathcart and I started from Charleston, I think it was; we were both bound for Liverpool with cargoes of cotton. Cathcart had a good-looking daughter on board, I remember."

Viola trembled from head to foot.

"We were separated in a fog one night, and I never saw Cathcart again, but I heard that he was captured by Money Marks the pirate."

After this conversation Money Marks was very guarded in his observations. He feared that Captain Parsons might discover his identity, and deliver him over to the civil authorities.

But it was not so.

The ship reached England, and Viola, Money Marks, and Cuffy were landed. The pirate had a large sum of money in jewels and gold, and he was rejoiced at the fact, because he wished to do as much good with it as lay in his power.

He had by a life of piety to atone for years of atrocious bloodshed.

Viola was an angel of light, and stimulated him in his efforts. They retired to the Isle of Wight, purchasing a small cottage in that delightful locality. Money Marks found great pleasure in contemplating the sea. He could not be far away from his native element.

Cuffy lived with his master and mistress, and was as faithful as of yore. The past was never alluded to; and the poor who blessed their benefactor never supposed for a moment that he was the once terrible pirate who had been the scourge of the seas.

*   *   *   *   *   *

Two years glided by, and they were years of uninterrupted happiness to Money Marks and his angelic wife.

But the vengeance of offended Heaven was not appeased. A cloud descended upon the little household near Blackgang Chine.

Viola had lately become a mother, and was nursing a fine healthy boy upon her knee.

Suddenly the deep boom of a gun was heard near at hand. A ship had struck upon the rocks!

Money Marks sprang up in great excitement, and dashed out of the cottage, in spite of his wife's entreaties to remain at home and not jeopardize his life.

He wished to save human life, if he could. He had shed so much blood in his time that he wished to make some reparation for his sanguinary career. Cuffy was with him. The sea was very rough and violent. A ship could be seen overwhelmed by the water. Men were struggling in the waves, and plaintive cries for help were borne faintly to the shore.

Without a moment's hesitation, Money Marks, with Cuffy's help, launched a boat.

They rowed gallantly to the wreck.

No sooner had they reached it than a tremendous wave overtook them. The boat was filled with water and capsized.

Money Marks endeavoured to swim to the shore, but a drowning man catching him by the arm, paralysed his efforts.

He sank to rise alive no more.

The negro saw the fate of the once famous pirate, and uttered a cry of despair.

It was his last. The next moment he was dashed against a rock, and soon lay floating lifeless on the surface of the ocean.

*   *   *   *   *   *

The little cottage in the Isle of Wight is still inhabited, but by a widow and her baby-boy.

When the wind is at its height, and the surges beat against the rocky shore, she gazes out into the stormy night and weeps.

The spirit of her dead husband seems to speak to her in weird tones, and beckon her to that land of spirits whither she is fast hurrying.

THE END.